The Panhandle

Paul Caddle

Published by New Generation Publishing in 2022

Copyright © Paul Caddle 2022

First Edition

The author asserts the moral right under the Copyright, Designs and Patents Act 1988 to be identified as the author of this work.

All Rights reserved. No part of this publication may be reproduced, stored in a retrieval system or transmitted, in any form or by any means without the prior consent of the author, nor be otherwise circulated in any form of binding or cover other than that which it is published and without a similar condition being imposed on the subsequent purchaser.

ISBN
    Paperback   978-1-80369-307-1
    Ebook   978-1-80369-308-8

www.newgeneration-publishing.com

New Generation Publishing

An Aside

Okay, this could be regarded as a book about teenagers, and of course besides the love/dread of sport, the survival of school lessons and simply being together, teenagers have three primary obsessions: who fancies whom, who is going out with whom, who has just finished with whom. This book has to pay homage to those legitimate concerns in order to aspire to its calling of being essentially a story of a school set in quasi-isolation within a British enclave situated in the south of Cyprus. However it also aspires to be something other and therefore I would encourage the reader to pay it more attention than just throwing in the direction of his or her daughter or sister.

Interesting teenagers are doomed to become boring adults by the necessity of social pressure. Many adults think teenagers are boring because of peer pressure. But hopeless cases of each transfer their gifts as teenagers to skills as adults at a price which, when looking back, seem a shameful waste or at best an excuse for nostalgia-inducing clichés such as 'youth is wasted on the young'.

The story, admittedly, does take place in the dark ages before internet social media, and begins on Thursday, 24 February 1972.

The Better Half

I realize now that throughout my life I've wanted two things: to get older and to stay the same. The inevitable against the impossible. How can I hope to live properly?
Rebecca Panhandle: Journal

Christopher and I hardly know each other. We are only brother and sister after all. We live in the same house, eat from the same table, attend the same school. When he looks at me it is because I happened to get in the way of his eyes. I doubt if he really knows anybody. It could be that everything gets in the way of his eyes.
Rebecca Panhandle: Journal

You know I've told you I play rugby for the school. Good game. Beats just running and it seems I'm still the school champion at just doing that. Rugby's a better game when you're playing against a good team, and our youth klub at Akrotiri (we spell it klub because of the K in Akrotiri I think) got together a two-bit team to play against us. I thought it'd be a walk-over but didn't the bastards go and beat us. One of their players is a little squirt called Panhandle. Can't stand the weedy bugger, although I fancy his sister. He always looks as if he's got better things to do. You know the sort.
Perry Stenfield: Letter to a friend.

CHRISTOPHER PANHANDLE ACTUALLY AGREED to become part of the team. Few people loved the game less than he. It was by consequence, rather than intent, but there was no surprise to him that he'd be playing. He had long ago resigned himself to being a victim to the natural sadism of games teachers. However, he had been the first some years before to make known an absolute. No way, under any circumstances, was he ever going to have anything to do whatsoever with rugby. His tendency towards research was limited and he reserved a mild acceptance of the many mysteries circling existence, one of which was the fact that, yes, many lads, even his size but usually greater, gained some fashion of fun out of the barbaric sport. Let them gambol away their spare time at the risk of ruptured spleens and fractured skulls. Self-preservation demanded more exclusive terms with fewer strenuous pursuits, such as mathematics, physics and the gathering cloud of important exams. In this he had the covert but acknowledged support of Wilfred George.

It seemed there was this unassuming but sublime calling to the partisan in every boy, and as such his religion became team sport. Christopher wanted to remain a stern atheist but appear agnostic (hedging bets being a constant in the now eternal process of teenage culture) and so, as a result, he was regarded as one of many sixth formers who missed out on the ritual pleasure of representing St John's but would be willing, by default to form one of the fifteen ready to take them on in the form of Akrotiri Youth Klub First. Akrotiri's was the only youth club capable of shaping a team from the left-overs at the school. Both Christopher and Wilfred lived in Akrotiri. This, as it stood, remained the only fact they had wished to have in common with the Youth Klub First. Neither of them were members of the Klub and both were happy to confess to a basic rugby-based incompetence, which included any attempt at understanding its cryptic rules, but as the team was being drawn up from *within* the school as an imperative push towards the first game *against* the school the following afternoon, some fanciful compulsion defying his less than ideal mathematical morale sparked off the challenge in Christopher. He did not immediately say no when asked if he would sign his name to the list. There was, after all, the impressive title: Akrotiri Y.K. 1st, which failed to be inhibited by the lack of a second team or even reserves. He chose his mild excuse: lack of experience – he hadn't played since lower sixth, and he took the precaution of reminding Colin Kamp that he was not and had never been and had no intention of ever becoming a card-carrying member of the Klub, but Colin with his clipboard, took needs before particulars, and interpreted these caveats as a yes. Besides, he liked Christopher enough to do him such favours.

'We've got no hooker, Christopher. You used to be quite good, so I was told.'

Christopher, who for reasons not of his demanding but he certainly endorsed was rarely called Chris, wondered who had been doing the telling but he failed to ask.

'What about David Bury?'

'He plays hooker for the school and, anyway, he doesn't live in Akrotiri.'

'Doesn't he?'

At which point Savina Markou heaved her solution sigh. Another impossible puzzle spliced together by the labyrinthine talents of integral calculus was untangled by what she would then consider to be a simple set of steps. Despite the energising effect this among many of her achievements had as a tonic to the sultry confines of prefects' room study, she sat back in the role of one who now deserved a triumphant rest. But would she slip her array of common figures and ingenious squiggles under Christopher's nose? No, she decided against doing that. Instead, she stood up and looked over his shoulder as he stared at Colin's list. He was not displeased to see that both Colin and his brother, Oliver, were leading the Akrotiri selection. And Francis Dorman too. Well, if he's crazy enough…

'What do you think, Savina? He wants me to play rugby against the school.'

'Have you played rugby for the school?'

Her enunciation of English was so good that it forced an honest answer.

'No.'

'Do you think it will help you in your maths?'

'Should help me take my mind off maths, especially those *Tranter* problems.'

'Which problems in particular? The one I just solved?'

'You solved it? Fantastic. Time for me to get a quick copy?'

Savina involved a good deal of her time with Christopher both resisting and loving the recurring need he had to copy her work. He often resisted it himself and merely asked for hints, but just now this rugby issue was too prominent for him to indulge in the luxury of analytical thinking.

'It was easy. You spend too much time fiddling your way at what you think you know instead of finding out a bit more of what you should know and what you could quite easily work out.'

'What I could work out, hey?' He looked at her work. 'But what about my fiddle factor?'

'It did not work this time.' She laughed. She could not remember a time when, whatever they happened to be, the factoring in of any of Christopher's fiddles actually worked, and neither could he. Neither could either of them, if pushed, come up with a reasonable description of what principles at this level remained from which fiddles were not totally outside the fall-back arc of reason.

Christopher had to be reminded of the list by staring away from her intelligent green eyes, behind which heated figures were often thrown against icy problems. For her there was never enough mathematical heat. What excited tension, frustration and impatience in others merely accelerated her fluent skill, and she was at her academic happiest when being impatient herself with the low level of contemporary work in progress – Christopher's work in particular. This may have led others to assume that both he and she were indirectly within the potential of becoming an item, but so far this failed to gather momentum on any level of the sixth form media.

'How come you're not playing for the school?' Christopher asked Colin.

'Youth Klub needs more support. We've got good players but the school has more. Anyway, I like the Klub better than I like school.'

This was easy loyalty and made adequate sense. It also had to account for inclusion of other names, such as William Grey who had often been lauded as the best rugby and football captain the school had never had. However…

'You're certainly counting on some dodgy players. I mean, I only survived the scrums because Wilfred George was the most powerful prop.'

'Yes, you're right, we could do with him.'

'I didn't suggest he should be included. Don't tell him it was my idea. He hates rugby and he's not that keen on the Klub.'

'Why wouldn't he be keen on the Klub? Does he prefer the school?'

'I wouldn't say he's in love with it.'

'Don't worry. I'll persuade him to sign the list.'

And he did, and not because he, Colin was a large lad. Wilfred was also large and shaped with the metabolic ability to be a good prop, but Colin had the confidence Wilfred lacked coupled with his inherent inclination to help others see things his way. Wilfred also lacked the necessary aptitude needed in resisting the broadside of a Kamp-contained request. Colin was larger than his older brother, Oliver, and, of course, his younger brother, Leonard – the scale in size to age was never a determining factor in sorting out the many rites existing within the first twenty years of life – and although he was not quite old enough to be given full licentia within the languid but studious, smoke-screened luxury of the prefects' room, he could with specified impunity, wander around this realm while distracting them from their many pleasures with the particular notion of his tasks. Wilfred had been sitting across two chairs, for all appearing to grapple with a hefty text on electronics but no doubt thinking instead about his afternoon walk to the Akrotiri lighthouse. The ensuing conversation would not allow him to wander far from either science or the sea before he consented to adding his name to the list.

'Great. We've got our hooker and loose-head prop. That's it. The team's made.'

'What about reserves?' asked Christopher, needing to say something.

'Oh yes,' admitted Colin, acknowledging a sound academic point. 'Reserves, hmm…'

And he walked away, happy (he was always happy, and becoming happier was not dismissed as a warning) and Christopher and Wilfred were left to worry about what they had done.

'What have we done?'

This forlorn, shared but rhetorical question allowed Savina to offer her futile attempt at cheering them up by calling them both stupid.

The next day Louding called him a fool.

'You fool. What have you done?'

'But you're playing as well, aren't you?'

Christopher's need for consolation was not assuaged by irony.

'That is true. I'm also a fool, but remember, I'm playing for the side that will win.'

'Yes, the school'll run all over us.'

'Running is what you've got to do if you're ever unlucky enough to find the ball in your hands. Just run. That's what I always do.'

Louding had a compulsory role. The school team needed him on the wing, and by a mixture of what he was willing to concede with Christopher as bad luck and speed, he had established himself with the unfortunate reputation for being the school's top try-scorer. He had to play. Not that he didn't like to play. Louding carefully enjoyed most of what he did which included being with Christopher and consolidating his need to worry about what he was going to do.

'But you can run, and stuck out on the wing you've got all that open space.' Christopher picked up a pebble and rolled it around his fingers. 'Actually I felt quite chuffed at first. Colin Kamp asking me and all that. He even pleaded with me, I think. I continued to feel quite chuffed about it right up until Perry Stenfield looked at the list and laughed loudly after reading my name. "Panhandle?" he shouted. "Not *the* Panhandle!" he announced to the whole bloody room. I mean, I know the Youth Klub's desperate, but he didn't have to emphasize it.'

'He's not so hot. You'll get your revenge, maybe.'

Such assurance, resting as it did then on the remote, was routine. It was usually followed by a change of tact, this time prompted by further company. Louding was not overjoyed at seeing Marion and knowing that she had seen him, not that he and Christopher were anything other than clearly visible. She was strolling across the yard towards them, and the timing gave the encounter the guise of a planned occasion. Christopher should have been at Physics and Louding at French, but both had finished early. This happy coincidence, seasoned as it was by worry, was not to be compromised. So why was she out now? Too young for the prefects' room but old enough to enjoy more schoolyard freedom than Louding certainly would have granted. Approaching thus, her saunter matched the gradual blush behind her thick, dark hair, long enough for her to hide the grins and grimaces generated by the love and hate she had for Louding and the many of her peers who fancied him. The two lads were sitting on the three-foot high wall which partially circled the main ground, and supported the embankment of a pebbled path and straggling Cypriot grass leading up to the isolated block containing the prefects' room. For the short duration of her company the three of them appeared to have the school to themselves, but for the occasional and faint scream betraying evidence of life on a higher, more motivated level than that perhaps portrayed by this listless pre-break part of the late morning.

'Hi,' she said, choosing to sit beside Christopher as a mark of coyness that all three regarded as fake. She detected Louding's scowl and received a pebble gently flicked from his double-jointed thumb. 'Shut up.'

'Bit early for break, isn't it?' asked Louding, looking at his multi-tasking watch. It gave him the time in Hong Kong and L.A. and was occasionally inclined to give the date in Chinese. They were no longer in the shade and he thought about moving but changed his mind as Marion, ignoring his question and the fact that they too were early, addressed Christopher.

'Where's your better half today then?'
'Good grief, you can't think much of me.'
Marion tried to suppress a snigger but failed.
'Do you not like her anymore?'
'She has her moments.'
'So when're you gonna chuck her?'
'She's not here today because she had to get her knee seen to.'
'Come on, Christopher, when're you gonna chuck her?'
'She's your friend. Why you asking me about that?'
'I'm interested because she's my friend.'
'No, it was a dumb question,' said Louding.

'Shut up. He was about to answer then.' She reached across Christopher to pinch Louding's arm, a habitual gesture of endearment and defiance, but this time she missed and lost her balance and position on the wall. She stood up straight and challenged them with a time-table fact they both wanted to postpone. 'You've got games soon, haven't you? You playing rugby, Simon?'

Other than his family, Marion was unique in her persistent ability to call Louding by his first name, and thus basked in the comforting belief that this alone established ownership over and above his following. The mystery of him allowing her to do so was never discussed.

'This afternoon we're playing rugby. '
'You mean a proper match? Who against?'
'Youth Klub.'
'What youth club?'
'Does it matter?' said Christopher, knowing forlornly that yes it really did.
'If it's the Island Disco Club I wanna see it. I wanna see it anyway. Can I come and watch?'
'We're playing in Akrotiri,' said Louding, hoping that this would answer all points.
'What's Island Disco Club doing in Akrotiri?'
'We're not playing the Island Disco Club.'
'What? You mean the Akrotiri Youth Klub? You're playing the Akrotiri Youth Klub? You'll get slaughtered. Can I watch?'

This delight in the prospect of seeing Louding getting slaughtered was a bonus.

'What makes you think we'll get slaughtered?'
'Most of the school's top players come from Akrotiri.'

Louding smiled at the potential confusion drawn forth from what truth lay in her haphazard perception. The fact that most of the school came from

Akrotiri added considerable weight to the evidence of what Marion said, but she failed to reckon on the fact that all of the top players *for* the school came from the school. He reminded her of this.

'Marion, most of the school's top players are playing for the school.'

'Oh yes, of course. Well, in that case, who's playing for the Akrotiri Youth Klub?'

'Well, er...' began Christopher. 'I am for a start.'

'You!' Marion's shocked stare gave him visions of her also accusing him of being the Panhandle. 'You're playing rugby for Akrotiri Youth Klub?'

'In Akrotiri Y.K. 1st, no less,' explained Louding.

'I don't believe it.' She returned to her seat on the wall beside Christopher and repeated the unbelievable. 'Christopher's playing against the school for Akrotiri Youth Klub.'

'What's so strange about that?'

Christopher discovered that his doubts on the subject were in actual fact inversely proportional to the strength of her exclaimed disbelief. She was looking at him as if daring him to confess to the joke he was sharing with Louding at her expense.

'Does Helen know about this?'

'I didn't even know about it until yesterday, and, as I said, she's away having her knee seen to.'

'You really are playing. Simon, he really is playing. Gosh, I've got to see this game.' She thought through the immediate geographical problem. 'Akrotiri, rats! I know, your parents can give me a lift, Simon.'

'My parents won't be coming. There's no need. I'll be going by the school's sports bus.'

This also, for some reason, assured his return to Berengaria, just north of Limassol, where he lived. Marion also lived there but that did not ease the situation.

'But what about me?'

'I don't know about you but I'm getting out of this sun. Christopher, you coming?'

Christopher forgave Marion's whimsical but mutual lack of confidence in his rugby-based fate by offering her a smile tinged with sympathy. He was mildly perplexed by Louding's dismissive attitude towards this relatively pretty girl whom was claimed by Helen, his girlfriend, as a best friend. He knew that Louding had the glorious, if often under-acknowledged, luxury of choice, and as he chose Christopher's company above the majority of circles, groups and routes his role as a favourite admiree could have travelled, Christopher was in no position to ardently question any scorn Louding casually presented others. He also knew that Marion would never give up. He knew that Louding knew this too and was willing to believe in the underlying pleasure Louding gleaned from her otherwise naïve tenacity.

The prefects' room suddenly burst into song. Someone had managed to screw together and wire-up a hitherto faulty Gerard record deck, but the choice of music was less than inspiring. 'I'd like to teach the World to Sing' was accompanied by those inside who first needed to be taught. The three walked in the opposite direction and took refuge in a secluded alley-way that ran between the main Admin Block and the Art Department billets. At this point the bells rang and woke up the entire school. Two thousand tweenies and teenagers were resurrected from the gloom of lessons into the sun-baked morning, and thus stormed forth into the compact skirmish offered by the qualified freedom of the main grounds.

'Timing, hey?' said Louding. 'We escaped the stampede.'

And he guided his two followers through the open metal and concrete hallway which, restricted from the clattering minions, possessed a public glory of its own, compared to elsewhere in the school, because of carefully framed and precisely hung, printed masters. For the pleasure of that minority willing to support an appreciative study of art's history, this area was deemed out of bounds during break to all but teachers and sixth formers: an oasis of silence walled in by the chaos of youth, with prefects employed to patrol and deter.

'Shall we share someone's prefect's duty?' suggested Louding as he stared through the stained windows into the studios, fascinated by the creatively disposed mess within.

'Why aren't you two prefects?' asked Marion.

'Ah well, we're the privileged few. We escaped the drudgery of enforcing law while, being upper sixth, gaining all the perks.'

'I don't think we were thought to be responsible enough,' explained Christopher with an honesty in line with his present mood.

'Gosh, how did you manage that?' asked Marion, knowing as she did many prefects, including Helen, whose response to their own ability she would mark as zero. She was now months away from joining the lower sixth whose only freedom differed from that of the fifth if designated with prefecthood, but she had had enough of authority to relish the dubious pleasure of instilling it. 'I think it's because you don't look tough enough.'

'Not ugly enough,' amended Louding.

'Not grim enough,' added Christopher.

'Yes, we lack that *je ne sais quoi* of direct attitude.'

'Direct attitude? Do you mean being open to people. You can be open to me if you like.' Marion offered this as a safe bet to Louding's usual rebuff, but nevertheless included one of her behind the curtain of hair smiles. 'I'll try not to mind.'

'All right then. Sod off.'

'What?' However, she was quite capable of believing in the reverse intimacy that, on any other scale, Louding would refuse to realize. 'I didn't mean that kind of openness. Be kind.'

'Marion,' said Christopher with a placid extension of Louding's curt demand, 'prefects aren't kind to anyone but other prefects and chosen members of the upper sixth, like us. We'll prove it. What better example than Gavin, and here he is.'

'Gosh, so it is.'

So it was. Direct from the comfort zone of the Post-Impressionists and lingering beside Manet's depiction of *Monet and his Wife in his Floating Studio*, and ready to give to each Goya, Blake and Delacroix ascending to where Louding, Christopher and Marion stood, a glancing, welcoming nod of more than the average three seconds bestowed on most paintings: Gavin Peters, the sixth formers sixth former, tall, thin, sophisticated in an awkward stance of constantly delving through what the historically embellished names wanted to have understood, slightly gawky and impenetrably gay.

'Is he really the head-boy?' asked Marion, not without concern.

Everybody knew that Gavin Peters was the head-boy but many asked the same question. He was part of that line formed by the outside world meeting the institution. He was supposedly looked upon as the complete student, but the aforementioned qualities of prefecthood – ugliness, grimness and directness of attitude – were as inconsistent in him as ice-cubes in a bowl of Scots Broth. And so it was to these three, standing as if ready for the discarded privilege of the glancing review, that he said, timorously:

'Oh, hi. Didn't notice you.'

'Lost to the world again?' asked Christopher.

'To be living in those times,' he replied, engrossed in the tangential romance of this display of many centuries worth of the visual arts.

'Why? Was there more chance of success in those days?'

'Yes,' said Louding. 'I can imagine having to write an essay on Peters thoughts about existence.'

'Doubt it,' said Gavin. 'I'm no philosopher. All I want is to become more than a mere critic.'

'And it the meantime you get A's for all your critical essays.'

But Gavin was as reluctant a candidate to 'A' level English as Savina was enthusiastic about maths and physics. He longed to compare notes with the great writers, add his weight to the eternal method of seeking truth through the written word and avoid this cause of analyzing style, diction and all the other stabs examiners made of quality books, poetry and plays. However, in order to strive later he conformed now and gained something of a dubious shade in being heralded a future Leavis instead of this century's answer to Henry James. "'A' level English is murdering English literature,' he proclaimed in despair, and he, like Brutus, was plunging in the final knife. Only hope: dive into the sea of art with the hope of pulling forth the worthy oysters. Christopher supplied the necessary grit.

'Art isn't that important.'

'It's vital. It's the only way to find out the real truth.'

'No great difficulty there. Hell is intense and pleasure is immense. That's truth.'

'It stands beyond suffering and pleasure. Truth depends on art to uncover it. It stands alone. It is a solitary station.'

But Christopher believed in God and all this meant including the monumental confusion of being everywhere at once. This did not necessarily match his notion of Jesus as standing alone. Meanwhile Marion was standing alone. She imagined Gavin suddenly noticing her there and informing her in his esoteric confirmation of imposed verbs to be off with herself. Did she not know that here, where the masters hung in their pictorial capacity of transforming colour into reason, only the reasonable few were allowed to roam? This meant being of the age of reason, i.e. sixth form and above, when reason usually became the victim of being kicked out of the same door through which all previous values were so suddenly placed beneath contempt. But this aloof time would have caught up with her sooner than any commands from Gavin as he passed her by to guide Christopher and Louding to the 20th Century: Picasso, Munch, Duchamp and Klee.

Louding, always amused by the many failures now breathing the open air of success, thought that much was not unlike his own efforts.

'I painted that,' he claimed. 'Last year, or was it two years ago.'

'Did you really?' said Marion, thinking it nowhere near as neat as the gothic calligraphy which, as memory favourably recalled, brought them together – almost a year ago now. 'Then why does it have printed underneath: "A Tiny Tale of a Tiny Dwarf" by Paul Klee?'

'Yes, he was a bit of a dwarf. Many think it looks nothing like him. I was a good friend of his, so he was willing to sit for me.'

'Who is he?' and doubting the wisdom now of such a question she went on: 'I wouldn't sit for you if that's how you'd draw me.'

'No, that's how I drew Paul Klee. I was too good for them,' and Louding sighed whimsically before walking on to where Christopher and Gavin were once again indulging the long argument on esthetics. 'I lost interest,' he added.

'Art is nothing but the decoration on museum wall,' said Christopher, 'And those who want to be in the "know" start going on about the way one line inclines towards another.'

'This inclination has more essence of quality than anything you could care to say against it.'

'What good will it do? There's more truth in a pan of frying eggs.'

Gavin wanted to be distinct about his answer, but was drawn to some vague lines used in criticism of modern music: '…is a truck in a music school?..' but the line of thought was blown aside by a stiff breeze in time: time for games.

Marion sensed the danger of impending separation, and with it the addition of friends from each corner, friends she could do without, and she caught hold of Louding's arm and pulled him away from the other two.

'Simon, take me with you to Akrotiri. I want to see the match.'

'Go with a friend on a school bus to Akrotiri. Go with Christopher's sister.'

'You mean Julie? She's not my friend.'

'Marion,' Louding began, almost softly and then reverted to type: 'you'll think of something. Other than that,' he shrugged: 'tough.'

He walked to where Gavin and Christopher stood waiting, only fifty yards from the entrance to the changing rooms. Marion wrenched herself free from the tangled toughness of how tough the word 'tough' was coming from someone as untough as Louding, and she ran after him.

'How can you be so rotten, you rat?' she cried.

'I'm not rotten. Only prefects are rotten. We discussed that earlier.'

'I'm not rotten,' said Gavin, taken aback. Then he looked at his watch.

'I want to go and see this rugby match and he won't let me go.'

'Not up to me,' said Louding. 'As I said, I'm sure you'll think of something.'

'What rugby match?' asked Gavin with total uncharacteristic indifference. Being head-boy he was morally obliged to play rugby for the school, and alongside such loyalty was contained the confidence displayed in his next statement: 'If you mean this inane match against Akrotiri Youth Klub, the result is an afore-drawn conclusion. The school couldn't lose if it played a three-legged game.'

The school lost. Many limped away as if from a one-legged game. The collision of the levelled youthful pride imploded into an all-out bout which partially crippled and bruised all but the referee, Reverent Galbraith, Anglican Vicar of Akrotiri. Christopher was both surprised by the result and his own performance. He had played a 'not bad' game. Not that I enjoyed it, he said earnestly to himself, remaining loyal to that which offered relief alongside closure. I'm still in one piece. My limbs, badly shaken, are still intact. I can still feel the end of my fingers, and my nose is still the same shape it was before I started. I did not enjoy the game. I did not enjoy it, he insisted. I refuse to believe that people play rugby because they enjoy it. Hard enough believing anyone understands the numerous off-side rules, created to compose more of a mystique than a method of harnessing any chance of real safety. Safety in number kept me from being crushed in the scrum.

School of thought suggests that rugby was a good game. University of thought implies the opposite. When 30 men run onto a pitch and provide organized battle for an oval ball the definition of good becomes universal. Christopher had been one of a recent band of 30 men and his team won. He now limped home with this new and not undisturbing experience of having been part of a team of winners. Had he lost, the limp might not have been there, neither the exclusive madness of agreeing to play another game for the same team on Sunday this time against a team belonging to one of the RAF squadrons. Akrotiri Youth Klub 1st was there to be reckoned with and, reflecting on where this could lead, he now wanted out. But I can't resign and leave them hookerless.

That was how he had touched the ball, by supposedly hooking it beneath his half of each scrum while the other simultaneously tried to barge its way over him. Wilfred's combined mass and strength tended to make each scrum rotate so when the resulting knot of writhing limbs released itself with the strength of fumbling forwards, many momentarily forgot which side of the pitch they were defending. For Christopher, the entire game consisted of constantly running after a ball he couldn't see. He could well have lost faith in its existence if not for the frozen aspect of something being guided by his feet a millisecond before the crunch, and as for actually holding it in his arms for longer than it took to get rid of it, he could sooner see himself scaling the conversion post. One and a half hours of wondering whether he was part of the game or just one of the million shadows fluttering gracefully out of the way except when needed, and in the meantime two tries were scored, both by the Klub, and Steve Galbraith, the vicar's son, who could have played for the school had he not been more devoted to soccer, converted both, almost sending one kick into an elliptical path towards the busy Friday afternoon Naafi. If this game ends with me being able to go to school on Monday, thought Christopher, as he staggered up from underneath one particularly messy scrum-down and attempted to follow in the floundering footsteps of those who, like him, were lost, I shall spend the weekend praising the Lord.

The game did end. One of the more pleasing promises in life is the eventual termination of each ordeal, and this was no exception, and as he shook and clapped hands along with the many shaking and clapping hands, and was heralded in with the heroes for a reception at the Flamingo Bar, he thought, not without begrudging some sense of being betrayed, how it now fell upon him to praise the Lord. He should have been on his knees, kissing the already abused grass and shouting: 'I'm alive! I'm still alive! Thank you Lord, thank you.' But he was also one of the victors in a dream-like carousel of having put the school in its well-determined place, and as emphasized by Julie and the girls, the gleaming white pints of milk, and the Akrotiri Y.K. 1st spontaneously composed chants, gratitude for the score was over and above any well-being of having survived.

'It does help to have some of our crack players nicked for your team,' said Gavin.

'What do you mean?' said Christopher, having joined him and Louding to console them on what must have been their shock of the season. 'You've got Stenfield and Innmaker, and even Louding here.'

'Yes, I enjoyed the game,' admitted Louding, who loved to run around the perimeter of the pitch with nothing to do rather than be expected to score tries after the ball cleared the often overwhelming prospects of being battered from the line. 'You played well, *mon ami.*'

'I can't remember playing at all. I just dived in there and somehow came out alive.'

Louding was suddenly distracted by the fact that he himself was a distraction – the sympathy and glee pouring in from a selection of his Akrotiri fans who had only just discovered the presence of their Berengarian hero. Christopher strayed away from this attention and shared in the mumbles of a much exhausted Wilfred George. They sat in the corner and watched Julie and her friends being entertained by the Youth Klub hierarchy. Anyone would think *they* had been the stars of the game: Julie's attention prompting rowdy adulations and victory cries from the local patch of well-in lads, including a few from the school's team: Nancy, silent and lovely, smiles and temptations being somewhat foiled by her puzzled response to their rugby-based jokes: Pat, laughing and talkative, exchanging raised brows with Christopher the few times their eyes met across the café.

As the buses pulled up to take the defeated and the deflated back to Berengaria, Limassol and Episkopi, the forlorn fans waved promises and sighs at the idols of any sixth form battle, which these said lads from alien parts gathered in a defeated heap of hanging shirts and duffle bags, ready to leave. So was Christopher who walked home with Colin, their houses being separated by a negligible piece of green adorned by a sap-sodden pine, while Wilfred, living elsewhere on the camp, wandered off in a different direction. Colin had received enough battering bruises to balance out the need to walk with a limp, but their stroll home together was careful. In the distance, closer to the angled plan of bungalows which included the abode of the Panhandle and the Kamps, Peter and Leonard, the younger brothers of Christopher and Colin respectively, were strolling back from an afternoon's bout of sea-fishing. The walk to and from the cliffs alone in the reliable Cypriot heat made them look as if they had gone through an equally trying ordeal.

'Who won then?' asked Leonard.

'Who else?' said Colin as if such a question had to be asked.

'Amazing,' said Peter, assuming Colin's counter question to have been the good news of a school defeat. He looked at Leonard. 'You owe me 50 piastres.'

They suddenly gained the energy bequeathed to such youth, despite the encumbrance of their fishing gear, and ran on ahead of the two, now established, fellow rugby players.

'Why didn't you stay at the Flamingo Bar?' Christopher asked Colin, both aware that Colin's other and older brother Oliver was still there attending to his share of female praise.

'Well, I'm working at the Families Club tonight and I'm starving. So, you'll be all right for Sunday?'

'56th Squadron,' said Christopher, suppressing a grunt of painful thought. 'Are we crazy?'

'We were crazy to challenge the school, but we won,' said Colin, confident that nothing could demonstrate better sanity than a game of rugby well played.

'Will we get crushed on Sunday?'

'Look, it's not as if we're playing the Colts or the Rock-Apes.'

'Well, you know, see what Saturday brings.'

'We need you as hooker. You did all right. Just get more into moving and you'll be fine.'

Which means, thought Christopher, I wasn't fine but I did as well, maybe better, than I had been expected to do.

Inside his bedroom, Christopher had to struggle to remove his boots. The easy swish of the overhead fan allowed him to sink back to the RAF upholstery, and on the dining table was a letter. His dad had arrived back early with the post, and his mum was preparing something in the kitchen which smelt good. Family comforts to Christopher were probably worth the ordeal of trench warfare. An armchair, much needed coffee, promised meals. Also the letter…

Larry Parthy had called around. 'He wants you to sit tonight,' was the message from the kitchen.

'Okay. Nothing happening tonight, I don't think.'

'And there's a letter for you.'

'So I see. Business letter from…' He held it up to the light still piercing the shutters. 'It's from Sheffield. Hey, it's the Polytechnic.' He ripped it open swiftly and read the brief, letter-headed contents:

> Dear Mr Panhandle,
> You will be pleased to hear that your educational reference has arrived from your headmaster.
> From his reference I see that you are to take A level examinations in Physics and Pure and Applied Mathematics combined. In order to satisfy the entry requirements, you need a pass in A level Physics and at least an O level pass from A level mathematics. I am pleased to offer you a provisional acceptance for a place on our H.N.D. course in Applied Physics commencing September 1972. Will you please let me know the results of your A level examinations as soon as they are available.
> Yours sincerely,
> E.M. Sissons.

It was interesting and not unpleasing to note that an 'F' had been partially erased over which the 'Ph' of 'Physics' was typed.

Peter wandered through and asked him what the game had been like.

'Tough…' he murmured and he fell asleep.

'It was about the craziest night yet,' said Larry Parthy as he poured out three glasses of brandy, topping each with generous portions of Canada Dry. 'When you go out with a large party I suppose you've got to put up with very trivial things, but very annoying. Oh yes, and big spending, small thinking and lots of noise.'

'I have to say I quite like the noise,' said Lorraine.

She was pretty enough to enhance any noisy, even threatening attempts at having fun. Christopher was never sure about noise, particularly of the sort Larry thought was the price one paid, but because she liked it he was now able to remember enjoyably noisy parties. What he particularly enjoyed was looking at her legs, and because his mother thought that her dresses were too short, he was ready with discreet notion of when not to stare to test the spirit of her judgment. He did not really want to think of such attire as not being short enough. After all, he was drinking their brandy in preparation for looking after their kids. Also short skirts and dresses revealing tanned and shapely legs were hardly within the general context a stare-at-now-or-never phenomenon befitting only those starved of such wonders. Within the British RAF enclave of southern Cyprus a fashionable majority of such alluring shapes was all but taken for granted and in line with the particulars of grace accorded to the heat. The exception Christopher secretly made of Lorraine had in its reasoning the age difference between them. She was cool and mature and seven years his senior and so he courted a fantasy barely akin to *The Summer Of '42* which he had seen a few weeks ago.

'We did spend a lot of money,' she admitted, 'mainly on taxi fares. We couldn't really bring the car. All that drinking and, do you know, one woman swallowed a bottle of perfume. She was so drunk she thought it was her drink. She said afterwards she thought it tasted a bit odd.'

'You shouldn't be telling him such things,' said Larry. 'He thinks we keep strange enough company as it is.'

'Didn't it poison her?' Christopher asked, believing every word.

'Well, hard to tell. I don't think so,' Lorraine replied carefully.

She stood up. He stood up. All three stood up. Larry stretched, his notional potbelly receding, and he flicked his fingers a couple of times and grabbed his cigarettes.

'You're getting disgustingly fat, Larry.'

Christopher enjoyed thinking that Lorraine, indulging such personal remarks in his company, did so out of the natural familiarity his presence imbued and also giving notice to her husband that unless the slight physique of their baby-sitter was something he could aspire towards matching then she had a right to look favourably elsewhere. The fantasy progressed.

'I could get rid of this after a three day work-out,' said Larry, another fantasy, as if ability alone was enough to solve the problem. Because he was questionably capable of working off a bit of flesh, he felt he had no need to do so. Theirs being a marriage of intent over outcome, despite the latter awarding them three children, this sort of sense was part of the bond Lorraine enjoyed with Larry, and Christopher begrudgingly regarded them both as the fulfilled couple.

After offering him more brandy they left. They left him enough cigarettes and drink for him to have his own party, but he wasn't inclined at present to learn how to smoke, and he was still of an age when alcohol maintained some of its mystery. There was never much food, no television and little reading material, apart from a cupboard shelf packed with imported copies of *The Sun*. There were three kids who kept him employed. They were always asleep before their parents left, but he could not remember a peaceful night. They woke up regularly – little Alan more than the other two. This minute hunk of cantankerous boyhood usually went through a ritual of calling for Larry and when such was determinatively ignored, there emerged a chronic plea for Lorraine. Christopher, on advice, sat through the lamenting until eventually Alan was compelled to climb out of his cot and enter the sitting room to find out why. This time his slightly older brother George joined him.

'You're not here again, are you?' he said scornfully, leading his brother by the hand and into the kitchen.

'You'll have a hard time finding any goodies,' said Christopher. 'I've already had a good search.'

'My mummy said that you're not allowed to come here anymore,' stated George.

'Yes,' said Alan, and both of them walked back into the sitting room and up to where Christopher sat.

'Are you two going to bed?'

'Don't have to,' said George. 'What are you doing?'

'Mathematics,' which was true and which was why he wasn't too displeased with the interruption. 'You can stay up if you like and if you're good I'll tell you a story.'

So they stayed up for a while, and they tried very hard to remain good and so Christopher assumed that they wanted to hear a story. He didn't actually have one at hand and so he looked around for inspiration. It was a blowy night and the shutters rumbled. The room echoed to an isolation which could so easily have undermined the fickle companionship of brandy and *Tranter* and now these two. Christopher started talking about the wind.

'What do you think the wind is?' he asked.

George took time to think.

'A wolf,' said Alan, 'and he is trying to go in to all the things.'

'Yes, is that right?' asked Christopher of George. 'I don't think I'd be much protection against a wolf.'

'Does the wind think of things?' asked George.

'Maybe. Shall we ask it?'

'Yes. Ask it for lots of sweets.'

'Ask it lots of pooh,' followed Alan with a giggle.

'Don't think it supplies either sweets or pooh. It supplies the cold though, and from the cold you have to get into bed to keep warm, don't you?'

'No,' said George, both defiant and puzzled.

'It can sing songs as well. It can sing about the frost in winter and the sun in summer. Can you sing with the wind?'

No answer. The question stumped them and for a moment all that could be heard was the wind. It was not without good reason that Alan began to want his father again. Christopher drew them a picture of the wind, first as a being doing a lot of blowing about, and then as a means of transporting a dead leaf from its tree to a point on the ground quite far away. He inserted the mathematical equations abided by a falling object undergoing the projectile's route to its point of rest, and George coloured in a few of the necessary clouds, while Alan added to the tree what looked like a couple of Lowry shaped men.

'I want to colour,' he demanded. He took up a few of the crayons but changed his mind and threw them across the room. 'I don't want to colour,' he said.

'No, George is going to take you back to bed, aren't you George?'

Oddly enough this is precisely what George did. The two of them actually went back to bed. Christopher began to doubt the magnetism of his company. Must have been the maths, he thought, and on this note he too had an early night, the guest room being on offer as part of the babysitting deal.

He dreamt of his sister, Angela, arriving in Cyprus, and Julie packing her bags to leave for England. This fare swap got no further than farewells and greetings because Alan's coughing woke him up. It seemed quite late. The Parthys must have returned by now. He fell back asleep. The room transformed itself into Louding's own at Berengaria. Within it the two of them sat. They talked and the usual quantity of Helen's presence materialized like words providing obscure plans for the future. Their conversation held less interest for her than the controls of her cassette tape-recorder, fizzing and popping beneath her fingers. An ex of Louding's, Grace Ford entered. This unexpected addition forming the foursome silenced the lads. Grace wanted Louding to stay and the other two had to leave and Helen grabbed at this chance to gain some time with Christopher alone. She led him by the hand and they entered a room which transformed itself into Christopher's own. Before leaving Louding he had noticed a knife clasped firmly in Grace's hand behind her back. He reckoned that if he was to see Louding again he should not have deserted him. All the same, he deserted him. The resulting frustration and anger had him turn against

Helen, and he ordered her out of this second room and told her never to return. This could well have been an agreeable time to wake up. The dream slipped from view, and he was travelling.

An underground system morphed his previous confusion to that of being lost. Rebecca was with him. She was also lost but they were not too worried about their plight. Only when they arrived at a junction of two caves was theirs a cause for concern. The hollow sound of Peter's voice beckoned them on, but it came with equal volume for each of the openings. He existed in both, and if the drone of his voice was anything to go by, there could well have been more. But there can only be one. It was unthinkable that there should be more than one Peter Panhandle. Unthinkable too that the two of them should separate, each to a different cave, but they did. Christopher followed a widening path to his bedroom. He remembered having ordered Helen to leave from that very place and he expected more than her absence to complete the picture. The voice of his brother continued to beckon and was very apparent now, but there was still Rebecca to think about. His correct choice was assumed from the familiar surroundings, but Peter's voice was not offering reassurance. It had grown no more in volume. Certainly no less, but was an indication of anxiety on his sister's part, still lost. It concerned him more to think of Rebecca alone and afraid than any danger she invariably faced. He sat on his bed to think over this problem and he was more than just a little surprised to find it occupied. Helen, of course, after all he could not remember her actually having left. He pulled back the cover and the woman he glanced at for a second turned out to be a man. This trick of the light all but subdued Peter's voice, and all other preoccupying mysteries were instantly wiped clean. One thing was for certain: he had no wish to stay around. The man did not look friendly. The fact that he was there, posing as Helen, added to the notion of evil, but he moved first, more startled than Christopher, and out of the room he ran. Coupled with this fright was the first indication of a solution which might have been more apparent had Helen been around. She had actually obeyed his request, his order and now he wanted her back, but more so his sisters. However, it was Julie who appeared. She was holding an LP cover full of pictures. It was her latest acquisition and if he wanted to listen to it, which he did, he should follow her. The pictures on the cover showed similar rooms through which they walked until they eventually reached the living rooms where the entire family of Panhandles, minus Angela, sat and ate. Peter was surrounded by technical drawing exercises. Plans and elevations were as second nature to him as a beautifully exploited cast from a first class rod and reel. Christopher plied him with questions. The test was complicated without logic. Assisting the challenge and decorating the walls, the solutions were revealed. To forestall further confusion, Christopher now knew that it was time to wake up.

Helen missed *Popaganda* for the first time in months. She was very unhappy because Duff Dill must have played her request. She was his special girl. Forces Radio had many special girls and she was one of them. Christopher was not expected to understand, and he didn't, but he could see that she was unhappy and to cheer her up he organized a picnic – just the two of them at the cliffs, with the sea and the sun and she had her camera so what more could she want? She had wanted him to listen to her request. She had told him before that there would be one.

'Well, what can I do? It's too late now. I was at the Parthy's this morning. I forgot it was on.'

'And my radio's not working.' He thought about his dream but her excuse was also one of omission – she had forgotten to renew the batteries. 'And it was such a good song. You would have liked it.'

'I see. What was it?' The 'would have liked it' part of her generous spirit also acted as a qualification which usually underlined their stark differences in taste. 'Are you sure it was the batteries?'

'I don't know. It usually works quite well on the bus, but it just started going wonky and it hasn't recovered.'

Christopher turned the hand-held radio on. He gave it a shake and then turned it off. That was the extent of his technical application to most objects carrying the promised utilities of audible or visible sensations which failed to be kept. The only noise this radio offered was the click of its dial. He placed it carefully by the sandwiches as if still informing the nation of Helen's love. Good to have a picnic now, he thought. At the cliffs, alone with her, only one Saturday a week, he thought, and he carried the two bags they needed. This gave her the time and space to skip ahead, talk with the vigilance of one wanting to voice every moment constantly, giggle at the remarks her friends made during the week, and then the full story of her knee and the doctor and the towelling bandage wrapped around it. They were soon well away from the married quarters and keeping to the narrow paths scoring through the long area of coarse and sharp vegetation – close to what Christopher's friend from last year, Henry, would have called 'thick bondoo' as opposed to 'brainy bondoo' (the noun itself he presumed to have being borrowed by the Brits from the Cypriot for grass). As it more intelligently thinned out Helen was able to walk faster still, the land applying with less intensity the obstacle to her skipping yards between her change of attitude to one of joy and his growing concern about tomorrow's game. Repeatedly she turned and stopped as if ready to shoot him down, and repeatedly she called for him to hurry up.

'We've all afternoon, Helen.' This thought consoled him. There were many many hours yet before kick-off. 'The sun is out, the breeze is fresh, the sea can wait.'

'I didn't bring my swimming stuff. I should have brought my swimming stuff. You should have told me we'd be going for a picnic and I'd have brought my swimming stuff.'

'I only just thought about it this morning. Too late then. You were on the bus.'

'You didn't think about *Popaganda*, and I told you I'd put a lovely record request on for you. He always plays my request because I'm Duff Dill's favourite girl.'

Christopher knew that Helen wanted him to retort that she was *his* favourite girl, but he was not ready yet to compete with Duff Dill. Instead he made the effort to catch up and she was tempted to remark on his funny looking legs. They were so white. Yesterday's rugby gave them their first real exposure to this year's sun, but she changed her mind and said how pleased she was to hear that he had played.

'More than I was pleased to play.'

'I like to think of you being sporty like the other lads. My friends are always wondering what you do and what can I say?'

Christopher had long since given up wondering who these friends were that Helen often referred to as hers in the context of sympathetic subjects surrounding music and boys. They did not seem to consist of girls he knew, such as Marion.

'You discuss me a lot, do you, with your friends?'

'Oh yes, Christopher, all the time. We talk about everything and of course I have to talk about you, but I only say good things, and how you remind me of a cuddly elephant.'

'Helen, how the hell can I remind you of a cuddly elephant? I look nothing like an elephant. I'm not large or anything. I've got more in common with mice, especially when it comes to playing games like rugby.'

'But you're my brave elephant. You should have told me about the rugby and I'd have come and watched.'

'But you weren't even at school. I wish I hadn't been either.'

'Yes, of course, I forgot. I went to the doctor about me knee. Silly me and silly knee. I always forget, not like an elephant who always remembers.'

'That counts me out then because I forgot to listen to your request.'

'You didn't really want to. Sometimes you're not nice at all. Not nice like my doctor who was very nice indeed. I'm sure he liked my knee very much. He kept stroking it.'

'Yeah, sure. Didn't prevent him covering it with a bandage.'

'That was to keep your hands off because it's not well. I've got water on it or something, so there. You like my knee, don't you? More than you like me.'

'Yes, you have nice legs, but I'm not too keen on those shorts you're wearing. I don't know why you go for such bright colours.'

'Because it's a bright day, silly. Bright days are for bright colours, and the other way round.'

She skipped off again. He looked around and was pleased. The houses were no longer in sight. They had walked further than he thought and the cliffs leading down to the sea were only a few more mounds of 'brainy bondoo' away. She would spot a good place for them to eat. The soothing sea breeze, the scent of various stray herbs, sanity at last and a couple of plastic bags of cold food – a singular Saturday. Plural Saturdays he knew as well. They resembled preparations for swimming.

She had her camera around her neck, having placed it there this morning and remained conscious of it ever since. She faced him this time from her ten-yard skip and shot him in his characteristic pose of impending boredom. Helen had a fancy for his serious face, enjoying the contrast with her own capricious nature. It presented no difficulty in allowing her to talk. Often it was very convenient, remaining quiet, and at the moment, although it seemed as if he was bored, he was ready to appreciate the whimsical quality of her company dancing around him. He had often passively contemplated the probable event of having to 'chuck' her, giving her what Louding coined 'the bronze kiss', but its smack could wait. Tolerance and timing evened out the stride, paced the distance between them. It was her birthday next Friday. He realized that if he finished with her then it would seem as if he was escaping simple obligations, and the move would be fraught with frivolous misconceptions. Mind you, he had been generous enough in his own fashion. I'm an adequate boyfriend, he thought. I can wait. After all, we only meet once a week.

Helen lived almost twenty miles away in Limassol, and for reasons more complex than the identity of these friends, school did not seem to count. She was a prefect but she seldom made use of the prefects' room. He was not a prefect but now, being in Upper Sixth he was there nearly all the time, outside classroom hours. For her, there were too many people to meet at school to make any single encounter shape up as a worthy break-time distraction.

She's oddly plain in a pretty sort of way, he thought, and she does have nice legs. She leant with them at a slightly provocative angle against a signpost which read: GRAZING BEYOND THIS POINT PROHIBITED.

'That's funny,' she said, reading the sign more than once. 'Will they say that we're not allowed to have a picnic?'

'I doubt it. With or without rules I hope we don't come across any "they". Listen, you stand there, right where you are, and I'll take a picture of you and the sign.'

'Oh good, yes of course, good idea. Me and the sign: *gazing* beyond this point prohibited.'

What point? he thought as he aimed the camera – those legs and where they lead? I wonder if it's frilly knickers beneath those terrible shorts.

It was not part of any semi-erotic plan to find out. Helen could be assured of his youthful innocence as the completion and maintenance of her virginal whimsy. They would kiss and he would stroke her unbandaged knee, and perhaps lay a hand on an outside thigh. Further than that did not match the contract between them as a going-out concern within their part of the RAF Cyprus culture.

He dropped the food, taking the camera and walking away from her. This was becoming quite a good arrangement. From fifteen yards or so her features added grace to the glaring fauvian colours which adorned her. Ach, she isn't a bad looking lass, he thought, from the correct angle. So he shot her against the grazing prohibited sign and ran off over the horizon of thorns which marked the beginning of the rocks blending into the sculpture of the descending cliffs. She called after him. Who was going to carry to food the rest of the way? But he didn't hear her. The noise of both the wind from the cliffs and the waves of the sea, far away the enthusiasm but solid the sound, intensified his love for the area. The cliff-face presented both terrifying drops and slopes that descended gently towards the monumental reefs upon and around only a few chose to swim. The beauty of the area was naturally enhanced by partial or complete solitude. The populous mainly kept to the bays which fashioned the resorts to the east. But here for him was an ecstasy of complete escape: a mighty bucolic and coastal simplicity of grey and white and green and blue. The climbing and walking and every new exposure to distance and height, plus the liberty of one who enticed the adventurous notion of no return countered the complex and compelling nature of despair. Only occasionally did he meet Wilfred George on one of his six mile hikes to the lighthouse standing now so very small and obsolete in the distance. Why ignore everything around and march relentlessly on, where before your nose and around your eyes and ears is the depth and meaning of an entire universe? But Wilfred George knew about loneliness and was able to gloss over its details with a contented smile.

Christopher stood where Copper's Rock, one hundred feet below, was a relatively straightforward, if less than gentle sloping, climb down. This place was the beginning. He did not strain his hopes between it and the end. The end was Akrotiri behind him, Episkopi further on and Limassol needed to form the isosceles. There was Helen behind him as well. She was carrying the food and she was now going to ask him why he had deserted her.

'...With my camera too,' she added.

'I left you the food,' he said, turning around, ready to greet her with a hug. He was happy. Copper's Rock was deserted. 'Listen, hold it. Don't drop the food...' and he shot her again. 'If you throw yourself over there I'll get a good action shot. Leave the food here, though.'

'Don't be silly. I'd kill myself, wouldn't I? There are too many things for me to do in life you know. Do you really want me to die?'

'One has to make sacrifices for art. Do you fancy having the picnic down there?'

He pointed down to Copper's Rock. It stood out far enough from the cliff face to dispel any immediate problems of access and space.

'It's a bit far down.'

'No it isn't. We can walk it. Follow me.'

And he took the food, kept the camera and she kept hold of him. He knew the correct route so well that very little effort was needed to keep them on the right path. She was worried about some of the steeper parts which they skirted around, and while he expressed severe doubts about being able to haul her back up in the event of her slipping and breaking a leg, he promised a kiss should they both manage to arrive intact.

'Why are you so rotten to me? I put a nice request for you on the radio and you don't bother listening to it.'

'You didn't either.'

'But I was going to. You didn't even think about it.'

They arrived and he kissed her, and for that reassuring post-kiss smile she kissed him back.

'What do you see in me?' he asked her while she shook the hair out of her eyes, her arms still around his neck, 'apart from some remarkably absurd resemblance to one of our larger four-legged friends.'

'You're silly. That's why I love you. Do you love me?'

He got away with his shrug by adding: 'Ask me again after my A levels.'

The Rock did not provide much by way of a flat surface upon which to lay the food. He sat on the edge and looked down fifteen feet into the persistent waves. There was enough spray splashing the height to enable him to feel the noise, and he ate a couple of sandwiches without tasting the contents. Helen sitting beside him, eased into him, and the music of the sea made them inseparable. For the half-hour of eating and snuggling, Christopher sat with her and conjured up one of his favourite images of bucolic freedom. If he was to realize this scene there had to be for some remote dream-remembered reason the need for a village stretching in its stereo quaintness from the foot of a wind-whipped hill. On top of this hill stood he, and while sitting at his side, curling into his legs for warmth, was the inevitable girl, thin in the face with bright intelligent eyes and long wind-splayed hair, like his own, long and curly, with the elements breathing into the locks the life of Medusa's snakes. He could just catch the statue's elegant power of admiration, not fear but the infatuated eternal stare, as the gorgon moves out of a benevolent healing of static beauty. And he with the girl looking down on the village below…

Helen could see seagulls and a ship on the horizon which she pointed out. The expansive, illusive blue of the Mediterranean sealed their thoughts. No talk about cooking, friends or her sister's new boyfriend. Soon it will be Easter. This pleasantly irrelevant fact occurred to him with a secondary wish not to remind her of this. Can't have her making plans for a future that won't exist between us. But the present is formless, like the sea. Only the past is solid and the future a goal, while now is all but a peacefully adorned calamity, and the two of us above it all. We're like the Greek Gods, albeit the lower forms with their constant leisure and useless gifts.

Saturday afternoon together: eating, kissing and taking pictures. Christopher took many of her with a view of an admirable pair of legs catching the lingering sun. Taking the chance to snatch back her camera she took plenty of his hair in the air, his feet clambering the slopes and his face and smile peering around the corridors of rocks, grime and hard gripping shrubs and thorns. The sea was certainly, for the two of them together, too rough for swimming. Christopher boasted about having made many splendid conquests of the rapid, crushing waves. She could not believe him. All physical attributes were already at odds with what he had said about rugby, although, embellished thus, he might well have got away with scoring a try.

'But didn't Louding score?'

'He could have done better being a spectator for the amount of attention the game gave him.'

'But he's so good,' she declared. 'I've seen him play. He's so fast.'

Quite unexpectedly she changed the subject. She talked about the cub-scouts' day venturing soon and she was responsible for part of the Pegasus Pack. No, she did not have a Jungle Book name. And yes, there was truth in the rumour. She *was* returning to England. What had that got to do with the cubs? 'Just for a few days. A week, maybe.'

'An interview?..'

'Yes, but not for a while, so don't worry your silly head about it.'

Christopher started to climb the up the slope towards camp level. They left the food bags behind and took pictures further on ahead. It was quite fitting to see them picture-postcarding the vast view. All part of his diet although her appetite afforded the more melodically volatile, and there was music coming from somewhere. Definitely, and it was while ascending from the depths, and peering over the edge, and watching through the leaves and cracks from their chosen hide above, that they saw a girl sitting in the sun on the turret of Subpoint. She had just been in for a swim and she was now wringing out her costume. The luscious benefit of the sun and the wind to dry her hair made the length of her dress unique. There were few covered knees at this time of day, and what she wore did not look like evening attire. It exposed the flimsy gaiety she imposed upon the serious tolerance of the rock turret, breathing the spraying salt, soaking in the blowing heat and studying the crinkling clouds as they back-clothed the very ship Helen had spotted. She was also sketching.

'No she isn't.'

'Yes, she's sketching all right,' said Christopher. 'Who is she? I don't think I recognize her.'

But Helen did. Anybody Helen did not know in RAF Cyprus either lived on the other side of the island or had just arrived. Apparently this girl had just arrived a month ago.

'She's only here for six months,' she explained, 'like a long holiday. She arrived three weeks ago and she's staying with Martin Clifton. Let's go and talk to her.'

'No, no!' Christopher exclaimed with a startling hiss. His last wish now was to invade her chosen Subpoint sanctuary. Had she been caught naked rather than fully draped within summer's idyllic material, he figured her embarrassment would have been the same. There could be no poetic involvement short of the unwelcomed visitor from Porlock. The romantic urge to leave as well as to stay staring at her turned against Helen's discouraging habits. 'Don't you dare call to her. There's obviously nobody with her so I'm sure she wouldn't welcome us.'

This line of thought was totally illogical to Helen.

'Surely,' she began, 'if there's nobody with her..?'

'It is strange that she's here by herself. Martin lives in BG, doesn't he?'

'No, he lives in Limassol, not far from the Naafi area. That's where I met her, at the Island Disco. She joined us because Marion started talking to her about something. Can't remember what. You know the way Marion goes on all the time about this and that with people, and she can talk to anyone.'

This was more of a brief description of herself while making light of Marion's more commanding virtues, but Christopher was too distracted to take note.

'What's her name?'

'Stella. It's a nice name, isn't it? She's a strange girl. She's always traveling about, so they say, and she's only eighteen.'

'What do you mean, only eighteen? You're eighteen soon I'm not yet eighteen – not for a while.'

'Yes, but you should know the places she's gone to: all over, especially Europe and different parts of Britain. She never stays with her family because they don't like each other. She said so herself, and she talked in a way that made me feel silly because of her knowledge, you know, of art and women's freedom and such like things. I laughed when I think of Marion too, not being able to answer her properly. All Marion ever thinks about is Louding.'

Christopher was willing to admit that this was less exaggeration – more the condition of Marion's teenage obsession.

'Oh, I see. So I presume she met Louding.'

'Who? Stella? How did you guess? Louding only ever stays at the Island Disco for about ten minutes, and that's only to keep Marion happy. They had a bit of a conversation, but you know Marion … won't leave him with another girl for long.'

'Not unlike you with me, hey?'

'Oh, you're very silly sometimes, Christopher,' and Helen got to her feet and walked away, maybe pretending to be hurt. He followed her, intent on hearing more about Stella, considering whether he should apologize for whatever he might have let slip. However, instantly cheering up, taking a picture of him and running off, she left trailing a few rather anticipatory words: 'Stella's a very strange girl...'

They walked home where Julie was saved from her turn to do something from a list of moderate household chores, this time drying dishes, by the arrival of five of her friends. This not unspectacular but standard event was greeted as a double bonus. She did not like Helen. She did not wish to spend any unforced minutes in her company, in the same house, in the same house where dishes were likely to be needing her help. So they, her friends, gathered around her and ushered her out. Her opinion and direction were wanted/needed on many matters, all likely to subdue mounting interest Christopher offered to his sister's command, impressed as he was, Helen or no Helen, by the physical emphasis of this perhaps excessive femininity. But Stella, he thought, and now there's something strange, or is it just something different?

Julie might well have stayed, although the dishes were a straightforward deterrence. Christopher and Helen left early after the family five o'clock meal. They walked to the bus terminus beside the Guardroom. There seemed little left to talk about, although they talked, little left to listen to, although Christopher listened. He listened without, he knew, the converging attention of a Louding, had he been Louding listening to Stella. It could only be guessed from his length of time with Helen walking and talking that Louding's time with Stella, pestered no doubt by obliging time with Marion and at the Island Disco, should well have been enough to engross all that he, Christopher, would have gained from any such talk. And had she, Helen, been Stella – Stella now with whatever strides she may have wanted to take towards the grinding, juddering efficiency of Cypriot single-decker transport through the white, official façade of British law – he had strong doubts as to whether there would any been any walking, just directly routed contact of voice crossing voice soaking in every second.

What am I thinking of? he thought. There's no such girl who seconds after seeing her nails me to a strong need to see her for a short time more. Yet now I feel insanely jealous of Louding.

'How long did Louding talk to her?'

'To who?'

'Weren't you talking about Stella?' Christopher asked, convinced in that second that she was.

'No, I was talking about my sister.'

Interested though Christopher had always been in this yet to be encountered quantity of a sister belonging to Helen, he considered it not beyond Helen now to understand why he had not been listening. But to suddenly proclaim his present greatest interest at that very moment reminded him of the bumper bungle usually committed by those who walk cheerfully in on a sudden bereavement. So he did not repeat his question.

He even hoped that Helen hadn't remembered what it meant. She stopped their walk and placed her gentle arms around his neck.

'You're going to miss the bus,' he said, responding with the squeeze necessary to take in her waist.

'Will you come to Limassol next week?'

'Of course. Bit early to ask, hey? I'll be seeing you at school.'

'You never talk to me properly at school.'

'I give you all the attention you deserve.'

'I don't think I really want it,' she reflected with commendable sense of proportional concerns. 'You'll be blaming me for failing your exams.'

But that's a luxury you'll hardly enjoy, he thought. By the time my exams arrive … God, I wonder if I'll be here, let alone here with Helen.

But there with Helen he was until the bus severed once again the Saturday's sealing of their suspect love. He was at least assured of some faith, as she with him, and he no longer resumed his thoughts of Stella on the walk back. All fantasies made grey by a complicated vision of impending homework.

Mathematics lay strewn on the table in the room he shared with Peter who was performing his fishing mime through the house while engaging Leonard on the subject of roach. It was soon time for *Marcus Welby, MD* on TV and Christopher knew what he was going to do, and it was not going to be homework. Sit down in front of the telly with a coffee and no more thinking. Enough is enough, he thought. I wonder really what that means and whether ever said when enough has been achieved.

Concentration practically nil. Poor lad. Me, I'm worried about this afternoon's bloody rugby.

Attempts to tackle maths had been on the level of theory on Sunday mornings, always peaceful and worth such advantage study required. The others, back from mass, continued on some manner of devotional themes by reading, cooking and making plastic models of fighter aircrafts. Except his father, still at the church, putting into an anti-clockwise order the neo-renaissance illustrations of the fourteen Stations of the Cross. Christopher could not worship and worry at the same time and so he opted out of the morning service. He was a bit puzzled – guilt and worry have the same symptoms.

What's it to be? he thought. Am I guilty because maths is as messy as ever and far from complete? Am I worried because I may not survive to sit through this evening's mass and finally carry out what I promised to do as gratitude to the Lord for surviving last Friday? Or am I just ashamed because I should be helping dad but having refused on principle I now wish I hadn't? Others should be carrying out what he so regularly reserves as his personal cross. There are plenty of able-bodied men of more compatible size to take on the task of reversing the circular order of the pictures. Fine time for dad to take up any cross now while his back aches and his night's sleep, as a result, had been ruined.

Tempers frayed and snapped and so as a result Mr James Panhandle stormed off with the conviction of one who would crawl to the confines of mystic solemnity, presenting thus to suffering souls such stations-of-the-cross duty as befits pride before the fall. And not for the third time, Christopher thought, wanting to gain compassion from what Christ himself illustrated just before spurning the women who wept for him. But such contemplation, as was his wont in the face of juggling figures and letters, left him mathematically blank, theologically reassured perhaps, but no pencil, ruler or rubber would act as crutch to a reality no less disabling as the image of himself crushed to the ground by the enthusiasm of sport.

An appropriated appearance of Barry Island cut through his moral dilemma. A routine call: the expected arrival of Angela from England kept him as a fairly regular visitor. He enjoyed the Panhandle reception. They employed an interesting variety of welcomes, from young Jennifer's giggling rapture to James' consistent choice of time to practice his guitar or make paper-shuffling noises behind a closed bedroom door. He refused to promote any time to this young airman who had attached himself, more in anticipation, to Angela's stimulating and often alternative affection the year before. He conformed to a serviceable distance between himself and the young single airmen as ruled by the nebulous code of respect running up the spine of the RAF. Christopher, too, entertained little to no time for the young professionals. He knew only enough to support popular notions of cropped, scalped morons implementing the uniformed wealth of semi-colonial defence which enabled them to steal all the best girls. What chance for the schoolboys in the distorted vision of the maturity race? Not that 'best girls' would have taken *him*, Christopher, up as a worthy alternative in the absence of airmen. But, thought Christopher (and others) sorting out the credits: sport, wit, good-looks, education and sense, pile them on the scales and see them ascend when set against the weight of wallet-filled wealth. Still, who wants women who merely want wealth? Be honest, he thought. Always honest, your honour, until faced with the truth.

Instead he faced Barry whom he liked. He liked him because he was the victim to an energy which pressed home friendly demands for others to listen. The world was overflowing with serious subjects that just had to be immediately discussed, such as rock music, Science Fiction and the noteable increase in graphic violence in films. Barry endorsed all three, and utilized through one visit a cross-section of charming illusions, and to the girls he was a definable hero interpreting the credits for each separate adventure (with the exception of Julie who thought him merely okay). Patricia Panhandle, the family mum, delighted in keeping him fed, feeding herself from his exuberant compliments covering the full virtues of motherhood, womanhood and cooking; hardly similar, Christopher was sure, to whatever wooing he may have presented Angela. Peter thought he was an ace swimmer and equal in weight with the fishing facts, and Rebecca thought he was genuinely funny. But with Christopher, it was Barry who wanted the opinions, comments on a definite code of ethics not generally practiced by school-kids, and today it was Christopher he came to see, knowing full well that Easter and therefore Angela had not yet arrived.

'There's more evidence that the Great Green Warrior does exist.'

'Has he been seen again?'

Barry stuck up two fingers.

'Twice, so when's it to be?'

'I'm not going. I conform to the notion that ghosts are scary.'

'You said you didn't believe in ghosts.'

'I only say that during the day.'

'It may have escaped your notice, Christopher, but it's still day.'

'You know, I've got a feeling that the Great Green Warrior presents himself so rarely that it wouldn't be worth our while just picking any night to go and find him.'

'No, I think he's out there every night. People just don't go out to the cliffs at night. I'm convinced he's there.'

'You're really convinced? A few green clouds and maybe a couple of hoaxed visions. So, what's this new evidence?'

There was actually nothing new. The Great Green Warrior had been seen again, only this time taking the form of a moving tree gliding around an area of rock and sea along which trees are not known to glide. A twilight concoction of party animals, so called because it was getting dark and they were having fun, did not stay around to distinguish between what may have been vegetable or spiritual. Christopher refused to associate the cliffs with any cold cover of fear, and for that reason did not welcome a future, albeit probably futile investigation. Barry would inevitably wander out that way alone but it would need further reluctance on Christopher's part to persuade him. They eventually moved on to the more, perhaps debatably, mundane subject of sport.

'I hear you're playing 56th Squadron this afternoon.'

'My God, then it's true. I'm playing 56th Squadron this afternoon. I was hoping it might turn out to be some bizarre joke, dream, nightmare...'

'They'll be quite amused about playing a school-boy team,' said Barry impassively and this evoked the extent of Christopher's defiance.

'Ha but, we're not the school team but Akrotiri Youth Klub 1st. Bit of a difference you know. Did you hear about Friday's game?'

'Hear about it? I saw it.'

'Oh dear.'

'But I couldn't stick around to congratulate you. You played quite well. Nobody told me you played rugby.'

'God, I wish nobody tried to tell me. I was persuaded against my better nature to take part. Because of my size, believe it or not. Nobody else was small enough for hooker, or rather they needed a small, weedy guy like me, crazy enough to be volunteered, and I was the only one available.'

'Magic game is rugby,' said Barry with what sounded like a nostalgic sigh. 'You talk as if you don't like it.'

Christopher laughed.

'Barry, nothing is further from my mind than joy when I'm playing rugby. Nothing is closer to my mind than survival.'

'Well, it's incredibly blowy outside, so you may have some fun keeping the ball in the right direction.' And Barry assumed the noise of the weather, shooting out his hand in a curved path, succeeding at the same time in grabbing a fly. It buzzed within his fist. Being in a Sunday mood he let it go.

'Mathematics, hey? Remainder theorem and all that.' Barry stood up. 'I was well instructed once. All up here, well stored away. Wish I could get at it.'

'I often wish I could get it in there to be stored.'

'Anyway, got to go. Magic coffee, Mrs P. Pure nectar as usual.'

He walked out and Christopher joined him. Mathematics could be justifiably abandoned for the day. They walked, talked and greeted those they knew who walked and talked the other way, and when they reached the Naafi they parted – Barry to the billets, Christopher to the church. Barry was not mistaken. The weather was very blowy. Warm force four, five, six... as pleasing to walk through now as the need for an extra coat in winter.

The grounds of the church looked out onto the sports field which stretched over to a formation of office blocks and airmen's billets, not to mention the Officers' Mess peering around at one corner of the horizon. The church was small but so too the number of Catholics who used it. It was a standard conservative shelter for the offerings made to the God who looked over the land of Lightnings, Victors, Rockapes and other squadrons, and the occasional DC 10 which circled and sank to be surrounded by on-duty NCOs. Christopher entered the church and its homely gloom welcomed him, as well as his father who was just completing the positioning of the final and fourteenth station. The required job had been easier that both of them had expected. It had also eased his back and reinstated the mood which for him made Sunday a communally richer day for the family. Christopher's picture of the ideal Sunday was the entrance to a placid café in the middle of a country afternoon. His entrance to the church, his father completing the job: rarely were diverse ideals offered such a blend.

'I couldn't let you do it by yourself,' explained Christopher, 'but, yes, I took my time turning up.'

'Well, as you see, there's no need. I've finished and if you did have homework you should have stuck to it.'

Yes, the whole message, he thought, the stations of homework: sticking to it and getting through.

'You know I play rugby this afternoon against your squadron?'

'Excellent. Physical exercise is good for the mind.'

'So is maths, and you know, many would think it was better. Times like this I'm not actually sure what it means to improve my mind.'

'Do you enjoy rugby?'

'I could stand and watch it being played. That much I could enjoy.'

'I can't remember the last time I watched it.' James had never played it. Hurling, many many years ago, was the nearest he got to the rough and tumble of team-based terror.

Yes, thought Christopher. Neither could he remember the last time he had watched a game. Neither could he remember the last time he felt so disinclined to eat Sunday dinner. It did not seem the correct ritual to perform before the game, but Patricia insisted he should eat. She had cooked, he would eat, but he was concerned about survival and his appetite took the first tumble.

Maybe very few would turn up and the game would be cancelled. Who wants to waste a Sunday afternoon scrapping and scraping the scorching grass? He knew, however, that if *he* turned up everyone else would. He had to be the most reluctant. To keep occupied the time left he washed the dishes, on average a slightly less than formidable task, took a second look at his maths, rarely for him the inspiration attached to an aimless glance, and then he got changed, pulling on the shorts and boots as if squeezing into death robes. The walk back to the sports field was too easy. The wind remained. In the midst of despair, he thought – what?.. Hope. What? I can always hope to break a leg. And he began to envy those few he never knew, barred by paralysis from ever testing their endurance through this barbaric trial by games. This is crazy. Like wanting to lose my legs because they're walking me to hell. But with each step his hyperbolic inclinations took on more bizarre shapes. Pray for the military coup in which all but terrorist oppression had to be cancelled, or even now, with this vociferously gentle weather, a sudden tornado, beaming as it sweeps as it cleans. What greater moment for a UFO abduction, and committing myself to anthropo-graphic experiments. I will kiss the ground and praise the Lord should I be instantly, right now, without further hesitation, transported through the light-years to my own private dome, to be or not to be shared with Hollywood's most voluptuous sex symbol. He thought of sex symbols and thought of himself playing rugby and he wanted to laugh. Light-years of difference. Finally, as a last resort, the wakening of the defossilized, prehistoric monster, raising its serpent-like snout over the agoraphobic airfields, picking off at random the swirling ant-like airmen as they scattered in the wake of their furnished filaments of defence, all set, ready to pound the monster with a colourful, Guy Fawke's Night variety of heat.

No monster, aliens or divertive acts of God. Just heat greatly eased by the stiff breeze, and he was early, knowing full well that a wait would do him no good at all. He was not the only one of the pitch. A few of the squadron's team were on the far side, kicking the ball into the wind and having it fly back into running, jumping arms. On his side, Perry Stenfield stood leaning against a post. As one of the best school team players he had honourable access to the Youth Klub side. Christopher now resented the accumulation of mundane chances which dictated this occasion of him and Perry being a few minutes alone together, waiting for the others. However, Perry employed some element of respect when greeting him, maybe as such a casual reference to the fact that they were going to die together, although this could not be judged as the norm. Christopher suspected that this lad actually enjoyed playing rugby, and mutual respect was now prompted by the game two days ago. After all, Christopher had been on the winning side.

'You hooker?' he asked. His overbearing grin now completely subdued, there was the breakthrough of him being serious. 'They're going to be difficult team to play, hey? Still, should be a good game.'

Christopher was now in despair. If Stenfield was endorsing the prospect of such a challenge what place did he, the Panhandle, have in even pretending perhaps that he could be wrong?

'I don't like this wind,' offered Christopher.

'You will when we're playing with it. I hope we're playing with the wind second half. We'll be more into the game, and we can get those tries going, because we'll know what they're like by then.'

'You think we'll lose.'

'What? Lose?' Perry reverted to form. 'C'mon, Panhandle. Don't be so weedy. I don't know the meaning of losing.'

In that case he had lived through what he didn't understand during the last game, thought Christopher. No time for profundities, just profanities, and besides, they were no longer alone. Others from the Youth Klub turned up, including Gavin Peters who, having been beaten last Friday and as the head-boy, felt he should be with the lads in order to be beaten again today. Christopher wondered, not without hope, that if enough of the school team arrived to help support the Youth Klub 1st, he could opt out of being anything other than a member of the latter's reserves. What he had in common with reserves had earlier been asserted in the length of time he could quite contentedly watch the game.

The Kamps were in a great mood.

'Just drank a pint of salt water,' said Oliver. 'Tasted fucking foul. Biology and me don't get on.'

'What made you do that?' Christopher asked, not really wanting an answer.

'Get your shirt tucked in,' demanded Colin. 'They'll kill you if you leave it hanging loose, flapping about.'

Christopher didn't think they'd be so finicky. They'll kill him anyway, tidy or not. Maybe a presentable corpse – at least he died with his boots on. More turned up. Wilfred George among the more, although he was undoubtedly among the less enthusiastically engaged. However, those who would have made reserves a numerical necessity were in Episkopi playing the inter-Youth Klubs soccer league, while those who were here and would otherwise have been over there playing likewise or making up their reserves, regarded rugby as the essential option. Christopher's in-built fear of rugby was second only to his almost complete inability to play football. And because of counter-size but partnered position, he and Wilfred were deemed irreplaceable (unless injured) and could therefore look forward to a full game (again unless injured which, Christopher was convinced, would be the case – to avoid injury was the reason why I want to avoid the game, he thought and now I have to play the game and the only way I can get out of doing so is by being injured, – all of which he found distressingly confusing). The arrival of the Galbraiths, Reverend for ref, and his son, Steve as the final forward, concluded the doubtful illusion of safety in number, and the squadron on the other side looked all set for the slaughter. The team's self-elected captain, Bill Grey, who would otherwise have been playing football as captain for a top Akrotiri YK team called the Magpies, gathered his team to offer firm advice.

'Kill or be killed. Don't just be scared that they're wide and tough because they can fall just as hard as anyone else. Try and get a system of passing the ball. The temptation to keep hold of it can be just as dangerous as throwing it wildly away.'

Christopher could not envision the former under the preconceived influence of the latter. The weather was also turning slightly chilly. To run like hell is definitely going to be my prime concern. The vicar blew his whistle; the men dutifully positioned themselves for the kick-off. The Youth Klub won the toss. Perry's earlier notion came within reach of Bill and he chose to play against the wind for the first half. Everybody ran to the opposite side and with equal duty repositioned themselves. Interesting, thought Christopher, looking now at the men he faced. None of them made any comments about his size. I wonder if they're as scared as me. Always be aware of the small rugby player, who, with fists flaying the air, will never fail to find the tender spots. He jumped up and down on the spot, kicked the air a couple of times and began to actually pray for victory alongside survival. In a manner which could have had him worship the long seconds before the ball was planted breathlessly in the arms of Francis Dorman behind him, he thought of his maths homework, and if he was crippled now...

They lost. He was still standing. The better half of his prayers had been answered. But they could have won. He could have been in a chair having splintered bones reset. He had spent most of the game trying to vehemently deny that he was enjoying himself. They scored the first and last try, their only tries, and both conversions with and against the wind went over the bar. Steve Galbraith had been practicing. The unlikely idea of actually winning began to go to the heads of those who played well. But the game was tough and the squaddies were better; not faster, but stronger, thicker and ruthless, utilising skilful tackles that the lads had rarely experienced. However, Wilfred's weight and strength gained Christopher most of the scrums, and from Oliver to Francis meant tentative seconds of the nervous eclipse breathing some freedom before and after the pounding crunch. Most in between were conscious of the size of the opponents thundering towards them. 'Just get in their way and try harder,' shouted Bill Grey, and Christopher actually obeyed, attempting something akin to the fearless while imagining that he could possibly floor one monster heading his way. He was dragged at some speed fifteen yards along the burning turf, ending in a loose scrum from which he emerged maybe wiser but defiantly wondering in which direction the wind now blew. No difference, it seemed, having it for or against them. Sheer effort to see through the two hours by playing reasonably well made weather problems shrink to a size few noticed. Gavin cracked his nose and blood sped from him like ketchuped saliva. He played on, oblivious to the impressive stains somewhat 'pollocked' against the mud-caked white shorts and striped shirt. Christopher grumbled, grunted and growled through a mutual affinity with the opposition's hooker. Both hardly got the chance to touch the ball once it was fed into the scrum. Urgent, crushing, front line strength complicated every limited method available of actually playing spot-the-ball before it instantly disappeared. There was little way of telling what time it was actually being handed down the line – rarely to reach Francis, and during one confused route someone actually tackled the reverend ref. With the type of concern soon made famous when confronted with hulk-sized onslaught one of the lads gave a blind pass. Reverend Galbraith, putting impulse before duty like any good Christian, caught it. This resulted in a loose scrum without the whistle to break it up. It only became obvious what had happened when it also became obvious that the ball was not going to trickle out. What did emerge was a dazed vicar and a weak whistle-blow for a scrum down. The ball was stampeded up and down with double severity followed by equal speed and a lot of indirect orders. The end is nigh, thought Christopher bleakly, imagining that essence forming the darkest hour. But the dawn came and went and it was suddenly over. Colin had scored the first try and Perry the last – an impressive line of tries to the squaddies in between and that was it. There followed a good deal of clapping and cheering and being required by this to feel no less than heroic.

 Christopher did not saunter home. Neither did he limp. He merely walked as if wanting to know why he wasn't satisfied. I certainly won't be satisfied with another game, he asserted. I've had enough. No girls to greet in us defeated exhausted lads. Nothing of Julie and her entourage of fan-based encouragement. She had known about the match, not least due to the usual and limited conversation with him as he may have reluctantly mentioned it earlier as a forthcoming event, but her loyalty remained soccer-based and at present in Episkopi, where the real flavor of youth versus youth was competitively installed.

'Thing is,' said Colin later on, 'we all played well but not well enough.' A dark threat of rugby practice was hovering over the hinterland of his meaning. He was, however, delighted with himself, having been one of those who scored. 'You must give extra push if the pushing back is hard.'

'What if it's too hard?' asked Christopher, maintaining the belief that it was always too hard.

'Rugby is never too hard,' replied Oliver in a sophisticated tone, 'that it cannot follow the trendy belief in the distribution of wealth.'

'Ignore my brother,' said Colin. 'He's happy he won most of the scrums.'

'I won most of the scrums,' said Christopher, assuming as he did that hookers and not scrum-halfs took credit for whatever could be defined as success from a scrum.

'Apparently we didn't do that badly in the soccer this afternoon,' said Oliver.

'You mean Akrotiri won?' asked Francis.

His enthusiasm was enough without Colin's answer. Christopher wanted to shrug – so what? he thought – but he did enquire after the score.

'We haven't won anything yet, remember,' said Colin. 'This is only the first round, but we did well.'

Sunday night was pay-night for the Families Club's doormen. This included Christopher and Colin. Oliver and Francis had tagged along. Thomas Rorner was already there. He was on duty, and from his official desk of guest vouchers and subscription fees, he supplied more news about the soccer. They were all set to regain the cup which had featured a disastrous humiliation of its twelve months' stay within the Island Disco. Almost as nauseating as the Families Club Sunday night teenage disco which was about to underwhelm all the regulars with the exception of the treasurer who was reluctant to wait around for the final doorman, Scott Juir, to arrive and collect his pay. He could pick up his packet from Thomas who picked up his own packet while he worked, while Colin and Christopher, with packages already picked were obliged to buy the drinks. Buying a round was listed fairly low on the generosity scale – a few steps below accompanying someone to the Families Club disco, held bi-weekly, Sundays, 8 to 10.30 pm.

The four of them were in possession of a confidence gained from the relief of a hard match well played. Thomas would have made a fifth but he had to stay at his desk. Besides, he had played soccer and that didn't count. Routine dribbling, passing and occasionally striking were naught compared to running the gauntlet of tanks. Christopher enjoyed a relatively rare facility for him of being one of the lads, and they strolled into the main bar, out of bounds to the kids at the dance, and took a table to themselves.

'Well, are we going in or not?' asked Francis.

'Possible there's a lot of available girls at these dances,' admitted Colin.

But neither Christopher nor Oliver was keen.

'Young women of the world can wait,' Oliver declared, looking at his drink. 'Let's stay here. I'm jiggered.'

'So the speaketh the old man.'

'And I agree,' said Christopher, but there again, he thought, I'm older.

He felt too worn out to dance and too stiff to do anything other than reluctantly move from where he sat.

'Who said anything about dancing?'

Eventually they did wander through to the hall, curiosity gaining a compromise in its favour, but fifteen minutes at the dance – an occasion that Julie and her followers held in sharp contempt – was enough to convince them that it was not worth their while staying.

The Gospel according to St John's

> If school is so bad why do so many endure it and, so it appears, survive? If school is so good why are so few happy?
> Rebecca Panhandle: Essay on Education

> They keep telling us that the school belongs to us and then they keep telling us not to do this and not to do that. I've known such people to say the same about freedom. You can't have freedom without rules. But who makes the rules? That's what I want to know.
> Leonard Kamp: Detention Essay

> Our school bus is great. Dot and me get to sit on the back seat now and our prefect Panhandle isn't such a pain as he used to be. Julie's still the boss. Did you really hate her when you were here? I don't think she's that bad.
> Doris Orange: Letter to her older sister, Debra.

SAINT JOHN'S COMPREHENSIVE SCHOOL, Episkopi, Cyprus – a haven set aside for young Brits to strengthen their faith in the drudgery of Monday morning, and it is now Monday morning. Christopher opened his eyes and attempted to move his legs, aching muscles competing with bruises to verify this undisputed level of morning existence. At the moment I feel like St John's – a less than comprehensive, confusing mess. However, head does not ache, but merely engages the eyes across a dazzling proportion of the light, like the vast portion of land upon which a military pattern of tin billets designate irregular areas to each subject.

Awake, young man to another dawn of freedom eagerly grasped by the youthful passion to learn more. Up and into these precious moments of making meaning out of an illusion of monotony. Don't feel jealous of the lazy warmth, or even long for the Friday afternoon sun. Think breakfast, and he thought breakfast: porridge. Oh my God. Monday morning, mum always makes porridge. Her mum made porridge every morning and is still fit enough to argue over the price of groceries twice a week. But that's too far away. This is Cyprus. One shouldn't have to eat porridge in Cyprus. All I want is chocolate covered toasted rice with milk followed by sweet coffee, and then I'll think of school and the maths I haven't done. God, I wish I hadn't played that rugby yesterday. My legs – wasn't like this on Saturday.

But this is Monday and all that Monday means besides the hangover, which, praise the Lord, I haven't got. So, I can count my blessings. What are they? Certainly not breakfast.

The Panhandles present a fairly average Monday morning breakfast message: choice above all containing the rare possibility of defiantly eating alone and in silence. For Julie, particularly, breakfast was not a communal meal. She would usually pass on the pleasure, being as during the week all but she were up before half-six. She gained her morning sustenance from the various offerings her followers donated on the bus and at school. Christopher needed time to get through breakfast, each mouthful and morsel of another week to go, and then another, and then another, to whatever it is I'm willing myself to work towards. Peter and Rebecca kept their distance from each other, table in between, she portraying the silent essence of undiluted hate first thing in the morning, he a hasty insistence on misplaced necessities. The four of them would usually leave together – probably the only time they did anything together outside the few family rituals dictating the terms of their routine. They hardly skipped down the road to where their particular bus would stop, but contributed instead the average example of trained but not un-tensed mutual tolerance joining the others their age, all compelled to such union by common travel.

Everywhere, the world over, on Monday mornings, children find their way to school. The fact that they do so equally as well on other days allotted to the school week says more for Mondays than any attempt to lessen its impact, and on their way there the planet throughout its twenty-four hour course, propels a universal hope that the lethargy of youthful steps would grow into confident, well-nourished strides. Hours later forms the world going the other way, and whether the time in between was used to learn or rebel, most accept the ideal of fundamental expedience: each day is similar to the last, and every changed circumstance is fixed to the eternal definition of the familiar.

Christopher hasn't worked that one out yet. He's still in bed. School has not vanished and no amount of philosophical pandering will make it so. Yesterday I stayed in bed wondering if I'd be doing so today. Now it's today I'm beginning to wish it was yesterday so that I can wonder about today just that bit longer. But I'm running out of time. I exist from day to day but I never really know if I'm going anywhere. If I make plans well ahead of immediate efforts isn't that where they remain? Wish I was like Julie, able to stay in bed and not think about anything until it's almost time to catch the bus, and then be incapable of thinking of anything because of the rush; a confident rush like a dance stopping just short of a keen reluctance to see anyone or anything other than her own reflection. Yes, always time for reflection. The amount of sleep (and everything) most girls must sacrifice because of mirrors.

Make-up, like smoking, was forbidden, but a subtle amount of each helped to adorn the edge of pupil-based sophistry, and Julie suffered no shortage of this prejudicially bestowed authority. Such was her leadership of a sizeable section of the youth within the RAF empire focussed without effort on a bus loaded with healthy kids whose primary call was to heckle each other every yard closer to a kingdom more measured and disciplined than that offered by the Pied Piper. It was hard to place her anywhere else but leading her own parallel solution, simplifying the complicated into trust and loyalty. And she's my sister, thought Christopher, and I've not yet being able to boast about this rarely considered fact. It's always as if she has to make do with me for a brother. Christ knows what she thinks of Peter, if at all. I just about live up to someone who may sit beside her on the back seat of the bus along with four others, chosen by such standards within our system of sub-cultural grading. Don't really know where I've been graded. Accident of birth – being born before her hasn't helped much.

Christopher was bus-prefect by dint of being the only upper sixth former on board. He was happy enough with the bus he had – number 27. None but the relevant authorities were certain how many buses covering Akrotiri, Limassol and Berengaria descended upon and ascended to (and from) Episkopi five times a week, and each bus had a prefect, deputy prefect and a backseat hierarchy. Bus 27 was comparatively peaceful, mostly late and so managed more times than not to avoid the inevitable confusion created by the school system of moving some fifteen hundred kids through the two hundred yards' walk from the bus stops to the main grounds. As the school jurisdiction covered all occasions when the buses were being used, the no-smoking rule was still supposedly employed and enforced by the bus-prefects. Christopher was not alone in allowing those who wanted to smoke to do so. He knew that there was little he could do about it anyway. It was the price he was willing to pay for acceptance on the backseat and a bus-load of play placated by demands more effective than his very occasional requests for less noise. Julie was an indifferent source of ash and dog-ends, but she commanded the most respect. She laughed only rarely and tended to speak quietly with the chosen few, and except for the occasions when he was in a position to do her a favour, this did not include Christopher. However, she allowed him the benefit by default of her command. Nobody questioned the early morning time when she obviously wanted peace.

Christopher Millings, a good-looking, boisterous fifth-former who, along with the many, was daunted by Julie but found it infinitely easier to flirt with the likes of the Orange twins, Dot and Doris, an identical duality of feminine attitude, mollified slightly during the ensuing year by the subtle but not insignificant notion of encroaching maturity, sat immediately in front of these girls who, perhaps alternating according to the day, sat beside Christopher who shared the middle of the back seat with Julie. Christopher Millings was called Chris because nobody ever called Christopher Chris and nobody really knew why, least of all Christopher or Chris, but most understood how to prevent confusion, which never seemed to occur when confronted with more than one John, Paul or even Colin. There was only one Colin, and he sat beside Chris and never flirted with the twins but argued sport and music with his brother, Oliver, who sat in a seat to himself on the other side and was above trying to find a place on the back seat, thinking that such means of measuring up logically absurd and paradoxically demeaning. Oliver was not a frustrated philosopher. True, there was nobody around to argue philosophy, except perhaps Christopher who was barred from such talk by Julie sitting almost in between, an obtuse angle to allow for errors of inhibition, but Oliver considered his environment of vacuous minds philosophically. It was fate that he too should fancy Julie, but was hardly willing to demonstrate an alternative by any sincere attempt to talk to Linda Keen, the fifth member of the back seat, a stringently beautiful girl who spent most of her sitting time knitting and smoking and shaking from her face her long bleached hair. It was often wondered if she actually went to school, sat in any classes, if she even existed outside the bus but merely maintained the rights of chief figment of general imagination. There was never any doubt about the existence of he who sat beside her claiming his window place as the sixth back-seat member: her brother Russell. He often felt the need to impress his independent opinions on those around, especially Oliver in front who often as not prompted his level inter-racial understanding. 'I hate those fuckers…' he would say, meaning all who were not British, and there were times when he confined his goodwill to only those from Scotland. He and Linda came from Fife, just like the Panhandles who mainly came from Ireland but had lived in RAF Leuchars, close to St Andrews before their move to Cyprus. So while in Fife they came from Yorkshire, and before that from Wales, until eventually Dublin which Christopher used as information set aside like certificates of confirmation and birth. Hardly worthwhile mentioning this fact to Russell whose concise solution to all political problems: '…drop the fuckers into the Dead Sea and force 'em under…' 'What does Russell think, then?' Oliver often asked. What could not be expressed with fingers was wrapped up within four to eight words and thrown out the window along with what remained of his cigarette and further discernible innuendos at tyres belonging to vehicles that dared to overtake. Russell has even less time for Cypriot drivers, except the one in the bus keeping the many others behind, and if a rival bus drew close he would mouth abuse and point at the wheels. This added a particular stretch to Christopher's already taut nerves, but putting up with Russell was an acquired art. Christopher, along with others, entertained the notion that Julie fancied Russell. It remained a suspicion bordering on an idea from a slight shift in her indifference. Julie had never actually made it known that she did not require a boyfriend; it was mainly her attitude which offered the ethereal medium of youth-bound enquiries the fact that one worthy of her particular attention did not at present reside on the island.

Today's bus was very late. The driver did not like Mondays either. Chris Millings talked about the football and Sunday's victory in Episkopi, and the Kamps talked about rugby and Sunday's defeat in Akrotiri. Christopher's thoughts had never really left his maths which he conveniently left at home. Oops, he thought, I've forgotten my maths which I couldn't do. What a shame? Very soon the entire bus-load formed a forlorn gathering and stood waiting a good ten minutes before the bus skidded around the corner and screeched to a halt. Christopher looked up at the sky from whence all the strength of his will descended. The sun was out. It was faithful enough. Another hot day.

The piling on was orderly enough, what with the elders at the back, Peter and Rebecca somewhere close to the middle with the many other middlings, and towards the front the first formers making irritable and playful efforts at pulling and pushing. The cigarettes were lit, some books came out and the journey began and ended likewise. Christopher was often at odds to remember what thoughts took up these excursions, and this morning's overall blank failed to take in the familiar houses and hills, mainly the latter, enveloping every conceivable shape of permitted distance. Getting so that going to school is like moving from one room to another and discarding the pictures hanging on the wall in the hallway in between. Something like that, he thought, and the bus arrived so late that they not only escaped the unbearably slow removal system, sparing Christopher the task of being the first at the exit in order to await staff-on-duty instructions regarding the alighting of his crew, but all suspected that the five minute warning bell had been and gone maybe more than five minutes ago. Christopher's Monday morning needs were many, and nowhere near the bottom of this list was the time graced in idle preparation for another sequence of tutorial events. But if one arrives late and forfeits drill one cannot expect the added bonus of a few minutes freedom. However, waiting outside, faithful to the final seconds if needs be, were three friends of the Orange twins. They now owned a spot where they waited every morning, system or no system, five minute warning or not. Throughout the sessions of this undemanded vigil in attaining a not so supreme privilege of walking the twins to school, they got to know Christopher quite well, well enough to address him as Christopher and ask him where they were on those not un-rare days when the twins were not where they should have been, on the backseat, waving to them wildly as if having survived a treacherous school-bound voyage. One twin never arrived without the other. True to their combustible nature which gained most energy in sharing events, every ailment was clearly contagious enough to always keep the two of them away together, and on such days their friends would walk away dejected as if the first few hours at least had been ruined. When was Julie ever shown such demonstrative respect? thought Christopher. And Helen, does she every wait for me, he thought, relentlessly, he thought, come rain heat or fog? he thought. Nowhere to be seen, and there was no-one nowhere to be seen but these friends of the Orange twins and members of his bus, some of whom had to rush, but most content to stroll to school.

He should have been late for registration but by all accounts he was early, one of the first few to stroll into Eric Hashfield's class. Eric's real name was probably Harold. His initials, H.P., before the Hashfield could well have prompted a more commercial-based nickname, as well from his surname any number of connotations re the growing of cannabis, but his appearance overshadowed such exercises in underlining with humour the serious task of teaching languages. He looked not unlike Eric Morcambe and was therefore doomed, but he was a happy man who could overlook the Eric in his life and willingly take up peripheral tasks such as marking the attendance of the upper sixth form lads. All of them were present unless proven absent, and this included those who preferred to remain for the first fifteen minutes in the prefects' room. He was not altogether pleased with this lack of serious support for registration and contrived various methods of enticing his form into his room –one of the few on an upstairs floor and therefore deemed as something of a journey for those long suffering nomads of the ground-floor level. The language department was in the main building (called main because it actually looked as if it had been purposely built, unlike the other departments dotted around the grounds as if the result of a random study in architectural and military expedience) which was not, unfortunately, a novelty inspiring enough to move any but the most expeditionary of the sixth formers from their prefects' room habitat. So Eric presided over rather one-sided discussions about world affairs and religion, politics and art, and he set up beside the blackboard a music system on the pretext of some academic attraction to the finer details of modern rock. However, the results were minimal; the same people turned up, usually late, and out of those were the few who never remained long enough to be reminded about the various house assemblies already going on.

Assemblies were there to be attended, and each person belonged to one of five houses – Canterbury, Durham, Exeter, Winchester and York – and each house held two morning assemblies a week. There was no particular system governing which house would hold its assembly when and where, except for Friday when no house held any particular assembly because the entire school would gather together out on the grounds, spread far and wide and mime unconvincingly to the taped hymns which echoed through the area from a couple of 150 watt speakers. This was the one time in the week when the headmaster could guarantee his appearance, and because the majority of the teachers were gathered around him, they had to sing. But they were provided with a roof which thwarted the sun's attempts at making the task intolerable, while others escaped obligations by posting themselves at various corners around the distilled pupils to urge authority and prevent the totally uninterested from totally escaping. It was even beyond upper-sixth form capacity to dodge this mass approach to Christian inaction other than the effortless slurring brought about by seven sharing one hymn-book, and moving in formation around the back edge of the pack, ready to pose as the rock of ages for any strolling teacher. So from Monday to Thursday five houses made the most of four days, with registration in between, not to mention the numerous exam-bound subjects.

Christopher attended registration because Louding attended registration, and also vice versa, Monday morning making no difference, the two sitting together when they could, everywhere else, different A level choices separating their selected seats.

'Louding, do you know a girl called Stella?'

Louding looked up from the sketch he was colouring of two red corpuscles slugging it out. He needed time to think. The girls he knew amounted to a list which took more than a few seconds of mental scanning except when dealing with persistent names.

'Helen told me about her on Saturday. We saw her at the cliffs. Apparently she's Martin Clifton's cousin out here on holiday.'

'Why not ask Martin then?' Louding suggested, still working on his list.

'He's here today.'

'But you're here now, and besides, it was just that, you see, Helen told me that Marion introduced her to you.'

'Aha, impossible. Marion would never introduce any girl to me. She has this idea that I'm interested in everyone else but her. Mind you. It's true. Wait a minute, wait a minute – Stella, of course – now how could I forget a Stella? Not many of them about. She was at the Island Disco, not too long ago, and it was Helen who introduced her to me, not Marion.'

'Well, we saw her at the Akrotiri cliffs. She was by herself. We didn't go down to where she was, but Helen talked as if, you know, this girl was something special. She's eighteen which I suppose must be quite young for a girl who travels without her family.'

Louding shrugged.

'I don't know. I didn't really get to know her. She works in Akrotiri though, which was probably why she was at the cliffs by herself. Had a bit of time off, maybe.'

'She works in Akrotiri? Are you sure?'

'Of course not. I'm only going by what she told me, and if you want to trust her then, yes, sure, she works in Akrotiri. She's got a temporary post as a clerical typist at the Sergeant's Mess.'

'I thought they were only allowed to employ Greek girls for jobs like that – part of the leasing contract or something.'

'I don't know. That's what she told me.' Louding stared at his work for a few seconds and looked up again. 'You want to get to know her, hey?'

'Without Helen knowing I want to know her. Listen, Louding, we could invite her out for a kebab. You could invite her and I'll take Helen and…'

'How would that prevent Helen from knowing? And what about Marion? She'd never forgive me.'

'I didn't think that would bother you too much.'

'True, true. I'll think about it. We could do with going out for another meal. Let's make plans later on, hey?'

'Yes, good. Shouldn't be too ready to inform Helen, though. She'd want to dispense with plans and go now.'

'What? During registration? Surely not.'

It was usually Savina who assured Christopher, whether or not he wanted assurance, that Helen was at school. The two girls shared the same school bus, the same job as bus-prefect, the same inability to control the noise which had offered Christopher, on one particular journey he made to Helen's place via this bus, bitter memories of the early days of bus 27. What these girls had in common, their despair at and eventual refusal to deal with the screaming, shouting, demanding, nagging kids, formed the defeated bond which sealed a good friendship. Savina was allowed to call Helen silly in a pleasing manner which aroused her faith in human nature when Helen started going out with Christopher. 'I am very happy to know this,' she said. 'He's just silly enough for you.' 'He must be very clever, doing A level maths and physics.' 'No, let me assure you, he is silly.' It was not an easy task for anybody to impress Savina in the context of her A level subjects which she shared with Christopher as one who shared a portion of a fruit cake with a poor man. Savina was a genius and Christopher had not yet reached the scientific stage of being able to remotely question this. Let him dispute instead what Brian Innmaker or Gavin Peters pronounced as creative masterpieces – he would sooner fight the wanton squiggle than the straight line or the strict angle, the latter bearing him through the stages of enlightened reality, the former offering the escape route he had little time to take. 'Give me rock music and red wine any time,' he said, but all they offered was the continuing saga of mathematics problems and a world in which Savina provided condescending help and Helen occasional bouts of comic relief.

Today Savina took Helen's role and made Christopher laugh. First lesson: physics and the study of static electric charge. John Warwick, their teacher, re-introduced them to the dubious pleasures of the Van de Graaf generator. Ha, thought all – O level piffle; all that is but Savina who expected great magic to be performed beneath the metal bowl. Tessa Miles, beside her, knew what to expect and kept away, while Christopher, who knew well what was going to be done urged Savina to take part. He abandoned the line-up from him to the machine just as Savina, on the other side, laid her hand on the bowl. So he escaped, with Tessa, a much greater shock than calculated, which would have amused John no end had he not been one of its victims.

'Jesus,' shouted Edmund Whitehead, and then realising that he had been the only one to cry out, stated: 'yes, well, somewhat more intense than expected.'

It was not so easy to subdue the humorous pain by calling to mind its serious association with scientific research. Both Steve and Brian bent double with laughter seemingly seized from the shock, Wilfred George wandered up and down the room shaking his wrist, and Savina stood on her spot, angrily bewildered and fuming at Christopher's all-knowing amusement. She wanted instant revenge, and was therefore very pleased when the chance offered itself so beseechingly. She flatly refused to give him a copy of the maths homework to be handed in after break. He wanted to know how he had offended her. It wasn't his damned machine. Maybe my damned luck, he thought, but there was some ironic consolation in Tessa informing him that he would never have had the time to copy it down anyway. He could resign himself not only to no help but no hope. Brian, who had likewise not done the wanted work, offered no care.

'There is no time to waste on homework,' he said. 'I've far too much to study, to see, to go...' and he put his hand on his heart, 'to love and to lose.' He dropped his head, looked longingly at the floor like a small man would look at the ceiling, and smiled. Brian, to Christopher, was a tall, on the edge of gangly, ego-on-stilts. Christopher, to Brian, was a normal guy while he, Brian, the Innmaker, was above normal, as represented by his height, his sharpened good-looks, his forward air of being in control and willing to share his flowing energy of promised achievement. He achieved his will by granting the school his time and thus, it seemed, excelled in most it offered. If he did not excel he insisted that he would. Nobody could honestly dislike the lad but most wanted to say that they did, including Christopher who had to sit with him at maths and learned more about magic and mystery than figures and facts. So Brian, in a rare moment of feeling, perhaps, responsible for the distraction he evoked, offered Christopher his assistance. 'Private study later on. We can work on the homework together.'

Just now it was break and the music in the prefects' room had already started. The Gerard deck had mysteriously disappeared without the added benefit of any asked questions, but Martin Clifton and Robert Johnson took up the available guitars and strummed and sang separate songs. This annoyed neither of them but bothered others, and the Innmaker, having almost reached the point of dishing out at random the energy of his mid-morning presence, picked up a long stake, pilfered from somewhere close to Dodge City, and swung what he defined as a perfect arc, missing by mere inches Robert's nose.

'Hey, what the fuck?'

'No, hold still,' said Brian during another exclaimed swing, this time just missing a pile of books and records, the community cigarette lighter and Linda Keen's bag of tangled wool. 'See, see, I'm the expert – the expert.'

He was not the type to leave anybody in doubt. All the same, Martin, who until then had imagined Rob's nose flying across the room to meet a innocuous poster of Mike d'Abo, asked quite knowingly the fatal question:

'What at?'

'Watch? You didn't see? You want me to do it again?'

'No way,' said Rob.

Too late. Brian very rarely frustrated his enthusiasm. With a leap in the air he held within a split second of swooping violence and crashing potential the living position of all just beyond the 270 degree swing. The two guitarists finally performed in harmony by leaving aside their instruments and jumping simultaneously onto Brian as he was regaining balance from the momentum he produced. All three, plus the stake, a few books and a chair suffered a startlingly loud crash.

'They are like children,' said Savina, looking on with Tessa from the studious side of the prefects' room. They were both about to leave and go on duty. Tessa assumed an element of concern about Brian's health beneath the scrum, and so their exit was quite a lofty affair compared to the scrap they left.

As they left Louding and Helen entered, sat on either side of Christopher who was staring wishfully at blank paper, hoping to magic up some convincingly mathematical figures. He knew where to start, but without direction and vague about where to continue the former offered no delights and could only match the latter insofar that it didn't exist, just yet. If Brian was not knocked senseless then there was a chance later, after maths, when homework wise it was too late.

'"Your face is a book upon which one can read strange matters",' said Louding carefully. 'Lady Macbeth, in a rare moment of uncertainty.'

'I wish my uncertainty was rare,' said Christopher.

'I thought Macbeth was a man,' said Helen.

'Fortunately, for both history and Shakespeare, his wife wasn't.' explained Louding. 'She was a lady of the unique brand of evil.'

Helen wanted Christopher to say that she herself was a lady of unique good. He was usually happy enough to follow Louding's less cryptic but to her unengagingly innocent remarks. But he merely continued to look at the paper he wanted to scribble up in the haste of algebraic inspiration but had not the will-power or know-how as to where to start. There was a danger of him cursing his lot, and so Helen decided to say something encouraging.

'Do you want anything from England when I go?'

Yes, a letter telling me that's you're not coming back, he thought. I'd even risk the chance of missing you.

He looked at her and was willing to surrender a smile.

'Yes, anything that is English, and that means nothing which has on it or looks like and can be reminded of an elephant.'

'Elephants can be English too, you know.'

'Yes, that's true,' said Louding. 'There's a place in London called

Elephant.'

'And I won't be going there, certainly not with Helen.'

'Aw, why not?' asked Helen, as if a definite future plan had been thwarted.

'Not if you carry on with this impossible notion that I look like an elephant.'

'I don't think you look like an elephant, silly. You just remind me of one.'

'I do not, I do not! I don't resemble in any shape or form an elephant. I'm closer to the size of a mouse. Just now I feel like one when it comes to maths.'

'There you go, Helen,' said Louding, 'problem solved. Buy him an English mouse. Apparently, from what I've learnt in biology, there are more of them than English men, and certainly more than English elephants.'

'Get me an Easter Egg – that'd be a good idea. It'll be close to Easter when you return, and I've reason to believe that elephants don't lay eggs. Is that not right, Louding?'

'I haven't quite reached that part yet. A level biology only teaches you about blood and goo.'

Yes, that's certainly what they'll be wanting in part, especially maths.

As it happened, Ken McGibb preferred to talk about rugby. Ken McGibb was not of that Scottish breed of mathematicians who displayed the rhombus by 'takking a square an' gi'ing it a bash', but he was still northern enough to accept the bait when Steve Galbraith insisted on the superiority of Welsh rugby over Scottish. There must have been a match televised last week. Christopher had missed it, and was not surprised to learn that rugby was played outside Cyprus. People are mad the world over, and while maths kept Ken alive, rugby, no doubt, tried to kill him. It was not unusual for him to limp into the class bearing the scars of a previous game. He played regularly for the Colts, notorious for being the best team on the island, and the hard road to this reputation had so far failed to keep him, even for one day, from the maths that many, such as Christopher, tried desperately to learn. Many thought that maths was not easy. It was not easy to teach how easy it was, and on those rare occasions when there was no need, the lateral edge of making maths the ongoing adventure in thought came up against the loyalty to a syllabus and occupational homage to the exam doctrine. This was known as cramming: cram in the facts and forget about the advantages of their exploratory nature. For Christopher it was cram facts and forget. He could not drink enough from the cup of knowledge before it overflowed and in his haste and need such quantities went up his nose, down his front, over the floor. Brian, beside him, casually dispelled the facts as if opening his throat, pouring them down, not bothering to swallow. With a bladder full of answers, exams to him were a natural means of alleviating much needed release. Christopher could not have partnered a more extreme opposite in attitudes even had he sat beside Savina. Brian was more concerned about what it meant to flow within St John's cultural concerns and having them adapt to his. Maths and physics – mere details through which he strove to assert his own adequately fleeting title. Because his interests were sailing on the ever fluctuating mode of universal events, he purposely walked the waves rather than electing to stand on solid ground. But only a few could actually see him rather than the Innmaker that possessed his skills. Where there was no faith there was little feeling and Brian was doomed to do much but achieve little by way of response. Christopher could well have worshipped him had he been given the time to grasp why he was so admirable, but from drawing to plan to story to text, Brian failed to be nothing more than the boastful giant of the many minor moments forming forgettable distractions. Ken McGibb could deal with Brian's quite frequent reactions to the mathematical rule with a sweeping smirk – youth speaks, maturity listens, silence wins.

But Brian was no mean mind at maths. He shared with Tessa and Savina a further seven periods of the subject under the tuition of the Departmental Head, Elliot Morrison, next door. A Level Mathematics was a strange, often cantankerous beast with at least two heads: Pure and Applied, and demanded abject studies from all on the syllabus towards what were known as Papers I and III. For those with extra aptitude, and Christopher had a few months since dissolved the illusion of being one of these, a further two heads, Papers II and IV were an option which when taken with I and II offered successful candidates two complete and separate certificates. In a sense the specialized uncertainty of how far maths could delve created from the latter papers a binding independence for the two categories. Christopher had never heard of applied maths until he had been asked to consider it as a separate A level. He had heard rumour of additional maths being tough, but he had been nurtured on a Scottish stream where O levels were O levels and nothing else. To confuse him even more after accepting, there would be two teachers: Ken McGibb for Pure/Applied (I and III) and Elliot Morrison for the extension to Pure and Applied (II and IV). So the system could only be understood if split into the categories of PAM and PAAM (pronounced palm); understood, that is, if one thought like Henry Dazel. And Henry hadn't even done maths, and Henry had long since left, and likewise, thought Christopher, I have long since left – left PAAM at the beginning of this term in order to push my way through PAM at the end of next term. What he had been left with was seven extra periods of private study. Lots of time but no excuses, especially in the case of homework. He prayed: maybe a subject of such colossal importance as rugby will all but make this lesson an instant appreciation of maths now, not maths that should have been done earlier.

But it was not to be.

'I left my work at home,' he explained, applying an unconvincing shrug as if evidence of the typical.

'Where, I suppose, it belongs,' said Ken, busy tapping into place the doubtlessly spotless work handed in by the two girls, Tessa and Savina, in front. 'Not Brian's influence, I hope.'

'What, me?' said Brian, giving himself time to apply a few finishing touches to a study sketch of his future 'Tree of Knowledge' painting before looking up: 'Hardly. I didn't leave my homework at home. I just haven't done it.'

This candour was not offered as a means of consoling the teacher.

'Don't you think the work I set is important, laddie?'

'With or without it I'll pass the exam. Apparently that's what's important.'

'I see, and who's to say I'll put your name down for the exam?'

Ken McGibb had no choice as Elliot had already put Brian's name down for papers II and IV. Brian had a ruthless confidence.

'I know you will,' he said, as if expressing faith in Ken McGibb's courage rather than integrity in terms of 'I know you can do it'.

'But I'm not to know how competent you are unless you hand in your work?'

Brian laughed and made a stressed effort at flicking through pages of carefully constructed classwork. And he stood up with the others as the class was about to adjourn and said:

'I think it's a fairly safe bet, sir.'

But hardly a safe bet to count on Brian's help during private study.

'Homework, homework?' he said. 'What's this I hear? Homework? The word means suffering beyond endurance and so begone. Am I not busy concentrating on my masterpiece: "The Tree of Knowledge".'

'You were going to help me,' said Christopher resisting, but only just, an urge to plead.

Brian picked up a guitar and was all set to strum his way over to the smokers' side of the prefects' room where he didn't smoke but did a lot of sitting around and sketching and strumming and thinking and singing.

'Help you with what?'

'With the homework we didn't do and should have been handed in last period and now I've got to hand in tomorrow.'

'I did it. Who said I didn't do it?'

'You did.'

'I did? I thought about it. That's enough. Such thoughts are usually reserved for other more important matters, like, for instance, which one of my many skills I shall devote to the House Handicraft this year.'

He had already thought of that and had already told many what it was to be – 'The Tree of Knowledge', but he did not want it to be expressed in a way which negated other options.

Well, if it's your skill at escaping obligations, you'll win hands down for Durham, and Christopher gave the matter some seconds' attention himself.

What can I do for the House Handicraft? He looked at his maths. He looked at Savina who was looking at her maths. Nothing. I can do nothing. I am totally incapable. Furthermore, I don't wanna do nothing, not even think in proper English.

He wished he had opted for English. This was a recurring regret, not least because then he would have been with Louding who appeared to undergo less stress in translating Chaucer than he, Christopher, did in translating *Tranter*. But he had chosen Elliot Morrison's option instead, and, after one and a half years of cascading despair, was awarded seven further periods of private study for his pains. Compared to the maths that was left, let alone the lot he had not survived and was long forgotten, English, for all its pandering to historical tongues, seemed like a wonderland.

'Hey, *mon ami*,' said Louding, while colouring a cholesterol cluster and whipping down notes from a monstrous book propped up against the window ledge beside him, 'don't fall into the trap of thinking that English is interesting.'

'But it is. It must be compared to maths.'

'English is dull, dull, dull, because A levels insist on everything being made dull, dull, dull, no matter how interesting a subject may be before or after.'

'Mathematics is not dull,' said Savina. 'It's you, Christopher. You have a dull mind.'

'Sparkle it with your light, Savina. It's not too late.'

'It is up to you to apply yourself and learn. Everything is easy, Christopher. Maths very much so. It is only because you have not tried to learn it.'

'I can't. As you say, my mind is too dull.'

'Talking of which,' said Louding, 'there is no chance of English being made interesting if you have a teacher who has a dull mind *like what we've got*. I agree with Gavin when he says that A level English murders literature. Mr Burke and teachers like him are the main murder weapons. What I really hate and what he is full of are these questions which give flowing quotes either from past critics or the books themselves and finish off with that dreaded word: discuss. Discuss what?'

'Discuss whether A level English murders literature?'

'Mock if you wish,' said Louding, almost returning to his biology. 'At least you have the definite purpose of what is right or wrong. For us "nothing is right or wrong but thinking makes it so", in context.'

And in line with the designated winter terms – September to March – Mondays at school were extended by an extra two hours. These two hours were called Activities and at the beginning of every academic year all were obliged to choose from a list of many, attempt to form clubs and learn much and mainly go home two hours later than the other days. Christopher had joined the tape-recorder club and as a result of which had met Helen. They were still recording sounds together. They spliced their tapes with loving care and engineered an orchestra of metal tinkling clangs and wooden knocks. Patrick Eve, with an RE teacher's special consignment of blissful enthusiasm, managed to organize many such works, all worthy examples of the alternative.

'We could hand ours in as a contribution to the House Handicraft,' said Helen and then remembered that they could not. She wanted to assure Christopher that he was capable of doing something exhibitory, even if shared, but she was in York and he was in Durham, and in the context of such competitions the twain could not conjoin. 'I don't think I'll be here for the House Handicraft anyway.'

'I could always have you killed, stuffed and put on display.'

'How could you think such a thing?'

'True enough, I doubt if we'd even get third prize.'

She stopped the rewind and gave him a hug. He pressed the play as if attempting to record the hug he happily accepted.

'You don't really want me to leave for England do you? - even although I am coming back. Poor Christopher will be all by himself.'

'Today is Tuesday, the 29th, leap year day,' stated Helen. 'People propose to each other on this day.'

Christopher, last night, had given up in despair, but now, this morning, figures were slowly starting to form, expressions were beginning to make sense, and functions he so wanted to have fit slotted into place. In spite of himself he was beginning to think like a mathematician, that part of his head which accepted maths having woken up. It would fall asleep soon enough, but while it was active…

'And then people have engagements which last six months and they get married in summer and have honeymoons in exotic places.'

'Do they now?' he said, looking up, looking down, writing some more.

'You're not listening.'

'I am. You said people have honeymoons in exotic places. Cyprus is an exotic place and we're here in Cyprus, so why don't we have a honeymoon?'

'We have to get married first.'

Maths firmly took hold and meant more than any comment Christopher may have made. Helen took his silence for an answer too delicate to express, and at first she thought that the mechanics of such a honeymoon did not necessitate the ritual of marriage in Christopher's eyes. She was prepared to take offence, but then the alternative meaning to the whirring scribble of pencil against paper as he jotted down one set of figures beneath another made her beam with delight.

'Is this your way of proposing to me, Christopher?'

'What?' He hadn't heard. 'I suppose so.'

'You mean it?' Her eyes almost shot out, and she was up from her seat ready to give a whoop of joy and announce to the whole world inside the prefects' room the great news had she not remembered that she had not exactly given him the required answer. 'Oh Christopher, my sweet, I will, yes I will, but when?'

'Oh you know,' he said, circling some numbers, fashioning a further idea from what he remembered as a Morrison trained route, 'it's up to you.'

'Wait 'til my friends hear of this.'

Helen's friends, the ones to whom she told everything she was later on to tell Christopher did in fact exist. Christopher was not sure who they specifically were. They remained a nebulous group of sixth form girls who partially enclosed Helen's school time within a world of keenly-focussed topical advice. This could not include Savina because she was too clever, too upper-sixth formish and ultimately too Cypriot, and therefore not fashionable enough for them, and it appeared to absolve Marion whom, apart from Helen, did not have girlfriends as such, only acquaintances she tagged alongside when not alongside Louding. Christopher suspected Sheila Millings, the sister of Chris Millings who sat in front of him on his bus – she was a bus-prefect of another route – as being a particularly vociferous member of this sisterhood. Helen knew her well. Sheila was a sixth former who rarely entered the prefects' room. She was mentioned by Helen many times as an intermediate source of information, and the final condition which made her perfect for the group was an underlying disapproval of Christopher as fitting decisively into pop-music-boyfriend fodder thus making him unsuitable for the top ten needs of someone like Helen. Helen had no qualms about telling Christopher what her friends thought of him. She was confident that he would somehow benefit from this and thus make efforts to improve his attitude towards her. No visible change had occurred as such, still hovering as he was between the extremes of frogdom and princehood, and the advice she could expect to receive from any immediate group session made her sit still for a while and think.

'Perhaps I should wait until I've finished my nurses' course.'

'What, to tell your friends?'

'No, silly. For us to get married.'

'Hmm, yes, perhaps you should wait.'

'You mean *we* should wait. Both of us get married you know, not just me.'

He looked at her. He was married to his maths which was beginning to look more like art the further down the page he went, but he could affably grant her the focus of his breather.

'Why not?' he asked, quite sweetly. 'Marriage would suit you quite admirably.'

'Do you really think so? You and me together? Of course, I realize that I haven't started the course yet, but I'll definitely be starting in July if my interview and whatnot is all right.'

But Christopher reverted to not listening. He was enthralled. For now his mathematics overshadowed Helen's otherwise more charming presence. He was actually getting somewhere and the result was beginning to shine in sight. Delighted, he reached across and gave Savina's hair a tug, but she was not impressed. Neither was Tessa. They had solved the problem long ago and in the want of sturdy academics of their age had moved on. Still, this time he had accepted no help – would have done so had any help been offered, but he could now produce his homework finished and correct for once. Break was a few minutes away and he would get the chance to hand it in then. He gave Helen a quick kiss. He was pleased with himself.

'Do you really want to marry me?' she asked, this time suspiciously.

'Now is a good time to ask a favour,' he admitted. 'I feel quite good.'

'But you should ask me. It's not right that I ask you, and you already did, didn't you?'

'Ask what?' He looked at her watch and kissed her hand and said: 'Listen, we'll talk later. I've get to get this work handed in.'

He darted up and out, almost colliding with Gavin darting in, his entrance shaped in the delivery of news that he, as head boy, was privy to and now allowed to share, and so Christopher remained on the threshold to listen.

'All fifth and sixth formers to meet in the assembly hall after break,' he announced in one breath. He then took two and said it again, requesting all prefects to spend part of their break going around with this news to the isolated groups of fifth and sixth formers. Thus it was that Christopher, along with many others, was informed quite a few times within the fifteen minutes which followed where he had to go instead of where he was scheduled to be. He spent his break walking to Ken McGibb's room, handing in his work and walking back; he had not planned on Ken McGibb being there. Most teachers spent their break, outside break-duties, out of the way in the staff room along the second floor of the main building. He would not have planned on the door being locked had Ken McGibb been out, but the door was open and the teacher was inside, busy marking some of the mountains of maths he had professionally invited into his already overloaded schedule of simply being a teacher. Christopher's contribution therefore was considered now by both to be a drop in the ocean – the teacher, understandably, not inordinately impressed. He stared at the shortish and sensitive looking student who stood as if ready to be dismissed, not wanting to believe that maths was beyond him, but ready to assume that neither was Innmaker's influence.

'Did you de this during private study?' he asked with the famous Ken McGibb smirk.

'Does it show?' asked Christopher, assuming concern but thinking instead how every hour's study was privation. 'Does it really matter?'

'It has to matter to you if you want to pass the exam?'

He wanted nothing more and Ken had put his name down with this in mind. At the assembly hall, in front of all those concerned, and a few who were not, such names were read out under the corresponding exams to be taken at O and A level standard next term. This took some time. Not that anybody really cared. Most were blissfully aware of the lessons they were missing. Christopher was happier sitting there with Louding, Marion and Helen than he would have been across the yard in the domestic studies department, learning how to fry fish and chips as part of a cookery lesson the two lads had chosen from a fairly short list of minority courses required to be taken every Tuesday, two periods between breaks, by those studying for O and A levels. Cooking, at the time, seemed a good idea. Out in the wild world people needed to provide for themselves, and much was already said about the student's stomach being the route to his brain. However, learning to cook was hard work and not the lark many of the lads who opted for this course thought they would have.

'I quite fancy fish and chips, though,' said Louding. 'I could chomp away during French, which I think is the right thing to do to appreciate a major cultural drive that defines that nation.'

He thought this every week, and every Tuesday's French was taken up by sampling his culinary disasters.

'Good job I don't do biology on a Tuesday. Not much difference between my goulash and those rodents we dissect.'

'I bet my name gets read out more times than yours,' whispered Helen.

'I should hope so,' said Christopher. 'I'm only taking two exams.'

As it turned out so was Louding. He thought he was taking three. He had almost dozed off to this idea and the waste of time it was reading out all the names and the more useful thoughts of fish and chips fizzing and smelling and frying across the yard. Surely everyone is well aware of what exams they'll be doing, even if not aware of anything else. Sam Emery, the deputy head, had not a boring voice, but his simple task did not help to enlighten this fact. However, when he stated: 'English A level candidates are as follows', pondering perhaps for a second on the nostalgic overtones besetting such deputy heads as he who had once been subject to this subject, Louding opened one eye and with one ear listened out for his name. He opened his other eye and his other ear as the list cited sounded alphabetically free of his influence.

'Did you hear my name just then?' he whispered to Marion.

'When?' she whispered back.

'Just then.'

'No, I don't think anybody called you.' She looked around to make sure.

'No, I mean on the list.'

'Hey, Louding,' said Christopher, cautious though he was about interrupting a whispered conversation, 'I thought you were doing A level English.'

He could well have been consistently misinformed all this time.

'So did I,' said Louding. He caught Gavin's eye a few rows up – an enquiring stare: what's gone wrong. 'I think Burke's whipped me off the list for this year. He wants me to do another year.'

He was shushed by a teacher standing on the side.

'Christ, my life is being compromised by some narrow-minded pillock, and I'm told to be silent.'

But he said this in a whisper to Christopher, and was silent. After a few more exam lists were read out he shrugged.

'I didn't want to do the A level anyway. His not wanting me to do it amounts to a mere insult.'

'In that case, give up English altogether and take another seven periods of private study. It worked for me when I chucked in PAAM.'

'Ha, but, *mon ami*, you were fairly well in with Morrison, but thou knoweth not the Burke as I. He loveths me not and likens me to a lazy lout. He won't grant my escape. It is to the bitter end that I am shackled.'

'But he can't stop you from…'

This time Christopher was shushed.

Louding did not want to have the attitude of a compelled failure and so he refused to accept sympathy from anyone, least of all Marion who thought that a catastrophe had stirred into her hero a more morose form of silence than usual. She accompanied him to the lists posted on the large board outside the hall. It was true. His name was not there under English.

'Gosh, Simon, what are you going to do?'

'Not much I can do except enjoy my freedom. I've achieved the ultimate. I'm not doing English A level.'

'You could always fight your case,' suggested Christopher. 'Make an appeal. I think that's what they call it.'

'To go above Burke's head I'd have to appeal to my maker, and I do that every time I sit through one of his lessons. I'm not really that bothered.'

'I'd be fuming,' said Marion, fuming. 'I'd be hopping mad.'

'I wouldn't be hopping mad over not having to do an exam,' said Helen, somehow clearing the air with her innocent transposition of what Louding had meant by the ultimate. 'I don't think it means anything really to do English.'

'Or not to do English,' Louding added. 'That's the answer.'

'I'd still be hopping mad,' insisted Marion, hopping mad. 'I don't like doing exams, but I don't like teachers pushing me around, doing the deciding for me.'

Louding agreed: 'But it's more a conclusion than a decision.'

He walked away as if enough had been said on the subject.

Such things are meant to be, thought Christopher. He thought this when Ken McGibb was late turning up. Brian was demonstrating his perfect arc trick with a blackboard compass. Edmund was noisily consuming a packet of ready-salted crisps. Savina and Tessa assumed the normal written discussion of numerical events, while Steve Galbraith and Wilfred George both looked large enough just ahead of the Innmaker's swirling spear to present a hefty siege once his guard was down. Christopher was busy doubting his existence while the Innmaker was steadily divining his own – into that of the Mighty Thor of Asgard. He was an avid fan and he swore Marvel-based oaths at his lingering, retreating foes.

'By my father's name, this lad will freeze before you demons exploit its verdant repose etc etc.'

But they attacked and he was down and the girls sighed and Edmund disposed of his crisp packet with a loud bang and all was well with the world when Ken McGibb finally entered. To him: the scene: the Innmaker pinned to the ground by a blackboard ruler, Steve and Wilfred George overcasting the fallen god, Edmund sniggering slightly behind a jotter of calculus notes and the Great War dogfight doodles, Savina and Tessa, loyal to the authoritative sense of prefect witnesses, and Christopher alone, daydreaming: not the ideal sixth form discipline to a subject requiring major forms of cerebral conviction.

'What's happening? Why aren't we busy studying? The A level exams aren't that far away.'

'In my capacity as the Innmaker,' said Brian, as he rose to his feet and carelessly dusted himself, 'I would have been devoted to the idea. But the almighty Thor has no time for maths. He is busy saving mankind from the evil of demons and the like.'

'Such as yerself.'

'I expect to be persecuted. That is my lot.'

So did Steve and Wilfred George, both of whom dramatically exploited the maths they had ignored by presenting particular problems for Ken to consider in his capacity now as 'revisions' tutor. Not that the syllabus had beaten time with a few months to spare. There were still a few grey areas. For Christopher they were generally black and revision often inspired little more than an undercoat of mottled beige. Edmund, on the other hand, regarded all the shadings pure until proven stained through the practical use of a far from ideal world. The world of maths did not fascinate the lad all the more for this. Steve may have been problematically competent, along with Wilfred George; Brian, Tessa and Savina gliding along a crest with Christopher floundering in the troughs below; Edmund did not care to associate his beliefs with any of these varied skills. He was in it for the want of doing something better. Science had that dignity lacking in most other forms of research, and he did not believe in the value of art. He did not believe in art.

Edmund Whitehead adopted the lofty view that allowed such expressions as 'Good grief' and 'Great Scot' to amplify his non-belief in many things. All concepts were dowsed by the cynical side of his sharp mind. He did not believe that action spoke louder than words, and he used this as a premise for the considerable amount he managed to avoid. His was a world wherein the duality of thinkers and doers maintained progress producing conflict, himself a thinker insofar as he kept his hands clean while being willing to provide the means, later on, for others to dirty theirs. He did not go through the process of disbelieving in God because of an intellectual trend. Besides, he could not abide philosophers and the minimal load they placed upon his worthy tax-collector ideal. He merely consorted with the easy life and from it achieved a few grades higher than those who insisted on struggle. He was the only one in sixth form who managed to escape the Friday obligation of games by means of conscientious objection – every sport is an attack on the dignity of being human; team sports in particular being obnoxiously abhorrent.

'You know the way they insist football's a religion?' he once asked Christopher.

'No.'

Edmund chose to ignore this unhelpful reply and stated: 'Well in that religion I'm an atheist.'

Christopher immediately saw the theological flaw in his argument, defaulting as he usually did, mainly because of his age, to the ontological definition of belief. Atheists refused to accept the reality of God, but like it or not football insisted on actually existing. Christopher liked him only because one could be assured that in his company there would be no sudden ideas about going and joining in a game of rugby. The experience of non-doers often favoured security. However, Christopher disliked him because he, Edmund, more than anyone, tended to expose in Christopher those areas of ignorance which undermined whatever freedom he may have earned through knowledge. Because of Edmund Christopher suspected that he knew very little about politics, Russia, World War II and the Apollo Moonshots. Edmund brought in books which could never have been read had Christopher even the time and the money spare to see the places the detailed prose described. But Edmund expected him to read and was happily disgruntled by the few pages turned and the rest discarded. He told Christopher that there was money to be made in solving world-wide problems. Christopher informed the Innmaker of this and Brian replied that this was what he was doing. But somehow the problems Brian tackled did not consist of the greater worries preoccupying Edmund's stress-free plans, and Christopher could not put his finger on why, and furthermore had little idea himself as to how he could swap any solutions with the ultimate sought-after cash. Christopher also found it hard to trust a lad more or less his age who took a contemptuous view towards Rock Music, preferring Bartok and Stravinsky over the likes of Led Zeppelin and Jethro Tull. Christopher was more than willing to indulge the esthetics of early orchestral stuff, only he wasn't sure who Bartok was.

'Who's Bartok?'

'Good grief!'

He dreamt of this, the physics class, John Warwick droning over past cases of failed inventions. Into this dream, into his class, came one of the heroes who carried with him a solid shaped like a Vulcan jet aircraft. It was small enough to hold and dip into a tank of orange liquid. Pulling the object out the place gradually turned crimson as if translucence had arrived by the red liquid flowing through it. John explained that this was the principle of day-glow, and that he, the forgotten hero, had invented it. The classroom underwent a change as was something of a habit befitting the narratives of Christopher's dreams. He was on a walk through the factory where the stuff was being processed. But had it not been a failure? They wanted to test out this day-glow liquid, a further level to its unexplained qualities which had yet to find a use in the artless world of business. They arrived at where a tank-full bubbled and puffed. Someone, either Brian or Edmund, or maybe both, picked Christopher up and chucked him in. And he bubbled and puffed and woke up.

What a silly dream, he thought. The strange sensation of having been 'day-glowed' left him with one foot still inside the dream and the rest became an orange relapse of bubbling and puffing and running circles which surrounded his semi-conscious welcome into not quite the Wednesday he was normally ready, if reluctant, to use. My experience is just a Wednesday and yet halfway between I could be totally renewed. Renewed and free in order to think. If I could be paid for thinking then I would come up with the ideas, and I wouldn't need Brian and Edmund to have me gape at the chasm between me and their inspiration. He did have inspiration. He once thought he was a prince of light. Not so long ago as well, and every Sunday afternoon I would walk three miles and join my princess, wherein the picture we painted together was royal and magic. But now, it's not more than common and flickering. God, how I loved those Sunday afternoons.

Poor Wednesday and even poorer Thursday. To what do they amount in the Universal week? Everybody is too busy hating Mondays. People (ie, in Christopher's world, the Rolling Stones and Moody Blues) write poetry and songs about Tuesday, and others occasionally bake pancakes, and then its downhill to glorious Friday. Every Friday is a good Friday. It pre-empts the weekend and often shapes an anti-climax out of the local leisure of which Saturday and then Sunday are supposed to supply in abundance. Quite a few people, (none that Christopher could readily name) dislike the idea of Sundays. If there was a six day week with four school days, and in effect no Wednesday, so as to lessen the afternoon boredom of the Sabbath, significantly out of kilter would be a bunch of mathematicians who would insist that an even number of days creates some sort of vacuum. So in effect Wednesday was created in order to balance a system which keeps Sunday holy and dull. And in order to appease any feelings of inadequacy and fight off bitterness in being the middleman, it was named after the father of the gods who appears now and again in the Marvel comics to warn his son against being too hasty. This isn't getting my physics done, he thought. But think of a Wednesday you can remember. And he thought and he couldn't. There was a likelihood that he couldn't deliberately. Maybe that extra-enthralling Christmas had fallen on a Wednesday. Now he was pushed to remember an extra-enthralling Christmas, and not many of his birthdays remained as highlights in his life.

This was not a highlight of his life. It rated maybe third from bottom. He was writing up the physics practical he did on Monday, all to do with an exciting concept called heat capacity. They had failed to teach him about such things in Scotland. Over there water was water, except a certain Cambeltown Loch which might have once been whisky and now was probably just sludge. He turned back in his book to his other practicals. Not a bad record, mainly Cs and he managed to achieve a B here and there, but also a D here and there with red-inked remarks. Savina, on the other hand, with half the effort and pages he used up was doing badly if she got a B. Warwick either approved of and practiced positive discrimination or caught the immortal drift of her Greek influenced English and rewarded the style as well as the results. Another reason could have been that her work was indeed spotless, and he, Christopher, with his strained and struggling load was unable to shape up to the genius in her brevity. Tessa also took her fare share of As, but with her it was effort whereas with Savina it was control. Control too in Brian's humorous scrawl which lashed furiously into the graph pages as well as the lined. He saw no reason why he should waste paper or be directed to where he could write, where he could draw and how far he could go. Edmund's work was a guarded treasure. What had been done could be left for prosperity next century which, as he was rarely tired of reminding others, was not too far away. But present tasks kept the secret grades a formal sounding board for most of the 'Good Grief!'s exclaimed when watching Christopher stumble over both simple statements and semi-complex conclusions. It would be a self-demoralising campaign ever to compare my work to his or Brian's. He knew well the sympathy he could expect from Wilfred George, and on a bad week Steve Galbraith was apt to swear at his lot.

But where is the comfort in imagining everyone doing as badly as me? he thought. Therefore, why should I feel bad when everyone does better? Because I could do better? Trouble is, there is never any sign about having done enough. Everything is compared but endurance. Endurance cannot be compared. It can only be lived – endured. That must be wrong. I seem less able to endure maths than Louding does his English, but he won't be doing it, and yet he has to do it, has to endure it, without the achievement. But am I right? I know I'm right. Christopher tried to think his way around to being right. Endurance is pure.

As pure as maths when the problem demands only one line of thought like one correct twig on a healthy tree pointing to the treasure, or one correct grain of sand among the mountains which have to be cleared – but it could be done and understood within four months – '"I doubt it," said the Carpenter, and shed a bitter tear.'

'Why seven maids with seven mops?' asked Brian.

'I think there's something mystic about the number seven.'

'And maids and mops, are they mystic, do you think?'

'Oh, without doubt.'

'Why the Walrus?'

'Why the Carpenter?' said Christopher. 'Why anything?'

'The carpenter is close to God – the Messiah's profession, and it takes a carpenter to make a cross. But the walrus is a beast with tusks floundering in the depths and looking like Churchill gone wrong on land. Where's the poetic grace in that? But there's my answer. Who needs grace when there is sand and oysters and plenty of sunshine making the billows smooth and bright?'

'Like your maths?' suggested Ken McGibb, having heard the final phrase which had crossed in passion the border between whispering and talk.

'Sir? Did you have any doubts?'

'Let me have the maths, first, laddie, and then expect an answer.'

'Pure poetry is maths,' explained Brian, looking down at his *Tranter* and then from the text book to the end of the desk, the on-going drama between paper and chewed pencils. 'Did you know, sir?' he ventured, looking up at the comically stern Scotsman who, for all the respect he may have gained, was unable to offer anything but disguised humour to the discourteously clever lad, 'that Lewis Carroll is more widely quoted than Robert Burns.'

'Rubbish,' said Ken McGibb. 'Is Lewis Carroll's birthday celebrated with as much intensity as Burns?'

'That's hardly the point sir?'

'I think you'll find it is. There's an American book called *Of Mice and Men* which is from Burns and that indicates how much Burns is respected and quoted in other countries.'

'O. Henry wrote a book called *Cabbages and Kings*,' said Edmund in his incidental tone which indicated another *Tranter* problem successfully solved and therefore, what next?

What was next was Elliot Morrison strolling quickly in on a loud abrupt tap, pointing at Edmund and asking him:

'Where's your tie, lad?'

Elliot Morrison believed that all the boys should be seen wearing ties during the designated winter terms. The tradition of Englishmen sweating it out under the collar was all part of the case of making irrelevant the fact that winter could be pretty much like summer in the few weeks prior to Easter. So Edmund couldn't argue and didn't. Instead he produced from his bag a tie which indeed seemed very worn, with the frayed edges forming the holes as well as the design.

'My war tie,' he explained, which probably meant his war against having to wear a tie.

Elliot Morrison had a problem. It was maths. He was head of the department but Ken McGibb was the acknowledged best. He had not entered on the spur of a tie-less purging moment, although none would have disagreed as to the extent of his entrance had he made his exit then with Edmund suitably shackled. But no, he explained, he had a friend in England who sent him a problem once a month and he would reply with the solution plus another problem, similar to Leibniz's correspondence with Newton which had simultaneously produced calculus on both sides of the Channel. Was what he had now something similar because he had worked on it all morning and was closer to despair than any form of a reasonable answer? It was closer to the end of the month. Ken McGibb did not mind his proceedings being interrupted by a Morrison pampering of a class who could probably learn more from the intrigue of what Morrison's friend would have to trust as being individual and solitary work.

First he and Elliot tackled the rudiments of his design, and eventually Ken McGibb had to admit to the unique nature of its twist. Unless a new branch of maths was discovered soon, and they had already covered the blackboard twice with all manner of suggestions thrown at them from the class, Elliot would be faced with writing defeat as a substitute for the solution and also the challenge of formulating an even tougher task. Brian offered a few routes all of which led to a strangle hold on logic. Edmund loosened his tie, Wilfred and Steve tightened the argument but whittled it to nothing, and Christopher sat, listened and got hopelessly lost. Even Tessa had to shake her head after discovering the misdirection compounding her initial agreement with what Brian was attempting to explain. Finally Savina volunteered the solution: it had taken her three pages which she whipped down during the many minutes of argument. She walked to the blackboard and rubbed clean the combined work of her teachers and colleagues. She then introduced her own theory and chalked up the problem from beginning to end, including a beautifully controlled twist which went straight for the answer. Ken McGibb looked at Elliot. Elliot looked at the twist which curved slightly because of the strain endured when reaching a metal slat of the rolling board. The twist was valid. Savina sat down and Morrison quickly took a few notes before bowing to her excellence and leaving. Edmund removed his tie.

'Mr Morrison is like a man who is fascinated by a growing shadow beneath his feet,' she explained to Christopher and Brian on the way out. 'He is always missing out on tiny things like looking up.'

'An example of very basic lateral thinking,' said Brian enthusiastically. 'When something seems to be moving beneath you, look up or be crushed.'

'I don't understand,' said Christopher, who was yet to understand the problem, least of all the solution. If the likes of Morrison was to be crushed, what about himself?

'What I do understand, though,' he added aside to Brian, 'it took one maid with one mop to sweep it clear in one minute.'

A wealthy Thursday and even more the wealthy Wednesday now that it's been and gone. It's not like I dislike Wednesdays. Just that I've struggled through one half of the week. Is it really fair that I should struggle through another? Suppose so, he thought as he stood and tried to catch up on the words of worship the other lads bunched around him had long ago lost. Or else it wouldn't be half a week.

It was *his* hymnal. All but he had lost their copies of the book he now held up for the others to read. He was expected to find the numbers and they were expected to sing. Safety in number at the back, hidden by the tall and muscular fifths, six of the sixth form lads from Durham House now paid for the mistake of turning up for registration and being told that there was a religious assembly for them in the hall. Each sixth former believed that there were too many members of his house, and Durham in particular could hardly fit inside the hall. Furthermore it was too annoying having a religious assembly on Thursday. After all, the entire school would be reminded *en bloc* about God, the God who existed for schools, the Great Headmaster in the sky who loved little boys with high voices, looked after the Queen and insisted on separate assemblies for Catholics. Christopher was a Catholic. But he still had to attend Durham assemblies because he was in Durham, and nobody could escape the mass, Friday morning stand-out in the sun. It was not decided as yet by himself or the authorities, of which there were many, what he was first: a Catholic or a Durhamite. The Catholics collected themselves one morning every week somewhere around the History Department billets. The morning varied, unlike Christopher who never went. Not now. He chose to think that those assemblies he did not attend did not exist. A sixth form luxury was vaguely attained in such philosophical assertions towards House assemblies of which there were two sorts: planning and religious, but those who attended neither, which were few and risked reprimand, were easily outnumbered by those who attended both.

Durham planning assemblies were called religiously at least once a week. The religious assemblies were not so consistently planned. The Durham housemaster was a man such assemblies could depend upon. It was not just a matter of form that he believed his house to be best. He was convinced they were best. In order for his house to sustain this conviction he thought it was a necessary part of the Durham durability to call regular house assemblies and to tell them that they were best. The religious assemblies at least spared them this exhortation of their own prowess. The process of praising God denied the competitive rights of one group over another, or even another four as in this case when, during planning assemblies, attended outside on a reserved spot in the main yard, those less interested and on the outside of the semi-circular gathering could stare around and catch the distant eyes of the similarly interested standing on the outside of other houses having their planning assemblies on their own reserved spots. To tackle the struggle common to the five houses a lot of talking and planning were construed to three simultaneous demands: take part, do well and win. The main participation, avoided by all sixth formers alike and gradually treated with contempt by the fifth, was the winning of house-points. All teachers could award house-points and did so liberally, and these tokens of appreciation for additional work done well were as much an embarrassment to the older students as they were marks of pride and achievement to the young. So the ultimate of either embarrassment or achievement according to the record of age and attitude was in the planning assembly ritual of awarding house-point certificates to those with ten or more points to their names. This meant the humiliating or honourable task of hearing one's name being called, followed by the straggle or march up to shake the housemaster's hand and accept in a shaken or proud grasp the invidious or compelling sheet of square-cut paper. Not that any sixth former purposely posted his own name to any house-point he might have accidently achieved. A victim was chosen with the conspiratorial stock of likely names, and each painfully concealed point had skillfully daubed upon it the forged signature of the unfortunate implant within a future honours' list. Most teachers, however, were aware of the sixth form reluctance to acknowledge house-points, and so the pleasure of seeing the unsuspecting student receive his or her unearned certificate was a rare event, rare enough to assuage any suspicions the housemaster may have had of contempt and rare indeed this climatic and united feeling of intent awarded inwardly to all those who had processed the happening. Who they were was not a likely preoccupation, even among those who feared the worse, like the Innmaker, convinced now because of his demonstrative skills, that a number of unlikely sixth form Durhamites had it in for him. It was indeed a well founded fear.

    The Innmaker was Durham's champion. He both enjoyed and encouraged this status on his own sustained impression that he had no choice. With the exception of house-points, he took part and did well. Louding was another Durham champion, something of a specialist insofar as his sporting devotions depended entirely on speed. A house-point certificate to him would fall somewhat flat within an anticipated abandon of jubilant girls who loved him ferociously. Louding would most likely rise to the occasion and, certificate in hand, stand beside the housemaster and wave to the fans who, with this more than mild incentive, scream for his already controlled attention. It would never do to have any member of their form so outrageously worshipped, especially as a result of a well-planned practical joke, and so, to the sixth formers, Louding was safe. Christopher's own security was never called to question but for opposite reasons. Nobody seemed to care what line of fire was directed at him, small and dreamingly insignificant as he was, merely dependable for such occasions as now when he and five others needed a hymnal and he, from his sturdy case of rare books, could produce one.

His doubts, fears and suspicions and a short following of double-edged faiths took on the more introspective slant of wondering why he ever bothered. He wanted to believe in God and so he did, and because others did not and as he was not like others he refused not to believe. There again others did believe but for reasons that did not conform to his own. Faith was in actual fact an adventure, or one of the few sources which could be counted upon as a promise. Today's adventure: a girl called Grace whose story was read out at the assembly. Along with her father she saved a boatload of stricken men from being dashed to death by rocks and waves. What had to be done took doubtless courage because no question was allowed to enter its realm of doubtful sense. When we offer a hand to those in need we should not hesitate or the trap of doubt is set, but that's not the same, he thought, because my trap has already sprung, and freedom is offered by questioning courage, accepting hesitation, regarding all acts (except that, of course, of saving men from drowning or similar exercises in the realm of International Rescue) as trivial compared to rebellion. Christopher was no rebel, not having the courage, but he understood what it was in the face of this one week's work only to be followed by another, and a string of Wednesdays like a necklace of bear's teeth made from plasticine.

But Thursday was more the plastic day, often shaped by the slide-show experience of invited speakers. The two periods between the two breaks on Thursday enjoyed the formless title of Civics wherein all the fifth and sixth formers were asked to attend a lecture in the hall given by one of many that the RAF had on call: men and women who had seen the world in all its cold, disease-ridden, colourful, grey, obnoxious and intriguingly hideous beauty, and did not mind informing these unassuming young adults as to what they were missing out on by being stuck at school – even a school stuck on the end of an idyllic island like Cyprus. Such stuff for dreams but not for sleep. Unfortunately a combination of late nights and the midday heat would catch up on the young minds pressed between droning paragraphs concentrating to the beat of changing slides. Anticipating the next picture, when it would arrive and what it would show, how it would blend in with the ruffling notes of the nervous or confident speaker had the predictable soporific effect.

However, today Patrick Eve presided over civics with a difference. His school role offered him the freedom gained from subtle differences between divinity, theology and RE, all three of which were represented through him by his ever-smiling face of Christianity. His smile actively allowed a large crop of the front part of his unruly hair to fall over and cover in total his beaming and enthusiastic eyes. Every gesture which followed the habitual movement of his right hand pushing his hair back into place was in keeping with the spiritual strength of a man whose principles demanded active questions, answers and further discussion. And on such a note did he form civics today. With professional proficiency he separated the gathered formers into groups of ten to fifteen. Each group of ten to fifteen went to a specifically available room or part of the hall and discussed a printed list of eight controversial school rules. Each group had to elect a spokesman who would voice to the other groups and a prepared panel of teachers, once they all gathered together again, the opinions and conclusions of that particular group. Christopher was obliged to assume the role for his group – but he couldn't remember why – and he quickly scribbled down what he could, adding bits and pieces of his own thoughts. Eventually all were back in the hall. Ready to face polite abuse and moderate to radical contention sat a panel of four: Patrick Eve, all ears for light-hearted battle, Sam Emery, the humanistic pose of a deputy headmaster, ready to concede momentary doubts in the system, Terrance Duncan, head of History and Geography, and the deputy headmistress, Juliette Neverland, resourceful, careful, composed.

Items for discussion were in the order of a list Patrick Eve had printed on the sheet each group had been given. However, an outsider without the list, on listening with interest to the cross-fire of comments both between the panel and the group spokesmen and between the spokesmen themselves, would have happily denied any particular system exercised in the promoting of the inherent controversy of living within this school's system.

Item one: the school was not democratic. Terrance Duncan stressed that there was no time for democracy within these few years of learning the ropes of life, to which the Innmaker retorted that the ropes were not even pulled until the school had become part of the past.

'What is part of the past,' he said, 'is homework. It is past and gone. We don't need it. It is an excuse for those who don't work to do no further work, and is a bane to those who want to do more.'

'There is an interesting theory,' said Patrick, with finger posed in the air just above his other hand about to preempt the fall of his hair, 'that pupils do not like doing study and therefore won't do it unless made to feel that it has to be done.'

'That's study is boring. School work is dull. No matter how fascinating a subject may be, the British system of education does its best to make it something of a yawn.'

'There is no trend more attractive than rejecting discipline for the easy life,' said Terrance. 'But there is no trend more disastrous and within youth it has to be thwarted before it takes root.'

'But I'm inclined to agree,' said Patrick, 'that under certain circumstances homework should be entirely optional.'

'To do away with homework is equivalent to doing away with lessons,' said Juliette Neverland, 'and education was never meant to be easy. If it is not interesting that is entirely the fault of the pupil.'

This resulted in lots of vociferous head-shaking accompanied by whispered versions of rubbish, Christ and one 'Good grief!' mainly from the back of the hall.

'The onus is on teachers,' said one, 'to make whatever they teach interesting.'

'There is too much pressure for teachers to follow exam syllabus to make anything interesting,' said another.

And then said another and then another, and Christopher wanted to be another but Patrick was too fast, standing up, throwing back his hair and bringing to light the next point on the list about missing lessons.

'Is is such a crime?' asked Steve Galbraith, 'although I wouldn't know. It may be something of a trend to reject discipline but playing truant has gone out of fashion.'

'Perhaps,' said Sam Emery, 'too much fuss is made of the truant. Many of the world's greatest men and women played truant, an occupation I don't in any way advocate but need not throw out of perspective. School was once much harder than it is now. In comparison there is really no need to exercise such an obvious means of escape when such escape in the forms which transgresses other rules is already supplied. For instance, the next rule of the list: You should not smoke in school…'

Christopher was pushed from behind. He did not really want to talk about this but had so far said nothing on behalf of his group. It was Oliver who pushed him and neither of them smoked.

'I … er,' he began and he looked at his notes and was unable to read the inch long scribble he had made alongside this point. O-ho, he thought, from-the-top-of-my-head time: 'I don't smoke but I believe that people should be allowed to if they want to. But …' he said over the supporting comments he immediately won for himself, 'there is a point of disturbing those who prefer not to smoke.'

'And the need,' intervened Patrick, 'of preventing younger pupils from taking up the habit which is now universally accepted as being damaging to health.'

'But so is drinking coke and 7-up,' said Robert Johnson, 'and eating cream buns and chocolate.'

'I think,' said Christopher, maintaining the floor and formulating an attractive idea from beneath the top of his head, 'that a place could be reserved specifically for those who wish to smoke. It will isolate the smokers from the non-smokers and lower the temptation offered to the younger forms, a temptation which is quite – is quite, er, there, present, when one considers how many really start smoking at school because it is forbidden.'

'Listen,' said Sam over the hubbub of engendered reaction to any idea that rules more than pleasure promote rebellion, 'on no account can I agree with young people smoking. It is anti-social…'

'No its not,' called out someone at the back.

'...And totally stupid.'

'Not as stupid as a lot of these rules.'

'I can sympathize only slightly with those who have to do without for the few hours of school jurisdiction – which I may add still covers the time that pupils are on the buses going to and from their homes – but it would take self-discipline and an overall cooperation to cure the smoking problem which I am well aware of exists within this school, rather than offering a sanctuary to those who wish to slowly commit suicide.'

'Tolerance is much more desirable than enforced abstinence,' said one.

'Why should we have to do without something which is done everywhere else?'

'What about coke and chocolates?'

'How many teachers smoke? And in the staff room?'

'You should not run down the corridors,' announced Patrick, reading part 4 of the list.

'That depends on what's chasing you,' said Robert.

'Or what you're chasing,' said Brian.

'Hardly relevant to this school,' said Terrance, and for once the majority there were able to agree with his statement. 'St John's does not provide the type of corridors usually associated with proscribed running. Of course the gangways between the billets are fairly narrow.'

'But they are also long,' said Brian, 'and who would want to run down them? They are usually only used as a route from one lesson to another.'

'But the next rule,' said Terrance, balancing his glasses in order to read from the list, 'is definitely disobeyed because it exists. One should not be of an unruly, untidy appearance: long hair, loose ties, etc.'

'Narrow-minded,' said one.

'Repressive,' said another.

'Absurd.'

'The length of one's hair does not necessarily endanger the soul,' said Patrick to the panel.

'That may be so,' said Sam, 'but I want to make it clear that although I'm not one for dictating individuals' appearances, appearance can be made individual enough without the extremes of unruly hair and wide open shirts, the latter point applying very much to the girls. As fashion still controls everything the youth of today wants to wear, I don't think I'm doing anything particularly new with my efforts to allow some credit for the neat and respectable turn out of the modern youth.'

'The robots of routine,' said Brian, and for the benefit of those not un-eager to move onto the next point he read out part six of the list: 'There should be no affectionate physical contact between members of the opposite sex.'

'What about members of the same sex?' asked Oliver, tempted again to push Christopher and fearless about popular connotations to do with his own surname. He gained the floor with this question, and decided to carry on with the relevance of the former point. 'If one is lucky enough to have a girl or boy friend worth constant hand-holding and physical affection, exercise of such affection should be left to the discretion of the couple involved.' Despite divided amusement he was allowed to continue. 'This applies to the holding of hands more than anything else, so teachers are led to believe. Emphasis against this has most members of staff sacrificing their break in order to wander the yards separating young lovers. This is senseless. We're in a large school and the variety of couples are such that it seems a measurable blessing that hand-holding is all the teachers are worried about. Go along with the tide. Don't interfere with what could be deep and meaningful.'

Juliette Neverland did not catch the hint of irony in Oliver's use of the last three words, not used to the philosophical overtone in his contempt for most of the trivia which to him lay like a carpet upon the school's otherwise frivolous existence.

'There is a time and place for everything,' she said.

'Yes,' said Patrick. 'While physical contact is very much a part of love, love need not depend on it.'

'Who mentioned anything about love,' said someone at the back.

Patrick's call for peace was cancelled by someone at the back shouting: 'Sex and violence. That's what this place needs.'

Thus ended the discussion which, because of lack of time, had to discard the final two rules referring to respect for teachers and the wearing of school uniforms. Sam Emery was no longer a member of the panel but the deputy head ordering everyone out except those at the back. But those at the back were closer to the front of the hall where the exit remained corruptibly impartial and they escaped first. The confusion assured by the immediate evacuation of the sixth formers left the panel harnessed to a notion that perhaps Patrick Eve's idea of dabbling in democracy was something of an undisciplined failure.

'Well,' said Christopher, sauntering out as the others rushed by, but catching up with Louding and Marion, leaving Helen to stroll around her area of scheduled prefect's duty, 'that made a change.'

Louding shrugged and then he remembered: 'Yes, I didn't fall asleep.'

'I couldn't. I had to stay awake in order to talk.'

'Yeah, and how come you defended the smokers?' asked Marion. 'I think they should all be expelled.'

'I was merely commenting on general feeling.'

'If Marion had her way,' Louding said as if realising a pleasing thought, 'that would be good-bye to half the sixth formers, including a good handful of prefects. Still, sixth form opinion will never influence school policy.'

'Yes, I agree,' said Christopher, but he disagreed with Julie who walked by saying that the whole thing had been a waste of time.

'All we heard was the Gospel according to St John's,' she said.

'But it makes those in power aware of what we want.'

'They're already aware of that which is why they won't give us what we want. You three wouldn't be heading towards the tuck-shop by any chance?'

Having her now as part of their company made them more than three times three. An entourage of pretty young things weaved the manifestation of her power about them. Marion, silenced by this rather solid circulation of her own sex, stayed at Louding's side as if stiffly resisting an overwhelming threat of deposition.

The prefects' room was fifty yards in front of them, the tuck shop was clearly out of their way, but what are miles even in the light of one request on behalf of so many fair females.

'I thought,' said Louding to Julie, 'that *you'd* be quite capable of jumping the queue.'

'But if I can get someone else to do it for me,' she said looking at her followers and then at Marion and then Christopher. 'Fancy saying that most people start smoking because it's forbidden.'

'Well, it's true.'

Julie smiled: quite a warm smile, but with it went the collected change that crossed her brother's palm. 'You *are* a fool, Christopher.' And to Louding, although it was to Christopher she gave the money: 'Just six packets of crisps, any flavor but cheese'n'onion, and four bottles of *7-up*, and you've done us a service. We'll wait over here.'

'You don't mind if I go with them?'

Pat Vendle, encouragingly both plump and attractive but often appearing modestly out of place by comparison to the beauties who at school seemed to remain relentlessly at Julie's side, gave an impression that it was now a relief to temporarily step out of the group.

'Of course, Pat. You can do what you like.'

Julie's methods of granting wishes usually compelled others to comply with her own. However, she quickly left Pat with the other three and accompanied her followers to where a section of the wall circling the grounds was blessed with a patch of shade.

Christopher looked at the money. Quite a tidy sum.

'We could always go to the prefects' room and keep it,' he said. 'They aren't allowed in.'

'Neither am I,' said Marion, recovering her voice first before her senses.

'But you wouldn't do that, would you?' asked Pat.

'Well, I don't know,' said Louding. 'We didn't actually say we'd go to the tuck-shop for them, or even if we'd go. Maybe tomorrow.'

'And what about me,' said Marion, convinced that in the confusion of the company she had been forgotten.

'Another good reason why we should go to the prefects' room,' he said, staring at her and feigning an initial jolt of surprise at seeing her there.

'You really are rotten to me,' she said with serious volume. 'Both of you.'

'If you don't like our company you can always go and wait with Julie.'

Marion took this as a malicious jab at her betrayed fear and awe of Julie Panhandle, and she stood her ground, seething slightly in a crimson build-up of what to say next.

'I hate you Simon. You'll see. I really hate you.'

Then she walked away, but not to where Julie and her friends were sitting.

'Er, Louding, I, er…' Christopher began, 'I think you really did it then.'

'Perhaps. Guilt will overtake me before supper,' and he smiled. 'Come on Christopher, come on, Pat, we're wasting time. Can't keep her ladyship waiting.'

'But she really was angry then, wasn't she?' said Pat as the three of them commenced their walk through the increasing density of break-time kids. 'I mean, I knew you were only joking.'

'Ah but, Pat, you don't know us like she does,' said Christopher.

'Yes,' explained Louding. 'We could very easily have been serious, not that we'd stoop to stealing your pennies or test Julie's access to the prefects' room. Actually what's really bothering her is Julie. She's annoyed that Julie can get away with so much and it must have rankled her to see Julie bully us into going shopping.'

'That's not true,' said Pat. 'Julie doesn't bully anyone. She's a great friend. She does so much for people, it's amazing.'

'It's amazing that you can believe that,' said Christopher.

It also amazed him now to think that where the crowd was at its greatest was also the place where he and Louding used to meet and entertain and be entertained by a well defined circle of friends and, in Louding's case, admirers, selected from provisional circumstances frequently occurring within a school year. Lower sixth form life was now nostalgia propelled at present by their direction, dispelled by Pat's reply.

'I don't think you like your sister, do you?'

'She's okay, I suppose,' he said. 'We don't have much to do with each other, that's all.'

'Well, I'd be proud if I had a sister like her.'

'I'm afraid Julie's not very proud of having a brother like me. She thinks I have a role to play because I'm her brother, and because I'm not playing it she's not happy with me.'

'I've never heard her saying anything against you.'

'I doubt if she ever discusses people behind their backs. She's certainly not scared of letting them know what she thinks.'

'She's probably talking about me right now,' said Pat as she allowed herself a quick glance back at Julie and the girls only yards away but beyond the vicinity of their present task. 'They're probably wondering why I wanted to walk with you two to the shop: anything to be alone with you two, they'll say.'

'What better reason?' asked Louding.

'But, do you two know that I'm leaving next week? – well no, not next week, but next week, next Friday, I'm having my going-away party. Will you two be able to come along?'

'A party?' said Christopher, as if such a phenomenon was constantly passing him by which, in many respects, probably was.

'In Limassol. We'll be going out for a kebab, a lot of us. Should be fun.'

'A kebab, hey? Yeah, that sounds all right. What do you think, Louding? Should be okay?'

Louding scratched the side of his face, looked at the crowded shop just ahead. The dense and anxious pull of wants against time helped bolster his characteristic uncertainty. He said he would have to see what was happening next week. This lack of immediate enthusiasm was a calculated plus by Pat's desperate love for him. The nourishment now needed was the chance within his doubt that he meant yes, he would attend with pleasure.

'But why do you need to be separated for Julie to invite us?'

'No, I'm not – I mean, it's not for that reason that – it's just that, well I wanted to walk with you to the shop, and while I was thinking about it I thought…'

Louding looked at her and awarded her a smile which Pat could hardly take in without staring away.

'Do you *really* want us two to go?'

'Why not? I like both of you, and it is my party. Please say yes?'

Her eyes wide open, there was everything inside their hazel glow which gave the ultimate charm to school-girlhood dreams.

'Sure,' said Louding. 'I love kebabs.'

'Well, don't tell Helen,' said Christopher. 'She'd never let me go anywhere like that without her along too, and she's away in England next week so she won't be pleased.'

'I won't tell Helen if you don't tell Marion. Pat, did you say next Friday, Friday week.'

'Yes,' said Pat. 'Tenth of March. Place booked and everything.'

Louding smiled again but said nothing. They were standing at the side entrance of the tuck-shop, the sixth-formers' route to fast service, guarded by prefects to keep the lower formers at bay. Queues longer than the time allocated for break stretched from the two front entrances, and these controlled by other prefects completed the tuck-shop duty. Pat was distracted by other friends. There were too many for her not to know a few if not more. Louding and Christopher entered by the side and were out by the front faster than expected. The lower formers who had queued for long minutes hardly noticed these intruders among the throng clambering at the counter, and the prefects were too bored to give them more than a nod. They bought the required amount of crisps and lemonade, and these they gave to Pat and friends who were on their way to where Julie and other followers sat patiently waiting. The lads were left alone. To one side the hot and frustrated queue slowly dwindled into an accepted despair.

'I may well be working that Friday,' said Louding as he stared after the departing girls.

'But you don't work,' was Christopher's impulsive response.

'What do you mean?' Louding asked, looking at him.

'You never told me you had a job.'

'Because I never had one. Too bloody lazy but now I'm becoming too bloody poor, so I've got myself a job at BG's Families Club as a waiter: serve the plonk and dispose of the slops.'

'And you work Friday nights?'

'Ah but don't worry about me not going to Pat's party. You won't want me there. I'd get in your way.'

'What do you mean?' asked Christopher. 'How could you possibly get in my way?'

Louding looked at him with a shrugged refusal to clarify his statement implying that if an answer was not already obvious it would be forthcoming soon enough. Christopher, not wishing to hazard a guess, changed the subject.

'Have you sorted out your problem with your English A level?'

'What problem? I didn't know there was a problem?'

'You not doing it – isn't that the problem?'

'No, don't worry. I'm quite capable of doing English A level.'

'Seriously, though…'

'You have to understand the working of Burke's mind, like I do. I don't understand what he's on about but I understand that he doesn't like me.'

'Why not? Why doesn't he like you?'

'A question I've asked myself many times.'

'But he has no right to dislike you and not include you on the list.'

'He does if I'm a lazy sod who never hands in homework on time and keeps getting E's for essays. I could make an appeal. I suppose, but it would be difficult at this late stage to justify why I should work any harder.'

'So you can pass your exam.'

'But that's just it, Christopher. I can work well at Biology, and French isn't that tough, but English…I suppose I could try harder. That seems to be a not uncommon solution, but really it won't do any good. I just haven't got what it takes when you're up against the Burke factor.'

'Surely it's not the teacher but the subject?'

By this time they were standing just outside the entrance of the prefects' room, neither really wanting to go in because it would just mean getting prepared to walk out again.

'Either way,' said Louding, 'English is too much for me, just like the maths was too much for you.'

'But it wasn't Morrison's fault. I knew that I was wasting my time doing PAAM instead of PAM, and those seven extra periods of PS are cream. Hey, you do English when I used to do Morrison's maths. Why not go for another seven periods of private study. It's the least Burke could do after throwing you out.'

'You mean it's the last thing he'll do. *Mon ami*, he hasn't actually thrown me out. He'll still expect me to turn up. He hasn't attempted to explain why he did what he did since last Tuesday. He's given me a meaningful stare as if to say: I'm ready for you, Louding – you just try to make trouble, but to his great annoyance, I'm sure, I've kept my peace.'

'But Louding, you should be kicking up a fuss. And if you don't want to do that you should walk out – come and do private study with me.'

'Yes, I'll see what I can do,' said Louding and he entered the room.

Louding was not prepared to do anything and Christopher knew him well enough to realize this. He won't fight, he thought. He just doesn't see the sense.

That night Christopher dreamt it was Saturday. He had missed the early bus to Limassol and Helen would be there waiting. While he was waiting for the next bus he went for a walk and came to a cinema where Ben Hur was showing, a film he wanted to see and an exclusive morning show was about to begin. But there was no time. He could not miss the next bus, but nevertheless he walked inside the cinema and was confronted by a vast courtyard where, plastered on the walls around, the forthcoming attractions could be studied like paintings at an exhibition. He met his brother and as Peter was going to see the film he persuaded Christopher to join him. But what about Helen? thought Christopher. She would wait for hours before being finally convinced that he wasn't going to show. She'd be furious, but he had no choice. The film skipped from modern times to frustrated westerns and their colourless display of speeded up stunts. Peter, this isn't Ben Hur, he wanted to say to Peter, but Peter was not Peter, nor was he to be seen. And the place was not crowded.

Just as he got off the school bus, just before he met the friends of the Orange twins and just after the attention he gave to his satchel while starting to walk to school, hitting his leg as the weight of books straggled along beside him, Christopher remembered what he had forgotten. He had left his games kit at the bus-stop in Akrotiri. Shit, three-fold, he thought: games master giving traditional ticking off for forgetting kit; games without kit like shower without water; and what a place to leave the stuff – would it remain there long before getting picked up? He had two periods of private study to think about this. Instead, like the good students Fridays often made of pupils, he completed his physics homework and read an essay from an anthology by C.S. Lewis which lay on the table beside the *Nelkon and Parker* A Level

Physics text. Lewis's subject was one of redundant context in which he stated that one did not need to be on the moon to die of starvation, or suffer from loneliness. It would be easy not to do otherwise, Christopher thought, if instant death by exposure and asphyxiation doesn't get one first. The moon is hardly what we'd recommend to our friendly Martians as the finest example of a pleasure beach. But bouncing about at a sixth of one's weight within a fluid suit of air, water and food could be an enjoyable way of passing a moon-day – which is how long? Forever, so long as you're on the bright side? All to do with the essential relevance of environmental hostility. Hostilities gape from without the suit, and from within, to soothe and secure, I take a suck at this pipe here and fill my astronomical palate with Cape Canaveral Candy, liquidized of course. And what matter A levels if I was suddenly whisked away to a new found freedom in the stars? Commander Panhandle will not pollute the ether with his source-based knowledge, nor shoot down stray aliens with the state-registered Apollo 101 stun-gun. I shall merely ask where it is that I may follow with the natural inertia of constant speed. However, I should think A levels are the bottom rung of gaining the chance to get up there.

'Gosh, this is the real stuff,' said Gavin Peters, emphasising from his eyes the Patrick Eve styled-hair he possessed which dropped like a dark silk curtain at every shake of his head. Christopher often wished he could do that with his own hair which insisted on staying relentlessly still.

'Really?' he said and thought: I wonder if you need to be on the moon to fall down a crater. 'What's the real stuff?'

'This.' Gavin held up a copy of Hardy: *Dynasts Part I*, and then from it he read: '"A local cult, called Christianity." Ha! Great, I like it.'

'But Christianity isn't a local cult.'

'Yes, I know that. Hardy's great sarcasm about something he could never believe in. He encompasses the entire faith into the scorn from the word "cult" and adds salt to the wound by saying "local". Is that not genius?'

'No,' said Christopher. 'It's very easy to be negative. Besides, one doesn't have to be on the moon to know when one is being dull.'

'Who mentioned the moon? I'm talking about literature.'

'No you're not. You're talking about faith. Christianity's about as local a faith to Hardy perhaps as the moon is local to where he lived. Where did he live?'

'Dorset, I think.'

'Never been there.'

But where, of course, he had often been and was often late for third period on a Friday was maths. Christopher did not own a watch. The prefects' room had no clock. A common and convenient prefects' room complaint was the inability to hear the period bell (nobody actually knew where it rang, so it seemed) and that included he who attempted to work intentionally within the time allowed. Christopher was not often very late for maths, but usually on a Friday, third lesson, the others were there before him, three having to simply remove themselves from the residence of Morrison's next door to McGibb's. Ken McGibb usually greeted him with his 'late again' smirk and allowed silence from his interrupted lesson for Christopher to sit down and clatter quietly his means of preparation before continuing, thus offering Brian the enthusiastic task of explaining to Christopher the subject so far.

Today, no smirk, no silence, hardly a lesson to interrupt; Christopher's entrance, if not for a glance from the class, could well have been ignored. Hardly worthwhile making the effort to be missed, but in the light of what he might have missed by leaving the prefects' room discussion with Gavin, shaded by what now entertained the others – a debate, and yes on rugby by Ken McGibb and Steve Galbraith – Christopher was pleased he had arrived. Brian quickly explained: a team calling themselves the Welsh Teachers had been defeated, but only just, by a team passed off as The Rest. This may only have been a term employed by McGibb and Galbraith in association with what happens when two splendid rugby forces clash. The Welsh and the Teachers combined forces to prove themselves outstripped by their own confidence. McGibb had played for the Welsh Teachers. Being un-Welsh was as incidental as various other contributory factors leading to their defeat, except for a try disqualified just ten minutes before the final whistle. The referee had seen a knock-on but the linesman had given no signal. Neither, of course, did the Welsh Teachers. Had the try been allowed they would have won. As it turned out the linesman had been Reverend Galbraith but one could hardly suppose that such a man would put patriotism above professional Christian ethics. Steve, son of Rev, maintained that all had been above board. His old man was getting short-sighted. Meanwhile Brian prettied up with final touches his latest masterpiece: 'The Motorway Junction', a potential secondary offering to the House Handicraft Competition. He had wanted to engage Savina in a private but not irrelevant discussion about the applied mathematics implied within the contours of the drawing but she was far too far in front, one seat ahead, her own mathematical patterns in constant need of foolscap sheet-based scribbling, while both Tessa and Wilfred were absent and Edmund was busy reading William L. Shirer's *The Rise and Fall of the Third Reich*.

'It is silly,' said Savina when later on the argument dissolved into fifteen minutes of revision, with Ken McGibb suddenly remembering a message he had to deliver, thus just before going imposing upon the class more problems from *Tranter*. 'We should be doing maths. The exams are very close. Not talking about stupid rugby.'

'I've been brought up on rugby and God,' said Steve. 'Not too keen on one now but love the other, if not playing it, talking about it is next best thing.'

Talking about and playing God, thought Christopher, and rugby is the local cult.

'And one doesn't have to be on the moon to be beaten either,' he said.

'You are on the moon, the way you think,' said Savina.

'It'd be interesting playing rugby on the moon,' said Brian. 'The conversion would probably go into orbit. We'd have very short games.'

'We'll ask Ken about it,' said Steve, 'the problem involved…' but it was noted then that Ken had not returned and it was time to go and so they went.

Christopher returned to the prefects' room and Savina was with him. She asked him whether he had any intention at all of trying to pass his maths exam.

'Of course I want to pass my exams. Wouldn't be here otherwise, would I?'

'Then why do you waste so much time?'

Helen marched into the room and, having spared Christopher the need to burden Savina with an answer, she announced, not so silently but mainly to Christopher, that it was her birthday and what was he going to do about it? What had he done about it? He had already thought that as a birthday present he would not finish with her until she arrived back from her interview in England. But it was easy to suppose that she thought herself worthy of something more tangible. Besides, there was still this distinct impression from her that their relationship was fairly safe, somewhat solid and also of that time-commanding stuff from which dreams were made. When he flicked his fingers and bounced his pen off the table, he was not acting out the frustrations of bad memory – he had sincerely forgotten to buy her a card.

'But we're in Limassol together tomorrow, aren't we. I'll get you something then.'

'But it's my birthday today, not tomorrow. I thought you'd at least remember a card. It may mean nothing to you, but to me it means a lot to have my boy-friend remember. But you forget, and then what do my friends think? Don't you agree, Savina?'

Savina rapped him over the head with her jotter and said yes emphatically that she agreed.

'See! And soon I'll be in England, and then what?'

'I've never been to England,' said Savina, 'and I'm hoping to go to Manchester University because they say it's best for maths.'

'But, Savina, you don't need the best,' said Christopher.

'That's a strange way of thinking, but I'll take it as a compliment.'

'One doesn't have to go to the moon etcetera. Helen, when do you leave for England?'

'There, you see, Savina. He forgets my birthday, but he knows I'm going away.'

'You just said you'd be going.'

'And you can't wait to see me leave. I'm surprised you don't remember the date. I'm sure I've told you more than once.'

'There's many things you've told me more than once. Don't worry. All filed up here.'

'I leave Tuesday, and I'll stay there for two weeks just to teach you a lesson.'

'Maybe I'll miss you.'

'You better miss me.'

'It'd be interesting to find out. One doesn't have to go out to the moon to be missed.'

'I'm only going to England.'

'England, the moon, what difference does it make. Two weeks without you will be like…'

He had to think of some sentimental means of redeeming his dishonoured memory, but she pushed him with interest for an answer by asking very softly:

'Two weeks without me would be like what, Christopher?'

'Like, er…' and he shrugged, 'two weeks without you.'

He had to leave to join the intrepid physics group who spent a period in a small room staring at the mirror projection of a ballistic galvanometer. John Warwick was doing his best because, although apparently favoured by the odds, he was trying to induce a current around a circuit with a magnet and a looped conductor, but the circuit wouldn't have it.

Christopher had a thought.

'Maybe the conditions are wrong,' he ventured unhelpfully.

He had been thinking about the moon again. Up there it would be easy to induce petty little disturbances like electric currents.

Conditions were wrong for games. He didn't have his kit. With luck his kit was still lying in the seasonal-rain drain he and the other bus 27ers had gathered around as a point of distraction during their morning wait for the bus. Without luck his kit was now part of some young lad's wardrobe pending future use in an English grammar school. Francis Dorman was also sans kit. His was under the breakfast table, so he said, and so they conspired to dodge the games' master by skirting around the far corner of the prefects' room building to where the tennis courts lay. There was not much doing anyway. Paul Fadpeel was merely indulging in the PE fetish for lists, this time detailing a future game of rugby that the school just had to perform as a replay against Akrotiri Youth Klub 1st. Christopher and Francis sauntered into the courts equipped with the necessary other than the conventional shorts and shirts. A shapely, very darkly tanned, and according to Francis (when they spoke about her afterwards), 'beautifully thighed and suitably mature but youthful' mistress commented on their choice of clothing, and Francis, one of many madly in love with her, quickly explained a conditions experiment he and his partner, Christopher here, were trying out. His partner too was suddenly also madly in love. He said nothing, love tightening his lips. She was not convinced. A dubious desire to watch her girls play no doubt, and when Francis offered to have him and his partner play them, she waved them away, pointing to the far court.

'It shouldn't be allowed,' said Christopher as they watched her walk away to where her sixth form girls were busy negotiating the drooping nets. 'She's too pretty to be a PE teacher.'

'She can teach me anything she wants anytime. I never thought I'd get the desire to be crushed by anything, but those legs are something else. Imagine the incredible mysteries to which they so obviously lead.'

To the far off court they went and they endured the sudden unbearable heat for no longer than ten minutes.

'Shall we declare the experiment a failure?' suggested Francis.

'One more game,' said Christopher, after all, in the distance, a few courts away, they were being watched.

Francis served and Christopher returned the ball into an orbit over the tennis court fence and into the wilderness beyond. Together they boldly traipsed across the courts, around the side where the girls bounced and jumped and swung and screamed, through the only exit, and back around the long way to where they reckoned among the jungle of thorn-ridden, heat-eaten bushes, the ball may have dropped. They found not one ball, but three, plus a shuttlecock, a plastic trumpet, the left leg of a pair of seamless stockings, the center page of a mouldy copy of *Titbits* and an empty bottle of RAF issue egg-shampoo.

'What a haul, hey?'

'One couldn't expect better if one went to the moon.'

'The moon? To find a thorny bush, let alone this lot, on the moon would destroy a few theories.'

Francis tried the trumpet, kept the balls, the shuttlecock and discarded the rest. The trumpet refused to work and so back into the thorns it went.

They had been scavenging the thorns for longer than they thought, but as neither had to get changed there was no usual rush for their respective buses. And they were both bus-prefects. What bus would leave without its prefect? They thought about this and so they quickened their pace. However, no worries, the football lot were late back from Happy Valley. Christopher had to keep his bus waiting for Russell Keen. Typical, he thought. Late away on the one day I need to get back to rescue my kit. Still, if it hasn't been nicked by now it never will be, and if it has then what does it matter how late I am? Fifteen minutes went by during which time the departure of other buses lengthened their privileged view of the daily partial congestion, of which bus 27 was usually an active member, the final squeeze of an ill thought out system drawing to an end yet another day, another week of school. Eventually, and not out of character, although maybe out of habit, his bus was the only one left.

'Why are *we* the only ones left?' asked Julie.

'Do you know what I'm thinking?' said Oliver.

'Okay, what are you thinking, Oliver?'

'I'm thinking that Russell can't have been the only bloke who played soccer. I'm thinking that he's on another bus thinking that we'd left him thinking that that'd be the type of thing we'd do to him.'

'And I'm thinking we should leave,' said Linda. 'He takes such a bloody long time to get changed, he deserves to be left.'

'Let's go,' said Dot.

'Not yet,' said Christopher.

'You wouldn't stay for us,' said Doris.

'That's not true,' he said, and he thought: oh yes, this time last year that would have been very true.

Russell suddenly climbed on board. He was followed by two other lads who belonged to buses not as faithful and which had probably followed up on their own versions of Oliver's theory.

'There, didn't I tell'ee Panhandle would keep the bus standing,' he exclaimed, obviously very pleased, more with himself than Christopher. All three of them swaggered down the aisle, the friends not uncommonly thrilled at the prospects of sharing a journey with Julie Panhandle, the Orange twins and Russell's considerably attractive if consistently knitting sister. There were enough seats near the back for them to sit and help convert this section of the bus into a smoke-screen.

The friends sat and asked the back-seat girls all sorts of inane questions. This appeared to bother Russell more than it did the girls, and both Oliver and Colin Kamp read Marvel comics with concentrated contempt. Chris Millings, feeling out of sorts among so many sixth formers, had obliged by moving further on up the bus to sit with a fifth form friend, while Julie merely sat and smoked and answered: 'Yes' and 'No' and 'Maybe' according to the unmoveable pattern of her mood. Christopher gained more of a response from her when he asked about Pat Vendle's eventual departure from Cyprus. Pat was considered to be one of Julie's closest friends, and there was no effort or reluctance to include within her answer the fact that there would be a leaving do.

'It should be next Friday,' she said. 'Just a small thing. We've certainly no intention of inviting the entire camp.'

Christopher's games' kit was still waiting for him where they had been left which, as he got off the bus, was a few yards ahead inside the rain drain. Not worth stealing are you? he thought. As secure as if you'd been left on the moon.

He might have been more pleased had he not been reminded that it was the family fast day: ie less food than usual for lunch and dinner.

'It's for a worth-while cause,' said his mother. 'The money I save will go to the starving people all over the world.'

'What? You're little contribution?' said Peter. 'How many mouths will that feed, especially if it goes all over the world? A few penny-chews here and there.'

'It all mounts up. Catholics all over the world contribute to this.'

'From what I hear,' said Julie, 'it's the Catholics who do most of the starving.'

Peter thought this was very funny, and Patricia told her not to be so silly.

'Yes, don't be so silly, Julie,' said Christopher – a rare moment, but Peter's laughter was decidedly infectious.

'All right, all right,' said Julie. 'It wasn't that funny.'

She almost smiled but then she looked at Rebecca who said:

'Laughter helps the appetite.'

Patricia started talking about reported troubles in Limassol.

'Why, only today,' she said, 'a policeman was shot. I've changed my mind about going there tomorrow. I'll wait until the trouble dies down a bit.'

'What are they fighting about now?' asked Julie.

'I don't think you should go in either tomorrow, Christopher.'

'Oh don't worry. Political ructions only concern those involved. And anyway, mum, nothing ever happens to me – ever. I'm only saying that to tempt fate, you understand. That way I can be sure of an interesting day.'

'Isn't Helen interesting enough?' asked Julie. 'When's she going to England again?'

Girls! Girls! Girls! (a)

The Circle

> People look at me and say: "Cheer up – it's not the end of the world", or "Cheer up – it'll probably never happen". Two truly amazing statements. The fact that this world will most likely not end and it'll probably never happen are hardly reasons for cheering up.
> Rebecca Panhandle: Journal

> Why am I so lonely? I have many friends. I am young and I know I'm attractive to men. Trouble is people never understand a girl who looks as if she had everything going for her.
> Debra Lester: Letter to her aunt.

> I miss the circle but it's good to be back in England. Nobody runs away from me anymore. There are lots of pretty girls, some of whom even laugh at my jokes (they were Henry's jokes, most of them). Is Christopher still trying to get off with that girl called Frances?
> Peter Christol: Letter to Louding.

CHRISTOPHER WAS OFF THE bus and immediately into Helen's arms. Something had made him slip. She supported him with surprising strength and while he soon recovered his balance she would not let him go.

'So, you're pleased to see me.'

'I thought you wouldn't turn up.'

'Did I say I wouldn't?' he asked concerned, wondering if he had. But then would she have been waiting for him?

'No, of course not. But there was a lot of trouble here yesterday. I was told about it, and do you know, a policeman got shot.'

'Was he killed?'

'I don't know.'

Typical, he thought.

The Bypass still looked the same as always with the Saturday morning crowds on both the road and accommodating happily the generosity of the wide pavements. Cars consumed the road space with sound European speed and the surrounding city distractions, being many, did not commission a distinctive feeling of the unwary. The Bypass, named thus despite its failure to allow the many vehicles it contained the luxury of urban avoidance, cut

Limassol in half and would, for British understanding, had made a conveniently contiguous stretch between the Greeks and the Turks, but for the fact that *if* having lived there for enough time to overcome subtle difficulties in distinguishing one race from the other, and being spared the burden of historical insight, it would have been logical to assume that they were on the best of terms. Christopher was not sure how far the Bypass stretched – probably like most things on an island, allowed to continue until the sea demanded otherwise – nor was there anything other than an impression of a city being cut in half to provide a broader sweep of cosmopolitan separation: the precious British from the splendid natives. The natives lived in abundance on both sides but the British were still able to maintain the standard of segregation which afforded them their tourist-colonial image once they emerged from their own dwelling areas. The Turks and the Greeks actually loved one another but a vociferous minority preferred it if they didn't, while both races loved the British and the British loved everything so long as it appeared to remain, as an abode, on the other side of the Bypass.

'Anyway,' said Christopher, 'I came because I knew you would be waiting for me. You're faithful and reliable and I still love you.'

'Oh Christopher, do you mean it?'

'Will that do as a belated birthday present?'

'No.' She let him go but then took his hand and led the way.

They went to a predominant RAF area of Limassol called, by the British, the Naafi Area. Its local name was no doubt sufficient to all who cared to wander around but it also contained a Navy, Army and Air Force Institutes store, and so the Naafi won despite the cafes, shops and one very popular discotheque nightclub called *C'est la Vie*. Helen wanted to explore the record shops. She had been given a few record tokens and there were still many singles needing to be added to the many singles making up her vast collection. Christopher browsed through the albums propped back to back in long racks. He was after the latest LP by Grand Funk Railroad, *E Pluribus Funk*, not only for the latinized title of 'Out of Many, Funk' which suggested, maybe within the forlorn friendship between hope and rock, a cut above the usual American beat, but also because the Railroad posed as a band which he longed to hold out as an extraordinary example of decent music; but he only had so much money and Helen still had to make up her mind how much of this money he was now going to spend on her. She could see nothing that she did not already have except for the rare singles she disliked (and with equal rarity he liked). However, she did not want a record from him. She had her tokens for that. She decided that his present had to be a St Christopher because soon she would be leaving for England and wouldn't it be nice to have Christopher with her dangling from her neck? So off they went to the jewellery shop which had plenty but not the particular one she wanted. He never thought there could be anything particular to want in a St Christopher, not anything that is which would warrant a fastidious quality from her otherwise undiscerning taste, but right now she knew what she wanted and it would mean a walk through the jewellery shops to find it, the only others being in St Andrews Street a good mile away on the other side of the Bypass. They walked briskly. There was not much of a bus service and Limassol tended to harass with its hailing taxis those who merely strolled. Christopher had not included a taxi fare in his budget. The day was shining and rich if only in colours and heat. A walk would be for them both good, bad and indifferent.

St Andrews Street, like the Naafi area, was a name of convenience. There was a flash quality of the street matching the name if only by a poetic coincidence. It was a place of embellished retail festivity where shops and abundant markets sold trinkets, rugs, clothes, lace, copper-craft, furniture and an impressive array of colourful oddities, lined and facing each other across a road so breathlessly narrow and crushingly busy, an extra wide kerb being the only protection afforded to the many pedestrians which the essential part of St Andrews Street souvenir paradox used to both excuse and alleviate congestion. A walk there took no time compared to the lengthy, task of penetrating the crowds, with a persistently polite effort which Christopher could only just about tolerate. Others could only just tolerate it too as they attempted to push him aside, while Helen, in her element, weaved through the cars and carts and shoppers as if having rehearsed the many manoeuvres needed to stop and stare at every attractive stall and window of which there were many. She also carried on a conversation unwittingly to herself about which one of her friends had what and where and when. 'A very long time ago, though, you understand...Oops, silly me...' and away she dragged him until, unable to take no more, he dragged her into the nearest most agreeable looking of the cafes where the white-haired, fat old men, dressed in combinations of grey and black, spent the rest of their lives playing *Tavli,* a popular board game resembling a cross between Go and Backgammon.

'We can get something to drink at my house.'

'It's not too bad here,' he explained, 'and I only want a coke and a cake.'

'But should I eat cake, I wonder?' she said, sitting down as he flopped down opposite.

'I'm buying, if it's any help.'

Outside the cars groaned and bellowed. One very bored driver pressed his horn to a set rhythm which ran from one end of the street to the other, and sweat kept the palm of his hand stuck to the hot roof of his over-gassed Colt. The café was very open. The old Greeks kept exclaiming with whoops of joy and a rather sad and plump old woman served them thick coffee while having plenty to say to whomever it was who lurked behind a hatch. The flies refused to go away. The wasps hovered longingly and curiously over the cakes and someone in the backyard made chronic the creaking of a rusty gate. Christopher was beginning to feel too hot to think of continuing with this relatively simple task of walking around both enclosed and exposed areas where stuff could be bought. Strange, he thought, how this side of Limassol is always more humid than north of the Bypass where Helen lives.

'I'd give anything for a cool breeze. I'd even welcome an ice-cube down the back of my neck.'

'Your nose is glowing red.' Helen laughed. 'It looks so funny.'

'My nose is rather sensitive to people laughing at it. It can't help looking funny.'

'You should put some cream on it.'

'I do and I have.'

Helen laughed again.

The cokes were warm, the cakes they avoided, and eventually they left, finally locating the jewellery shop which happened to have, within a limited collection, the correct medal, after which it was with relief that they caught an available bus heading all the way to Helen's house. A lemonade at her place did not go unwelcome and she was happy enough to arrive in time to tape the last fifteen minutes of *Popaganda* on BFBS. Duff Dill, who sounded remarkably like his name, only managed to squeeze in a few words on her tape before she cut short his between-record rant. Obviously they were too late for her request and she only wanted to record the music.

'Are you happy now?' she asked.

'Are you happy with your St Christopher?'

'Yes, Christopher, it's beautiful. Thank you, thank you, thank you.' With this she showered him with kisses and he endeavoured to shower back. This dual shower of gratitude lasted a good five minutes before being interrupted by Duff Dill playing an actual track from the Grand Fund album, and Christopher just had to stop everything and listen to it. He was pleased that she was taping it although he rarely listened to any of her tapes. The track was very good.

'It's very good,' he said.

She shrugged.

'Better than me?' she then asked.

'Simply no comparison.'

Lunch was announced from down the hall.

Helen's mother, jollity itself in her ample ability to bake pleasingly good cakes, and someone who sincerely thought that Christopher was the ideal lad for her Helen to be dating – better than those skinheads and scruffs who made so much noise at night – was very excited about Helen's interview in England. They both talked rapidly and both went rapidly through departure plans as if she was leaving that very day. Helen showed off her St Christopher, swinging it pendulum-like from her neck.

'This will protect me.'

'Oh, silly charms,' said Mrs Margate and she laughed.

'But it will, mum. These types of things do work. My friends always go on about tarot cards and reading palms and objects of luck. They convince me all the time about how some of the things, you know, that we think is just superstition is true. That's very true to do with one you love.' She stared at Christopher who chewed and swallowed some salad and changed the subject.

'Helen, how far away does Martin Clifton live?'

'Not too far away? Why do you want to know that? Do you want to go around and see him?'

'I wouldn't mind meeting his cousin.'

'Who's his cousin? What's his name?' And then it occurred to Helen that a cousin of a male mentioned by a male need not necessarily be male. 'You don't mean that girl, Stella?'

'Well yes, you see, I was asking Louding about us two seeing her last Saturday – remember, at the cliffs? – and we had this idea that we should go out for a meal, you and me, and Louding and "that girl" Stella.'

'Why Stella? She's a real snob you know.'

'What makes you think she's a snob?'

'She is. Most of the girls think she's very standoffish and she doesn't want to make friends with anybody. She spends a lot of her time with Greeks.'

'That certainly doesn't make her a snob.'

'She's strange, but it's okay, Christopher, us going out for a meal, even with her. I'm sure she'll fancy an evening with Louding. Marion wouldn't like it.'

'Marion needn't know.'

'But won't you have to wait until I return which won't be for two weeks? We could go when it's *your* birthday.'

'That's not till August.'

'Gosh, I thought it was sooner.'

'We could always celebrate it sooner.'

'We'll have to celebrate it before July because I might have to start my course in England in July. Silly time to start a course. It's not fair.'

'What's not fair, darling,' asked Mrs Margate who was now so accustomed to the lack of justice in Helen's world that it made little difference if Helen supplied an adequate answer.

Helen supplied no answer. A thought occurred which propelled her up, and out the dining room she danced. This usually meant that she was going to dance back in with something to show Christopher. Seconds later back she came with a packet of photographs: prints of the pictures they had both taken the previous Saturday at Akrotiri cliffs. Well, this was something of ready interest, and he was pleased to note no grotesque results but a lot of hair blowing in the wind, over his face, around his eyes, and the cliffs, the sea and the twisted paths all captured in squares not instantly recognizable.

The picture of herself leaning against GRAZING BEYOND THIS POINT PROHIBITED was actually not bad and worth keeping and he said so knowing that she would happily part with it.

'I don't know how you think so. I look almost goofy.'

'I like it.'

'Very much to keep it?'

'By my heart.'

She laughed delightedly, she kissed him and she said:

'I think you're a liar, and I think it's very silly, but here, take it.'

'And look at this one here.' He held up a picture of himself peering through a sharp, stone passageway, clinging to the fern with an effort that rolled all his serious expressions into one thoughtless pose. 'You're not a bad photographer, Helen. Maybe that's your thing and not nursing.'

'I can be a nurse as well,' said Helen, 'and do photography and take pictures of lots of things when I want to. I'll get all the stuff you need when I start getting that type of money and I can do it as a hobby.'

'What type of money?' asked Christopher.

'More than the type of money I get now. More than you get as a doorman.'

'I should hope so.'

'And she'll be spending it on all types of rubbish,' said Mrs Margate, 'instead of saving it as I advised her to.'

'I can buy records and go to concerts and take pictures of pop stars and famous people.'

'Until you yourself become famous,' suggested Christopher as if fame and pop-stardom was a natural progression of the norm in England, 'and pictures will be taken of you standing beside a sign stating "gazing beyond this point prohibited".'

Lunch was over and an afternoon with Helen was usually three hours and a multitude of records long. He eventually left and it took him just short of half-hour to stroll to a Bypass bus-stop named after an adjacent but indefinable British institution building called Unicorn House, and there he waited for the bus to Akrotiri which more than likely would turn up but sometimes, disturbingly, didn't. There was nobody else waiting at the stop. The bus company probably sent out scouts to report on the situation, deciding from the data gathered whether it was worth providing a bus. As the sole representative of the 5 pm Akrotiri-bound Christopher did not feel that important. The street was packed with ethnically tanned people and he was very conscious of his red nose. He tried to look at it and managed to catch a distinct shine at the side of his eye, while many Greek and Turkish young men strode past in boisterous groups, now in charge; both determinedly and aimlessly disposing of the Akrotiri British image. Might well be trying to get to the moon, he thought, considering how easy it is now to die of loneliness here. Even a place like Limassol must have its victims, although most here are happy with the society of the same sex grouping, the fairer linking arms stepping along the pavement as if ready to float on air with their purity intact, and the men are singing songs that the gods have chosen to ignore. The gods are ignoring me, and then he thought, why do none of those girls look like Savina and yet Savina can easily look like any other Greek Cypriot lass, less likely to allure than to elude? Savina is a genius. She may look like them, dress like them and her hair is long and black, but she stands out because she *is* something. All these crowds, they're all nothing until someone stands out and proves he's something, he thought, like me and me red nose, waiting for a bus that is determined not to come, not yet. People are as meaningless as empty buses unless they do something amazing and then they're either free or messed up. Savina, however, did not really strike him as being either.

I've known Savina for almost two years, Helen almost one. I knew Savina because she's on my course, Helen because she's on my course – tape recorder course – our effort to play and rewind and fast forward and... I liked her then but not so much now. I do like her now but I don't want to go out with her anymore. He had argued this out many times with himself. He was constantly going to finish with Helen. Serial postponement always sets a definite date. But then I'll have no girlfriend, and she does cheer me up, and A levels are so difficult. I thought they were so difficult at the beginning. Half way through I knew I was right, and now I'm thinking of finishing with Helen before they finish me.

The previous year, his lower sixth year, long before he knew Helen and at a time when sixth form registration had been divided into the various houses and so the only sixth form girls he got to know were the ones from his own house and the few on his course; a time when neither he nor Louding had access to the prefects' room and all private study went on in a special private study room beside the library across the other side of the school; when St John's was a new experience for Christopher especially when compared to the more stuffy but less congested school-life he tried to enjoy at Madras Comprehensive, St Andrews, Scotland from whence he and his family had hailed in their previous posting; when all the lads had short hair and the upper sixth really did look upper sixth, with the lower sixth striving simultaneously to appear moderately upper as well; Christopher was not happy but happier. He was happy that neither he nor Louding had been made prefects. Henry Dazel was also not a prefect and proud of it. Who needs a room when there are plenty of rooms, he said. Give him and them the circle anytime, formed as it had been by a selection of friends every break-time just outside the tuck-shop. Henry coined the term, and Christopher emphasized its definite article when he wrote to Henry about its present non-existence. Henry had avoided upper sixth by joining the RAF and leaving for England, and so it was easy for him to write back to Christopher and assume that it had been he and not Louding who supplied the binding strength holding the circle together. Louding had never given himself this credit but the circle had originally formed around him and, to some extent and despite Christopher's letter to Henry, continued to do so.

Louding, during lower sixth, had a very faithful and loyal friend in the form of a small and slightly deformed lad who would, if he could, have followed him anywhere. This lad's size and distortion, made him eminently eligible for school-yard cruelty. His name was Peter Christol – not Peter or Christol but Peter Christol – and having taken him under his wing, Louding was unaware of how much he protected Peter Christol from his peculiarly abrasive conditions of being part of the school. Louding's conditions were ideal: simply stand near the tuck-shop area with Henry and Christopher on one side, Peter Christol and Peter Christol's other adopted friend, Colin Jottrell, on the other, and let the few girls who stayed to talk form the circle. No one could actually see that a circle existed except those who were part of it, the blending in process of blues and whites and khaki making up the colour-coded crowds which formed the massive queues stretching patiently into the tuck-shop. It had not been Henry's idea to stand near the tuck-shop. Neither had it been Louding's. Colin blamed Peter Christol because, although he was regarded as Peter Christol's friend by association from the previous year, in truth he despised Peter Christol. To Colin, Peter Christol constituted all the irritating aspects that consistent friendship had to offer, and so if life was a drag it was Peter Christol's fault and if a place was too crowded that too was Peter Christol's fault. The friendship had initially maintained momentum in the lower sixth form by one running away from the other, and it was during this exercise that Colin met Henry also running away, and so together they ran from Peter Christol until Peter Christol met Louding and Louding stayed put. Louding either stood or walked as if unable to understand why everybody was in such a rush. When Peter Christol walked by and Louding was asked where the big lad had gone, Louding assuming that Colin was he because he, Louding, already knew Henry and Henry was many things but not big, Christopher beside him eased the confusion with the assurance that being here, at school, they had gone nowhere special. Christopher also stayed put and as all three were staying put beside the tuck-shop, as independent a place as any and well within the shade, Colin and Henry had to return and say: 'Oh, there you are, Peter Christol. What kept you?' It became the gathering girls that kept them and so really the girls were to blame, and of course girls were always to blame everywhere, even near the assembly hall, for keeping people where they were. What was so special about the tuck-shop area was the density of third and fourth formers who made up the majority of Louding's rapidly growing fan club, although the circle itself never consisted of more than ten and ceased to function below three.

Despite odds against this happening, Colin, who was notoriously plain but enthusiastically deluded with ideas of personal magnetism, had an exceedingly pretty sister called Sarah, and of course she fancied Louding. But left to her own devices she would not have fancied Louding. He was too popular, had the adoring attention of too many, and as such her membership of this club would have compromised an equal share of respect, after all many were the members of even the upper sixth who made it known that they were agreeably distracted by her walking by? But now she fancied him because now Colin allowed the means of grabbing him from beneath the noses of mass devotion. Colin was her key to the circle and with his twist and her entrance Louding left with Sarah but not for long. While he was away with her, girls forlornly asked where Louding had gone, but despite his charm and good looks and under-squandered fame, Sarah took a sudden interest in airmen and smartly finished with him for one during a racing meeting at the Akrotiri Go-Kart Klub which they had both attended to support Henry's and Colin's participation there as a class-one drivers.

One of the circle girls at the time was Henry's sister, Rosemary, who was not beautiful, not really very pretty but possessed an attractively humorous gaze which she lent to a chosen few of the boys around; and Henry's other sister, Gale, who was not even that attractive but better looking than Henry. Rosemary fancied Louding and so did Gale although Gale insisted that she really fancied Christopher. Henry did not fancy either getting into the circle – they were his sisters and should stay that way, away from him – but their entrance was guaranteed because of a friend they brought along. Grace Ford was neither beautiful nor pretty nor better looking than any – but she had learnt to acquire a Henry-alluring quality, employing answers to most of his quips that did not even emerge as questions, and so eventually membership was assured. And anyway, sisters who were not *his* sisters were no problem to Christopher. Henry's resistance was at first based on equity.

'You bring your sister to join the circle and mine may join too,' he said.

'My sister doesn't want to join the circle,' said Christopher. His certainty on this score had not been backed by any actual enquiry.

'Older brothers have no authority,' said Grace who had no brothers but a quasi-brotherly share of confidence.

Christopher was willing to second this, and so Gale and Rosemary joined without the need to call upon Julie's highly unlikely help. In a fantasy world of Julie's actual membership hers would have been an overwhelming presence. Christopher's initial impression of Grace was subject to the usual teenage method of grading peers: not very pretty but okay. However, despite the beautiful and the pretty which St John's and even the likes of the circle could provide in sometimes immaculate abundance, he began to detect within himself symptoms of love for this Grace Ford.

'I may fall in love with Grace Ford,' he said with an air of having nothing better to do and not really seeking Henry's advice and gaining no more than an opinion.

'I don't think that'd work,' said he. 'I'd go out with her myself if she wasn't so cocksure of herself. And anyway, she's not very pretty.'

Had she not been so cocksure he would not have thought about it. As it was Louding went out with her, just after his session with Sarah, and then lost her to another airman at the twice weekly sessions of the Akrotiri Folk Club. As he never attended the folk club at any time, he therefore had to be informed by Rosemary who went to both whenever she could and then by Grace herself who continued going to most events, including the circle, as if nothing had happened. Grace had set Louding free but Rosemary was not pleased with her method. How could she chuck Louding and yet turn up now? she thought. Louding had, in his way, turned Rosemary down by not considering her an eligible substitute for Grace. She had made no mention of wanting to take her place except to Henry who laughed, and to Gale who advised her to go out with Colin – he having mentioned a time-honoured and fool-proof method to Gale of gaining Christopher with the simple usage of sister and sister's boyfriend whom, he hoped, would be he, as he quite fancied her, her sister. Problem was, Christopher also fancied her, her sister, and not her, herself. Such potential for upset would have passed unnoticed had she, Gale, not announced to her world that Christopher was in her heart. As it was she failed and she even had to adjust to the startling turn of events which brought Rosemary and Christopher together, and just one short week after Colin (and his sister Sarah) had left Cyprus for good. Gale wanted to leave for good but contented herself, instead, with leaving the circle just as Rosemary was to do a little while later, much to the delight of Henry. Rosemary, who had been disappointed in Grace and having disappointed Gale went on to disappoint Christopher by telling him of the airman in *her* life, thus making their brief romantic interlude briefer than even Christopher had expected. She left the circle as a point of honour but Grace stayed, while Louding and Christopher suffered little if any resulting despair. They certainly felt better informed.

Some time before the departure of the Jottrells, three of Grace's friends, Frances Smith, Wendy Lester and Heidi Innmaker had also joined the circle. Heidi was the rather subdued sister of the then up and coming Brian Innmaker. She disliked this association of being an Innmaker as if she had doubts as to how to live up to it. She wasn't too keen on the name Heidi either, stating that it made her sound like someone from the hills of Austria,

'What's wrong with sounding like someone from the hills of Austria?' asked Wendy, being able to recall as a relatively recent memory the glory of having seen *The Sound of Music* and assuming therefore that such hills were very much alive. 'I'd rather be a Heidi than a Peter Pan side-kick.'

'What about my name?' asked Frances.

'What about your name?'

'You can boast of having a very saintly namesake,' said Henry.

But Frances had never heard of Saint Francis, and when she did so from Henry, it verified the point she was trying to make. 'I have a man's name.'

'No more manly than Lesley,' said Grace, and she was asked if had ever met a happy Lesley; to which she answered that she was sure she had, many times.

They could imagine too many happy Graces and they accused her of having an inherited advantage. Heidi would not even have objected to being called Ford.

'Better than Innmaker. Can hardly imagine what my ancestors got up to to get *that* name.'

'Well they obviously made inns,' said Henry unable to detect irony from a female source.

'What about Smith?' said Frances.

'Common as houseflies,' he said. He was yet to meet another Dazel beyond his own family and, being Henry, he was proud of it.

They asked Louding why he was always called Louding and never (or hardly ever) Simon, but he said he didn't know. People tended to ignore the fact that Christopher was rarely called Chris; hardly ever Panhandle unless he was accused of being one, in which case he was called 'The Panhandle' in a pejorative manner which tended to distinguish him from Julie who, naturally enough, was also a Panhandle. Frances thought Christopher was a splendid name.

'If I had a son I'd call him Christopher,' she declared. 'Your second name's not Robin by any chance.'

They were both somehow pleased it wasn't, especially Christopher, and not wanting to place too fine a point on the unexpected compliment, and gaining the idea, mainly from Colin, that her questions were directed at him in a way indicating more than casual interest, he asked her out to the next Akrotiri Youth Klub dance. She said she'd meet him there but she failed to turn up. She did, however, turn up to the next one but arrived with a lad almost twice his size and, of course, better looking. Christopher had never really considered himself to be boy-friend material but then again, as it turned out, neither was this lad; well, not for longer than a week. So Christopher forgave her and continued to do so throughout a session of similar hardships, because every time he decided to listen to Henry who told him that he was probably wasting his time, Frances made it known that his presence was needed. They took to arguing, mainly about music: she being loyal to the skin'ead, moonstompin' quasi-reggae cult while his leanings were strictly 'Rock with a capital r'. Variations of a mutual contempt and favour carried on into the early weeks of his Upper Sixth form experience until she suddenly left.

'Now where's she gone?' he said, as if once again discarded for preferable conditions.

'UK,' said Wendy. 'Didn't you know?'

'Oh...'

Wendy was more of a Debra if such a name called to mind someone of definite desires, to be entertained where she stood rather than seeking out her wants. Debra, her sister, did the wandering, never happy where she was, temperature never right, people too few or too many, different worlds shaped by similar shades, and always wanting to be enticed away rather than persuaded to stay. She was living in the cliché of never being around when she was wanted, perhaps overdoing the effect of never being around at all. However she managed one session with the circle and left in her place, as a substitute to the fast fading memory of her having ever been there at all, a rather awkward and physically ill-defined creature of plain-day charm, William Meald. Nobody could dislike him although many girls tried their best to do so by acting as if ready to accuse him of deliberately looking ugly. He was deliberately pleasing to know. The Lester girls knew him well. He was one of the few sixth formers who travelled on the same bus as them to and from BG before moving with his family to Akrotiri. They liked him well enough to bolster his faith in human nature by encouraging his company at various social dos, even such functions that stretched its fun into the Limassol night-life. Debra, at times, could be particularly demonstrative about his inclusion by linking her arm with his and sticking out her tongue at those detractors who stood ready to lay on the whispering scorn. People warned her about raising his hopes too high as if he did not deserve a garden path or two and a friendly female hand to lead him along its borders. Her answer was simple: 'I don't care what you think.' However, William cared. He knew she was being kind, and to prevent this from being a duty as opposed to the occasionally welcomed devotion, he remained part of the circle when Debra left. He was doubtless saddened by such fast departure, but relieved that from her passing speed no nagging shape of feeling, hard or soft, could form. Wendy remained. By the time Debra and William arrived she had been a long standing member, and so she was able to bolster William's confidence by telling him that he had no chance. Wendy was emolliently indifferent to the point of being oblivious to obsessive debates about who was taking an interest in whom other than a nod at the well acknowledged fact that Louding was worshiped by many, but she was able to inform William that Debra could never remain anywhere with anyone long enough for her to feel committed to a monotonous routine of 'going steady'.

 William could so easily become part of anyone's routine – therein lies a sad story, thought Christopher as he tried to remember the first time William and he actually became good friends. There was one particular mutual friend, of no consequence to this immediate story, that perpetuated extra-school encounters. With regards to the circle, there was no particular friendship in sharing the same allotted area, crowded as it was, during a fifteen minute break from school-work. I know exactly how I befriended Henry, Louding and … well, try as he might he never really could like Peter Christol – a rebarbative element in his otherwise reasonable demand for fare treatment stretched Christopher's attitude in the direction of sympathy for Henry and Colin's purposeful desire to run away from him, subdued substantially since Peter Christol gained protection from being in the shadow of Louding's care. Christopher nurtured mixed feelings about Colin, probably having resented the jealousy Colin had nurtured when Frances had paid Christopher the attention that admittedly neither he nor Colin thought he, Christopher deserved. Colin also wanted Wendy and thus submitted mutterings against the smiling grotesque always standing on her left. Of course, such mutterings were confined to Henry who would duly inform Christopher as they shared the on-going debate over who stood what chance with whom. Why is Colin taking Wendy's indifference out on William? he thought. He usually blames Peter Christol for all his woes. During Louding's brief courtship with Grace, it was covertly accepted that he presented no obstacle in the way of any of the girls who stood alongside them in the circle. Frances never expressed any interest in Louding – she had merely played various anodyne tunes to the instrument of Christopher's infatuation. Wendy, who still lived in BG and therefore had more chance than other girls to work on the Louding prospect, seemed likewise devoid of that particular interest he must have grown accustomed to receiving, if not accepting. Perhaps by the nature of their mutual consent to be within the circle both Wendy and Frances were magically immune to the Louding spell.

However, the one caught under it and particularly well tangled, was Heidi. Heidi had this brother who insisted on being the best, so what could she do to keep up but aspire to going out with the best? She was still flustered by her name and not really wanting to give it the credit it was due – Heidi Innmaker: quality control would give it one star at least for purposes of aiming towards a famous future – and she asked Louding why he was called Louding. Surely that wasn't his first name, but if so what was his surname, just out of interest?

'Louding,' said Louding.

'Sorry, could you say that louder, Louding?' said Henry pre-empting the response which from Heidi could well have been: 'But surely you're not called Louding Louding.'

Louding had always been called Louding as far back as he could remember. Only his family (and Marion – but she was a later presence) called him Simon, but this never complicated a life implicitly free of tackling underlying concerns with the mysterious powers of the universal nomenclator. This, to Heidi, was the strangest thing she had ever heard. (Actually it wasn't. She heard stranger still from her brother and would probably continue to do so.)

'What's wrong with the name Simon? It's a perfectly good name.'

But Louding did not have to answer that because whatever was wrong and missing with Simon was missing and right with Louding. Heidi became almost obsessed with the name. Was it spelt with an a or an o? Did it really end in ing? And what was it like living out present participle of the verb loud? She had consulted her pocket English Grammar but Henry corrected her:

'Not the present participle but a cockney expression of the present tense participle…' and he pointed an academic finger in the air. 'For example; "Ere Bert, wot y'doing?" "Wot y'fink. I'm louding the van wiv the goods."' But Louding did not look like the type of person who would readily 'loud' vans with 'the goods'. He looked as if he had the goods and from the name, having written it in a modest abundance around her exercise jotters, Heidi became obsessed with the guy. She very suddenly left the circle, unable, it was supposed, to conform to tuck-shop ambience. However, at maths, Brian happened to mention to Christopher as a point of incidental interest, that his sister had taken a funny turn. She was not longer enthusiastic.

'About what?' Christopher asked.

'About anything. My sister is an enthusiastic girl. Everything she does she does with enthusiasm. If it wasn't so annoying I'd say she's almost like me.'

This was the new Heidi, perhaps. Had she discovered her age? Less annoying and yet somehow less amusing. Days later Brian continued the report.

'She's beginning not to eat.'

'What? How can one begin not to eat?'

'Simple. You look at your food, you half-heartedly swirl it around the plate, you put your elbow on the table and sigh and then not eat. One can either say "I'm not hungry" or "Yuck". Funny, I don't think she said either.'

Next report progressed from not eating to not sleeping and then not waking up.

'She's also turned quite pale and is beginning to insist that she's dying.'

'Has she woken up?'

'Oh yes, many times. Enough times to say that she's ill and she wants to stay in bed and die. Interesting. Not wanting to appear indifferent I started to look into the matter and in the course of my investigations I discovered the name Louding and matters referring to the same within the thrown-about realms of my sister's belongings. Now, what do you make of that?'

'Hard to say.'

'Yes. My very first thoughts: is this an ancient incantation against some bizarre spell? "What's all this about Louding?" I asked her and she groaned. She was still in bed at the time with her face to the wall and was unable to turn over which helps to demonstrate inner pain. "Does the name hurt you?" I asked. She suddenly sat up. "I'm in love with him, dammit," she shouted. She was annoyed with me for taking so long to discover the truth.'

Her mother had called the doctor the day before and the doctor said she was ill. One didn't need a doctor to diagnose this but it was helpful to have it confirmed. So Heidi had two weeks off school.

'Did you know Heidi is off school because she's lovesick?' asked Henry of Louding.

No, Louding did not know this.

'Who's she in love with?'

'Well, we all have our theories and all of them coincidentally suggests that it's you.'

Louding refused to believe this, even when Brian said out right that his sister was being slowly killed by Louding's uncaring attitude.

'Such an effect from unrequited love is probably more common that we think,' said Brian. 'I wonder if it will take its full course and actually kill her.'

Coming from him it sounded more like a conspiracy, but not being one to take such risks and opposing any notion that he was uncaring, Louding called around to the Innmaker's accompanied by Peter Christol (a perhaps successful method of lessening compromising retribution). By this time Heidi was too ill to appreciate the visit from her possible cure. She had, in actual fact, caught a not uncommon version of glandular fever which offered her the recurring symptoms of being in love with Louding from then until the following Summer. The poor girl was hardly given the chance while healthy to state how her love for Louding had been a contributing factor – love now withered by an image of herself as a shadowy being gaining little strength from the light of his cautious visit. Peter Christol started reading *The Almighty Thor* taken from the top of a pile of *Almighty Thors* left by Brian in a last minute before-rushing-for-the-bus act of sibling affection. Louding gave her the latest news fresh from the circle and then he started reading *The Almighty Thor*. She didn't want to read *The Almighty Thor*.

'Thor's such a bore,' she said.

'The artwork's good though,' said Louding, not noting a universal excuse.

It was during this first bout of fever that Louding had started dating Sarah, Colin's sister. Just as Heidi recovered he was ditched for an airman and both he and Heidi returned to the circle to continue in irony what had been lacking in drama. Her enthusiasm replenished and chances ripe again, he went out with Grace Ford who had introduced her in the first place. A second relapse arrived just as Rosemary Dazel explained to him in Grace's well-chosen absence, the intricate nature of the fickle fancy of feminine and folk club whims. Heidi's intermittent bouts of glandular fever had her constantly returning to school as well as could be expected, and she was wondering if it was now Wendy Lester or even Frances Smith who was intervening or not on her behalf. No, neither, but finally instead a third S, this time in the form of a Sharon Wendrake.

'Who?' she exclaimed when having asked why he wasn't around. "Who the hell is Sharon Wendrake?'

The answer was somewhat vague. The girls could only shrug and pull faces at the idea that this Sharon, who was at least a year younger than any of them, had sneaked in from the third form and stolen the lad from right under their noses. Henry sort of remembered this happening, and, if they tried hard enough, so did Christopher and Peter Christol. Heidi looked around for a comment from Colin but he was busy courting Rosemary at the other side of the school (out of the range of Henry's scorn), and so the circle's principal absentee was Louding-and-Sharon shaped, an achievement for Sharon as she had never joined the circle in the first place. Henry explained: Louding had met Sharon at the Go-Kart Klub. 'She crashed the fun-cart and he fell in love.' This had been some time ago as if the interesting combination had to be given time to blossom. Heidi was annoyed that something which occurred in the past, as it always did, should now have such a drastic effect on the present, as, to her, it also always did. Henry shared her loss at understanding the process between the first dramatic encounter and Louding and Sharon's present courtship. Maybe it was her youth – hardly fourteen – but Christopher disagreed.

'No, it's because Louding's now in love.'

'But what difference does that make?' said Heidi, outraged.

All right, the lad had every right to fall in love, but not to make a scene out of it by abandoning the circle. They had not actually placed themselves into the category of missing persons. One only had to stare across the yard at the masses of blue and white and khaki adorning the more revealing array of summer's influence, to understand what it was, this thing called love – Louding in love: a bonding of hands, a silent conversation and the much treasured seclusion within the framework of such-like couples consorting in their own company, which, although not stated, included Colin and Rosemary. Louding and Sharon sat together thigh-to-thigh on the thigh-high wall, a wall which bordered two sides of the main yard and possessed an important role in developing youthful days of contemporary romance. Its love-charmed utility was also, more prosaically, converted to a platform upon which house-masters stood and announced house-matters to the gathering pupils making up their respective houses first thing in the morning. Really, all that mattered to the many couples decorating its healthy strip of shade and fresh air was the being together for now and all eternity during both first and second break.

'But Louding's in sixth form,' said Heidi.

Henry agreed.

'How could he do this?' she asked, although she would do something similar if given the chance to swap places with Sharon.

And given the chance to swap places with Louding '…I'd straight away swap Sharon for Chantal,' said Henry, referring to a lower sixth form prefect whom he believed was rarely to be seen outside the prefects room, and whom he once had the audacity to date and, although she declined her further part in the forming of an item, to whom he remained forever smitten.

He was also willing to believe himself grateful enough to see no more of his sister at the circle even if just now the cause invited the slight risk but not undisturbing thought of a Jottrell contamination of the Dazel species (notwithstanding Colin's own above average looking sister, Sarah, now long gone).

'It's outrageous,' said Heidi. Henry, still lost in thought, agreed.

But, what was more outrageous to Louding was Sharon's departure. This time the fault was not an airman but the Air Force itself. The Wendrakes' three years were up and their return to England was due. In fact the return came and went and took her away before Louding had a proper chance to appreciate the fact that he was now in Cyprus for another two years without her. He had only just started writing Sharon's name in every known style of English calligraphy including the then vague idea of computer notation. He did not know much about computers but soon mastered the method of writing in their popular font, squaring off the curves and doubling by parallel the vertical strokes. Before her departure and while she was still at school, he could spot her from a distance of 200 yards and the height of the language balcony during registration in Eric's classroom. From such a distance all girls looked adequately attractive, but for him Sharon glowed as if covered in Tinker Bell's fairy dust. And she was staring and waving and he was smiling and staring and waving back and '…now look, she's smiling, see.' But all Christopher imagined he saw were lots of girls smiling back, all at Louding, some even waving. Every girl is irrelevant compared to the one now chosen, especially Sharon and especially when she left. Louding left too, that summer during the holidays, to go and see her, but he had to return.

He's thinking of leaving this summer to go and see her again, thought Christopher now, still waiting for the bus back to Akrotiri from Limassol. But Sharon to me is hardly relevant because I hardly knew her. I remember she was young and very pretty and Louding prefers her still to every girl he's ever met. He talks less about her now than most of the girls he meets, and only then her name is mentioned when he refers to England.

Louding's return to the circle after she had gone had been as if a slight illness had caused him to stay away but now he had recovered. But their lower sixth form career was drawing to a close, and very soon, after the summer holidays, after Louding had returned from his first sojourn abroad to see Sharon, upper sixth came upon them in all its glory, represented by the prefects' room. So much for the ivory tower complex – just one year deeper into mature conflict. More enduring is the dust and grime of those formative years culminating in both an allegorical and actual random stress of the tuck-shop circle, and thankful that they had not been made prefects they resumed, for a short time, their lower sixth way of spending the breaks. The bachelor pad of the special private study room beside the library could now be commendably abandoned in favour of what the prefects' room dubiously offered as work space. But too much play and not enough work made Jack not a very bright lad, although it did not occur to either Christopher or Louding to complain. Work was far from lacking, and play could not be totally renewed from old distractions. Henry, who had accused everyone at some time of being a mad fool, demonstrated how he too was part of this social side of insanity. He had left to join the RAF. Peter Christol and Colin Jottrell, within weeks of each other and possibly in similar mileage, had also returned to England. The shifting sands of Cypriot time had fallen through its fill for them, and Christopher was just less than saddened when eventually informed that Frances had gone.

Grace and Heidi advanced onto a level of affable constraint. They both had better things to do, their tour at the tuck-shop circle silenced by the brighter wider world of the main yard where gatherings of greater abundance and more imaginative shape were transporting like a field of negative ions the individuals of tomorrow. That was not to say that Louding and Christopher were to them yesterday's men. But Grace and Heidi had taken to the stage. What other way was there for Heidi to live up to her brother's standards of variety? And the school offered its own form of variety in a range of break-time rehearsals, each containing enough encounters for Grace in her turn to use as a means of forming other circles, which Heidi used, both from behind and in front of the curtain, to seek help in her need to escape the strangle-hold of loneliness.

'She just needs to be more like Debra,' said William when the subject of Heidi's misery arose.

'Don't think so,' said Christopher, thinking that few can be lonelier than she who was rarely there but elsewhere. And what about Wendy? All Christopher could remember of her departure was that William remained while she didn't.

'It's a funny thing,' said Christopher, 'but there's only three of us and yet we're surrounded by thousands.'

'What?' asked Louding, distracted by thoughts of Sharon.

The crowds surrounding them were a conforming illusion. Yes, many girls still wanted to know Louding but only if he became the statuesque legend in the middle of crunched crisps and chewed cream buns. Christopher saw Louding's contemplative solution to the distraction of this ready-made attention as one admiring the dignity of a featureless desert figure astride the patient camel looking at life which lay just beyond the final sand dune. He became frightened of losing Louding, and so he said: 'Nothing, nothing,' to his friend's enquiry and made an awkward sideways suggestion which happened to fit.

'Let's go to the prefects' room. Read *Charlie Brown*, listen to music, play cards…'

Sing, dance, rant and rave, anything but this. So upper sixth took them in, William tagging along as if without choice, his age having fooled him again into accepting another following from the previous one he could not remember rejecting. And eventually Christopher met Helen. They shared the same Monday afternoon activity, being part of Patrick Eve's tape-recording club, but it was in the prefects' room that they actually met, that they said hello and cheerfully participated in the exclusive time they had together which included picking up litter during the headmaster's campaign, sharing various aspects of her prefect's duty and laughing simultaneously at the same Snoopy cartoon. He could not remember her from lower sixth although he may well have seen her then many times, the choice of familiar faces remaining tight in those days. However, he did remember Marion from the first time because she had been keen on Louding's calligraphic skills in the art of Gothic script, keen enough to sneak away from the library into the lower sixth private study room where he and Christopher, during that year, had spent a good deal of their time playing three dimensional noughts and crosses while waiting for Mrs Burlington to arrive and invigilate their study. Marion had a gift for gaining attention even if authority threatened to roughen the smooth edges of her intrusion, and Christopher remembered how he lost his game because he thought she was freckly and pretty. Louding was accustomed to pretty girls, freckles and all, and merely explained while winning that the calligraphy he had promised her but forgotten to do, had been left at home and was on top of his bedroom table. Next time, he assured her, and she seemed happy with that, having to go anyway because Mrs Burlington at that point arrived and pointedly stared at her presence until she became absent. Christopher never saw her again until months, and another form, later, another age, the age wherein this girl was forever Louding's Berengaria companion – she and he, as it happened, sharing the same street.

'Not quite,' countered Louding to an understated accusation that she was now his girl, 'but she's in easy walking distance and she's around almost every day.'

And the calligraphy never had been done, but Christopher could tell that she never really cared. With equal suddenness, donning an extra layer of identity she became, as if she had always been, one of Helen's very good friends. Helen had that many good friends it was easy to be unwittingly included, but Marion's manipulation of established affections had about it the ability of one taking short-cuts. Debra and Wendy may not have known her from Eve, but Marion was well in with William – had been friends for years, although it came as a slight surprise to learn that he was now living in Akrotiri.

'Do you think maybe,' Christopher asked, 'she wants to join our circle and she knows she's too late and the prefects' room is out of bounds, poor girl?'

Louding suspected that the manifestation of Marion occurred because the circle had been disbanded and she was now taking what chances were available. He was soon to learn that she disliked Heidi, Grace disliked her and as for Frances – she closed her fists, closed her eyes and seemed to close her mouth as she breathed: 'I never understood what you saw in her, Christopher.'

'How do you know I saw anything in her?'

'Everybody knew you fancied her. I'm glad she's back in England.'

The connection between these two statements was something of a prolonged illusion. Marion had no intention of taking the place of Frances but was delighted when Christopher started dating Helen.

'And what about Wendy,' he asked.

'Who?'

Marion loved Louding. No girl had ever, has ever or will ever love Louding the way Marion did and still does, thought Christopher. She refuses to give in despite the fact that Louding doesn't treat her that well, hardly thinks about her until she's around – but then, she is around a lot. Maybe, but not believing for one minute that it is true, no less false than an image of both girls marching down the bypass beyond or behind any combination of Cypriot youth, that Marion's love for Louding caused Helen to go out with me. No! Caused me to go out with Helen, and its relentless adherence is keeping us together. But Savina didn't invite Marion to the engagement party: it was Helen who invited her after she herself had been invited by Savina and then only as a comfortable arrangement for accommodating Louding in the deal so that Christopher could stay with him the night at BG. Girls have been known to work together to construct these matrices in which us dauntless lads find ourselves entangled. What an arrogant thought, Christopher thought. Who the hell's going to work with who to get me?

But there was nothing complicated about the plot. An engagement party was in the offing – the lucky couple was irrelevant to the story other than one side being distantly related to Savina. Savina assured the presence of British guests, and it now occurred to Christopher that maybe Savina measured up to something extra special among her own Cypriot friends. She certainly measured up to something extra special when he saw her at the party. She swapped the white knee-length socks and navy blue skirt for a skin tight wrap around of silk and lace which hung gently from her shoulders and stretched to her naked feet. And her hair, freed from the plats, danced lightly over the disciplined cloth with a complementary sheen. He danced with this new Cypriot goddess to the slow crooning of Aphrodite's Child.

'May I tug your hair now?' he whispered, his mouth pushing against the strands in the way of her hidden ear.

'Christopher, you should be with Helen.'

'Why?'

Helen was with Marion. The two girls sat alone on a couch near the balcony being ignored while Louding was elsewhere in apparently ardent conversation with a few delightful looking Cypriots of his age. Helen and Marion drank Cypriot sherry, avoided the cheap wine popularly referred to *cockanelly* and wondered why the many Cypriot lads were not living up to their British made reputation of not leaving them alone. Such lads seemed happy enough standing aside in this business like groups laughing constantly at one line jokes or singing alongside their balalaika songs. But with arms folded and eyes peeling everywhere through the mesh of the party the two British girls encouraged the type of challenge only inflicted on the restless Saturday night mind. Nobody was restless. Everybody ate, drank, danced, talked and consigned the evening to a success for all but, it seemed, Marion and Helen. Louding entered, staggered for a second over the contrast of their sober glare and informed the girls of the excellent Olympian red wine from whence he'd just come, and did they know the whereabouts of the nearest loo? Christopher, meanwhile, was being taught to dance like Zorba while Savina joined her British friends on the couch to watch.

'You'll have to watch him,' she warned Helen. 'He becomes amorous. Is that the right word?'

Not for Helen, although on the balcony without the Cypriot girls and with maybe a drop of wine things could be different. The stars were out. They could count the falling ones and luxuriate together in the comfortable evening heat. Marion, at that moment, was busy falling out with herself. She wanted to search for Louding, guessing that he was no longer elsewhere having a pee, and just as she gathered the courage and will to do so he appeared, full of intoxicated energy, ready to demonstrate variations of the dance theme from *The Fiddler on the Roof*. Zorba was all very well but anyone could do a half-hearted tiller-girl kick. 'Watch this,' and that part of the party made space and clapped the rhythm and he was quite good. Christopher joined him and so did a few of the other lads and the balalaikas never gave up until Savina arranged with another young lady whose father probably owned the house, probably the one shouting above the riot and demonstrating with his insistence that young men in his day had more dancing pluck, for the music to suddenly change.

'This sounds familiar,' said Christopher who fell over in his attempt to pick Louding up. 'The British charts are invading.'

'I've made up my mind,' said Louding very slowly and carefully, 'never to do that again. I feel funny.'

He walked over to the couch, sat down beside Marion and asked for her shoulder. He then fell asleep. Helen went with Christopher to where sobriety now ruled with the standard of evening bopping. She slipped her arms underneath his, looked at him straight, smiled, blinked, inhaled and said: 'Christopher, go out with me please.'

'Well, of course. When?'

'What do you mean, when? Now!'

'Oh, I see. You mean *go out* with you. Not just take you out but really go out with you.'

And he tried to figure out the difference and its whereabouts within the

English language which allowed for this. But they both knew what this meant and he brought her closer into a hug and asked the usual as if doubt was a necessary part in order to have something to overcome.

'Do you really mean it?'

Helen nodded her head. She said: "Yes! Yes! Yes!' She meant it.

'Do you think so?' asked Louding the next morning.

He was suffering. His world, dazed with doubt, was as if his entire head was pressing its contents into the small space just above the eyes and there was only enough room for the light to get in. Christopher, on the other hand, the least companion needed by a hangover, was 'full of the joys of spring' – an out of season gesture of certainty considering it was the middle of the mild Cypriot winter and just under a fortnight before Christmas.

'I'm in love,' he insisted.

'I'm in hell,' said Louding. 'Why do I always get drunk on wine? Why do I never remember about the previous times I got drunk on wine? Truly truly never again.'

A challenging season for such a pledge, and no sooner did they meet Helen and Marion again, this time at the top of Louding's road, Christopher having taken his crestfallen friend out for a remedial spot of fresh air, then plans were being made regarding their part in the sixth form kebab.

'What kebab?' asked Louding, extra hesitant about remembering future events. 'What sixth form? We're on holiday.'

He was reminded that it as it was Christmas and all this had been arranged. Christopher, still making the most of his time on cloud nine, promptly went home and fell ill. First the sore throat, then the shivers and then the full force of flu. Poor Tessa, he thought, transferring his self-pity of yuletide ailments to last year's story of her and her entire family having gone down with the same ailment on Christmas Eve. At least the advantages to being laid low was the guiltless excuse to do nothing coupled with the goodwill of others. Helen arrived. A welcome visit at first.

'You have to get better for tomorrow's do.'

'When I'm better I'm better,' he said, still not feeling at all well as he lay on the couch and did the requisite amount of groaning. She wanted to lie there with him, keep him warm, but there was really not enough room and he was sweating enough within the confines of his accepted plight. In fact he began to resent Helen's interference. She became, as if an extension to his flu, an example of what, on the other side health and happiness, was fastidiously expected. And thus, at first hand, he experienced what Heidi must have gone through when Louding paid her a call during her bout of illness. The next day he discovered that this did not apply to all because Louding himself actually came around having been dropped off by his parents on their way to Dreamers Bay. There was an invigorating sense of deliverance in the underlying command of his casual enquiry after his health. What was not feeling too good now started climbing the hill, throat still sore, arms still over-aware of every movement but the spirit no longer weak.

'Louding, you have the gift of healing.'

'Well thanks. Good to know I can do something right.'

'So why didn't it work on Heidi that time? Why wasn't she cured?'

'Well, I was intending to cast away the evil demons of glandular fever but *The Almighty Thor* got in the way.'

A few hours later Christopher was fit and Louding, with the help of his parents, whisked him away to BG, health and all, leaving the flu on the couch to compose itself for the inevitable Christmas relapse. At BG Christopher patiently sat through the ritual of his friend choosing which shirt he should wear and fighting all efforts to prevent his shoulder length hair from curling 'out-the-way'. Marion arrived with Helen and applied the curling tongs in the way girls knew how but also as a means of one task mounting with others to secure her hopes of a lasting friendship.

They were late. The majority of sixth formers had already taken over the Britannia Restaurant and places together had to be inordinately pursued somewhere at the end of a horseshoe design of tables, taking the shape of a medieval courtyard without the benefit of straw and hounds.

'Don't go near my brother,' said Julie on one side. 'He's ill.'

This did not part the waves, but it helped, as she said hello to Louding, asking him when *she* was to receive his festive kiss.

'Well, yes. Whenever you want.'

'Before the onions please.'

Christopher could not remember much about the meal or what he said to those on either side or how he managed to stay ahead or behind Helen who seemed to spend her evening leading him or pushing him along. Neither did he remember at all any actual effort in filling his glass. Every time he looked at it, it was full of *cockanelly* and every time he drank from it, it returned to the table almost empty. Such is the cycle of liquid lingering through the night. He did, however, remember all the kisses and all the girls to which they were given as if, without having to move from his seat, he assured their unconscious desire to be given the flu for Christmas too; Helen, in particular, who eventually had to sit on his lap to prevent him from wandering off for more kisses elsewhere. Outside the rain clattered, the mud splattered and the two hired buses shattered the illusion of heaven being just next door for many. It was miles across the other side of the bypass. Onward to the *C'est la Vie* disco but with everything spinning around and lurching forward many were the young stomachs that insisted on going no further. Those who made it to the disco, still feeling reasonably in balance, had to persuade those paralysed to their seats to get up and out, although most denied responsibility for the few and crowded in through the doors by some system of disorderly payment, out of the pelting rain into the flashing lights and pumping beat. The place was full of more of the young and festive. Drinks were through a maze of crushing shoulders and out-raised arms. Everyone wanted to remind everybody that it was Christmas, although Marion could not find Louding and she dared any other lad to try and compensate the loss. He eventually emerged from out of the rain with four others, all totally soaked. Better wet than stinking although each still had their suspicions of a lingering stench to their troubles. The bus drivers had demanded all off the bus so that they could park elsewhere, and a few of the more noble, including Louding, dealt with an easily ignored need, that of assisting the sudden profusion of paralytics who needed prompt attention and propping up where it was relatively dry, and a projectile spray of vomit from one hit all those within range which covered a good few feet from the bus steps to the disco door. So Louding and his assistants stood in the rain and only considered themselves adequately sociable when waiters and bouncers from within gathered up what they could of this invasion of the youth from St John's, and politely but firmly evicted the sixth formers.

'Hello again,' said Julie, taking his arm, discarding the confused attention she always received and handling with dexterity a dignified form of exit, 'I think we're leaving. Some of us,' she explained with affected surprise, 'are infringing the local rules of decency.'

Louding certainly welcomed this unexpected affection more than he welcomed a return to the wet, although he wondered what part of the game held Marion in check. She was somewhere still in the depths of the club, most likely by herself and being guided with others to emerge. Also at the back Christopher and Helen who, ignoring all, even those assuming quite correctly that they should be with the many now leaving, danced their slow dance, said to each other again that it was Christmas and asked each other what it meant.

'Snow and presents and lots of colour and much to eat,' said Helen.

'Girls, girls, girls,' said Christopher and he added, in order to be prophetic about his present rapture, 'flowing with the wine but never mine.'

But Helen insisted that she was mine and I'm now, a couple months later I'm beginning to insist that she's not. Although I'm not really, am I? Have I told her that we should finish? Are we finished?

'It is Christopher. I told you it was. Hey, Christopher...'

Christopher looked up. A woman's voice, and Limassol usually only offered taxis by way of unsolicited agents.

'Lorraine, Larry, hello. What are you doing here?'

'Driving back to Akrotiri,' said Lorraine.

She popped her head back in from the window on the passenger side and opened the backseat door of the car. Christopher would have to jump in smartish as Larry was aching to get going. The bypass was no place to remain stationary for long, and in Cyprus, in order to out-snare the snares, one had to drive like the Cypriots. This Larry often did and better, but without second thoughts to the hazards involved, Christopher jumped in and away they went.

'Dreaming as usual, what?' asked Lorraine, turning around and stretching across her side of the car, indifferent to the speed and the fact that her seatbelt, redundantly dangled beside her. 'What could a young man like you have so much to think about? I bet you were thinking about romance.'

'Sex and violence, actually.'

'Good,' said Larry. 'You had us worried there for a second. We thought maybe you were concerned about the state of the world. I gave up doing that years ago.'

'That's why he joined the RAF,' explained Lorraine.

She looked again at Christopher, and Christopher, always looking at her, widened his eyes to listen.

'Do you want to baby-sit for us tonight?'

'Oh, I don't know. It'd take some thinking.'

'Good then,' said Larry. 'We'll expect you at eight. The kids should be fairly knackered. They're staying with friends who have very climbable trees in the back garden, and lots of other kids around who they find and kill all the time.'

'We told them to try and break a leg each as well,' said Lorraine.

'Well, in that case it should be all right,' said Christopher. 'You'll have to put barbed wire around Alan's cot. He can climb out of it now, and how about gagging George so he doesn't cough so much. Fancy calling your son George. Only adults are called George.'

'It was either that or David. St George for England, you see,' Larry explained, letting go of the steering wheel to put his fist in the air. 'And Alan's St Alan for ... where've they adopted Alan?'

'I wish someone would adopt ours,' and then Lorraine again looked at Christopher. 'Do you like the name Carol?'

'I like Carol. She's the only one who stays asleep.'

'Takes after her mum,' said Larry. 'D'you know, Christopher, it takes a high pitched scream from Alan when his vocals are in spic condition to wake this woman up.'

'How would he know? You should see the machines Larry here's rigged up to get himself up. Books and gears, saucepans and tape recordings of seven different types of hospital alarms. Wakes the entire street but himself.'

Their conversation lasted to Akrotiri during which time the three of them faced and all but nonchalantly escaped death on more than one occasion. One look at Larry from the security guard at 'Checkpoint Charlie' was enough to allow him through. He was part of a team looking after the pharmaceutical interests of the hospital and so he was well known.

'I have my own particular operations going on,' he murmured once. 'I specialize in synthetic aphrodisiacs.'

'What are aphrodisiacs?' asked Christopher.

'Methods of persuading nature's little ways to show a bit more oomph.'

George's intermittent bursts of anguished sounding coughing went through a rhythm of desire, demand and pause. Christopher lay awake listening, wondering if he could put music to the beat and thus lull himself to sleep. He had gone to bed early having felt the effects of brandy mixed with maths. He knew the kids would not allow him to sleep in. They would throw *Lego* bricks at him, they would scream at each other and they would want breakfast without having to wait the hours before either one of their parents would be up to make it. He began to dream that Alan was crying. He knew he was dreaming because he had his doubts about being awake. Always a good sign, and besides Alan never cried before a good few minutes of calling for his dad. Christopher's dad entered the dream in the form of a voice reciting definite unwritten rules about babysitting. This troubled Christopher. What could his father possibly know about babysitting? Being a parent he was obviously and totally inexperienced in the task, and did he not know he was at the Parthys' where the manner of babysitting was somewhat different from the rest? And he reminded his father that the Parthys were now back, and it was clearly stated on the unwritten contract that his responsibility as an employed guardian did not run into any particular time following their return. His father said that this was maybe so but a good guard always remained at his post until he was properly relieved, and was it not true that both Larry and Lorraine were very strong sleepers? This frightened Christopher and he woke. Alan was screaming. George was no longer coughing. Christopher got up and went into their bedroom.

'Why are you screaming like that Alan?'

Alan continued screaming and somehow managed to include in the uproar a demand for Christopher to go away. It was then that he started wanting his dad.

'Is that all? I thought something was wrong?'

Christopher checked George who was asleep. His coughing had stopped because Alan's screaming had taken over.

'Do you want a drink of water?'

'Go away!'

Christopher went away. He was very tired and he slept through to being woken up by the many attempts the children made to wake up their parents. They ran about and kicked over furniture and kept shouting that the house was on fire. Christopher lay on his back wondering how much he could tolerate before getting up. The final act, like an exclamation mark to their plans, was an explosion from the kitchen which nearly blew him out of bed. George was the culprit because he ran through the hallway crying and shouting that it wasn't his fault. Christopher quickly got dressed and went through to the kitchen to investigate. The already embittered linoleum floor was almost entirely covered in a layer of rolling and hissing and bubbling *Cocoa Cola*. The smashed bottle, family economy size, also lay claim to the area, and he and the three kids stared at the mess with different modes of fascination: George still crying, Alan screaming and laughing and wanting to play in it: Carol very much wanting to wake Larry and Lorraine so that she could tell on them both.

'Did you get cut?' asked Christopher.

'Yes,' George mumbled through his tears but he changed his mind. 'The bottle was too high for me to reach and Alan and Carol wanted to have a drink and ...'

'I did not,' said Carol.

'You did, you did, you did!'

'I did not and I'm going to tell on you both. You really done it this time, George. Larry will stuff you in the dustbin.'

'He will not,' he screamed and this refuelled the strength needed to run off and cry in a different part of the house.

'Alan, don't you dare walk in there,' said Christopher, pulling the young lad back. 'I don't want anyone in this kitchen until I've cleared up the mess.'

And he ventured into the black and seething pool and searched for and found an adequate cloth and basin. What seemed like a losing battle, while all three kids looked on with a mixture of admiration and envy, became a gradual process of rounding up the coke and glass, squeeze by squeeze, persuading its ebb from the floor, but wiping around the refuge points, underneath the fridge and oven, was not easy. Finally he stood up and back like an artist begrudgingly satisfied with his work, and he washed his hand. He wished he could wash his hands of the three behind but he set about making them their breakfast.

'You're no good at making breakfast,' said Carol when she realized what he was doing.

'I am. I'm better than you.'

'No you're not. You're not better than my mother and I'm still telling on George.'

But with all the evidence cleared up and he and Alan busy emptying the sideboard, George didn't care. After breakfast, Christopher left them to it, left the house and their parents inside it to their mercy, and left in good time for 10 am mass.

Girls! Girls! Girls! (b)

A Party of Select Friends

> The world is full of men and women looking for men and women and finding men and women and avoiding men and women. When all three occur in a tangle of magic and tragic moments the confusion can be sickening. I often wonder why we bother. My sister adequately deals with all three by including a fourth, which is controlling men and women.
> Rebecca Panhandle: Journal

> I sometimes wish women weren't so sexy and then us men can get on with life without having to be so sexist. Takes some effort...
> Robert Johnson: The Girls that Got Away.

> The way I see it is: if they come down and sort us out and tell us what we shouldn't be doing then they'd be confessing to the mess they caused in the first place. Mind you, perhaps they're quite happy to have us carry on the way we are. Wouldn't we if we were in their place?
> Simon Howard: Essay – "What's Probably Up There Looking Down On Us Here".

ERIC STARTED HOLDING TALKS. He wanted his registration form to transcend that which would be remembered as a mere ticking-off of names and the repetitious but, yes, necessary rendition of Morning-Orders. Morning-Orders was a daily bulletin of information and general requirements. It told of which assemblies were where and who had to attend what, and in all it was infuriatingly dull. So was registration – fifteen minutes a day, an hour and a quarter a week, a long time to be spent by twenty odd lads already accustomed to doing no more than the schooling required. Not so odd to assume that some only stayed in the prefects' room because they preferred doing only what was required there than here sitting opposite him doing nothing at all. The very nature of a language department premises strengthened the urge to discuss. Communication generated opinions which had to generate interest especially if arousing that which generated the controversial.

'All right, lads, we're going to have a discussion. Ten minutes' worth.'

The last phrase compelled Eric to look at his watch to check. 'Let's begin by talking about the meaning of life – interested? To get us started – the meaning of life is community, us, being together, and in a way we have no choice.'

The lads were interested but they found this hard to believe.

'We find it hard to believe, sir,' said Bill Grey who spoke with a class-representative confidence equal to his ability in directing his team at rugby.

'How many of you choose to be educated at school? It is part of human nature to defy this lack of choice. We group together to maintain the fact that we're free and tend to dislike other groups. Reconciling different groups is politics. Would it interest you to know that we're living in a country that's on the brink of political turmoil?'

'It's the Turks, sir. They say the island belongs to them,' said Robert Johnson

'But the Greeks say the island belongs to them.'

'Isn't that why we live here, sir?'

'What? To prove that the island really belongs to us? This country is a spotlight on the Middle East where most of the oil comes from. The Arab states own the oil and Arabs and Jews cannot get on. The Jews live in Israel – very small but very much there, just south-west of here. Apart from the sea Israel is completely surrounded by Arab states. We're in the middle of a hot bed of radical nationalism, while we're basically here because of what is called a cold war.'

'Is there going to be a war, sir?' asked Steve.

'Everything depends on politics. What is politics?'

'Boring.'

'No, not at all. It's very interesting. You'll be surprised how quickly you'll all be caught up in it when you leave and go to your respective colleges and universities. You'll receive such a sudden dose of political urges that for a while little else will seem as important. The music you listen to will be political. The clothes you wear: the clothes you wear now when you're not at school, and for some of you here, the fact that your hair is considerably longer than mine.'

But most teachers had hair longer than Eric's. However, they understood and listened but some agreed that everything was still dull because adults were intrinsically dull.

'Bring back the feudal system,' said Edmund Whitehead.

The next day religion reared its weary head, not so much as the intruder but with the recognized stride of one invited. Eric, despite himself possessing the faith akin to more forthright Christianity, had about him something of the well-travelled and the ardent observer, and he attempted to draw them into the usually ignored phenomenon of religion without God or gods. Unheard of – like a beach without the sea ('Wasn't that a desert?'). But he assured them that such religions did exist.

'The battle for truth is the battle between God and cause and effect.'

If this didn't confuse them – time not allowing for further analysis into who was fighting what, whether it was cause fighting effect and God, or cause and effect fighting God – Eric added another limbo for logic: all they did either pleased or displeased God, or alternatively created means for doing or not doing more in the future.

'You have control of your future or God does.'

'Isn't it both?' asked Christopher, not wanting to deny his own influence on his events but certain from his Catholic upbringing that in the long run God would have his way.

'No, I'm afraid it can only be one of the other. Think about it. Either God exists or he doesn't. If he doesn't you're in control, if he does then he's in control.'

'Maybe he exists but doesn't control.'

'That's what's known as deism, but then what's the use of such religion?'

Most in the room could think of no use for it whatsoever.

'All right then, what is religion?'

'Boring.'

'Come on now, lads. Don't just associate religion with Friday morning assembly and going to church. As a matter of interest, how many go to church on Sunday?'

He may as well have asked them how many received house-points recently. Very few were willing to volunteer such information. The hands that hesitantly rose quickly went down when discovering they were a minority.

'You see, you cover up the fact that you're embarrassed about religion or being thought of as religious by saying it's boring. It is an essential part of life. Man is a religious animal. He does things religiously. Your beliefs, no matter what they are, form your religion.'

'You said the same about politics yesterday,' said Brian.

'Yes, precisely,' said Eric, wondering if he should be pleased that the awkward lad was paying attention. 'What you believe is political insofar as it goes towards one group or another, but I'm not talking about party politics which we will probably go into some time later. How those beliefs form your life is your religion. Politics and religion are very closely related, that's why people endlessly battle to keep them apart. Religion is how you guide your individual life, politics is how you guide your social life.'

'It's just a case of being told what's right and what's wrong,' said Steve.

'And it's usually not what we think is right and wrong,' said Francis.

'And what if I was to tell you that religion is there to help you work out for yourself what is right and wrong.'

'You're saying that there is no God, aren't you sir?' asked Steve. 'My father's job depends on the existence of God. God's his ultimate employer.'

'I'm not here to say whether or not there's a God in the Christian, Jewish or Islamic sense.'

'Do you believe in God, sir?'

'I believe in religion.'

But that was confusing because the existence of religion was a verifiable fact and the lads were unaccustomed to the philosophical scope of the word 'believe'.

It did not take long, next morning in fact, for sex to rear its governing head.

'Desires are the driving force of life. Sex is one desire which adds to or takes away the strength of other desires.'

'Therefore girls must be the gods of the world,' said Brian.

'Maybe, but then, what is a woman?' asked Eric. He got up from his seat and sat against his desk and asked: 'Are we to suppose that women are there specifically for sex?'

'Yeah, like, wow, why not?' said Robert as he looked around and summed up what the others were thinking.

'Do you lads really try to understand the girls you constantly see around you?' asked Eric. 'Really try and understand them, rather than class them the way you want them to be?'

'I think they're more guilty of not understanding us,' said Francis.

'In what way?'

'They always think we're only after one thing,' said Steve.

'That's because we are only after one thing,' said Perry from the back of the class. This was a rare visit from him at registration and so he felt obliged to say something. 'A girl is definitely made for sex, and you'd think that's all they're made for. *They* think and talk about nothing else.'

'Oh yes, and what do you lads think and talk of then?' asked Eric.

'Sport and sex, the wonders of the universe and sex,' said Brian, 'more sport, Led Zeppelin, more sport, bikes and cars and sex, Deep Purple, more sport, Black Sabbath and then, if there's room, more sex.'

'Many are formed in order to fit the role they play in life: Edmund Whitehead, 72,' said Edmund Whitehead.

Christopher, startled and from his silence compelled to look around the class in order not to appear shocked, was actually surprised at himself for being disturbed by the manner in which the subject was discussed. Much as he was interested in sex, and interested in taking on a third party discussion in the ethical merits of its mechanics, his level of appreciation went not much higher than the petting particulars of a good kiss. Holding hands and kissing has to be as far as it gets, he thought, remembering last Thursday's civics debate about whether such activities should be approved of in the playground – and then it was not even kissing, just holding hands. It had never really occurred to him that girls were made for sex other than vague elements of faith in the maturing quality of life after school. At school, on camp, in Limassol or wherever, our thing with girls is one of talk, and to try and make them look amused by us doing the silly things in the hope of being rewarded with nothing more than an encouraging smile.

'Walk the happy gauntlet?' asked Henry once, referring to marriage. 'Not for me.' Of course he had a different, no doubt fully aspirant attitude towards sex, implying therein that a full flourishing of the youthful frolic was part of that need to appear mature but remain young no matter what. But then he went and joined the RAF and in a way turned against the attitude of eternal youth not to be discovered within any institution. But I don't want eternal youth, thought Christopher. I just want to be eternally stunning, but of course I'm not, far from it. I'm not even just stunning – not like Louding there, or Martin Clifton over there.

Just now, perhaps, for Helen he had a possibly low to average reading on the stunningometer, like last Monday afternoon when the tape recorder club and all other activities had been cancelled because of the annual opening day. Parents of their world united, students stayed away, teachers maintained the identifiable focus on their calling. James and Patricia, accepting a lift to Episkopi from their neighbours the Kamps, went to school, while Christopher, Julie, Peter and Rebecca stayed at home with Jennifer, none of them really caring about any of the negative or affirmative interest shown in their educational progress. It was enough to worry over the end of term reports without these additional hazards.

Helen was also at their home having arrived in Akrotiri by means of bus 27. Chris Millings was delighted to swap seats so that he could sit between Dot (or was it Doris?) and Julie, while Christopher and Helen had a seat together. She was amazed at how quiet the bus was compared to the monstrously noisy thing she and Savina tried to rule. She had resigned herself into thinking that such peace as presently enjoyed by bus 27, measurable to the school standards expected on a school conveyance, was for herself and Savina forever impossible.

'I rule with the art of gentle persuasion,' Christopher explained afterwards, 'but it does help to have Julie sitting beside me.'

Now he and Helen were accepting the rule of the house which really amounted to little Jennifer and her demand to be taken to the shops. Julie went out to rule some other part of the camp. Peter had gone fishing with Leonard, and while Rebecca, although in, was busy with friends, records and cooking – she did not have time for Jennifer-sitting – but no matter, Helen was very willing to take Jennifer to the shops and she reminded Christopher of the engraving on her St Christopher that *he* said he would arrange. There was a little man beside the Naafi who would do the job just as efficiently as any of the specialists in Limassol. Helen was leaving the very next day and so, for Christopher, it was a small price. He worked it out while the little man took away the medal, made a lot of grinding noises behind a curtain which worried Helen into saying that surely such a small thing would not need so much effort – 'Is he reshaping it?' – and returned with a job as delicately finished as the actual portion taken up by the little lad perched on the right shoulder of the big man with his sturdy staff. There was enough money left to buy three ice-creams as well, so all were happy.

'I'll have the name 'Chris' beside my heart protecting me when I'm travelling.'

'And on the other side, St Christopher, what's he going to do?'

'You're St Christopher,' said Helen, and then she laughed as if the concept was clearly a joke.

Christopher laughed because he hoped that what was backed by jest would become a slice of truth.

Jennifer laughed too. She thought they were laughing at her because of ice-cream on the top of her nose. Helen asked her what she would like to be when she was older.

'Rich, with lots of money.'

'Gosh, you learn quickly,' said Christopher. 'What will you do with the money?'

'Buy lots of ice-cream and not give it to the people I don't like.'

'Sounds reasonable.'

'Best way to become rich is to marry a rich boy,' suggested Helen.

'I will not marry a boy,' said Jennifer, quite shocked. 'Boys are horrible.'

'Not all boys are horrible,' and to use Christopher as an example she put her arm through his. 'When are we to get married?' she asked, half understanding that he might have forgotten.

'Well, we must take our time, save and learn and live a bit, and so give or take a year or two, I'd say in about twenty years time.'

'Twenty years? I'd be an old maid by then. Twenty years! That's just silly, isn't it, Jenny?'

'My mum said not to be called Jenny because it's not nice to have names shortened.'

'Yes it is. It's friendly.'

'It'd be an unfortunate thing if people decided to shorten your name,' said Christopher. 'Not at all friendly.'

Helen thought about it.

'Now you're both being silly.'

'I don't really mind being called Chris,' said Christopher thinking now that this unknown part of him had no choice in its italicized fate to be dangling between her breasts forever. 'But I can't help thinking that instead of adding to my character it takes something away. But you want to take part of me away, don't you, in order to travel with you?'

'I want to take all of you away. I wish you could come with me tomorrow. I'm going to feel awfully lonely by myself.'

'I shouldn't think so. The excitement of going back to England will easily wipe me from your head.'

'Is that where all those white people come from?' asked Jennifer.

'What do you mean?' said Helen, looking at the little girl holding her hand with playful concern. 'You're one of the white people. You come from England.'

'I am not white. I've got the best suntan ever in the whole of my family. Much better than Christopher with his red nose. Like a Red Indian.' She pointed at him, laughed at her joke and, letting go of Helen's hand, ran on ahead.

'How old is Jenny – Jennifer?'

'I can't remember. Five, I think.'

'Surely she's not that young that she can't remember England?'

'She's never been in England. She was born in Scotland. Maybe part of the same place but to her England is an obscure land full of people with whitewashed skin who arrive here all the time and become newcomers. She has this sneaking suspicion that we'll be returning there one day and she's not too keen.'

'I'm not that keen either. I bet it'll be very cold. We have an afternoon together. What shall we do?'

They opted for kissing and listening to music. Having passed Jennifer over to Rebecca, they repaired to his room. There was reel-to-reel taped music and parallel beams of sunlight piercing through the shutters. There was always one cricket out on the veranda keeping up the chirping competition for the Moody Blues. Their differing tastes for music met and remained on *The Threshold of a Dream*.

'No don't, Christopher,' she whispered in a gasped interruption, one of many, most of which advanced further on the theme of how she would miss him and how nobody else on the island could possibly gain her love. But this time she took his hand and made it jump the area to where it had been slowly sliding. 'We're not married yet.'

'Well, what's twenty years?'

'I'm still a virgin. One of the few left out of my friends.'

Christopher wasn't quite sure how this statement was supposed to grade her prospects.

'So, do you want me to do something about it?'

She laughed and kissed him and said he was being silly. He got up and changed over the tape which had reached the end of the reel and was flapping like a frightened bird against a church window pane. He then turned around and looked at her. She lay on the bed and he sensed the slight struggle she had settling her purple dress while he had been settling the music.

And that was Monday afternoon? he thought, looking around the class on Wednesday morning, and I was thinking of sex and Helen, but hardly expecting it to be the encapsulated subject for Eric's discussion. Is it just Eric or the others or even myself which makes this shocking? because he was still shocked, and he didn't want to be but he was. Helen told me she was a virgin and I should have said (in Henry Dazel style, although he wouldn't have confessed as much): that's a coincidence, so am I.

Thursday morning he had to leave registration early, as did Louding and a few others. Eric only just remembered to read out the Morning Orders: outside assembly for Durham. By the time they arrived it was in full swing and it was rarely worth catching the tail-end of such rallies. However, Emily Burlington, the housemistress, would have delivered a part-empty speech without them, enough having been announced about of the subject the previous week. She was talking about the Inter-House Handicraft Competition and this time she wanted sixth formers to pay particular attention. She always wants sixth formers to pay particular attention, thought Christopher. What type of attention is particular attention if one always has to pay attention anyway? He was mildly interested in art and handicrafts, being subjects all but unrelated to his chosen field of study, and if the houses insisted on constantly having competitions then he could think of no better method of enduring the fetish than the idle viewing of a few paintings followed by watching the performance of one-act plays and maybe reading a short story or two. However, he held in no esteem his own practical abilities that could result in exhibited examples of anything reflecting his mild interests. He suggested to Louding that he could contribute some of his Gothic calligraphy and supported Brian's confidence in the masterpiece he had in store. Brian was concerned about a more 'domestic' element of competition, wherein it was noted that Jane Sellers, also a Durhamite, had her reputation of the school's most promising artist to maintain.

'What makes *her* the most promising?'

'Her paintings,' said Christopher dryly. 'They're weird. It helps, you know. Don't ask me why. Personally, I prefer my sister's work.'

Brian gave him a hard stare. He had no need to be reminded of other threats. Julie was also in Durham.

'What did you say?'

'I think Julie is a better artist.'

So did Julie, and to install the artistic merit along with her flourishing reputation she was ready to contribute a work doubtless demanding some prize. Christopher wanted her to call it *The Power of Prayer* but she could not see the connection, the subject being girls trapped in perfume bottles curving upwards to brown shapes longing for freedom through tiny holes.

'We are praying for freedom all the time,' he explained.

'I'm not.'

She covered her painting, suspicious of such thoughts and any such allegorical promotion. Rebecca showed them the model Peter had made and discarded. It was a Bristol Bulldog and she painted it in rainbow colours, 'As camouflage on a rainy day,' she explained. Peter and Leonard weeks before had informed him of the real thing and its Douglas Bader legendary fame. Christopher's mood, set to the struggle of physics had him thinking how typical it was for the British to make a hero out of someone who had crashed – twice. Peter and Leonard were not interested in his physics, although a similar problem as to the dynamics of a Bulldog, maybe the canine variety, going through a projectile flight had been drawn and scribbled on screwed-up pieces of foolscap lying on the floor around his chair. He thought about them now, strung together to form something as equally as promising as any work churned out by the Jane Sellers' studio. But such problems were not for his brother and Leonard Kamp. They were not going to lose their legs or their sanity – just where to put the glue and paint, door-handles usually. Rebecca took up the work where it had been left, somewhere close to the bathroom, and planned out her own display. Peter was not that bothered about having part of his idea stolen. He never had any intention of painting it weird colours and most likely dangling plastic models of fighter planes would festoon the occasion, and his modest effort would have been lost in the display. 'It's silly anyway' he said, 'the amount of things this school expects you to do.' But he was only sore about not making a recent catch large enough to enclose in a glass case, unlike Leonard who, with his fish, was not sure what to do next.

Christopher's contribution to the contest concerned Durham's entire display. Competition points were to be gained by this as well, and where will it end, he thought as he listened to Emily Burlington explain to the house that overwhelming could be the odds against other houses winning. Why are teachers, he thought, always full of confidence? Do they get taught that at college – confidence? Then why stop at being teachers? If they're going to win all the time, lead the country or something. He used to think that teaching had to be the most attractive job in the world – as jobs went, but he was inclined to think differently as his age increased in direct proportion to the rigour of the subjects taught, shooting into the exponential stars with A levels (so long as the years are on the X axis, of course, he thought, otherwise flattens out like an infinite plateau). However, he tended to toy with indefinable admiration for Emily Burlington and wondered if *she* had not been made primarily for sex. She was a healthy woman enjoying middle age as a standard for prime, and with remaining good looks and such independent grace about her otherwise pedagogical motivations she could not help but garner respect and obedience. Christopher knew that she could order any fifth or sixth boy to service her every school-based whim, but fortunately she did not know this, or if doing so held it in esteem which ruled out tasks not affiliated to the well-being of Durham House. She now wanted all sixth form Durhamites to spend the first break of Thursday in her classroom, ready and equipped with ideas.

'While I realize that we are capable of winning the fight, we must not be complacent. We must not underestimate the abilities of other four houses.' This was something she did constantly, and coupled to which now was the over estimating of sixth formers expected. Christopher, Louding, Brian and Wilfred George joined Wilma Carter and Jane Sellers for a first break session of Burlington views.

'Is that all?' she remarked. 'Where is the support we need? To think that some cannot give up fifteen minutes break to organize something that will be both interesting and of lasting good for the house. Togetherness is the only road to victory, but still we shall trudge ahead despite our number, or rather your number, because I am assigning the entire task to you. I'll be available for advice, of course...' of which she continued to give including a comment on Wilfred's tie which was loose and twisted. 'A smart appearance is necessary for ready ideas. You will find that true later on in life, but now use it to furnish our house with strength and meaning, and you, Christopher, you walk around too much with your hands in your pockets.'

He had to smile while displaying a clean pair of palms, thinking better of remarking how the school, having recently forbidden the hands of boys being grasped by girls, left little by way of choice as to where such hands should be. Despite the wide awake glow to her face her humour was not to be tested. She was proud of Brian and Brian was slightly embarrassed by the fact that she was proud of him.

'But can I help it?' he explained. Not his fault if he was the lad who towed the line with a willingness not usually offered by others. 'Maybe she'll remark about my hair getting longer or the rumours and reports of my otherwise wholesome neglect of homework.'

Louding, on the other hand, was thought of by Mrs Burlington to be a slouch – 'admittedly,' she said to other teachers, 'a remarkably good-looking slouch, but nevertheless, a slouch' – and many times during the previous year when she had been allotted the task of supervising his and Christopher's private study, did she not tell him to stand up straight and both of them to take their hands out of their pockets? She despised the lethargy of youth. She had perfect posture and thus was able to offer perfect advice.

'You're far too indifferent,' she once said, 'and that will never do because you will never progress. I have noticed your name written on books and shoes and satchels of many of my girls, and yet you looked so bored.'

'Really, is that true?' he said. '*But* I'm not bored. I'm suffering.'

'What, a young lad like you, suffering?'

'That's not unusual.'

'And what could possibly make you suffer?'

'School?' he suggested, but she refused to listen to him. Besides, suffering was a sign of aristocratic ill-breeding. They had no room for such nonsense at comprehensive schools.

'It is completely up to you and whoever else you manage to press-gang into our little scheme as to how you organize the display,' she said, now sitting on the edge of her desk and staring hard at them all with a slow swerve of her head. However, she had made out an exact list of what they would need and she now held it out in front of her for the benefit of those close enough to read. 'Cardboard Boxes' was written in thick felt lettering and heavily underlined. 'As you can see, these are of prime importance. You must collect as many as you think will be able to support the contents of our display. Have a note put into morning orders requesting cardboard boxes to be left outside my room, and I'll supply you with written permission to leave the school premises during break either tomorrow or Monday so as to go to Dodge City and see if you can rummage them up from the Naafi there.'

Dodge City, a term of implied affection by British standards, was the shopping area next door to St John's and therefore strictly out of bounds to pupils during school days. With this in mind they settled for Monday, not without her help, and were willing as well to remain behind after Monday afternoon activities when they could paint the boxes black and white – the Durham colours.

'It'll be all there in black and white,' said Brian, posing a Burlington style quite magically with his method of taking the lead in the walk back to the prefects' room. 'That woman is close to psychotic.'

'I think she's demandingly charming,' said Christopher. 'Such confidence.'

'Not in us. What can we do with black and white cardboard boxes?' Brian usually answered his own questions: 'I know, a chess board. Chess boards are black and white. Three dimensional chess board.'

'Doesn't that limit the display to sixteen articles?' said Louding.

'I think you'll find it's thirty two, which is a good enough number. I don't want my painting overcrowded, and Miss Sellers behind us, her work can be the opposing king if she so wishes.'

Miss Sellers behind them was not listening and was confidently ignorant of any concern. To her, all related activities in the production of her art, even if this entailed the display of other works, were incidental parts of a retrospective of her latter days at school, and but for the immediate future, mere shapeless struggle. Wilma, beside her, who talked a lot and got on very well with Jane because she could merely but attentively answer yes and no, was more anxious about practicing her jiving for the forthcoming and end-of-school-year production of *West Side Story*. She always thought that Jane must know something about anything because Jane seemed the type who possessed a sensibly acquired practice in attracting exclusive knowledge.

'I mean I didn't even know jiving was called jiving,' said Wilma. 'I just thought it was the way they used to dance and it wasn't called anything.'

'Who's they?'

'Well, I don't know – everybody.'

But she couldn't wait for Jane to reveal now what may or may not have been universally known. She had to involve the lads who until then had thought less and less of the jive, more and more of the songs, 'Officer Krupke' being of particular interest. To all those who hadn't seen the film, this song was not a displeasing surprise, a little gem in fact within a midst of splendid but dated melodies. But Harry Henley, the maddeningly ambitious and successful producer of school epics, was above being guided by the screen. His only apparent interests, drama and school and the seasonal grand mixture of the two, had been called upon and he responded with the drastic energy of suggesting to the all but ignorant that such affairs as *The Royal Hunt of the Sun*, *Oliver*, *Becket* and *The Crucible* were well within the production capabilities of St John's. He was already enjoying the energy and frustration gained by rehearsals of *A Man for all Seasons* to be performed just prior to Easter, and there had been early stirrings of much greater plans for next term. Last month he had announced to the school assembly what had previously been paraded as a passing thought, and now he assumed the more generous tone of his ideas by calling for a full sixth form meeting. Tuesday minority subjects bowed to this superior intention, and all the sixth formers gathered for a sing-song inside the assembly hall. They all sang, more than once, 'Officer Krupke'. They were divided into groups and each group again sang 'Officer Krupke'. The music head nodded to Harry and shook his head and the two of them went to a corner and whispered away a few discerning seconds. He then asked everybody to sit down.

'We need people who can sound American and how many of you lot can jive?'

A few hands, none of which shot into the air but wavered over an attempt to actually understand what he had said, formed a doubtful consolation to his usual optimism. They were, he announced, definitely and without doubt or any sort of flagging or messing around soon to produce an outdoor performance of *West Side Story*. By outdoor he meant the main yard, by soon he meant the last week of the next term, the last week of the school year, a splendid conclusion to the year no less, and by they he meant most if not all of the sixth formers and a sizeable chunk of the fifth. If they were game, which they had to be and most were – by the last week of the year, who cared? – it would be necessary for all to learn how to jive. Thoughts varied, ranging from what was so difficult about jiving to what the hell was jiving.

'Is he totally blind to the fact that we're doing A levels next term?' Christopher asked Louding. 'Maybe I'll tamper with a light of two, but A levels are A levels and that plus rehearsing for a bout of rhythmic gymnastics will equal failed A levels.'

It occurred to him that even without tampering with a light or two he could fail his A levels, and therefore depending on his shade of reality, it was not *West Side Story* that presented a particular threat to the course of his career. But there were times when he emphasized the anti-social argument that school only existed for him to sit exams so that the rigid philosophy if not engaging his will would hardly show up any weakness in his wants. He was, in his way, using school to reprimand school.

'But it could be fun,' said Louding, and together with the rest they sang

'Tonight' followed by 'When You're A Jet'.

'My throat is sore,' said Christopher. 'It'll be so exhausting and it'll take up too much time, and further more it's far too ambitious a thing for a school production. I mean, have you seen the film? All that dancing.'

Christopher cheered up. He suddenly remembered that he had a Mars Bar in his bag: a bastion indeed of British know-how. Forget these dancing Americans. Back to the prefects' room where he revealed the bar and shared it with Louding. They ceremoniously cut it in half and took their time chewing around the chocolate edges.

'So, Helen has gone,' murmured Louding as if contemplating a thought as satisfying as the taste of the chocolate. 'Has she?'

'Has she what?'

'Gone?'

'Yes, today. It is Tuesday today, isn't it? She may even be in England by now. I'm free for two weeks. How can I handle this freedom and not go mad?'

'Take a cold shower every day.'

'I was thinking of having a good time actually.'

'Yes, that as well.'

Eating a Mars Bar was having a good time. There was simply nothing left to be said. Besides, the lads on the other side were making a racket from what was supposed to be 'I feel Pretty'.

Christopher had a dream of Helen in a large hall full of students his age and older. At first he recognized no-one. They were all playing many simultaneous games of tennis which converted the hall into a confusion of running figures and fighting shadows, with tennis balls to and fro everywhere. The chances of being hit by any one of the many projectiles only prevented paranoia by contagious indifference, and the dancing dodging dealing of separate blows issued from the tangled games an excellent sense of control. Christopher's control was in full form. There was no opposing shot he missed although no shot he gave rendered his random opponent at fault either. There were no courts and no nets, but a spaghetti route from dodge to hit forming a violent coalition between art and speed. More students entered the place and set about erecting rows of tables upon which they placed large pots of soup with bowls and spoons. The game did not cease, they merely became more congested, but soon everything was ready, the soup was to be served and so the tennis had to end. All closed in on the tables and from the other side of the hall appeared Helen. Christopher until then had found it impossible to notice anything but that which threatened to either hit him or have him miss what he intended to hit. But now she walked towards him and her tennis whites glowed like a reflecting spotlight of the full day sun. The many other players had to make way as she walked through, and at first it was his recognition of her and subsequent surprise which made her all the more dazzling. However, as she walked closer he sensed less need to guard his eyes. He had to look otherwise the shine would take her away, and the stillness, heavy from the former speed and confusion, framed the picture as they sank into the glow together – she descended, he followed and the ground covered their grip. They kissed lightly but his hands were heavy, not caring about what remaining answers lay beneath the physical lust as to why she should keep prone this power until then. The hall was not servicing their need, but instead that of the heavily organized catering clattered overhead and they rolled around the jungle of legs and feet until finally, or just before finally, he woke up.

'We had a discussion about women,' said Steve Galbraith. 'Eric thinks we should try and understand them.'

'I thought it was impossible for you men to understand us women,' said Tessa.

'What is there to understand?' asked Edmund emphatically. 'Women are basically stupid.'

'What did you say?' Savina turned around to face him where he sat in the other row.

'It's an historical fact. Women have been intellectually inferior to men since history began.'

'Yes,' agreed Steve. 'Stupid.'

'It's men who to do all the stupid things,' said Savina.

'We like to play along, after all, we understand,' explained Edmund. 'It must be very difficult keeping up with us.'

'Ha! Now I know you're being silly.'

'Not at all. We cannot defy the facts. Think of all the famous and enduring figures of history. All men…'

'With a few exceptions,' said Brian, 'like Madam Curie and … and … Mary Shelley and another Mary. Whatshername? You know the … ' He flicked his fingers. He was actually stuck.

'Jane Austen,' ventured Christopher.

'Yes, I suppose so, but she only wrote romantic comedies. Any fool can write a book. Yes, I must say, Steve and Edmund are right. Women *are* intellectually inferior to men.'

'I'm not saying that,' said Steve. 'I'm saying that they're stupid.'

'There are many things in the world that women have been better at than men,' said Savina. 'The sort of things men never recognize as important but without women there to do them …'

'And what self-respecting man would wish to boast of such skills.'

'The reasons why women have not made much of themselves in the past,' said Tessa, 'is because they were never given the chance. There were many subjects actually forbidden to them because the men thought that female interest in such things was not natural.'

'Rubbish,' said Edmund. 'A bit of oppression here and there and you've been using it as an excuse ever since.'

The argument continued until Savina became so infuriated she had to resort to violence. She clouted Christopher, who had said nothing since 'Jane Austen', over the head with an exercise book.

'Ow, Savina. That hurt.'

'That's for being stupid yourself.'

'Don't listen to those three. Anyway, what does it matter if women are stupid? You and Tessa are exceptions.'

He received another clout and decided to shut up. Ken entered and Savina was so flustered that she was unable to put forward her solution to a problem which had foiled them all since Monday. However, Ken already had the solution set down on notes in front of him and he went about copying them onto the board. It was a faster method than hers and she became so angry that she had to get up and leave the room. Tessa would have left with her had Ken's method not been so interesting.

'What's wrong with Savina?' he asked.

'She has one of those things women get,' said Edmund.

Christopher thought her anger would have cooled somewhat after she had delivered a record number of names for detention as a result of her prefect's duty during break, but she refused to talk to him throughout the first period of private study. He said that her solution had been more artistic than Ken's, but she looked at him without warmth in those dark eyes and her hair was stretched back, ready for war if he dared to touch it. So both of them delved into their separate tasks of writing up their physics practicals. Brian and Steve arrived and the two of them sat on either side of her. Christopher looked up from his work and she looked at all three.

'Go away,' she said. 'You three are not wanted at this side of the room. Only people who work go to this side of the room.'

'But we are working,' said Brian, 'or we will. Work is a means of refreshing the mind as well as taxing it. Isn't that right, Steve?'

Steve was still greatly amused and Savina, without his answer and without her rebuke, sensed this. She almost clouted him but instead she threw her rubber at Christopher and managed to hit him between the eyes.

'Ow, Savina, that hurt.'

'Work,' she ordered and he was shocked into obedience.

Brian offered his party-piece impersonation of Spike Milligan being Eccles but having no effect other than perhaps risking the wrong idea he tried closer to home and became the headmaster addressing assembly. He went further than the usual '…theme of this morning's assembly is drone, drone, drone…' and went on to say that smoking was a filthy habit and something of a perversion among innocent pupils. Instead of the wrong idea that an Eccles may have directed at the previous argument on the gender of mental apprehension, a reverse response was conceived not from a headmaster mocked but a subject implied and a rule enforced. At the other side of the room Rob Johnson, Dave the Bury and Rick Chinner, to name only a few, were smoking, strumming guitars and singing bits of 'Stay Cool Boy' and accompanying their efforts with inadequate reasons for laughter as well as the occasional slaps. Savina stood up. Her eyes were fixed particularly on Rob whose voice alone was an adequate source of focus within the mist which wandered over as an antidote to the dissipated lull on the workers' side.

'All of you,' she announced and she announced well in her clear English and Greek tone, 'would you please stop smoking. This place is for the private study and not a smokers' den, and it is very difficult working when you're being choked.'

All those she silenced looked at her with a mixture of resentment and respect. Rob even went as far as stubbing out his cigarette. But Rick Chinner, who regularly confiscated the smokes from the other formers so that he could add to the prefects' room's rapidly diminishing stash, and having little to no experience of Savina's personality, assumed that being only a bit older than he and an intrinsically un-English girl, she was powerless to do anything.

'Kindly sod off,' he said. 'Who d'y'think you are?'

'Give me those cigarettes,' she demanded with a relentless and controlled rage of purpose, and she ventured over the border line into the smokers' realm. Those behind her were stunned into a silent line of staring support. Brian could well have reasoned with her, while Christopher would have been more willing to accuse Rick of being mad.

Rick stood up to face her. Christopher then thought he *was* mad, followed by other considerations, saying to himself, Rick you're a class-one prick.

'Are you gonna try and take the fags away yourself?'

Rob wanted to intervene, but so did the girls around and for differing reasons. He kept himself on this level of flickering peace partially out of a relentless fascination for upended consequences.

'I want you to give me those cigarettes,' said Savina, 'all of them, or else I will go to Mr Emery and report you all.'

Rob intervened: 'For Christ's sake, give'em to her. She'll go'n'do it you know.'

When it came to calling bluffs Rick was a weak judge of character.

'Yeah, sure,' he said. 'No bloody wop's gonna tell me what do to. Go on, fuck off to Emery. See if we care.'

'Ah but we do care, we really do,' said Rob, overstating the obvious and thereby understating his sincerity as few took him seriously on most issues.

'Hey, Mr Rickydickylous,' said Brian, with his elbows on the bookcase partition, his head looking over into the smokers' section, 'say anything more like that and we'll drag you to Emery, won't we Steve.'

'I'll certainly give it some thought,' said Steve.

And Louding emerged from the outside as promptly as a man of the moment and stopped by the threshold as if trying to sniff the atmosphere.

'What's going on? Why the silence?'

Tessa stood up and told Savina that if she wanted to go and see Mr Emery she would join her. Louding wondered if he was late for an appointment with the great man himself while Savina turned and left the room with Tessa. No-one followed and so he ventured further into the room, and before asking what had happened became witness to a scene which explained all.

Rob jumped from his seat, snatched the cigarettes from Rick and called him a pillock.

'She's bluffing,' he replied as he sat down and took a couple of drags from the cigarette still burning.

'Maybe up to the point where you called her a wop.'

'She's a strong minded girl,' said Brian, delighted with this outcome. 'Both of them are. You don't have to work with them.'

All on the smokers' side started clearing their supplies, stashing most of the boxes into one of the guitars and leaving for display purposes half a packet to keep the deputy head reasonably in line with his expectations of strong disapproval bordering on mild reprobation. He arrived rather ruffled looking around the edges, as if having been disturbed from a nap. Rick handed him the half-empty packet and said that it was one he had confiscated. He was asked if he had taken the names of the culprits but Rick said he had forgotten. He could now look forward to being de-striped of his prefecthood – a singularly displeasing thought especially in view of Rick being lower sixth and therefore not eligible for the prefects' room without the stripes, but on the other hand, Sam Emery appeared willing to forget this little scene and so it took Savina's insistence that smoking was a continual habit within the room to finally wake him up.

'It is very hard to work here because of the smoke and now is the last straw,' she said.

Sam looked at her and then looked at Rick.

'Well, is there smoking going on in this room?'

He wanted to look and feel more shocked but he was not in the mood. Rick was equally reluctant to come up with an affirmative answer.

'Maybe,' he muttered.

Sam asked Rick to accompany him.

'Anybody else here willing to share the blame?'

Rob stood up, ready to follow, and then the Bury plus a growing enthusiasm to a similar response from the girls on their side. This was getting a touch embarrassing. However, Sam left with over half the occupants of the prefects' room following him, and Savina and Tessa sat down. She did not sit down in the same way as Tessa demonstrating a job well done. She was still too angry to gain any satisfaction out of a room half-emptied by the effect of principle.

'Do you think the prefects among them will be de-striped?' asked Tessa with an academic tone to her interest in the outcome.

'God, I hope not,' said Louding. 'That'd make a shortage of prefects and the school may feel compelled to request my services.'

'Mine too,' said Christopher, realising how his elevation to being bus prefect had been due to the results last year of smoking infringements on bus 27.

'Is that all you can think of?' said Savina. 'Yourselves?'

'Well, actually, I was thinking of the school. I'm not cut out to be a prefect.'

'Me neither,' said Christopher, also realising how un-cut-out he was to be bus prefect considering the smoking was still very much part of the bus culture.

'Neither are ninety percent of the prefects,' said Brian. 'With a bit of luck they might all get expelled. We could do with a bit of scandal to liven up the place.'

'Do you think they'll actually get expelled?' asked Tessa, this time slightly anxious about what she and Savina had done.

'Expel the lot,' said Steve. 'That's what I say.'

Nobody said much more before all those who had left with Mr Emery filed back into the room without him. They went straight to their side of the room, sat down, looked at each other, a few giggles and whispered impersonations of what they had been told and a contemptuous air of all being well with the world.

'For the benefit of those wishing to work,' said Rob, standing up and facing those on the workers side wishing to listen, 'if we get caught again, and that means anyone, the prefects' room will be closed down. He went and called out Gavin Peters from wherever he was, history of art or something, and told him that as head boy he was to keep an extra eye on us. That's made us all very scared – this extra eye from Gavin.'

'Satisfied?' asked Rick. 'We won't be smoking anymore, so you can get on with your work and breathe your precious fresh air.'

'Didn't he de-stripe you?' asked Brian.

'No. We're obviously too valuable.'

'Didn't he even threaten to expel you?' asked Steve.

'Yes, sorry to disappoint you – we tried our best.'

'Still, well done, Savina, that's what I say. About time someone made a stand against this filthy habit.'

'Hey, who's the greasy garbage talking,' said Rob. 'You're one of the heaviest smokers here.'

'You mean, I was. Because of our Savina I've seen the light. No smoking now, remember, and next time, when she tells you to do something you jump to it.'

He was answered with an orange peel.

The bell went. Louding and Christopher walked Savina to her bus. They were both experiencing irregular feelings of guilt and Louding explained to her that what she did was right but it took more courage than he possessed.

'I suppose I put you both in a bad situation. I'm sorry,' she said.

'Don't start feeling sorry,' said Christopher. 'Brian and Steve were on your side, and us two, and of course there's Tessa. It's true, there shouldn't be smoking in the prefects' room. It's crazy because…' But reasons did not arrive so readily. He thought about his own bus and how the regular few would light up at the back seat as soon as Episkopi disappeared behind the hills.

'It's just one of those little things that amount to nothing,' said Louding, 'but it seems to mean a lot at the time. You'll see, they'll all have forgotten it by next week.'

'They better not forget what Mr Emery said. They better not start smoking again.'

Isolation such as hers was worthy of the risks which would not compromise the issue even if it meant losing the prefects' room.

Julie, for one, knew just how important the issue was.

'I heard about what happened today,' she said, 'all about Savina reporting the sixth form smokers to Emery.'

She mentioned this just after lighting up a cigarette herself. She had persuaded Christopher to join her in a walk to the chippy beside the Flamingo Bar. Their part of Akrotiri was suffering from a power-failure which went on into the evening. Apart from patches bathed in candle-light soaking almost every house, the streets were in darkness. It was Rebecca who suggested fish and chips. Just the thing for such a family crisis - no TV or stereo – and, unusual for Wednesday night, or any night, all were in. Julie volunteered to collect the goods, disturbed by the environment of a self-imposed curfew and wanting to get out. She would also need help and she was also gasping for a smoke. She exhaled a straight beam of smoke into the cool twilight with an audible sigh of relief.

'You were there, Christopher. It seemed as if you were involved in it somehow.'

'Circumstantial,' he replied, still feeling somewhat low about his lack of involvement.

'I was told that it was you who put Savina up to it.'

'Who told you that?'

'That's hardly the point. You know that nothing of that nature escapes my attention for long.'

'Well, you were misinformed. It was Rick Chinner who put her up to it.'

'Rick Chinner!'

'Rick Chinner refused to hand over his cigarettes when she told him to.'

'She's no authority to tell him to do anything. She's not head girl. What she did was stupid.'

Christopher was not in the mood to discuss the finer details of Julie's opinions but he was disturbed by the manner of reporting that eventually gave her the news.

'Who told you I'd put her up to it?'

'Did you agree with her, reporting the smokers to Emery.'

They both took about five more steps before Christopher answered.

'I wouldn't have done what she did. I would never have had the guts and being a girl she can get away with things that I would never have survived. But if you're asking if I agree with her, I'd have to say yes.'

'I thought so. You understand very little. She was stupid.'

'I don't think so, Julie. She gave the warning, she made her just demand and she was in the right. Also she carried out her threat. To me she showed character.'

'The character of a fool.'

Julie smiled at her brother and her face hardly matching the arrogance of her words. There was affection in her eyes as they shone above the gleam of her straight, white teeth, and this startled Christopher. Maybe warmth escaped like a valve expelling air to be tightened.

'You say you dislike St John's, Christopher, because of this, that and the other, but there can be no go-between for those who control and the people like us who are trying to get what is ours out of life.'

'Rather dangerous talk. You sound as if we're in the middle of a military oppression.'

The melodrama was entertaining enough to make her laugh.

'We are,' she said quite brightly. 'Take a look around you. Not now, of course, in all this darkness. We're in the middle of an RAF camp, and look, the chippy, an area immune to power failures.'

The shop was standing close to the border where possible neighbouring grids met but remained independent. It was still in business as too was the Flamingo Bar from which emerged a group of youths who, having spotted Julie's arrival, wanted to welcome her. They wanted her to follow them into the bar but instead they followed her into the shop where Neoklis, the fat Cypriot chippy, expressed regret at seeing her so rarely.

'What do you expect when you always serve recooked chips?'

'That's not true. Cruel lies. Would I serve you anything but the best?'

'Well, do so now. Big order tonight: seven of each plus scraps.'

'What's happened to the camp?' asked one of her followers.

'The beginning of the end,' explained Julie. 'Are you all gonna buy fish and chips? You see, Neoklis, I bring you many customers, so you needn't charge me.'

Christopher could easily imagine her driving some sort of bargain with the proprietor who appeared to know her well, especially when a large, black cockroach fell from the ceiling and landed with an audibly though soft thud at her feet, allowing one of the girls beside her to cry out. Julie looked down, just slightly startled by the combination of unexpected noises, and crushed the stunned creature into a dry powdery part of the floor's already present dirt. She was constantly pestered with questions, mainly regarding the Youth Klub and its many subsidiary ventures which apparently kept the place ticking over. She was in her element but inclined towards a weary anticipation which, like the death of the cockroach, was part of the burden such inexplicable power accrued. During the time taken to serve them Christopher himself was accumulating an element of kudos by association, but he was pleased to eventually escape the attention and he commented on her popularity as they walked back.

'I keep my nose clean,' she said.

'Does that imply that I don't?' he ventured to ask.

'You annoy the wrong people.'

'Such as?'

'Perry Stenfield.'

'Stenfield? What does he know about what happened? He wasn't there.'

'Well, he knew enough to keep me informed – second hand information is usually all I have to work on. Remember, I wasn't there either. Usually I'm not there but usually I get to know about things.'

'Why does Stenfield want to lower me in your opinion?'

'Because it's the one thing he doesn't have to try so hard to achieve. I don't think Stenfield's trying to impress me – if so there are more effective ways of doing so, but I've been told he fancies me, therefore going against you, perhaps, somehow makes it bearable.'

'Fancies you! So do half the lads on the island.'

'Yes, pity it's only half. It's said that Sonja Stirling's fancied as far as Istanbul. You see, Christopher, even I have my limitations.'

'And who do you fancy?'

'It's a strange thing – I get informed but I don't inform anyone, not like that. But it pleases me to give Perry the idea that he has a chance – small chance. Here, you carry these and I'll carry the fish. That's better. I didn't just bring you along for the company. You'd have me carry the lot, wouldn't you, Christopher?'

'You carried the money.'

'Yes, I know, and I did most of the talking. I'm too good to you.'

Suddenly she stopped and looked at her brother as if the two had only just met after weeks apart.

'Christopher, what do you think of me?'

'What can I say? You're Julie Panhandle, the most powerful girl on the camp…'

'On the island,' she said, as if the requirement for some modesty had been overstretched. 'I often feel I'm on an island, all by myself, somehow managing to learn how to survive. But don't get the wrong idea.' She tried to express a measure of herself as transcending the usual vulnerability that went with the job of being powerful, but all that resulted was her shaking her head. 'Okay, I'll tell you. Dave the Bury, he was there, wasn't he?'

'What, in the prefects' room? Yeah.'

'He told Perry Stenfield that you put Savina up to the idea of reporting the smokers, saying that you were too cowardly to do it yourself.'

'Why should the Bury do that?'

'Well, I doubt if it's because he fancies you. Maybe you're a better hooker.'

'Oh God, don't remind me of rugby. I've a game this Friday.'

They continued walking and Julie continued talking.

'Pat wants you to go to her going away kebab this Friday night. I think you already know about it.'

'Oh yes, of course, I'd forgotten about that. This Friday night hey?'

'It's all been arranged. Just the select few. Don't cripple yourself at the game and tell Louding not to cripple himself either if he's playing as he's invited too. Pat's fallen for this now boring business of fancying him.'

'Oh, in that case he's not to bring Marion.'

'Marion? Marion Shoremichael? God no!'

'You know what Julie, you make a habit of disliking the girls I befriend.'

'Aha.' She shook her head without looking at him. 'You make a habit of befriending the girls I dislike.'

That night Christopher dreamt about being late for the school bus. When he arrived at the stop he was by himself. However, the bus turned up driven by the usual driver, but it was of such a size that thousands could have sat comfortably within its steel-plated walls. There was nobody on that he recognized and as he sat down amidst this crowd of strangers he woke up.

Could do with being late for Thursday morning, he thought, and enter at an advantage the morning wade through the sludge of monotony: physics and the realm of *Nelkon and Parker*, only to be relieved by a quick kip during civics. As expected, the school rules discussion was not continued. A mountain-rescue expert, who probably spent most of his working time maintaining the large yellow RAF choppers, spent a contented one and half hours showing slides of a recent Himalayan expedition. Christopher wanted to be interested. This *is* an interesting subject, snow, deprivation and friendly Sherpas, but he dozed off. No chance of doing likewise in front of Mrs Burlington, with her display discussion and Durhamite enthusiasm forbidden to diminish.

All houses were by now severely hampered by handicrafts. Sorting the wheat from the chaff was a major affair. Mr Penhurst of York house sacrificed half his classroom to this formidable task. He was head of the art department and a natural York enthusiast as well as the school bus coordinator and, a major plus in St John's-based hegemony, a first class rugby player. He was one of many elements Emily Burlington referred to in her exhortations against underestimating the strength of the opposition. Tessa was his right hand girl, efficient and systematic, and so he put her in charge of York's handicraft and she took into her temporary possession the accessible portion of the rejects, storing them in an unlocked cupboard of the prefects' room. They appeared there like a silent display of moral culprits as if waiting for their turn at detention. They gained attention – Perry Stenfield's in particular. Both he and the Bury found fascinating what had earlier been regarded by the chosen experts as undesirable.

'Look at this. A pyramid. What's wrong with a pyramid?'

'Old idea. Been done before. By some prat called Cheops wasn't it?'

'No, he was the one they put inside. There he is, there.'

Perry picked out of the box he took from the cupboard a long knot of pipe cleaners shaped like a man and wrapped in sticky plasters. Tessa returned from a rapid route around her prefects' duty as Louding, Christopher, Steve and Brian entered the room still discussing what one could do with a variety of black and white cardboard boxes apart from utilising them somehow in a probable future need to practice jiving. Savina, who was studying for O level French, and used this as a means of occupying what would have otherwise been private study for the last two periods on a Thursday, did not make an appearance. Nevertheless, the time did not pass without problems. Perry, trying to launch the model mummy off the top of the cupboard with the use of a rather fancy but dilapidated elastic band missile launching pad, aiming for the room's empty goldfish bowl, missed, and mummy plus elastic band landed safely on a padded seat beside Tessa. She took possession of it, stating that it belonged to someone and was going to be returned in one piece.

'Christ, woman, you like messing things up, don't you?' said Perry, annoyed that he should be reprimanded for doing something which he, himself, would have thought as childish from anyone else.

'Yes, and so do you,' was her sharp reply.

Steve laughed, Christopher had to smile, and Perry was by now not amused at all.

'Ha, Panhandle. You're always on *her* side' he said, addressing Christopher and ignoring Steve.

Christopher could hardly deny this, especially in front of Tessa.

'We're on the side of truth and goodness,' said Steve.

'Talking of truth, Perry,' said Christopher, indulging a moment of somewhat rash bravado, 'is what you rarely do concerning my sister.'

Matters concerning his famous sister were also rarely subjects of conversation from Christopher and so everyone in the room looked up to listen.

'What d'y'mean, shortarse?' demanded Perry.

'You know what you told Julie. Afraid you've landed in her bad books. What gave you the right to discuss me with my sister anyway?'

'What gave you the right?..' Perry mimicked and the Bury laughed and answered the question for him.

'You were just about to go and tell Emery yourself, Panhandle. I could see it. You get the girls to do your work for you.'

Christopher thought: Is he referring to maths? He was now not sure what was more disturbing. The unjust accusation levelled at him by David Bury or this strange extension performed by some prefects' room media hype which allowed academic assistance to encroach upon decisions asserting authority.

'You're a liar, Bury. And you lied about me to my sister, Stenfield.'

'Oh wow,' said Perry. 'Mr Tough Guy Panhandle, accusing us both of lying. Fighting talk. Do you want to make something of it.'

There was a difficult anguish within Christopher's rage because, while remaining on Tessa's side, he could hardly decline the challenge and still honour unwritten rules. Christopher was far from the fighting man the present culture recognized in line with him being his sister's brother, and Louding, realising this within the few seconds of heavy silence stepped forward.

'All right,' he said with a mild firmness fortunately persuasive enough within the limits of himself being able to consolidate the physical attributes needed for a fight. 'Come on, hey? No more.'

He had approached Perry from Christopher's side and stood between them. His benign but serious stare was enough to convince both Perry and Dave that an honourable retreat on their side had about it the taste of victory – that plus an assumed solidarity in the presence of both Brian and Steve. Christopher was so infuriated that he found it impossible to make any start on the physics homework set that morning. Louding sat down beside him and continued working on some pictures of flabby looking chromosomes, and he mentioned, without looking up and with the joining of two curves, that he had met Stella again. It was Christopher who looked up.

'You never, did you?'

'Aha, thought that might interest you. Wouldn't let that betray you when we eventually get to take Stella out, unless of course you want her to know your feelings, but with Helen there...'

'So you mentioned a kebab?'

'No, that would have been a bit too quick, but I'll get to know her a bit more at the Island Disco tomorrow night. Marion's dragging me along again, and Stella could well be there. She said she would try to turn up but discos, so she said, were not really her scene. Then she hopped on a bus going to Akrotiri.'

'When was this?'

'Last Saturday.'

'Last Saturday? How come you've taken so long to tell me?'

'I was meaning to. I should be able to tell you more next week.'

'But I want to know more now,' said Christopher.

He was happier. He found it much easier to tackle his physics problems but had no less that average difficulty sorting them out. Brian assisted him where he could without any intention of actually doing the work himself. Louding continued with his art work, scribbling pieces of notated wisdom underneath each crayon coloured globule.

'Louding,' said Christopher eventually.

'*Oui, mon ami*?'

'How can you go to the Island Disco if you're working tomorrow night?'

'Aha, good point. I don't start work tomorrow, as it happens, but next week.'

'In that case there's nothing to stop you turning up at Pat Vendle's going away kebab.'

'There is. There's Marion and the Island Disco. Where's this kebab being held?'

'That's also a good point. I don't know.'

'You're a great help.' He shook his head, resigned to his fate. 'Don't bother finding out. I'll stay with Marion and talk to Stella and you have a good time.'

But Christopher was of the belief that good times were better with Louding than without, but for now there was too much time ahead, a good day and a half before the event, to concern himself with any but immediate details, such as the physics which took him all afternoon and on into the night. He was on doorman's duty at the Families Club. He sat at a desk opposite the entrance and for a fee of one shilling he wrote out tickets for what Thomas Rorner called 'bonny fiddle' guests. The money would go into a cashbox beside the phone and thus help assure funds from which would emerge the doormen's pay every Sunday night. He worked from seven to ten most Wednesdays and Thursdays as befitting a schedule drawn up by the manager. The other nights and two afternoons were covered by Scott Juir, Colin Kamp and Thomas himself. All four, however, swapped their sessions frequently, and as Christopher had worked last Sunday afternoon for Scott he missed out on last night's shift which possibly had about it candle-light elegance because of the power failure. Scott told him later on that the wives club had not taken place as usual and, as if the postponement had rallied the men, the evening had been quite busy. He was unsure of which to prefer. Scott was not lazy, just indecisive about earning his pay, and already the system of swaps were against him as now he would have to make up the balance of nights by working his usual Friday as scheduled instead of going out with Pat and her select friends.

'It's not fair. All the doormen have been invited,' by which he meant that Christopher having, unexpectedly, been invited, spoiled his, Scott's, plans about making a further swap with him. 'How can she do that?'

'An unfortunate coincidence. We are all loved alike.'

Thomas was loved all the more by one particular girl who, aware of his employment at the Families Club at least twice a week was careful not to visit the place (Sunday Youth Dance nights excepted when she would nonchalantly press her urgent entrance through the protection of the youthful crowd) unless Christopher sat at the door. She was so much in love with Thomas, she explained, that she could not possibly share the same room with him or share this information with Thomas's mates, i.e. Scott and Colin, and least of all with Thomas himself. There was a kudos missing in her thinking but Christopher did not mind *not* being thought of as a mate. He liked Thomas and Thomas liked him, and he supposed it was true. What he lacked in mate-ness he had gained in the undeniable charm of her company. Christopher was able to assure her that Thomas knew nothing. She was always hoping that he might suspect something, and Christopher wondered, looking at her, pretty enough as she was, if in this case ignorance remained bliss.

She was Gavin Peter's sister although Christopher knew her better as Pamela who sat a few seats up on Oliver's side of bus 27. Why she was not part of her own brother's bus was not important enough to even define as an anomaly. It had been some time before Christopher discovered that she was part of Gavin's family – not that she was a quiet girl like her friend Eve Sholts who, indeed, said very little but was nearly always by her side. Being Pamela's bus prefect as well as doorman to a fairly popular club, Christopher was suitably designated, if only to compliment their visits with drinks and the occasional kebab sandwich, as the ideal confidant. Pamela was in love with Thomas Rorner and she wanted to know more about him but only from Christopher. Apart from Eve, only he knew of Pamela's passion, but of Thomas he knew even less. Thomas, not unlike Christopher, was called Thomas and not Tom although he had never been known to specify a preference. More than likely he would have welcomed the freedom implied by the shorter name because he was the outdoor type, with cycling and soccer and chasing up every available Youth Klub activity. If this was America, thought Christopher, he would have been thought of as a regular guy. As it was his standing remained a popular contribution to the youth culture of the southern RAF kingdom in Cyprus. This, of course, included school of which he was an ardent fifth former, like Scott and Colin and Chris Millings, all four very good friends. Pamela merely wanted to know if it was wise of her to love him so. But Christopher knew even less about such wisdom.

She also merely wanted to know, why *him*, Thomas? Yes, why not me, thought Christopher, but then she'd be visiting Thomas. He was attracted to this young lady who found life such a mystery like a social ladder leaning away from the grace of her existence. While he was already on fairly good terms with her head-boy brother and like so many others found it hard to believe that he, Gavin Peters, was head-boy anyway, he wondered if Pamela also found it hard to believe that she was the sister of the head-boy. He might have asked her had it not seemed out of place to assume Gavin's influence, the Gavin side of her Peters potential, although he too was after the enlightened state which for her possibly crystallized into the solution of infatuated causes.

One cause was Eve who was a mystery all set to melt into the shadows if Pamela vanished. Pamela wanted Eve matched up with a particular lad who seemed set on making the task difficult. Christopher knew this particular lad well but it was of him that they rarely talked because Eve rarely talked and Eve did not seem so interested. Christopher remembered Eve from Scotland. He never got around to enquiring but her father must have been stationed, like his had been, at Leuchars in Fife. He remembered a vague association with the girl he thought of now. He had finished his homework while at the Club, Thursday being a quiet night, and he had enough time left to complete a letter to Ronald Arteeky, a friend from Fife. He examined his address book list of correspondents which had dwindled considerably over the past six months. Henry could still be relied upon for a line or two, and this was all he ever offered, just a line of two, mainly about the money he was now earning and the various assets he was adding to his stock. Christopher then thought of Mary-Ann Sheen, his very own major love story that, unfortunately, had not been ideally balanced on the mutual side, and it is true, he thought: Eve did know Mary-Ann. I saw them together once and it's there in the fog of my memory. She's given up writing to me – and so too has the more successful rival to her love, Mark Langford, but understandable as he's a guaranteed presence in BG every holiday. Below Mark's name was Brian Reem, another good friend from Leuchars who, like Mark, was no longer there. He and his family had moved to Germany and he was now part of some boarding school system there. From scanty reference to conditions and work, Christopher could only assume that he was content.

That night Christopher dreamt of Mark sitting with him in a cinema which suddenly erupted into a state of panic. Men and women, children and dogs, the mice and the cats and little sections reserved for cockroaches started leaping all over the place. Mark sat still and advised Christopher not to move. It was only the effect of the film they were watching, he explained. But Christopher could not help himself. He had to jump up and down as well. The film was piping out a tune which was driving everybody nuts. Maybe Mark had cotton in his ears.

Patrick Eve, with his bright new morning voice, read out a story to the entire school.

'Once there was a quarry man who hated his job. But there was no way he could get out of it as he had a wife and a family to feed and it was either work on the quarry or starvation. Suddenly a genie appeared to him and asked him what he would like to be. The man replied that he would like to be the leader of men having power over the type of men who worked in quarries. So the genie made him into an emperor, but on one occasion, when this emperor was about to have a large procession, a black cloud came over the place and caused a storm. The emperor was mad about this and said to the genie: "I wish I could be like that cloud as clouds rule over emperors." So he became a cloud and he floated everywhere, looking down on the lands and life below, until one day he ran into a mountain. "This is no good," he said. "I cannot move now. I wish I was a mountain as mountains have power over clouds." So the genie transformed him into a mountain, and he stood up so majestic over all and resisted with ease all storms and weather against him. However, as fate would have it, he saw a quarry man working down at the foot of him and finding that the quarry man was doing considerable damage he called for the quarry man to stop. "This is no good," he said. "I wish I was a quarry man again as they rule over mountains." So the genie transformed him back into a quarry man and the man grumbled no more about his job. This oriental parable teaches that no matter what part of society you serve you are the master no matter what you do.'

'What a load of bull,' said Steve Galbraith later on, but considering it as something his father should spend more time reading out on Sundays he added: 'It was interesting bull. It means you've to be satisfied with your lot and not complain.'

'Like a monk in a monastery,' said Brian, 'where continual silence is practiced. He is allowed to say something every five years, and after five years of saying nothing he gets his chance for one sentence and thus announces to the abbot: "The food is lousy." Five years later he says: "The rooms are all cold." And then another five years of silence and he says: "The work is too hard." The abbot has had enough of this and states: "Ever since you've come here you've done nothing but complain."'

'Satisfaction is apathy,' said Edmund. 'There used to be a lot of apathy but now nothing much is done.'

'Nothing much is ever done when I walk in here,' said Ken McGibb who had just entered. 'Aren't you satisfied, laddie?' addressing Brian. 'Is your lot not worthwhile?'

'Shouldn't satisfaction,' said Brian, 'come at the end of a struggle and not during it? Just now we're struggling with A levels and…'

'Ha! I don't think I've ever seen you struggle over anything,' said Ken McGibb, 'and I don't mean that as a compliment.'

'But I shall accept it as such. You see, I speak for my poorer brothers,' upon which Christopher made his entrance having failed to hear Friday's third period bell again. 'Now, there's one who suffers the pangs of outrageous problems.'

'A problem arriving on time,' suggested Ken McGibb as he looked at his watch.

'Well actually,' said Christopher as he sat down beside Brian, 'I was following you up the gangway, and so technically I haven't missed anything, have I?'

Ken McGibb shook his head, more as a shrug of despair than an affirmative answer. He risked no further comment but started the lesson.

'What were you going on about?' whispered Christopher.

'We were talking about struggling,' Brian whispered back.

'Don't use me as an example. I'm not very good at struggling.'

'But you're pretty good at suffering.'

Not much of an aspiring gift, but it is true, Christopher thought. I suffer well. And then between credit and credence, like a slice of light through a crack in the blinds, came insight. Truth failed to flood the room inside his head. Too much mess with maths clustering the available space, and more was trying to push past what had suddenly occurred in the beam weakening with refraction. It was crying for help and Christopher became momentarily desperate. He opened his eyes wide and stared forward, following without reading the lines on the blackboard. He repeated in his head the two inclined versions of his present situation: I don't struggle too well but I'm pretty good at suffering – therefore struggle is strength and suffering is weakness. I doubt if Christ would agree because he suffered for my sins and I'm struggling to understand why. Don't divert the argument, but I've lost it. What was it I thought just then? For a second everything was clear. Didn't the Buddha do something similar three thousand years ago while sitting beneath a tree? Eric mentioned that version of religion – the perfect insight, and maybe it is a common insight and the Buddha merely lengthens it from a split second to a lifetime. I'd have been quite happy with just an afternoon – a few hours. Wouldn't serve me too well to know it all from now on – I might well suffer universal disappointment. But…

Christopher was not all that great with the buts, which was why he was playing rugby in the afternoon. At a precise time he had but failed to challenge the positively reluctant and reluctantly positive decision to give the crazy game a go and now, two games later, with a third one on the way, many were the buts dragging behind them quite relevant excuses: I'm sorry and I understand it would be fun but I'm allergic to male sweat. I have to stay out of the sun in case I come out all blotchy which I do anyway, right at the end of my nose. I suffer from the royal disease – what's it called? Internal bleeding? Broken bones? I bruise with such astonishing ease and the colour purple does not become me. Alternatively, the good draft dodger: I am in actual fact, and having tried to think otherwise for many years, homosexual. I wonder what school rules would have to be passed to discourage that confession, and it would never do to have a homosexual hooker – a real bender to the name, the position, the centre bearing to all that masculine sweat. Wisdom is rarely related to rugby but they'd soon have extracted me from the list. The game has a hard enough time making up the type of songs needing to keep its image intact. Never do to derive from its complicated means of mashing one's opponents into the mush any form of dubious pleasure. But I don't want to be mashed into the muck. I want to go out tonight and have a good time. That to me is pleasure which can be cancelled at the break of a leg or the rupture of a spleen. Christopher had no idea what a ruptured spleen meant by way of cutting short pleasure, but it sounded horrible enough to be part of rugby's plan against him. I could always back down with stomach pains now rather than waiting for them to be afflicted – but then go ahead and eat a kebab? Sod's law teaches that dragged on kicking and screaming or marched forward to victory or defeat, a coward dies a thousand deaths and the hero is soon forgotten.

Akrotiri Youth Klub 1st beat the St John's yet again. This time they played away at the school's home ground at Happy Valley in Episkopi. The school used Happy Valley for all its major sporting events as well as a multitude of minor games. To lose two out of two matches was more than just careless and being as it was on their home ground the record receded towards humiliation. Christopher felt guilty. I should be playing for the school, he thought. Most of the school team are much better than me and yet we ran roughshod over them again. Is this not treachery? But the school means nothing to me, and so he limped off the field and onto the bus back to school with a modicum of head-held-highness. However, he thought, the Youth Klub means even less. I'm not even a member. Question: did I play well? His side won every scrum. The Bury, the school's hooker had to be carried off. Wilfred George trampled over him. A good exercise in leverage and confusion, with one injured Bury buried to the ground. I hope he didn't rupture his spleen. After all, I don't dislike him that much, but I played a satisfactory game. I must have done. My ankle hurts abominably.

Because he was now obliged to limp Christopher assumed that he had paid the price and was eligible for a good night out, sod's law on this occasion having come down on the mild side. Not on all – the Bury apart, three players had been injured, one with a crushed foot, one with a dancing form of impact weaving him around the spot before having him pass out, and Bill Grey rebroke his nose, an inconvenience which made him mutter a harsh 'damn!' And no one on this occasion watched the heroes win and lose. They played each other for each other. Grey, Galbraith, Kamp, Stenfield and Louding scored tries all of which could only be applauded or cursed within the field. Christopher cheered when Louding scored. He wasn't on his side but he cheered all the same and he cheered all the more when he scored again. The school could well have won. Stenfield was tough and Louding fast and on the wing they worked well together, but the Youth Klub had a lined performance of a sword sweeping the field. We sliced resistance, said Christopher to himself, and at the end, at the tip, the ball went where we wanted it to go. First Colin and then Bill and then Bill again and then Steve and then Colin again, and in between each Steve, Steve, Steve with his immaculate conversions. I'm thinking as if I've been converted, but I could be lying on my back with crushed balls. Instead, my ankle smarts and I'm happier now than before when I was a healthy victim for Mr Sod. He was happy to sing the songs, clap the backs, cheer and stagger like a soldier homeward bound.

He was so happy that he kissed the letter from Helen as he swept it up from the kitchen table where it had been waiting.

Dear Christopher,
As you can see I arrived safely. I eventually took off at 12.15 instead of 9.30 which meant I arrived at Brize Norton 5.15 your time. I also just missed my train and had to wait over an hour for the next.

Anyway, it's done nothing but rain since I've been here.

Would you believe it, I was awake at 6.00 our time (8.00 your time).

It is also very cold. I am going shopping today so I might just get your Easter Egg and something else for you.

Would you believe that I miss you lots and can't wait to see you again. I sit and look at my St Christopher, mainly 'Chris' on the back.

Well, I will have to write off as I have a bus to catch 9.20 (our time) and I have letters to write.

Take care and God bless,
All my love,
Helen.

He read this in the bath. His ankle still hurt but it was like a pain signifying life at the tail-end of luxury. The water was a liquid blanket and it caressed as it soothed as it cleansed. Tonight I shall live like a king. Do I miss you Helen, having just been reminded by this letter that you are four days gone? Do I hear fair maidens giggling and dancing along the corridor?

'Christopher, are you going to be long?'
'Like a tower stretching to the clouds.'
'Sorry.'
'I'm having a bath.'
'I'm not interested in what you're doing in there. I just want to know if you're going to be a long time doing it.'
'No longer than you usually take with your ablutions.'
'Oh, Christopher, that's a long time and I need that time now.'
'Julie, I've just had a hard game of rugby.'
'Yeah, sure. Ablute yourself quickly. We've got to go soon.'
'Not for another hour at least.'

But with two girls needing to use the bathroom an hour to go was sailing close to the ablutionary wind. He had guessed correctly that there was someone else with Julie and he called after the stranger, requesting an introduction.

'Not until you come out,' Julie replied.
'Hello, Christopher,' said a friendly voice beside Julie which Christopher

did not recognize and Julie did not expect.

'Hello to you. I'm Julie's brother. I think she wants me out of the bathroom and you sound as if you're worth the effort.'

'Get dried and dressed though,' said Julie. 'Too early yet to make us both laugh.'

Christopher got dried and dressed but emerged with soaking hair and a damp offer of a handshake. Laura, who was sitting now in the living room flicking through the pages of an abandoned fashion magazine, received his welcome with a contented smile suited to her making room for him on the sofa. As it was he left the room almost immediately and returned with a hairdryer.

'You don't mind if I dry my hair in front of you, do you? More sociable.'

'I'll dry it for you if you like,' and she stood up and confidently took the appliance from his hand and efficiently sprayed his head with hot air.

'You look as if you're ready to go.'

'You must be joking. I'm a mess.'

'No you're not. You look fine.'

He had to turn around to verify his statement but she told him to stay still. He sat looking at the door which, wide open, gave full view of an empty kitchen across a narrow hall. This reminded him now of what was missing. The rest of his family.

'Where is everybody?'

'Julie's having a shower, I think.'

He laughed.

'My sister's quite a personality but even she doesn't amount as everyone. I'm sorry I'm being sarcastic and you're doing a great job with my hair. It feels quite bouncy.'

'It's very curly. Where do you get the curls,' and she combed her hand through his elastic locks to test how much of the condition was merely due to moisture.

'Swap you for your long straight hair.'

'Oh, you wouldn't want to. Mine always needs washing. Horribly greasy.'

'You're good at handling hair. Are you going to become a hairdresser?'

'It'd be fun but I think I'd be too nervous to cut other people's hair.'

'What d'you wanna be?'

'Oh, I don't know.'

Why are girls always so modest about their ambitions?

'What are you best at at school?'

'Games, I suppose. I enjoy art and geography. I quite like French. I hate maths.'

'That's a coincidence. So do I?'

'There you are. Finished.'

Christopher felt his hair. It was spongy, comfortable and dry. Pity. He could have sat with her handling his hair for hours. He almost forgot that they were going out. She was probably meeting her boyfriend in Limassol. Most of Julie's friends had boyfriends who lived in Limassol.

'Where do you live, Laura?'

'Episkopi. Julie invited me to stay the night. It'll save me having to catch a taxi back to Episkopi. Two other girls from Episkopi are staying with Pat.'

'The three of you'll have to catch a taxi back to Akrotiri,' he said, testing the full sense of the otherwise very agreeable arrangement. 'Limassol is equidistant from both Akers and Epi.'

'It's what?'

'Never mind. Good news that you're staying. I never object to addition to the many girls already in this household. You know there's quite a few?'

'Yes, I've been told. Where are they?'

'I was just wondering the same myself. So, who are the other two girls from Episkopi?'

'Sonja and Mary, I think.'

'Sonja and Mary? Do I know them?'

Laura shrugged. She was not sure how much Christopher knew of his sister's world. She had only just realized that he would be joining them and so maybe he knew more than most would suspect.

'You don't mean Sonja Stirling?' he asked.

'Yes, and Mary Orris.'

You mean I might get to know Sonja Stirling tonight? he thought. Our very own Miss World. Laura, you're truly delightful and very friendly but why isn't Sonja staying here and you with Pat? Still, could have been Mary Orris – whoever Mary is.

He was soon to find out. Just as Julie left the bathroom and disappeared for further renovation of her appearance into the room she shared with her sisters, announcing in her stride that the place was free for Laura, the front door became surrounded by a bevy consistent with whatever was needed to form a short list of a beauty competition. Christopher straightened his back, opened the door and smiled, and they filed past, Pat first who stayed by his side and introduced him to each as Julie's brother. Not one said: 'Oh, you must be Christopher. We've heard so much about you.' He failed to bask in the reflected fame that being related to Julie should have endowed. He knew Nancy Lynson, and was thus able and confident enough to apply a quick kiss to her cheek, especially after having just played a hard game of rugby and his ankle still hurting, and so he felt somewhat elevated to the level of being worthy. Her sister, Angela, equally as pretty but in a younger and more contained way, he didn't know so well, and so the eligibility of a similar peck was not forthcoming (had he been a try scorer then maybe things would have been different). However, he said:

'I've a sister called Angela.'

'Yes, I know,' said Angela, 'and she lives in London, doesn't she?'

To these girls, living in London was comparable to sharing residence with the rich and famous, and being constantly immersed in the world of fashion, music and movies, and Julie probably exploited a fantasy image of Angela's impeccably trendy lifestyle.

Christopher looked at Sonja and said: 'So you must be Sonja,' before Pat could repeat the phrase: 'This is Julie's brother.' It seemed so important to look like the name Sonja and Sonja succeeded. As he shook her hand he wanted to totally register its touch. It is not absurd to believe that the hand of a beautiful girl feels better, softer, different than the hand of anyone else. The other parts were the engrossing secrets of ecstasy now tastefully covered by garments so carefully chosen without danger of overdoing her appearance. She did not have to say anything that was not already mentioned by her smile. All the same she said: 'Yes, hello,' and was directed by him into the living room where the girls sat and waited. None touched the fashion magazine recently discarded by Laura, and who among them, he thought, would have volunteered to dry his hair? Maybe Mary who took an interest in the photographs on the mantelpiece. She is nice, he supposed, whereas to say nice about any of the others would expose a gross lack of imagination. She benefits from the beauties by being the least of the lovelies and gaining therefore from a more individual style to her dress and pose. I bet she dances well. He looked at Pat (reassuringly attractive in the design of what could have been regarded as passably plain and plump) who still stood beside him while he still had the front door open.

'Are you expecting anyone else?' she asked.

'I was about to ask you,' he replied. 'I'm now beyond expecting. With you, Pat, I wouldn't be surprised if Nana Mouskouri walked through the door.'

'Nana Who?'

He shut the door. 'I was being sweet. Are we late?'

'Where's Julie?'

'Administering to her ablutions.'

'You've a funny way of putting things, Christopher. We may be early,' she added more as an afterthought than an answer to his question. She followed him into the room where he asked the young ladies if they would care for drinks. All he could offer was lemonade or milk, unless someone wanted coffee or tea.

'My parents don't encourage indoor boozing,' he explained, 'but had I known everybody was going to meet here I would have got in some wine at least.'

'Actually, we're meeting at the Families Club,' explained Pat. 'The coach leaves from there.'

'The coach? How many of us are going?'

'Just us lot, I think, oh and Chris Millings and Paul Begman. Most of the other lads already in Limassol.'

The Limassol boyfriends, he thought not without a slight droop in his spirit. He had relished even for fraction of a second Pat's explanation outlining a fabulous impression of himself as the only male among this lot for the entire evening.

'Lemonade would be nice,' said Nancy and Sonja agreed. Christopher said that he could make it more interesting by adding either blackcurrant or orange, both if anybody wanted to be outrageous. Pat helped him. She lined up the tumblers on the kitchen table and said:

'Oh Christopher, I'm so nervous. I feel as if I want to run away. It's terrible.'

'Why, what's wrong?' She isn't dying with the anticipation of an evening encounter with Louding, is she? he thought while she paused to catch her breath. I'd hate to disappoint her.

'Gosh, I'm with all my very best friends. What if the entire evening is a terrible flop? What if nobody enjoys themselves?'

Christopher was very touched. Fancy choosing me, he thought, to be the one to whom to confess this fear.

'That's up to them. If you enjoy yourself then the others have to.'

'Oh, I can't enjoy myself. I feel so bad.'

'Why, whatever for?'

'Everything is wrong. This is a new dress and it's so uncomfortable. My shoes don't fit properly. There's a blister on my heel already. My hair feels all out of place.'

'Pat, you look great.'

Which she didn't compared to the others because she was plain, but by her own usual standards she was next to stunning.

'Do I really? I don't believe you.'

'Here, start pouring the lemonade. Take your mind off your worries.'

'Christopher, stay with me tonight.'

'I wasn't planning on going anywhere else.'

Pat did not fumble with the drinks. In fact, as the liquid fizzed its way from one container to another she started laughing at herself and wanted Christopher to share in the hidden joke behind their task.

'Your right. This will be a great night. Best in my life. Wish I was just like Julie. She's always so relaxed.'

'She's only relaxed because she doesn't care.'

'Oh she does, Christopher. She cares very much. If it wasn't for her this evening probably wouldn't be happening. She's done most of the organising.'

'Well, I may stand corrected, but I do prefer you the way you are.'

'Oh, Christopher, you're so sweet.'

I was expecting you to say that – as sweet as this lemonade perhaps, he wondered.

Julie and Laura made their ready appearance – a colourful and close to protean transformation in each which, based on the matching presence alone, assured the evening its success. Christopher was hardly given the time to introduce the guests to the photographed and mantelpieced members of his family, before these two, who had been first but were now last, entered. Laura, who had spent less time doing so, concocted her appearance to the almost total conviction that Christopher had been wrong in his earlier impression of her having already looked ready to go. She was certainly ready to go now, like a princess to a ball, and from here to the Families Club he was to escort them all. These women, he thought, how do they manage it? And then there's me – one bath was enough, plus a splash of smellies and a change of clothes. On the other hand he was too accustomed to Julie's cosmetic encounters with the before to ever really be stunned by the after. There is, he thought, a lurking constant about the appearance of sisters.

Julie did not actually enter the room. She was accustomed to having those waiting for her to move on her arrival.

'Come on everybody,' she said, 'we better go. Coach to catch.'

It was a glide to the Families Club, not a walk, although Christopher failed in his task of accommodating any need for a male escort. He limped and lagged behind, but so did Pat; one bruised and the other blistered, while those on ahead looked so self-contained in their cluster of beauty making Pat conscious of being left out but not conscious of precisely what. She blamed the time which always rushed towards the brink of a beginning as if somewhere in the middle impatience ruled.

'Perhaps we're late,' she said, 'but I can't possibly walk any faster. These shoes…'

'How could you possibly be late for your own going-away do? It doesn't make sense.'

'It does,' she said and she looked at him as if she had forgotten some small but vital part of the evening. 'You're limping.'

'So are you.'

They laughed and limped together arm in arm to the Families Club where they could be assured of respite on the coach. Christopher said that he would never again play rugby. Pat said that she would never again buy a new pair of shoes on the very day of an evening out. To limp again would be mockery of this precious moment together. The blister would fade, unlike the memory.

The coach was not waiting for them at the Families Club. Everybody thought it would be but it wasn't. They were late when they arrived and now it was getting even later. Scott, who had been sitting at the doorman's desk since seven, said that there had been no sign of a coach. But what did they need a coach for? He didn't say that, but he did want them to remain in need without which they would not remain, the girls, that is, standing around his desk, each in her turn refusing his offer of a seat. Chris Millings and Paul Begman were at the bar buying drinks. They were so well dressed that the small detail of them both being clearly underage was overlooked. The girls would not enter the bar themselves, having faith in arrangements which would whisk them away as soon as Julie and Christopher finished phoning. Julie was phoning. Christopher was just standing beside her in the manager's office as if, being an employee, he was consolidating her right to be there.

'There's nobody answering,' she said.

'Don't they realize who wants to talk to them? But who's them?'

'Aristos Coaches. It was only a 17 seater,' she said as if this made its absence more of a mystery. She put the phone down. 'I wonder,' she thought out loud with the air of someone incapable of being perturbed by any upset in arrangements, 'did I give them the right time? Can't wait much longer. We'll have to go by normal bus.'

'That'll mean more walking.'

'Yes, and those waiting in Limassol will have to wait a bit longer.'

'Who's actually waiting for us in Limassol?'

Julie shrugged the answer to this question into another mere detail but then replied with surprisingly few names.

'Let's see: there's Laura's boyfriend, Simon. Then there's Oliver and Colin and also Perry.'

'Perry?'

'Yes, Perry.'

'Perry Stenfield?'

'Yes, Perry Stenfield. He *is* a friend, Christopher.'

'A select friend?'

'I can see you're not overjoyed, but don't worry. I have everything worked out. However, that did not include the coach not turning up...'

When Julie asked them all to drink up because there was a bus to be caught Pat was miserable. A further walk did not help, and to think of catching a Friday night bus which would be packed with all sorts of who knows what kind of kids pandered to the prospects of torturous indignity for her friends. She spent the walk pondering this potential pandering.

'What if they don't get a seat and have to stand all the way?' she asked Christopher who opted once more to limp beside her.

'If there are not enough seats, people will have to stand, sure enough, but it won't be Julie and her friends.'

He was right. The Friday night Limassol bound youth were in awe of the unexpected presence of Julie Panhandle, and she and her friends were provided with back-seat spaces as they were simultaneously surrounded and allowed their separate space. Christopher sat beside Pat who was still unhappy.

'I love Julie so much,' she said as if caught in the act of being faithless. 'She really is something when she's angry.'

'She's not angry.'

'She is. She hates being in situations like this.'

'No she doesn't. She never invites any situation upon herself which she hates. Remember, I'm her older brother. I've known her all her life. And anyway, look, your friends are getting plenty of attention.'

Chris and Paul, standing at the front and who were both significantly put out about being separated from the others so soon in the evening, suffered seclusion from the mass of attention being paid to the bevy. Although time dragged somewhat for these two, Limassol made its promised appearance and nearly all who had flocked around the girls got off at the main stop opposite Unicorn House, assuming that the girls would follow. However, on Julie's order, her party remained seated, but too late to warn Chris and Paul flowing with the crowd, and as the bus moved off without them Pat had to ask why.

'Oh Pat, you'll never learn will you? Do you want that entire rabble to follow us to the Moonlight? They're obviously going to the Island Disco which is such a dive that it wouldn't take much to change their minds. Chris and Paul know where we're going and they can do without us for now.'

'Not having our own coach means it's going to be a longer walk. Christopher and I are in agony.'

'Well, good for you. We'll see what the evening can bring for the rest of us.'

Their walk to the Moonlight had a so-far-so-good harmony from an evening still impressed with its Friday night energy and youth, and Pat clung onto Christopher, exchanging an increasing affection for the rhythmic weight on her blistered heel. She was definitely going to miss everything she saw especially the Moonlight Restaurant, eventually in sight, glowing in the fantasy of an oasis within the desert of grey, secluded as it was from the other restaurants which completely lit up the street around the corner.

'What are you going to do in England?'

'Everything,' said Pat so enthusiastically she failed to remember why she was holding onto Christopher as she let go to let swing a gesture of defiance against fate. Fate directed her full weight where it hurt most and she winced with her sudden happiness. 'England has everything. Good clothes, music, everything. But I do love Limassol.'

'Yes, with nothing it is so defenceless.'

Someone, was it Mary, stood outside the Moonlight and waved at them to hurry up. She vanished and they ventured on.

The Kamps and Thomas Rorner had been waiting for some time. They had thought they were late leaving a popular pub on the Bypass called Andy Capp III and then shortly after arrival had begun to wonder if the Moonlight had been the arranged rendezvous. More importantly, money was not in abundance and this lack demanded slow drinking – not an easy task. As expected, Perry arrived even later, strolling up to the large table specially set as if testing the quality of his entrance with an accompanied concern of what until then had been missing. Christopher harboured the reverse proposal, seeing this tall lad as in a dampening light.

'You and I will not drink *cockanelly*,' Christopher said to Pat who sat with him at the far corner, opposite Laura and a rather sophisticated looking Simon who shook hands with people he didn't know and said that he was pleased to meet him and her – not the simple 'hi there' or the more mellow but mature 'hello'. 'Simon, have you tasted *Mavro*? Excellent red wine.'

'I prefer white but I'll give it a try.'

Christopher, until then, had no idea that preference for white had been an option. One bottle of wine for four produced one specific group out of perhaps three groups along the table. The settled conversation commented on the warm night and the day's rugby.

'Did you play?' asked Simon who was a self-confessed enthusiast.

'Yes, and never again. I have an agreement with Pat here. I'm not going to break my ankle for anyone else.'

'Did you break your ankle?'

'Came pretty close. I think the game's crazy. I don't need to play rugby to prove that I can get hurt.'

'I think it's a marvellous game, with real teamwork. I wish I could play for the school.'

'I'm glad I didn't. They lost.'

'But you played this afternoon?'

'I was on the winning side. But that doesn't make me feel any different about broken ankles and ruptured spleens.'

'What's a ruptured spleen?' asked Pat.

'I don't think I want to know,' said Laura, forestalling from Simon any description of the spleen's function just as the kebab began.

The sausages were served first. The chicken would be last and in between three more meat courses, along with the salad, sour yoghurt and garnished oil, would stretch the meal with its gradual servings into a two hour feast. Laura said that the sausage part was her favourite – something they did with herbs…just right – and then referred to her boyfriend's interest in astronomy. He could name all the stars.

'Not all of them. There are more stars up there than there are people on this planet.'

'Never seems to be that many when I look at them,' said Pat.

'Too much light pollution and the naked eye can only see so much.'

'Light pollution?'

'That's what you get when you see women dressed in purple and green,' said Christopher.

Pat quickly examined the colour combination she had chosen and someone put money in the juke-box.

'Noise pollution,' said Simon because, and Christopher readily sympathized, he was not so keen on reggae.

'Simon saw a UFO,' said Laura.

'A what?' asked Pat who was now paying more attention to the music and tended to resist interest in anything involving abbreviations.

'A flying saucer.'

'Well, it didn't actually look like a flying saucer,' Simon explained, refilling his and Christopher's glass. 'More like a ball of light which zigzagged across the sky. I believe we are constantly being visited. This sighting was nothing special compared to other sightings. An actual encounter with aliens is not uncommon.'

'But if they spend so much time, trouble and their form of money getting here,' asked Christopher, 'why don't they make themselves known?'

'They will when the time is right and suits their plans.'

'What plans?'

Simon laughed at the unwitting irony of this question.

'If I knew that there'd probably be no need for plans. I believe Christ was a spaceman. It would explain quite a few of the things he was able to do.'

'It wouldn't explain the crucifixion.'

'Maybe his timing was off.'

'Come on, Christopher,' said Pat, pulling his arm, taking advantage of a pause he made in his eating to think about Simon's theory, 'let's dance.'

There was a dance floor. There was nobody dancing. Had Pat forgotten about his sore ankle and her blisters?

'I love reggae,' she explained. 'I must dance.' She unshod her shoes and he hobbled up behind her, but he too enjoyed dancing despite the chosen music and was soon able to null the ankle pain by carefully copied reggae steps. As they danced she said: 'The waiters want to get rid of us. They're serving the food too fast.'

'I hadn't noticed.'

He had hardly finished his sausage, but now on the floor he was given the chance to see how the others were fairing. 'Sonja's getting a lot of attention.'

Oliver and Perry sitting on either side of her seemed to focus more attention on her plate than their own, and they told competing stories and both succeeded in making her laugh. Pat pulled Christopher closer. There was a lot more she had to say on this subject.

'Poor Chris over there. Look at him sitting there looking so miserable. Don't look now. He's staring at us. He's madly in love with Sonja.'

'But who isn't?'

'But I mean it, Christopher. And someone told him that Sonja quite fancies him, secretly, and so you can imagine how he feels.'

'I'd feel pretty damned good if someone told me that. Why isn't he talking to her?'

'He's too shy.'

Paul was also too shy to talk to anyone, and Julie sitting beside him only succeeded in making him blush with comments no more suggestive than him testing his ability to pass the salt.

'Are neither of you two going to ask me to dance?' she enquired.

Chris Millings stood up, welcoming this chance to avert his eyes from the giggling goddess opposite. On the floor he and Julie talked and Julie nodded slowly while Chris sent a few shrug-cast sighs after further glances at Sonja. Thomas and Nancy joined them on the floor while Paul joined Colin at the bar maybe because Mary, sitting now by herself, had unsettled him with her silence.

'Where's Angela?' asked Pat, and as she spoke Angela appeared from the other side of the table where Laura and Simon still sat and ate. She was engrossed in whatever it was Simon had to say. She was disagreeing with him and finally had to pull him to the juke-box. Pat and Christopher sat down and Laura explained that Angela was now showing Simon how much of the record choice was not manipulated by the monotony of the reggae beat. 'I don't think reggae's monotonous.'

'Neither do I,' said Laura, 'but Simon's a Pink Floydy and he needs his regular dose of Emerson, Lake and Palmer. She says she'll teach him how to reggae dance if she's right.'

'I'm going to teach Christopher how to smoke a cigarette,' said Pat as she handed him one which he accepted with the innocence of a child gaining a first sip of whisky. 'You've got to lubricate your throat first,' she said, pouring half a glass of wine into his mouth. 'Now, try and inhale.' He couldn't think how to draw in the smoke after the initial cause of bringing it into his mouth. The vapours crowded around his teeth and came out like a weary sponge of disenchanted mist.

'This must be the most useless way of gaining pleasure,' he said, staring at his cigarette. He tried again and suddenly succeeded. His head immediately span, his eyes shot open, the smoke emitted in a straight line left not a displeasing flavour around his throat. 'How did I do that? I can't remember.'

'Are you trying to corrupt my brother?' asked Julie as she joined the group, having sent Paul and Colin to gather her flock so that all would return to the table. 'Fill the glasses, Laura.'

She walked around and stood behind her own chair. She waited patiently for Angela and Simon to realize that they were wanted in order to complete a circle ready to listen to what she had to say.

'She's a funny girl, that Angela,' said Simon as he accepted his glass from Laura.

'Don't get too entertained. You're with me, remember.'

Julie requested attention and gained as much silence as could be made available in their spot of the full restaurant. She then pulled from beneath the table a cube shaped gift, wrapped in yellow crepe and red ribbons, previously smuggled there by Thomas who, with the Kamps, had arrived in Limassol early in order to keep the pretty container from Pat's perceptive gaze.

'This, perfect Pat, is for you. It is a small token of our appreciation, affection and esteem.'

Pat, transfixed, managed to mutter a feeble: 'For me?'

'I'd like to drink to your future health and happiness wherever you go, so everybody raise your glasses to perfect Pat.'

'Perfect Pat,' they all agreed and drank their wine.

Perfect Pat was given her gift which she opened carefully, willing herself to slowly unravel its mystery, seeing it soften beneath her shaking hands until silk and satin scarves sifted forth a string of delicately coloured wooden beads. Also inside: a tie-dye t-shirt.

'Gosh, I don't know what to say. Thanks ever so much everybody. These scarves are beautiful.'

'And now,' said Julie. 'Pat is going to go around and give all the lads a farewell kiss.'

'Oh yes,' she said. 'I quite forgot.'

This she did, hobbling around the tables, leaning on each recipient to help ease the pain of her nagging blister. While attention was on her Julie took Sonja to one side.

'Do me a favour, Sonja, and ask Chris Millings to buy you a drink. He's so madly in love with you that there's a good chance he may die tomorrow if he doesn't talk to you tonight.'

Sonja looked at her and then at Chris who was laughing with Paul at a joke Colin cracked. Pat wanted to know what was so funny and refused to give Paul his kiss unless he told her.

'Are you sure,' said Sonja.

'He's a good-looking lad is he not?'

True – Chris Millings was good-looking. Not so true, she was sure, the theory of imminent death through unrequited love. Hardly her fault, but the upward twist of Julie's lips and the slight gleam from her sharp eyes betrayed the depth of the favour requested. So Sonja asked Chris after Chris had followed Paul in Pat's round if he would care to buy her a drink. He nearly jumped to attention. He was without much money, but she had actually approached *him* and talked to *him* and asked *him* for something that the other lads could have and certainly would have provided, and so matters in order of direct importance, the cash balance had to suffer. They walked to the bar together and while she wanted ouzo with coke he wanted to check if he wasn't dreaming but was too scared to risk the reality of anything other than a straight brandy for himself.

The meal continued with many courses seemingly involved on the same plate at the same time. Julie observed the scene, studying it carefully. Sonja and Chris remained at the bar and they were talking and Sonja was laughing. Very good. Thomas and the delightful Nancy would have stayed on the dance floor but for her speech and now they were back, occupied in a slow dance to a relatively fast record. Colin was using toothpicks to play pick-up-sticks with Angela, and each turn shaped the collusion of smiling eyes and steady hands flickering at longer, less lighter touches. The four at the far end were discussing the concluding scenes of *2001: A Space Odyssey*, or at least Simon was discussing it, the others were listening, while Pat had the potential of concluding her own scene of the Odyssey she might have endured and enjoyed in the less confusing scenario of staying with Christopher. I always thought those two would get together, thought Julie, even at this late stage. She had not seen the film itself and was told that if she wanted to make a big deal out of a black slab then she would enjoy it. They were talking about white rooms and the forbidding embrace of the relativity of time. Time to get a few relationships stirred, she thought, and decided that although Mary Orris was still alone, and Paul Begman on the other hand was trying to make some sense with his *cockanelly*, it would be a bit much on both to ask one to pair up with the other. She was in a good mood and knew the benefits of making a sacrifice herself now and then.

Oliver and Perry were disagreeing with each other.

'Balls!' said Perry.

'I can only go by the facts,' said Oliver.

And so they were obviously discussing rugby with particular reference to the afternoon's match. They possessed a combined confidence mixed with indifference about girls falling like flies to the swatting of their competitive masculine charm. Julie ignored them for a second and went over to catch part of Simon's description of Ligeti's music.

'A what poem?' she asked.

'Symphonic poem,' said Simon. 'Ligeti wrote a symphonic poem score for metronomes and it was supposed to be some sort of musical criticism.'

'Who doesn't criticize music?'

Julie did not wait for an answer but stood up and walked to the other end of the table, catching Oliver's eye and demanding his presence with a flick of her lashes.

'Quit wasting time arguing over why you won the match and ask Mary to dance. She didn't come all the way over from Episkopi to sit by herself.'

'Look Julie, if you want to give match-making a try, Paul's sitting by himself and he came all the way from Akrotiri.'

Julie gently took hold of the lapels of his wine-coloured velvet jacket and went so close to his eyes that their noses only just escaped touching.

'Oliver, you don't understand. All the other girls except Mary and me are paired off, and so my advice is to grab Mary while you can. Apart from that, I'm not asking you, I'm telling you. Say no and I'll bite your nose off.'

'That may be more enjoyable than dancing with Mary,' he whispered and she whispered back:

'Do you really want to find out?'

He shook his head.

'Perry spread malicious rumours about my brother and I want to teach him a lesson, so please ask Mary to dance or buy her a drink. Use your irresistible charm.'

'I don't understand you, Julie. You're in one of those moods.'

'Just do it.'

She let him go and he walked over to where Mary sat, leant over her chair and whispered into her ear. She looked at him, tried to make an excuse and then thought better of it, standing up and accepting his hand as he led her to the floor. Julie returned to her seat and asked Perry to fill her glass. He had to reach over the table to do so.

'Where's your girl, Perry?' she asked and he smiled in symptomatic response to what he thought was a taunting hint.

'What's wrong, Julie, hey?' he asked. 'You lonely?'

'Not I. Not at all. I'm with Paul.'

And Paul heard this and he eyes shot up from the cloud clusters of his glass. He gave her a hard stare as if hallucinating.

'Paul!' Perry exclaimed with a laugh loud enough to slice through the layered intrigue of Simon's knowledgeable dialogue, and from abstract to silence the music of the entire place seemed to pause for breath.

'I don't think you heard me properly, Perry,' said Julie. 'Paul asked me to be with him for the evening, didn't you Paul?'

More to accompany his bewildered stare Paul gave her a slow nod.

'Which is more than you did, so...'

She brushed him back with a delicate gesture of her free hand and with her glass of wine in the other she went over and sat on the other side of Paul.

'You'll protect me, won't you, from that nasty man.'

Paul was probably more in need of protection and so Julie took his hand thus protection assured. Perry, isolated, defeated, still sober enough to take a snub without an option of resorting to violence, gave, instead, some money as his contribution to the bill, and retrieving his jacket said goodbye to Pat.

'So soon,' she said, standing up, wanting him to sit, forgetting once again that she had on her foot a blister which intermittently hurt a lot. 'Ah no,' she groaned, 'do you have to go?'

'Seems like it...'

Amused by the rhyming invasion of her pain he almost relented, and Julie suffered slightly for a few seconds, not having accounted for anyone actually persuading him to stay. He must go, he must go, she thought, feeding this insistence into her grip on Paul's hand. Perry's pride had taken a jolt and retreat was the only means left for maintaining an integrity tested by Julie's stare. If intuition could travel like the message from one ironic smile now firmly coating the delay in Perry's decision, then he might well have stayed in order to spite this valued respect. However, with this smile directed at her, with a glance at Paul, Perry muttered audibly: 'Girls, girls, girls – one thing's for sure, there's many of them everywhere,' and he left. Julie, encouraged by the predictable smile at Paul, called him a brave boy for risking so much for her. Paul was still silent, more so than a statue of Paul would have been, and so Julie poured him a glass of *cockanelly*, placed it in his hand, clinked her glass with his and said:

'Here's to us, for this evening, okay?'

He nodded as he drank. It was difficult enough raising the glass to his lips.

'Where's Louding?' asked Pat, not pretending that she was pleased about Simon's sudden silence, having himself harnessed to a net of thoughts which now seemed so clearly irrelevant. Laura wanted him to dance with her and Christopher, almost, wanted another cigarette. 'Seeing Perry leave has reminded me that he hasn't turned up.'

'He couldn't make it,' said Christopher, settling for more wine instead. 'The Island Disco has a more pressing engagement.'

'Is he going out with that girl?'

'Which girl? Marion?'

'The girl with the freckles.'

'I think so and Marion thinks so but he doesn't.'

'Doesn't he have to think so to make it so?'

'Don't know. Didn't know there were any rules.'

'Are you really still going out with Helen Margate?'

He also didn't know if any definite answer would engage such rules forbidding possible disloyalty, and gathering that a complimentary response would follow a negative reply Christopher saved face without denying Helen by giving Pat a choice:

'Not if you don't want me to.'

'Ha!' she said, enough wine inside her to display Julie's influence. 'You, my lad, can do what you want.' She raised her glass to make an announcement. 'To the Calypso Disco.'

Her real meaning referred to a definite place to go, the need to go somewhere else, not to mention a few minutes in the powder room, but the others thought that she was offering a toast to the nightclub.

'We're not in the Calypso,' said Laura.

'Aren't we?' said Simon, now tolerating the over-exposure to such music which fashioned for him the universal disco of disdain.

They did eventually go to the Calypso but the place was packed and so Pat's party opted for the Prison Disco where the drinks were expensive and the management were not at all keen on the necking that they suspected the ambience of cobwebbed-themed alcoves with its subdued lighting tended to invite.

'Christopher, am I drunk?' asked Pat.

'I can't see you, Pat.'

So they sat closer, so close that Christopher smelt from her breath and kissed from her lips the answer.

'Pat, remain with me forever.'

'I'm going to England and you're not, so there.'

'Why should that stop you from remaining with me forever?'

'I cannot begin to think of an answer to that question except that you're drunk now and so you must go and get me a drink.'

'Can't afford to.'

153

'Get me a bloody drink. You have to buy drinks or else you get thrown out of here.'

Simon was actually dancing with Laura and Pat laughed because Simon had gained from his predictable taste in music a peculiar dancing technique. Thomas suddenly blocked her view.

'We have to go, you two. The management wants us out.'

'What? It's my going-away party and I haven't gone yet. Have I, Christopher?'

'Not without me you haven't.'

He looked at Thomas who looked like a silhouette of Thomas with ultraviolet splayed around his outline.

'Can't Julie arrange something?'

'Well, to be honest, I think we should leave now. We're all broke. Me and the Kamps are going to hitch back.'

'What, at this hour?'

'We do it all the time,' he said, confidently assured of having gained with Nancy a kissing-based relationship that would last at least a week. 'There's plenty of British servicemen heading back to Ackers about now. Wanna join us?'

'No thanks.'

It seemed likely that the Kamps were just as unwilling, Oliver informing Thomas that he could take himself and his hitching idea to hell where, at such a moment, he and Mary were as far away as decently possible. Colin was not around to give a similar reply. Neither was Angela. They were still part of the crowd at the Calypso. Paul was sent off with instructions from Julie to find them and she was so pleased with Thomas's offer to hitch back that she arranged the taxis and eventually persuaded the Kamps to join him. They were, in actual fact, going to anyway. The intrepid three, having arrived together, always left together, unless persuaded otherwise by offers impossible to resist. None were forthcoming, although Mary was willing to hitch with Oliver. Oliver was more willing to travel in a taxi with Mary. But with Oliver there would not be enough room and without Mary there would not be enough funds. They were outside and there were two taxis, all they could now afford, and they were discussing this fact.

'What are we doing out here?' asked Christopher, suddenly forgetting why they had left the comfortable confines of the darkened disco. The evening was mild, but it had been so much warmer, so much darker, so much on the eternal side of Pat's company from within the Prison to contemplate freedom so soon.

'I think this is where I leave,' admitted Simon, and he shook available hands, kissed Laura, promised to see her during the weekend, and walked away.

Christopher looked at Laura who had been so suddenly deserted. He then searched out for the sake of comparison for any similar tendencies in Pat.

'The three of us are to be separated?' he asked and he took hold of them both.

'Christopher?' said Laura. 'What are you doing?'

Simon had hardly gone. He was still visible, just about four shops away, but Laura did not want to show up her best friend's brother by vehemently wriggling free.

'We shall stick together and fight this plot,' Christopher explained.

However, his fears were ill-founded. All three piled into the back of the same taxi, guided by Julie's ability to speed them up. She then kissed Paul goodnight.

'Thank you for a splendid evening, my lad,' she said quite softly and ordered him into the front seat of the second taxi while she joined Pat, Laura and Christopher by sitting in the front seat of the first. Chris Millings and Sonja Stirling were so much in love that entering taxi number two together was as if part of a Prison Disco inclined reality. Mary joined the lovers, longing for Oliver to join her, only just accepting the need in order that all could afford the wheels which were to sweep them away. Nancy and Thomas shared an attitude of an everyday departure as she slipped in beside Paul and asked him if he had enjoyed his evening, and he, Thomas, pulled Oliver and Colin away from the Mary and Angela who were so suddenly consuming their lives. Angela took her seat in the first taxi beside Julie.

'Isn't he the sweetest thing?' she said, referring more to the hunk of Colin's striding charm than the haphazard shape which had him towering over his older brother and friend.

'Who? Colin? I've fancied worse.' Julie then addressed the driver as if disposing of any comment on affection with the perpetual cause of more important things to do. 'We can go now.'

Pat was happy to travel, happy to have Limassol travel by on both sides and she wanted to go to Episkopi so that Episkopi could travel on both sides as well.

'I'm staying still and the whole world is moving,' she said. 'Isn't that exciting?'

'Aren't you likely to be left behind?' Christopher asked.

'I want to be left behind. I don't wanna go to England. I don't wanna go to Akrotiri. Why are we going to Akrotiri?'

Julie turned around to face her friend with an answer not as worldly-wise as being in more than one place at once without apparently moving but socially practical, just as Akrotiri itself was socially practical from their travelling point of view.

'You're hostess for Sonja and Mary. You have to return.'

'But they live in Episkopi. Why don't we go to Episkopi and I can be hostess there?'

'Where would Christopher and I go?'

Pat looked at Laura who was looking out of the window as if associating the diminishing lights with a phantom of defected love. Her silence seemed quite sad, but she smiled on the instant her name was mentioned, when Pat reminded all, including herself, that she, Laura, also lived in Episkopi.

'Sorry?' she said, paying attention to this flurry of distance. 'I was miles away.'

'Pat's just being delirious,' explained Julie.

'I am not being delirious. Christopher, am I being delirious?'

'I don't mind if you are or not, but just now I'd say no. Delirious is when you don't know what you're saying.'

'And she doesn't know what she's saying,' said Julie. She turned around, faced the windscreen as if by the power of her gaze alone the taxi was determinedly Akrotiri-bound.

Being delirious was perhaps not such a bad idea and so Pat started being delirious. She laughed and sang and told the driver to go faster, overtake the one ahead, after all, it was supposed to be taxi number two.

'We should to be in the lead.'

'Shut up, Pat,' said Angela. 'I don't want this car to go any faster.'

'Johnny Reggae, here comes Johnny Reggae, Johnny Reggae Reggae lay i'on me. Common, let's have a party in the car.'

'Shut up, Pat,' said Julie, turning around again. She was laughing herself, but seriously wanted her to calm down. 'Checkpoint Charlie' was just about on the horizon.

'Shut up, Pat,' said Laura, catching on to the tail-rhythm of Pat's voice as she repeated:

'Lay i'on me...'

'Shut up, Pat,' said Pat and she shouted into Christopher's left ear: 'Christopher, tell me to shut up.'

'Shut up, Pat.'

But she was disabled from doing so by a combination of her happiness and the car's constant speed.

'Pat, you've got to calm down. The MPs at the checkpoint aren't going to be overjoyed at us lot rolling in drunk.'

'To hell with MPs and BPs and ODs. Your boyfriend has a funny way of dancing, Laura.'

This sudden non-sequitur confused Laura and for a moment she was not sure who Pat was referring to.

'My boyfriend? Oh, you mean Simon. He doesn't like reggae.'

'Then I don't like him.'

Christopher laughed and sitting between the two girls gave him the excuse not to take any particular side, if there was indeed any side to take. Laura was less likely to comment, amused by the candid condition of Pat's mixture of late evening and red wine.

'Well, I don't,' Pat insisted, more to Julie because she was doing the staring having turned around again. 'He knows too much.'

'Talking to you,' said Julie softly, 'that's not a difficult impression to make.'

'Very funny. He does know too much. He tries to make me think I know nothing.'

'No he doesn't,' said Laura. She was not offended and she was also spared further attempts from Pat at making her so.

Their taxi overtook the other and Pat gave a whoop of joy, waving wildly at the vague outline of the occupants inside and then waving into the headlights of the receding car. She sang again and then announced that she wanted a drink.

'No bar in the car,' said Christopher.

'Can't we stop off and get one?'

But the checkpoint gave them no choice and just yards away Christopher discovered not only the absence of but also the presence of a bar, the latter assuming greater potential the more pockets he searched.

'Christ, I've forgotten to bring me passport.'

'Oh, you fool, Christopher,' said Julie. 'I was depending on you remembering it.'

'Were you?' He searched around his person some more. A passport was of a size too awkward to melt into his sitting shape, but there had to be evidence somewhere of his British dependency. This is crazy, he thought. We all look British, except the driver of course, but most MPs look Greek and to them we could be American reporters trying to undermine this hook of a British colony by driving in drunk and making for the Victors on the other side of the camp. What am I thinking? What am I finding? No card. Maybe a tag somewhere suggesting ownership by the Archangel.

'I've my Youth Klub card,' said Angela, shining it through the growing security light into Julie's eyes. 'This should get us in.'

And it did but only just. The MP stared through the window on Angela's side as she waved the card in front of him as if trying to shield herself from his torch. He ignored her at first. He shone the torch along the back row. Pat wanted to smile at him because he looked quite cute beneath his stern cap but she didn't because she wanted to show to all in the car that she could be quite capable of being sensible if needs be. The needs were being quite provocative as Christopher pressed her hand and whispered sense into her right ear. He was then asked his name.

'I'm sorry?'

'Your name, son, and your passport which I'm guessing you don't have.'

This MP was not Greek. He was the worst type, English and sarcastic.

'I have my card on me,' Angela announced hesitantly. 'Youth Klub card – see.'

'Don't you lot realize that there's been a lot of trouble in Limassol recently,' he said as if the entire tenderness of the island's political sores would have been soothed and disposed of by Christopher producing what was now wanted by all. 'Without proper identification you can get yourself into serious trouble.'

'We have identification,' said Julie. 'Are you deliberately ignoring her? She's showing you her Akrotiri Youth Klub card.'

The MP shone his torch at Julie's face and she shone her eyes back at him. There was a conflict of silent wills for a few seconds before he took Angela's card from her, examined it under the same light used to challenge Julie's authority, and then gave it back. It looked like a Youth Klub card. It felt like a Youth Klub card and there was no denying that Angela looked like a youth.

'All right, carry on, but all of you, next time: passports.'

And he let them through, ready to do the same to the other car which had by this time caught up and was preparing itself for a similar torchlight interrogation.

'Let's blow up the guardroom now – we're through,' said Christopher.'

'Just a bunch of uniformed men playing soldiers,' said Pat. 'That checkpoint should be blown up. That'd show 'em. What's so special about Akrotiri?'

'Nerve centre of the western world,' said Julie.

'Mind you I thought he looked cute.'

'How could you?' said Angela, instinctively feeling that through her card she had been abused by the unknown forces of her father's world. 'What did he mean about trouble in Limassol?'

'Greeks and Turks not getting on too well just now,' explained Christopher.

'Seems hard to believe. I can never tell the difference between them.'

This conversation was obviously exercised within earshot of the taxi-driver who may have had partial comments to make himself about the security man's definition of Limassol-based troubles, but Julie was directing him to the Families Club where they stopped, and after brief confusion with money and tips they walked back to the Panhandles'. It was once again a longish walk for Christopher and Pat. However, one ankle and one heel did not hinder them now. They took the wrong road.

'Gosh, I'm suddenly sad,' said Pat. The road they took was to her Akrotiri in its entire tranquil splendour. 'I'm leaving here.'

'Not as sad as me,' said Christopher. 'I'm staying.'

'You'll be leaving soon. You'll be able to drop by and see me. I'm going to Wales.'

'I might be going to Sheffield.'

'Sheffield? Where's that?'

Christopher had to stop and think. It occurred to him that he did not actually know where he was going, pending agreeable exam results, except that it was called Sheffield. Was it close to Driffield where he had spent the first five years of his life?

'Where did you spend the first five years of your life, Pat?

'At home. Spent the next eleven years there as well. Isn't that funny? I'm now sixteen, soon to be seventeen and I've been all over the world, and yet I've never been away from home. Let's go for a swim.'

'We could swim away from home and camp in the desert down south.'

She stopped walking and she looked at Christopher who stared back and saw that the glitter in her eyes were no longer the exuberance of a wine-enhanced evening but tears ready and willing to flow.

'Life outside home must be a desert.'

'Why are you so sad, Pat? You're not leaving home.'

She shook her head and said no more and together they walked to the Panhandles' where they fell asleep in an armchair. Everybody drank coffee except for Julie who said that she had had enough.

The Beauties and the Best (a)

Art and Crafts

> What is Art? All right, all right, an easier question: why are we here?
> Rebecca Panhandle: Letter to Angela
>
> Snake wraps around the stalk of a flower,
> This is the gentle hug of life's love.
> Forgive me, said the snake,
> My life lies beneath the rock.
> Forgive me, said flower,
> My life is still.
> Gavin Peters: Poem

GAVIN WAS TAKING A special interest with a view towards making an artistic study of snakes.

'Have you lost something?' asked Christopher.

'I've taking a special interest with a view towards making an artistic study of snakes,' he explained and the darker grey of a circle around him illustrated that few stones were left unturned.

'You might be bitten by such art,' said Christopher as he crouched down beside him and looked where the stones had uncovered the remaining dampness of otherwise lifeless ground. He also noticed a paperback copy of Hardy tied to a notebook by an elastic band. They were both close enough to the edge, the sea pounding below, the one ship on the horizon gliding along the peaceful day. 'Still reading Hardy, I see.'

Gavin stared away from the ship and looked at his book. Possibly he had forgotten it was there. 'You say that as if it's a bad habit.'

'No, a hard habit – a Hardy habit,' and Christopher, despite himself, giggled.

Gavin shook his head, released the book and leafed through it.

'"I have always heard, Sansho, that doing good to base fellows is like throwing water into the sea,"' he muttered.

'I'm sorry?'

'Cervantes' Don Quixote,' said Gavin. 'I was quoting from it.'

'Oh, I thought you were reading from the book – *Tess of d'Urbervilles*. Title's enough to put me off, but you may read me a passage if you insist.'

'Oh all right. Let's see. Are you sitting comfortably?'

He himself was not even sitting. He stood up from his crouching position of attempting to show interest in the underside of upturned stones and stared at the ship which only moved when unobserved.

'A passage at random,' said Gavin and he began: '"He paused in his labours for a moment to lean with her against the banister. Was he going to throw her down? Self-solicitude was near extinction in her, and in the knowledge that he had planned to depart on the morrow, possibly for always, she lay in his arms in this precarious position with a sense rather of luxury than of terror. If they could only fall together, and both be dashed to pieces, how fit, how desirable." Perfect love, hey?'

Christopher looked at him, realising that he was no longer reading.

'I should think not, if he was about to throw her down the stairs.'

'Yes, and then throw himself – to die together and – well you know, it's perfect love.'

'A perfect waste,' said Christopher and he laughed. 'What a waste.'

Gavin closed his book with a one-handed clap.

'Yes well, I hardly thought it would mean much to you.'

'You Hardy thought, you mean.'

'Why are you such a pleb?' asked Gavin, expecting an answer and standing up in order to gently tower over him.

'I don't know. It could just be today. I feel hopeless today.'

'That's nothing new.'

And neither was the ship on the horizon, a thought they both shared as if rather than a passage which could mean more merchandise for the Lebanon, a fantasy repose of the distant sea constructing for them both a definite object of Saturday's early afternoon.

'Are you worried about exams?'

'No,' said Christopher, turning to walk, compelling Gavin to do likewise, thus freeing the snakes or blessing the area as snake-free. 'It's just that I'm wondering what the hell I'm doing anything for. This whole education lark, and going to school and being part of the school, and doing this and doing that for them. What's it all going to lead to? Just death in the long run.'

'In the very long run. Despair has made you miss the stops.'

'What do you mean? I stopped here and all I could see was a ship on the horizon. What's it mean to me? For those on board it's everything. Everything is so different. Everything is here, everything is there; it all comes and goes, but where's the value?'

'Individual value,' said Gavin. Not unlike the snakes, he was going to say, but that would have left little impression. 'We have to have standards and once we've made those standards then you can define your values.'

'You've learned that through being head-boy? Your values are to the school.'

'That's like saying I'm a professional sixth-former. I have to have reasoning which'll take me much further than that.'

'What do you mean by reasoning?' A question Christopher had asked the

Innmaker and was now to offer his answer. 'Why is there so much sand on the beach?'

'What beach?'

The nearest was Banana Beach, and Dreamers' Bay was a distance but not as far away as Buttons, but Christopher persisted.

'And "If seven maids with seven mops swept it for half a year, do you suppose, the Walrus said, that they could get it clear? I doubt it..."'

'My God, Christopher. Are you well? You're quoting literature.'

'No, "Walrus and the Carpenter".'

And they walked on together like the Walrus and the Carpenter, thinner versions.

'Brian Innmaker says it's a perfect poem.'

'What does he know about poetry? "Walrus and the Carpenter" is a children's nonsense verse.'

'Maybe, but I'd sooner regard that as a perfect poem than falling down stairs as perfect love.'

Christopher left Gavin because he now had to walk to the Post Office, across the other side of the camp, about as far away from the cliffs as the ship had been from the pounding waves below the snakeless rocks. The afternoon could only be taken in with a long stroll through what he felt to be a silent and empty culmination of non-events beyond his control. My death, he thought, but more. Who would mourn me if I died? I am the hopeless part of my planet. He stopped to think: it was the Walrus who cried for the oysters who died so that he and the Carpenter could eat their fill. So they were hungry and had to eat or they were greedy and they had to kill, and before that, crying over the senseless waste of sand, just like the sands of Buttons Bay which I frequent almost as rarely as I do the Youth Klub.

He really wanted to know if he was happier by himself but he was led to thinking about Frances Smith who was certainly less happy with others but with equal certainty wanted to try them out. She wanted to try me out and both Buttons Bay and the Youth Klub were offered as suitable venues. He was not a member of the Youth Klub. He went to the dances hosted by the Klub but only once to its twice weekly social events of youth sifting its way through the accompanying indoor games. Only once because Frances had only called around once for Christopher to take her there. She was with Colin Jottrell who was a member and was therefore able to get them both in. He was able to get her in anyway without Christopher having to tag along, but she wanted Christopher because Christopher was a good friend of Colin's and as she did not fancy Colin she decided, correctly in this case, that the friendship offered, by them being together, a zone of protection. Besides, Christopher had never joined the Klub in the year and a bit he had been in Akrotiri and she wanted to know why. All the other members of the youth became members of the Youth Klub, a belief she was inclined to accept simply because of her youthful desire to be with youth.

'So, why aren't you a member?'

'Yes, why aren't you a member?' repeated Colin, a question posed in realising about Christopher something he had hitherto not known.

'Henry's not a member either,' said Christopher as if this fact alone would dispose of non-membership as being a strange thing.

'He's too busy go-carting and being a prat.'

'You're also busy go-carting, and he is not a prat.' Christopher thought about this. 'Well, maybe he has bits of pratness about him. He and I haven't joined the Youth Klub because we just haven't got around to it.'

'You mean,' said Frances, unable to understand the subtlety of the conversation but catching up on the last comment, 'you haven't thought about it, you and Henry.'

'They mean,' said Colin, 'they have better things to do – better fish to fry.'

'In the words of Henry,' said Christopher, misquoting no doubt but not misshaping what would have been Henry's attitude if asked, 'we're not members and we're proud of it.'

Colin's accusation of contempt was carried as far as the Klub itself, and once there Christopher spread out his arms to Frances and said: 'Look and see.'

All the necessary facilities were provided: a disco at one end which bellowed right through to the other, and in between, within the hall, one table tennis table and a trampoline. Another room housed a full-sized snooker table.

'So,' asked Frances, 'what's wrong with all this? Seems okay to me.'

And there were enough youth about to make a popular sport out of staring at the most time-consuming and available activities. A few couples did a bit of cavorting around excess tables and chairs and there was a lot of laughing and a few curses.

The three of them wandered from one large room to the next together. Colin was happy enough to show them around, cheerfully resigned to Christopher's presence although realising that for him his guided tour was redundant. Christopher was familiar enough with the premises and could not really put into words what he disliked about the place, after all he didn't really dislike the place. He just felt that if this was where it was all happening, why had he left Scotland? Of course, he had had no choice, but there had to be a better reason for the compulsory. He could sense Colin's natural pride in being part of the established community which allowed him thus, a superior view of youth culture by dint of Frances's fresh arrival and Christopher's compulsion towards that of the curmudgeon.

'The disco's not bad,' said Frances as they moved closer to where they eventually had to shout at each other.

'Nobody's dancing.'

'Of course not. This isn't a dance. It's just a Youth Klub social night. I think you must like complaining, Christopher.'

'Yes, he's just an old moan,' agreed Colin.

They stood around the trampoline and watched various kids bounce up and down. There was an implicit dare to see how high one could go without hitting one's head against the ceiling. Colin asked Frances if she wanted to have a go. Frances said she couldn't. She was wearing a skirt. Colin did not regard such modesty as an endorsement to her defiance, pointing out that so were many of the girls either already bouncing about or ready and willing to do so. Legs and knickers with a sporting excuse to show off both were essential ingredients to many examples of exuberance and high energy. Frances walked away, quite offended by Colin for having reminded her of this. Christopher was also unwilling to have a go, his excuse being the ceiling challenge and the fact that he wanted to keep his head for other more metaphorical heights.

Frances was new to Akrotiri and in this Klub it was easy to sit down in a corner and look new. Nobody cared. There were a few she could talk to and Colin had his friends and surely Christopher had means of introducing her to the community. Wasn't his sister, Julie, the community? And where was his sister?

'Where's your sisters?' she asked them both as he and Colin joined her.

Colin gave a shrug for his answer but added: 'Sarah's with some airman I suppose.'

'I never know where Julie is,' said Christopher, but confident in the knowledge that airmen did not feature in that answer. 'Do you want to play table tennis?'

'I can't play table tennis.'

'One of the easiest games in the world to play,' said Colin.

'Then you two play and I'll watch.'

And so they played a few games and they soon discovered that she wasn't really watching. Colin asked Christopher, during the points Christopher seemed to consistently lose, how it was possible to get through to such a girl.

'I shouldn't bother. You're not her type.'

'Oh, and I suppose you are.'

'I can assure you; she doesn't fancy me any more than you. She just needs company and we just happen to be around.'

Colin was not put out by being defined in this case as a convenience. This occasion being prior to his romance with Rosemary, his desire for a girlfriend accommodated whatever chances he thought he might have had with Frances but, like Christopher, he was suitably enchanted by her membership of their school circle to understand that such conditions for her probably required a recognized but unmentioned loyalty to the platonic. For Christopher there were enough mysteries in life without having to question the loyalty Frances bore to his acquired status of being her guide to Akrotiri.

He was happy enough to be with her but he did not particularly want to be at the places she chose. As for his choices...

'Why not the cliffs? Copper's Rock, Subpoint?..'

'Because they're boring.'

'So's the Youth Klub but we went there.'

'There's people at the Youth Klub. There's nobody at the cliffs. I went there and all I saw were anglers. I'm not interested in catching fish.'

'Neither am I.'

'I'm interested in having fun.'

Christopher almost said: So am I, but thought better of it.

And so they went to Buttons Bay where people, many their age and a bit younger, were admittedly having fun. If not to be alone with her as offered by the cliffs, he could at least hope to help her sunbathe and swim. It occurred to him that she could probably do both reasonably well by herself but she did insist on his company – moral protection perhaps in the midst of this desire for the company of others – more as a concern than anything prized from the Youth Klub. Society at the Bay was a bronzed energy beyond the contrived means of exposing the occasional pair of coloured or white knickers. Here was an abundance of well honed flesh only just modestly clad in tight trunks and skimpy bikinis. However, on arrival, Frances refused to get changed. The strong breeze whipping up the surface sand drove most into the large pavilion as an excuse for shelter. She and Christopher were too late to gain any of the crowded tables, and Frances stood on the side and compared the whiteness of her legs to the shining brownness surrounding her and was therefore reluctant to emphasize this basic colour difference. She accepted a lemonade and the two of them looked in on one group of people playing cards. This soon began to bore her and she was already over conscious of herself as a pale dressing surrounded by bikini dishes. She was also annoyed about having forgotten her sunglasses, and there were, of course, a few girls there whom she particularly disliked with the accompanying horror of realising now how much they existed outside the confines of school.

The sun fought and won against the wind. People started to venture onto the different stretches of beach which made up Buttons Bay.

'Now we have a table,' said Christopher. In fact they had many to choose from. She sat down, looked at the other tables and shook her head.

'I don't want to stay, Christopher. I feel odd.'

'Why, are you not well?'

'No, look at me and look at them.'

Christopher looked – an easy option when there was so much to delight the eyes.

'Is it because you don't have a tan? Neither have I. I'm just a darker shade of pink.'

'I look like death warmed up with all these brown people about.'

But all the people were on the beach, and this included Rosemary and Colin who saw them, waved to them and then joined them. What were they doing just sitting there? Why weren't they on the beach soaking up the fabulous sun while it was around? How about a swim? Come on, Christopher. Look at all those people on the raft and Rosemary could see her friends waving to her from this point a hundred yards out to sea, and ... Christopher was persuaded. He wouldn't be long as he walked towards the changing rooms and in no time he was in the sea, and in no time being at the Bay did not seem so bad. Company served its purpose within the swimming scene of British life in Cyprus, but one part of his company did not seem to think so. Frances was more than just annoyed at Christopher for getting changed and going into the water and, in effect, deserting her. He eventually emerged, dripping and happy, and because of this she accused him of practically betraying to all why she had been so shy about exposing her white skin. Although her clothes still covered most of this, she included him in a plot to uncover her sense of shame and this preceded a few lines of what she thought of him and his Buttons Bay.

'Listen,' he explained, 'I feel the same about the Bay and that's why I suggested we should go to the cliffs.'

'Cliffs, Akrotiri, it's all boring.'

'And you're being silly.'

'I hate you.'

'Suit yourself,' he said with an angry shrug.

He was about to walk away and so she slapped him across the shoulders with her towel forgetting that it held together the two-piece that he had wanted to see hold her together. The two-piece became two pieces which flew apart and across the pavilion. They were picked up by some airmen who started playing catch, adequately preventing her from taking part. It was only when they saw that her rage was for real, bringing her close to tears, that she received half her costume back. The other half came by way of Christopher who managed to take part in the confusion for her sake. She snatched it from him and walked away towards the buses returning to the camp. She chose her bus, sat inside and wanted to die. Five minutes later, fully dressed, partially dried, Christopher sat down beside her.

'I'm sorry about what happened.'

'Go away.'

'I am, Frances, but it wasn't my fault really. We came here to swim and that's what I did.'

'I hate you.'

She said that before and I think she said it again but I don't think she really meant it at any time. That's why it didn't bother me, he thought. Now she's gone. In what seemed like a premature act of defiance, Frances abandoned her family and Cyprus in order to set up residence somewhere within the confines of a UK sixth form college. Further details drifted into the cloud of her self-imposed mystery.

At Mass the parishioners were read the story of Christ forming a mud paste mixed with spittle and curing a blind man – apparently the only miracle wherein some form of medical procedure was implied, as well as one which caused more than the usual amount of controversial grit to the theological mill. Within this story was the conceit of knowledge embellishing faith, according to Father Fullman's take on ex-blind man's powerful statement which, when paraphrased meant 'Not sure about all this business of sinners, prophets and miracles. All I know is that at one time I could not see and now I can.' Christopher was quite taken by this evidence-based backing of the supernatural and thought about this in connection with the Great Green Warrior, encountered by possibly the chosen few and sporadically haunting, or at least wandering around (only at night) the cliffs of Akrotiri. People say they've seen things or experienced things which most other people say cannot be so. Nature and scientific studies do not allow for this, but he consoled himself, within the midst of his semi-forthright scepticism, that such phenomena until now was always within the realm of others, separated even from those he actually knew. This did not include any conflict with his faith as such – he remained a Catholic because he was brought up a Catholic, and was not apt as yet to consider the paradox of his position.

    He had spent the day doing physics problems before going to mass which preceded payment at the Families Club where Julie, much to the amazement of many, for the first time in months, almost years, partook in the Club's Sunday night youth disco. She did not like the Families Club and their 'poxy' disco dances and for that reason neither did many of her friends. But she went now for Pat's sake as, poxy or not, the dance would be the last one Pat would be able to attend on the island. Unfortunately Christopher could not join them. He had agreed to babysit in place of Julie for Mr and Mrs Heinz who left him a large supper and two very quiet kids. Julie obviously has them well trained, he thought. But there was something missing from all this prepared comfort. He preferred the Parthy's spirit of mystery, the search and grab he could make of any food and drinks going, and the interesting reading material they left around or the ultra-soft porn he could rummage out from one of the cupboards in the sitting room. Still, the question is, he thought as he sat and watched a Cypriot play performed in Greek without subtitles, why did Christ form a mud paste mixed with spittle? Why didn't he just cure the blind man by using the old hands-over-the-eye trick?

    And he thought over what happened yesterday when walking to the post office. He had cut across the sports field and encountered what looked like, from a distance, a breathing clump of muck on the ground. On closer inspection he discovered that it was alive, but not breathing as a whole entity but consumed within its body the movement of many. This scared him at first and he wanted to walk on – run away in fact. The clump consisted of numerous large and hairy caterpillars crawling through some primal confusion forcing them to constantly slither over and under each other. He became transfixed by this process which neither tried to prove nor construct but merely exist as a necessary means of a collective act. A few managed to escape and crawl away, never to be missed. It occurred to him that his real fear was of these few gaining the open ground. He walked on quickly, shivering in the afternoon heat.

'I'm mum today,' announced Julie as she poured into Christopher's bowl a sludge of lumpy Monday morning porridge. 'Mum's in bed not well.'

'What's wrong with her?'

'Don't know. Maybe touch of flu, and anyway, Pat's still upset about leaving today and so it's obvious I can't possibly go to school.'

'Of course,' Christopher murmured, staring at the porridge and thinking: with this porridge another week I do begin.

Pat, who had stayed overnight, had returned from the Families' Club disco dance in tears into which she burst again at the mere mention of St John's.

'I'll never go to St John's again. I love that school, best school ever and this is the best country in the world and it's not fair. I hate England.'

'I thought you were going to Wales.'

Pat was in no mood for quibbling.

'I hate Wales – I hate everything because I don't want to go. I'll never see my friends again.'

'Yes you will.' Christopher sat on the sofa beside her. His cup of tea rattled on its saucer as it descended with him down to the consoling level of where she sobbed. 'We all have to return to Britain and because it's the RAF it makes you sense you'll see someone again, quite soon even.'

'But not everyone here and I love everyone here.'

That's nice to know, he thought, regarding himself as a qualified member of everyone here.

'I have to go,' he said. School instead of England – Wales – wherever – what a drag.

She did not throw herself onto his neck with a beseeching need for him to stay, her crying did not increase into a wailing volume, she was not even stunned into staring at him for a silent second of seeing him for the last time. She blew her nose.

'Pat, if I had a choice of going to England, Wales or wherever, or going to St John's, I'd definitely, without hesitation, ask to be directed to the airport.'

'I know nobody in Wales. I know everyone here and it's so impossible to think of leaving, but I have to leave because of the stupid RAF thinking three years is long enough.'

Their departure, which he made first, leaving the house to stroll towards to bus-stop, followed a two second handshake and kiss, and a slight belch brought about by Julie's porridge.

A constant whiff of xylene during an experiment in physics practical made him even more conscious of the porridge and he may well have fallen ill had Louding not been on hand afterwards to offer remedial help by way of mentioning Stella.

'I did get the chance to ask her,' he began, 'but it wasn't much of a chance. Hardly time to talk to her at all. Marion made her usual demands.'

'She's a pest that girl. Why don't you tell her to sod off?'

'I do, but she thinks I jest – either that or she's used to it. But don't worry. Stella was very charmed by the idea. But now you can worry because it seems her Saturday nights are used up by a certain lad who takes her out.'

'What?..'

'Afraid so, Christopher. It seems that Stella is already spoken for, and by a Cypriot lad too. Surprise surprise. She says she thinks the Cypriots are very friendly and, you know the way it is, this guy's probably a great example.'

'Yes, but does she fancy him?'

'What level of information do you expect from me? The amount I got from the time allowed was quite good, wasn't it? This young Cypriot works every other night but Saturdays and Sundays, and he uses those nights to take her out. Apart from that Martin and Zoe have arranged a few things for her. Very little of her time is actually on her own because, remember, she works in Akrotiri, so…'

'So I begin to feel unwell again.'

'Ah but, *mon ami*, don't forget one thing – two things in fact. One, she was sincerely charmed by my offer, and two, I didn't get much of a chance to be persuasive. When I get the chance I shall call around to Martin's one night and who knows?' He offered one of his more hopeful shrugs. 'Leave it to Louding.'

A West Side Story meeting was called. All those interested, that is all who had signed the West Side Story list which few could avoid on its way around last week's meeting, were obliged to devote second break to the cause.

'Almost like rallying the party,' said Brian.

'The party?' asked Christopher.

Brian looked down as his unlearned friend.

'"Now is the time for all good men to come to the aid of the party."'

But those good men of Durham House had other plans. They were supposed to be collecting cardboard boxes having gained permission to go to Dodge City for that purpose. Thrills, thought all, but it *was* for the more immediate cause, and when they discovered that the meeting was merely to advertise a larger meeting to come they were not very pleased. They were also puzzled. Who would be included to make the next meeting larger?

'Everything gets larger,' said Steve. 'It's all part of growing up.'

'But it's already grown out of proportion.'

Not unlike, perhaps, the number of cardboard boxes collected by the young ladies compared to those gathered by the lads who, on entering Emily Burlington's classroom, bearing their result of a semi-illegal raid Steve and Brian had made on the backyard of the Naafi in Dodge City during private study, were not as delighted as the house-mistress to see half the room covered in all sizes and representing a comprehensive range of the retail trade, piled up and even (over the head or under the feet) worn by the waiting women.

'Is that all you could get?' Mrs Burlington asked the lads. She was puzzled but pleased that the girls should quite characteristically excel in such matters, but concerned that likewise social character influenced apathy in whatever the male mind considered more mundane than meaningful. Cardboard boxes were like tyres. Few would be capable of suppressing frequent yawns if subject to a lecture on their use but none she knew would deny their importance. 'It's a good thing the girls did so well because I think we've got enough in spite of your efforts.'

'Not our fault if we've picked an off-day for Naafi sales,' whispered Steve to Brian.

'Don't make excuses among yourselves. It's not as if I'm asking for your blood – not yet. Everything in Durham is clear, black and white. So that's all you have to do. Choose which boxes will be which, the paint and brushes and all you need, including lots of old cloth which you'll cover the tables with before you start, are in the store-cupboard, so get going. Should only take you about an hour.'

That was all the time they had before the buses, which always left late on winter-term Monday afternoons to allow for the activities missed by most this afternoon because of display preparations, departed. Mrs Burlington had to leave early, but they were sixth formers now well able to look after themselves in the face of this anti-chromatic task (a trust which from her tended to patronize more than award their present stage of maturity). 'Use your time well, create action and let's see what the results will be,' were her departing words. Within minutes after preparation, distribution and applying of paint, these sixth form Durhamites, managed to create a very definite action of colour change: brown boxes to black and/or white.

'I think Exeter are thinking of building a hardboard castle,' said Steve. 'What can we do with these things but make building bricks?'

'So we lose,' said Brian. 'An everyday event, and we lose with the Durham spirit and Mrs Burlington showing the ranks what effort and dedication can do to change the face of failure.'

'No reason why we should lose,' said Jane Sellers who, true to the artistic greatness thrust upon her, was making more of a mess than anyone with the swishing to and fro of the chronic black. 'What's so special about a hardboard castle? Probably as tasteless as something out of Hollywood Tinseltown.'

'Which has more going for it than Toytown.'

'I know,' said Wilma. 'We'll use spotlights.'

'Spotlights?'

'Yes. It'll be great. Spotlights spotlighting the interesting angles of our work.'

'What's interesting about right angles?' asked Brian, 'unless of course we're thinking of hiring a couple of near-naked models to stand in shapely positions over these things.'

'That's not a bad idea,' said Steve.

'No, I'm serious,' said Wilma. 'Both you and Louding, Brian, should be able to swipe a couple of spotlights from the assembly hall.'

'Can we?' said Louding.

'You've worked on the lights for *Oliver*, and you Brian, you were up there doing it for *A Man for All Seasons*.'

'Ahah, wrong,' said Brian. 'It was during *The Royal Hunt for the Sun* I was busy, as you say, doing it. Well, I suppose we do know how the lights work, don't we Louding?'

'Do we?'

'And how they can be disconnected, taken down and then used for the display.'

'I only know how heavy they are. Distance between assembly hall and display is a good fifteen billets.'

Not an accurate reckoning but it mattered little. Brian was not listening. Instead he was seeing it all:

'I can see it all now, across the wall: 'Durham Wonders' in shades of green and pink and purple splendour.'

'Green and pink and purple?' said Christopher. 'But we're black and white.'

'You know, that reminds me, but don't ask me how: Bill Grey wants all us lads to remain behind tomorrow and run ourselves into the ground for rugby practice. We've all been volunteered for the Durham seven-a-side team, plus a few others – in fact many others.'

'There's usually only seven in seven-a-side,' said Steve, slightly hesitant in case he was wrong.

'Correct, but we need reserves because, I mean, who's gonna play in place of you when you get crippled? They're out to get you, you know.'

'Who's they?' asked Christopher with even more hesitation.

'The other houses of course.'

'Not another bloody inter-house contest.'

'This one could be bloody and this one we will win. All the star players are in Durham.'

'That case there's no need for me, is there?'

'Or you,' said Stephen.

'Very funny,' said Brian.

'Or me,' said Louding.

'I'm afraid you're considered to be one of our star players, Louding. That's what happens when you score tries.'

'Not my fault. If I didn't run when I had the ball I'd just be ploughed into the ground.'

'I get ploughed whether I run or not,' said Christopher.

'And Brian,' said Steve, 'gets ploughed whether he has the ball or not.'

'You better look out for yourself,' said Brian. 'Your big mouth has invited untold violence.'

Wilfred George was saying nothing. Maybe, with luck, they had forgotten to include him on the list, main plougher or not. It concerned both himself and Christopher how such acts of madness could be formulated beyond the courtesy rule of gaining the victim's approval. Definition of victim perhaps: no approval necessary. It was not the games which bothered them so much as the training. They had heard of many horror stories relating the rugby practice.

'All this black paint,' said Christopher. 'It's a bad omen.'

But it was not such a bad display. It took time to form its message – all of the first three periods of private study the next day and well into the minority subjects. And true enough, there was a hardboard castle being built but not by Exeter.

'Shit,' said Brian. 'It's Canterbury.'

'So?' said Steve. 'Still a castle.'

'But it's beginning to look good compared to this mess here.' Brian had reached this opinion some time before the mess reached something of a desired message about Durham and Wonders being on friendly terms. 'You know, of course, they're sure to win and I've always been certain we could beat Canterbury at everything.'

They were standing in the middle of the new assembly hall. It was called the new assembly hall because it was an extra large tin billet erected at the end of many smaller ones and around the maths area. This made it, by process of historical authority, younger than the now old assembly hall but under-used; instead of its youth perpetuated there was an image of scholastic age ideal for playing host to external exams and similarly frightening functions. The old assembly hall was part of the main building and being the centre of action was versatile as shelter for religion, theatre, discussion and civics. At Christopher's previous school in Scotland there had been the luxury of a separate hall for each one of these occasions. St John's covered twice the area taken up by Madras Kilrymont in St Andrews, but in gathering the hordes together there was an economic sense of booking ahead or gaining priority perhaps through divine right, and the new assembly hall was merely out on a limb. For security reasons, as well as the time allotted for the colour and shape about to be prepared within, the new assembly hall finally gained the full attention of the school. All those free to prepare for the displays as well as the materials needed, in Durham's case black and white cardboard boxes, focused on the disturbed layers of dust and allowed the sun to glow around the gutters. To add a timely insult, especially as *A Man for All Seasons* was steadily delving into the corners and around the sides, the old assembly hall was deprived of three spotlights. This had not been easy. The place was rarely deserted and if so only for minutes and so the success of the theft depended upon an efficient means of handling the chains and pulleys which kept the spotlights attached to the ceiling, spotting down, and when questioned as to what they were doing, which they were by no less than Mr Emery, Brian added the professional touch by saying the magic word:

'Maintenance. We're the maintenance crew, sir. Spotlights are very important and need constant servicing.'

He was playing an easy gamble. Sam Emery, being deputy head, knew nothing about the practicalities surrounding thespian science. His appreciation of the production lay in the esthetical elements within the limits of what he knew about politics, economics and philosophy. Therefore all he could do was to tell them to carry on and be careful, while forgetting to ask who had given them permission. Brian was all set to throw the buck at Mrs Burlington, but instead he, Louding and Steve staggered away burdened more by the conspicuous and awkward shape of their load than its weight. However, none of the other houses questioned Durham's use of spotlights. What good were a few heavy torches among a mountain of black and white boxes and a couple of rolls of yellow crape?

'What do we do now?' asked Jane.

''You're the artist,' said Steve. 'Get artifying.'

'I know,' said Wilma. 'We need tables.'

'Tables, tables?' said Brian. 'Are we going to put a mountain of boxes on tables just to make them more visible?'

'At least it will give us something to put the crape around.'

'True. Christopher, Louding. Wilfred – go get tables.'

'Where from?' asked Christopher.

'Where from! The school's full of bloody tables.'

Louding led the way. He knew where to go. Mrs Burlington did give them the liberty to use what they thought would be necessary – within reason, a cliché which they understood to have arbitrary definition. Tables were rarely without reason and an empty class made them look almost shameful, and so two journeys to and fro and three tables and one large pair of scissors later, the Durhamites stood around their black and white cardboard boxes and stared at where the tables looked less shameful but somehow more useless. Jane and Wilma started putting the boxes on the tables, the other girls began to help, authority was established, groups were divided according to regulated size of box and distance, height and clever manipulation of tiers being calculated. Christopher and Louding picked up a lot of floor dust crawling around the table legs, taping the crape from behind into a covering: curtain-styled slats beneath the girl's work, and helping Brian to hide the spotlights in places which enabled them to shine up from behind with glowing eloquence to the outstanding works such as his masterpiece.

'My masterpiece,' said Brian as he uncovered his painting, propped it up against the inside corner where two tables met and flicked the switch. The effect was beyond reproach.

'Not bad, not bad,' said Jane. She took a closer look. 'Bit too much of a message.'

'What do you mean – bit too much of a message?'

'Could have done with being toned down a bit.'

'With some black paint,' suggested Wilma.

'What do women know about art?' Brian picked up his painting as an act of reassurance. 'Brilliant, almost painful in its considerations of the conditions involved.'

'It's only a tree,' said Steve.

'It's more than a tree. It's the tree of life, the tree of knowledge, the downfall of Adam, the ultimate destruction of the world.'

But it was indeed a tree. It was cut in half by yellow and red and it held a blue and green world in its branches shaped like a human grasp. It grasped also its corner beside the tables, in front of the yellow craped-filtered light, and began to resent the gradual invasion of many other works which arrived by the trolley-load.

There were many airfix models, too many for whatever space had been made available for them.

'A ceiling job,' said Louding, and off he went to acquire some twine from the Burlington supply. He arrived back with blue and white crinkly paper upon which the patient warships either balanced or fell. Overhead were hung all known British, German and American fighter-crafts, including the Bristol Bulldog made by Peter and contributed colourfully by Rebecca.

Before long what had not been an inevitable problem because few could see further than the cardboard boxes, began to take over. There was more work than there was space to display them. Brian's tree was really suffering from the distractions of such that surrounded its frame and so he moved it, cleared the space and put it back.

'This is intolerable,' he said. 'There are too many artists in Durham and not enough cardboard boxes.'

I must be one of the cardboard boxes then, thought Christopher.

'Why not let the works overtake the display until they become the display themselves?' he suggested.

Everybody looked at him. His suggestion sounded so simple and obvious that none were sure what he actually meant.

'What I mean is…'

But then he realized that he didn't know what he meant either except that he suspected that he was right.

'Just keep piling the stuff on,' said Brian. 'Is that it? If there's an award for quantity then at least we'll be sure of getting somewhere in this bloody contest.'

However, they started piling the stuff on and it worked. The works did overtake the display and it was not long before, with some initiative and care, all the contributions were somewhere on top of something over and above and through and within the various shades of glorious light. They had finished before the other houses. This gave them the satisfaction of being the first to stand back and compare their display effort with others while admiring at least some of the individual pieces of work. It also supplied some concern. Why were the other houses taking so long? Canterbury's castle was not yet the robust feature it hoped to secure within its battlements, Exeter was propping up ladders and the distinct sound of sawing and planning could be heard going beyond the borders of Winchester and York

'All we did was cut papers and paint boxes,' said Wilfred.

'And steal three spotlights,' said Louding.

'Well there doesn't seem much room for improvement,' said Brian.

'I don't see much room left for anything,' said Steve.

But Jane Sellers proved them wrong. She arrived with an enormous cat made from, it seemed, a Cheshire smile, lots of corduroy, buttons and fluff. Unlike its fictional counterpart there was less chance of it losing its body – more likely the tree upon which it had famously perched. However, the only tree around was Brian's, and it was too small and flat and made of paint. No good – it would have to rest beside it.

'Gosh, that's brilliant,' said Wilma, picking it up, giving it a squeeze and then a hug and then looking at it from arm's length.

'I don't know,' said Jane. 'It took me some time.'

Wilma put it down.

'Not there,' said Brian, simply horrified by the inclusion of this cat within the realm of his message. 'Not under my painting.'

'It's not under it, it's beside it.'

'Well not beside it, under it or anywhere near it.'

'Are you afraid people won't even glance at your work due to the brilliance of this cat?' Wilma asked standing gently between him and it.

'No, of course not. I'm talking about subject matter. Mine is a work of serious thought and method and whatever you artists go on about. It cannot possibly be displayed beside some reject from *Watch With Mother*.'

'How dare you,' said Jane and she walked away, taking Wilma with her.

Brian, of course, moved the cat, only to see it back in its place beside his painting when it came to his turn to guard the display later that day. He moved it to where he considered it would offer less aesthetic harm, where matchbox furniture, pink paper flowers and dried grass gave it some sense of belonging out of scale to whatever adventure it wished to observe.

All sixth formers took turns in guarding the displays. Some missed out on lessons and therefore this not totally necessary precaution became a fairly pleasing task. However, Christopher and Louding, who were on guard together, only managed this arrangement during the last two lesson periods on Wednesday when they were both officially at private study. Unable to decide what was better, standing around or sitting around, looking at art and crafts or listening to songs now mainly chosen from *West Side Story*, they opted for where there were coffee facilities provided specifically for the few teachers who were using their spare time to add to the security – one could not even trust sixth formers, so it seemed. The judges wandered in and out all day, recognized by the marking boards they carried and upon which, in pencil, they wrote their secret comments, and escorted at all times by various leaders of the school, including one obviously bored Gavin Peters.

'I'm playing at being head-boy today,' he said, given the chance to loiter with his two friends. 'Those judges seem to think that children's art has a lot to say. Looking around me I can't think where they get that idea from.'

'The art of adolescence,' said Christopher as if realising an excuse without knowing how to explain it.

'There very little art. There's just construction.'

'"There's no art to find the mind's construction in the face",' said Louding with an academic impulse verging on triumph. He knew that Gavin did not like to be quoted at, especially when playing on what he had just said. It implied that he was jealous, and to prove the opposite Gavin walked over to where Brian's tree lay tangibly free of the Cheshire's influence.

He picked up the painting.

'This is good,' he said. 'Is it sixth form work?'

'Yes, I painted it,' said Christopher. 'Took some time.'

'You painted it!'

'I may only be a philistine scientist to you but I do have some artistic talent.'

Gavin looked at Louding.

'Did he really paint this?'

'Can't you tell,' said Louding. 'Has all the hallmarks of a Panhandle during his allegorical period.'

'My what period?'

'Well, it's very good. Should win a prize.' Gavin carefully placed it down where a rectangle of light had previously escaped from behind the yellow crape. Then he carefully stood up and carefully looked at Christopher just prior to noticing that he was required elsewhere. The judges had arrived at York. 'Liar,' he said and he walked away.

The deputy headmistress, Juliette Neverland browsed in while the intrepid Durham guards were on their third cup of coffee.

'Drink the coffee outside and not in here,' she said without looking at them, staring instead at Brian's tree.

'But we're here to guard the display, ma'am,' said Christopher.

'Well, don't drink coffee then. It's up to you.'

'But in that case we'll fall asleep. Sleeping guards are no use.'

'Despite historical and Shakespearian value,' added Louding.

This time she looked at them.

'Are you two are being impertinent?'

This was another way of asking them to drink outside or guard a coffee-free zone. Juliette was professionally impervious to Louding's charm. This applied to the entire staff, but she in particular. She examined the works as if they were set before her like men on parade awaiting inspection. She was not tempted to take a gentle swipe at the dangling plastic fighter planes and neither did she squeeze the cuddly toys or consult the oracle like slices of glass constructed into a maze of colourful reflections. But she was interested in Brian's painting because she stared at it, stepped back and stared at it again. She became self-conscious of this fascination, aware that she herself was being stared at, and so she began to touch this and pick up that, replacing all she moved where all had not been, including Jane's cat which found itself back beside the tree. This pleased Louding so much that he offered her some coffee.

'Please,' she said without thinking. 'You lads do anything in this lot?'

'I did the cat,' said Louding.

'You mean this cat here?' she asked and she was impressed and in order to prevent her from touching it and thus moving it again Louding continued:

'And he did the painting.'

However, she was not as willing to believe this and so Christopher added: 'And we also did the taping behind the table.'

She walked behind the tables fully expecting to meet another masterpiece. She returned with hardly a change of expression.

'I often think that the sixth formers are apt to be more stupid than sensible in spite of everything they're taught at school,' and she accepted her cup of coffee and walked away.

'I don't think she believed us about the taping.'

'You know, looking at her from here,' said Louding, 'and if we didn't know who it was, er well – perhaps not.'

'Perhaps not what?' asked Christopher and he looked at her from 'here', raising his cup to her not unshapely form as it repaired into Canterbury Castle, and he tried to pretend that he didn't know who it was but it didn't work.

'You know, I've always fancied Miss Neverland, and there's something pleasing about the fact that she's a Miss. I mean, who knows…'

'I quite fancy Mrs Burlington and I don't mind she's married.'

'How can I make Miss Neverland notice me?'

'Help me elope with Mrs Burlington.'

'She would never elope with you. She's a Catholic.'

'Well, so am I.'

'She would never elope with a Catholic. Isn't it a sin?'

'I don't think so. I can't remember the subject of elopement being brought up in catechism.'

'I wouldn't mind eloping with that games mistress whatsername.'

'Yes, I know who you mean, but neither would every lad in the school and perhaps a lot more besides. It's the way she plays tennis, I think.'

'And hockey.'

'And rounders.'

'And swims.'

'Swims? Swimming! When have you seen her swimming? I've never seen any teacher swimming at any time. I've never ever been swimming at this school.'

'Shows how much it sets her apart,' said Louding. 'Did you know, Christopher, that that English teacher with the dandruff who took us for rugby practice yesterday is the school's most fancied man?'

'I thought you were.'

Louding smiled and thought about this.

'I'll be happy if I'm in the top twenty,' he said modestly.

These details which could well have led to misguided associations in later life were more than he and a few others would care to remember about rugby practice. Rugby practice was harder than any game of rugby he had yet played. Still, rugby was full of surprises and maybe the real thing pared down to seven-a-side was death on fourteen legs or, with fate conspiring, twenty-six not counting his own soon to be laid to rest – another of those ill-recorded casualties fallen for the school cause, the house cause, the hindered cause for growth. I will not grow another inch past five foot seven, he thought, no matter how much rugby I don't play. On the other hand, if I keep doing these crazy things like towing the line, I'll be deeper by six feet and eventually regarded by less, remembered by none and chosen by God as yet another short outcome.

Each house had their space, time and specific teacher for rugby training and Crycton was allocated Durham's coach. Yes, true enough, Mr Henry Crycton did have dandruff. It speckled his fading tracksuit like his own private snow-cloud, a climatically impossible downpour of which all would have welcomed after the afternoon was up. He had them running from one side of the pitch to the other, and then again and again and again, and then on one foot and then the other, and then press-ups and handclaps and variations on taxing calves and thighs, and then a game and again another game followed by what could have been another game but was in fact a rest.

He gathered the lads around, and despite the usual sadistic element contained in any enthusiasm for rugby he was generous with praise, more so than Fadpeel, much more so than Morgan before had ever been. He thought that Christopher was one of the best hookers he had seen in a long time.

'Why aren't you in the school team, lad?'

'Well, sir, I…'

'Never mind. You're playing for Durham and that's what counts.'

Counts for what? Recognition or death? Both? Christopher could hardly see himself while he hooked but still thought he was the better judge of his game and therefore considered his hooking no better, in fact quite a bit worse, than he had seen elsewhere. I just want to get away from the ball both mentally and physically as fast as possible. There is no object in the universe more attractive and repulsive at the same time.

Mr Crycton did not think the lads' tackling was up to scratch.

'You see, in seven-a-side, one guy could very easily get an open space, run like the clappers and score before you know what's happened. You've got to learn to tackle quick, firm and without fear, because, like any other battle, it's kill or be killed.'

So they all practiced this special tackle he devised: leap from the top, hit the middle, force down but weight up to move away fast. He thought Louding's speed was first class. Kamps, Innmaker, Galbraith and Grey: second to none, and with the mighty front-line weight of Wilfred George, how could they lose?

I'm not interested in winning, thought Christopher. Just surviving. All to be seen next Monday and he was now convinced he was going to get killed. A sudden need arose. Before death and dishonour, I must go out this Saturday night.

Wednesday night at the Families' Club and Pamela asked him what was wrong. He was sitting at the doorman's desk looking worried instead of intelligently concerned.

'I can't decide whether to go out this Saturday night for a meal in Limassol,' he replied. 'You see, I'm going to die on Monday, so do you think I should go out this Saturday?'

'Die on Monday?'

'Yes. I'm playing seven-a-side rugby for Durham on Monday afternoon.'

'Oh good. Can I come along? I love watching rugby especially if its school rugby.'

'Of course. I'm sure there'll be plenty of supporters. What house are you in?'

'York.'

'In that case I don't suppose you'll mind watching me get killed.'

'Of course I'd mind. Who else would get the drinks for me and Eve here?'

Hearing this, realising what he and others stood to lose should he lose his life, he made up his mind to go out on Saturday night. Louding could be relied upon to give Stella a bit of short-notice persuasion. Helen'd be delighted, he thought, what with her returning Friday all ready to see me Saturday. Louding too: he's collected enough worry necessary to living it up before impending doom. Although we can't both die during the same tournament, thought Christopher, loyal to the locality of logical probability. That'd be too much of a coincidence, and as I'm the one with the really bad feeling about this he's nothing to worry about. Mind you, if any of the other sides were to utilize Crycton's tackle, at Louding's speed and open runs, if he was caught it would be instant death.

Pamela reminded Christopher of this common death awaiting him. She wanted to talk to him as they left the bus the next morning. A shorter walk to school this time. Bus 27 arrived so late, long after the second bell, that the bus drove right up to the main grounds to prevent further delay and left standing the faithful friends of Dot and Doris Orange. This was a forbidden route except in heavy rain, but Christopher risked the chance of reprimand over and above the reprimand he did not want to receive due to his entire bus-list being five to ten minutes late. There would be no actual ticking off to cover the faults of many but he felt morally obliged to weaken its potential made symbolic by a silent school scowling upon the empty yard as it patiently awaited the stragglers. He would be all right himself. Eric would consider him early because he actually turned up. Pamela was oblivious to the walk she did not now have to make and the more important issue of avoiding the comments Mrs Clancy dealt out to her consistent late-comers. To her, because of her subject no doubt, domestic science, those who were not punctual could hardly expect to excel in the bounteous glories of house-wifery, and would therefore always fall behind. Pamela did not care about being behind or forward so long as she was beside the person she wanted to talk to, and Christopher remained this person from the bus to the main building. There he would have to leave her so that he could make his way to Eric's room. She asked him whether it would be possible to persuade Thomas Rorner to go with him to Limassol and, if so, would it make any sense to imagine him taking her and if so…and would Thomas be playing rugby next Monday? Christopher avoided the last question by offering her mere whimsical allusions to Rorner's present relationship with Nancy Lynson as compelling comments on the first two.

'Who's Nancy Lynson?'
'A friend of Julie's.'
'Your sister?'
Christopher slowly nodded as if to say, 'I'm afraid so.'
'Oh, I see.' She was now ready to go and face Mrs Clancy.
'You're not going to allow this to bother you, are you, Pamela?'
'I think so.' And she nodded as if to say, 'Typical!'

John Warwick received a nasty shock from a capacitor. His sentence gasped in mid-flight as his hand absorbed and flew from the full power of an unhealthy looking arc activated by a rusty switch. This unforeseen part of the experiment, a misdirection of current registered on both the meter and John's face, introduced an element of courage needed to carry on with what he now considered to be a failure. Most thought that any mishap which made others laugh could hardly be regarded as a failure. Edmund also had his own theory and showed his usual faith in self-inflicted plans in the face of severe odds by volunteering to handle the fateful capacitor. Christopher was not willing to hero-worship this particular colleague but he could not help admiring such conviction. He later found out, from both Edmund and Brian, that the capacitor proven to be damaged, had released the shock during the process of that damage.

'Therefore,' Edmund explained, 'any subsequent use of the capacitor was useless. It did not form a circuit. I was in no danger.'

'And you knew that beforehand?'

'Of course he did,' said Brian who was sore at Edmund for beating him to it. 'Only a fool would have thought of that later.'

'Maybe, but I wouldn't have been foolish enough to place so much trust in my knowledge of physics.'

'But don't you see?' Brian continued dramatically, 'One day you might have to. I mean, aren't you working towards that field of study?'

'You must be joking. I'm not working towards anything except A levels. What I do after that has not entered my head. One thing at a time.'

It was more than one thing at a time with dismantling the handicraft display. Durham was taken apart in no time with ownership ravishing the tiers and leaving naked, crinkled and dusty the black and white boxes and torn, draught-blown crepe. Julie, who had been the stand-in Panhandle mum since Monday, had managed to find time to go to school and see the display. She was not disappointed. In fact she was so certain of Durham's victory that she refused to participate in its collapse. It was not right to take apart the mountain she had only just managed to admire. Brian agreed with her, but all the same he carefully wrapped his tree in velvet and threw Jane's Cheshire into Canterbury castle. It was soon returned, thrown back over the hardboard wall with granny-knotted ribbon and a bouquet of sponge flowers. The cat and its accompanying missiles scattered boxes laden with airfix models, much to the angry distress of those who had turned up to collect their work. It could not be concealed, least of all by Brian, that Canterbury had committed their cat to the projectile act alien to its design, but the cat went back over the wall and into the castle along with many boxes. Safety in number enabled most of the works to escape unharmed, but the siege of Canterbury castle became quite serious, the dissipation of Durham into Canterbury a spectacle for the other houses; spotlights on tables emerging like stretchers from a battlefield and the hardboard walls which took the brunt of projectiled art, irreparably damaged. A few fights among the lower formers ensued but the prefects moved in to keep the peace, and those who stayed searched for their wares among the rubble.

Jane Sellers had to remain to look for her cat which she eventually located four days later in a dustbin outside the Naafi in Dodge City. During its travels it had collected enough rubbish in place of the stuffing it had lost to make this final home sadly appropriate, but it appeared to be quite content. It stared up at Jane, its blue eyes still intact and bathed with the sweetness of its Cheshire smile, the eloquence of silent suffering and the ubiquity of innocence abused. She left it there. She never did like it anyway. All the same, Friday assembly (the morning after the siege on Canterbury Castle) she was one among the few awarded special prizes for outstanding work. The headmaster was kept out of cold storage for a good fifteen minutes longer than usual to announce the winning house and the worthy contributors who earned his handshake and fifteen pounds worth of book tokens each.

'Fifteen pounds!' exclaimed Brian, and he had been happy enough to announce to the maths class earlier that week the successful sale of his tree for fifteen pounds. There was Sellers, catless, walking up to receive the equivalent of this gain just for displaying her work. He suspected her of having displayed another piece of work on the quiet and using her cat as a smug-smiling decoy deliberately dispatched to undermine his tree.

But the headmaster then announced with regret the loss of the cat. The culprits had all been severely dealt with. The school had this mysterious method of severely dealing with culprits which, when now announced, left Brian slightly more subdued. He had to remind himself that *he* wasn't in actual fact a culprit, because to become a culprit at school you had to get caught, and to get caught it helps to be not in upper sixth and a prefect. Wonder what did happen to her cat? he thought, while the headmaster surpassed his usual Friday morning drone with a three minute speech on the importance of respect for other people's property and how he was totally, yes totally, shocked to hear about the dreadful chaos that drone ... drone...drone. More winners were hastened up from their houses, one of whom, from Canterbury, was Savina Markou for her excellent example of Cypriot lace.

'That was piss all compared to my work,' said Brian.

It galled him to think that that girl, and she was, let's face it, only a girl, but already superior to him in maths, could reveal enough creative palaver to convince the critics of her artistic merit. Of course, it always helps to be ethnic. He was then actually called up with the second-prizers, each awarded a five pound book token, but this only partially cushioned the blow he somehow took personally when it was announced that Canterbury, with their excellent, but sadly demolished castle, won first prize for the actual display while for overall entries, imagination and art, Exeter were the winners –

cliff-hanger victory – Durham just behind in second place.

'I want to weep,' said Brian among the cheering. 'Black and white bloody boxes.'

'I think we won a moral victory,' said Christopher.

'What do you mean?'

'I'm not sure.'

It was the assembly that was morally victorious with its recorded song from *Joseph and His Technicolour Dreamcoat*, a studio version of the rock opera played over the speakers followed by a loud 'Aww...' as it was suddenly cut short for Patrick Eve's: 'Let us pray together.' He was a particular fan of the work of Lloyd Webber & Rice and thus a keen promoter of *Jesus Christ Superstar* which he regarded as an audibly stunning rendition of the Christian message. God's help only received minority support. The others cursed the sun and wished for something closer to shelter than divine covering from sins and Canterbury Castles. Patrick was so fond of *Jesus Christ Superstar* that it made him deaf to the actual sounds and singing needed to prevent the opera from abusing the message of John's Gospel any more than numerous critics had already accused it of doing. He wanted Harry Henley to back up his enthusiasm with an actual attempt at a performance. It was well within his scope and all he needed were the necessary singers which unfortunately Harry didn't think the school had. It was all he could hope for with *West Side Story*, but Patrick offered enough support a drama teacher could expect from the energetic grace of a parallel profession. They both specialized in alternative streams of communication, and so together, the day before, they organized a civics sing-song.

'What good news,' he said to all his sixth formers, and his sixth formers said 'What good news?'

The lads sang 'Officer Krupke'. The girls went elsewhere to sing 'Tonight'. After civics the prefects' room became a soundbox variation on these themes. 'Officer Krupke' had been analysed as a song containing odd expressions beyond the region of Patrick's attempted explanations, but all the same he had done his best. Harry with Hilda Ferguson, the principal music teacher, listened closely for those voices that remained in tune. They then divided the lads into groups and had the individual groups enter a separate room one at a time to sing lines from the song. The two of them seemed satisfied, the major names were to be picked later on, and so long as agreements could be made with all those chosen then rehearsals would soon begin.

'He won't get my consent,' said Christopher. 'I'm having nothing to do with any of it.'

'I've got to avoid becoming Tony,' said Louding, not without a bit of mock concern. 'I was told that Henley was giving me that infamous "I think I've found me a leading character" look.'

'Avoid becoming *anyone* – like me.'

'Tony has too many lines to learn and he has to sing by himself more than once.'

'He gets to fall in love with Maria and, you never know, she might turn out to be Sonya.'

'Christopher, you know what, I think I might try and become Tony.'

'Better still, don't bother, like me.'

'After all, what's a few extra lines. Beats having to learn Chaucer.'

'But you don't have to learn Chaucer.'

'I do.'

'You're not doing the exam.'

'I'm morally obliged to act as if I am.'

'You think you've got it bad. Look what I've got to learn.' And Christopher showed Louding what he had to learn: e=2i-ifNABsin2i-ift.

'E equals to I minis if Nab sin to I minus iftee? I thought e was equalled to emcee squared.'

'Ah, that's old hat. E has evolved into a monster. It's quite thrilling actually. I mean, if you do this to e and then that, look what happens.'

Louding looked.

'Yikes. Give me "unknowe, unkist, and lost that is unsought' any day. Better still, lead me to Maria.'

'I'm still waiting for you to lead me to Stella. Have you seen her yet?'

'Have you seen Helen. She's back.'

'What? When? Yesterday? She arrived back? She wasn't supposed to return until today.'

'Marion says she's back.'

'Hardly makes any difference when she returns, I suppose. One way or another I'm bound to meet her before I get killed on Monday. I'm more interested in meeting this Stella, preferably Saturday night across a kebab table for four.'

'Well, you'll have to dream it or survive Monday, because she can't make it this Saturday.'

'Louding, you're not telling me you failed to persuade her?'

'I never got to see her. I'm going by Martin on whom my persuasive powers are not so effective. Stella'll be in Famagusta on Saturday through 'til Sunday.'

'Shit!'

That was Thursday, the day before Jane, Savina and Brian were due to collect their prizes, the fateful day of the Canterbury Castle siege and the Cheshire Cat smite. It had been a dry day but not hot and the next morning there had been a sudden downpour, evaporated before the solar might of assembly, but enough to soak what spirits remained through the quarter mile walk from the buses to the school – no shortened route based on popular notions of what weather overruled, and no Dot and Doris to greet their faithful, patient, long-suffering and now somewhat drenched friends.

Everybody seemed happy enough because it was Friday. Even Brian had to eventually submit to the small printed conformity which went with five pound book tokens. One could only scoff at reward and success for so long, but at the beginning he did have it in for God and all the other directors whose handicraft decisions had been final. Christopher reminded him that, five pounds or fifteen pounds, in either case they weighed the same.

'What type of logic is that?'

'Whereas,' said Christopher, philosophically, 'a walrus weighs far more.'

'Then perhaps I should have been awarded a walrus for getting rid of the Cheshire Cat.' He took from his bag and laid across his *Tranter* text maths jotter his second masterpiece: The Motorway. 'What do you think? Judging from the results this would have stood more chance.'

'More style,' said Edmund, 'than that your preposterous tree.'

'My tree is not preposterous. My tree is power, meaning, knowledge, escape and hope with a peppering of despair. Arty people like to see a peppering of despair. Still, there is more to art than slapping colour onto paper. I shall recite lines. I shall employ the basic precepts of the Mighty Thor. Henley's searching for those *West Side Story* characters. I'm too tall to be Tony I was told or else there I'd be negotiating demanding contracts. And I'm sorry Christopher. I think you're too small to be Tony.'

'Yes, has to be something there for Maria to fall in love with,' said Edmund. 'But generous of you, Brian, to consider his size the only impediment.'

'Shut up,' said Christopher. 'I've made up my mind. I'm having nothing whatsoever to do with the damned play.'

'That's an odd coincidence. Neither am I.'

'I'm going to be Riff,' continued Brian, ignoring those who didn't care, 'the leader of the Jets.'

'Oh good, he comes to a nasty end,' said Steve. 'And you're such a popular part of the school, Brian, I'd watch out to see who's to be your killer first.'

'Yes,' said Christopher. 'Could be Steve here.'

'It'll be the ambition of seventy per cent of all who know you.'

'Only seventy. Didn't realize I was that well loved. Do you love me, Savina?' Brain asked, tapping her on the shoulder while she was creating from the top of the page down a mountain and fountain of equations.

'Yes, yes,' she said irritably, not having heard the question, thinking that the only way to get him off her back was to agree with him.

'Will you marry me then?'

She heard that. She turned around.

'Marry you? Marry you! You must think I'm crazy.'

'Yes, after all she's going to marry me,' said Steve.

'You must be joking. I wouldn't marry any of you for any money.'

'Of course we realize that in your part of the world such things are well arranged and that the money usually comes from your side of the family along with a house and many brothers threatening castration for any extra-marital flings, but...'

'I don't have any brothers.'

'Your father is therefore a sorry man.'

'My father is a very happy man, thank you very much."

'Is he rich?'

'I still wouldn't marry you, Steve, if he was poor, rich or anything. If the whole thing was arranged since my birth I still wouldn't marry you. I wouldn't marry any of you.' However, she changed her mind. 'I'd marry Christopher because he doesn't laugh at me so much.'

'But he tugs you hair,' said Brian, 'and don't deny it because I've seen him do it. It doesn't turn you on does it like one of those string switches in a bathroom?'

He tugged her hair, she clattered him with her *Tranter* and he reckoned his question had been answered.

Ken arrived. Christopher's possible engagement postponed, but discussion about Savina's future husband and him filling this role was continued during break.

'Isn't there a law against a Catholic marrying a Greek Orthodox?'

'Should be a law against Catholics marrying.'

'Do you realize, Christopher, you'll never have to study maths again.'

'Actually, I thought about that,' said Christopher, 'and I doubt if she'll have any effect either way. We won't allow maths to come between us, will we Savina? We haven't yet.'

'I've had a change of heart,' said Savina. 'I don't think I will marry you.'

'Oh, I see, I get the picture.'

'But I do prefer you to these two.'

'Don't worry about it,' he said. 'I wouldn't have married you anyway.'

'What?' She was taken aback, physically, removing her elbows which she had dug into his shoulders when standing behind him as he sat and while supplying her consolatory note, and he waved his head about the pivot bone of his neck with some relief. 'Why not? I think I'm more than worthy of you.'

'You are, you are. I thoroughly agree. I'm not fit to sharpen your pencil. And I'm not the marrying kind. I'm too sad.'

'You're not sad. Why should you be sad?'

'I keep thinking about death.'

'Death? A young man like you thinking about death.'

'Death on a Monday afternoon.'

'Death on a Monday afternoon?'

'There are Monday mornings,' said Steve reflectively, 'when I would have preferred to have woken up dead.'

'It's almost Friday afternoon,' said Savina. 'You lot are crazy.'

'Savina is right,' said Brian. 'We have reached the Friday afternoon of our lives. The Saturday night is around the corner. How can you be thinking of death now, Christopher?'

'Because nothing is more certain and yet so unpredictable.'

In actual fact Christopher was not thinking of death. There was no Grim Reaper tearing apart the Canterbury Castle in his head. He did not really consider himself a victim of the oyster plot, and that Cheshire smile was not the remaining part of a carefully worked out scheme for fading away. He was simply wondering why he was so sad. Why am I not happy? Even when I'm experiencing happiness I'm not happy. However, he promptly went home and dreamt of death – not his own – no hollow smile piercing through a dark hood after answering the door to a brittle knock. There instead stood his friend. Are you coming out to play, said his friend and Christopher was back to the age when friends would ask this, and he of them. He was back in Leuchars and he and his friend went out to play, a form of play called travelling, sitting on top of a train. They were too young to buy tickets and so it was a case of legs over the side, rushing lampposts and strolling hills, screaming air and judging a dogfight among the seagulls. The clouds travelled with them but offered no warning of what should have been inevitable. A tunnel knocked the friend off the train while Christopher jumped. His friend was surely dead but the lad stood up, not even shaken. Christopher wondered what he himself found more shocking: the horror of it happening or the horror of nothing having happened but a smile of recovery. Christopher was so shocked that he instantly fell ill and was put to bed, his friend returning to his side, wanting him to play again. There was an anxiety about his need to play and Christopher, being ill, was unable to share in the emotion. But he had to get out and play, leave the house now. No, I'm too ill. But the house is crumbling. No, I'm too ill for this house to crumble. However, the house did crumble and fall and the two lads escaped just in time, everywhere cascading around their ears as they flew. The lad, his friend, was killed by an overhanging branch which played him through the contortions of an expanding and contracting spring. When everything settled and Christopher walked back the next day in his dream to where his friend had died, he found nothing there, not even a tree.

The Beauties And The Best (b)
Dreams and Schemes

> Sometimes it seems obvious that God must exist and just keeping out the way. Other times it's all a nonsensical part of our desire to always attach the blame to something else. But nobody nowhere is ever totally to blame for anything anywhere than ever happens.
> Rebecca Panhandle: Essay on Cause and Effect

> I fell in love once. Once! It certainly taught me the distance between the one who loves and the beloved. Never again.
> Rebecca Panhandle: Books I have Read – *The Ballad of the Sad Cafe* by Carson McCullars

> His name is Christopher. When I was told that he was to become part of our lot I threatened to leave. I hate him. Don't ask me why, I just do. But I can't just part from my friends like that. Maybe he is not so bad, but I don't think so.
> Jane Anderson: Letter to her pen-friend in Australia

> Life is so boring. Nobody ever does what I want to do. Nobody ever listens to me. I feel as if I'm just tagging along. It's all Mark's fault. After all the arguments and especially after last night I think it is only right that I should never associate with Mark again. My mother thinks so too. I'm awfully sorry, Flan. I hope we can remain friends.
> Sarah Shellcross: Note to Mary-Ann Sheen.

ST PATRICK'S DAY OCCURRED during the week and would have passed by unnoticed had not the Roman Catholic Club felt the need in mid-Lent for a do: Friday night, mass beforehand, and then a drink to a sound and popular saint and a few Irish songs and maybe a bit of food to follow. This would be followed by more drinking, of course. Larry had to make it quite clear that this was not his incentive for going. He was a good Catholic Irishman, maybe not a saint, but the next best thing to him was the ability to recognize a saint and stand sufficiently in awe if this saint was privileged with a special day.

'Wasn't he a Scotsman?' asked Christopher.

'Now, where would you get a ridiculous idea like that? It's us who brought Christianity to the heathen Scots – not the other way round.'

'I'm sure I read somewhere…'

'Okay, he may have had to convert the Irish but thus the saint.'

'Always easy to be a saint,' said Lorraine. 'If you want to become one, Christopher, just don't do what Larry does and do what he doesn't.'

'You wait. I'll surprise you yet,' said Larry while simultaneously staring at his watch and drinking down his brandy. 'I'll go off and convert a nation, rid the land of a few snakes and then you'll be sorry you didn't listen to me sooner.'

'But Christopher and I are already part of the converted.' Lorraine looked for encouragement from Christopher while he was wondering why they hadn't yet gone. Mass began five minutes ago, but he didn't care. He was babysitting and thus was willing to sacrifice the devotions and mirth. His babysitting did depend on them leaving but he was always happy to have them delay on that part of the deal. He could drink more of their brandy, share a few laughs and look at Lorraine's legs. 'You see, Christopher, he wouldn't marry me unless I became a Catholic.'

'You were already a Catholic,' said Larry.

'No I wasn't.'

'Well, quite right too,' said Larry and poured out three more brandies before raising his glass: 'The Catholics! The only religion on earth that really knows what it means to have fun.'

'Larry, we must go. Look at the time.'

'And the Irish: the nation of saints and scholars.'

'Of scholars maybe,' said Christopher but still he raised his glass.

'What do you know about scholars? You're only a schoolboy. I'll admit though, to be totally Irish and a saint at the same time is quite an achievement. Maybe St Paddy wasn't Irish after all. That Scottish temperament kept his saintliness from going astray in the face of all that temptation: all that first class whisky and those pretty Colleens.'

'And there he is drinking Greek brandy and he married me,' said Lorraine, 'a Londoner.'

She said this while walking across the room and throwing her husband his coat.

'Don't become too English, Christopher. Very easy in this day and age.'

'Too true, Larry. I've often been on my guard against that danger.' But Christopher could not remember distinct evidence of his own overt Irishness. To him the Irish shared a curious accent, nurtured a streak of anger shaped like a smile and bred priests. To him, to be totally human without having to think about it was to be English. 'I'm an Irishman through and through, just like yourself.'

'Christopher, you may have another brandy for that.'

'Larry, you'll be turning Mrs Panhandle's son into an alcoholic and you are now deliberately trying to miss mass.'

'Don't worry. It's not a holy day. It's not even St Patrick's day.'

'Makes no difference. The sin's still the same.'

'Christopher'll forgive me.'

'Certainly,' said he, 'but I don't think I have the same say in the matter as God.'

'True, true.' Larry turned around, his coat strewn over his shoulders. 'Woman, where are you? Your lord and master calls. Don't you realize we're late? If we delay any longer we'll miss communion.'

Lorraine appeared from in front of the mirror in the hall having given her hair a final pat.

'We can't have communion after all that brandy.'

'We'll discuss it on the say, my sweet. A couple of mints and no-one will know the difference.'

'But darling, that's not the point.'

And they departed. The brandy was still out but Christopher put it away, already left as he was with half a glassful. He thought about the kids who had not been mentioned by either parent, which was not that unusual. It was not unusual for them to be actually asleep when he arrived for the ordeal of keeping them so, and if he was a good babysitter he would now risk all by going to each bedroom to check if each child therein was okay. Only two rooms. Alan and George shared a large one next door to Carol's further down the hall and if he was an even better babysitter he would not even risk waking them up so silent would be his care. However, he settled down to an evening of maths until Alan wandered in all forlorn, searching for his teddy again. He took one look at Christopher and started crying.

'What's wrong, Alan?'

'Go away. I want Larry. I want Larry.'

Carol appeared, not quite the same but she would do and Alan stopped crying. She accused Christopher of stealing Alan's teddy.

'What would I want with Alan's teddy? The last thing in the world I'd want to steal is Alan's teddy. Alan's teddy with Alan is the number one example of Peace on Earth.'

Little Carol in her nightdress stood like a forbidding Wendy just daring anyone to cover her with fairy-dust.

'Where's mum and dad gone?'

'I'm sure they must have told you. They won't be back until much later tonight and I'm looking after you.'

'You can't look after us.'

'Yes I can. So go back to bed.'

'Don't have to. You're not my mummy or daddy.'

'I believe I am by proxy.'

Carol stared hard as if waiting for this proxy to cast a similar spell to that in which Disney's Tinker Bell was snatched from her Carol-like pose on the window-sill. Christopher was suddenly reminded of the film and in particular the scene in which this highly irate, very jealous little fairy betrayed Peter Pan to the pirates.

'Do you have a boyfriend, Carol?' he asked, walking over to her and then crouching down to her height.

'Yuck! You must be joking. George does though. He has a girlfriend and I saw them kissing.'

'Gosh, and when was this?'

'Is it a sin to kiss?'

'It's a sin to kiss and then go away and hate.'

'Tell story,' said Alan, and he sat down where he stood with an audible bump. Carol sat down with greater care beside her brother and she gracefully crossed her legs, allowing the hem of her nightdress to touch the floor and curve up in symmetry to where her feet popped out.

Christopher looked at them and then over his shoulder as he looked at his maths. Ah well, why not? he thought. Peter Pan is more important than calculus.

'Once upon a time there was a little girl called Wendy.'

'Like in Peter Pan?' asked Carol with enthusiasm.

'Oh, you already know the story?'

'Not very well. My teacher tries to read it but it's full of big words.'

'I should be the last to invade your teacher's territory. So, better still, and again, once upon a time there was a little girl called Alice.' He held his breath. They both stared up at him waiting, bated breaths perhaps, hardly a 'oh well, so what' between them. 'She was walking on the beach which was very sandy and there was lots of sea and blue sky and she met a walrus and a carpenter.'

Christopher had to explain to Carol what a walrus was. Alan didn't mind not knowing that or the carpenter, but after Christopher's description the walrus became even more confusing for him than the original and enchantingly vague premise of being partner to two things encountered on an otherwise deserted beach.

'"Oh, good evening, Alice,' said the Walrus in his rather deep and gruff voice. 'My friend, the Carpenter, and I were just talking about all this sand. We think it's rather a mess and we're sure you must agree."

'"Yes, yes, yes, we must get rid of it," the Carpenter said in a voice so fast that he seemed to be wanting to get rid of his words. "Have you got a mop?"

'"A mop?" said Alice. "I'm sure that wouldn't do any good."

'"Well, if you haven't got a mop then it certainly won't do any good," said the Carpenter.

'"Have you got a mop?' asked Alice.

'"Alas, no," said the Walrus. "That is why we are discussing the problem rather than dealing with it."

"'And if I had a mop I think you would have me deal with it by myself,'" said Alice.

"'We'd be sure to give you advice,'" said the Carpenter.

"'There's too much sand for just your advice,'" said Alice.

"'With my advice in addition,'" said the Walrus, "it may not be too much sand for your mop. However, we are considering the idea of there being six other maidens, which would make seven mops in all, and we think the seven of you should sweep for at least half a year."

"'I have better things to do than the sweep sand for half a year,'" said Alice.

"'But I'm afraid that as it's only you,'" said the Carpenter, "you would be sweeping for seven times half a year which is…which is…" He clicked his carpenter fingers and the Walrus clarified the problem.

'"Seven times six months, and if two times six months is a year..."'

'Three and a half years,' said Carol, and she laughed when she knew she was right and Christopher was pleased that she was paying attention.

'Very good. Could you mop up sand for three and a half years?'

'It's impossible.'

'Isn't that one of the large words in Peter Pan? Never mind. Alice thought it was impossible too and was quite pleased that she had not been carrying a mop when she met these two. They were probably in the mood to begin at least part of the experiment but it would have been a safe guess to assume that after an hour they would have got bored. However, the Walrus carried on with the argument: "If you did have six helpers and there happened to be seven mops then it is hardly likely, Alice, that there would be better things to do."

"'That is not logical,'" said Alice. "The reason for carrying out a useless task is not improved simply because the means of doing so are made more available." Did you understand what she meant?'

Carol shook her head and Alan gave a slight sniff but sat as if alert to the predicament described.

'A useless task is a task which need not be done because it has no value. For instance,' and Christopher tried to think of a 'for instance': 'If I try to roll a rock up a mountain but I know it is too heavy for me to move and the mountain is too high for me to climb, it doesn't follow that with more help..' and then he decided it did follow and so he thought for a second and said: 'But maybe it doesn't really matter. We'll get on with the story. At that very moment there happened to appear six other maidens. They all had mops and there was a spare one for Alice. Gosh, she thought, perhaps there isn't anything better to do. The maidens started mopping the sand but it seemed that the more they mopped the more there was left to mop. "In six months surely," said Alice to the Walrus and the Carpenter, "there will be so much sand that this place will be more like a desert than a beach."

"'We are not in the business or mopping up the sea," said the Walrus

with a deep huff. "After all, I myself have a vested interest in this medium.""

'That's a silly place to have a vest,' said Carol, 'whatever it is.'

'Not very comfortable indeed for us but walruses are strange creatures. They go around with Carpenters and persuade oysters to take walks and then they eat them.'

'Eat the Carpenters? That's not very nice.'

Alan, totally delighted with the macabre image, laughed out loud.

'Carpenters taste nice,' he said.

'Yuck, I don't think so,' said Carol. 'All that wood.'

'No, no, you've both got it wrong. It was the oysters that were eaten.'

'What are oysters?'

'Little sea-creatures that make pearls.'

This seemed to say it all. Carol had no further questions.

'Well, after an hour the six maidens with their seven mops, seeing that they were making matters worse, went on strike. That means to stop working.'

'Yes, I know that,' said Carol. 'My mother's always threatening to go on strike.'

'Good for her. The Carpenter was not very pleased. "They've only worked an hour," he said very crossly. "They've got another – how many hours to go"

'"Yes, well, quite a few I'm sure," said the Walrus. "Of course their job is useless because there's only six of them. We are missing a maiden." The maidens agreed. They were missing a maiden. The Walrus and the Carpenter and the six maidens with their seven mops all stared at Alice, who, despite their number, was of a different opinion.

'"I don't agree at all," she said, "that there should be seven maidens doing the job. After all, you two were assuming earlier on that I could do the job myself only it would take seven times as long. It should only take these six seven sixths as long. And how long is that?"

'"Too long for us, I'm afraid," said the Walrus, totally aloof now that the problem was getting arithmetically confusing. "We have oysters to take for their afternoon constitutional."'

'Their what?'

'That's a fancy word for a walk. The Walrus like to use fancy words because it concealed the fact that he didn't really know that much at all. "Mr Carpenter," he said. "We must go. You did bring the salt, didn't you?"

'"Yes, yes, of course," the Carpenter snapped. They walked away.

'Why should they need all that salt? thought Alice. The sea is full of it. The six maidens took her away and made her the Queen, but that's another story. So, come on, bed.'

'Aww, that wasn't a very good story.'

'I'm sorry, but there was no previous deal made about only going to bed if you heard a good story. Besides, Alan enjoyed it, didn't you?'

'Are there any dragons and monsters?' asked Alan.

'Later on, maybe. Another night. Come on.' Christopher clapped his hands and guided his two listeners to the door. 'Bed, right now. It's getting late.'

That story was so confusing, he thought, I doubt if I would have understood it had I been the listener. Telling a tale makes it clearer than having it told. He looked at his borrowed watch which agreed with the clock, which might well have agreed with the Cypriot scheduling of TV had there been a TV. But instead a large reel to reel and endless recordings of James Last doing endless recordings of other people's hits. Carol and Alan went to their respective beds without fuss and the house sank to a silence ideal for Christopher to look at his maths, circle a 5, cross an X, scribble a few more hopeful lines and go to bed. Once in bed he thought about Alice and dreamt that he was sitting opposite her at a table in the Buttons Bay pavilion. They were both fully dressed but surrounded by the scantily clad and dripping sun soakers. There was little chance of any of them wondering what they should do about the problem of so much sand and little chance of any of them thinking it was a problem.

Christopher recognized Alice from the books, the most memorable picture being of her receiving from a dashing looking dodo her own thimble, the remaining article out of possessions she had awarded to all who took part in a race won by all.

'I once ran a race which nobody won,' he said.

'I'm sure that's not possible,' said Alice who was, it had to be admitted, a very clever girl, 'unless the race was not totally run.'

Christopher could not remember and so he changed the subject.

'The beach is lovely. Why did the Walrus and the Carpenter think it was a mess?'

'They didn't say.'

'I would have questioned the need to clear it, let alone the method.'

He looked at Alice and Alice wasn't Alice anymore. Neither was the pavilion the pavilion. They were sitting in a café in the middle of a city, he and Mary-Ann Sheen.

'Mary-Ann! It's you! Gosh, I thought you were…'

'No, Christopher. It's me, Mary-Ann,' she replied, 'and it's good to see you again. I really missed you.'

'Where are we?'

'In London, of course. How could you not know that? London is many things to many people but to everyone it is always London.'

'It could be many more things to me. I've never been here before.'

They were eating a meal which he couldn't taste. It was quite natural now that Alice had gone with Buttons Bay and Mary-Ann, in her way, had returned as part of an alien race.

'Mary-Ann,' said Christopher, 'When I used to know you in Leuchars I was a fool.'

'So was I.'

She poured the coffee. It was tasteless. He should have realized he was dreaming but he was too stunned by the unpredictable blow of a dream fulfilled. His longing to meet again and be with Mary-Ann made up for London looking like a freshly painted neo-Impressionistic canvas: the café focused on a table for two suspended by its white covering of explosive dots, the other customers frozen by the danger of sudden disintegration.

'But I acted such a fool.'

'Don't think about it. It's all over now. We are together.'

'That's right.' He sat back. He laughed. He shook his head. 'I can't believe it.'

'It's easy not to believe in many things, but I don't trouble myself by not believing in something that is obviously true.'

She looked like Mary-Ann but she sounded like Alice. This is not reasonable doubt, he thought. It is merely a case of adjusting: adjusting to London and adjusting to this café with its tasteless goods. She stood up and she left and of course he followed. There was no bill to be paid.

London had wide streets and was packed with people all walking by. They were all motionless unless he moved. She moved fast and the effort to keep up prevented him from paying too close an attention to the many who were left behind. Nobody recognized him. She did not look as if she was walking to any one particular person or place, but there was definitely a direction chosen. Had he realized the dream he would have feared the appearance of Mark Langford. Anyone can manifest the shattering effect of rapture destroyed, and Mary-Ann marching into Mark's arms would have had him, Christopher, disintegrate painfully along with the innocents on either side. However, she stopped and when she turned around she was still smiling.

'We're going home,' she said.

'To your place in London.'

'No, Limassol. My place in Limassol and over this wall is Limassol.'

'Limassol, on the other side of a wall in London? That's incredible. But Mary-Ann, we can't go there.'

'You believe in so little I doubt if you really want me back.'

'Of course I do. I love you so much. More than any girl anywhere. But it's not over. Don't you see, Mary Ann? There's still Mark and he's living in Berengaria just now, or he will be, maybe soon. Do you think more of him than me?'

But Mary-Ann was distracted by a problem immediately presented to them both. The wall was too high for them to climb. She stood beside it and it stood high, disappearing into the clouds above.

'We must wait until it rains. The rain will make us shrink. After that, without difficulty, we should be able to fit through the hole at the bottom there.'

He looked for a hole at the bottom and sure enough, from its appearance, it penetrated the wall. He looked up at the clouds. They did not look grey. It was hard to dream of rain and had he been aware of the dream he would have despaired. To enter the tunnel with Mary-Ann and emerge into Limassol at the other end was worth the risk of any form of Mark's discouraging presence. Waiting by a large wall in London and wishing for rain dampened nothing but the romance of a specially prepared occasion. I would have indeed travelled thousands of miles to be with her, and now that we're together all I want to know is why. She answers the question with how.

He grasped her, a hand on each shoulder.

Years ago in a similar situation, not waiting for parents to return but knowing in front of each moment of them eventually doing so, he had pinned her to one of the walls surrounding their joint babysitting task, a hand on each shoulder. In his dream he remembered that particular moment and half expected the identical response: 'Christopher? Really, we are only supposed to be good friends.' He never understood her doubt in that statement, as if further courage from him, not forthcoming, could easily have swayed her reluctance to be anything else but good friends. Now, good friends they were, he only half expected her to say the same, because the doubt contained an element of identity as if the girl he clasped by the shoulders was only acting as Mary-Ann for the sake of memory.

'If you're trying to dance with me I'm afraid I'm terribly clumsy without the music. My teacher even said how little rhythm I have even during the most gentle waltz.'

'I want to kiss you but you're not Mary-Ann. You're still Alice.'

'I'm not Alice. I'm Mary-Ann. I *am* Mary-Ann. Why can't you believe in me?'

'I do. I always have done. That's been my downfall. I can accept anything in my love for Mary-Ann.'

'Then accept me. Poor boy, Christopher. You were in a race which nobody won. Please take this. It's all I have but it has its sentimental and practical value.'

She turned around, freeing herself from his grasp. She struggled for a few seconds with a tight pocket. She looked at the sky.

'Not raining yet.'

She faced him and gave him a thimble. He snatched it from her.

'Where did you get this? This is Alice's thimble.'

'It's my thimble. It's always been mine and now it's yours.'

'Is this all I mean to you, Mary-Ann? I worship you and you give me a thimble.'

He pressed his fist and wanted to crush it in his grip but instead he woke up. He still felt within his fist the impression made by the thimble. He was convinced for a full second that this gift had travelled with him from the dream by the wall in London to here in bed. What bed?

'Mary-Ann?' he called.

He groaned and agony within increased as the sharp evidence of having been with her declined. I'm by myself in bed at the Parthys' and there is no thimble in my hands. I could quite happily accept nails instead, driven hard through my palms, if only for proof of her…pain to beat me senseless into seeing her. A mirage now would be worth all the thirst of the Sahara. He tried to sleep. He wanted to call back his dream. He wanted to use it, but he was wide awake. Why did I waste the dream?

'Mary-Ann,' he called in a whisper. 'Why have you forsaken me? Not for Mark. It can't be. Mark is too perfect. You said that yourself. How could you trust perfection? You wanted me to tell you that Mark could not be trusted. Maybe she still needs convincing, or maybe Mark should be told that Mary-Ann is not to be trusted.'

Actually Mary-Ann had never at any time admitted that Mark was too perfect. In fact very rarely had she talked about him, least of all her feelings for the boy. Alone with Christopher had differed totally from Mark's welcoming world which had insisted on both of them and more sharing in its abundance. I want my life to be full of everything that can be done and said by me and I want everybody to share in its abundance. Needless to say this was hardly achieved although no deadline had been set for its infinite potential, and guaranteed failure was directly credited to Mark's ability to do too much; thus the doubtful side of perfection with those closely involved feeling more frustrated than the creator of its strain.

Mark had many plans for Christopher, himself and Mary-Ann. The common theme was growing up and working together as a team.

'I say, we could become teachers in the outback of Australia and run a school for kids specially flown in. We could run a private detective agency in the States and handle all the messed up cases that must thrive there. We could become fruit farmers owning vast stretches of powerful land in one of the southern African countries. Take your choice.'

Christopher wasn't fussy. Any adventure would do. All he wanted was to be with Mary-Ann. In her presence, for him, the enchantment was total, all else they did subsidiary and all they saw as stemming from the sparkling situation of the formative years peripheral. Following instructions, mainly Mark's, he was as enthusiastic as any best friend could be, and effortlessly resisted any cause to betray his desire to do little else than gaze at Mary-Ann, talk to her in meaningful ways, maybe even touch her hand.

Mary-Ann was Mark's girlfriend. Mark introduced her as such. Mary-Ann did not deny the honour and so that was it. Christopher refused to doubt this bond although looking back he remembered nothing ever happening throughout their association which suggested more than the mutual friendship he also enjoyed with this totally delightful girl. He remembered quite clearly the time it occurred to him that she was a totally delightful girl.

Up until then she was one among many good-looking but somewhat unobtainable and therefore substantially forgettable girls on camp, which accounted for all the good-looking girls his age, although had she been seen less then she might have been remembered more, the first occasion only stamped by the absence of a third, but Christopher must have seen her some thirty times, only as an incidental part of the camp collection to or from school in St Andrews or the Naafi in Leuchars. He saw her a few times with Eve Sholts, but Eve at this time meant even less and with Mary-Ann appeared to dissolve more blindingly into the shadow she now, in Akrotiri, assimilated as Pamela Peters quiet companion. It was hard to imagine Eve conforming to the society surrounding Mark and so because her best friend had been chosen it was never questioned how Eve, with natural volition, simply disappeared, only to reappear years later and then be remembered as the girl who was with Mary-Ann through her forgotten days.

For Christopher any girl at that time out of Julie's sphere of growing influence, and quite a few within, merely impinged upon him the discomfort of a vaguely important problem yet to be challenged, not unlike feelings of guilt associated with totally lazy afternoons. He conformed to a fairly average case of being shy with girls his own age. He mistook this for indifference, even distaste. When he was very young he enjoyed the company of girls, preferred it to the confusion caused by the boys who wanted him to join their exhausting games. But eventually his childhood caught him up and relegated this phase, even the rather touching memory of a primary school courtship at Driffield in Yorkshire with a bespectacled girl wearing a kilt, to that part of the past one includes among the trivia of thank you letters after Christmas and essays on what one did during Easter break. They met every break for a full three weeks. They stood together where the far corner of the playground wall protected them from those playing tig. She was short-sighted and had an attractive squint to her smile. She wore a tartan skirt but was not Scottish, but how would he know as he had never heard of Scotland then. He was only just learning how the world was made up of more than the area covering the three miles between camp and school. There were fields beyond and much more beyond them as well. It was of this much more beyond that they talked. The beyond they could not see produced crisps and chocolates which they shared and with the crisps and chocolates were dragons and towers, production of all four perhaps dependent on intervals between battles. He said that he would do battles with any dragon to protect her and she said that if her hair ever grew long enough she would let it down for him to climb any tower. But it was not for him to benefit from that persistent promise of growth. She probably cut it short in protest because she fell ill, was away for a month, and returned to his complete indifference. He became old enough now to discard girls, after all, he was almost six and there were too many guns to fire, troops to support, Indians and Nazis to kill, and such dragons which existed dealt out fire more threatening and alluring than Rapunzel's pull of fancy. He wanted to explain that the world was full of important matters and he simply couldn't waste his time standing in the refuge of her far corner. She didn't want to know. She didn't talk to him anymore. She didn't cry either and so he didn't care.

There had been that other girl in Driffield who, falling in love with Christopher, wanted nothing more from life than to have him beside her to kiss. He had to deny that she even existed but she called around and she took him out by the hand and was kissing his face in no time. Her kisses, first on the cheek, then on the lips and then on the other cheek, were sandwiched between statements of how she loved him more than anything in the world, even more than mummy and the dog, and even more than her best friend who was ever so good to her. He wasn't quite sure how to avoid being kissed. He wanted to run off and play battles with his friends but he couldn't risk the danger of her running after him and declaring her love in front of a pack of battled-hardened eight to ten year old lads. So rather than die from embarrassment he stayed where he was and was kissed. This was an excruciatingly dull way to spend a free afternoon, but what could he do? The RAF did it for him. She and her family left, and months later the Panhandles moved to Scotland. This did not necessarily weaken their chances of meeting again. The RAF shrank the world into constant upheavals from one camp to the other. Maybe they did meet without realising it, her devotion having been transferred to another boy who might have deserved the attention because of what he was willing to give in return, or maybe it had undergone as drastic a change throughout the years as her facial appearance, ironically blotted from his memory due to its very proximity within the experience. She probably feels as much a fool as me, thought he, but for opposing reasons. Right now, any girl wanting to spend an idle afternoon kissing him would be very welcome to give it a go.

Of course it did occur to him that girls had better things to do. He accepted the transience of such longings as the consoling virtue of having to get on with life. Maybe this young lady had been enlightened before her time, but as wisdom became clouded by the existing trial of things to do and learn there was little chance of her improving the image she needed from Christopher as her object of unconditional worship. To Christopher worship became more a matter of distinguishing good from bad and right from wrong than natural loyalty to partial causes. He was an old hand at these matters by then. He was eight. He had lived in England but now he was in Scotland, and he went to a primary school in St Andrews. The school was run by nuns who taught spelling and grammar, arithmetic and how to avoid getting caned across the hand for mistakes. The canes were flat wooden sticks, custom made for rapping palms.

Christopher quite liked these odd set of elderly women who dressed no matter what the weather in black with black and white hoods; who were constantly yawning, praying, smiling, and telling their classes about unbearable ordeals the saints had endured. Before it had just been a case of living through the fact that God made him. Now he could feel proud of the reason why. To love Him and to serve Him in this world so that he could be happy with Him in the next seemed, at his age, a reasonable deal. He was told about his Guardian Angel which for him took the form of a floating Madonna slowly revolving the area governed by his bed. He imagined the Gospel writers getting together to discuss what part of Christ's life each would tackle although there was enough importance in various aspects of the story itself for it to be told almost exactly the same way four times round. He didn't think that one would copy from the other, all stemming from Matthew's inspired hand. They just brought the matter before God who said: 'Look here, just tell what you can and make it honest.' He prayed to the saints: asking St Paul how he managed to write his letters and send them off – in an envelope marked 'The Corinthians' – to St Clare because she was the patron saint of TV and he admitted to enjoying TV more than he enjoyed praying, and to St Dominic, the Dominic who died at fourteen and was everything Christopher thought a schoolboy should be but couldn't if he wanted to have fun and avoid being bullied. He also prayed to his namesake until he was told that this saint was nothing more than a myth whipped up by tradition to please a few travellers.

Christopher became an ardently devoted altar-boy. He lit the candles smoothly, without fuss, and rang the bells not too loud but clear and never presented wine when it should only have been water. When he was about to leave the nuns and move onto better things initiated and compromised by the failing of his eleven-plus he was given a wooden crucifix which he nailed to his bedroom wall and to which he offered prayers for family peace. He could begrudge the livelihood of his sisters, quite individually and not on the collective basis of conflicts stirred up by the sharing of a few rooms in a house. Angela was bossy, Julie was rude and arrogant (although at that time the word arrogant was substituted by a range of feelings surrounding the fact that life was unfair) and Rebecca was unfeasibly quiet. As for his brother, Peter, – he was of the squittish age which needed to be all but totally ignored. Jennifer had yet to arrive. But he could love them all for being God's children along with all the other boys and girls, men and women he encountered, whether or not they appreciated their lack of choice. Love and hate had no experience other than contributing to his Catholic state. A passing fancy saw such priestliness solving the problems of many. Fight for the good of all – this time the dragon sweeping down upon a village, more nourishment than a stranded princess, and as a warrior of God with his wooden crucifix he would be ready. But why wait for sainthood. Dispense with the middle man, forgive all and, yes, die at fouteen.

But having failed his eleven-plus, nothing more devastating happened to him than being sent to Madras Secondary Modern commonly known then as The Burgh. This could well have formed the impression of being buried away as a failure for convenience, however, the Burgh wasn't such a bad school and the secondary contract not such a bad method of advancing in years especially has he had started his first year there in the A stream. It soon became Comprehensive, and the entire school as an institution rather than the locks, stock and blackboards left at the old place, moved to a sturdy display of brand new buildings where facilities increased as well as the number of teachers, pupils and classrooms, and the change in name triumphed from the downtrodden to the uprisen: Madras Kilrymont complete with everything a twentieth century education demanded and more (including the share of a minority percentage memory of a nearby industrial computer). But the Grammar School part of Madras, commonly known by its location: South Street, stayed put in South Street and thereby maintained its pedagogic air of superiority. As for the Burgh, that was handed over to the nuns of Christopher's primary school education.

This all resulted in Christopher's loss of urge for sainthood. He discovered maths and physics and he became conscious of a need to save the world by other more secular means. He did what he could to do well in exams which he reckoned were on the right path. He remained in the A stream and was proud of possessing what he thought was a better than average ability at utilising the school subjects. He did not, however, enjoy games. He was not made of such stuff which manufactured heroes. He was not unpopular but this drawback underlined the usual reaction he stirred in others, with a few peers regarding him as puny. However, he had his friends, two in particular: one he never saw outside school and with whom he shared all the urgency stemming from force times distance, the other he met more times at home, being as he, the friend, was a good year younger and therefore academically almost a generation behind, having never endured or enjoyed the Burgh in his brain. Both were best because neither ever compromised the beliefs Christopher struggled to maintain within himself. Without these beliefs he was thinking that perhaps he was a very dull boy indeed. Nothing special maybe about being set apart when others made the noise, did the deeds and won the acclaims, unless chance was preparing him for a task of greater glory. He wondered what it was to conquer the moon and strike out for the stars, a noble future as a Doctor of Science applying research to the necessary ingredients of a fantastic expedition, all resolved from the humble beginnings as himself, a pupil, alongside Ronald Arteeky, as together they worked and joked their way through the struggle of text book problems. At home, with Brian Reem, the moon was theirs. They only had to climb the nearest climbable tree, alongside which they also enjoyed cycling, trespassing and fishing. They caught nothing but their choice of imagined achievements which, when left alone together, were vast.

Christopher was not totally without the sporting impulse. Just a bit of persuasion and he was part of a team, a small one, sometimes only made up of himself, Brian Reem and Colin Pritchard who, throughout the season, sang, played and pulsated soccer but never seemed to consolidate his enthusiasm with any form of victory. Colin did not despair, but gathered other friends, gained support, played games, lost pride, made enemies and finally left. There was the impact of control which Christopher hardly realized he was under until he was set free. Because Colin played soccer, so did he, and they shared their enemies and friends, no longer the indifference but a champion of causes which from the immediate attention harped back to the dragon and the towers of old. If I'm to be different it may as well be for similar reasons. Christopher conformed to the appeal of living according to the instructions of others about making fun while the day shone.

Throughout the time of finding himself but losing the ideal it again occurred to Christopher that girls had better things to do, although to him, judging from his sisters Angela and Julie and their friends, they did nothing that special. They followed fashion, the charts, and they acquired and disposed of boyfriends. Not for one moment did he ever think that he could be one of the latter. It was as if boyfriends were a different breed of boy, specially hewn from the rock of modern times from which he had escaped by means hardly worth consulting. Looking back he could not decide whether he was interested but shy or aloof but curious. There was a lot of evidence to suggest that really he just didn't care. He was not famous for having sisters but he realized that he had more than most. With such sisters, particularly from the older two, a society of girls was inevitable, but the brother he remained implied a separation because of impartial rights concerning domestic imperatives. He could never imagine Angela or Julie actually going out with one of *his* friends and so it became, for him, ridiculous to think that he could have any inclination towards theirs. Colin did say that he thought Angela was pretty. Julie once remarked on Brian's odd and not unattractive quality of smiling constantly without looking like a moron. Julie would have gone to South Street had the Burgh not turned into Kilrymont, and so there was a post eleven-plus ability to discriminate against morons and to such an extent this remained the story of her life which she exploited with the admirable expertise of a world leader emerging from the ashes of some bloodless revolution. Christopher was not a moron but his status, in relation to Julie, up until making good friends with Mark Langford was to remain worlds apart.

At school Ronald was known to associate in hand-holding terms with the occasional female, but Christopher managed to maintain his separation from the world of boyfriends, and the girls hardly bemoaned their loss. In fact if he was thought of at all by those girls who knew him it was only as a pathetic object who cut for himself the indefinable image of the class weed. Christopher did not lose sleep over this but every so often he wondered where he might have gone wrong. His year at the Burgh had been colourless, and three more years at Kilrymont had only helped to enlarge on a rumour that he was in actual fact, believe it or not, although not just a few were astounded, Julie Panhandle's brother.

Julie knew of Mark Langford long before Christopher had heard of him. Being Christopher's age, almost to the month, Mark escaped the humiliation of the Comprehensive pull by remaining a South Streeter throughout the time of his family's posting in Leuchars, and once a year he displayed a school report consisting of A's in everything but modesty. He developed and maintained all the candour and fame, outside the sixties meaning of the term, of a legendary freak, disliked, despised but admired in proportion to his success. He left with his family a year before his O levels and took the equivalent in GCEs at a boarding school in Newport, Shrewsbury, Shropshire, but the disruption of leaving Leuchars, and in effect St Andrews, all but destroyed the impression of his power, the effect of which on Christopher's life, up to that point, had been profound. From the outset and by default Mark was disliked because he was so demonstrably good at whatever he chose to do. Also Colin disliked him and so Christopher had to follow suit. However, Colin moved with his family to Singapore before too much damage had been done, and supported by Brian's passive concern with just getting on and having fun, Christopher and he had to admit that they found admirable Mark's ability to do just this.

Mark's idea of fun was to create a world in which, although contained in Leuchars, was completely independent of almost everything but his enthusiastic control over those who were not his deadliest enemies. He guaranteed fresh ideas, presenting the challenge of a pioneer as if entering for the first time rather than returning to the glory of outdoor youth. He was emotional, passionate and proud, always with a consistence and relevance to the joy or anger, energy or turmoil, stimulated by the adventures he created for his disciples, and this energy was called to task and passed around like graded rewards.

Mark was a legend a short time before Christopher got to know the lad. Julie only made it to cult-figureship which was preferable insofar as it lessened the chance of acquiring enemies and the burden of proving her status, both qualities in which Mark was particularly skilled. It was actually a touch redundant to say that Mark was especially skilled at anything although most got to know him through what others were saying with reference to some particular achievement. Colin probably resented having his team-making thunder stolen despite Mark's almost zero interest in football, but this was a probable part of a general case of disliking the lad on principle which was a pity because Colin's departure was just prior to him being given the real chance of entering the exclusive, but nevertheless Colin friendly, wonder of Mark's world. Christopher, convinced that Colin would have gained something, thought that the process at least would have been interesting to watch.

Is that it? thought Christopher now. Do I just read the reaction others have on each other? That's why I'm so content with my nothingness. It was certainly the reason why I was so interested in Mark meeting Louding last summer. I wanted them to live up to an expectation I avoid in myself by being the means of making people I invest in so much meet. But there had been no chance encounter. It was Mark who had introduced me to Mary-Ann and this immediately confused the issue. Okay, his girlfriend, and that's what he said and she didn't deny it, but it was as if he wanted me to look and live, and I looked at Mary-Ann and I fell in love.

The circumstances were not so usual. Christopher had never played tennis before. He had never any designs on the game, not even as an attempt at something which admittedly would make a change. Mark, however, loved the game. It was shaped by his enthusiasm into an art form presented thus: the game of games, although it turned out, to the immense surprise of all apart from himself, that he wasn't really that good. He organized a Leuchars youth-based tournament, and was knocked out in the second round. Christopher had hardly won a point, didn't really expect the ball to clear the net more times than was necessary to complete his own frustration and so assumed that Mark, excellent in every shot, was merely taking it easy, the allusion of ownership sharing all including the victory. Mark's victory had been the success in getting so many kids together, and in order to make up the number he had actually called around to the Panhandles in person. If truth be known, thought Christopher, he probably wanted Julie because her attendance would mean others would come, but he settled for me and Brian (who happened to be there at the time) because there were already just enough kids waiting for his return with their rackets at the courts. However, underlying Christopher's doubts was the mystery of Mark's preference for him which he, Christopher, would learn about but never quite resolve. After all, he, Christopher, expressed reluctance to play. Despite past experience he had yet to grow accustomed to making a fool of himself. He explained, out-right and in Brian's presence, that he couldn't play, but this was after inviting Mark in, pleased as he was that such a media-giant should take the trouble to actually knock at his front door. Mark was slightly smaller in height but was contained in a proportionate build which displayed an aristocratic confidence. This confidence disposed of others who only had to hint at what Christopher insisted was lacking in himself. But instead of disposing of him he disposed of his excuses. Mark entered the house and waited, with Brian, for him to get ready. He and Brian talked about a time in early years when they happened to be part of the same team playing rounders with a bunch of short-term friends at Treetops, the Officers' Married Quarters of Leuchars where Mark himself lived. The previous week the three of them had shared the same field (along with many others) for the highly finger-pricking task of picking gooseberries, and Mark asked the two of them if they could recall when, the previous year he and one of his erstwhile friends had helped Christopher and Colin to finish off patches of potato picking they had found difficult to clear in the time allowed by the coming and going of the oppressive potato scattering tractor. Christopher preferred not to think about it. He had almost fallen out with Colin when the combination of potatoes, money and broken backs had left their friendship almost in 'tatty'-based tatters. They had planned to pick their patch together but each resulted in accusing the other of not picking enough while Mark and friend, both super-fast and some furrows away, instigated further conflict by their available assistance. Christopher wasn't sure what had happened, but humiliation was closer than the horizon, and now here in his house, sans Colin, Mark was extending his friendship like an unwrapped gift, not so new as matured, locally imparted on the chosen few.

Many had been called and many did attend. The tournament lasted all afternoon which meant that Christopher sitting down nearly all afternoon watching kids his own age, whom he was familiar with but hardly knew, playing tennis. Mark soon joined him. He was laughing because he had lost, a situation to which he was jovially unaccustomed. The matches were only one set long and so he might well have won a second set and said so. Christopher tried to remember whether he himself had won a second point, so devastating had been his defeat, so conclusive now the imposed condition of being a spectator, all but justifying all the initial reluctance about attending. However, one of the girls, having lost her set like a breeze of careless beauty gently putting aside a task naturally beneath her, was called over by Mark in between games on the court which separated them. Christopher, having seen her often enough within the camp, occasionally at school and almost always with Eve, now looked at her for the first time. Gosh, she really is pretty, he thought. But it was something else. There were many girls and as girls go many were pretty. The lads were joking around because of their prettiness, and so the difference with Mary-Ann, defined later by Christopher as natural grace (and years later by Mark to Christopher as the Goddess in Residence) transformed the entire afternoon, transformed tennis, transformed Christopher's under-polished view of girls and basically transformed his life. She also consolidated in Mark what Christopher had to admit was lacking in everyone else he had ever known, a flowing unit of confidence, influence and class. Within the seconds it took her to cross the court Christopher had to reconsider his entire attitude to life. Absolutely nothing he could remember up to this point could equal the marvel of this encounter, and all she did was walk towards him in her well proportioned but modestly lengthened whites and say hello.

'This is Mary-Ann, my girlfriend,' said Mark without standing up in order to support the moral absolutes of this outrageous claim. Christopher was unwittingly impressed by the absence of any apparent gesture of ownership, an absence he would have registered as arrogance in others. But had Mark stood beside Mary-Ann so as to offer his friend the benefit of social perspective Christopher might well have seen this as a nervous reaction. Mark was the master of reaction, matching fire for fire and voice for voice, filled with a healthy laugh and not too proud to avoid the occasional scream. He was packed with a tireless supply of emotion which, filtered through his will, enabled him to direct others with ease, and steer all the action with an elegant flow of firm control. 'Mary-Ann, meet Christopher and take a seat. You lost? I had such strong hopes for you.'

'Well, that was more than I had,' she replied. 'You lost as well.'

'So did I,' said Christopher, as if to his credit.

What a gentle voice, he thought.

'Are you Christopher Panhandle?'

She had heard of him – Mark perhaps had arranged for him a formation of unusual praise.

'Yes,' he said with slight over-emphasis on the positive.

'Julie Panhandle's bother?'

He nodded. The under-emphasis had returned. Mark came to his rescue.

'He doesn't like to be reminded of that doubtful privilege.'

How the hell did he know that?

'Isn't it true,' said Mary-Ann, 'that even teachers are scared of her?'

'I've yet to meet a teacher who is scared of anything but time,' said Mark with an insight beyond his age but evidence of training he gained at South Street which, to the likes of both Christopher and Mary-Ann, was a mystery beyond contemplation.

'This bloody tournament,' he suddenly exclaimed as he raised his arms in an effort to underline the injustice, but sharing with them a moment of the affable disingenuousness about his act. 'How could I lose in the second round? Okay, I don't want to win the final. After all, I don't organize these things in order to win, but the second bloody round.'

Christopher was surprised that Mark was so familiar with Mary-Ann that he could swear to such effect in her company.

'I lost in the first round,' she said with her impulsive nature for attempting to console.

'So did I,' said Christopher.

Mark looked at the two of them, he stood up, so did Christopher, they formed a triangle of both self-assuring and self-conscious stares, and for a moment the tournament was no longer there.

'I can see the three of us are going to go places,' said Mark with a prescient generosity which Christopher would spend years attempting to unravel.

It was as if everything was planned to get the three of us together, he thought, so that, yes indeed, we could go places. Separated now, we were without direction. Mary-Ann apart no longer exists unless she's floundering like me, and as for Mark, the great Mark of genius – but analyzing what actually went amiss created the usual complications which Christopher found easy to put aside. He returned his thoughts to Mary-Ann whom he met at a tennis tournament which, to the best of his knowledge, had never actually been won, the few still to play the final sets promising to return the next day but didn't. Neither did most who were no longer playing – a threat of rain perhaps, and besides, as it turned out, lads like young ladies had better things to do than kowtow to the pulling power of Mark's directorial demands.

Mark did not apply much energy to increasing his flock once the faithful had been found. He wanted to start the tournament again but on the second day the tennis turned into a talk-in during desultory shots over the nets about the many events the gathered, predominantly female lives individually, collectively, regionally and scholastically revolved around. Few seemed that interested in becoming actually better at the game, although Mark shaped most of his subsequent ideas around an image of endless sets under a steaming sun.

'It's those bloody girls,' he said to Christopher and Brian while the three of them played separate games on the far court. 'All they ever do is gossip. Talk, talk, talk, chitter-chatter and then make some facile attempt at whatever the reason for us being together. And where are all the others? Don't you find? – people are bloody useless.'

Christopher, always impressed by Mark's vocabulary, asked what facile meant. He may as well have questioned what it was that had brought them all together. Certainly Mark had not been including his girlfriend in his general statement as to why he and therefore they should so innocently consider the fairer sex to be bloody. Mary-Ann had a holiday job as a shop-assistant at Leuchars Village newsagent, and so she was not around to risk loss of grace by participating in needless particulars. Furthermore, after a couple of points, when Mark established how totally bored he was at the fact-finding obsession with what others not around were doing, not doing, going to do and not going to do, he himself a highly probable victim of many deluded presumptions, witnessed an exit from the court confines, the wonder of which could well have undermined Mark's moral and powerful influence on all of which he now regarded with contempt. This contempt was a half-acknowledged need for a teenage media to fuel the process of his on-going adventures. What people thought, with or without bitterness, he needed in order to focus all his engrossing strength of purpose on those who needed him. Julie Panhandle, on the other hand, cared little and needed even less the opinions of others to support her unique fame. Her power remained absolute in its independence of her action. She merely attracted the attention of others, especially the girls of her age group in the camp and at school, and because they were already prepared by what they already knew, the girls and a few of the remaining lads, other than Mark, Christopher and Brian, left the court to join her as she made her appearance some yards down the road.

'Now where they all going?' asked Mark.

'Oh look,' said Brian, himself more than half interested, 'it's Julie.'

Christopher was not displeased. He wanted Julie to meet Mark although he knew that they had met before but that had been prior to Mark's new role as his very good friend.

'God knows what they'll find to talk about that could possibly interest her,' said Mark, betraying preconceived notions of someone whom he would be not unhappy, if challenged, to regard as an equal.

You, of course, said Christopher to himself. Mark's a worthy rival, and as Julie always appears so consistently boyfriendless, and unique in making this lack a badge of honour, who knows? And then Mary-Ann, innocent of all intrigue, can follow up a fascination she may have in me being Julie's brother.

The girls were pointing at the tennis courts and had Mark been on the moon, no doubt they would have pointed at the sky. They were hardly trying to impress Miss Panhandle with news about how thrilling they found the game, but a game with Mark, perhaps? She started walking towards the courts, forming behind herself a V shaped entourage. Her entrance was quite sublime. The gate was opened for her and she did not mind stretching the moment to its extreme. Reality was rarely extenuated by the pampering she received. She looked at Christopher first and for a moment it seemed as if she had entered the court, the very vicinity in fact, with the sole purpose of talking to him. He could well have been asked to excuse his presence and no doubt he would have done so with Brian in tow, but Julie was never that insensitive. Neither would she have introduced any element of the bathetic by referring to a message from parents or home.

'You're full of surprises, Christopher. Playing tennis. I'm impressed.'

Mark walked over to the net which was about as far as he was willing to get to the invasion and announced quite firmly:

'Listen, you lot, we're in the middle of a bloody tournament. Can't we get on with it?'

'We haven't even started yet and we don't know who's playing who,' said a girl called Sarah.

'Whom, not who,' said Mark deciding that Sarah was near the top of his increasing list of things being bloody. 'You can join us if you want, Julie.'

'I've never played tennis before,' said Julie with characteristic honesty about her limitations. 'You'll have to teach me.'

'Yes,' said Sarah. 'Hey, everybody, Mark's going to teach Julie tennis.'

'Mark cannot remember saying yes he would,' said Mark.

Nevertheless he realized that he would not necessarily undermine his agenda to comply with her wishes, and Christopher, along with the others, knew that Julie would gain her lessons, and for one displeasing moment Christopher exercised an idea that Mark's entire approach at friendship with him was so that he could bring about such a situation. But then it occurred to him that if Mark had wanted to gain Julie's attention, maybe even her esteem, befriending her weedy brother was the last method he would have chosen. That alone amounted to common enough knowledge. Christopher and his friends were not part of Julie's world. Mark was about to cast himself in the role of an exception.

Perhaps the most annoying but enlightening aspect of having a sister like Julie was seeing himself in her actions, but a self that was ideal had he the universally beseeching gift of recreating action based on hindsight. Julie, in her attempts to demonstrate her inability to play tennis, misread the ball, mis-hit her returns and failed to clear the net with her many reserved and timid shots. In fact she did everything Christopher had done the day before and she even had the dubious benefit of a crowd of spectators egging on the none too subtle impact of humiliation, while the only person who had taken notice of Christopher's clangers had been his rival. While he had felt a fool at not doing at all well at something he had never done before, her obvious gift for staying on top lent her an air of victory mounting up in lost points. The only distinction Christopher could discern was that of attitude, and he understood that he enjoyed her style mainly because it was appreciated by others. As for Mark, he was given the chance to display a definite skill not yet developed but certainly apparent, and was appraised accordingly. Thus the two leaders complemented each other. He did not play an indifferent game, and every unforced mistake he made was followed by at least a characteristic grunt if not a scream. She just placidly did the wrong thing in the right way.

'Bloody hell,' he shouted, standing his ground, refusing to believe in distance as the ball went out.

'Your serve, I think,' said Julie and she failed to clear the net in her attempt to pass the ball to him and so she said, with a wonderful shrug in her voice: 'bloody hell.'

Everyone laughed. Mark was being mimicked.

'Madam,' he said, 'are you by any chance taking the micky?'

'I'm trying to give you this ball. Are you sure these nets aren't too high?'

'Too high for you maybe, but of standard height for the rest of us.'

'Julie's above standard,' shouted Sarah incongruously.

'You know, Christopher,' confided Mark later on, 'I'm beginning to dislike Sarah. She answers back everything I say. Is that right? Is it the normal practice?'

'Not everything you say.'

'Nearly everything. Too much anyway.'

But Sarah did remain when others had left and she was an ever enthusiastic part of their dwindling group. She was also, now, with Eve no longer around, Mary-Ann's best friend, or at least she could claim that Mary-Ann was her best friend, and when Mary-Ann finally turned up on that second day of the tournament, when there was a hint of twilight and the courts had been abandoned for a game of rounders on the adjacent field at Julie's request, it was Sarah who shouted: 'Look, its Mary-Ann.'

'It thrills me to think that Sarah's my girlfriend's best friend,' said Mark sourly as Sarah abandoned her position on the second base and ran off to greet the strolling goddess.

After the intermission that Mary-Ann's arrival caused, the game of rounders continued. She was happy to watch and so Christopher was conscious of her watching him, as indeed she watched them all with equal concern, but he felt compelled, especially with Julie present, to avoid watching her watching him (and the others). But it was hopeless. Julie did not gain her reputation of control for nothing. She read almost every situation impeccably.

'You fancy Mary-Ann, don't you?' she asked him while they were walking home together, game eventually abandoned because of lack of light.

'Oh come on, Julie. What lad doesn't fancy her?' But Julie received this mundane observation by returning an intent eye-brow curling stare. 'How do you know?' he asked.

'I could tell. Yes, she is a very pretty girl, isn't she?'

'Like I said, every lad fancies her, but she's Mark's girlfriend.'

'And what if every girl fancies Mark?'

'I see. Do you fancy him yourself?'

She awarded him with one of her 'you should know me better than that' looks and Christopher was quite content. He knew that his secret longing was reasonably safe with her.

Julie perhaps saw in Mark something of a refuge. As leaders of quality they separately secured company for themselves from miles around, but a happy paradox involved in their matchless attraction towards each other deterred all but those particularly strong in faith. During a summer full of tennis and rounders with the occasional day off for picnics and walks, the odd game of Risk played in the equally odd situation of being on top of Sarah's porch roof – she owned the game, the sun owned the roof – Julie and Mark had accumulated between them a well diminished count of five followers: Christopher and Brian, Mary-Ann and Sarah, and girl called Jane.

Where had all the others gone? thought Christopher. Even more interesting, why did Jane stay? After all, she hated me, and in her silent moods as well as the couple of tantrums by which she all but broke up the group, she hardly struck people as a bastion of loyalty. I bet she wrote in a letter to her pen-friend in Australia about how much she hated me as if it was all part of being up north. Like a devotion which scribbles my name on wrapping paper and burns it, and in the absence of a waxed image, she actually did one time score a twisted safety pin through my flesh.

Christopher had to think now. Maybe Jane had really loved him. Jane was at heart a quiet girl and it was hard to recall whether anyone actually liked or disliked her, Christopher's stifling indifference accusing his flesh with a compulsive need to be stabbed. He felt obliged to avoid her because she stared at him with accusing eyes when he was thrown back into an intense horror by what was assumed by others to have been an accident. It had been one of those picnic days and he was so intensely in love with Mary-Ann that try as he could there was no way of overcoming the need to stare at her or move that bit closer to where she sat, or where he could comment, instinctively veering towards the foolish, on much that she had to say. He could not understand how Mark could pose this superior guise which enjoyed such immunity to her glory. It could have been that in an attempt to cover a mutual feeling of hope with Julie he granted to all an equal measure of his generosity in enthusiasm and joy. The two leaders displayed an easy-going respect for the freedom, mainly from choice and attention, which they effortlessly offered each other. A good deal of their fans remained outside this arrangement. What was attainable had been attained by their partnership from which there was no longer the pulling incentive for the erstwhile follower. It seemed that in the short duration of their friendship Julie and Mark had cancelled out for each other the calling power they both possessed in being surrounded by many who for different reasons needed one or the other to be an inspired source of admiration, respect, and even worship. Julie enjoyed a holiday gained by tagging along with Mark, remaining together throughout the summer months, gaining from each other the novelty of inner peace located in a circle of the chosen. She would certainly never admit to that now, but Christopher remembered a different girl, perhaps a different Mark, and maybe it was true that those two offered each other security of tenure not allocated to their separate modes of leadership. Happiness is stripped of ownership. Mark could not see Mary-Ann through Christopher's eyes, no more so than he could feel the pin which Jane plunged into Christopher's side as he reached across the blanket and across her for some more cake. He cried out, the pin was withdrawn and the stare offered by Jane appeared to accuse him of having committed the crime.

'What happened?' asked Mary-Ann having held her breath with the shock that replaced the answer Christopher had been about to offer to a previous question.

'She stuck a pin in me,' said Christopher. He was still in some pain.

Mark laughed but was the one to ask the relevant question.

'I say, whatever made you do that, Jane?'

'It was an accident,' she said. She stated this as if identifying a course of action and there was not the slightest hint of sorrow in her voice. She looked at Julie and then said, as if to her, 'I'm sorry.'

Christopher was sorry now that he had lost his cool under such duress. This did more than the pain to undermine the miracle of Mary-Ann's almost tender attention. She asked him if he was really okay – if he was bleeding, did he need a plaster, and he actually showed her the mark in his side like a feeble Christ to a glorious Thomas. They had all been talking about jungle cats – the difference between jaguars and panthers and the amazing speed of cheetahs and the laziness of male lions. Christopher knew precisely nothing about the characteristics of jungle cats, least of all jaguars and panthers. He had always thought a jaguar was a car and wasn't a panther some sort of bear? All the same, even with Mark at his side to expose such elements of ignorance, Christopher knew everything about everything that Mary-Ann wished to include in their conversation. She talked well, she hardly gossiped and she listened with the intention of learning. And then Jane goes and sticks a pin in me. Why?

'You're okay,' assured Julie. 'She hardly scratched you.'

Later on she confused matters by telling him that there was jealousy because of Mary-Ann.

'Why me? If it's because of Mary-Ann why doesn't she stick a pin in Mark?'

'Christopher, she's jealous of Mary-Ann, not you.'

Christopher tried to work this out but had to laugh at a not too humorous conclusion.

'Then why didn't she stick the pin into Mary-Ann?' he asked with an innocent sense of his own answer.

'Would you have let her? Would that have improved matters for her? After all, you're in love with Mary-Ann.'

'Jane doesn't fancy me, does she?' It was conceivably possible. 'And if she does it certainly not making things better sticking pins in me.'

'If you love someone who ignores you, you'd stick a pin in him too.'

'It wouldn't be a him, and I don't ignore Jane. But I think I might have to avoid her.'

Christopher could only see the clear distinction between love and hate. Julie saw how they were related and the line between them was as thin as a pin. This pin was not a final achievement. Jane hardly said another word to Christopher, refusing to partner up with him at tennis, opting for Brian whose game gratifyingly enabled Christopher to notice improvements in his own.

Mark took his flock all over the camp. They explored the woods at Treetops, made a HQ out of an abandoned air-raid shelter, mapped out farms and counted hills, giving to each a fictional name denoting countries in a world of magical conflict. There was even an enemy gang called the Black Guards, and it was difficult to refute their reality as Mark had them so intensely involved in his list of precautions. Throughout all this Jane did as much as she could, without actually hurting him again physically, to make Christopher understand how much she despised him. If his comments were apt she un-apted them, if his ideas were sound she unsounded them, from one direction he met with resistance, from the other persistence if only by the vigour of her brooding silence.

'Christopher, you're a pain, a real pain,' she said. A longer sentence would have taken so much effort and he had merely walked in on a structure she was making out of twigs for their HQ.

'What have I done now?'

'You don't have to do anything to be a pain. You just are.'

She longed to attack him. Her hatred was at a peak. At that moment Brian walked in with more twigs and she screamed at him. Brian was too innocent to survive and so he walked out and did not return, having been isolated enough times by the conflicting elements within the group. All he really wanted was to kick a ball around a field. It was better in the Colin Pritchard days. Christopher also left. He went straight to Mark and in his way offered his resignation from the club to be rescinded on condition that Jane stayed away.

'She's a bit of bitch, isn't she?' agreed Mark, not for one moment believing that he was going to lose Christopher. 'We're going to have a party in a tent at Treetops. I'll supply the tent and the drinks and a few cakes, and we can bring along a radio and more food and have a bloody good time.'

Brian did not want to join them when Christopher called around to see him. He said nothing against Jane, the club, the way things were. The summer was almost through, the end days too close for comfort and he had been given some homework etc. Besides, his sisters wanted him to help with the in-garden tree-house. Couldn't Christopher stay? In earlier days there would hardly have been a choice: fine trees in the Reems back garden, plenty of facilities for constructing tree-houses, and Brian's sisters were good fun if only a bit young. However, who would hold up the chance of sharing a tent with Mary-Ann even if space had to be made for others including Jane the pain.

However, Jane was suddenly quite friendly. She offered Christopher the rest of her lemonade, agreed with him when he said that the Beatles were and always would be far better than the Monkees, and laughed at a joke he made about Sarah's toffee which for attempt alone Mark had actually praised, resulting as it did in a gooey, dry tasting mess which alongside the rest of the food, remained mainly ornamental. The tent was small but large enough for them all to crouch and circle an appetising spread. Mark and Julie brightened the beginning with stories, rumours and ideas, but still Mary-Ann looked too wonderful for words and Christopher felt too urgently his need to stay only with her or get away.

'I'm going to climb some trees,' he said.

He was prompted to this by the thought of how much better it would have been had he stayed with Brian for the afternoon, and every afternoon for the rest of the summer. He was disillusioned. Mark with Julie was merely Mark and Julie. Mary-Ann was clearly out of reach. He was pleased that no-one volunteered to join him. He suspected some sort of perverse colour to Jane's good nature and would not have been surprised had she said yes to the idea in order to hasten some devastating plan of final destruction. If indeed she did fancy him, surely to share a simple tree and progress from branch to branch together, as he would have longed to do with Mary-Ann, would have been the peak of her then subsiding happiness.

He climbed higher than before and attained a view of all of Treetops and most of Leuchars. The furthest sight was a flagstaff planted in what looked like the middle of an abandoned ammunition dump, presenting an odd perspective of early afternoon peace. More unexpected although not so out of place was the nearest and most attractive sight. Mary-Ann was playing at skipping with Mark's younger sister, Kate. Nobody else was around. She was happy because the child loved her tuition almost, perhaps, as much as Christopher loved her now, as if by herself she was a newly discovered treasure. This was a rare and, from his height in the tree, literally a heavenly moment. He climbed down and walked over to where they were playing, nervous about intruding, but offering to be the third person needed to hold the end of a rope. He and Mary-Ann circled the young sister with the whirling rope, the girl concentrated on the rhyme depicting her survival in the middle. He had sap on his jeans. His nose was red. He was staring at Mary-Ann as a mystery of shape with long fair hair. The others had dispersed like the mist of morning and this was an afternoon without an evening to follow – an immortal moment. Like most such moments dipped in eternity it did not last long.

Jane emerged from the forest. She was crying. She was very angry. She was ready to hit something hard. Her thumb was purple because of a bee-sting, and the thick, sticky, gooey toffee was all over her blouse. Julie and Sarah followed her, both equally annoyed, Sarah also in tears, Julie just written up with her unique facial version of fury and distress, her skinny-ribbed t-shirt having suffered the same fate as Jane's blouse, and the toffee marked all three with the evidence of a conflict totally alien to those within the confines of the skipping. Had they been there they would also have been marked, and where was Mark? The girls had obviously not found what they had been looking for, but something else instead. Mark had thought he heard some Black Guards roaming through the cover of trees. Julie warned Christopher now that Mark was clearly a headcase although she too had joined the search, Mary-Ann having wanted nothing to do with any hoot or call of a rival gang. Something had happened involving a liberal use of Sarah's toffee. Mary-Ann was obliged to join the girls now and help clear away their food and dishes, while Christopher went into the forest to find Mark. He was sitting on the remains of a fallen tree which, although almost fossilized into its position, gave an impression of having come down as a result of the commotion. He was trying to scrape the toffee off his shirt with a flat piece of wood.

'I think Sarah's invented a new type of glue,' he said when he looked up and saw that it was Christopher who sat down beside him.

'What happened?'

'I'm not quite sure other than discovering that they're a bunch of bloody, bumptious bitches. You made no mistake about Jane. What a cow.'

'I think they're a bit annoyed with you. It's dangerous to set Julie against you.'

'I'll let them know what's dangerous. All this fuss about a bit of toffee, and I didn't secretly instruct the bloody bee to go and sting Jane. Bloody good choice. That's all I can say. I know where I'd have planted the sting if I'd been it. As for your precious Julie, she and I are through.'

Christopher laughed. There was something funny about Mark and Julie being through. What was it had they had actually been through?

'I thought Mary-Ann was your girlfriend.'

'Yes, and it's only Mary-Ann from now on. You, me and Mary-Ann.'

Mark set about this with malicious skill. The three girls, Sarah, Jane and Mary-Ann played tennis together quite frequently and with the summer holidays over it was during the evenings after school while daylight permitted. On one such evening, when Mark called around to see Christopher after having suffered a furious argument with his father, the girls enjoyed a good thirty minutes worth of the game before being joined by the lads. This was the first Sarah and Jane had seen of him for some time, Mark having confined his activities to Christopher and Brian, undergoing a form of cheerful resignation after the downfall of his empire. Jane was very cold. The two lads were not welcome. Her playing appeared to concentrate on this bitterness. Mark's comments, usually witty and caustic, began to evoke a dangerous element into the style of tennis played until he was laughing at every mistake Jane made. He could erupt into a spontaneous and hearty laugh which convinced all around how seriously amused he had become. Christopher started laughing too but not at Jane's mistakes or the increasing anger which increased her mistakes. There was an infectious strength in Mark's laugh which weakened Mark so much that he was practically rolling over the neighbouring net. It was a sound which killed other sounds. It made him groan and gasp and played beautiful havoc with his smart handsome face and wide-awake eyes. It was not the escape of imbecile amusement but an intelligent if unsuccessful effort at trying to take in the seemingly observed stupidity. So every time the ball was misplaced the laughter, controlled, fled free again, and Jane easily assumed that Christopher was laughing at her too. He was laughing at Mark laughing. He was wanting him to stop. It was getting painful, but nowhere near as painful as the fast smack from the ball as it hit his thigh. Undoubtedly a direct aim, this was an exceedingly well placed shot from Jane, and Christopher hopped around, crippled for a few seconds. All three girls packed up and walked out.

'Anyone for tennis?' Mark shouted after them, and he sat down on the bench where Christopher eased his burning leg. 'I say, do you think we went a bit far this time? Not the recommended route for kissing and making up.'

Christopher looked at him. His leg was suffering the loss. You've bloody well ruined my chances of ever getting to kiss Mary-Ann, he thought.

Neither of them ever saw Jane and Sarah again, not on the way to or from school not on camp, anywhere. It was as if their fury had whisked them to a different and probably better world. Mary-Ann, however, was still around and Christopher met her during that week. She sat down beside him on the school-bus going back to Leuchars. He couldn't believe it and neither could he work out whether the overwhelming pleasure was pride at having such a girl sit beside him in front of all the other lads there, or that this gesture alone meant that she had forgiven him. He was sorry and in their whispered conversation, both equally self-conscious of their travelling company, he apologized for his and Mark's behaviour.

'It wasn't your fault and Mark does get a bit... a bit...much.' This was the best Mary-Ann could offer by way of criticism. It would never have occurred to her to use the word 'stupid' or 'annoying' in conjunction with whatever threatened to undermine her loyalty. 'Anyway, Mark wants the two of us to visit him tonight at his place and so if you call around for me we'll walk to Treetops together.'

What, me alone call around to see her by herself, and just the two of us walk the mile or so to where Mark lives? And so he did call around and they, just the two of them walked the exquisite distance which graced them with the first of many walks they would in solitary companionship take together. Mary-Ann's house was just down a neighbouring road whereas Mark lived at the other side of the camp. Mary-Ann had a younger sister who looked very suspiciously at Christopher while he waited in the hall.

'Are you Flan's new boyfriend?' she asked as if remarking on the boring and recurring situation with older sisters and their range of male hopefuls hanging around.

'No.'

'Yes you are. Flan's got a new boyfriend and she's chucked that silly Langford.'

'Who's Flan?' Christopher asked as he was quickly whisked outside.

'That's me,' said Mary-Ann.

'Flan?' Christopher repeated with off-hand fascination.

'Even mum calls me that now.'

'And it seems you've "chucked silly Langford".'

'Don't pay any attention to my sister. She and Mark don't like each other. In fact she hates Mark, just like so many people seem to hate Mark. Mind you, most of it is his fault. He's told me what he thinks of my sister and I bet he's let her know as well.'

The subject of Mark, falling somewhat short of any special understanding Mary-Ann may have held dear, suddenly ceased. She wanted to know about Christopher. She had never really talked to him before, not outside the group. Where was he born? What camps had he been to before Leuchars? What O levels was he doing and what did he think of the illustrious Madras Kilrymont? She didn't like it at all although she enjoyed cooking and biology and track events in athletics. She was doing hockey now. Which did he prefer: rugby or football? What did he think of various teachers? Did he have a favourite? At school she had no real close friends and even here, in Leuchars, it seemed likely she would fall out with Sarah over Mark.

Christopher, for the first time since seeing her in the light of his love, thought about Eve, although at the time he didn't know she was called Eve. He wanted to ask Mary-Ann what had happened to this diminutive girl, but became so busy answering her questions he was hardly given the chance to talk about anything else except himself. He was now confronted with a new Mary-Ann. An enhanced Mary-Ann who was spreading her verbal wings having been set free from the cage of characters who had, until then, mainly through Mark, surrounded her and her ability to be known as someone within herself. Maybe, with Mark ridding them of all the others, she was at her happiest and exploring this unknown terrain and coming across Christopher as if for the first time, she wanted to know everything. She would certainly get the chance to know this and more because Mark could no longer leave Treetops, on his father's orders, not until he had completed as series of studies the basics from which he had fallen behind. Almost every night they took the same walk across camp, and within the distance, slowing down when necessary, they tackled and formed and weaved up and displayed in memory a matchless conversation about themselves, the warp of hope being crossed and tightened by a weft of modest dreams and facts. Christopher was completing his love. That was it. Mark was always pleased to see them both. He did not ask for them separately. Christopher knew of no particular time which Mark had deliberately set aside for Mary-Ann. She remained in a way his girlfriend by appointment to Christopher's protection, and on the few occasions when Mark was not available, they still completed the walk and had a game of basketball in the sports' hangar next to the Officers' Quarters.

Basketball was a new part of the scheme of things but only as a rest from their adopted studies. Mark wanted to write books about their eventual success, their international adventures, their spreading world from schoolboy's study to a universe of experience. They completed several first chapters. They gathered facts in order to make a card-driven computer, and they studied poetry. There were more cards than facts and Mark's poetry was full of Tennyson:

"'The old order changeth, yielding place to new,
And God fulfils Himself in many ways,
Lest one good custom should corrupt the world."

We live through constant variations of that theme,' he said but his two friends did not understand. 'It's like a train. The same train passes through many different scenes.

"Give me the call to take from my mind the train that will sprawl through the mess of mankind."'

'What have you got against mankind?' asked Christopher with a naivety embracing an aesthetic class difference between the two.

'Nothing. I love mankind. It's just people I can't stand.'

'I read that somewhere,' said Mary-Ann accusingly. 'You're stealing other people's thoughts.'

'It's the only way I survive.'

But Mark as a Leuchars legend did not survive. He left just before the Christmas holidays. The Langfords were uprooted and they moved to RAF Shawbury, Shrewsbury, Shropshire. Mary-Ann and Christopher had been well informed about this event. Mark was never short on producing itemed results of his research, having removed from the South Street library a few books on that part of England, and they had practically the full scope of his new environment-to-be before them. But it was beyond the two of them to plan so effectively ahead that they could make do without their leaving leader.

Without Mark there was no direct reason for them to continue their evening walks across camp, although Christopher could think of many formed from a deep desire to shape evidence of a mutual need. All he had to do was to call around, say to Mary-Ann: 'Let's go for a walk, we have much talking to do,' and they would have gone for their walk with or without a planned destination, they would have done much talking, independent of any courage needed from either to convey to each state of mind as talking was the natural framework in which they existed together. But Christopher was only too aware of Mary-Ann's sister who knew only too well that the Langfords had left. It was more than his moral courage could sustain, to knock on the front door and have that insidious girl answer it. Such a sister takes the place of demons. Whatever was wrong with fancying Mary-Ann, let alone being in love, the sister would eventually taunt out from his simple but strained act of asking if, by any chance, Mary-Ann was in. Christopher's own collection of sisters did little to sustain the psychological abundance of such an approach. Julie for one knew of Christopher's longing, but since the breakdown of her friendship with Mark she no longer saw any need to share with her older brother her casually observed advice. Although he was too young to realize the obstacles he was inventing for himself, his phobia was that of playing out a hubristic role in which steps taken to secure more than just ambivalence in Mary-Ann's regard for him would result in total rejection. Like all those who love, he wanted more than his life's dreams to be loved back but feared more than his life's nightmares to be despised as a result. He was too shy to consult the oracle of fate and so, with a philosophy entailing a reunion with Brian Reem, he let her, Mary-Ann, go.

Away from each other their past companionship was imprisoned in the forlorn world of what could have been, trapped by the scheduled removal of the one person who had brought them together but on the initial basis of Christopher's longing had really kept them apart. The walks had established that basis as one of trust. Mark may have been a meaning but certainly was not intended to be an end. There had been no question of deceit. Mark himself had remained silent on the subject of fidelity as if to acknowledge a situation he had created for them to play into each other's hearts, and Christopher had begun to suspect the reward due to relatively long service and friendship. But now that he was gone the truth remained that there could be no rights of bequest. Mary-Ann was part of the complicated rules of freedom and Christopher, cowering from the game, achieved nothing except a new course in being alone.

It was no good. What Mark had given Mark had taken away. Christopher did not have the strength to force Mary-Ann from his mind, but fear disguised as apathy took her place, and it was only Brian's friendship that stopped him from developing a slightly prior to post-adolescent death-wish. He had his religion but every prayer was part of a heed to self-pity. He did not know the meaning of the word and even less did he realize any meaning to life other than a vague idea of what might happen afterwards. He made a pact with Christmas and was happy for a few weeks, and after the festivities attained some balance with the urgency of O levels and the rumour that the family were to be posted to Cyprus. Such rumour spread discontent as well as hope. The Panhandles had never been sent abroad by the RAF and Cyprus was a wonderland compared to the prospects of Suffolk where they thought they might be going next (always better than RAF Valley in Wales – the renowned dustbin of the forsaken ones.) Who needs women when there is the world, and was it not true that he was still attempting to save it by progressing in the field of scientific research in which passing a number of O levels was but a detail? Yes, he was convinced now about how foolish it was to pine after someone who, with her outstanding good looks, fair hair and accompanying grace, could with conviction gloat over the ownership of many friends and fans. It was certainly no secret than many lads, much more inclined to membership of the boyfriend club than he, included Mary-Ann within the top-ten, top-five, top-three most fancied girls both at school and within camp. What possible improvement to her life could he hope to offer by way of any declaration of his feeling over and above that of being a friend? It was hardly likely that after the charisma of Mark he could be the part of a worthy replacement.

But what friends? She had said that there were no friends – just herself. What he saw at school was usually in the process of avoiding her eyes and therefore something of a peripheral picture. Mary-Ann did not care to have people around her all the time. Very similar circumstances, maybe a different story – he had remained by himself but for Brian who arrived with a football or cricket bat and eventually a new tennis racket, and so it was he who accompanied Christopher when eventually he called around to Mary-Ann's on the off-chance that he could borrow her racket. The warmish days of April allowed tennis to re-emerge in his world as a past-time of choice. It was her and not her sister who answered the door. Her eyes emitted a joyful sparkle of recognition and it was the accompanying delight at seeing him there which suggested that within five minutes she would have been out to join them, but because she was going elsewhere with her family she couldn't. However, she handed over the racket, he and Brian spent a promising afternoon of improving their game, and that evening, a soothing passion whispered to his legs: walk around, return the racket, see her again. If it was her sister he would just hand back what was hers and so he did and it was *she* who answered.

'I believe this is yours,' he said, having rehearsed the line.

'Thanks. Was it a good game?'

'Just Brian and me. We're getting better. I can do a fairly good first service now, I think.'

'The three of us must play tennis together some time.'

'Or the two of us could go for a walk.' The removal of the safety in number found Christopher indulging more courage than he was often reluctant to use and so he accompanied it with an immediate get-out clause: 'only if you've nothing better to do. I mean, it's up to you.'

'Wait there. I'd invite you in but my sister is lurking.'

Fear of her sister was a common factor between them and Christopher was delighted. Mary-Ann hastily put on her coat and she was standing out in the porch beside him, ready to leave.

'What happened to you?' she asked as they set off. 'I thought you had left but then I kept seeing you at school.'

'I wouldn't ever leave without saying goodbye.'

'You hardly say hello. I thought I did something wrong.'

Yes, you took a step up onto the level of the totally unobtainable, he thought, but there again you were always on that level.

'No, not at all. It was me, and you know, the way things were, Mark leaving and all that, and I naturally thought you had better things to do.'

'I've done nothing since Mark left. Apart from going to school I've stayed in.'

They walked a couple of blocks and back, in which time she explained that in Leuchars she had no friends and although she knew that this worried her mother, she, Mary-Ann, had been quite happy without them. She then said the words which Christopher stored in a special place in his exclusive box containing those rare moments of complete magic.

'*You* are my only friend.'

They were not holding hands. Christopher could have secured this blessing but let the moment pass. Besides they were almost back at her door, and both were separated by *Top of the Pops* about to begin and Mary-Ann was too inhibited to invite him inside. But she wanted to see him again. She enjoyed walking with him and so he called around the next evening. He thought this might be a bit soon but he could not contain his desire to make up for what he had neglected since Mark left. This time they walked as far as the village cemetery and back, and their power and compulsion for reminiscence was such that they could still complete the task without the glorious burden of physical contact. Christopher also failed to find out why Mary-Ann did not have any other friends, although when calling around again, a (decent) few evenings later he was welcomed into the house by her mother in order to do so. Mary-Ann was out delivering a message but her mother said that she would be back and invited him in. No sooner was he sitting down and refusing tea when he was informed of her concern. Mary-Ann had no social life. She no longer went out unless it was to the shops or to school. Worse still, nobody called around to see her. Christopher wondered how that actually categorized him, but of course he was now the unmentioned (but not unmentionable) exception. Her mother was perhaps hoping that this message Mary-Ann was delivering on her mother's behalf would in itself and in a minute way, impress upon her the need to be with others.

'I suppose my mother's been telling you that I should go out more,' said Mary-Ann in their first few yards away from the house.

'Maybe she's right.'

'Why should I? I'm just not interested.'

'Why not?'

She gave him a gentle look which had within its secret a warning against such an inquisitive direction. But she had brought up the subject. He was allowed to ask how she was, what she was doing and maybe where she was going. Encroach upon the motive against radically changing her social situation and there lay an element of danger, and within this element a darkness coloured the promise of his actual position. He now felt that Mary-Ann was protecting him from a truth regarding Mark, but naturally enough throughout their walks, of which they had countless, they talked about Mark, but only surface details which featured him less and less until it became only a routine matter to mention that he had written.

Mary-Ann probably had a deeper understanding of loneliness. She just had no use for the conspiring persistence of group company. Christopher was different because he was there and there was only him and in no way did he align their walks to conditions which dealt specifically with the society of others. He became part of her solitude and offered to it from the exercise they gained in walking many stories which honestly amused her. She laughed because he was funny and it pleased him because she was not just laughing to please him. She was not just walking with him to please him. When it rained they stood inside a bus shelter along their route until it stopped. Rain was therefore always to remind him of Mary-Ann. The glistening creation from the grey clouds evoked shine to their love which went no further than the deeper stares they offered each other and the musical crisscrossing of voice with voice.

One Saturday afternoon Mary-Ann asked him if he would go with her to Dundee. She had some shopping to do and on this occasion she did not want to go alone. There had been no need for her to make an excuse – he would have gone with her to the North Pole. For them Dundee was the metropolis of Fife, and the crowds were large and the roads were busy and they both became irritated by each similar street being totally and wearisomely congested by this unaccustomed maze of life. They got partially lost and actually exchanged angry words as they contradicted each other's attempt to get their bearings. For a good fifteen minutes during the train journey home Mary-Ann refused to say a thing. He attempted to caress her hand and she whipped it away and rebuked him with a stare that made all forms of impurity and any slight hint of lust stand accused. He realized with terrible despair that there was no going beyond a point he had reached. Dundee had thrust them through the world together and neither of them could handle each other's extra-companionable demands. There was for the first time he had known her a danger of seeing her too often, whereas before it was merely the compulsive anxiety of never seeing her enough.

His visits had not gone unnoticed. Julie made it known that she was happy for him.

'You've become a topic of conversation. My brother going out with Mary-Ann Sheen.'

'I don't think I'm actually going out with her.'

'What do you mean, you're not sure? That means you're not going out with her.'

'We are very good friends.'

'Now you're being pathetic. You should go out with her. You deserve her much more than Mark ever did. I could make it known to her that...'

Julie was offering her unassailable services and Christopher was horrified.

'You will do no such thing. Mary-Ann isn't part of your circle anyway.'

'Oh, Christopher. I don't have a circle as such. You should know that. But it's true. She seems to be alone and you are doomed to love her.'

'If I love her I want her to be happy and not to be told what will make her happy. Please tell your friends that it's not the way it seems.'

'The way it seems is often the way it is,' said Julie enigmatically as she left the room. 'It always seemed to me that Mary-Ann was meant for you and not for Mark.'

Whatever it was that had come between Julie and Mark might have supplied that element of uncertainty which for himself and Mary-Ann embellished rather than corroded what could be defined as a mutual love. Many of the kids in the camp and those from there who went the same school, Madras Kilrymont, St Andrews, nurtured and gossiped their way through a powerful belief that incongruous though it was, Mary-Ann Sheen was actually going out with Christopher Panhandle, even although in the camp the sightings of them together did not entail cinema and youth club activities, and at school he and Mary-Ann had little if anything to do with each other, their separation in forms and years dictating a distance that even romance found difficult to cross. Christopher occasionally enjoyed the respect by association which came from being Julie's brother, but for something as big as being a boyfriend to she who had recently turned down a request to represent the school at St Andrews University rag-week beauty and fashion contest, he found himself deflated to the status of 'Who does he think he is?' The same question was asked of Mary-Ann when it was made known that her refusal to be part of the cat-walk celebrations came about in part from a contempt she had for such occasions rather than a supposed but very real modesty instilled by any hint of honour and privilege. They also put it down to her being shy.

'What's it to me?' she said to him when he asked her why she had refused. 'I'm simply not interested. Gosh, there are so many girls who are better at such things.'

'But doesn't it please you?'

'Only when I don't have to think what it is that people really want from me.'

'People want what people want,' he said not really understanding the use of the tautology within the quota of privilege he had in her sharing such thoughts. 'They also think that we're going out with each other.'

She stopped, he stopped and she looked at him so that he could clearly remember the rebuke when he had tried, in an attempt to ease her previous anger, to touch her hand.

'Well, we're not,' she said emphatically, and then she eased the tone and smiled at him. 'Christopher, you are my friend. We are together. Don't make it something it isn't.'

'I'm not. It's not me that's making people think that.'

'Oh, I don't care what people think. But I do care what you think, and I care what you want.'

In that instant Christopher questioned what it was he wanted. She was offering a unity that played towards the unique, and he was judging his love for her on the basis of her physical beauty. There was no other girl that matched her presence, but she was like liquid gold capable of flowing away because of a misalliance of expectations. Maybe all he really wanted to do was give her a kiss and hold hands and dispense with the finer details of the conversations that such actions threatened.

One special occasion he was invited by her to share an evening's babysitting for friends of her family. It was at the price of having to sit through a Frank Sinatra concert. He did not share Mary-Ann's musical tastes, having recently been introduced to the before-and-after phenomenon of Cream while she was inclined towards such diverse elements of swing as Sinatra, Presley and more recently Engelbert Humperdinck, and so they were willing to indulge in and enjoy what amounted to not unheated arguments about music. If it didn't contain the rock sound of an electric guitar backed by drums he wasn't interest, while she wasn't interested in the great unwashed and raucous energy of much that lay outside the strains of direct pop. This discussion was sustained by wine and a brave demonstration of appropriate dancing until he concocted a situation whereby he had his hands on her shoulders and her back against the wall. Within the next half-second his thoughts amounted to the following: 'Yes, we are great friends and you value what you have with me only because you have, through your own choice mind, no other friends, and yes nobody does compare to Mark, but I, Christopher Panhandle, am going to kiss you, Mary-Ann Sheen.' Their lips met, there was response, it lasted only another second before she pulled away but as such the response could not be denied, gainsaid or forgotten.

'No, Christopher. Don't.'

'Don't what? Kiss you.' He did not want her to answer that because no words would convey what she had to say in order not to hurt him or in any way compromise what she felt. 'Let's fight out our musical tastes with cushions. Choose your weapon.'

The contest lasted no longer than falling over each other and together across the sofa. His head was suddenly too light to support or avoid a fall which caught hold of her, and together they fell and together they lay, she supporting him, both unhurt.

'Are you alright?' she asked.

I cannot imagine a moment when I've ever been more alright, he thought, or a moment when I will be as alright.

'Sorry about that,' he whispered.

She must have been aware of their position especially so soon after making it known that a kiss was not part of the deal, but she made no move to convey physically a message to release her. It was up to him, and standing up he supported her outstretched arm and pulled her to her feet.

That evening, as represented by my dream, thought Christopher now, she gave me her thimble.

Christopher and Mary-Ann continued their walks, the youth based media continued their talks although it smoothed out to a case of Christopher not having the characteristic instinct towards being a better boyfriend, and eventually the Panhandles did take off southwards to Cyprus, while the Sheens went no further than Norfolk. Since then Christopher had met Mark whose family was now living in Berengaria. It was pretty much the same Mark, charming, funny, very expressive and present, but one and a half years had given him size gilded with sophistication and style indicative of his time at boarding school. He was now a public schoolboy, allowed out of his Castalian gaol three times a year, while Christopher merely remained the good friend from a Comprehensive (some three thousand miles away) and worth a visit or two when he happened to be around. There was a gap prized by experience of which Mark was unwilling to credit this friend – after all, the lad was still a cherub while he, Mark, was fast compiling a list worthy of any aspiring Don Juan. At first a passing mention of Mary-Ann hinted at indifference: no, Mark had not seen her since he had left Leuchars – how could he? – he was at bloody school and while there were available girls she was across the other side of the country. Her letters were short and sweet but at least he was still receiving them. Those few Christopher kept in his own collection were shorter and maybe not so sweet in their casual reference to how she was getting on without him. But if such epistles were evidence of endearment, by now Christopher had apparently been forgotten. However, it was while he spent a few summer days at Berengaria with the Langfords that Mark read to Christopher parts of a three page letter he had recently received, the written contents hardly consistent with her neat but monotonous hand. She wrote of her persistent faith in the idea of seeing Mark once again and because of this she had chosen never to take an interest in other lads. She went on to express how the years had been long without him, as long as her memory of those golden months when they had been together. There was enough in just those few lines to have driven Christopher wild with ecstatic hope had he been their recipient, but Mark tempered what joy he gained with contemplation verging on doubt – why was she writing this now, choosing this 'fine time' to reveal her love when he was too far away to do anything about it, and besides there was and had been other 'fish to fry'. He talked about the early days with Mary-Ann. It was great to be with her and to be seen with her and to be talked about as the boyfriend fully, he believed, within the league she represented, but she was this goddess who threatened to fade into nothing if you went too far. Their first kiss: he had to actually ask her:

'"For God's sake will let me you kiss you – what's the deal here?" We were sitting on a bench together. Bloody stupid place to have a kiss.'

'Why?' Christopher associated Mary-Ann and kissing as totally transcending any drawback offered by the setting.

'You have to be opposite each other to have a good kiss, not sitting awkwardly side by side and not as a result of me asking her if it would be okay. It's embarrassing and that's what it was. But, remember, this is Mary-Ann, and embarrassing or awkward or not, kissing Mary-Ann at the time was far above snogging any other girl. We did a few more kissing and petting and that sort of thing but really, Christopher, I felt belittled by her when we were alone. Gosh, have I ever progressed from there. I was thinking of chucking her but, it's Mary-Ann Sheen, the best-looking girl from here to wherever. And then I thought about it again when your sister joined us for that short time.'

'Oh no, Mark, please don't say that.'

'She may only be your sister, but it was Julie Panhandle. I knew I could get off with her and I knew she fancied me while being Julie Panhandle she makes a big deal out of fancying nobody. But what could I do? Mary-Ann was there, and you know, it occurred to me that she fancied you.'

'She did not. She liked me because I was your friend.'

'Yeah, maybe so, but I thought at the time – me and Julie, you and Mary-Ann. Why not?'

Christopher smiled with an assured sigh as if the idea had about it a summer's day option equal to other Langford inspired activities, rather than a cascade of undreamed of parallels shaping paradise.

'You really wanted to get off with Julie at the time?'

'For God's sake Christopher, apart from you who didn't?'

This hyperbolic answer contained much about it that was true although, as far as Christopher could remember, not once did Brian Reem state anything amounting to a preference regarding Julie, but there again Brian had not been one to state a preference for any girl. Still, as the laws of exceptions dictate…and Christopher was still swirling inside with the noted possibility of him and Mary-Ann with the hinted blessing of Mark and Julie.

'Mark, why didn't you tell me this at the time? I would have gone along with any of your plans although I don't think we could have counted on Mary-Ann's full participation. So why didn't you try and get off with Julie – if you thought she fancied you?'

'What makes you think I didn't?'

'What?'

'I was going to talk to you about it. I was going to say to you at the time: "Listen Christopher, who doesn't fancy Mary-Ann? – so don't tell me you don't – and who doesn't fancy your sister? – because I certainly do, and I think she fancies me, because, let's face it, what girl doesn't?"'

'And I would have said, with reference to latter point, Sarah Shellcross doesn't fancy you and Jane Anderson doesn't, and…' Christopher attempted, but in vain, to think of other examples.

'Ah, they were all crazy about me and you know it. Jane just happened to be a head-case and as for Sarah…'

'Sarah was overwhelmed about the fact that she was constantly in the company of both Julie and Mary-Ann and, let's face it, you. So, okay, you would have concocted some plan to ease Mary-Ann over to me thus making you available for Julie, but it depended on Mary-Ann wanting to be eased over to me.'

'You said it, and I just couldn't do it because, let's face it, it was Mary-Ann. But then it was Julie and so I messed up and took Julie off into the woods that disastrous day of the toffee and…'

'Yeess... and..?'

'Well, she is your sister so I'm not sure how far I can go with this story. Suffice to say it resulted in toffee over everyone.'

'Suffice fuck. What happened?'

'Okay, you want to know the sordid details. Julie and I sat on a log. Same situation, side by side and not opposite and therefore just as awkward, but I didn't have to ask for the kiss this time. We just kissed and – I know you could never understand what this means being her brother – I was *kissing* Julie Panhandle. Man! *Kissing* Julie Panhandle. Now, you know me: not one to deal in clichés, but that rocks! You sister was the ultimate – still is I suppose, but for God's sake don't tell her that and don't let her know *you* know about me and her. Anyway, we were caught by Sarah and she got angry because she was always Mary-Ann's "best friend", and she called over Jane who for some reason was carrying the toffee. One thing led to another and we threw toffee all over each other, and Julie, for some reason, became unreasonably angry with me. What I think it was, she hated the indignity of being caught by someone like bloody Sarah. So, thus the split. Just as it began so well – but still, *I*, Mark Langford, kissed Julie Panhandle and she loved it.'

'What do you mean it began so well? You got your kiss but what about Mary-Ann.'

'I know, I know. Anyway, I thought, that was it. Sarah would tell Mary-Ann because girls do tell each other things and I'd never see Mary-Ann again. That's why I was such a bloody bumptious bastard at the tennis court that day, laughing the way I can at every mistake Sarah and Jane made. I was certain all three of them hated me anyway and so it was my little revenge. But if Sarah had told Mary-Ann, Mary-Ann never made it known to me. I called around to see her because I had to make sure she wanted nothing to do with me. I had a bit argument with my parents at the time over something silly about the amount of effort I wasn't putting in to my schoolwork, and so I stormed out and thought I'd complete the misery by being told to go to hell by my ex-girlfriend. Only it turned out she wasn't my ex-girlfriend. She was very pleased to see me, but I felt constricted by what she did or didn't know about me and Julie. For some reason I thought it would make things better if I included you in the equation, although don't get me wrong, that wasn't the only reason I wanted you around. I really didn't want to lose you as well. I knew I was to be definitely grounded by my dad so I suggested you both coming over to Treetops.'

'I wouldn't have minded not being included; after all surely you wanted time alone with Mary-Ann.'

But Mark shook his head.

'I wanted it but I don't think she wanted that. God, sometimes she was worse than a cryptic crossword puzzle to figure out. And now she writes to me and says she wants to see me again. You know what it is?'

'What?'

'I think she's met somebody else.'

No! thought Christopher in a hopeless rage which he kept from disturbing his pose of just being a bit more than mildly interested in what Mark was saying.

Mark continued: 'And she doesn't think that I may have met somebody else. Hah, I've met a crowd since her. Let me tell you, Chris, I'd be more than happy to have her back but I'm not likely to practice the same faithful task of abstaining from the fruits which Mary-Ann had then forbidden herself. Huh, she can have me or keep her virginity. The two, I'm afraid don't mix. That is if she *has* kept her virginity.'

She was trying to keep her sanity, thought Christopher. The virginity bit was by default.

Mark never had cause to suspect Christopher's true feelings over and above being a member of the universal club who would naturally fancy Mary-Ann, and since that conversation all suspicions of feelings, such as they were, became part of a complacent decision to let the entire matter lie, not like the lion with the lamb, but with acceptance of a civil truth that the beautiful are for the beautiful.

But not now. Not now that I've dreamt of her and am thinking of her again. The laws of life may be simple, unjust and harsh but not the laws of such granted dreams. He lay in his bed in the Parthy's house, listening to George's coughing, the silence of the early hours awakening a refusal, dormant as usual but stirring now, to accept defeat. Mary-Ann was never for Mark. She must have known about him and Julie and therefore perhaps welcomed all that talk about her and me. But why did she want Mark back? She was too pure and that purity, the essence of her private perfection, can only be captured and appreciated by me. Mark barred himself from the chance of meeting her on this level.

Since last summer he and Mark had given up writing to each other. Christopher had made the effort to visit him last Christmas, but there was about that encounter an image of strangers meeting for the second or third time. No doubt there would be a fourth this Easter. He'd go over to Berengaria to be with Louding and it was only correct that while there he and Louding would call around to the Langfords. He realized now with refreshing analysis how between them both and away from each other there lay the track towards Mary-Ann along which Mark, himself, would not want to race.

However, all his big talk about other girls – let's face it, it *is* Mary-Ann and she did write to him saying that she longed to see him. So, what if he's already won?

The Beauties And The Best (c)

Victory and Defeat

> It is difficult to meander like a stream upon the face of youth. We take everything at once from the shock of impact and then act as if nothing extraordinary has happened.
> Rebecca Panhandle: Essay on Cause and Effect

> We dropped a clanger. It was Thomas's fault but Thomas blames me. Of course we both tried to blame Colin but it just didn't seem to work. Easier to blame Christopher but I suppose he was innocent. Neither of us won the cup. We were both in the wrong team. Classic case of always being somewhere else at the wrong time. Are you confused? Not half as much as me I bet.
> Scott Juir: Letter to Thomas's brother, Paul Rorner

> I know I shouldn't be a bad loser but I know for a fact that I'm much better looking than that poxy Ellen Oldfield. At least she didn't come first. A really lovely girl came first. I don't know her, she's from St John's, but she looked great.
> Teresa Donglesh: Letter to a friend.

'SHOCK DELAY,' SUGGESTED CHRISTOPHER as, without delay, they left the house.
 'What? The Clock?'
 'You weren't going by that clock were you? It's always slow on a Sunday. What's happened to your watch?'
 He now noticed Louding's naked wrist which was usually ringed and loaded by Louding's easy reference to 21st Century technology.
 'I forgot to put it on.'
 'Impossible.'
 'It's true. I was in a hurry.'
 'Now that is impossible. And here's me thinking that the watch was there. I mean, how could it let us down? Even tells the time in Chinese.'
 'No, it could give you the time in China, not Chinese. Subtle difference, *mon ami*. It only gives the date in Chinese and that's 24 hours ahead.'
 'What? The Chinese are 24 hours ahead?'
 'No, my watch is. That way I'm never a day late for anything.'
 'So long as you go by the Chinese calendar.'

'No, I never go by the Chinese calendar. I can't read Chinese.'

'But you just said you're 24 hours ahead in Chinese.'

'I've never said anything in my entire life in Chinese, at least not to my knowledge.'

'Mr Louding, you're deliberately confusing the issue. A point I'd like to raise is, if you're 24 hours ahead in order to prevent yourself from being a day late, isn't there always a danger of you being a day early.'

Christopher was four steps ahead before he noticed that Louding had stopped walking. He looked back.

'Today is Saturday, isn't it?' asked Louding, his eyes looking as if he was trying to come to terms with some chaos of the past. 'We're not 23½ hours too early?'

'Without your watch you can only be half an hour late if you go by my clock.'

'True, true. What are we standing around for? We're now 35 minutes into the first half.'

As expected the match did not wait for them to turn up. But as they were not playing, their irrelevance was emphasized by the crowd standing between them and the pitch. Louding did not play soccer but coming from Berengaria he had a team to support. Today was the inter-Youth Klub soccer tournament final: the Akrotiri Magpies against the BG Fliers, and so with others he had arrived in Akrotiri specifically to see the match. Unlike many others he had arrived early so he could pop around and visit Christopher who had been expecting Helen and was delighted to see Louding instead.

'I was expecting Helen.'

'Oh well then. I'll go away.'

'No, unless I can go with you.'

'I'm going to see the match.'

'What match?'

Louding had been in a hurry. His father said he would give him a lift to Limassol so long as he didn't mess around trying to choose what clothes to wear. Out of bed, into clothes, he forgot his watch, but managed to catch the Akrotiri bus. Christopher, on the other hand, had an easy morning conforming to his own rules of what he should do if he had time on his hands. Very little – a bit more sleep and maybe he'd read. He was only expecting Helen because he had been told she was back. He had not been expecting Louding, least of all because of soccer, but it was a final and his afternoon was free – if Helen arrived it was nearly always morning, and really he should have known that such an important match was on. Plenty of time, time enough for lunch, coffee, conversation, records...

They walked slowly around the edge of the crowd. It was hard to decide which gaps showed them the best football, but somehow, even only after five minutes and an enquiry which had the Magpies ahead, it was easy to say which direction the competition lay. There was confidence in the chant:

'One for joy, two for zest, three for speed, Magpies are best.'

'What's the score?' Christopher asked Louding who had asked one of the BG fans who may have lost interest and was wandering like them around the edge.

'Two nil. Need I say more? It isn't our home ground, you see.'

'Let's go and watch the other match.'

On a neighbouring pitch the cubs were playing an afternoon tournament. This unlikely clash of sporting schedules attracted a slight off-load from the crowd at the Youth Klub final, but at least the pitch was available and there was room to actually sit on the dry grass. They found their patch, sat down, heard a roar from the crowds – 'Three nil,' muttered Louding – and met Helen.

'Hello Christopher, and Louding too. Golly...'

'Helen!' Christopher stood up. 'What are you doing here?'

'I'm one of the organizers although I'm not really organising anymore because my pack were knocked out.'

She was semi-surrounded by a bunch of grubby kit-clad kids who made up part of her pack called Pegasus and they had lost. They were all chewing their way into oranges and they all looked equally ugly. The colours she wore and held glared out against this background like fire across a grey sky: over her arm a red leather mac and wrapped around her a bright green dress with short puffed out sleeves. Such a clash made her look delightful for many of the wrong reasons.

'Like my new dress and coat? Got them in England. Cost me £15.'

'What, in weight?'

'Shut up and give me a kiss.'

'Not in front of these innocent cubs.'

'I've been away for almost two weeks,' she said indignantly. 'You don't look very pleased to see me.'

'Of course I'm pleased. I'm just a bit ... dazzled.'

'I had a great time. It's very cold in England and there's so many silly things going on all the time, but lots of lovely shops and plenty of music. Do you know they've got a radio station which plays pop music all day long? I've still got your St Christopher, see...' She dug into the recesses of her dress and produced it, demanding, so it seemed, credit for the remarkable achievement of having kept it on herself for over a fortnight. 'And I've bought you an Easter Egg. The cup... The egg's on a cup and the cup's got elephants on it.'

'Helen, you've made my day,' said Christopher and he kissed her in preference to her producing the cupped egg in front of everyone. However, this only delayed the moment. She wriggled free in order to pull it out of her bag.

'There you are, see. Elephants.'

He did not want to see it let alone accept it if she handed it across. She handed it across. Christopher accepted it just as a small fight erupted among the cubs and Easter Eggs with elephants did not look appropriately part of Helen's required authority. She walked away with her pack after telling Christopher and Louding not to go away.

'What am I supposed to do with this?'

'Eat it, I suppose,' said Louding.

'It's not Easter yet. It's embarrassing, holding onto an Easter Egg with all these people about. Didn't I say I'd do something if she bought me something with an elephant on.'

'Can't quite remember. Wasn't it scream? With this crowd I'd rather hold the egg.'

'You can if you want,' said Christopher eagerly.

'I'll help you eat it.'

Christopher looked at what he held, a pretty egg made of chocolate underneath its patterned foil, the elephants on the cup looking sweet enough despite appearing like rejects from a Dumbo factory. He looked at Louding.

'Shall we?'

'If we don't the chocolate will melt in this heat.'

But Helen returned. She was alone. She had disposed of her cubs and she now disposed of the egg by returning it to the cavernous entrails of her bag.

'It'll melt otherwise in this heat,' she explained, and she should know because she had been in England.

After an evening meal at the Panhandles when Helen managed to all but exhaust the subject of her two weeks at 'home', the three of them listened to *The Yes Album* in Christopher's room and, in the light of the magnificent music the record succeeded in putting across, they discussed the chances of a night out together in Limassol.

'Must be next Saturday for definite,' said Christopher who always liked to improve on what was perhaps just possible, maybe even probable.

'By which time,' said Louding, 'I'll know for certain what this Stella really thinks of me.'

'Why Stella?' asked Helen. 'Why not Marion?'

'I already know what Marion thinks of me, and, anyway, why not Stella?'

'Well – Marion's my friend, and she and my other friends, they don't like Stella. They think she's a snob. I hate being with snobs.'

'Do you think she's a snob?'

'You fancy her, don't you, Louding?' And with equal impulse Helen added: 'She must fancy you. All the girls do.'

'I don't think so – not all.' Louding was not sure how to handle such a sudden check on his modesty but he was rescued by a knock on the door.

Thomas Rorner walked in.

'Your dad let me in,' he explained and then thinking, when he saw Helen, that he was intruding, but he relaxed when he also saw Louding. 'Watcha Louding. How's tricks?'

'Better than the BG Fliers.'

'What a massacre, hey? Five nil – five bloody nil, maybe even six. I lost count.'

'Did you score any?' asked Christopher.'

'Would have done but I wasn't playing. I'm a Starling – we got to the semis but you gotta give these outsiders a chance. Anyway, Christopher, you may have guessed – I'm not here to talk football with you. Would you do my job tomorrow night and I'll do your's Thursday? Fair?'

'Doubt if I'd benefit from that,' said Christopher. 'I could well be dead by then.'

'What do you mean?' said Helen, who until then had been in silent awe, cast thus, the only girl within a circle of containing Louding and Thomas. 'You're being silly. You don't look ill to me.'

'Who knows?'

'True,' said Thomas, his only answer to most philosophical comments, but Louding dispelled the air of existential angst by revealing Christopher's chief concern.

'He's playing rugby on Monday and he always thinks the next game's going to kill him.'

'Well, if you're gonna kick the bucket then I'd better take advantage of you while I can.'

Scott too's taking advantage, thought Christopher as he woke up Sunday morning. He remembered the afternoon stint at the Club he had arranged to do in place of him. Doorman hours had been arranged specifically to suit the bar. This did not always suit the four doormen and their jobs underwent a constant process of swapping set nights. Rules of employment stated that no swapping of shifts was allowed without the Club Manager's permission, but they worked according to a deceptive adage about the bliss of ignorance in the face of the wisdom's folly, and so today Christopher was able to wrap up his full week's whack in one go. Or so he thought until Colin Kamp turned up during his evening shift and asked if he would work in his place on Tuesday night.

'Not the dreaded Folk Club night?'

'It's not that bad. You have to check everyone or nearly everyone who comes in. Quite a few non-members arrive for the Folk, but it keeps you busy and it really passes the time.'

'I prefer to pass the time not being busy.'

Colin had seen an interesting film the night before. The modern age of extreme violence on the screen was enjoying some measure of critical acclaim and Colin had a passion for describing particular details in particular detail and on this occasion it was the scene depicting the massacre of the Cheyenne in *Soldier Blue*.

'You played a good game yesterday,' said Christopher, not intentionally trying to change the subject.

'Yeah, thanks. It was a good game but we were lucky. The Fliers pulled off some close calls and they're a good team. We had to fight for those three goals.'

'Three? Thomas was saying six.'

'When he talks about scores you've gotta divide his numbers by two. Still, rugby tomorrow, hey? and when you think about it Durham just can't lose. Just impossible.'

What was impossible was neither very consoling, especially after the gory contents of Colin's film.

'I wish I had your confidence.'

'Not confidence, Christopher, just fact – pure fact.'

It's becoming more of a fact that I'm gonna die, he thought. Imagining his death to be one of the sudden impact sort, he thought that that at least should take away the fear of pain. I should be rejoicing. My religion is based on being on the right side of death, hell being shaped like an oval ball and heaven free from exams. What is maths in the face of suddenly being pushed into the immortal?

But he was mortal and that meant suffering. First physics – there was no better way of making Monday morning more like Monday morning. Edmund had brought in his portable steam-engine. He had apparently been promising to do this for some time, and here it was, the size of a fat hamster. They used it to run a dynamo to light a tiny light bulb. It did its best, pushing itself in and out so fast that the fly-wheel demonstrated the stroboscopic illusion of reversing direction. The steam hissed, the body rattled, it threatened to blow a piston but no way would the bulb fully wake up.

'Just like my brother on Sunday morning,' said Christopher.

'The piston does slow down once the bulb's connected,' said John Warwick. 'Definite evidence of a current.'

'The bulb is obviously US,' said Edmund.

'And his little engine's getting shagged,' said Steve. 'Yet another failure.'

'How dare you. My steam engine's a great success. It's a symbol of everything we enjoy in the modern world.'

He took it away and during break in the prefects' room he set it up again and it spluttered and bounced, sounding as if stretching towards the wrong side of not blowing up. It was certainly intent on throwing itself off the table. It scared a few of the fascinated girls who wanted to know what it was and why it was so angry and so for a few moments, rarely to be repeated, Edmund found himself the centre of girl-based attention. But he was under no illusion that they fancied him more than it given its hamster-proportioned size.

Christopher thought about writing his will. He told Savina that she could have his Nelkon and Parker and his pencil case.

'But the book belongs to the school,' she said, 'and what would I want with it anyway. I already have a copy. As for your pencil case, I've seen better ones in dumps.'

'Don't I get any sympathy? I'm going to die this very afternoon.'

'God, Christopher, you'll do anything to get out of doing homework, but you won't escape your A levels that easily.'

She could be right, he thought. All the same, he bequeathed all his elephant-stamped belongings to Helen and Louding could have his records. Oddly enough Louding was not as worried as he had been last week.

'Seven-a-side's easy,' he said. 'More room to dodge the killers and you can stand around for a second or two and think about what to do with the ball.'

'Me, I'll just stand around for a few minutes and think about what I'll do *if* I get the ball.'

'When I get the ball I never think. I just run like hell. It's the only thing about rugby I know how to do. Seven-a-side's fast moving, but the game only last's ten or fifteen minutes.'

'Ten or fifteen minutes?' Christopher exclaimed.

'Well yes. How long did you think each game would last?'

Christopher didn't say. He only thought: maybe I have a chance after all.

More arrived in Happy Valley to see this contest than the many who had stood around Saturday's soccer final. There was the Durham banner on one side of the pitch: 'Durham Works Wonders', designed in the format of the two D's of the Double Diamond advert. The word 'Wonders' had caused controversy because Winchester had adopted it too to describe their side: 'The Winchester Wonders', and thereby presumed they had copyright because of alliteration. It was said that the two housemasters almost came to blows over this one issue. 'Canterbury Can Do It' faced 'The Excellence of Exeter', while York, somehow out on a limb in the corner, had nothing to say for itself. Instead, a large flag depicting a white rose, billowed in the rising breeze.

Durham faced Canterbury first and after a ten minute scrap won the game, 20 points to nil. Christopher couldn't believe it. Each time a member of his team touched the ball a try was scored, and when he himself placed the ball down over the line, to the vindicated cheers of 'Durham Works Wonders' way across the other side of the pitch he felt an exhilaration unique to his usual sporting inspired attitudes. The separation between Colin Kamp's confidence and established facts began to contract and Christopher thought to himself, not bad this seven-a-side lark. Any longer than ten minutes, he thought, and we'll be losing count, and I wonder if Thomas, playing for York, will be as willing to double the telling of our score. Durham defeated York who had defeated Exeter who, after Winchester walked over a worn out York, went on to be honourably disposed of by the well-rested Durham. Christopher thought that the league system was too complicated to be considered fair, could not understand why the school did not stick to a conventional tournament, but by then was not complaining. From what he was told if a team lost twice it was out. Exeter was the first to be faced with this threat and so during play they had resorted to a few tricks. Dave the Bury was Christopher's opposing hooker and the Bury would have won every scrum had it not been for the remarkable power behind the combined push of Colin Kamp and Wilfred George. Exeter's loose-head prop kept covering Christopher's eyes with his free hand just as the ball entered and both sight and speed were essential. Fortunately, the Bury's hooking was not as fast as the overall push. Exeter weaved around in all directions. Straight line passing to a direct score became essentially impossible.

'What do you mean, essentially impossible?' asked Christopher of Brian, who had studied the form, having reluctantly accepted a place that time in the reserves if guaranteed a role in the next game. 'Isn't it essential that we don't get crippled?'

York, knocked out by Canterbury, followed Exeter only to be followed by Canterbury whose main achievement had been to lose by 20 points to nil yet again, this time to Winchester.

Winchester had not lost a game. They had beaten York, knocked out Canterbury and now faced Durham, again well-rested. The word 'Wonder' was chanted clearly within the mess of combined slogans issuing from both sides of the pitch.

'This is where I get killed,' said Christopher, 'mashed up by the potential of what we're supposed to represent.'

'They're pretty big aren't they,' muttered Louding, 'ah but, we should be able to run circles around them.'

'That to me is essentially impossible.'

And then Bill Grey gathered his team and told them that essentially it was impossible for them to lose because of their combined skill. Winchester was just muscle. Christopher did not want to be corrected and so he said nothing, but he was under the impression that for rugby muscle was all that was needed, and they also needed Wilfred George, now quite willingly in the reserves for this game, and not him. His dispensable qualities as a hooker must surely have been noted by now. The starting whistle blew and if Christopher was ever to be asked to describe the following fifteen minutes he could well have related it to everything which combined him to elephants. The ball was probably the safest object on the pitch. Each minute was a ferocious battle before each team scored, and each team scored again. Their ten minutes was up but one team had to score more than the other and so they played on for the golden try. Scrum-down, this time Colin and Bill Grey gave adequate support to Christopher's advantage, and Oliver passed the ball to Steve who passed it back just prior to being made part of the pitch. Oliver weaved around the confused scrum, passed the ball to Brian who then demonstrated some surprising speed, so much in need of the honour of the winning try before being forced by opponents to allow Louding to take over. Louding was the hero although he had hardly worked for the final try, having scored three seconds after handling the ball. He became the call of victory under all but one of the banners. Brian was probably not best pleased at this detail in the outcome. Yes, indeed, his team had won but he could hardly count on his name being chanted had he scored. But he hadn't scored and Louding had, but not without his help, and the combination of glory was a combination his pride was unwilling to unravel.

Christopher fell flat on his back. It was over. He had survived and Durham had won. Furthermore he had fun. The impossible along with the inevitable. He did not kiss the ground or praise the Lord. He was a bit sore around the ankles and when he stopped to think about it, such as now upon his back, he was *very* sore around the ankles. In fact it was as much an effort to stand up as it had been to earn the privilege of lying thus. Here was me thinking I'd be carried off by stretcher and I'm beginning to think I should be carried off by stretcher.

>Dear Christopher,
>
>Sorry it has taken me so long to write but I have been busy lately. I don't know if I told you of my acquisition – a stereo record player. It only set me back £40 and it has separate speakers – the lot. Likewise is my record collection growing or is my record collection growing! Deep Purple have a new record out – but I haven't found it yet.
>
>I went to Sunny Scunny (Scunthorpe) with my fiancé – Oh, I forgot I am engaged. Don't tell anyone. We are getting married in August next year (1973).
>
>I've got a great Sci-fi collection now. I have got the other two to *Makers of the Universe* – the one you read. Perhaps you'd like me to send them to you?
>
>How is everyone out there? How are you're A levels going? Or have they gone? Knowing you, you're still there, struggling.
>
>Don't go near my sisters because I sent them a reggae record (how sickening).
>
>Well, must close now.
>Write soon.
>Henry.

A more detailed letter than usual from Henry, his news, leaping from one possession to another, spread further as if attempting to thin out without the camouflage of previous information, the threat (as Henry would normally have put it) of impending marriage. The brevity of the news fueled many questions surrounding what now could only be regarded as astounding: Henry Dazel to be married! There is in existence a girl willing to put up with his self-raising wit for the rest of her or his life, and become a chosen example of the extent to which women were willing to be tolerant. Henry's level of tolerance had to have some account as he had always regarded marriage as being man's first and final big mistake. Christopher did not think for one moment that he was doing this to demonstrate his theory. Henry would never feasibly pass as the guinea pig in life's capable traumas, but it was strange that so short a time should elapse between his leaving home to this: the edge of his sharp scorn now blunted by enchantment. Maybe, Christopher thought, it's an excuse.

He read the letter at work. It was all he had time to do. All day he had time to read a letter volumes longer but post never arrived until late afternoon, and it was not until late afternoon that he remembered that Tuesday would not be totally deprived of effort. He had spent the morning in bed, having given himself the day off school so as to appease a now very painful ankle. His mother was also in bed. She was actually ill, he was injured (a bit) and Julie, off school to look after them both, was ironing most of the time, indulging in a spot of midday cooking and listening to one of Christopher's reel-to-reel tapes. Occasionally sharing his taste in music, especially since the discovery of Groundhogs *Split*, was a concession that Julie offered to the notion of common ground. He did a bit of doodling with physics in the afternoon, but was reasonably settled into the torpor of his ailment when he suddenly remembered, almost as he received Henry's letter from his father, the work expected from him in place of Colin at the Families Club.

Tuesday night, Folk Club night, the hardest night of the week. The doorman, usually Colin, had to check the membership whether to the Folk Club strolling in by his desk on one side of the bar or simply to the bar on the other, unless such members were known by sight. Those Christopher knew consisted of the loyal few who ventured in for a drink only when the Club was quiet. It worried him to think that he almost forgot that he was on duty. All four doormen understood the chances of there being one night when no one would turn up due to a complicated mess they were making of their swapping system. Christopher was determined that he wouldn't be the first, and now he just remembered the one night in which his absence would have caused a disaster. But up he turned, limped into his chair and then actually earned his piastres through an evening of being a doorman rather than just a man (or boy) sitting beside a door. He had to fill out tickets for many *bona fide* guests, or 'bonny fiddles', a term of endurance rather than endearment coined by Thomas. There were subscriptions, a couple of renewals of membership, and the telephone rang more than a reasonable number of times. Who are these creatures who folk-club their Tuesday evenings and leave behind so many messages needing to be relayed? He hated the phone. To answer it at all was for him an ordeal, and the calls were usually for anyone, anywhere, whether during a song, a round or an entrance. He became a sudden slave to tolerance.

A man entered with a tall blond woman by his side, and he and blond strode past Christopher, grunting at him when asked to see his membership card. So Christopher left his busy post and walked through to the bar to confront him. He had the weight of bureaucracy on his side and he was intent on using it, and indulging in this pleasure of the official demand he was reminded of the MP and his torch,

'Listen, I want to see your card,' he said as the man walked from the bar with a couple of drinks.

'And you listen: I'll knuckle you if you don't get lost.'

'And I'll report you to the manager and the treasurer and the officer in charge who are all sitting over there and they'll have you and your girlfriend out.'

The mention of there being an officer in charge was a powerful argument. Now the entire weight of the RAF was on Christopher's side although the said officer was nowhere to be seen, very rarely did he actually enter the Club. The man took out his card. It was not an easy task while carrying two drinks but he managed it and it was valid with many months in his favour.

'Every week I get asked for my bloody card. You think I'd be recognized by now.'

But Christopher pretended not to listen, thinking as well that by now the usual doorman would have been recognized by the man. He wondered if Colin was given this similar hassle or was Colin's size a recommended part of the job, especially on a Tuesday night. He stared across at the girl. She was sitting patiently isolated among the men.

'It's a shilling entrance for the girl unless she's your wife.'

'You little…' But the man shook his head slowly, the drinks ready to boil in his hand, and this time he had to put them down in order to take from a tight pocket a 50 mil piece.

And Christopher smiled.

'Always glad to be of service.'

They went their separate ways, both thinking: prat!

There was nobody at the desk when he returned. The hall was full and the bar was packed, but his little area was at last a haven of comparative peace. He remembered the letter, took it from his pocket and opened it up. It was of course not easy to believe that Henry was actually going to get married. Not that nobody would want him: it was just him defying the temporary in order to sort out the permanent. Maybe it's an excuse, he thought, just like that blond. The comparison was hard to justify as the man had used his fancy friend as decoration for the arrogant stride past Christopher's desk. But it was seeing her sit there by herself among the men which made him think of Henry's decision as an excuse. He was pleased for him. It was, with or without tradition, good news. He imagined Henry's sisters being over the moon, his mother perhaps a little concerned, his father glad it would be a son and not a daughter about to be married off. The news would have been no great surprise. Mr and Mrs Dazel both thought that Henry was very level-headed, intelligent, mature, but inclined towards the unpredictable. Christopher thought that Henry could not admit to a loneliness most of his friends endured, even if couched as classified news. 'I am engaged. Don't tell anyone.' And so Christopher, always honoured by secrets, especially one so devastating to Henry's previous philosophy, decided to go right ahead and tell Louding.

Louding read the letter.
 'What do you think?'
 'It says here not the tell anyone.'
 'Well that obviously means tell Louding.'
 'Doesn't it make you jealous?'
 'Jealous that he's engaged?' He was about to meet what he considered an absurd point with a definite no, but instead Christopher found himself muttering, 'You know, I don't know.'
 'I wasn't referring to him being engaged, but that he's got a new stereo and by now he's probably bought the new Deep Purple album.'
 'Oh, that goes without saying. Steaming with envy. Only reason why he writes to me. He seemed to add his fiancée onto a list of recent things he's got. Join the RAF and you too can suddenly get engaged. It seems like such an excuse.'
 'Excuse for what?'
 'I don't know. When he told me last year that he was joining the RAF I had the same feeling.'
 Louding looked at the letter again.
 'Funny he should go to Scunny. I've got relatives in Scunthorpe.'
 'Have you?'
 'So has she.'
 'Who?'
 'His fiancée. They went to Scunthorpe to meet her parents.'
 'How do you know all this?'
 'I can read between the lines.'
 'That's very clever of you. Of course. Why else would they go to Scunthorpe.'
 And Christopher said this without a trace of irony.
 'Actually I received a letter from him as well. He went into slightly more detail. He wrote something like: "I've just met my future in-laws. Relief to know the mother is very friendly and quiet – hardly says a word unless it was asking me if I wanted more cake. The father [get this] speaks fluent Esperanto. I don't so we had to speak English although I used a bit of my

Cypriot Greek which he didn't understand. [I think he wrote 'hee hee' after that bit of one-upmanship.] They both live in a terraced house in Scunthorpe.'"

'He wrote all that? Compared to what I usually receive that was microscopic detail.'

The prefects' room was starting to fill up with prefects. It was getting close to break. William Meald entered, sat down beside them, gave them each a cream bun and asked them if they had seen this new film making the rounds of the Astra circuit.

'It's incredibly violent. A whole Indian reservation is massacred in full gory detail.'

'We were just talking about detail. You could say I've more or less seen it. Colin Kamp told me the entire story, leaving out the boring bits.'

'Tell us about the boring bits,' asked Louding. 'Why is it called *Soldier Blue*?'

'I think it's because it's a love story,' said William, having to question any sense of poetry reflected in what was blown out of proportion when he thought of what might have happened, not having seen the film himself, and annoyed that he hadn't asked those he knew, who had, that very question.

'Good enough title,' said Christopher. 'Were the lovers killed?'

'No, or wait a minute, were they?'

'They didn't die together in what Gavin Peters would have us believe is perfect love. Speaking of which, Louding, any news on Stella?'

'Stella is Christopher's perfect love,' Louding explained to William.

'Who's Stella?'

'She is not,' said Christopher, annoyed about having to be defensive instead of indulging the need to shape a fascinating form of denial. 'I'm just interested in getting to know her better.'

'Who's Stella?'

'Well I'm afraid the news is not good,' said Louding. 'She won't be able to make it this Saturday.'

Christopher took a bite out of his cream bun. It had that flavour of resigned acceptance which went with a disappointing but expected fact.

'You see, *mon ami*,' continued Louding, 'it's not particularly because of her Greek boyfriend, but she's been invited to a wedding with him and she's obliged to attend – besides which she really wants to as well.'

'Come on you two, who's Stella?'

'So when did you meet her?' asked Christopher.

'I didn't meet her. Yesterday, here, in this very room, almost at this very table and at this precise moment in time, I asked Martin to ask her if she would be interested in going out for a meal with myself and you and Helen. I invited Martin along too – him and Zoe Holland – and then he told me about the wedding. Not that he'll be going. He won't be going with us either. He's going to the football dance.'

'What football dance?'

'Akrotiri Youth Klub are hosting this year's football dance, and there'll be the presentation of the cup to the Magpies plus shields for the Fliers of which Martin is one.'

'I see,' said Christopher. 'Another function remarkably well advertised.'

'To be attended by representatives of youth teams all over the island, including some from King Dicks. You just don't keep yourself in the know.'

'Did you know about it?'

'Possibly. Football's not really my thing and so I wasn't that interested, but I might be now though. Apparently there's going to be a beauty contest. Zoe Holland is the only contestant I know of so far. She's going as Miss BG Fliers.'

'She should win. She's very pretty.'

'I should think they'll all be very pretty.'

'I rather be with this Stella than all the pretty girls. And Helen – how can I say that Helen isn't pretty? Red mac and green dress and all, plus Easter Eggs, but yes, certainly not beauty contest pretty. Well, shall we go to this dance?'

Louding shrugged, not inclined to being so decisive this early in the week.

'What do you think, William?'

'Who's Stella?'

Christopher's mother was still ill and his father, who had stayed off work a couple of days, managed to take Julie's place as mother and allow her to go to school. Barry Island called around when Christopher had returned from school, as he had done so a few times prior to Angela's arrival, not because he was excited but there was something of a preparation in his pre-Angela visits. On each occasion James Panhandle kept his wife company in the bedroom and practiced his guitar. What a dedicated guitarist Barry must think dad is, thought Christopher. Barry beat him at chess and later on Christopher was defeated by physics. But physics and chess were no great concern. All were expecting Angela to arrive on Wednesday evening when they received news from sources totally unknown to Christopher that her plane was due in to Nicosia midday Thursday.

'Why not here? Akrotiri's an airport.'

'Such are the powers at be,' said Barry as he left.

Such powers at be cause a lot of unnecessary effort, thought Christopher. Totally ridiculous that his father would have to hire a car to go to Nicosia, a method of fetching the young lady which was slightly more expensive but much more convenient than travelling by bus.

Another source of a lot of unnecessary effort wanted to see him the next morning.

'Mrs Burlington wants to see you, Panhandle,' said Eric.

'See me?'

'That's what she told me to tell you.'

'Just me and nobody else?'

'She didn't give any other names.'

'Not even Louding, here.'

'Go on, get going. Also there's a Durham outside assembly. That should cheer you up.'

What have I done wrong this time? Maybe I've done something right. More than likely it's about something I haven't done.

It was the latter and she wanted a reasonable excuse, nothing new. He was tempted to say that a good friend of his was getting married next year. She was referring to the RC assemblies and his non-attendance. His plea of total absence from school would not work. Thursday did not allow Tuesday to be yesterday.

'Every Wednesday morning in the private study room beside the library, and Rebecca and Peter have always attended and so from that it's easy to assume that both you and Julie are Catholics.'

Keeping tabs on the siblings was quite an achievement and Christopher was tempted to compliment her on her powers of observation.

'Yes,' he said. 'I do my best. I haven't lapsed – yet.'

'You say that as if you're thinking of doing so.'

They both started walking across the yard towards the Durham outside assembly. He put his hands behind his back to make his private participation in what she had to say something of philosophical importance. The reprimand took on the appearance of a five minute walking conference.

'Christopher, your religion is the backbone of your life. Every effort to strengthen your faith will strengthen your character. Try not to forget that, and tell that…' she paused in order to choose an adequate adjective but failed, '…sister of yours that I want to see both you and her at the next assembly.'

'But you see, ma'am, it's Father Allsort…'

She looked at him, her piercing eyes outlining the symmetry of her finely drawn nose off-setting the sternness of her otherwise annoyingly handsome face.

They had stopped walking.

'Well, what about him?'

'Nothing personal, of course,' said Christopher who then proceeded to contradict himself. 'He's so boring. He makes Wednesday morning Catholic assemblies tedious.'

'I'm caught between telling you off for being disrespectful and acknowledging your honesty. Yes, perhaps Father Allsort does fail to exude a *joie de vie* one expects from the Catholic faith. Nevertheless he's inspiring enough and he's all we've got at present. However, I should think by now, Christopher, that it is up to you to make interesting those aspects of your life you cannot or rather should not avoid.'

Yes, by avoiding them, he thought.

'Progress is fashioned by such attitudes,' said Mrs Burlington with her glorious eyes pointing to heaven. She looked at him and instantly read his thoughts. 'We're certainly not here to grow stale, I know, but avoiding this does not mean literally avoiding everything that happens to bore you. If truth be known, the boredom comes from you, no-one else. You're very fortunate to have the luxury of boredom and doubly fortunate to having been born to the true faith. Many Catholics fail to understand that it is the core of Christianity.'

'Yes, ma'am,' he muttered, and he thought: has anyone ever told you you have the most beautiful eyes that gleam in the sun?

'There are a lot of house-point certificates to be handed out at this assembly, and I may as well tell you that you have not won one. Are you relieved? When was the last time you actually posted a house-point? It's beneath fifth and sixth form contempt which is a very silly attitude. Supporting the house is remarkably good training for life. Life out there has many principles which need supporting, and without principles you have nothing and you are nothing.'

'Yes, ma'am.'

Twenty house-point certificates were awarded. This meant that since the last outside assembly, notwithstanding those previously accumulated but added to the score, 200 house-points had been posted, and not one, so it seemed, by a sixth former. There were a few who thought that house-points were being posted in their names, a fraudulent infiltration of the system which had Brian, in particular, conscious of a unique fear. He did not regard his participation in almost everything the school did outside the mundane tasks of lessons and home-work as outrageous, but he knew of a few who did. For him, as with others, death on the spot was optionally more attractive than walking up to where Tony Sealhard, the housemaster, stood ready to shake his hand and offer him as an award a remarkably bland looking sheet of paper. House-points were usually awarded for such acts often regarded as being too agreeable with the teachers, and to be too agreeable with this housemaster, bearded, proud, enthusiastic and assembly-loving, injected within Brian something of the care he was not used to employing as part of his anxious road to future fame and fortune.

Physics was marginally more entertaining. The class was shown a couple of school films: one about the diode and triode valves, another about the cathode ray tube. They used one of the few video recorder/playback systems belonging to St John's and inconveniently housed in the biology department, thus interrupting a class of fifth form biologists who had to chop up their gooey menagerie elsewhere. The inside of a television consisted of a spot travelling at such an incredible speed that its after-image formed the picture. Christopher refused to believe this. He was willing to believe in the omnipotence of God but this was far too much work for one little spot. Why not employ thousands staying still?

He managed to stay awake and also kept his eyes open during civics which discussed, with the use of cartoon slides, the importance of a good career; the general advice being that as there are usually very few vacancies for world leaders or managing directors one had to make do with a job further down the ladder. The first few pictures compared the illusive freedom of the tramp to the solid security of the businessman. While the tramp had flowers and fields, heat and cold, and a spot of hunger, the businessman was in his castle made of affordable insurance, loving family, up-to-date technology and efficient transport.

'I'm not asking you to choose either,' said the careers master who was also Mr Sutherland, a language teacher, fluent in most of the European tongues including Cypriot Greek. 'It's just that happiness is security and security is freedom. Correct?'

There were no comments but a piece of paper was passed from one person to the other until it was destroyed at the end of the second row by Patrick Eve. On it had been written: 'Career is what you do when you go out of control.'

During private study, trapped by yet another physics problem with Helen sitting beside him and sowing a pocket to a dress she was repairing for a friend, it occurred to him that now was the chance to obtain from his not unreasonably pretty girlfriend a reasonably intelligent answer to any question he cared to ask, while with her tongue slightly adrift from her lips she attempted to thread the needle.

'What do you think freedom is, Helen?'

'Uhuh?' she asked.

'You know, at civics, with Sutherland going on about the security of a good career being the road to freedom and all that – what do you think?'

'Well, he's right, isn't he? He has to be because a good job gets you money and you don't hate doing it because it's good, and with the money you can get on and do other things you don't hate.'

So, he thought, freedom is the simple but all-enveloping disposal of hatred.

'Helen, you're a genius.'

'It's obvious. If you don't like doing something then you shouldn't do it and then that's freedom. Do what you want to do and don't do what you don't want to do. Oh hell, this thing is so awkward.'

She pulled at her sowing and began to mutter curses upon her craft.

'I don't particularly like studying for physics A level. Maybe I should stop doing it.'

'Yes you do.' She looked at him. It spared her eyes to study his face rather than the thread and material below.

'No I don't. I hate physics. I really do.'

'But you can't hate physics, Christopher.'
'Why not?'
'I don't know. It's too late.'
But she believed him and she was suddenly very concerned.
He was beginning to believe it himself.
'It's just one problem after the next. The experiments are boring, and the only field I'm really interested in, Einstein's theory of general relativity, doesn't really make sense. Apart from which I believe that physics will eventually destroy the world.'
'No it won't,' she said, and then realising that she was hardly qualified to defend the subject, she reverted to her earlier argument. 'You can't hate physics, Christopher. How can you hate it and do an A level in it as well?'
'I haven't done the A level yet. All I seem to be doing is struggling and what good will it do me if I do pass? I'm losing faith. Mrs Burlington told me this morning that my faith is the backbone of my life. My physics in that case has become spineless.'
'Oh Christopher, I'm so sorry for you.'
He looked at her. She had abandoned her sowing. She really was undergoing some form of compassion for his plight.
'You shouldn't be. I really don't care.'
'But you should care. Why don't you care? You could be ruining your whole life.'
'Helen, if my life depends on success at physics then I prefer to see it ruined.'
'Gosh, Christopher, that's terrible.'
'Don't worry about it, Helen. I don't mind.'
'But you should mind. A levels are important.'
'But you're not doing any.'
'I don't need to. I'm going to become a nurse.'
'I don't need to either. I'm going to become free.'

It was five pm. The Panhandle household had been steeped in quiet anticipation, and now suddenly it was full of the exuberant arrival of Angela. She was followed by her father heaving in two suitcases packed with clothes and books. Her excitement at being in Cyprus for the second time was equalled by their excitement at seeing her, so white, so healthy, so full of London, the alert, naïve but sophisticated experiences of a city girl abroad to see her family.
Angela was more the elderly relative, the favourite eccentric aunt, than the sister two years ahead of Christopher and three years beyond Julie and very much the adult to her younger siblings, although her bright simplicity underlined by a less than conventional understanding of others gave her a very youthful appearance – apart from which she was only slightly larger than Rebecca. She always wore long and loose clothes. Their throw-together

appearance was the first to prevent any compact image of Angela being merely a fashionable girl, the second being her impartial practice of listening to what others had to say before chancing a delightful opinion often independent of conditions topically concerned with youth and struggle. But she was very much part of the youth of her day and she was struggling, with what James Panhandle thought of as unnecessary problems. She introduced them all to the need for identity. The phrase: 'I have to identify with what I'm doing', baffled her parents only slightly less than when asserting the individual part of her role: 'As a woman I need a definite identity.'

Christopher's love and fascination for her was totally different from the affection he sometimes felt obliged to offer his other sisters. He loved her flexible freedom, and in his own way, like just now relating to the fact that the entire family was sitting around the table having dinner, he thought of her ability to mix anywhere as being similar to best butter, spreading with even flavour over all edible surfaces, smoothing away all the complexities contaminating the contingent interests of enchantment. While for him it was difficult to judge sisters from the point of view of what other boys probably thought, but he was certain that although she was not as pretty as Julie she was definitely more attractive, and apart from his mother, she was the only member of the family who could develop the even tan demanded from the sun, adding thus a natural attribute to her gift for travelling. She can mix anywhere, thought Christopher, and still remain Angela.

His father worried about her a lot. Patricia remarked quite often about how selflessly happy she always seemed to be (which was the cause of most of James' worries). Julie wanted to see her new clothes (if anything different she happened to bring could be regarded as new rather than just original) and talk about what was happening in London, and who she may have seen and where she may have gone. Rebecca wanted to show her some poems she had written and some drawings she had drawn, and see for herself the photographic art Angela had mentioned in her last letter as being a turning point in her life. Jennifer were merely too excited about the difference she made to the house to be resolute in specifics that Angela could offer, both looking upon her as a queen from some far-away land. Peter was the least affected by the arrival because he had failed before to impress her with his accomplished record as one of Akrotiri's leading young anglers. She considered angling an inexplicable blood sport and said so, but nevertheless had bought him a book on sharks and whales as a tangential offer of her affection for a growing lad who had a lot to learn. Her gifts consisted mainly of food, flowers and cosmetics: the flowers pressed and part of printed patterns, the food generally sweet but, she assured, nutritious, and the smellies of a quality free from the trappings of animal testing. Still smells the same to me, thought Christopher, as he took a whiff of the after-shave she presented to him in a fancy bottle. She ruled the talking as they all sat and ate and listened. She said that the flavour of food 'out here is so distinct.'

She loved the chirping of the crickets and there was something wonderful about the early nights being so warm. She then mentioned her recent 'turning point' which was to lead in time to a course in photography. The word 'course' was the only hint within recent events in her life which her father considered promising.

'So, you've given up dress and design altogether?' he asked, thinking her only capable of handling one subject at a time.

'No, of course not, dad, but fashion is very frustrating, whereas photography could open out much more for me as an artist.'

'Oh, it's an artist now you want to be?'

'Angela's always been an artist,' said Christopher.

'You don't have to paint pictures to be an artist.'

'Yes, that must be true,' said James, laughing. 'You don't even have to be *able* to paint pictures judging from modern art nowadays.'

'Well, yes,' said Angela either refusing to take the bait or immune to irony. 'You can actually do anything nowadays.' Her gentle tone suggested that although she understood where her father was coming from she was also somewhat apologetic about her present mood of being prepared to do anything. 'Even what you eat and what you leave can be considered as art.'

'And when it's not considered art it is just food left on a plate?'

'When it's not meant to represent anything or a range of particular human feelings. But don't worry. I don't have the aptitude for that particular type of sculpture. Photography is something I feel is special. I've a good friend who uses the camera for artistic expression, and he actually thinks that I'm gifted enough to do something in that line. Look, I'll show you.' She pulled from one of her canvas carrier bags a folder containing some of her recent work: black and white shots of buckets, railings, the sea and a white-cloaked figure sitting on a chair. To her father they all meant as much as they showed: buckets, railings, the sea and a white-cloaked figure sitting in a chair. 'What do you think of them, Christopher?'

'They're very clear,' he said slowly. 'There's something very definite about them, especially the buckets.'

Rebecca wanted to have a good look at them, but she went to answer the front door because there had definitely been a knock. She returned and sat down and started to look at the pictures and mentioned quite nonchalantly that the boy who lived next door was at the front door for Christopher.

'Who? Colin or Oliver?'

'No, next door on the other side. I don't know his name.'

Christopher, convinced she must have been mistaken, went out to investigate and, true enough, it was the boy from next door on the other side: Russell Keen. Is this an honour, he thought, or a warning?

It was in fact a request.

'Hi, Christopher?'

'Well, hello Russell. You coming in?'

Russell was actually quite nervous. He felt much better standing outside as to enter would go too far beyond the rule of rarely calling around anywhere, accustomed as he was to friends calling around to see him.

'Na, jist here to ask ye somin'. Won't be long. Yer no going to the fitba dance this Saturday neet, are ye?'

'At the Youth Klub? I only just got to know there is one. Julie never tells me anything and not being a member I don't keep myself informed. So this dance is more or less news to me.'

'Which means yer no going?'

'Why do you ask?'

'Well ye ken, I gotta be there 'cause they're handin' oot the awards to the Magpies, but I need someone to de me wai'in' job at the Families Club.'

This was also news to Christopher. Never having been to the Families' Club on a Saturday night, he had no idea that it employed waiters as well as doormen. Least of all did he expect Russell to have such a job, but now it was easy to guess what he was after.

'You want me to do your job for you, is that it?'

'Aye, if it's nay a problem.'

But the meal out in Limassol is planned for Saturday, thought Christopher, but there again I could do with the money.

'Won't there be other waiters? Is it necessary that someone should turn up in your place?'

'Only me, Ben Stevenson and Oliver de the job Saturday neets an' we all ha't' turn up at the dance. Oliver's got his brother to de his job.'

Christopher wasn't sure who Ben Stevenson was but there was a more imposing question regarding Oliver's brother.

'You mean, Colin? But he's in the Magpies too.'

'Yeah, but he dinna care.'

'And who's doing his doorman's job?'

At this precise moment Colin arrived as if to answer that very question. He was carrying a bullworker, having just borrowed it from Thomas, and on passing Christopher's place to return home and try it out, and seeing him and Russell standing at the Panhandles' door, he decided to join them and ask Christopher if he would care to do his doorman's job on Saturday.

'Te late man. I got here first,' said Russell. 'He'll be daying ma job. Berrer money wai'in' than bein' a fooken doorman.'

'Well actually,' said Christopher, more inclined now to disoblige both than just one, 'I may be in Limassol.'

'Wot, this Saturday?'

'It's all been arranged.'

Had it been arranged? he thought. But his mind was made up. I really don't want to work this Saturday night.

'There must be others you can ask.'

All three quickly exhausted a short list of names. If Bob and Oliver could get replacements then two waiters could cope, but only one of the four doormen could do the doorman's job and so Colin had to accept a usual clash of events which would make things difficult for Oliver and...

'But Thomas isn't in the Magpies?' said Christopher. 'At least he said he wasn't'

'He's taking Nancy Lynson to the dance,' explained Colin as if to add: 'Who wouldn't?'

'And so why haven't you got similar arrangements with her sister, Angela?'

'Wish I had but that short romance fizzled out.'

'You weren't given the bronze kiss, were you?'

Colin, confused by this question, said nothing.

'Hey,' said Russell, delighted. 'He got chucked. Welcome to the fookin' club.'

Angela's probably a serial 'bronze kisser', thought Christopher.

Colin decided to ignore Russell's comment, not in the mood at present to explore Russell's dalliance in this area, but acknowledged by his stance that there was certainly no dishonour in being a member of the Angela Lynson ex-boyfriend club.

'Anyway, I need the money,' he said emphatically.

'So that's ye fooked, and Oliver too,' said Russell, analyzing the problem, 'Ben Stevenson can't de it on his ain, an' I still ain't anybidy ta de ma job. Christ, ye'd think they be able to de without their bleedin' wai'ers for once. Shit, I'll ge an ask Paul Begman. Whether Bob and Oliver get other people is their problem. Fookem.'

'Spoken like a true friend,' said Colin and he turned to Christopher and gave him a get-ready-for-more-news look. 'I've just come from Thomas's place,' he began, brandishing the bull-worker as evidence, 'and he says he doesn't want to do the Families Club shift tonight.'

'What? He has to. He said he would because we swapped.'

'Well, that's what he told me. Something to do with Nancy and maybe he's trying to avoid Pamela.'

'God almighty. That's his bloody problem.'

'Aye, reet on, Christopher,' said Russell.

'Don't worry,' said Colin. 'He said he'd turn up just to see if you'd be there, so just don't be there and you won't have to work tonight.'

'Too right I won't be there. I'm never at that place unless I'm working or I go to one of the Sunday night dances or something.'

'Wot, ye go t' them woosey dances?'

'Yeah. Occasionally. So does Colin and others...'

'Anyway, reet on, I say. Fookem.'

One way of concluding matters as they stood was to accept Colin's bull-worker challenge. The power-meter on it was graded from ten to a hundred and Colin's record for pushing the machine in while holding it out in front of his chest was seventy-five. Christopher could only manage fifty which, they all agreed, was adequate for his size. He was always willing to acknowledge Colin's superior strength and to this he added the excuse of having just eaten.

'Yeah, you've gotta choose the right time, but after a workout on this thing, so they say – I've not tried it properly before – you feel as strong as an ox. Come on, Russell. Have a go.'

'I thought ye *were* as strong as an ox, Colin?' said Russell, taking the bullworker from Christopher.

'Okay then, powerful enough to pull out trees by their roots.'

'Better not try that out on the few trees we have around here,' said Christopher. 'Protected species.'

'Ha,' said Russell, 'sa are the lassies under sixteen but they still get fooked.'

And, unable to refuse a challenge, he remained for the time it took him to shove the bullworker to a mark of ninety before handing it back to Colin and walking away.

'What did he say just then?' asked Colin.

'Something about young ladies being pulled out of the ground by their roots. Means something different in Scotland. I've lived there. I know.' And both he and Colin looked at the power-meter together. 'Hey, Colin, I thought you were the strongest guy around here.'

'Proves nothing,' said Colin, and sliding away the evidence he walked off.

Christopher wondered now if he had made the right decision about Saturday, keeping to tenuous plans, losing out on the chance of making some much needed cash. True, all he would have gained by swapping a night with Colin would have been the money saved by not going to Limassol, whereas on accepting the job as a waiter he would have saved and gained extra cash. Russell was giving him an evening's work and not merely swapping it for one he could supply, but now he could do neither and as Limassol was re-formed into a final decision, he was determined to have something worked out with Louding. Louding would, no doubt, call him a fool if he got to know about what he had turned down to be with him, but of course there was Helen to consider, just like Thomas giving time to Nancy.

Thomas, he thought: that sod better turn up at the Club tonight.

Back at the table there was an active sharpening of opposing opinions. James and daughter were arguing about the ethics and practicalities of squatting in London and living in a cave in Crete. Angela had friends who did and were doing both, and they seemed to prosper in terms of what was now considered by her age group as the Good Life. Barry eventually called around and father and daughter went their separate ways for the evening.

Christopher stayed indoors. He forgot that he was supposed to hate physics. He was so determined to stay away from the Families' Club that he fell upon the best excuse available, and he studied physics and worked on physics problems right through the evening. He was invigorated by the soothing effect this struggle had upon a slight and out-of-focus but nagging desire to walk purposely to the Club, creep up to the entrance and just to check to see if the doorman's desk was in fact occupied. He pictured Mrs Burlington telling him that one's duty was the blood coursing through the veins of one's life. But on any night the desk could be empty. What was it to him? He had done his work for the week. What was it to him compared to this physics which on any night he was more than likely to forego? So he stayed where he was and he continued studying and struggling and feeling good and determined and justified.

He was still in a studying and feeling justified mood when he stepped on the school bus the next morning. He breezed on in front of Oliver who swung himself along the aisle by supporting himself upon the corresponding edges of the seats until he eventually claimed his own near the back. It was a cloudy day and Oliver suggested that they perform a rain-dance there and then. He was one for getting cheesed off with all the chronically sunny weather. However, on a seemingly more cheerful note, he stared at Christopher and then at Julie, both sitting together in the centre of the back seat, Linda and Russell Keen to the right of Julie and Dot and Doris Orange to the left of Christopher – all as it should be. Oliver was wondering how and to whom he should break the news. The news was primarily for Christopher but Julie had been known to take an unusual interest in his misfortunes. But whether to one or the other, they were both going to hear what he had to say, and it was to Christopher he stared at when he spoke.

'Nobody turned up to do the doorman's job last night.'

'What? You're kidding!'

Oliver then stared at Julie who had to look at Russell because he started laughing.

'Weel, I did warn ya,' he said.

'No you didn't. You said "fookem".'

'What's this about?' said Julie who was not accustomed to being out of the loop especially if it concerned Keen-based expletives.

'Yeah?' asked Linda, agreeing with Julie and looking at her brother.

Dot and Doris said nothing but listened in, fascinated.

Oliver called Colin over from the middle of the bus and when the situation was explained to him – Christopher being surprised that he didn't already know – he too laughed and repeated word for word Russell's reaction.

'Well, I did warn you.'

'No you didn't,' said Christopher. 'You told me Thomas didn't want to turn up but you also said he'd turn up to check if I was there.'

'But he didn't,' said Oliver, delighted at the contrasting motives cancelled out any real exoneration. 'And you didn't, but I did, although not to do the job. I just happened to be there with Francis and we took it on together, which of course means…'

'It means that Thomas owes you a night's pay,' said Christopher.

'I don't care who it is that owes me so long as me and Francis get paid. But it was your shift.'

However, it was mere seconds before the jury at the back, including Russell decided upon Thomas's guilt. Julie pronounced that it was definitely fair – Thomas had to pay.

Thomas, however, did not think so. He discussed the matter with Scott and the two Kamps during the first break at school and then the four lads entered the prefects' room to confront Christopher who was sharing a guitar with Louding. While Louding plucked the strings Christopher pressed a few familiar chords, mainly D, G and A, and between many mistakes and an odd acceptable 'I woke up this morning' tune they talked about Saturday night. They looked at the four who semi-circled them, and the smile Louding offered was all he could at first contribute to the confusing debate about who was or had actually been in the wrong. To Christopher it was an open and shut case: Thomas should have been there having agreed to the swap; but to Thomas, confusion was necessary until his own method of persuasion almost had them thinking that Oliver had been in the wrong for actually being in the Club at the time.

'It's my old man,' he explained. 'He can be a sod at times, and he got this idea that I was going out more nights than is good for me. I've got to get to see Nancy, haven't I? But you know, once he gets an idea into his head – and he forbid me, out right, to go out last night.'

'Even though it was necessary for you to be there.'

'Yeah, but I thought Scott was going to turn up because he owed you a night too, but I wasn't sure.'

'Like hell you thought that,' said Scott.

'Thomas,' said Christopher, 'Scott worked instead of me on Wednesday.'

'No he didn't,' said Colin. 'I did. You worked for me on Tuesday, remember.'

'Yeah, but Scott said he worked on Wednesday, didn't you?'

'I know,' admitted Scott, 'but then I asked Colin to do it because it didn't suit me to work Wednesday. I thought I'd work in place of Colin this Saturday.'

'But Colin, you told me you couldn't get anyone to work Saturday. I mean, you were wanting me to work Saturday.'

'Ah well, that's because it no longer suits him to work Saturday,' said Thomas. 'Starlings have to be at this dance as well as Magpies, and we need to form a foursome or else, poor lad here, being lovesick, can't get off with the girl he's after.'

'Don't bring girls into this,' said Colin. 'Confusing enough as it is.'

'Maybe so, but it ain't my fault nobody turned up yesterday but noggins here.'

'I don't care whose fault it is,' said Oliver, 'just so long as I get paid.'

'Listen you,' said Thomas to Oliver. '*Spiskay ffokay.* You'll get your money.'

But Oliver had to stay because he shared with Louding an outsider's interest and amusement in the confusion.

'You see,' said Thomas. 'I thought Scott would turn up last night.'

'Like hell you did,' said Scott. 'Why should I turn up?'

'Because, pillock, I told you to tell him that I couldn't make it and you told me that you also owed him a night.'

'But it was Colin who told me you might not make it,' said Christopher.

'Ah yeah, well you see, that's because Scott told me,' explained Colin, 'when he asked me to work for him on Wednesday, or for you rather, if you know what I mean. Then Thomas told me again yesterday.'

'I have to admit,' said Scott, 'I did forget to tell you. Good job Colin did.'

'No it wasn't,' said Thomas. 'You still didn't turn up.'

'I wasn't gonna turn up. I never had any intention of turning up. My desire to turn up was even smaller than yours.'

'Which means you're the one to blame.'

'I am not,' said Scott. 'And anyway, why didn't you tell Christopher yourself?'

'Tell him what?'

'That you weren't gonna bloody well turn up.'

'Because you were gonna bloody well turn up and tell him.'

'But,' said Christopher, 'you, Colin, said that Thomas would turn up to check whether or not I had turned up.'

'Oh boy,' said Louding, 'this is more complex and intriguing than Chaucer. Listen chaps, the way to solve this is to write everything down so that we know where we are.' So, from his pocket he took a piece of notepaper and his parker pen. He clicked it, licked it and was ready to take notes. 'Right now, when did all the confusion start?'

'Ages ago,' said Thomas.

'Last night,' said Christopher.

'Let's start from the beginning of the week,' suggested Colin.

'No, Saturday,' said Thomas, 'because I worked then instead of Colin.'

'Yeah, but that was covered last week and has nothing to do with this week.'

All the same, Louding wrote this fact down and followed it with a list of other weekend activities:

Saturday night: Thomas worked instead of Colin.

Sunday afternoon: Christopher worked instead of Scott.

Sunday night: Thomas worked his normal night.

'No, Monday's my normal night,' said Thomas. 'I don't think I worked

Sunday.'

'No, I worked Sunday,' said Christopher, 'in place of you.'

'Start again,' said Louding, screwing up his first attempt. On another piece of paper he started the list off with Sunday afternoon.

Sunday afternoon: Chris worked instead of Scott.

Sunday night: Chris instead of Thomas.

Monday night: Thomas worked his normal night.

Tuesday night: Chris instead of Colin.

Wednesday night: Colin instead of Chris.

Thursday night: Oliver worked...

'And who works tonight?' he asked.

'I suppose I do,' said Thomas, 'because I only worked one night.'

'Like hell you do,' said Scott. 'It's my turn. I haven't worked one night this week.'

'Ah so,' said Oliver with unmitigated delight, 'there's a great danger of more than one of you turning up tonight.'

'According to these notes,' said Louding, staring down at them as if he was scholastically staring through a pair of bifocals, 'Christopher has worked three times, you and Colin have worked only once this week, and you, Scott, haven't worked at all.'

'And it's my normal night tomorrow,' said Colin, not only resigned to work it instead of being a waiter in place of his brother, but quite happy under the circumstances that it was there, available for him to clear his allotted shifts.

'And it's mine tonight,' said Scott.

'When was the last time you worked Friday night,' said Thomas. 'My bloody night is Friday night, the amount of times I've swapped with you for Sunday.'

'Well, not this week it isn't. I know your bloody game, Thomas. You'll say that Friday is yours, then you'll have worked your set nights and that it was me who should have turned up last night.'

'But it *was* you who should have turned up last night.'

'Like hell. You swapped with Chris and you should have turned up. Nothing to do with me.'

'But you ain't worked at all this week.'

'That don't make any difference. If it's my fault, which it isn't, and I don't work at all this week, which I will, tonight, how the hell am I gonna pay Oliver. I won't get any pay myself.'

'He has a point,' said Oliver. 'It seems to me that not one of you is going to pay me fully, so why don't you all share the cost. I mean, it seems to me you're all to blame for fucking up the system. And I'll share what you give me with Francis, who by the way has never done the job before and thinks it's a doddle.'

Somewhat more in the guilty zone than the other two, Scott and Thomas agreed to do this. Colin was not so sure. The only blame attached to him was evidence under Louding's pen of incomplete work. Christopher appeared to be the only innocent party – in fact, over innocent, having worked one shift more than his scheduled week.

Break ended and the four lads left.

'After all, it had been your night,' said Louding as he with Christopher prepared to vacate the prefects' room, in a more dilatory way marking out their official right to actually be there.

'I don't understand it. I'm still confused as ever, more confused than I'll ever be. I work three times this week, and had I agreed to work for Colin this Saturday that would have been four, and yet somehow I'm losing out.'

'I'd forget about it. You stand to lose the least.'

'How did you work that out? We'll all have to pay the same.'

'Yes, but you'll be paid more.'

Somehow the logic stuck but Christopher resignation went elsewhere.

'I should have said yes to Russell. You can earn good money being a waiter.'

'Can you,' said Louding. 'Every Friday night I'm a waiter at the BG Families Club, but it's news to me that I can earn good money.'

'Well, you know what I mean. Better money than being a doorman, especially when you start owing. So what we going to do this Saturday? I've sacrificed a night's work. We've got to do something. Why can't Marion make it?'

'She's babysitting and she says she needs the money.'

'*She* needs the money! What does she need money for? What does anyone need money for? Why do people argue so much over money? Why do we miss out so much because of money?'

'She didn't really argue. I mean I wasn't that pushed to persuade her. There were hopeful signs that maybe she's actually going off me.'

They were both outside. They were both walking across the yard. Their waiting lessons, both different, were studied in the same vicinity. Christopher stopped and looked at Louding.

'If I didn't know you better, Louding,' he said, 'I'd say you were being serious.'

'I am being serious.'

'You think the world of Marion.'

'I have to admit, her departure from this world would leave a strange vacuum.'

'And despite the fact that I know you better, I'm still wondering why there isn't another young lady you can take with you.'

'Maybe they all want to go to this football dance at the Akrotiri Youth Klub.'

'All except Helen. Her father doesn't like her going to Akrotiri dances. She told me that he thought there's always fights going on there.'

'I've yet to see a fight anywhere on this peaceful island, and the best dances are at Akrotiri, so you Akrotiri lot are always telling us.'

'She's over eighteen, and in this world of age discrimination that makes her capable of thinking for herself.'

This time Louding stopped.

'You know, Christopher. That's the nicest thing I've heard you say about Helen.'

When Christopher told Angela that a friend of his called Gavin Peters, whom he had met almost right above this very spot two weeks back, had insisted that 'Tess of whatever it was' represented perfect love or at least the passage taken from the book referring to a death-wish and leaning over banisters did, Angela stared at her brother and said:

'Had he read the book or just the passage?'

The cloudy, miserable morning which had successfully rained off the school assembly as well as other outside activities, turned into one of Angela's longed for glorious afternoons: simply splendid. She and Christopher went for a walk to the cliffs and climbed down to a large clear area beside the sea. There were plenty of rocks dry and smooth enough to use as seats and they spent the bright hours cutting up strips of leather, Angela's ability being above that of Christopher's when it came to keeping the strips straight and narrow, he discovering yet again the drawback of not possessing the knack. These strips were then to be knitted into the dress Angela was making for a friend.

'All part of survival,' she explained. 'If I didn't need the money then the dress would be for me.'

This topical need for money was not something that Christopher wanted to explore.

'It'll look unusual having all this leather knitted in with it.'

'I think I'll present the design to *Spare Rib* for publication. Should be accepted, but one can't forecast magazines' response to anything nowadays.' Angela suddenly, for a moment, abandoned her work in order to lie back and praise her surroundings, a habit she adopted from trying to perfect her notion of the good life. 'This sun, my God, and all these cliffs.... This is what I love most about being here in Cyprus. You're so lucky, Christopher, to be able to enjoy it here every day.'

'No. You're the lucky one. You can appreciate it more. I love these cliffs but they can depress me.'

'Oh? Why's that?'

'Because being here, everything else I do seems useless compared to this. I feel wasted, except when I'm here, and then I can't really have this as my kingdom. It wouldn't work.'

'What's the matter?'

'Nothing seems to matter. That's what the matter is.'

'But all this is so beautiful. I love it.'

'So do I. I love all this, but I wonder if it's because I can't love anything else. Everything is so meaningless.'

'Aha, I see. Nothing is real and not much is enchantment. Is that it?'

'Not compared to when we were kids.'

'Yes, true,' admitted Angela.

'Strange, but I never thought of you as a child along with me. I always thought of you as someone who was older and that sort of negated your childhood as far as I was concerned.'

'Oh come on, Christopher. I was never the stereotype older sister.'

'Well no, but you were always older.'

'Of course. What did you expect?'

'You know what I mean. I think you let go. I always tried to hold onto the adventure of childhood instead of letting go. We all do, I suppose. That's why we offer all this praise to one ball of fire in the sky and that monotonous stretch of blue sea. Look, two kids.'

Angela looked.

'They have arrived at your request,' she said and she laughed.

Two lads of primary school age were climbing down towards them. The one in front confidently skipped over the rocks and looked back, occasionally waiting with impatience for his friend who was gingerly taking his time. Both of them jumped onto the sand together and then walked to where Angela and her brother sat. They all noticed the seagulls, hearing them just above the waves.

'Hello,' said the first one. 'My name's Andrew and this is my friend, Mark.'

'Yes. Hello to you,' said Angela.

They were good friends: Mark'n'Andrew. Andrew was active and energetic and full of ideas, and he clambered down to further sections of the cliff towards the sea. He was paddling and splashing through the soft waves before Mark had followed half-way. Mark was carefully tracing each step Andrew had taken. He was to Christopher an example of what he had been like at that age: the inspired follower, gaining from what he preferred to observe: mainly the backs of others moving forward. Reality is always at arm's length, ready-made, and the many dreams of a ruler sitting alone, always alone, alone but ready. Andrew was different because what he saw had to be used, remade and changed, reality being flexible, pliable and usually under his control. He started to build a dam across the miniature bay formed by a separation in the rocks.

'Come on, Mark, you've got to help me,' he called. 'We must make a castle here and then lead the sea around it so's to have a moat.'

They set about doing this without much success. Christopher hopped from one rock to the other and gained a better view of them and the foundations of their work. He found an empty milk carton which he threw down to Andrew so that he could use it as a moat scoop. Andrew was pleased but it made little impression on their attempts at guiding the water. Their castle, rather innocent looking and very small, had little chance of withstanding the excess water that insisted on going the wrong way, and eventually they abandoned the project, or rather Andrew did and Mark followed. Andrew found a very short part of what looked like garden hose, picking it up and sucking on it, hoping to drink the sea which, he informed Mark, was a very nice thing to do. Christopher called down and informed him that he was likely to draw into his mouth more than just salt water – maybe even a family of cockroaches. Andrew looked into the pipe, saw nothing, but blew through it instead and was overjoyed at seeing so many bubbles being given this chance to escape. He called Mark to come and look. Mark, however, was busy cleaning his feet so as to put his shoes and socks back on. Andrew did not notice the change in the weather until the falling rain informed him of water from above being slightly more interesting than the rising bubbles of air below.

'Shit,' said Angela. 'Why is it I never escape changeable weather?'

She quickly packed together her leather, wool and knitting accoutrements.

'Yes, we better start making tracks,' he said, 'before it really starts pouring hard.'

And then it really started pouring hard.

'Anywhere we can shelter? Might just be a five minute shower?'

'Yes,' said Andrew, having reached them before Mark who was still struggling with his socks. 'There's a cave 'round the corner. I know these cliffs ever so well.'

Christopher also knew about the cave but he would not have described its location as simply around the corner. Nevertheless the two of them followed Andrew whose route entailed some slightly tricky climbing, particularly so for Angela as she held onto Christopher as well as her lightweight bag of material. She was also concerned about Mark who was apparently quite happy to get drenched so long as he managed to get his shoes on. But by now they were all getting drenched, including Andrew who had left his shoes and socks outside somewhere above their floundering castle, and assured his followers that his friend knew about the cave too:

''Cos,' he explained, 'it's our special cave where we can hide from bandits and fight sea-serpents and things.'

The cave, just large enough to fit the four of them, hardly supplied the elbow room needed to fight it out with any denizen from the Mediterranean depths, but after the effort taken to reach it, its very existence was a timely and well-positioned find. Mark surprised them all by managing to reach the shelter just before the rain displayed its total wrath – bandits all right, robbing them of space and clearing, cleaning the wilderness hastily vacated, as cursed as the castle soaked to the ground, the cliffs converted to a thousand channels, each a faster route to the final getaway, camouflaging, merging and swallowed into the home of every bandit everywhere, just as the orchestra becomes the home of every theme played everywhere. The strings flurried, the woodwind brightened, the brass to the rescue, the drums overhead and life goes on, first with Andrew creeping out to collect fresh water in his hands. Angela sat down beside Christopher within the cave and continued the now therapeutic task of cutting leather into strips. Christopher still struggled to acquire the knack as he tried to help her.

'Nature hates a straight line,' he said, 'and maybe I do as well.'

And he presented his crooked effort.

'How are you getting on with your maths?'

'Surviving. Keeping my head above water.'

'The rain is complete,' she said, quoting her thoughts as if reading from a book. 'Let my mind fall like you over everything. Let me understand the ways and shapes of life, as here the ways of rocks and grass, fields and woods, houses and castles, from the strong clouds to the weak below. Between us and the rain is love for life. I always think that but only when I'm under shelter.'

'Yes, there is something about it. I wonder if its security. It can hardly be freedom.'

'What, the shelter?'

'Both. There's no shelter without rain.'

'Ah yes, that maybe so. But there's plenty of rain without shelter. We've all experience that. The rain represents freedom, Christopher, because it brings on change and freedom is change. Without change there is no life.'

'So what's security?' asked Christopher.

Angela thought about this for a while and then with a shrug said: 'It's whatever you want it to be.'

'That can't be right.' He did a bit of thinking and said again: 'That can't be right. It isn't a case of want. I mean, I always want to be secure but that doesn't make me secure. I feel secure one day in one situation, but the next day, the same situation, I don't feel so safe.'

'That's because you limit yourself, Christopher. To remain secure you've got to throw back your shoulders, stretch your lungs and breathe in life and don't let it defeat you.'

'I wish I could. Oh yes, I can throw back my shoulders. I should do more often, I agree. But so can the man who wants to fly: so he throws back his shoulders and throws himself off the cliff and gets killed. Maybe that's perfect security, going by what Gavin said.'

'I'm sorry?'

'A friend of mine from school, although I met him just above this very spot – well almost, and almost two weeks ago – Gavin Peters. He was searching for snakes and he was reading Hardy.'

'An odd combination.'

'*Tess of whatever it was.*'

'You mean *Tess of the d'Urbervilles*. He must be an English student. I can't see any lad your age reading that book unless he has to.'

'He said it represented perfect love, or rather the bit where she leans over the banister with her lover and has this death-wish that they should both fall together. He read that bit to me and then he said something about it being perfect love.'

'Had he read the book or just the passage?'

'Well, he must be doing an exam in it as you say, so I suppose he's read the book.'

Angela stopped what she was doing and shook her head.

'I don't think so or else he would not have said that it represented perfect love. Certainly the book is a good picture of twisted love. Well, the idea's a good picture of twisted love. The book itself is one of many that Hardy's off-loaded onto English literature.'

'You sound as if you don't think much of Hardy.'

'His plots are annoying and when I read him I wish that someone else had written them down. I tried to read that book last year. It's not about perfect love at all, Christopher. Tess falls in love with this utter prick called Angel Clare, who loves her at first and then abandons her because she tells him that she is not in fact the maiden he thought she was. I almost threw the book at the wall, I was so angry with the man. I was angry at her too for continuing to love him and indulging in a sort of masochistic devotion which had her doing degrading work in order to punish herself. Perfect love is to, is to…' Angela tried to pick at her thoughts by gripping at the air: 'is to accept and understand what a person is. Simple, sound and very difficult.'

'Gosh, I'm quite distressed about poor Tess,' admitted Christopher. 'What happens to her?'

'I don't know. I'm afraid I did, in a way, throw the book at the wall. Actually, I left it at a station waiting-room when rushing for a train, so someone else can then enjoy the benefits of Hardy's methods of making you forget about time. You know, time's a funny thing. What seems a blessing on Sunday turns out to be a curse on Monday.'

'And on Wednesday it's my birthday,' said Mark.

Christopher and Angela had not been aware that he was listening. It was doubtful if Andrew had given them any more attention than he now gave the weakening weather condition. He was outside the cave making waterfalls.

'Oh, is that so? And how old will you be then?' asked Angela.

'Eleven. Same age as Andrew.'

But Andrew, his friend, was not interested.

There was something different about Helen. She was exposing an inch of flesh, a belt of skin, from the fancy stitched finish of her small jumper to the fraying top of her English jeans, her navel completing the design like a tasty but self-conscious buckle. That's it, thought Christopher as he followed her through to the kitchen. Her jeans are tight, her jumper is small, her clothes actually suit her. So, in addition to the usual response to her usual welcome, he circled the exposed inch with his hands and kissed the back of her neck, pushing aside with his nose her freshly washed hair.

'I've had to wash my dress for tonight. It's in the machine and it's got some stain on it which I hope it washes out.'

But Christopher was not interested in any dress which had to be washed. He was interested in the way she was now dressed and the way she could possibly recline, thus dressed, upon the sofa in the living-room. But with a simple twist she was free from his grasp and into the kitchen she did dart. With a usual sigh, more from direction when following Helen, he entered the kitchen, sat down on his usual stool to await his usual coffee. The unusual was dancing before him and he half expected the navel to wink. However, she was not making coffee but cleaning the kitchen which meant drying the dishes, slamming the cupboard doors and clattering the cutlery. Every noise she made in time with the already compromised peace, hastened through its process the Saturday morning fare of her favourite radio programme: *Popaganda*. But it was noise with an efficient lack of hesitation, quite indifferent to fondling and whispering endearments of mutual ecstasy, and he snapped out his 'yes' when she eventually asked him if he would care for some coffee. She slammed home the last cupboard door and started clattering the cups and saucers, milk, sugar and a badly dented kettle. The coffee was made, short of mishaps but also the concern needed in accompanying finesse with the pleasure of service. On the pretext of having to go and check her spinning dress she rushed to her bedroom and changed her jumper for one which, to her, seemed more homely. The girl returned – no more flesh but mounds of jumper disposing of the curves which the flesh had pronounced. For Christopher, with Helen, disappointment would always be on his side and for reasons he assumed were hardly his fault. After all, his expectations made few demands – maybe I should make more, he thought. This presence, so suddenly charmless in comparison to before, was hard to forgive. Lust was stunted by her deliberate act of removing all which permitted fair play, and in order to be on the safer side of her distracting test of love she pulled from the fridge a slice of processed cheese which she slowly, with relish and devotion matching that which he had earlier wanted to have as his own, ate it in front of him.

'I think we will be going to Akrotiri tonight by a special bus being laid on for those going from Limassol and BG,' he said slowly, hoping to maintain some control over the previously un-proposed schedule, enlarged now by the need to avoid any possibility of breathing in the cheese. 'Do you really have to eat that stuff?'

'Yes, I really do. I love cheese slices. It's good for a girl in my condition.'

'What condition?'

'You shouldn't ask such questions. It's a girl condition and I can't tell you.'

Just now he would have gone along with any method of springing upon him further news of the actual difference England had meant to Helen's immediate life; Helen being in the mood which usually mixed along with anger some interesting if not devastating fact. However he realized that she was merely annoyed with him because they were not going for a meal in Limassol but to a dance in Akrotiri.

'But we don't have to go to the dance tonight if you don't want to.'

'It's all right. I don't mind. See, I'm washing my dress specially. We can't do anything else can we? After all, Louding hasn't got a partner. But dad will get angry with me, but I'm eighteen so I don't care. I can think for myself.'

'It's a dance with a difference. Not only will they be presenting cups and shields to various football teams, but there's a beauty contest.'

'What? For the most beautiful girl at the dance?'

'Not necessarily,' he said, and either way, he thought, what with floppy jumper and processed cheese, it wouldn't make any difference to you. 'Each team has nominated a beauty to represent it and they'll parade under such names as Miss Magpie, Miss BG Fliers etc.'

'In their swimwear?'

'If it's in their evening wear,' he murmured thoughtfully as if given the chance to forget the grudge and perhaps accompany his idea with a hug, 'then with you in your freshly washed midi-dress, you would have stood a good chance. We must get a Limassol team to nominate you.'

'Not likely,' said Helen. 'Me in a beauty contest. I'd be too shy. I'm not the type otherwise I wouldn't be going out with you.'

'What's that supposed to mean?'

'You don't play football or things like that. Beauty contest girls go out with football players. Anyway,' she said, before sliding another slice of cheese into her mouth, 'who will be in it? You must tell me.'

'I'm not sure. Sonja Stirling, no doubt. Zoe Holland, so I'm told and I should think Nancy Lynson among others.'

'Not your sister?'

'Who, Julie? No – like you she's not the type. Anyway, she wants to give the others a chance.'

And Christopher could well have believed this, inconsistent though it was with his general opinion of Julie's physical charisma. Her force of character was capable of winning for her much that may have been lost to others due to a relative lack of the required looks.

'She says Sonja will win. I don't think so though. Do you?'

'Who's Sonja?'

'Sonja is very beautiful and she had incredible legs but if they're to parade in evening dress that'll hardly do her much good other than get her onto the platform.'

'If she's very beautiful then she had a good chance of winning.'

'Beverley Janek might be one of the Episkopi girls, and then there's Nancy and Zoe – hard to reckon between them. If a St John's girl wins it probably will be Beverley. Either way, King Richard's lot gonna have to pull out a few Aphrodites to stand a chance against our beauties.'

'And Christopher, you think I'm beautiful as well,' Helen asked, forgetting about her not-the-type assertion as she placed her arms around his neck and gave him the benefit of realising more readily what she had just eaten. 'You think I'd make a beauty queen.'

'No,' he replied without hesitation.

'But you said I would.'

'I'll reconsider you if you put that other jumper back on.'

'I don't want to. It's too chilly.'

'Ah but, Helen, I'd soon warm you up.'

'You can warm me up tonight at the dance. Wait and see when I wear my new midi. You'll love it.'

And the non too subtle scent of cheese deterred him from persisting.

Christopher left Helen's soon after dinner. He explained that he was expected at Louding's quite early and as if to help him believe that this was true he was able to catch the bus which took him from Helen's to where the number 15 to BG could be caught. Helen said she didn't mind, having lots to do, always lots to do when the basis of her action, stimulating or otherwise, was that of being cross. He wasn't quite sure why she should be angry. He wasn't quite sure if she was angry. He just caught a sense of scorn which entitled him to gaze more independently upon the afternoon and make good his escape. There was never much likelihood of him desiring Helen's company less than when, thrown from tracks of affection, he was still required to make use of a few hours of her time.

Perhaps I am unfair. Maybe she has a right to be angry and I should treat her with more respect. Perhaps the number 15 bus will never arrive he thought just prior to it pulling up from around the corner.

This BG bus appeared to be the only one the Limassol transport authorities had bothered numbering. All other buses merely wandered around displaying the Greek alphabet as evidence of random access, but because plenty of Brits caught the number 15 and due to their nationalistic fervour for numerical systems, inherited no doubt from the Greeks themselves (although at the back of Christopher's mind was a notion that the Arabs had something to do with it), this fairly decent digital duo became a facility laid on at no extra cost. It was not a regular service, but enough to deter the taxi-drivers who hailed the waiting and wandering Brits as if accusing them of taking too much exercise and risking sun-stroke. This number 15 rumbled to Berengaria, a journey broken by screeching brakes and cartridge taped balalaikas.

It was just possible that Mark was 'back in town' and Christopher thought about calling around as he walked past the quiet road leading to the Langford house. However, he quickly reasserted that any surviving friendship depended completely on Mark's efforts to contact him. Christopher had called last Christmas, and although very pleased to see him, apologising for not writing and promising a definite visit to Akrotiri some time, there was something in Mark's attitude which indicated strain.

'I'm glad you arrived early,' said Louding who *was* glad he arrived early. A mere matter of routine classified the timing of any of their meetings, and beyond this Louding and Christopher were glad to see each other under any title, early or otherwise. 'I want to show you something. My new method of cleaning records.'

Louding had bought a new stylus for his parent's stereo. An improvement of quality enabled him to hear sounds on his records previously gone unnoticed. He wiped a film of water over the surface of *Humble Pie Rockin' the Fillmore* and then placed it on the turn-table.

'Now, the needle will pick up dust easily but it leaves it to one side, damp enough for the duster to collect afterwards. Clever, hey?'

'I suppose so,' said Christopher, 'but I always thought the object was to prevent the needle getting anywhere near the dust.'

'Lateral thinking, *mon ami*.'

'What thinking?'

'It's an art of being able to solve problems by looking around them rather than at them, or as in this case, getting around a problem by perpetuating the nature of its existence. That sounds clever but it's something I read.'

'Would it work for math problems? If anything perpetuates the nature of its existence...'

'Hard to say,' said Louding as he placed the needle carefully onto the edge of the revolving record. 'I'm just a beginner. You see, there exists the dust, somewhere, and there exists the needle. They are both enemies but together they help the duster do its job. Meanwhile, back at the ranch...'

The speakers burst forth loud music. Obviously there was nobody but them about. The house was subject to the sound-proof benefit of its detached isolation. Louding loved to listen to rock music at a volume which enabled normal conversation to be held at shouting level.

'Doesn't sound any different to me,' bellowed Christopher.

'It wouldn't would it?' said Louding who rarely needed to shout at anybody to make himself understood. He looked at his friend as if he had much to learn about the finer points of hard distortion. 'It's only your bloody record.'

'Oh yes, so it is,' replied Christopher who was happily surprised that Louding could sound so much like Mark even if it took Humble Pie to make the difference. But Louding was himself again, which pleased him even more, when from out of the fridge he pulled two cans of beer. 'How long have you had it now?'

'Long enough for it to be mine, I think.'

'Can't remember you paying any rent.'

'I pay it in beer,' he said, throwing him a can, 'and I pay it in wisdom. You learn a lot from me, a lot money can't buy.'

'I see, and what part does Stella play in this course.'

He sat down and Louding said, after an 'Aha' with his finger in the air and a pause to scan the mental list: 'Stella is worth more than an 'Umble Pie record.'

'How about Wishbone Ash and I'll throw in *Cricklewood Green*.'

'That plus Moody Blues' *Question of Balance* and I'll teach you how to tolerate Marion as well.'

'I'm already fully versed in tolerating Marion.'

'Ah but, *mon ami*, there are realms of toleration beyond your wildest dreams.'

'She can exercise that much tolerance can she?'

'A class of her own.'

And Christopher looked at his now half empty can of beer.

'Tell me a bit more about lateral thinking and Stella.'

'And how the twain may mix?'

'Well, yes.'

'Lateral thinking is a means of approach,' explained Louding. 'Looking at a problem from all angles rather than from the angle dictated by logic. How can you get to know Stella? Logic suggests that you should take her out. But what is the problem? Surely you can turn it around and say: how can Stella get to know you?'

'Yes you're right,' said Christopher slowly, thinking about it. 'That does put a different light on it. The solutions are already of a different kind. So…' and he thought some more before looking up at Louding who was still standing in his role as the teacher staring benevolently down upon his eagerness to learn. 'How *can* Stella get to know me?'

'Advertisement.'

'What?'

'Advertise yourself. Be where she is and make sure she notices you.'

And Christopher stood up, put down his beer and walked out of the room.

'I realize of course,' called Louding through to where he went, 'it won't be easy.'

'Nothing worth having is ever easy,' said Christopher gaining philosophical reassurance as he relieved his bladder. The general excuse for accepting struggle only became part of his beliefs on those days, such as today, when life was quite agreeable and furnished with events tailor-made for his enjoyment. He returned to the room and Louding had to ask him who or what had given him that piece of twaddle. 'My sister, yesterday.'

'Who, Julie? I can't imagine her allowing any hardship getting in the way of what she wants.'

'Oh you'd be surprised, but Julie's struggle is with herself.' And Christopher, glancing at his album cover added: 'It's hard to be humble when you know you're the best.'

He retrieved his beer and stared at the reflection of the room curved around the silver tone of the can. 'Actually it was my older sister, Angela, who said to me yesterday that I should learn to enjoy life by challenging it. It is the struggle of challenge which makes one rich with happiness. What do you think?'

'I think it's time for another record.'

They spent the afternoon listening to and cleaning records. They saved on the beer by drinking coke instead, and they ate a few sandwiches before thinking about going to Andy Capp III.

'If we leave now, give or take quarter of an hour to get ready, we'll get in an hour's drinking.'

'Remember, I've got to collect Helen.'

'If you get a taxi from the pub it shouldn't take long.'

They bussed it to the Bypass and arrived at Andy Capp III in good time despite the lack of space, having not been the first by any means to regard this pub as the ideal place to prepare for the evening out. There were many of the Limassol and BG British lads anticipating the Akrotiri-dance bus, but requiring time to drink and talk and play darts. Louding and Christopher were invited to take part in a game with Martin, Rob Johnson and the Bury. There were very few girls among the mob which layered the standing room around the bar. Most were already at the Youth Klub including Martin's girlfriend, Zoe, who had to make an early appearance along with the other contestants for the Football Team Beauty of the Year – such being the preparatory formalities of what they assumed was an annual event, although this had to be the first time such a contest was taking place – that or nobody could remember who won last year.

Christopher asked Martin about Stella, the Greek wedding she was attending tonight and whether he would have preferred to have gone there himself.

'Stella's getting on fine. I think she's coming out of herself,' he added as he took aim and missed by an arm's length a passing tray of lager. 'She was very shy at first but now she's enjoying herself more.' After his shot he looked around as if anyone even close, other than Christopher, could hear what he was about to say: 'Actually, I'd sooner be at the wedding getting pissed than trudging off to some lemonade dance just to receive the runner's-up shield, but – ' and he looked around at his mates, 'you know the way it is. Anyway, I suppose I've got to go and see Zoe win the beauty contest, although I know that she too'd rather be at a wedding.'

Martin could have done worse than attempting to win the contest himself, possessing something of the sturdy expression in feminine beauty only just concealed in his finely cast masculine frame. He was one of the lads who took his full quota of natural gifts: broad shoulders, brown skin, trim physique, blue eyes and an enthusiasm for sport. Needless to say he was immensely popular, but under it all and perhaps as a result of conforming to social demands, intrinsically nondescript.

'Beverley Janek of Epi Eagles'll win,' announced Louding having overheard his reference to Zoe.

'Not a chance,' said Rob who was handed the darts – himself a casual combination of teenage will-power and extrovert grace. 'Has to be Zoe.'

'Just because she's Miss BG Fliers.'

'That helps.'

'What about Sonja?' asked the Bury, smaller but as keen, and implacably part of the set.

'Yeah, what about Sonja?'

'Yeah, what about her?'

'Yeah?'

'Yeah?'

'Yeah!'

There was no further comment forthcoming as Louding, with his placid ability to sweep the board of character, looks and deeds, scored two sixties and a bull. He only wanted to escape being asked about Marion, assuming that most were under the impression that he was (still) going out with her. Nobody asked after Helen, not even when Christopher lost the game and bought the next round, costing enough to cause him concern about the taxi fare. He was also worried about the time, and before long and with a bit of fast drinking and the assurance that, twenty-four hours fast or not, Louding's watch was correct, he was out of the pub, ready to fetch Helen but wondering if it would not be wise to return and go to the loo. Limassol taxis are never available when wanted, he thought while walking quickly up the Bypass, calling for what he could see but missing quite a few before one eventually stopped.

Helen was outside and ready and because her mother had rushed her she became annoyed with Christopher.

'You always do things to suit Louding,' she said, a statement she may have been preparing all afternoon and sounding suitable enough now as she settled inside the taxi. 'I think I would have preferred to go for a kebab tonight – just the two of us.'

'Don't you want to find out who'll win the contest?'

'It'll be a King Dick's girl and anyway, we'll find out on Monday at school.'

'But don't you want to dance with me?'

'Yes, but we could have gone to a disco after the meal, just you and me.'

'Are you hungry?'

'Yes.' But she wasn't. Christopher knew her well enough to know that, unless planning for a meal, she would have eaten before venturing on an evening's voyage to Akrotiri. 'I'm angry. You've got to do this, you've got to do that, but when it comes to what I want, oh no, it has to be next time.'

'Are you really annoyed with me?' Christopher had a forlorn faith in asking questions as a method of soothing her vexed notion of having been wronged.

'Oh no, Christopher. I'm over the moon with joy.'

He was surprised but not displeased by her uncharacteristic sarcasm. He wanted to kiss her, he wanted to promise her that tonight would be her night, but she sat against the door as if ready to push him away.

'And you've drunk too much beer. I can smell it.'

So he sat back and thought about the cheese she had eaten earlier but said nothing.

The taxi pulled up at the Unicorn House bus-stop. They had seen a group of girls waiting there, a few of whom Helen recognized as a separate collection of her many anonymous friends, and it was obvious to all that that was where the dance bus would stop. When he had paid the taxi and watched it leave he remembered a duffel bag containing clothes he had changed out of. He had left this under Louding's supervision back at the crowded pub. I should really go and collect it, he thought. Can't really expect Louding to remember it?

'I just have to go to the Andy Capp III,' he said to Helen who shrugged her response as part of her nurtured indifference to what pleasure could yet be salvaged from the evening thus far, despite the presence of friends some of whom were walking towards her. It suited her conviction to see him desert her now. 'Don't worry. I'll be back in a jiffy.'

'Don't bother. I might not be here.'

'Oh, come on, Helen, don't be like that.'

It occurred to him that he was beginning to fancy her more now that she was prepared to end an evening that had hardly started. Maybe all along, what they were waiting for from their relationship was such an evening, and with strength on either side increasing to where their needs would meet as one, all would have been rejected except each other and a kebab table for two. As it was, Christopher's loyalties were based on a utilitarian calculation, whereby from one place to another he could please most but maybe assure only limited value for some.

He ran to the Andy Capp III and was welcomed with another beer, purchased by Dave the Bury who had lost the last game of darts and hadn't realized that he had gone. He, the Bury, would certainly never have paid for the extra beer on the off-chance of this early unlikely return. For a few moments Christopher's inconspicuous absence had caused him to curse, but when the very lad stepped inside girl-less they all assumed the worst and thought he, more than any of them, was in need of a drink.

'Where is she?' said Louding as he was handed his pint.

'What's this? I…er…I left her with friends at Unicorn House.'

'Quite right too,' said Rob. 'Perfect place to leave one's lass. Bound to make many more friends there.'

'What do you mean? I'm going to return to her now, forthwith and without further delay, so…cheers Dave.'

Priorities assured – the music and such friendly means of available conversation – there arose within Christopher an increasing reluctance to immediately withdraw. If he returned to Unicorn House now he would be waiting for a bus which, according to Martin, was not due for another fifteen minutes.

'What should I do, Louding?' he asked while staring at his beer. 'Should I stay or should I go?'

This prophetic question enabled Louding to return to an earlier subject.

'A bit of lateral thinking: don't do either.'

'How can I do that? That's no solution.'

'In that case, do both. Go back and stay – sorry, that sounds wrong. Bring Helen back here.'

'She's in a slightly off-putting mood. But I better collect her. There isn't much chance of her getting on the bus without me, even if I can catch it opposite here.'

This was precisely what they all planned to do.

'Christopher, you must return with Miss Troy,' said Rob who managed to overhear part of their conversation. 'We're lacking glamour. But before you go drink this.'

'And also this,' said the Bury as he and the others poured the remnants of their drinks into one glass and presented the concoction as an offering to a task none but Christopher was brave or obliged enough to complete.

He stared at the glass of mainly ouzo and coke and suspected a conspiracy. We must get Panhandle drunk – a plan obviously endorsed if not initiated by Louding.

'To the greatest hooker ever to face the school team,' said the Bury.

'To hook well with Helen, hey?' said Rob.

'What?…' Christopher spluttered, opting for his beer and then feeling less likely to resist whatever else was prepared as the four lads lifted him bodily and carried him outside.

The fresh air forced his eyes to focus on everything at once, and setting him on his feet they convinced him that he was now wavering in the proper direction. They also waved him goodbye.

'I'm surprisingly tipsy,' he said to Helen as he approached her, remembering as he looked into her stare the bag he had intended to pick up but had forgotten. He also thought about the parting request for him to return with some of her friends should there be any around.

But she was standing alone and, being close to tears, was determined now to walk home. She was so angry, even more so than before, that she found it difficult to talk. Apparently a bus-full of the Akrotiri-bound had just gone. It had stopped to collect what friends there had been. Her frustration had exposed the other edge of loyalty. She stood firm on a mounting grudge and unwittingly verified Christopher's belief by refusing to step onto the bus alone, with or without friends, despite strong fears of him catching the bus with his friends at the next stop opposite the Andy Capp III without her. She was not, however, relieved to see him walking towards her now. She merely directed his eyes to the back-end of the distant bus going the other way.

'What, the bus has gone!' he exclaimed. He had indeed noticed a bus going by as he took his walk towards her from the pub.

She stood quite cold and hard against his disabled grasp of the situation. They were alone outside Unicorn House on a busy Saturday night. But without the element of sympathetic tenderness this was not the ideal she had been hoping for.

'Louding would never leave without us,' he said, thinking: with those other lads that's exactly what he'd do. I mean, I would, he thought.

'If you mention Louding once more I shall scream!' she screamed.

'Okay, okay. What's wrong with you? So we missed a bus.'

'And I'm glad. I'm glad we missed the bus. I want to go somewhere just with you. I want to go somewhere just with you now. If we don't go somewhere, just the two of us, I shall go home and you can walk to your stupid dance.'

The taste in his mouth complemented the distortion of moving lights which pulsated the Bypass in all directions.

'Helen, I know you're upset about something, but you're being unfair.'

'Me unfair! Unfair! Me! It's you who's being unfair to me.'

'Listen, quite frankly, I can't afford to pay for a kebab or whatever, and I left my bag with...' He was for once reluctant to say the name.

'Okay, I'm going home. Goodbye.'

She walked away. He did not ask if she was perhaps going to walk all the way and if so, by herself? Neither did he call after her by saying: 'Now wait, let's not be too hasty.' He did not even mention her name or bid her good-night. She did not turn around to evaluate the silence, and as the distance between them grew so too did the mutual feeling of having underestimated each other's moral endurance. Christopher rejected time to think about how much he wanted her back. To him the only notion needing to be tackled through the eerie zest of the city was total desertion emphasized by a bus now long gone. Louding might well have left without him. Christopher, deluded by a world apparently racing backwards, was now convinced that he had.

Not only had Louding not gone but neither had half the pub. Nobody told them that the bus was going to be quarter an hour early. When Christopher returned there again and to his relief discovered he could tell his four what had happened, glossing over his failure to be accompanied by Helen, word quickly got around until all who were going to the dance made a swift exit and stood anxiously at the second designated Bypass departure point. They unanimously rejected the tentative suggestion of hiring a fleet of taxis and they demonstrated a collective urge of youth and distance by convincing each other that there had to be a second bus.

'All your fault, you know,' said Rob to Christopher. 'You made us miss the bus.'

'How did I manage that?'

'We waited for you.'

'But it was me that told you the bus had gone, and are you telling me now that the entire pub were waiting for me?'

'And you said you were going to bring some nice friends of your nice friend and you haven't even got your nice friend.'

'Change of plan, I'm afraid. My nice friend didn't turn out to be so nice after all, and her nice friends caught the bus we just missed.'

'Not to worry,' said Martin, worried that it had actually been his fault, having instigated the fifteen minute theory which he now whittled down to five minutes. 'In five minutes we can catch the BG bus. The one just gone was obviously for the Limassol kids.'

'That's us lot,' said Rob. 'We're *in* Limassol.'

'I know that. But we're not from Limassol.'

'You are.'

'I am not. I lived half way between BG and here. That makes me neutral.'

'So you can catch the neutral bus.'

Christopher was happier now that they all seemed to have lost out together. He cushioned his guilt with regard to Helen by an unexpected consoling quality of a shared experience. He tried not to be concerned for her walking-back-home-by-herself safety. He should have seen her to her door after having taken her for at least a drink, which he could just about afford, and thus steadily mollify her rage by sacrificing the dance. But then what? – such an option would have resulted in him being stranded in Limassol. She gave me no choice – totally unreasonable, but what a girl to become so suddenly different from the Helen I usually know and hate – well not hate, not even despise – just not really fancy. There had simply been no pleasure in his normal reaction to what he had usually disposed of as stupidity, but in so short a time she had dug into a sensitive area, stunned into an unusually pleasing dilemma of restricted impulse.

Louding, who throughout this time had returned to the pub to retrieve a bag he only just remembered had been left in his care, ambled across the treacherous road, took Christopher to one side and asked the inevitable, naturally taking it for granted that Helen was not in momentary hiding:

'What happened?'

'Remember I said she was angry?'

'I think so.'

'Well, I was wrong. She was very angry.'

'Why?'

'Because she couldn't get on the bus with her friends because I wasn't with her. I had left her but said I would return – she didn't know what to do, and because she didn't really want to go to Akrotiri anyway and because of a million and one things girls get angry about. It could be also because she has this condition.'

'What condition? Not pregnant is she?'

Christopher's eyes widened.

'Louding! I'm lucky if I get a hug and a kiss. No, you know, that thing about girls.'

'Oh yes. Well that explains it. But do you think we should go and find out how she is?'

'What? She's probably back home by now. She's being unreasonable. I've no money to take her for a meal. I don't believe she wants a meal. She's just being awkward. She would have loved the dance, but sod her! Let's just go ourselves.'

The bitterness failed to make him feel better even if most of its impetus was taken up in being boyishly jovial with the others in the increasing hope for the magic BG bus. Louding was never very good at making any of his suggestions stick, even when faced with the arrogance Christopher displayed in sweeping aside his idea. If Christopher had said yes, and Christopher knew this, the two of them would have left the others and the promised fun of this Saturday evening, bus or no bus, and gone to search out Helen. But it came to pass that they all stepped onto the bus which was, as predicted, only five minutes behind the other and, in the light of BG preference, not as redundant as the one which had been hired for the local British youth. It was crowded and being the final ones on board they had to stand. Martin suffered no further lack of confidence and thereby regained his status. This was the BG bus and they were merely stragglers rescued on route from being stranded in Limassol, and heading now for a heavenly evening within the confines of an RAF superstructure. But Akrotiri was many miles away. The road was bumpy. The bus creaked and jolted and suffered the pains of never having seen a garage in months, maybe years. And it occurred to Christopher, as the un-dipped beam of wilderness was replacing the lights of Limassol, that he had not yet gone to the loo.

He began to understand the intensity of one problem being replaced by another, a civilized solution to which would create for him a new life without any fundamental change in the old. No matter what spiritual, financial or potential burden pressed on the task of living, the physical demands were always in their bullying authority totally paramount. Forget about Helen and the hurt you caused, he thought, or any of the work awaiting to accuse you of failure – all this is nothing compared to the need, the growing painful need to go for a leak. He looked around. There were definitely no seats. He was convinced that if he sat down life would not be half so hellish. His bladder would even out the pain along its reactionary system so long as he rested the weight on his butt. A mixture of diffidence and pride prevented him from crouching on the floor and it was totally beyond him to even consider going to the driver and suggesting he should stop the bus. It was too noisy, too active, too full of the enveloping influence of tribal haste for him to ever disturb its pleasure. Had it been revealed to him alone that the bus was on a collision course, still, notwithstanding the motive of self-preservation bolstered by definite evidence of danger, the indefinable defect in his character would have held sway – the coward racing to his death rather than initiating any change in the present calamity of the excited and deluded doom. But at present he was convinced that he was alone in standing uniquely desperate and release in death appeared an enviable course. And in the chaos of his thoughts, keeping them frantically around the top of his head rather than venturing into the lower regions where one mention of water, one solitary sound of escaping pressure and hopes for release would have opted for new fathoms of humiliation, an absurd idea stemming from an earlier question offered with horrific relish a new awareness bringing punishment into form. He recalled that he had been quite distressed about Hardy's Tess and wanted to know what had happened to her. The pain should be beautifully just, he thought, because I am that utter prick called – what was he called? It was like Angela's name but *she* didn't like him, not at all – in fact in the form of a book he was all but thrown against the wall if this is comparable to being left in a railway waiting room. But the pages were protected by literature. No-one would think of burning Thomas Hardy even if he is something of a dead weight on the minds of A level English students. I shouldn't have abandoned Helen, especially for this. I should have begged her company, taken her away, kissed her hard, kissed her hardy. Don't smile – makes it worse. I am not worthy even to tighten the buckles of her shoes. This is one hell of a time to discover than I'm in love.

'Louding,' he whispered.

Louding stood behind him, quietly, motionlessly demonstrating how to be part of a crowded bus but remain isolated by a terminal stretch of nature's violent call.

'You too?'

'I think so.'

'Shall we stop the bus?'

'We should be there soon.'

There was little comfort in suggesting that the ordeal was almost over simply because the definition of heavenly there as opposed to hellish here was merely separated by a purgatorial soon.

Louding looked over his shoulder. Martin appeared quite content but Rob was studying with tense fingers the method his jacket buttons underwent to pierce their respective holes. He caught Louding's sympathetic gaze.

'Shall we stop the bus?'

'Let's stop the bus.'

'Yes, the bus must be stopped,' said Martin.

'For fuck's sake stop the fucking bus,' suggested the Bury.

'*Alla Ray*,' shouted Rob in his confident default tone of addressing Greek bus drivers. 'Stop the bus.'

'Some sick?' the driver asked as he looked from left to right of his headlights.

'Not yet, mate, but us five about to explode if we don't get off.'

'All five of you sick?'

As he asked this he pulled the bus to an obedient and immediate halt, jostling all the occupants and almost offering immediate relief to the five who demonstrated the art of the hasty exit. They were followed by a sixth, then a seventh and the a few more until those left were momentarily deluded into thinking that perhaps they had actually arrived and the Youth Klub had magically transported itself into a more congenial place within the wilderness.

Christopher ran into the pitch black. He was part of the instinctive split in all directions governed by the boundaries of a fairly busy road upon which the bus remained, droning quizzically into the surrounding, chirping and flying insects immediately attracted by its lights. A fan had formed made up of the many ahead and behind him all individually searching for their treasured but as yet unknown spot. He fell down a hole. He thought that that might happen and so he did not scream in surprise. The fact that he had yet to relieve himself had removed most of the fear. He may have been hurt but his bladder demanded right of way. It was not a deep hole, but wet and finely furnished with thorns, and into these thorns and contributing to the sodden aspect of their hostility, our hero silently peed.

Now what? Where am I? He could just about hear the bus. He had no idea how many were still outside. If the bus was waiting for him alone there was every reason to believe that the evening was a complete shambles. I have lost Helen. The bus has lost me. I should be making money doing Russell Keen's waiting job at the Families Club. I may as well remain here and make this hole my home. He moved from where he had contorted his body in order to avoid the liquid he had lost. No broken bones. His ankles were still intact. Where's the drama in that? A broken bone would offset the rather distressing fact that I have made a mess of my clothes. He clambered out of the hold and Louding was there to help him to his feet.

'Hello. You all right?'

'I'm a walking disaster area. Look at me, messed up in muck and thorns.'

'Bit too dark to see,' said Louding who, nevertheless, had noticed Christopher's sudden descent just prior to his own ecstatic stand over a small dispassionate but probably not very grateful bush.

'What am I gonna do?'

'Get back on the bus, I think.'

'I mean about my clothes? I can't go to the dance looking like this.'

'It just so happens I have over my shoulder a duffel bag containing your clothes. You can change when we arrive.'

'But I only just changed out of those for the dance.'

'I know, that but nobody else will.'

'But they're not smart clothes.'

'Probably lot smarter than you look now. Come on, let's go.'

Those who had taken the longest to return were applauded back in. Christopher was quite astounded by this attention and assumed in his case that it was drawn from the state he was in. He was pointed at by one of the girls at the front. There were a few leaves in his hair, and his clothes, quite clearly soiled by his brief encounter with the wilderness, felt as if they were dropping off him from within. He was now thinking it would have been less embarrassing to have peed himself on board. Better now, perhaps, to take the bag from Louding and get changed on the spot, space permitting or not. He took the bag from Louding – after all it was his bag.

'As soon as we arrive,' he said, 'I'm gonna race home a get changed.'

'Get changed in the loo in the Klub.'

He did not want to be informed of the existence of loos. They represented the reward for those who thought they could wait and did wait. He could have waited, now that he thought about it, but didn't. Like the sinner I am I go after what I want and gain a half-measure of what I have to learn.

'I'm not thinking of getting changed into these clothes. I'm going home to get completely changed into completely fresh clothes.'

In other words, very similar, he wanted a complete change. He was quite willing to cancel the night, enough having happened to make it an evening to remember but one he wanted to forget. However, Louding was with him. He had gone to Limassol because of Louding. He had, in effect, abandoned Helen because of Louding. Louding, of course, could catch the designated bus back to BG after the dance, but it had been arranged that Louding should stay overnight and that was precisely, after everything that had happened, would happen. And under it all, with truth defying every aspect of honour, emotion and hope, he just had to find out first hand who was going to win the wretched beauty contest.

Amazingly, it was only eight thirty when the bus pulled up outside the Klub. He abandoned the immediate proceedings taken up by everyone else who disembarked and he ran home. Although it was a warm evening he was not sweating when through the hall he rushed and on into his bedroom. His mother thought that the dance must have finished early. He explained that as far as he was concerned it hadn't started. He just had a slight accident and what was the clean clothes situation? He didn't really need to shower but he quickly showered. He never really needed to shave but he shaved. Being the youth he was he overdid the aftershave. He asked his mother if perhaps he had overdone the aftershave and she said no while both Peter and Rebecca said 'Pooh.' He cleaned his teeth, dragged a comb through his tangled mop, pulled and pushed himself into the clothes his mother laid on the bed and left. Despite it being still quite early he had to will himself not to run. It took only twenty minutes to walk from his house to the Klub. Everything that was anything on the camp only took twenty minutes to walk to from his house; either that or one had to use a bus in order for it to be sensibly reached. One does not have to be sensible to exist within the RAF, he thought, but it helped. He thought about Angela. She hadn't been in the house. Was she at the dance with Julie or had Barry taken her to somewhere sensible? Maybe he was being both sensible and at the dance as well. He thought about the word sensible. What did it really mean? Not the same as sensitive – in fact to react in a sensitive manner would possibly negate the sensible use of a situation. Doing what is right and avoiding mishaps like falling down holes in the pursuit of a piss seems to be the sensible way of passing one's time. To fall down a hole, he thought while insisting on the hidden beauty of events, is an immaculate act of sensitive abandon, so long as one survives. I can't imagine Angela or Julie falling down a hole. Well, Angela perhaps, just like Alice, and yes, I can even see her contemplating the thrill. It's Julie who's immune to the universal prospect of sharing her air with a hole. Somehow she's missing out on an important part of living. Me too by not chasing after Helen because I loved her when she left me.

The Klub was pulsating with the basic mixture of music, people and steam bellowing from the open windows. Many had arrived from the north of the island, resident within the catchment area of King Richard's where the best athletes (but for this year not the best footballers) were nurtured along with a myriad of curious looking strangers, all alluring in their totally British cloak of difference, and pertaining to what was suspected as an air of Oxbridge hopefuls, all but absent at St John's. King Richard's (known in the west as King Dick's) was much smaller than St John's but it shared the same problems, the same variety of characters and the same wealth of different shapes and average sizes. However it had gained a mysterious reputation for higher standards of learning.

Christopher recognized nobody at first and could have been persuaded that the space/time warp of parallel universes was alive and kicking. Then he met very suddenly and unexpectedly (but then again, why not?) William Meald.

'William!'

William actually looked as if he was waiting for a young lady to emerge from the cluster of girls in order to take her by the arm and lead her away through the crush at the entrance and into the crush of the hall. In a parallel universe such would naturally enough have taken place, but in Christopher's world William would remain forever girl-free. However and indeed a young lady did emerge and it was she who took William by the arm and was about to lead him away when she recognized Christopher.

'I know you,' she said. 'William, it's your funny looking friend. I recognize that red nose anywhere.'

'Thank you, Debra,' said Christopher, impulsively feeling his nose to check on its independent emission of heat. 'Nice to be noticed. You're looking smart, William.'

'Isn't he lovely?'

Lovely was never a word one associated with William, but Debra Lester, his temporary mouthpiece, always did regard this ungainly creature as her special pet and hugging his arm really did want to take him away into the fray where many would be unable to understand why a sweet lass like her was beside this ample example of ugliness.

'How's Wendy? Is she here?' asked Christopher, determined now, until he met Louding again, to stick with William, being as he was, in his way, a good friend.

'They're all there,' William managed to say, having gained some confidence from the effort needed to follow the route of least resistance through the crowd.

All is certainly the right word to use in this case, thought Christopher, as he followed them and listened to a list of names, a few of which he could not remember. He half expected William to include Frances, Henry and Colin, so intense this palace of people meeting people, distance under most space/time warp conditions being negligible. He referred mainly to the present members of the disbanded tuck-shop circle who considered themselves old friends as such, despite the daily risk of chance encounters at school. Christopher could confidently count the weeks since he last saw Grace, and when was the last time he remembered how much he had forgotten Wendy?

'Where's Helen?' asked someone.

He turned around as best he could to answer a voice he took for granted within this promise of being with so many people he knew.

'Marion? What are you doing here?'

'Well, why shouldn't I be here?'

'You should be babysitting.'

'Why should I be babysitting?'

'Louding said you were babysitting. Louding said you couldn't come with us because you were babysitting.'

Marion looked from side to side. All she saw was a field of faces that he saw when looking from side to side as he followed her eyes. She looked quite inspired and almost radiant with the thrilling aspect of being an unexpected event. So she was willing to let him into a secret.

'My plan backfired.'

'What plan?'

By now they were alone and yet about as far from being alone as physically and audibly possible. They were practically dancing with each other; the crowd swelling to a point were any movement to the loud pop music could only amount to a wave from the middle rippling out and disturbing the edges where they stood.

'I didn't think Simon would take me here and I wanted to go to this dance.'

'So did everyone else, so it seems.'

'I told him I was babysitting because he wanted to take me for a kebab with you and Helen.'

'Why didn't you just tell him you were going to the dance?'

'How could I go to a dance and he go to a kebab?'

'Why not?'

Coming from Christopher this 'why not' situation imposed a different light on Marion's mixed up motives. She shrugged as if to say that babysitting spared the suspicious mind. Christopher knew instinctively that Marion's clumsy attempt at intrigue was merely to avoid tainting the image she and others had of herself as Louding's most loyal fan, and to this extent her plan did backfire. The more successful outcome from manipulating events had actually occurred – she was at the dance and so too, somewhere, was Louding; Louding, himself, free of any element within his relationship with her that could have promoted even a tiny slice of jealous suspicion. Marion, of course, would like to believe that this was not true.

'Anyway,' said Christopher, following her shrug with a shrug of his own, reserved specially for this mild turn of events in his favour, 'at least you're here and, you know, I'm always pleased to see you.'

Marion had perfected the modest but coquettish move of partially hiding her face behind her hair. It was at times like this that Christopher experienced the mixture of joy and puzzlement which came about by such friends. Why was Louding so noticeably indifferent to her affections? She cares, he thought, but in a carefree sense of happiness which makes her more attractive than many of the girls around who are, yes, prettier. Louding is the lucky lad if he can gain half of this attention and loyalty from the girl he eventually chooses. But, of course, he had chosen Sharon only she definitely wasn't here, living now three thousand miles away in England.

'So where is Louding and the others?' he asked.

She pointed over there and said: 'Over there,' and he looked over there and over there looked like every other over there elsewhere. It was certainly not the direction he had been following just before losing William and Debra but looked very much the same. It occurred to him that William must have been on the inside before to realize how many of their mutual friends were around, and so how had he, on Christopher's arrival, looked as if he had only just arrived himself? And had Debra always been with him or had she just spotted him from a distance and prized herself through the crowd in order to pull him back into an area of social tolerance? Debra was from BG. William lived in Akrotiri, so they must have just met now. Surely it hadn't been arranged, and why was it bothering him so? And was Marion alone or merely avoiding friends for the sake of Louding or Louding for the sake of friends, or both for the sake of her own perplexed sanity? Did she see in Christopher the delightful means of becoming part of Louding's society, compounded slightly by the apparent absence of Helen?

They remained where they were. They looked at each other as if fighting back an urge to laugh out of shared comfort and self-pity. She managed, however, to repeat her opening words.

'Where's Helen?'

'At home, I suppose – I hope.'

'But I thought she was suppose to be with you tonight, and neither of you were supposed to be here.'

'I'm afraid we had a bit of a disagreement and we've fallen out.'

'What? For good?'

Christopher thought, I hope not, but he said: 'I suppose so. Hard to tell with these type of things. Problem is, because we've fallen out, which I never thought would happen, and the way it happened, I think I've fallen in love with her.'

'You were always supposed to be in love with her.'

'No I wasn't.'

'She was always in love with you.'

'No she wasn't. Did she say she was?'

'She actually talked about marriage to me. Anyway, now you've fallen out and you've fallen in love. Christopher, you're a fool.'

'Well, Marion, if you want Louding to fall in love with you maybe you should fall out with him.'

'I don't think that would work.' She was silent for a few seconds. 'I'd be too scared to give it a try. So, anyway, what happened? Why did you two fall out?'

'She didn't really want to come to this dance. Her dad doesn't like her going to Akrotiri.'

'I know – he's just stupid. Has stupid ideas.'

'Well, I think it influenced her although she kept saying about being eighteen and all that. She wanted to go out for this meal but it was agreed about the dance because I told her that Louding couldn't get a partner because you were babysitting and…'

'That's never stopped him in the past.'

'Well, Marion, it stopped him now. So the dance was the next best thing. I wasn't with her when the Limassol bus turned up at Unicorn House and her friends got on and she didn't because I had gone to Andy Capp III to collect a bag of clothes, and when I got back she was very angry and she stormed off.'

'She walked all the way home at night in the middle of Limassol by herself?'

Christopher thought about this afresh in the light of Marion's surprise. 'Sort of.'

'And you didn't run after her?'

'What could I do? I can't stay at her place. Louding would catch the bus to the dance. I'd be stranded. I know, I know, I shouldn't have let her go. I feel bad about it but everything, as always, happens at once. But it was so unlike her to walk off like that, and yet it was so wonderful that I'm now in love with her, I think. Don't tell anybody.'

'Why not?'

'I don't know. Just don't. I may feel different about it tomorrow.'

Marion was all for having a detailed account of this everything that always happened at once which so magically resulted in an apparent turnaround of Christopher's attitude to his now perhaps erstwhile girlfriend, even when everything seemed to be happening at that very moment to prevent normal conversation. The crowd were a jostling, close to the uncomfortable, sensation of making one feel in the way and out of place. The music was persistently loud and the generated heat was beginning to impress upon him the sensation of not being in or out of any place whatsoever. He was fascinated to realize that he was undergoing the symptoms just prior to fainting, and she held onto him and asked him what was wrong.

'I'm not sure. I've had quite a bit to drink this evening. I think I'm beginning to feel the effect.'

'You can't go and faint on me. You're not allowed to faint. I'm the one who's supposed to faint.'

Marion had strict rules governing social upheavals and in order to prevent them from being infringed she took Christopher by the waist and half-danced with and half-supported him slowly out to where fresh air could actually be seen. They reached the entrance where the crowd in comparison was a mere handful, mainly couples into which it was possible the two of them would merge, and the steam from the windows floated gracefully into the starlight. By now Christopher was feeling quite ill and this change in noise and space was merely part of a dream to be vanquished by a seat outside where he could rest and lay his head in his hands. He hardly heard Marion's apologies as she left him to see the promised show, get help or refreshments or participate in the shuffling dance. She would be back to see how he was soon, so she said.

What's happening? he thought. I'm trying to enjoy myself, that's all. I don't ask for much – but first Helen, then the bus, then the hole, then the crowd and now this. What *this* was was not easy to define. He did not want to throw up but neither did he want to stand up, check his degree of physical stability and then re-enter the arena. He had been given the thumbs down by fate and left outside by a delightful lass to die.

Perhaps this is death, he thought, and he opened his eyes and looked up and saw that to the best of his knowledge this was not death but the outside of the Akrotiri Youth Klub wherein all was happening and out here all was (not quite) lost.

'Hello, Christopher. Had a bit too much?'

It was Gavin. It was Gavin in need of fresh air which was fairly typical of Gavin. Christopher wanted it to be typical of Gavin. He certainly did not want his sympathy, and to avoid it being in anyway applicable to what Gavin could and usually did provide as a tonic, he felt suddenly better and was prepared now to act as if nothing had happened. Here was Gavin who was about to sit down beside him and share an outside reprieve. The presentation of cups and shields followed by Miss Youth Klub Football Team of the Year or some such title would soon begin.

'I've no time for all this gobbledygook,' Gavin explained. 'There's far too many people and the one person I wanted to see isn't here.'

It was hard to imagine Gavin having, like his sister Pamela, a romantic goal to his private life, especially existing beyond the academic appreciation of what he was willing to share with Christopher. But here he was waiting for someone he despaired about seeing.

'Are you sure?'

'Am I sure of what?'

'Are you sure she isn't here?'

'How do you know it's a she?'

'I think I've a better than fifty-fifty chance of being right,' said Christopher in all innocence.

'I rather not discuss it.' Which meant that he would if pressed.

Poor Gavin, thought Christopher. Frustrated by the fact that he's not a genius, or the genius in him will never emerge because of this heavy cloud of geniuses everywhere having emerged before him. So now he feels he needs to suffer and what better way than waiting for a girl who probably doesn't realize he's waiting. He'd prefer to think that she is deliberately making him suffer, just like Helen thought that I was deliberately going against her. Like everyone else I'm just trying to follow the path of least resistance.

'She may arrive at any time. The night is still young,'

Gavin looked at his watch which did not look like the type that offered the condolence of being twenty four hours fast. He knew by its efficient face when it was late and when it wasn't. As far as his rendezvous was concerned, it was late. The youthful pursuit of any evening depends upon action. It could age rapidly within minutes of waiting. Gavin was ready to go home.

'Aren't you interested in seeing who will win the contest?' Christopher asked, asking himself the same question which Gavin perceived in the friendly glance returned as consolation.

'Are you?'

'Maybe. I'm not sure if I want to see Sonja Stirling lose.'

'And you think she will?'

'If she does Julie will be in a bad mood. That usually has a dire effect on my outlook for the week. But more than likely Beverley Janek will win.'

Gavin had his suspicions that Nancy Lynson would probably take the title and failing this there was always Zoe Holland. And anyway, what about the beauties from the other place.

'Would it not feasible to give the title to one of their girls by way of purely being polite to our King Dick cousins.'

'Was Tess beautiful?'

'Tess?' asked Gavin and he only managed to prevent the obvious question as to who Tess was by looking at Christopher and wondering if indeed he was all there. 'Do you mean Tess of *Tess of the d'Urbervilles*?'

'Certainly do. The only other Tess we know is Tessa Miles, the genius at A level maths and physics but beautiful she is not. What's the name of Tess's lover in the book?'

'Angel Clare,' said Gavin, delighted by his own complete lack of hesitation.

'That's it. I knew it sounded like my sister's name.'

'Doesn't sound anything like Julie?'

'I *am* blessed with other sisters, you know. And this other sister, whose name is Angela, does not like Angel Clare. In fact she hated him and left him in a station waiting room.'

'What do you mean: left him in a station waiting room?'

'The book, that is. But that's what she thought of him, and she said that the book does not represent perfect love.'

'Nobody's saying it does.'

'You said it did.'

'I did not.'

'You did. You read me a passage and then said it represents perfect love.'

'But one passage does not make a book. The book is an angry statement against the hypocrisy of the time and it managed to rock the religious foundations of a repressive class of people. Angel Clare is a very fine character because he is a man of principle who becomes enlightened to the error of his ways although at first he is spiritually unable to handle it.'

Christopher sighed. This is becoming a drag, he thought. When anybody talks of anyone else like this it always reminds me of me but I don't learn anything new. He looked at Gavin who was, as it were, looking into the definition supplied by his present staring at the open and relatively deserted road.

'The book is a masterpiece,' he continued. 'It is a torrent of life without the usual distractions of offering a way out or a way in.'

'That's all very well but what happened to Tess?'

'Oh, I shouldn't tell you that. It'll spoil your enjoyment of the story.'

'I've no intention of reading the story.'

'You say that now but... Anyway, why not?'

'I don't know. It may leave me in a station waiting room. Come on, Gavin. I've just gotta know. What happens to Tess and I'll tell you what happens to Alice.'

'Who's Alice? You don't mean Lewis Carroll? What's she got to do with it? Everyone knows what happens to her. She wakes up.'

'Ah but, when does she wake up? On falling down the rabbit hole – going through the looking-glass?'

But on attempting to understand the mundane intention of Alice's outcome as regarded by Gavin, it suddenly occurred to Christopher that the poor girl had to wake up and remove herself from her enlightened road in order to avoid the consequences of finding herself on trial in both cases.

'That's it,' he said.

'What's it?'

I've been punishing myself, he thought. All this time I've been my own judge, jury and accused. I'm really no more on the outside looking in than the next man and yet inside there are the beauties and the best.

He stood up. He looked down at Gavin. He felt so elated, so much better than five minutes earlier that he wanted to shake his hand.

'I'm going back in.'

'I see,' said Gavin without understanding.

'Are you coming?'

'I think I'll go home.'

One of Gavin's many determinations was to actually read *Tess of the d'Urbervilles* and find out what actually did happen to Tess. He was also determined to find out why the mystery lad he loved and whom he had been waiting for had not turned up. Why people refuse to turn up is an exaggerated drama in life. Christopher had no time for this now. Too much was happening in too short a time for him to ever wait for something else.

He plunged back into the throng. The first person to recognize was Paul Begman. He was standing on the fringes of a mini-crowd around the soft-drinks table. What's he doing here? thought Christopher. He should be doing Russell's job at the Families Club. Maybe Russell is at the Families Club and I should be there in place of him so that he can be here to receive his cup. He earned it. More right to be here than me. Not wishing to learn the truth, thinking that Paul would hardly be in a position to allocate answers, and not really wanting to attach himself too closely to Paul for the rest of the evening, he nevertheless made the otherwise chronically forlorn lad welcome. He also needed a drink and it took time standing behind so many in order to get served, and so curiosity driven by forced patience supplied the conversation. He asked Paul if Russell had approached him about the Families Club job.

'Oh yes, he did. Yes,' said Paul, absurdly excited and grateful that Christopher should actually talk to him and also know of such a happening. 'But I've never been a waiter before. You know. I don't think I'd be very good at it.'

The one thing Paul was very good at was in portraying the type of lad who thought he was not very good at anything. People forgave him and liked him for being a blunderer, and so he continued to blunder, grateful that people liked him at all. As he was nearly always around those who did not blunder, information from him, as Christopher was about to learn, was in good supply and forthcoming.

'Chris Millings said he'd do it as he needed the money,' he explained, 'so I gave him the job. I said I'd do it for Russell and Russell was very pleased, but I didn't really want to do it and I'm glad Chris is doing it for me.'

Christopher imagined Paul's mild amount of courage failing in the face of saying no to Russell as opposed to quaking with the prospect of undertaking a not unformidable task he had never done before.

'Thing is,' said Paul, 'if Russell sees me here he'll think I've forgotten or something.'

'Yeah, I told Russell I wouldn't be here but in Limassol which was why I turned him down. He came to ask me first before he asked you, so I'm glad Chris has filled the spot. Mind you,' said Christopher, thinking now that Sonja may just happen to pull off this beauty title, 'I'm surprised he's not here to see his girlfriend win the contest. Thomas is here to see Nancy…'

'Who? Chris's girlfriend? You mean Sonja Stirling? Chris isn't going out with Sonja anymore.'

'Gosh, that was quick. I mean, I wasn't that surprised about the Colin and Angela split, but those two looked as if they were madly in love.'

'Sonja's like that, apparently. She never has a boyfriend for longer than a week. Same as Angela. Can't see it lasting long between Nancy and Thomas either.'

Therefore, thought Christopher, based on this logic why should it be so bad that I'm no longer going out with Helen.

'But you're still going strong with Julie?'

'God!' and Paul laughed and said 'God' again and laughed some more as if Christopher had suggested the funniest thing ever.

'Julie! Your sister you mean? God!'

'But you were getting on very well with her at Pat Vendle's going away do. She even kissed you which I know is the ambition of nearly every lad on the island that knows her which is practically every lad on the island.'

'She did, didn't she?' said Paul contemplating and just about remembering this stunning event.

He looked around to see how close he was to the table and Christopher was conscious of the thought that he had probably suffered as much as Chris and Colin, if not more so, having been used as a convenient substitute for Perry Stenfield. But here he is while Chris is working as a waiter with Colin at the door because neither of them need the money so much as grinding from their system the effect of their loss. Thomas won't care if he loses Nancy. Being him, he cares more about what he stands to lose if justice was served and he actually paid Oliver for the shift at the door that he should have done. And what about Oliver?

'What about Oliver?'

'What about Oliver?' asked Paul and then he remembered. 'Oh yes, he's still strong with Mary Orris. Look, see.'

And Paul pointed into the dance hall where Christopher could just about make out the reclining form of Mary apparently asleep on Oliver's lap as he sat on one of the seats along the wall. He'll have to wake her up to collect his cup, he thought. Ah well, so much for lonely hearts and local gossip.

'I wonder who's doing Oliver's waiting job at the Families Club.'

'Ah, that must be Francis. Those two are the best of mates – always doing things for each other.'

Could Francis Dorman be the latest victim to be thrown aside by love? Being a waiter at the Families Club on such an evening as this is our answer to the Foreign Legion. Nancy'll be on the platform soon as Miss Starling, while he, Thomas, a starling, gets no cup, no shield and soon no girl but lots of friends. Friends everywhere for everyone – such is the benefit of our enclosed youth.

Christopher bought a *7 Up* and, with Paul tagging along, he walked into the hall and had no difficulty locating his own particular friends, the circle consisting of Louding, Marion, Grace Ford and the Dazel sisters, and an apparently abandoned William Meald, all of whom welcomed him and Paul within their enclosure. It was at this point that when further explanations of Helen's absence was touched upon and avoided, plus some reassurance about his health, the presentation began. The music stopped and the eye-opening plunge into unexpected silence allowed the full hall's attention to be focused on the officer in charge of the Youth Klub as he walked onto the platform and twisted a bit of inevitable feedback into the freestanding microphone. He was a handsome and well-meaning looking man who was obviously always polite to his non-commissioned subordinates and never endured any fear about public address. He began by praising the virtues of sport and in particular the ever popular game of football. Soccer was the sport of sports and it was a definite feature within the spirit of the game that the Inter-island Youth Club Soccer League would grow from a small but ambitious idea into such a magnificent event, culminating in this wonderful dance that had brought together the two sides of the British colony.

'Two sides of the one side,' said Grace, who stood on one side of Christopher in order to have a good look at him. They had somehow managed to avoid seeing each other for months and this time lapse added to the ease of separating the old from the new. 'Heidi's in love with Bill Grey, and he's going up there to collect the Magpie's cup and she's going to swoon. You just watch.'

Grace had a mild habit of accurately predicting the worst, and Christopher, on looking at her now, a normal, well-built girl with a round, intelligent face, capable of passing unmoved through some quite shocking acts of deceit, he wanted to seek out her particular advice on how he should deal with Helen. But Grace knew practically nothing about Helen. She always gathered her material first hand and never paid conscious attention to gossip that failed to include her interests. How the hell she gets on so well with the Dazel girls I'll never know. I suppose it helped that Henry fancied her, and this unrequited admiration kept the bond of friendship going. Come to that, how the hell do I get on so well with the Dazel girls, but needless to say, I don't as much as I used to. Life is full of social wonders. Rosemary and Gale are sturdy parts of a definite scene of choice; as too is Marion, ready to marry Louding tomorrow should he suddenly see sense in her love the way I've seen sense in Helen's anger. And the two Lesters, Wendy and Debra – just over there with their cluster – why shouldn't William be loved by them both simply because, let's face it, he's ugly? Why shouldn't I love Helen even if most of the time she's not my type? And there she is, poor, puzzled Heidi Innmaker. Will she really swoon?

No. She survived the ordeal of watching her ultimate hero Bill Grey going up to collect the team's cup and then his own cup, followed by his team accepting their cups, the Fliers following them for their shields, and following this the Youth Klub manager, Warrant-Officer Orange, vouching for their collective enthusiasm by announcing:

'And now, what we've all been waiting for – first may I present...' and he looked at his list, not counting to memory such an important task, 'Miss Nicosia Knaves.'

Forgetting that this was apparently the name of a team from up north, Christopher thought for a moment that she had been called by her actual name, a truly splendid catch-phrase for such a nervous beauty as she took the first step onto the platform now allocated for the beauty queens. What a beautiful name, and because of this he fell in love with her. She was indeed exceptional even although, as revealed seconds later, her real name was Teresa Dongleash. That, he was willing to admit, had a certain ring about it. However, she ceased to be exceptional when she was joined by her competing colleagues, each called to her place beside each other in the order of the teams on the list, and having their real names revealed alongside their ability to remain smiling, without laughing, as the cheering began and increased. When Sonja stepped on the stage as Miss Akrotiri Magpies the crowd responded with an exceptional roar, but Nancy, as Miss Akrotiri Starlings gained more by way of whistles, and Beverley Janek, who until then had been something of an unknown factor within St John's, residing as she did in both the fourth year and the other side of Episkopi, but representing now the Epi Eagles, took in what could correctly be described as a response remaining only just on the sane side of hysteria.

'*Very* pretty,' said Louding.

'Yes, maybe,' replied Christopher including the discerning subjunctive so as to improve upon a nonchalant shout to his friend's stressed whisper as he added: 'I'm still drooling over Nicosia Knaves, and look at Larnaca Larks. Where do all these beautiful girls come from and where do they go?'

'Miss BG Fliers,' announced the manager three girls after Beverley, and one could almost feel the sombre weight of Berengaria taken upon Zoe as she intrepidly stepped into line to add in her own way to the already dazzling light, 'who is Miss Zoe Holland.'

And from the back of the hall a banner was hoisted by Martin and Rob sitting on the shoulders of a couple of BG giants, and they and a fairly large group gathered for this one act, including all members of the Fliers, started chanting: 'BG is best! BG is best! Give us a Z, give us an O, give us an E: Zoe! Zoe! Zoe!'

'Well they had that well organized,' said Louding. 'I should be with them.'

'Something tells me they want her to win.'

'God she must be embarrassed,' said Marion who was longing to be up there with them but was realistic in such assumptions about herself to understand why she wasn't.

Zoe, in fact, had been the last to form the beauty line-up and Christopher looked at them all, one by one, and loved them all one by one as did all lads like him who looked at them all one by one, and they all looked the same because they were all so lovely, and yet each had to fight a smiling battle to proclaim her individual difference that would make all the difference to this onslaught of the male gaze and win. Despite support, despite the doubtless impact of her model appearance, Zoe did not have a chance. Neither, it seemed, did Sonja who merged too much into what had been expected and therefore did not stand out as exceptional. The judges took as little time to do their judging as considered feasible, taking into consideration the overwhelming fact that this was a youth club dance. The officer in charge again walked onto the stage. He announced the three winners in reverse order and for his trouble could look forward to giving each a peck-like kiss on the cheek. Nancy came third. She was so delighted she almost tripped up as she walked forward to where the officer stood to deliver his kiss and award her a cheque for £10 plus a certificate. Ellen Oldfield of Dhekelia Doves was given a cheque for £20 for being second.

'Miss Cyprus Youth Club Soccer Team of the Year,' said the officer, 'our very own Miss Epi Eagles, Beverley Janek.'

At first Beverley refused to believe it. She had to be informed by the two girls on either side of her that she had actually won, and phenomenal cheers greeted her stunned effort to collect £50. She had received many kisses from the girls who had lost and therefore were left to make a worthy fuss of her, crowding around her victory as if wanting to touch its essence, and she also enjoyed joint hugs from Nancy and Ellen.

'Gosh, imagine being in the middle of that lot,' said Christopher.

'There, what did I tell you?' said Louding as he clapped and whistled and happily nurtured an indefinable feeling of being sorry for her. 'You know, in a way, I feel sorry for her. She's the most magnificent example of a fish out of water.'

This was only meant to be heard by Christopher who would, in his way, understand, but Marion issued a hearty slap across his shoulders and said:

'How about feeling sorry for me for a change?'

'You don't win beauty contests.'

'There's nothing special about her,' said Heidi who had joined Grace and the Dazels to share their opinions of the event. 'That girl there was far prettier.'

Heidi often thought it was a great mystery why anyone should be considered pretty enough to win money, honour and the accompanying wealth of friends.

'Dance with me,' said Christopher as the music started again.

She looked at him and for a second he was a complete stranger.

'‘Christopher Panhandle – it's you. Where've you been? Yeah, okay.'

Christopher danced with each of the girls in the now increasingly crushed circle, including Rosemary and Gale. The exception was Grace who said she was tired. He asked Heidi if she was happy and what her ambitions were. No, she was not very happy and she wanted to be an actress. Actresses who were not acting were not, so she believed, very happy. But she could look forward to a part in *West Side Story*. Rosemary was writing letters to Henry as part of the many plans surrounding an impending wedding and Gale was busy being crazy stupid about Marc Bolan. Christopher ventured beyond his circle to where Wendy and Debra shuffled in their own formation, and he asked them both what they were doing with themselves these days. Trying to get a tan and saving to go on holiday around the Greek islands was foremost in both activities and plans.

Eventually the music offered the comfort of slow dancing which he managed to time and share with Marion.

'Forget about Louding, Marion. Marry me.'

'Oh, Christopher, that's very sweet but I don't think we're suited. However, if you can get Simon to ask me the same question I will love you forever.'

'That won't do me much good.'

'I say, Christopher, you can't be in love with me? You just told me you love Helen.'

'I also love Miss Nicosia Knaves – so what difference will that make.'

Louding decided that he should do the decent thing and see Marion home, which meant that he would have to pass on the very tempting invitation to stay at the Panhandles even if it meant the possibility of a swim at the cliffs as a method of dealing with what would definitely amount to a hangover. Anyway, he had failed to bring with him the appropriate staying out gear, including casual clothes into which come morning he could comfortably change

All this he explained as they walked towards the buses. He delayed getting on board in order to stand beside Christopher and share in his reluctance to see the eventful evening end. He also stared studiously at his friend and finally asked: 'what's wrong now?'

'Louding, why am I not satisfied with life?'

'That, *mon ami*, is an age old question. I think that as soon as you start feeling satisfied then you should start worrying.'

'Now who's coming out with twaddle? I *am* feeling bad about Helen and all sorts of things. You know what? I think I've fallen in love with her.'

'And I think I've fallen in love with Marion.'

'I'm being serious.'

'And I'm not?'

'No.'

'Yes, I suppose you're right. Christopher you have a school-boy's habit of feeling bad about too many things at once. You love Helen and you feel bad about her. Great – leave it at that and make it up to her on Monday, and if you're still in love you'll be happy and you can move onto something else to feel bad about.'

Christopher walked away from the departing bus and joined William for part of their walk back to the married quarters. They would have to separate soon enough as William's dad was officer status and therefore lived in an area designated as such.

'Had a good evening?'

'Yes,' said William. Had he not had a good evening he still would have said yes, and so Christopher had to trace his certainty by remarking on how well he had been getting on with the Lester sisters now on their way back to BG. 'Yes, I like them very much,' said William, not believing for one moment that they perhaps liked him to this extent and more. 'They thought I was still living in Limassol and was wondering what had happened to me.'

'But you haven't lived in Limassol for months.'

William thought that it was perfectly natural for people not to take any notice of his departure.

'I'm shattered,' said William, further implying that his evening had indeed been a success.

'So am I.'

Christopher looked at those in front of them and then glanced at those behind. He could join most if not all of these groups and still be recognized, mainly if not only by association with the camp's most powerful girl. But nobody really cares, he thought. If nobody cares then why should I worry?

'By the way, William, where was Stanley?'

The Other Side Of Silence (a)

The Acquiescent Fold

> Simple minds explore what's new and complex turn to old.
> Rebecca Panhandle: Essay on Education

> I have not read a book which has moved me more than The Outsider. When you understand the way others look at life, especially if it is different from your own view, then you must be moved.
> Wilma Carter: Thoughts on Camus

> The Young Man jumped into the haystack
> And the needle got stuck in his back.
> An instant halt to the fun.
> I've found it! he said,
> Before he dropped dead,
> But unfortunately,
> It was the wrong one.
> Stanley Palloway: Diary of Cock Robin.

'TIME TO GO AND see Stanley. Definitely no other course to take.'

Christopher had had enough. He could take no more.

Stanley remained the only option because of the impression he gave of someone who had had enough and could take no more since the age of ten. He was now seventeen. He did not reject life but his attitude only calmed the cynic within by training the Bohemian without. He often slept in a tent at the back of his garden and would have moved onto the sports field over the fence if not for fear of authorities, grasshoppers and the morning dew.

Christopher was trying to ignore what was not quite a hangover. Its function was to keep him from feeling at all happy about life. He was prepared to blame the night before but for reasons not necessarily associated with his mixed intake of booze. He was up in time for the afternoon but did not want to go out. He did not want to stay in. He did not want to sit for hours on the sofa but neither was he keen on standing up which would mean moving to where he would have to sit down again. He did not want to do any school-work – that was a given – but felt guilty all the same about wasting time. It took him some time to arrive at the decision mentioned above although it appeared as if on an instant beam of hope and so he said it out loud.

'Who?' asked Julie.

'Stanley. You know Stan? Stanley Palloway. Postman Stan.'

Stanley was not really a postman. He worked for Akrotiri post office, and because he had a full time job and could so easily have been at school he was known, not without envy, by the profession suggested by his work.

'Oh, that moron.'

'He is not a moron. He's merely misunderstood.'

Christopher was rather fond of Stanley although if pressed he was willing to admit that the guy was weird. Julie was in no mood to defend her opinion.

One thing that was not to be misunderstood: Julie did have a hangover. To her, just now, everyone was a moron. She had stayed late after the dance and with the YK Committee, of which she was an important member, she shared a bottle of scotch. She hated whisky and then she began to like it. Now she was back to hating it. She faced a very sober breakfast of coffee and toast, but without the toast, and now facing her was a white cross taped to the sitting-room door.

'It's not Palm Sunday is it?' she asked Christopher who shared her sofa as well as her sorrow. 'Have you been to mass yet?'

'Hardly. I've hardly got up.'

'If you've hardly got up then I'm still in bed. God my head. Christ had it good.'

'He probably suffered a few hangovers in his time, all those feasts he was invited to. He even invited himself to a few, and a pretty good party trick that, changing water into wine.'

Julie looked at him – being reminded of such a miracle was not consistent with her immediate needs.

'I could do with a donkey, myself, to take me to mass. See if it can be arranged. They can dispense with the crowd waving palms.' She sat back and sighed and then said, as if having second thoughts about a possibly advantageous appointment: 'I think I'll risk my mortal soul and not bother going.'

'You had a busy time last night?'

'Busy, yes busy.'

'I didn't see you anywhere.'

'That's a coincidence. I didn't see you either. Lots of people I didn't see. Too many people I did see. I'm getting ever so slightly fed up with it all.'

That sounds hopeful, he thought, but could not think why. He asked her if the night had been a success referring quite naturally to the dance as a whole. She was in a position to give an expert opinion because she had helped to organize it. But she looked at him as if he had been questioning a media view of her personal failure.

'Well, all right,' he said, reading her stare, 'so Sonja didn't win.'

'She didn't even come third but she was by far the most beautiful girl there. I spent some time helping her look as magnificent as she did. She outshone them all like a Goddess. What were they thinking of?'

'Perhaps they were not ready for divinity. But it wasn't so bad. Nancy came third.'

'Third? Hah! I don't know what's worse. And I almost promised Sonja this victory I was so confident she'd win.'

'But even you can't fix the judging and it included those from King Dick's.'

'Wish I had fixed it now. Wouldn't surprise me if it was fixed the way the Epi lot went crazy over that cow Janek.'

Sounded to me as if the whole place went crazy over her, he thought, except for the band of Berengarians cheering Zoe.

'Oh come on, Julie. Beverley Janek is not a cow and she looked great.'

'Bev Janek is a cow and she looked like a reject from a *Harmony Hairspray* advert. She looks down on everyone. Everyone! She's the most unbelievable snob. Sonja is lovely, graceful, makes everybody feel at ease. Janek is nothing compared to her.'

This is not like Julie, he thought. She really is fed up. Poor girl. She needs a fella.

He did not really believe this but it was pleasing to think of this powerful girl being no happier, no more fulfilled and in no better shape health-wise, perhaps a bit worse on all counts, than he who had lost Helen and gained a sore head. And so he thought it would be a good idea if at that point he resisted the urge to argue in favour of Bev and, not wanting to risk his immortal soul, although in greater need of fresh air than spiritual assurance, went to mass instead.

Lord knows what she'd think if I told her I've fallen in love with Helen, but of course I would add, that on the plus side she's probably finished with me.

And after all, who knows, perhaps this Beverley Janek *is* the most unbelievable snob. I hardly know the lass.

'She's very, very sensitive – hardly talks to anyone,' said Stanley. 'Keeps her head to the ground. You know, a case of being privileged if you get to see her eyes.'

He, of all the lads he knew, actually *knew* her. Christopher, who was by now accustomed to this remarkable side of Stanley actually knowing people – people whom Christopher, through school, saw many more times than he – was astounded. He wanted to know more. Snobs were not usually so sensitive and shy that they kept their eyes to the ground, at least not in his experience. In fact, snobs, being driven more by confidence than class, were usually interesting and talkative, if not pleasant, to be with. When he was in a good mood and self-respect was an on-going session between talk and opinion, he would happily accuse himself of being a snob. And it pleased him to think that maybe others thought so too. Stanley, even more so. Anyone who thought that people were a classic example of an observable set of worthless habits could not be anything else but a snob. And it only improved Christopher's self-image to agree with him.

Stanley did a lot of observing. He had an eye for shapes and sizes, each form compared to what he called 'the acquiescent curving fold' of its neighbour. His work at the post office started him off on his theory of influential shapes, although he gave full credit, as he nearly did everything else, to his golden age of ten when he had both had enough and discovered a love for doggerel-based wisdom.

'That time I thought I can't escape, and now I never will.
'The guards that rule my sense of loss, only time will kill.
'But time takes time to tick things off, and now I cannot wait.
'The trap has closed around my life and freedom is my fate.'

He never specified the trap (Christopher assumed it was normality) or the turning point experience which offered him advanced warning of its approaching claws. It was not beyond his imagination to come up with the credible bluff, as nothing had happened to him then beyond going to school, studying for his 11-plus which he eventually failed as if choosing a popular option. His experience could be regarded as an existential leap except that very few people, and certainly none within the trial and error age-group of ten to twenty, can say with any clear certainty what is and isn't existential from a point of view of people being free to determine their own future. If Christopher knew anything about philosophy, which he didn't, the subject being sadly ignored by every curriculum he encountered, he would have accused Stanley of being a perverse form of a Hegelian rationalist. All Stanley wanted (from, as he would claim, the age of ten) was to define the truth in his own words, and so he began to accept the possibility of lies, the premise being that truth was deliberately kept hidden by the mysterious few for reasons best known to economists and philosophers. One could assume the former grudge to be political, the latter religious. Stanley's own form of solipsism prevented him from being either. But he was an activist, only insofar as quoting from his own experience, usually in verse, of what he had learnt for himself. To successfully fail the 11-plus one had to endure a grounding of what was not only essential for avoiding civilized harassment, the three Rs being the first wall erected (besides clothes) to keep embarrassment at bay, but totally adequate for surviving the rest of one's academic existence. Once in secondary school Stanley had free reign over actions according to his choice of control. He accepted the authority of co-habitable ethics and rejected everything else, beginning with algebra where he insisted that the distributive law was a load of crap. 'One plus two was not equal to two plus one. Two have fun while one with none is done.' The balance was only apparent. To say that an equilateral triangle had to be constructed from lines at sixty degrees to each other was an act of deception beyond endurance. Christopher insisted that it had to be so, but geometry had long since been kicked out. In fact maths and he, Stanley informed him, only met on a battle field of failed problems and bad reports. The same applied to English when the division between plural and singular started him on a course which ran roughshod over both grammar and vocabulary. In Geography he refused to believe in the existence of America, but this was a default mechanism of the flat-earth society of which he was ardent member, and so for him the land of chewing gum and the Monkees had become the monster of successful conspiracy. As for History – 'Why aren't we speaking French Italian? Why did it take twenty and a half centuries to invent the jet engine? What's happened to all the dead? And how could civilisations have survived without a Mars a Day?' He enjoyed art because of an understanding he had regarding shapes, but the lessons had still compounded from him enough controversy regarding anything that was definite about the subject.

'Shapes that shift upon the sands are not like putty in my hands.
'Art is beyond the empty sound of any battle cry
'There is more my friend in a dead-leaf sketch
'Than an ocean of fish to fry.'
'What are you on about?' Christopher had asked this question long before his thoughts about Alice being one of the seven maids with seven mops, and now, had he given some thought to Stanley's versified statement, his enquiry would have been coloured by sympathetic resonance.

'I've been carrying out some experiments,' Stanley said at the time, and this time thankfully not in verse, 'and I've come to the conclusion, the future does not unfold; it merely improves on the folds already made and reforming. Each moment, however, is free to form its own conclusions.' Thus the Hegelian element in his means of confusing his friend.

He slept outside in a tent, he took long circular walks around the neighbouring blocks shaping from the routes a chosen sequence of patterned events, and took up what appeared to be a normal interest in the watching of birds. He bought books on birds, collected a week by week encyclopaedic magazine on the subject, gave generously to the RSPB and attended ornithological exhibitions. He even supported a quasi-radical campaign to stamp out the use of Cypriot vineyard traps which killed by the hundreds wrens, sparrows and starlings, and worked for some weeks on his own composition, in prose, of 'On Hearing the First Cuckoo in Spring.' Naturally enough his parents were please because thanks to this and employment with the GPO, sanity was assured. Christopher, however, was given a glimpse of the other side of this interest and it helped to be at that time as ignorant as Christopher was on birds and their habits. Although not once did Stanley disagree with anything he heard or read about birds, anyone as equally as furnished on the subject as he would have accused him of deliberately twisting the facts and totally creating a new set of reasons as to why birds did what they did. He even added names to those already suitably endowed with titles. To Christopher it was quite feasible that such splendid creatures and Lapwing Souchongs and Dovetail Joists and Lesser Spotted Lemars should exist. The content of his ignorance was a marvel to behold. But he questioned Stanley's theory on the justification of elaborate nests.

'Some birds are just good at building nests and some aren't.'

'Why?' asked Stanley.

'Evolution?'

'No, no, no! The acquiescent fold! The house martin makes a nest of architectural standard matching the house upon which it's built. The cuckoo doesn't even bother making a nest. The shape or lack of shape is everything. But the most important thing about birds are the patterns in their flights. I watch them mostly because of this.'

'And can you see the patterns?'

'No, not yet.'

'Then how do you know they're there?'

'There's no knowing about it. The patterns I'm talking about are not like normal patterns. They are a flow and the only way we can understand them is to trap them into form. Gosh, I wish I was a bird. Despite the hardships, hazards and having to feed their greedy young, they're so close to the truth that its worth everything a human life has to offer.'

'But only humans can appreciate truth.'

'My God, we're the ones who can't. We have to constantly justify ourselves. Therefore we make up bastard truths, like one plus two equals two plus one.'

Christopher was no longer willing to defend basic maths or assert that it was not Stanley-dized truth which was making him think differently about the very foundation of his number crunching experience. He was, however, more interested in Stanley's theory about animals, in particular birds and grasshoppers. Stanley had a fear of grasshoppers, crickets and the like. Christopher got to know about this because Stanley told him about the tent.

'I have spent

'Time in a tent

'In order to repent

'The time I haven't spent

'In a tent.'

He continued in prose: 'I sleep in this tent in order to break a pattern restricting me from seeing other patterns.'

Christopher looked at the tent. It was small, simple and pitched at the back of the Palloways' garden.

'What?' he asked. 'Every night?'

'No, not every night. Do you think I'm stupid? I like my comforts as well, you know. But if you sleep more nights in a tent than in your bedroom then you'll know what I mean. I wanted to break away from the garden but

I'm scared of grasshoppers.'

The sports field was full of grasshopper-type chirpy creatures that only emerged at night in order to help remind residents that they were no longer in England. This was no hallucination conjured by the inconsistency of this fear with regard to natural history matching the exigency of theory. If sanity maintained a healthy distance from phobia his theory was hardly a redemption. However, the fear itself offered him the human touch more approachable to the society he seemed to reject. If hell existed in the middle of a locust storm, heaven, the peaceful gyration of the sky-born, afforded him the space to see and hear shapes and sounds totally free of any austere distractions. He went on long walks, took Christopher with him a couple of times, explaining from the build up of shapes made from the routes they took the events occurring within – very mundane events, such as people washing cars or walking to shops or talking to each other over garden fences while flopping flags of washing gave forth an encouraging chorus like the cryptic ingredients of a Gilbert and Sullivan operetta. Christopher no longer believed that Stanley was dotty, just on the right side of being 'strangely strange but oddly normal', a quote that Stanley himself was happy to process from one of his favourite singles.

He first met Stanley with William at the Families Club Sunday night disco. Stanley was actually willing to patronize these events especially if it meant little more than sitting at a table and watching what was going on. He first went by himself and then with William whom he had known since living in Limassol. Christopher took to joining them a few times to see films at the Astra, but more often to attend these fortnightly discos which none of the three really enjoyed with any negotiable enthusiasm. It became beyond all three to understand why they went. Even Stanley and his acquiescent folds or his venture into verse could not explain it. 'This disco is a pisco that rarely goes balisco.' The three informed each other about how reluctant they were to go when they went, and throughout the evening the collective reluctance, instead of abating apiece, increased to the final opinion that yet another Sunday night had been wasted.

Christopher always went to the Club on Sunday evenings to get paid and so it was merely a case of deciding every two weeks whether or not to stay. Before he knew Stanley he used to venture in and then, minutes later, venture out. Now he waited for Stanley and if he didn't show he would call around, the Palloways' house being on the way back to his own, to find out why. The reason usually remained on an optional basis where there was close to a fifty-fifty chance of him returning with Stanley to the Club, often with William tagging along, himself a frequent visitor to the Palloways and, apart from Christopher, Stanley's only friend. Stanley never mentioned his theory when both William and Christopher were there. Christopher was under the impression that he enjoyed the privileged post of instruction. William perhaps maintained a balance for Stanley to step out and become for others a normal, unassuming character quite in line with the down-market level of the Meald and Panhandle society. And what could be more down-market than supporting the Families Club discos? Is that the impression? Christopher thought without undue concern, three lonely lads looking at dancing girls. He often marvelled at his own loneliness and how it differed from Stanley's; both inclined towards self-imposed isolation. As for William: some had it thrust upon them.

Stanley was forever reluctant to break any agreement he might have made about being by himself. To him, loneliness was a gift and possibly perceiving its value within Christopher, he befriended him at a dance a good year ago, a friendship resulting from a warning about Frances Smith. The girl was only interested in herself he said, which, being a safe assumption entailing ninety percent of all known girls, would have sounded as such from anyone else. From him, accompanied with advice to Christopher about better things to do than wasting his time chasing her, it sounded as if being presented with a new angle to be examined in the light of social experience. But Christopher, who did not believe for one moment that he had been chasing Frances (after all the girl had been constantly pestering him – 'ask Colin Jottrell'), continued chasing her. Then he went out with Rosemary whom Stanley thought was a better match but gave him the benefit of another warning: this Dazel sister now despised her previous boyfriend (that being Colin) and Christopher was probably a classic case of rebound and the sounding board of moral revenge.

'I know that,' said Christopher. 'I *am* being used as a sounding-board for her moral revenge.'

He was not quite sure what this meant but thought it to be consistent with the facts. Rosemary would not shut up about how much she had detested Colin. This worried Christopher because, although he too had also detested Colin, no longer around to offer a Jottrell means of defence, he began to think of himself as the main subject to be brought under attack should she move on to another boyfriend. All along there had to be another boyfriend because he had more horror of permanence with Rosemary than he ever nurtured with Helen. Rosemary was quite pretty and vivacious and, along with her sister, appeared to conform in a fanciful way to all the innocent delights of being young and looking for love. But as part of a team with Grace Ford and others, there formed a conspiracy to undermine rather to encourage pride in sound friendship. Besides which, Christopher, having lost Grace Ford (after persistent thoughts of worship from afar) to Louding (who lost her to some round-faced skinhead in uniform) and feeling the pressure of Gale's attention insert unnecessary seeds of guilt, had a hunch from the beginning that going out with Rosemary as her replacement for Colin – even just going out with her – was not totally correct. It went against the grain of his friendship with her brother Henry who, at the time, had not quite left to start his career in the RAF. But then Stanley thought she was a better match than Frances, and to add to the confusion, because for Christopher, Frances had never been a match, had taken a dim view of Christopher's designs on Grace. She did not fit the pattern, the fold, of what was acquiescently available.

Stanley thought that the Dazel girls were okay. One just had to be firm. To prove this he broke the reclusive side of the pact he had with himself and suggested to William some months later that *they* should take the two girls out. William could only see the falling flat part of the idea's outcome, but the girls actually did agree to go out with them. A meal was planned in the café called Half-way House some miles beyond 'Checkpoint Charlie', and while this offered little by way of after-meal night club options, all four enjoyed a reasonably fun night out, and a further two weeks of brisk and daylight association which ran into Christmas and on to the New Year. Gale still wanted Christopher so badly during the former days of his courting Helen that she was willing to compromise by taking up with William, the good all round friend, an established proxy whose close to complete lack of looks was to her a temporary assurance. Once Christopher was free William would surely do the right thing and stand aside. Rosemary always did fancy Stanley who was, to all intents and purposes, despite his reputation for being a loon, a fine looking lad. She hardly knew him personally which helped; and so he became Rosemary's boyfriend after Christopher – some three months after Christopher – enough time for Christopher to all but forget that he had gone out with her let alone nurture forebodings about how she would treat him as a conversation piece. The airman she had deserted Christopher for had very soon deserted her. She did not have the flourishing touch to a deception which kept Grace's love life alive, and this was just as well because she and Christopher remained on good terms. Grace, although part of the circle surrounding Louding, apparently had to forfeit by mixture and usage, her role in the group. She was a natural born leader, not in Julie's league and therefore no imperative threat, but devoid of her outlet because of her betrayal, she lost interest and the loss was mutual. Christopher, who fancied her once, as did Henry and Colin, hardly thought about her now, and seeing her last night at the football dance, once more in the circle, made little difference. From a spontaneous list to Stanley as to who had been there (his own absence due to unknown quantities and the clash in experimental time) he only just managed to fit her in, a name most likely to precede a grunt from Stanley by way of response. But there again Christopher had hardly thought of Wendy, Debra, Heidi and any number of girls he may have seen and recognized from long ago in the halcyon days of Henry, but brought back together for one complete evening. The fact that he had fallen in love with Helen, in a way, funded the vacuum.

'So, the Dazel sisters were there,' said Stanley, 'with you lot? I'm glad William made it. He enjoyed himself?'

'If not the man's a master of deception.'

'So he and Gale are back on talking terms.'

'He wasn't actually with Gale. Gale and Rosemary just became part of our group like I was part of the group.'

The fact that the folding events allowed Gale and William to share the same space, irrespective of groups, was to Stanley reassuring enough. He did not blame himself for the downfall in William's short-lived romance but it hardly helped matters to remember that he had fashioned the necessary fold which got them together. Rosemary, in a style exclusive to those who try to mean well but wander into areas beyond this plan, had fashioned a fold which broke them apart. She had organized a New Year's party and invited the wrong people. Her friends on one side did not like her friends on the other. They said that Gale had been making a fool of herself by going out with someone as gross looking as William, and for a different but not unrelated reason, Stanley quarrelled with Grace and walked out. The gentle art of maintaining the correct attitude was tough even for one who understood the right folds. The right to conflict could not easily be set aside, deliberate in its folding as fun, and Stanley relished within this one evening the chance of severing himself forever from Grace's society.

'Ever since I was ten I've never met a girl like her,' he said implying, of course, that before the age of ten he had met many.

'No different from any other girl,' said Christopher who at the time of hearing about the event was trying to figure out why he had not been invited. Maybe Rosemary thought I'd be sensitive to any affectionate display she was willing to demonstrate towards Stanley.

But as it happened she never allowed herself the chance to display anything other than a mild form of hysteria – fifty minutes before the midnight hour a nasty quarrel erupted on her premises; the cakes had been burnt earlier that day and someone had stolen a couple of her favourite records, and it was all enough to make a grown girl rush upstairs and weep. However, there was no upstairs up which to rush. She ran along the hall and Gale followed, while William thought that the best thing for him to do was to follow Stanley. Gale ran after William to inform him that it was all Stanley's fault because Rosemary said it was all Stanley's fault and Gale was that type of sister. William insisted that it had been Grace's fault and that Stanley was his friend. Grace, by this time, was with Rosemary, talking her into hating Stanley. Gale and William managed to do something similar into hating each other while still, those who were left got on with having a party.

'And I wasn't invited,' said Christopher. 'I can sort of imagine Grace getting up your nose.'

'She's very destructive.'

'No she isn't. Actually I think she's quite delightful.'

He was just remembering then that he had spent his Hogmanay in bed suffering from intermittent bouts of flu which had jiggered his Christmas and all but put an early halt to his blossoming romance with Helen. And now the blossoms have faded, the petals have dropped, and every time now a record is played which reminds me of her I'll be convinced that she was the treasure I've been too blind to see.

It was fitting that just as Christmas should create, despite the flu, a beginning, the passion of Christ, under the religious delusion of Palm Sunday, should mark what had to be an end. It was not very refreshing to be reminded about the consequence of debt which he and many others of a similar religious bent felt that they owed to Christ. When he thought about what it meant to have someone die for him without being asked, he wondered if Christ really wanted him to do likewise. Mass was lengthened by St John's Passion being read out in full by Father Fullman, James Panhandle and Larry Parthy. Christopher's dad did the narrative and as if indulging in the special magic of this office pronounced each word with the precision of one actually expecting magic to result. Father Fullman filled in for Christ and all he said, while Larry gave a fitting rendition of an Irish Pilate, Irish Caiaphas and an Irish crowd calling for their adopted hero Barabbas. Having recently seen Anthony Quinn play the part, Barabbas was now something of a hero to Christopher. It was a long reading throughout which the congregation was expected to stand unless special needs demanded otherwise. Christopher longed to sit down. He was still suffering which was probably appropriate given the story he was listening to. My head aches, he thought, but I disagree with Julie. Christ in comparison did not have it easy. All the same, he could have done with sitting down. Not like the children in front, bored and restless, still to be instructed in the restrictions of history, religion, legend and tradition.

'So you have not the strength to keep awake with me one hour? You should be awake and praying not to be put to the test. The spirit is willing but the flesh is weak.'

What is there about this story which always needs to be explained? If Christ did suffer to such an extent by the hands of those who revered him earlier and, like many, were led astray by more fashionable events, can I ever be thankful enough? But Christopher was unable to feel any gratitude. He carried his white cross all the way to the Families Club where he was paid and where he sat patiently waiting for Stanley, patiently contemplating the effect a brandy-lemon would have on his now mildly throbbing head.

'What do you think of this?' he asked Stanley, handing over the palm cross with a drink of coke.

'Smells nice. Good Catholic incense, no doubt.'

'Is it a good form? Does the cross have a special fold?'

Stanley held up the white cross. He examined it closely. He saw that running down the stalk were lines so temptingly placed that it was all he could do to resist folding it and having it crack at the surface.

'Brittle stuff.' He handed it back.

'Stanley, I think I'm in love.'

'Who with?'

He asked this without any urgent sense of expecting something new. It was not every day that Christopher fell in love, but he seemed to exact a fancy for girls which were, to Stanley, so erroneously favourable. Love was just part of the game.

'Helen.'

'Oh come on, Christopher. Surely not Helen? You're going out with her. Mind you, if you are going out with her and you've just fallen in love with her then what's the problem?'

'I'm no longer going out with her. We fell out last night just before I was about to take her to the dance. She walked off in a huff, big-time huff and I ended up going to the dance by myself – well not actually by myself. I was with Louding and I met William there and others, but my point is, during the dance I discovered that I loved her. I fell in love with her, I think. I'm still in love with her – I think.'

'That makes as much sense as anything else I've heard recently. What did William think?'

'Well, I didn't actually get around to telling him. But I told Louding.'

'Of course you told Louding. I don't hold any illusions about being the one friend you confide in.'

Christopher looked at him. He was not sure if this was the response he wanted to hear.

'Don't you want to know what Louding thought?'

'Not particularly. With all the women who love him what does he know about love?'

'A lot. He said I was loving like a school boy.'

'But you are a school boy and, you know what, so is he.'

'Do you not like Louding?'

'I don't know him that well to give an honest answer. I suspect he's a self-satisfied prat.'

'You're talking about my best friend, I'll have you know.'

However Christopher was not offended. This was the first time he had encountered a negative word about Louding and Christopher knew well, by now, that Stanley's distaste for Grace was deeply imbedded in his own struggle with unrequited love, and Louding had been one of her many romantic interludes. But Christopher was still frustrated by the way the conversation was veering. He had wanted a Stanleynized explanation of it all – best way of escaping the sacrifice involved in the Christian view as gently and persuasively laid down by the agape symbol of the white cross beside Stanley's glass.

'Anyway, Stanley, how can my being in love with Helen make sense after finishing with her, after we'd been going out for so long?'

'Yes, true, it has been quite a long time. But it's quite natural for people to suddenly miss and value what they took for granted but now have to do without. Even I can't dispute that foible in human nature.'

'I don't *just* miss her. God in heaven, I may have missed Rosemary but I never ever loved *her*. I do now love Helen, which means I want her and I don't want anybody else.'

Stanley looked at him with an air of defiance as if Christopher had declared that a much-needed bunch of keys had been lost but in reality he just hadn't searched hard enough.

'How do you know you've finished with her? If it was last night you could easily make up again. She isn't going with another guy, is she?'

'No. She isn't going with another guy. She's going to England soon, that's what's she's doing.'

'For us lot here, going to England soon is as inevitable as death and tax. How soon? Too soon for you tell her you love her? Have you told her you love her?'

'No, of course not. I only discovered I loved her after she stormed off.' Christopher thought about this. 'Do you think I should?'

Stanley shrugged. This meant yes – the obvious solution – and the disco had started, the sound from which was plunging its way into the bar from the adjacent hall. He had lost interest in Christopher's freshly sprung love-life in the ardent face of more trivial parts of his studies in the art of elucidating acquiescent folds. The dance and all it meant was too nebulous and covered in such a vast range of sins against the golden mean of clarity for him to resist being the mannered observer for the purposes of justice and reason. He was as fascinated by the means of love and being loved as the next lad but could not approach the element of its rhythm with any reasonable degree of success for himself. It was not his fault if people decided to love him – he was not going to love people.

As it happened the only person to fall into this category was Eve Sholts. Pamela Peters had told Christopher that her best friend, Eve, loved Stanley. What could they do?

'Nothing,' said Christopher, 'except hope that Stanley falls in love with her and then all will be well with the world.'

But Pamela was reluctant to relegate matters concerning others to the feckless area of hope. Eve was frightened that she, Pamela, might do something drastic like demand from Stanley some sort of response. All Stanley had done was to walk the shy girl home after one particular Families Club dance when both she and he had arrived at the venue alone. He admitted to Christopher that Eve was indeed a very nice and totally inoffensive girl.

'But not my type.'

Christopher had his doubts, but even if Eve was unable to fit the type suitable for one busily rearranging the laws of the cosmos, it would have been a supporting testament to Stanley's rejection of the apparent truth if he had gone out with the girl. But he would not go out with her and neither would he avoid her, not contemplating the risk of her worship becoming a special issue. He still turned up to the dances where she was likely to be. In fact there seemed to be little chance of him not attending the Families Club discos. He was not there particularly to emphasize his ability to cope, but he was insensitive to Eve's ability. She was possibly pulled along most of the time by Pamela who longed to see her friend matched up with the arrogant lad.

'Teach him a thing or two,' she said, but following Christopher's advice she did not pre-empt any situation. Christopher was a great believer in the natural outcome when it came to matters of the heart.

He was not testing this belief in his compulsive telling of the events of last night as he and Stanley walked into the disco and took their usual table on the far side of the speakers and sat ready to observe the flood of young teenagers who would eventually cover the floor.

'I wouldn't concern yourself too much about Helen,' said Stanley, basking in a rare moment of Limassol-based reminiscence. 'I never did and I went out with her, remember.'

This, even for Stanley, was not far from the truth. Stanley's stay in Limassol had been just long enough for him to get to know Helen and have himself subject to attentions Christopher had tragically, so he now thought, taken for granted. Helen skipped her way in the class of folds Stanley had been happy to place to one side for the sake of future reference. She believed herself to be universally adored, and because Stanley moved to Akrotiri before he was ready to make her think differently, she continued to regard him with some esteem. She now very rarely saw him which helped to create an illusion of his authority. If anyone knows about Helen, thought Christopher, having heard Helen exhort Stanley's virtues as a contrast to his own, Stanley does. And so he gave Stanley the benefit of this latest revelation only to have it cast to one side under the guise of indifference.

Christopher adopted another approach.

'Is it possible to fall in love with Helen?' he asked.

'I shouldn't have thought so. But there again, there you are, in love with her.'

'So you don't think this is remarkable? Doesn't this shake at the foundations of all your talk of patterns and form?'

'No, not at all. If anything, it verifies its immaculate twists. Who won the beauty contest then?'

Christopher, having just described the dance or, as he called it, the undulating crush, and thus given Stanley the pleasure of not having added to its effect, had omitted this one detail due to a difference of opinion concerning Grace and the blessings of her still being around. It reminded him of Helen having not been around and in the light of this such matters as the all important beauty contest paled.

'Beverley Janek. She did look super. I fancied a girl called Nicosia Knaves.'

'I know her,' said Stanley.

'Who, Miss Knaves?'

'No. Bev Janek.'

And he was surprised. Not that her obvious beauty could be easily surpassed, but on saying that he knew her he exposed the challenge. She was sensitive. She, like Eve, was shy. But she, unlike Eve, was not, at present, in love with Stanley, but, be that as it may and notwithstanding the fact that she lived in Episkopi, it seemed likely that he really did know her (but of course – much beyond Christopher's reasoning – such knowledge 'in the biblical sense' was inconceivable).

'I met her in Limassol in an ironmonger's shop. She was so shy and nervous as we entered an alien land of Cypriot artisans that she was unable to ask for what she wanted. I remember I struggled to make myself understood, my Greek not being up to much and we always expect them to speak English. I wanted a curtain rail and a roller for the wringer on our washing machine and she wanted picture hooks. I somehow succeeded in getting what I wanted and so she tentatively asked me if I would come to her assistance.' He shook his head as if to nostalgically grasp the magic of this arrangement which, for him and his out-of-this-worldly experience with retail therapy, had amounted to a once-in-a-lifetime experience. 'So, I did most of the talking and she was impeccably grateful. I have to say, her gratitude, which in broken bits of conversation, lasted all the way back to the street where I lived and to the bus which she caught, swept over me not unlike your revelation of love last night.'

'You mean you fell in love.'

'Certainly not. I was smitten because she was that rare combination of being charmingly shy and exceptionally beautiful. So, of course, she has the power to do that to any boy of any age. I was fascinated because she couldn't talk without blushing and staring at the ground – however, I can imagine that sustaining such fascination could be something of a strain. She's very, very sensitive – hardly talks to anyone. Keeps her head to the ground. You know, a case of being privileged if you get to see her eyes'

Christopher consciously fingered the money lying in loose folds within his jacket pocket. He wanted another drink. The hall was still half empty and so it was probably worth going back to the bar without risking the loss of their table here, but then he remembered that part of the money belonging to Oliver. None of the other doormen had arrived. It was not unusual for them to be late, especially if incentive was being hindered by debt. He was in no mood for another financial wrangle almost assured in such a world where minor-level justice was constantly pursued. He was resigned to paying the cost of their collective carelessness but not now. Wait until tomorrow. A few girls were dancing. The coke and 7up were out in crates on the far table, and there, quite close to where these refreshments could be bought sat Pamela and Eve. Shall I will them to come over here? he thought. Poor Eve. Pamela loves the intrigue. I can tell by the way she knows we're here and she'll look in every other direction and talk rapidly to all her many lesser friends and leave Eve beside her sitting in silence. And Gale – Gale was sitting with them and she did indeed look in their direction and point to them and wave.

'What I'd like to know,' said Christopher slowly as he waved back.

'Uhuh?' murmured Stanley unable to notice the girls on the other side because of those dancing in front to which he gave his studious but un-rapt attention.

'Is, who persuaded Bev Janek to represent the Epi Eagles, you know, being as you say she's so shy and withdrawn? Taking part in the contest must have been a very nerve-wracking occasion for her – let alone winning it.'

'You know, you've got a good point there. Who talked her into it? Perhaps we shall never know.'

'I did,' said Brian.

It was Steve who had asked the question. It was not because of the persuasion needed that he was curious. He had played a couple of disinterested games for the Starlings who had survived a couple more. He had been more enthusiastic about victory represented by a beautiful girl than a silver cup and was surprised to the point of being highly vexed that King Dick's could produce someone better looking that Nancy, and it pleased him slightly less to see the Eagles leap in with their fancy-piece and in effect score victory without having produced any great results on the pitch. He was only incensed because Brian, who had led the Eagles from one defeat to the next, entered the physics class with fists outstretched chanting: 'Bev the best, Bev the best.'

'You did!' said Christopher, after following him in and chanting likewise. He who is truly neutral can wholeheartedly appreciate the best.

'Pillock.'

'Be Steve a sore loser?' enquired Brian, going around the front of Warwick's lab. He was going to write on the blackboard: 'Bev the best' but John Warwick entered and almost immediately, without saying hello, without the hesitation needed for Monday mornings, demanded Brian's homework. 'But, sir, it be the last week of term. Besides weren't the problems meant for this Thursday?'

'No they were not.'

'Weren't they?' asked Christopher.

'No, Panhandle. For today.'

He honestly thought that the problems set last week had by their very weight a week's allowance. As far a Brian was concerned it could well have been Thursday of next year.

'I've been too busy studying for my exams,' he explained nonchalantly, 'in order that I might gain a place in a good university and carve out for myself a career which will shape the rest of my otherwise luckless life.'

'I'll shape the rest of your luckless life if you don't sit down.'

Christopher wanted to find out first-hand how Brian had persuaded Bev to become a beauty queen but they were given experiments which separated them by four benches. He set up what was known as Searle's Bar and for the next two hours progress towards world peace depended on him determining the thermal conductivity of water. Ten minutes into the fun and he had a disaster. He had before him a funnel up to the brim of which the level of water was kept constant by slight adjustments of a tap and a red rubber pipe. Constant water flow was as significant an outcome as the electrical measurements he needed to make, and all at first made the picture of a pretty practical. But no sooner did Christopher take his eyes off the funnel then the entire apparatus toppled over and into the sink which was primarily there in this case to catch the water arriving from the red hose at the other end. It was this red hose which flew out of the sink and flew around in a generous semi-circle soaking Christopher and risked all within a three-foot radius.

'Somehow,' said Edmund, shaking his head and scratching his chin, giving the panicking Christopher the benefit of his intelligent stare, 'I don't think that's what's supposed to happen.'

'Panhandle principles at work,' announced Brian. 'Could you do it again? The crash sounded great but I didn't see a thing.'

'Action replay coming up,' said Steve as Christopher struggled with his pipes and funnel while desperately trying to remember how to turn off the tap.

'Well, come on, give us a hand,' he said.

'Savina, your closest,' said Mr Warwick. 'Go and give the wretched lad a hand.'

'Why me?' asked Savina, looking at her own work in a manner which read her presence alongside it as indispensible, but for the benefit of all she left her own work and aided Christopher's drenched recovery.

When they had finally sculptured a secure arrangement of retort stands, adjusted pipes and flickering meters, Savina asked him if he was okay.

'Have you seen Helen at all?' he asked. 'Was she on your bus?'

'No. I was told by her sister that she is not coming in to school today.'

'Why not?'

'I do not know. Helen maybe thinks that as it's the last week of term and she's leaving soon it's not worth bothering with school.'

'You mean she might not turn up at all?'

'You should know better than me, Christopher. And now, if you think everything is okay, I have my own experiment to do.'

'Savina, what would I do without you? Where would I be? You are adorable. I'll take back what I said about not marrying you.'

'I think you will find that it is me not marrying you.'

'Be mine and we can dilly-dally over experiments forever.'

'I am not interested in your dilly-dallying,' she said in her prefect tone, and she walked away, aloof but highly delighted.

Christopher, however, was not delighted. He was wet through and bereft of Helen. He looked at his funnel, he adjusted his tap and he asked himself why life was for him such a monumental cock-up. I could go to Limassol, he thought. I could see her tomorrow. I could see her this afternoon. But she is deliberately avoiding me by taking the week off, and it's the last week of term. Nobody takes off the last week of term.

Dot and Doris did. Only Monday morning saw their exuberance fill the bus.

'Last week of term! Last week of term!' they sang together from the back of the bus. 'Let's have perm and swallow the sperm.'

'What?' said a chorus of others at the back.

'Last week of term! Last week of term!'

And then for the rest of the week, no Dot and Doris. This was highly annoying for their faithful friends who waited past the first bell every morning at school. They did not want to see Christopher shake his head at them as he stepped off the bus, always the first to do so being the bus prefect and therefore he being the first they saw after the bus pulled in, but he shook his head at them on Tuesday and Wednesday and then he himself stayed away on Thursday. Savina, in her turn, had shaken her head at him. No Helen. No message? Christopher did not know Helen's sister. Somehow, maybe miraculously, they had been circumstantially kept apart during the months he had been going out with Helen. Even so, if her sister was available to comment on what Savina implied by the head shaking, it could be that no message was better than any endorsed reason for staying away.

Brian also had his troubles. He confided in Christopher who only approached him while alone on Monday because he wanted to know a bit more about Beverley Janek. Who knows? he thought. Something on the sparkling side maybe going on between her and the Innmaker.

'Is something on the sparkling side going on between you and Bev Janek?'

But this was not a happy Brian despite having declared jubilant triumph for the otherwise defeated Eagles just an hour and a half ago. In fact he had not expected anyone to interrupt his solitary flow of worry. Christopher was a sympathetic, regular type of fellow who surely understood even if he had not experienced the pressures one such as he had to endure. Not easy living up to an image of being perpetually above average. Christopher, of course, did not understand, but as nobody else did there was a chance, perhaps, that he could start.

'The world's about to collapse. In fact an imminent collapse would be a blessing.'

Poor lad's in love, he thought. Like me, he thought. Although maybe not like me because she's a beauty queen whereas Helen's – well Helen's Helen – free from competition.

'How can the world collapse, Brian?' he asked, 'when you're equipped with the Innmaker powers of persuasion, charm and charisma?'

'It's Jane Sellers upon who my many gifts are null and void.'

'Jane Sellers! You're in love with Jane Sellers?'

'Good God no. I'd sooner fall in love with her Cheshire Cat. I'd sooner fall in love with Canterbury Castle. Whatever gave you that idea?'

But Jane is not without charm, Christopher thought.

They both thought this but for different reasons. Christopher thought that his love for Helen was comparable. Brian thought that his love for himself, its dignity and honour, may not be undermined. The alternative was too shattering for his now delicate ego to endure.

'But, you know, Christopher me lad, you've just given me an idea. If I was to declare my undying love for her how could she possibly carry out her threat?'

'What threat?'

'She wants compensation for the cat.'

'What cat?'

'That cat that sat on the mat beside my painting and then went splat into Canterbury Castle. Wilma Carter put her up to this. She said I was the one who threw the cat into Canterbury Castle and they're blaming me because it didn't return.'

'Yes it did. I saw it return.'

'Didn't I throw it back again?'

Christopher could not remember. He looked at Brian and thought that perhaps he did.

'Well, what if you did? What do they mean by compensation?'

'A signed apology and a declaration of how, because of the superiority of her cat to my tree, I was compelled by artistic temperament to launch it forth into oblivion and into what became the Canterbury Castle siege.'

'Oh, I'd leave out the bit about the castle, Brian. The beak's still after the people who started that.'

'I doubt it. All he ever worries about when he's out of cold storage are VIP's. But don't worry; I intend to leave out the bit about the castle, because I intend to leave out the apology and everything.'

He was pleased now, having given voice to this assertion, and he sat back as if the problem had been solved. But then he remembered the real cause for his despair.

'You know what they're threatening to do.'

'Shudder to think.'

'It's truly horrible, devious and absolutely despicable. I'd sooner face electric shock therapy, incarceration, the lot. I'd sooner have each one of my lovely locks pulled out one by one while the rack is stretching the Young's modulus out of me. I'd sooner be…I'd sooner be…'

'Castrated?'

'Aye, castrated. Well, no, perhaps not castration. Maybe shaking Sealhard's hand and collecting a house-point certificate is preferable to being castrated – but only just.'

'Never. They're not going to…Brian?' Christopher gasped. He was deeply shocked. He also wondered why it had taken so long. This had been a threat hanging over Brian since he had made it known that the Head Boy's job should have gone to himself and not Gavin Peters.

Christopher was also wondering why Louding was taking so long, and if it would be better now to start on his Searle's Bar write-up during private study so he could justify zipping across to Limassol for the afternoon in Louding's bus (not Savina's – too much of a give-away) or, if it was worth justifying, worth going at all, after all pride also had a stake when it came to declarations of love.

'I'm astounded. Could it possibly be true?'

'It will be done. The only consoling point is that at least I won't be the first sixth former to be publicly humiliated by being congratulated for scoring ten house-points. It happened to some poor bastard around about this time in 1970, so I'm told.'

'Who was it? Is he still here?'

'The disgrace must have been too much to bear. I'm sure he took the only honourable way out – a bottle of brandy and a 45.'

'Makes me feel all oogly inside thinking about it. Brian, you've got to fight this. You must not be made the second one to seek such an honourable solution. You haven't seen Louding at all today, have you?'

'What can I do? They say that unless compensation is forthcoming before the end of the week, and of all the weeks in the term this one has to be the four day week…'

'Good grief, yes, Good Friday this week. Hah, it's the end of term.' He and everyone else had known this already, but it was always worth reminding oneself and others of this inevitable fact. Terms, by definition, came to an end. 'How can they amass enough house-points in four days, and then after that you've a two week reprieve.'

'Women have methods of making anything happen. That's why they're women and not men?'

'What's to stop you threatening them with the same thing?'

'What, me actually score ten house points and post them in their names.'

'Well, for it to work on Wilma and Jane together you'd have to score twenty.'

'I wouldn't have the slightest idea how to go about scoring one.'

'You could always start by doing your homework. I wonder what happened to Louding.'

'You know, Christopher. I think you may have hit on something there. What's it matter if I don't get a sausage so long as I threaten them? They're not to know. For all I know they're probably bluffing me. They have to be. How can any sixth former score ten house-points and maintain self-respect, especially within four days?'

Brian stood up. He was happy again. Christopher was expecting him to call him a genius.

'Christopher, you're a genius.'

'Always glad to be of help. Obvious really. Have you seen Louding at all?'

'I don't even have to declare my love for her, the bitch. Fancy imagining for one moment that I would.'

'I don't think she did.'

'What?'

'All she wants is a declaration of her artistic superiority with reference to her cat as opposed to your tree, and an apology. You can insert love as you think best.'

Christopher thought now that he was sounding distinctly like Stanley, but quite basically Brian before him was an emotional man quite capable of slotting such a girl as Jane into what or who should or should not be loved.

They were not only ones in the prefects' room. Break was almost over but still no Louding, or for that matter, no Jane or Wilma. They were on prefect-duty. Helen, who was rarely on duty on a Monday would have been with him now. I'll see her tomorrow, he thought. Who knows, she may actually be ill?

'You know what,' said Brian, sitting down and reaching over for the guitar. 'What's an apology from one artist to another? After all, has it not been said, Jane is an artist? Perhaps the best we have, and the Cheshire Cat is part of a wonderful story about such things as walruses and carpenters and babies and pigs and pepper and people getting their head chopped off and somewhere in there is Humpty Dumpty. And I can't explain. Sold my tree for £15. Hah! All she got was a lousy book token.'

'Worth £15.'

'I shall draft the required declaration and apology right now. Least I can do.'

And he started plucking the chords to 'Little Tin Soldier'.

'Clever of you to persuade Bev to represent the Eagles last Saturday night.'

'Bloody clever of her to win.' He was in a modest mood. Credit would not be denied but shared. 'Lovely girl, isn't she? Bit shy.'

'So I'm told. In fact I'm told she's very shy. I'd like to know where she hides herself at school.'

'Wouldn't we all? Especially now that she's a celebrity. "I'm just your little tin soldier…" Clever Bev, becoming a celebrity.'

'How did you do it, talking her into becoming a beauty queen?'

'Simple. Of course it helps to be me, but I just asked her if she would become Miss Epi Eagles and she said yes.'

'Just like that?'

'Just like that. She thought I was joking.'

Christopher also thought he was joking. Team effort had probably been used. Poor Brian, he thought. He'll probably still have to shake Sealhard's hand no matter what he does. I know that Steve's already used his name on a couple of points he was awarded for library work, and Savina's constantly doing what she shouldn't if she wants to avoid the dreaded ten, and under Steve's influence her name won't be on all of them, and even Gavin and Louding have contributed to the effort of Operation Innmaker. Where is Louding?

Louding had fallen ill on Sunday and had stayed off until Tuesday. He would have stayed off until Thursday had he been told earlier what was to happen on Wednesday. Nobody had known until Tuesday but to the enthusiasts it had been a planned rumour for some time.

'There, you see,' said Francis, 'you're on the list.'

The lists were on the sports board. They had been pinned up without any special ceremony but within hours it had been examined by hundreds.

'You think it may have been possible to ask me first?' said Louding.

'You weren't here to be asked.'

Christopher, who stood behind the others at the board, had to admit that this was true. The default mechanism had kicked in and it had been assumed that Louding wanted to play. Christopher, himself, wasn't on the list and try as he may, because of this omission for which he was thoroughly grateful, he could not sympathize to the point of disputing ethical details.

'I may not have been here at all to play,' said Louding. 'Time for a relapse, I think.'

He walked away. It ceased to amaze Christopher the amount of people who were compelled to follow Louding, including, of course, himself, especially when such walking away was driven more by determination than talking. For the first time in hours the lists were almost deserted.

'You don't think we were going to leave you out of the team. You've scored more tries than anyone else here ever in the history of St John's.'

Francis was attempting to remind Louding of his self-respect which had been convincingly exercised on himself by the likes of the Colin Kamp, Bill Grey and the other usual suspects making up the sports-crazies. They all would have considered any departure from what was expected on the field as a gross affront to nature.

'Can I help it if I'm in the right place at the right time I can run fast?'

'Come on, Louding, anyone would think you didn't like rugby.'

'I can think of no better way of spending a Wednesday afternoon, especially the one just before the holidays, than being mashed into the ground by the staff team.'

Anyone would have assumed from the way he played that avoiding such a mashing was his chief skill. But Louding was not that upset. His reluctance to play was now a formality. He knew he was good. He knew he'd probably score not one but maybe even three tries. In fact he often harboured ideas, at the expense of his better nature, about being the best. For my age, of course, he thought, and on this side of the Middle East – maybe on the other side depending on how far the Middle East stretches. Not so deep down, in fact quite close to the surface, he knew that had his name not been on the list wondering why would have preoccupied him much more than concern about being injured before Easter. There was the common worry of total devastation. The annual inter-staff pupil rugby match had always resulted in total devastation for the fifth and sixth formers who played. Most of them facing this year's result were now following Louding back across the yard to the temporary sanctuary of the prefects' room.

Brian had to run to catch them up. He had sneaked back for a second look at the list. First time he had been so certain that his name would be with the forwards – and he would have settled for a position in the line, even on the wings – he did not at first take in the fact that he was to be one of the reserves. Having had this verified he was now annoyed. He called Colin by his second name and wanted to know why.

'I've played for the school every time. Dammit, I've even scored tries.'

'I don't organize these things,' said Colin, mild-manner enough to assume that Brian was exercising justifiable anger and not needing to add that, after all, he, Kamp, was only a fifth former.

'Bill bloody Grey and the rest of the bastards – they've always had it in for me. Bloody reserve. What do they think I am?'

'If they had it in for you,' said Steve, conjuring for himself ideas of an alien position granted to him because of a tactical reshuffle, 'they'd have made you loose-head prop.'

'That's what I am. I'm one of the forwards. Bastards…'

'Sorry about that, Brian,' said Colin sounding genuine. 'There's just too many to choose from. If I had my way David Bury wouldn't be hooker. Poor Christopher here isn't even in the reserves.'

'Yes,' said poor Christopher. Dave the Bury was not with them and so he spoke in his defence. 'Dave's a very good hooker though. I'm quite happy to see him do the job. Just out of interest, who's reserve hooker.'

'I'm not sure, but as I said we've that many good players and Bill Grey, well he doesn't know you that well.'

'Knows me well enough,' said Brian who was thinking of making an appeal. 'I'm thinking of making an appeal.'

'You can't. You're in the reserves. You can't just take someone else's name off the team list already made.'

'You could always think of taking my name off the list,' said Louding.

'What's the matter,' said Francis who by now was actually concerned about Louding withdrawing from the game. 'This will be the game of the year.'

'Slaughter of the year.'

They were outside the prefects' room. One could catch from where they stood a glimpse of the activity in the staff room on the far side of the Language Floor of the main building. It was at this room that they stared as they talked as if the place conspired from its refuge definite plans for their collective demise.

'We're going to be the best team the school's ever had,' said Francis, instantly devising from his own experience a potted history of the game as seen and played by the youth of Happy Valley.

'Staff's not only got a crack team,' said Steve who, having lost his scrum-half privilege by the necessity of one deemed to fulfil the role of star-player, was inclined to take Louding's side, 'they're made up of players from teams supposed to be the best on the island. Ken McGibb plays for the Colts and they're touring Nigeria next week.'

'So what?' said Francis. 'What's Nigeria?'

'And then there's Penrose, Warwick, Crycton, Fadpeel and Sunspire and and … condition of teaching at this place, if you're a man that is, is to be good enough to play rugby union for the country.'

'But we're getting Gary Edmunds,' said Colin who knew about such things but, fortunately for Christopher, did not carry with similar knowledge influence necessary to argue in favour of individuals not considered by the sixth form sports committee to be list-worthy. 'And we are the best this school's had for years. We'll clobber the staff. We'll clobber them like we've never had the chance to clobber them before.'

'They've never had the chance to clobber us before,' said Oliver who, although older than his brother, did not possess his physical confidence, and like Steve, would have to make do with a position certainly second best to the much-coveted scrum-half or suffer the humiliation of being placed in the reserves.

'Gary Edmunds definitely playing?' asked Louding.

'Pity it'll be for us,' said Francis, inserting an element of the kamikaze. 'What an honour to be mowed down by him if he was playing for the staff.'

Gary Edmunds also played for Wales. He was on holiday in Cyprus but being Gary Edmunds and also the bulldozing scrum-half for the Barbarians, he was asked to play in a few friendlies within the RAF league. He had indirectly pushed the rumour of his participation in the staff v pupil match into reality when Grey, Stenfield and Peters, forming a delegation from St John's, received an affirmative answer to their request for him to play with the lads. It had been, according to Grey, an eager yes. This bit of rugby union work would be what he saw as a possible holiday escape into a novel form of taking part in that which he excelled. Merely to watch him play, a privilege now handed to the entire school, would be considered a master class in the kinetic construction of the game.

'Watch him play,' said Grey later on that day. 'You'll learn a lot. He's playing for the Hospital against the Chairman's Committee team in Akers this aft'.'

Bill Grey's advice was usually structured on semi-abbreviated pockets of information which improved his ability to portray the stereotype sports' hero into which slot he was, while in Cyprus, permanently entrenched. Bill Grey was Gavin Peter's burden because most including Gavin thought that he should have been this year's head boy. The respect he garnered was part of the discipline maintained by frolicking less with the imagination and following a steady set of commands and action to which those on the disparaging front would have regarded as culturally barren. To him, the view of culture was within the hair-lines of sport, and on that count there was always a definite sight before him. He was therefore highly predictable, trustworthy and, as a bonus, very good within the narrow field of activities he chose to pursue. Had he been so inclined his scholastic achievements, although not promising enough to stir, let alone change, the course of history, would have been profound. As it was, ninety percent of his energy was confined to sport. He would make an excellent military man. He did not dally long from these arenas from where he gained nearly all his fun, and he was saved from being, in Christopher's eyes, totally dull because of his cheerful smile nearly all of which was American-styled teeth glistening with the warmth of constant encouragement. He did not harbour the slightest grudge or exercise any scorn at what must have been clearly inferior within his world of guts, pig-headedness and strength, but gained his very fuel from the giving of support and advice. Everyone liked him although Brian tried his best not to. Heidi (among many girls her age) loved him.

'But he's a screw-top with muscular legs and arms. He's programmed to carry, hit or kick a ball.'

'I think he's the best yet. Better than all of you put together.'

'Better than Louding?'

'Don't talk to me about Louding when I'm thinking about Bill.'

Brian and Heidi always argued in a manner which led them to compare the qualities, virtues and values of others. Just now Heidi would not hear of anything against Bill Grey. Brian was in no mood to hear anything for him. Louding was somehow wedged in the middle only by credit of his influence, not yet dissipated (or proven), on Heidi's health. He was, during this conversation, nowhere in sight, being on a different bus but they were all heading for Akrotiri. They were going to see the match and so were a good proportion of the fifth and sixth formers concerned with the lists.

This was all very annoying for Christopher. He had not planned on spending a perfectly decent Tuesday afternoon watching rugby. He had wanted to go to Limassol. He wanted to see Helen. There was now desperation lurking behind the desire as he imagined her impatiently waiting for his visit. It was bad enough impatiently waiting for her to return to school, and why should she? while she was thinking: why should he? I'll teach her to think I'm not faithful, he thought, and was about to ask Louding if he could use his bus when Louding asked for a place on number 27.

'We could always swap.'

'Don't you want to see the match?'

'I want to see Helen.'

'Helen doesn't live in BG.'

'She doesn't live in Akrotiri either. I can be dropped off at Limassol, assuming your bus goes down the Bypass.'

'What do you want to see Helen for when you can see Gary Edmunds play rugby instead?'

'I can see him play rugby tomorrow when the staff mash you lot into the ground.'

'True. Wouldn't you like to be mashed into the ground with us? It could be arranged.'

'I doubt it. No one's likely to do anything to raise Brian's masochistic hopes, so why should strings be pulled for me?'

'I see – and if they could be pulled would you have them pulled?'

Christopher did not answer. He laughed. He walked away and shook his head. He stopped and looked at Louding and laughed again. Why not? he thought. I'm getting desperate enough as it is. He was surprisingly reluctant to explain to Louding the insistent extent of his newly established love for Helen. There was also within a reluctance to explain this to himself lest it fall victim to a severe bout of doubt. He knew he had no choice concerning this perfectly decent Tuesday afternoon. It was not often that Louding went to Akrotiri and never before had he opted for the daily available method of bus 27. Christopher could hardly allow him to venture onto this relatively unknown terrain by himself although Louding would be certain to receive a welcome not likely to be enjoyed by many others.

As there was no Dot and Doris (and wouldn't they be mad at missing him?) he had a place on the back seat. In fact, there being two places allowed room for lounging against the corner if he so wished. But Julie did not so wish. She wanted him to sit in the middle with her and Christopher could do the lounging. However, he sat upright in order to talk. Quite a few eyes from the front were down to the back and so he could hardly lounge in view of the attention given to his guest, but neither could he talk, overwhelmed by the many questions offered to Louding from all directions. Was he really called Louding (yes, but his parents called him Simon)? Could he run hundred metres faster than anyone else (depended on who was chasing him)? Was he out to beat Gary Edmunds (merely to see him play would be enough)? Did he play for the Larks or the Fliers (he played for neither – football was not his game)? Was it true he had a sister and did he have any brothers (one older sister, married and with children which actually gave him the remarkably mature status of being an uncle)? Was he really going out with Marion Shoremichael?

'No, I'm not going out with Marion,' he replied. 'We're good friends.'

It was Chris Millings who asked this last question. He was now not going out with Sonja Stirling, and a tight comparison between her and Bev Janek steered him towards a mysterious form of jealousy. He did not want to think it possible, but one day someone like Louding would be on display as the successful candidate to her heart.

'I should think,' said Julie, 'that the word millstone comes to mind when Marion is mentioned to Louding.'

'Well, that's not fair,' said Christopher, risking an area of conversation to which Julie would inevitably install Helen. 'Marion's okay. She's a laugh.'

'You do spend a lot of time with her,' said Julie not unprovocatively to Louding.

Louding did not reply but gave Julie the full blessing of one of his alluring smiles which stirred well the melting of a host of female hearts including, to some extent, Linda Keen who had for the duration been furiously knitting beside her stoney faced brother. Julie remained untouched.

It was Russell who brought up the subject of rugby.

'Sae yer off ta see the game then?'

'Aren't we all,' said Colin jubilantly. 'Gary Edmunds – what a star!'

'Ye gonna pick up some tips before being slayed by the staff t'mmara.'

'Yes,' agreed Oliver more inclined to this morose fact than his brother. 'We'll be *slayed*, indeed, but with luck we'll take some of them down with us.'

'Ahh it's a poofta's game, rugby. If us real men were gi'en the chance to play the staff at soccer, aye…' And Russell displayed his fists as if pulling a piece of rope in front him. 'Fookem – back'o'net all the time.'

Few were sure what this was supposed to mean other than Russell's belief that the fifth and sixth formers would actually do well if the chosen game was soccer. But for some reason this did actually seem to move the subject onto that of the lists.

'I hear Innmaker is mad at being put in reserves,' said Chris Millings.

'Why isn't your name in the reserves?' Julie asked her brother.

'Ask Colin.'

And she did. She asked Colin with Oliver sitting across from him and with Louding in full view of the proceedings and dark metaphysical tug between fear and longing swept through Christopher's stomach.

'We've enough rugby talent to fill out three lists,' said Colin.

'But he should be on the reserves at least.'

Colin looked at Oliver who looked at Louding who then looked at Christopher.

'Er... it's okay. I'm not that bothered,' said Christopher, knowing that Julie could read him like an open book mysteriously closed to many others who were willing to accept this as an answer. 'So where is Marion?' he asked Louding, hoping to revert to an earlier subject.'

'I think she's decided to take the week off.'

Louding was not certain. He had already disorientated his share of local knowledge by the one day he had taken off himself. His illness was self-inflicted, he said. A ham sandwich in the open sun.

'God, that could have killed you.'

'Put it this way. I'm not longer in love with ham sandwiches.'

'Me neither,' said Julie, who was not in love with the topic but was willing on this occasion, being as she was sitting beside Louding, to add her own ideas. 'I'm not in love with food full stop. Bad planning, this business of having to eat.'

'She makes a rare bowl of lumpy porridge,' said Christopher.

'If we didn't eat,' said Oliver, 'if we didn't have to eat there'd be no progress. We'd still be in the caves and you wouldn't be enjoying the luxuries of the modern world.'

'What luxuries? Give me a cave any day and a bit of fur.'

'Ooo a bit't'fur,' mimicked Linda beside her. 'What bit where?'

'Enough to keep out the cold. That bit there.'

And Julie pointed to her middle and everybody looked at Julie's middle already covered as adequate protection from the heat by the plain blue of her school dress.

Everybody looked out for Gary Edmunds. Those who knew who he was had to point him out to those who didn't and the latter were surprised at how unprofessional he actually looked. He did not have that haze of super-star gold around his frame. In fact he looked less professional than almost every other man on the pitch. He was a bit on the short side.

'Bit on the short side,' said Brian.

'Shows how good he is,' said Francis, 'if despite his size he plays for the Barbarians.'

The first quarter of the match appeared to weigh in favour of the Chairman's Committee, and Edmunds, with the Hospital staff, was playing a low-key game. Oliver and Steve studied his scrum-half technique and scrum-downs, of which there were enough to eventually bore the girls whom, with most of the fifth and sixth form lads from St John's, had arrived after the game had begun, thus removing from their initial appreciation the excitement of anticipation. Apart from always managing to retrieve the ball from the mess that the scrums became and then immediately passing it down the line, Edmunds had failed to really, convincingly touch the ball. And then suddenly, as if sensing an air of disappointment among his would-be young fans, he caught the ball, kicked it down the pitch and followed it with such remarkable speed for his size that he managed to catch it again on the first bounce, and in a few seconds it took to perform this manoeuvre the spectators around the edge of the pitch was subdued and then illuminated by a rousing cheer. In keeping with the spirit of actually having a holiday, and in a modest manner of stressing the professionalism of his play, he had proffered the understanding that he would certainly play a few games but that on no account would he actually score a try. This condition proved to be detrimental to his team because he turned out to be too good for them. The opposition, on the other hand, were mutually bound by their comparatively efficient means of sticking together on a lower level of play. It was they who highlighted the team skill of the game. They performed a dummy dance down the line which suspended Christopher's attitude to the game. Seeing them play it was no longer a case of barbarism encased in complicated off-side rules. Art had infiltrated the determined mangle of men otherwise fighting for space.

'What's the difference between rugby league and rugby union?' Christopher asked Brian, somehow thinking that he would know.

'Ah well, you see,' he said, thinking that up until then he had never known there had been a difference, brought up as he was to regard the fifteen men in rugby union as paramount to any real sense of how it is played. 'One is professional and one is amateur. The union must be professional and likely to go on strike.'

'Other way round,' said Francis. 'The game we're watching is union. It can be cumbersome and slow while league has far fewer scrums.'

'Doesn't look cumbersome and slow to me.'

'Compared to the league it is. Instead of a scrum-down every time there's a foul they do what's known as the chicken-scratch. That keeps the game on the move.'

'So when *do* they scrum-down?'

Francis had to think about this.

'Another difference,' he said, still thinking, 'is that there's only thirteen players in rugby league. Fifteen in union.'

Christopher did not for one moment believe that two players, missing or added, could make that much difference. Bit excessive as it is, he thought. Three in the front row and two behind and one behind that, that's five. Scrum-half's six. That leaves seven more at least. He forgot about the three quarters and he had effectively forgotten about Louding stuck out there in the wing, but Louding, at present, was standing beside him. They oohed and aahed every time the crowd oohed and aahed. They jumped up and down every time the crowd jumped up and down, and Christopher, realising the formation of crowd reaction thought about acquiescent folds.

Not bad this rugby lark, he thought. I could stand and watch it for hours. Probably just as well I didn't go and see Helen. Why should she expect me to chase after her? I didn't ask her to storm off. If she misses me, huh, she can come here and I'll forgive her. And if she doesn't miss me, she needn't come here, and I'll work out my own reasons for loving her alone.

Chairman's Committee won 25 points to 7. It had been a rough game handled with finesse. Not for one moment during the appreciation of the game displayed before him did he think that, okay, if Julie can pull strings, I'll be happy to be on the list of reserves.

'Now that's what I call rugby,' said Colin. 'Any chance of us doing the same at Happy Valley?'

'Good chance of us watching the same,' said Steve, 'once the staff get going.'

'I've no bloody choice, have I?' said Brian as an aside to Christopher who wanted to sympathize with his cause but for once felt lonely and lost among all the concern that surrounded him but remaining outside that which they was able to share.

But, he thought, thinking of Brian, he may well be shaking Sealhard's hand before the year is up. He should be given the chance to kill Sealhard first, legally that is, in a manner expressed within rugby's complex rules.

The lads all moved to where they could gain a good chance of greeting Gary Edmunds who, if not kept in sight, was likely to be whisked away by the chosen officers-in-charge only to vanish forever until tomorrow's appearance on Happy Valley's pitch. They gathered around him. He was no taller than most of them, smaller in fact than quite a few. Christopher had the impression that he was no taller than himself but he remained on the edge of the group who, for a short time, had been allowed to surround the man. Edmunds was cheerful and laughing at remarks Bill Grey made, despite having helped the Hospital staff team to lose. Christopher caught a glimpse of this joy shared among the lads all of whom were anxiously catching Edmunds' every word about what would happen tomorrow. As he, Christopher, would not be playing for the school he suffered doubts about his rights to even stand where he was, helping in this sports-bound acclamation of a hero. He wanted to go home and forget that there was such a thing as rugby and not because of what he usually considered to be its deranged method of defining fun. For the first time since seeing the lists he was sincerely wincing at the regret he always thought food for scorn, and for his emotional experience reminding him of Julie's roundabout hint at helping him out should he wish to see his name somewhere in the reserves.

'I shouldn't be here,' he said to Louding.

Despair was like a confession. He was willing to release the hitherto bearable trapped passion for play, smothered before him by his own style of common sense.

Louding looked at his twenty-four hour fast watch.

'Yes,' he said. 'I should be off as well.'

'No, I didn't mean that,' said Christopher, but the two of them sensed a stepping away from the inner adulation of their group as if parting was inevitable.

'Bit of work to do,' Louding muttered, not really wanting to stay in Akrotiri longer than necessary, but finding it difficult to explain why he should want to leave.

'Not homework, surely? Not the last week of term.'

'Oh, good lord no,' said Louding, and they were back to normal as they paced a distance between themselves and the group.

Their friendship was not on a level which depended on individual grey areas remaining concealed. But neither were there skeletons gathering cobwebs in cupboards. Louding already knew that something splendidly deeper than not playing rugby against the staff was bothering Christopher. Christopher knew he knew, while between them matured mutually shared suspicions of Louding's ill-defined problems.

Louding was unhappy. He was still officially and, he believed, wholeheartedly going out with Sharon Wendrake but she now lived in England. He was still not eligible to sit the English exam and yet translation of Chaucer's *Troilus and Criseyde* bothered him. He was still the central figure of an admittedly diminishing fan-club but he found little pleasure in being fascinated by what it was which fascinated others about him. Marion loved him and this could only be sieved through the Wendrake factor as a strain. He and Christopher understood each other because Christopher, for what appeared to be different reasons, was also unhappy. There was no need to communicate these facts and inwardly there was a lack of faith in anything other than the growing lack of love for and commitment to themselves.

'When I read Chaucer,' said Louding, 'I wonder how the hell we made it to the twentieth century. And yet Chaucer is the beacon of hope in the horror of the Middle Ages.'

'We only think it was horrific because we think we're safe. Planned it nicely, didn't we? Born after the Second World War and with enough time to appreciate rock music. I think in those days they were just more tolerant and a hell of a lot more intolerant. We might revert back to the way they were this time next century. On the other hand people in the future might think that we had it extremely tough, mowing each other into the ground playing rugby.'

'But that's a matter of choice.'

'You know, Louding, I'm beginning to wonder if we really can live by choice. The Middle Ages probably had as much choice as we have now. Stanley says – you know Stanley Palloway?...'

'Is he William's friend? I think we've met.'

'Well, he doesn't believe in what he calls fundamental choice. He believes that everything is ruled by acquiescent folds.'

'Acquiescent folds – that's a new one.'

'Yes, and I've had quite a few explanations but I'm still not sure what he means. But he told me of a sure way of seeing it demonstrated. He said: "The next time you're asked to do something, no matter how important, refuse to do it and then you'll witness a complete set of acquiescent folds."'

'And did you?'

'That's just it. Would I recognize them if I did? Nobody's asked me to do anything important yet and I'm not sure if I have the courage to say no. I did think about it though, what the reactions would probably be like and whether anything could be regarded as a definite fold simply because you've psyched yourself to see it, and I found myself caught up in this business of what it means to say no. We very rarely say no. Did you know that?'

'No.'

'Louding, people change the world when they say no, according to Stanley.'

Hours later Christopher was obliged to attend an emergency meeting. The manager and the treasurer of the Families Club asked their four doormen to do something of particular importance and none of them were prepared to say no. Christopher only found out about the meeting thirty minutes before it began, Thomas having called around to collect him. He was in his militant mood which, in its last-minute need to act, took for granted Christopher's total lack of any pressing alternative plans. It had been left to Thomas to tell the others about the meeting days earlier. As he was almost always with Scott both at school and at home he could not avoid fulfilling a third of his assignment. It was Tuesday night, Colin's shift, and so he was already at the club. Christopher felt himself being propelled along by a minor example of changing tides.

'The club's finance is in the red,' Thomas told him while they walked from his house, and he followed this statement with a searching nod.

'What's that mean?' Christopher asked, subject to an immediate, literal and bizarre image of blood money.

'I don't know but I don't think it's good news. Something to do with no profit, but you'd think they'd scrape up enough from Tombola nights and dances and all. According to Colin – bit of a prat with his stats – he says that we doormen make seven pounds a week for the club and that's after you've subtracted our wages. Not bad is it? Seven pounds. I've a feeling they want to lower our wages, but I'm not gonna take a drop in money. Six hours a week's a lot for thirty bob, even if we don't do that much.'

'Yes, I agree. Shall we go on strike?'

Thomas looked at him as if to say: I'm feeling militant but not that militant.

'Do you think that'd work? I don't think they need us that much.'

It turned out that they didn't. The manager informed his four men of the problems from above. He pointed his finger up to heaven but they understood that he was not referring to God. The officer in charge wanted to politely sack them all. It was called redundancy which meant that they were not needed. They were now being educated in one of the first laws of life not taught in school – thou must always overcome the question of not being needed or else thou will always be made redundant. Colin already knew about such things, being a student of economics, and he interrupted the manager with an unexpected question of rights.

'If we're to be made redundant doesn't that mean we're entitled to redundancy pay?'

'Not unless backed by a union who has negotiated with the management insertion of such rights in the memorandum of association,' said the treasurer. 'I'm afraid you bunch are only entitled to remuneration on the hours you've worked. Redundancy need not always be paid for.'

'But who's being made redundant?' said the manager. 'I only mentioned it to give you an idea of how the officer felt. I managed to persuade him to think otherwise. We do need you as doormen. This club needs to have some form of entrance security, but we also need to make money. I know that all four of you could make more money during your shifts than you are actually taking in at the moment. There are probably many members who are carrying out-of-date cards and you're letting them in because you recognize them. From now on I want you all the check the membership of everyone who walks in, no matter who it is. Even mine, even his, and especially the officer's if he ever decides to come here.'

'Don't know who the officer is,' said Thomas.

'Which is all the more reason for checking his card if and when he arrives. Another thing: all four of you, very popular lads and you have many friends which is great. But while you're here working I don't want to see those friends crowding around your table. This is not a youth club. I've had complaints about too many youths hanging around, and it does look bad if your table is surrounded by your mates. Could put people off going to the bar. Which brings me to the next point. I know that not one of you is eighteen yet. However, every time I come here there's a drink on the doorman's table.'

'Can we help it if people buy us drinks?' said Scot.

'Yes you can. You must refuse any offer of a drink. Not only is it not allowed while you're on duty but it is actually against the British law, and this camp abides by the British law. Good idea would be to put up a notice – you know, a polite humorous one stating your case. And bringing friends into the bar is really not on. I know you've done this before many times and by now you probably consider this something of a perk for being doormen, but I'm afraid you have to lead by example. Other youths your age do come here to drink and it upsets the members seeing under-aged drinkers at the bar. It would certainly upset the officer. He has the power to close the place down.'

'Seems to me,' said Scott later on when the four of them were left to discuss among themselves what had been said, and they retired as it were to their now famous table where Colin was enjoying a relatively quiet Tuesday evening, the Folk Club having closed for Easter, 'seems to me that officers only exist to be offended.'

'I used to think that of all adults,' said Christopher, not remembering when it was he had actually stopped thinking this.

'Not bloody fair being asked not to use the bar again. What bar can we use?'

'I don't know what part of the sentence "it's against the British law" you don't understand,' said Colin, 'but we're not supposed to use any bar. We're all under-aged.'

'So we break a British law,' said Thomas. 'We're in Cyprus.'

'But we have to abide by British law when we're in Akrotiri.' Colin offered them one of his optimistic sighs: 'Still,' he said, 'little has changed. Just check a few people's cards, keep'em happy, throw out our friends, fill up the tin box and in a few weeks thing's'll be back to normal.'

'Yes, but isn't it strange,' said Christopher, 'how things like this get harder and yet life's supposed to be easier than it was?'

'Nah, all it means is that we have to do what we've been paid to do.'

'I'm just glad he didn't say anything about the way we've been swapping our nights about,' said Thomas, and he looked at Christopher in a prepared move to depart on a thought-provoking statement. 'You owe me some money.'

'You've paid Oliver?' Christopher asked, not ready to conclude the proceedings.

'Don't listen to him,' said Scott. 'You don't owe him a thing.'

'Shut-up,' said Thomas and he walked away. Scott followed, leaving it to Colin to explain how matters stood.

'Yes, Thomas did pay Oliver in full.'

'Impossible. In full, and you and Scott didn't pay anything?'

'We would have done, just like you would have done, but it seems that your sister intervened. She got wind of what was happening and as far as she was concerned Thomas was to blame for the cock-up. Open and shut case.'

'One assumes of course,' said Christopher slowly, 'that you're referring to Julie.'

'Of course. Who else?'

'Well, it's just that, you know, people do tend to forget that I have other sisters all graced in their ways with feminine powers of persuasion I'm sure. Except perhaps Rebecca – she's just weird.'

'But what other girl anywhere on the island could do what she does?'

'But how did she do it?'

'Dunno if you don't know. Seems like she just told him to cough up the cost.'

Anything else referred to in that salient statement was contained in Colin's shrug as if to say that methods used on higher levels of the Youth Klub influence were not for him or Christopher to discuss.

'She rarely tells me anything of importance,' Christopher muttered, recognising from this a wish on her part for him never to refer to the matter or attempt in any clumsy way a means of saying thank-you. Julie loathed gratitude. She did what she did independent of a third party's horror, appreciation, anger or esteem. Her sense of purpose was not in the business of accumulating credit. All the same, he thought, I feel I owe her something. It's getting a bit embarrassing. 'Embarrassing having a sister like Julie.'

'I should say it's great. All the lads envy you being her brother.'

'But all the lads fancy her as well. Something mixed up about that.'

'Anyway, here's something else to think about. Don't get your hopes up too much,' and Colin looked to either side as if such hopes, not yet clarified, were likely to be shot down, underpowered as they were by definite facts. Christopher immediately thought: I don't think I'm going to like the sound of this. 'I'd advise you to bring your rugby boots and stuff to school tomorrow. There may be a chance of you getting in the team.'

'In the team. You don't mean the reserves?'

'I don't know much about anything until it actually happens,' said Colin in all modesty. 'Just you bring your stuff, just in case.'

And he stuck his thumb in the air and with this meaningful gesture of good will, power and success, once again Christopher saw his longing for the peaceful life severely compromised.

I am happy to play rugby, he said to himself as he walked home. I am happy to play rugby because everyone else is playing and I don't want to be left out. I am happy to play because Gary Edmunds is playing, and we're playing against the staff and with him on our side we can give the staff a sound thrashing. I am happy to play rugby because I am mad and it's the last week of term and I'm to be wiped off the face of the earth.

He knew that it was not his role in life to be brave. He toyed with the desire to be famous. He wanted to somehow influence the flow of events, but outrageous bravery had at no time been part of the deal. He dreamt that he was a famous writer who achieved immediate popularity by writing the number one world best-seller, *How to Avoid Rugby*. Have you had enough of honour? Does the idea of courage make you crease with laughter? Cowards of the world unite. You knight, he wrote, me wimp. And it's the wimps who get the women. Watch any Bob Hope film. And so he dreamt that he had written this book and that people loved him for it but he still had to go to school. You still have to become a man. Cliché or not there is still only one method. Hard work. Work is never just work at school. It is always accompanied by the word hard as if to acknowledge that there was reluctance on the pupils' part to take advantage of what the school offered. Miracles in the latter days were contained in the success of having fun and working hard. Christopher could not understand how both managed to co-exist. I rather have fun but if I work hard I can make something of my life so that I can have fun. But what does this making something really entail? Service from others, the privilege of being in society without wondering why, the chance to express an opinion and not only have it heard but also titled and considered as the school of thought from which doth evolve more exams. So Christopher gave up school, withdrew from the staggering publicity of his book and took to hitchhiking around the world with a friend. The friend had a unkempt beard, scarred face and long straight hair, thus encapsulating for Christopher the ideal example of travelling freedom. He knew a good deal about art, thus lending magic to much they encountered by calling it such. Christopher wanted to paint ambition. He had already dealt with knowledge and, like the true artist he was becoming, gained little satisfaction. His friend told him that whatever ambition he had in mind so long as he chose the right colours he was sure to succeed. They had travelled far, experience having eaten into their eyes, attitudes beaten into an enlightened shape, and so Christopher started painting a picture. He chose his colours with care, and people applauded his work and offered him vast sums for his canvas. Why had he called it ambition? Cherry-blossoms falling from a tree? Ambition does not float in the air. Call it happiness instead and Christopher shrugged and asked: 'What's the difference?'

'The difference between student's poverty and ordinary poverty,' said Eric, who was informing his registration class of the treachery of false economy, 'is that the student is occupied, or at least he should be, by what makes him a student. Everyday poverty has no occupation. It is just meaningless struggle. Economics could be thought of as a method of making struggle into occupation by a planned use of money. There's not much I know about economics, but the Western world is ruled by it and there's very little we can do at the moment to change this shift in power.'

Eric had worked in Africa and had seen first-hand how economics had ruined a continent while attempting to teach it to cope. He was convinced that economics had been the cause of the Jewish Holocaust, and the Third World was a euphemism for the failings of economics on a grand scale.

'We worship economics,' he said, 'and we are sacrificing the world to this arrogant, insatiable god.'

All the same there was a side to the subject which had to be understood in order to gain a reasonable degree of existence.

'We all need food, clothing and shelter. It may seem a great pity that food is not like air, always in great supply and freely available. Clothes as well to keep in the heat and other things you lads are always thinking of, and shelter

– you may think that because we live in the civilized world of high technology we don't have to concern ourselves with these three necessities for survival, but it's not true. All of us have to live within our means. To succeed beyond this is not easy and fraught with risk. What do I mean by means?'

'Money,' said Rob.

'Yes. There are three sides to economics, like the Christian trinity I suppose. *Fuel*: oil, coal, nuclear power; *manpower* which is the labour force and employment from which we derive our resources and food; and as Johnson so characteristically but correctly stated: *money*, as represented by gold which is, for all intents and purposes, quite useless, but nevertheless the one substance just rare enough to be of the right value. It may be a mystery as to why we use gold as the basis of our monetary wealth. You could, if you wanted to, use art treasures or buildings, but these are subject to fluctuating rates of value and they fail to melt down and remain art treasures and buildings. So, let's pretend I'm going to give each of you a slice of gold worth ten pounds in order to survive for a week.'

He looked at his watch. This even distribution of virtual wealth was in danger of running out of time. To each he handed a sheet of paper with '£10' written on the top line. Each line below this represented a channel through which part of the £10 above had to run. The very bottom line said 'savings'.

'You'll notice the word "savings" at the bottom. Now if you manage to reach savings – if you manage to, in other words, accumulate part of your wealth and invest for the future, it is then that you are invited into the complicated world of high finance. If this works for you then eventually all the other channels work for themselves. I think you better go now. It's getting late.'

They left, each taking with him his would-be survival list. Christopher also reluctantly pulled along his duffel bag containing boots, socks and rugby shorts – the shirt to be supplied in conjunction with the colours chosen. As it was not a house matter it would make little difference. Colin's the only person who's advised me to arrive fully laden for battle. If I am to play then there's been a singular absence of honest warning. He was embarrassed about revealing that he was ready if the other lads did not want him ready. What a cheek they'd think, he thought. And me not even in the reserves. He had already gone through a complicated process of mixed motives. After all, when all's said and done and at the end of the day, I really do not want to play rugby this afternoon. I really do not want to play rugby at all ever again. And here I am, with my kit, ready to go down with the rest of the fools, working on a chance that there's a place for me in the team, looking at Louding and loving the glorious moment we could spend together getting killed.

He looked instead at his survival list and with Louding later on, in the prefects' room, he compared notes.

'Ten pounds is a lot of money,' said Christopher.

'Not when you have to buy everything our parents usually get.'

'Well, look at it this way: four pounds for digs. The six pounds left covers food during the day, clothes, transport and entertainment.'

'Two pounds enough for the food, leaving another two happily flipped aside for my future closet.'

'You'll need more than that for clothes.'

'*Mon ami*, I'm not even banking on a closet. When I get out there I'll be happy if it's just a drawer.'

'I'm putting five bob on the bookshelf and ten to bridge the gap from A to B. What is it about B that's so good that people from A want to get there?'

'Riches beyond whatever I suppose. Anyway, that leaves a quid. Yeah, that might do it. And there's also five shillings for song and dance, wine and women, but what about really vital, important and essential things like records and a stereo.'

'Well, that's what the quid's for. We're gonna save that. Purchase a few shares here and there, you know, and before long we'll be able to buy our very own studio.'

'Depressing though,' said Louding, looking at his sheet which, apart from his handwriting being more refined, styled and likely to break out with the occasional notation, was similar to Christopher's. 'Ten pounds a week – bloody little.'

The place was filling up. With a few of the usual exceptions the lads looked dejected. Not one member of the staff destined to help mow them into the grass had stayed away. The game was definitely on. It did not look as if it was going to rain. Not that this would have made a deal of difference, but the sun was doing its best and it would soon be mid-day.

'Magic,' said Francis, an exception. 'We're gonna do it lads. We'll make mince-meat out of those podgy adults.'

His enthusiasm, shining through the prism of advantageous distortion, was followed by the entrance of the four rugby greats: Bill Grey, Perry Stenfield, Martin Clifton and Gavin Peters. Gavin was only part of this brotherhood as an example of the latter side of greatness whereas Bill, Perry and Martin had all been born great. Martin, in particular, was part of the soccer greats as well, this time alongside Bill Grey again, Russell Keen and Rob Johnson. Both Bill and Perry exuded the substantial call of competitive winning, living on the physical side of life as if it was the only just reason for breathing. Their company was matched with Gavin's final desire to be remembered somehow for his sporting prowess, and he was now one of the greats because of this quality of sixth form pride inserted in the status of being both British and head-boy. He merely lacked that final charisma of knowing you were good without having to be told, and people immediately sensing something special without it being demonstrated alongside the promise that, despite everything, it would certainly entertain. And so it came to pass that this glorious gang sat around the table where Christopher sat. It was they who had made out the lists. They had seen fit to exclude him from the reserves and now they wanted him to play in the team.

'I was told this might happen,' said Christopher as he looked at Bill Grey and instinctively felt the stirrings of something akin to pride and passion. 'I've brought my kit.'

'Great,' said Bill. 'I don't know why we missed you from the reserves...'

'So why am I now in the team?'

'You can thank Colin Kamp for that.'

I'll never forgive you for this, Colin, thought Christopher, and on the other side of his mind as he realized the attention he was being given, how can I express my thanks – Colin, you're a brick. Colin you're a prick. Why do you have to open your mouth? Great that you've got such influence. What are friends for? With friends like you...

'What position am I playing?'

'Well, hooker of course. That's been your position for the Akrotiri Youth Klub First.'

'But the Bury's always been hooker and he plays for the school.'

'Well, you see, Christopher,' said Martin. 'Dave's not playing.'

'Yeah, if he was playing, you wouldn't be,' said Perry with a strain that reminded Christopher of the early days in his rugby career when Perry had laughed and mockingly called him 'The Panhandle!'

Gavin was the only one who, in his manner, offered him apologies for being inconvenienced. He understood the trap. So did Louding who sat back and listened, pleased that Christopher was not part of a sacrificial ritual. He was being asked to play for the pupils because there was nobody else within the entire school suitably experienced enough as a replacement hooker. It was not un-similar to being the last person chosen for a team, taken because there was no choice, but within this he had the chance of relishing the honour of being unique. Either way it was promotion, recognition, a turning in the tide. A few weeks back Colin Kamp asked if he could add his name to a list making up an opposing team and Perry had laughed at his inclusion and then went on to play for the losing side. Now Perry, among others, wants me as part of their only hope for victory, although to look at him complete now with feet up and the Stenfield smirk, you'd think the only thing that matters is how he appears to the few girls wandering in and out.

Where are all the girls? Are we left to contemplate glory without them?

'So why's Dave not playing?' asked Christopher, looking at Martin who was perusing his own copy of the lists, preparing perhaps for the next question. 'And what about the hooker in the reserve team? Shouldn't he be given the chance seeing as his name is down?'

'Who is the reserve hooker?' Bill asked Martin.

Martin looked down his list and sighed in a studious: 'Let me see now.'

They both knew who it was. They enjoyed putting on an act of confidence. The indifference this expressed was not as arrogant as Perry's but just as politically sound. They had to give Christopher the impression that they were doing him a favour, not the reverse.

'Yes, of course, a fifth former: Simon Howard. He was willing to give you, Christopher, being as you're upper sixth form, the chance.' Martin looked at Christopher to see how this chance was being registered. 'He thinks, and so do we, that you're a better hooker.'

He bloody would, thought Christopher. He did not know Simon Howard and he did not think that Simon Howard knew him. Who else do I know called Simon?

'You know him,' said Perry, with a remarkable capacity for reading his thoughts. 'He was at that kebab at the Moonlight. Pat Vendle's leaving do, remember?'

'Not Laura's boy-friend?'

'Yes, that prat.'

The bastard. I told 'that prat' that I'd promised faithfully to Pat that I wouldn't risk a broken ankle, a ruptured spleen. The fact that I've broken the promise once for the sake of Durham makes no difference.

Christopher smiled. He sat back to complete his look of thoughtful resignation. He looked at Louding who could offer him no further hope. He only smiled back in his particular way of welcoming him to the fold.

'Great,' said Bill. 'Great' was Bill's favourite word. 'You've got your kit. We've got our hooker.'

'So, Dave's just not playing?' Christopher looked to Gavin for the answer.

'He's ill. He's been ill since Sunday.'

'Aha, like me,' said Louding. 'Only he's had the sense to stay ill. Nothing quite like being ill to avoid marching off to war.'

'Don't you start,' said Martin. 'We're gonna pulverize the staff this afternoon and none of us can wait to get out there and make it happen.'

'Yes, great,' said Bill. 'I don't understand this rumour going around that we're gonna lose. We've an excellent chance of winning. Great team complete with Gary Edmunds.'

'And now with the Panhandle on board,' said Perry, 'it'll be a dead cert.'

And he laughed, not with any particular contempt as his respect for Bill and Martin subdued the sarcasm. But Christopher sensed the implied abuse even if it escaped the others.

'Fine by me, Perry,' he said. 'If you don't think I'm needed I needn't play.'

'Course you're needed,' said Martin. He looked again at his list to make sure. He looked at Christopher. 'Don't worry, mate. You're playing. You're definitely on the list.'

'Then you can scrub me off. I'm not playing. I don't want to play. My answer to you for me to play is no.'

'What!'

Bill looked at Martin and they both looked at Perry and then back at their lists.

'What's wrong? You've got to play,' said Bill. 'We need you. You're on the list.'

'Who needs him?' said Perry relieved now that in the process of standing up and knocking over his chair he could make his feelings known. 'Anyone can play hooker.'

Christopher hated Perry intensely especially now as he realized how he was doing more to actually persuade him to play through this hatred than anything the other three could say in friendship. On the other extreme was Gavin who was also ready, for the opposite reason, to accept his refusal. Martin and Bill remained astounded.

'We're offering you the chance,' said Bill, 'to play hooker for us with Gary Edmunds as scrum-half, and you're refusing.'

'That's right.'

Come on, Stanley, where are those acquiescent folds you promised me. All I sense is a confusion of friendly and unfriendly reactions. Christopher knew that he had to play, but by refusing now he had gained some manner of control. Not so ready to take me for granted. Leaving me off the list and then using me like some oversight.

'Yes,' he said. 'Like Brian, I'm not playing.'

'Brian? You mean Brian Innmaker,' said Bill. 'What's he got to do with it?'

'Why's he not playing?'

'He is,' said Martin, again looking at his list. 'He's in the reserves.'

'But he's good enough to be in the team.'

'Ha!' said Perry. 'He thinks he's good enough. He's just a pillock who thinks he's best at everything.'

'And you think you're not?'

'I *know* I'm the best.'

'Not better than me,' said Bill stepping beyond his usual mode of avoiding the self-referential argument. He laughed with a relaxing sigh of understanding what it was Christopher was getting at. He often saw Christopher and Brian together. They were good friends. 'You think Innmaker should be in the team?'

'Well, put it this way,' said Christopher, 'I don't play, I don't even think about playing, unless Brian's name is put on the team list. He's on prefect's duty at the moment. When he comes back you're gonna tell him that he's in the team, not the reserves.'

'Fuck that for a lark,' said Perry. 'Who are you, Panhandle, to say who should be in the team? You're lucky not to get your arse kicked from here to Dodge City.'

'Well, I won't be getting my arse kicked in Happy Valley, will I?

Because I'm not playing.'

'Listen, Christopher,' said Martin, becoming the nominated list-based voice of reason. 'We can't put Brian in the team. He's in the reserves. It's all been arranged. If he goes in the team somebody has to be taken out.'

Christopher looked at Perry. He knew it was impossible, after all, Perry was probably the best, but it was a pleasing thought. Gavin saved him from making it anything else.

'He can take my place.'

'No way,' said Bill. 'You've got to play. You're on the list.'

'Why? Brian's my size and I think he is probably a better player than me.'

'Bloody isn't,' said Perry. 'He's a wanker. Anyway, why should we let this prat blackmail us? We don't need him.'

'Suits me,' said Christopher.

'Shut up, Perry,' said Bill. 'Listen Christopher, we can't just take someone off the team so that Brian can play. But we do need you. We need a hooker.'

'Use Simon.'

'What if we were to promise to use Brian as first choice soon as we need a swap,' said Martin, sweeping through the names before him, wondering who would probably be first to succumb. 'Can't say fairer than that.'

'True,' said Gavin. 'I mean, I suppose I better play being as I am head-boy.'

'He could always take my place,' said Louding, something now of a forgotten witness, sitting to one side.

'You keep out of this,' said Bill. 'I said we've got a good chance of winning, but not without someone to score the tries.'

'Sorry, no compromise,' said Christopher. 'No Brian no me.'

And Christopher stretched his arms back and yawned a victory yawn.

'You little bastard,' said Perry and he walked out of the room and slammed the door.

'Don't know why he did that,' said Christopher. 'He doesn't want me to play anyway.'

To affect the grand exit he made Perry had to push his way through a gathering of the team who already occupied the room and had closed in around the argument. They all gave their comments now until it was finally put to the vote. It was reasonable to suppose that Brian could not play, the list being what it was, definite and rigid in the priority of its players, but it was right to think that he should because it was right to think of them each being able to opt out or opt in as individual entities of sellable skill. Christopher looked at Martin and then at Bill and said: 'Okay, I'll play.'

'Great!'

Brian heard about this during private study when he sat opposite Christopher and they had the table to themselves. He was not sure what to say.

'I presume you've brought your kit,' said Christopher.

'Yes, of course. If you're in the reserves you've got to bring your kit. Anyway I usually keep mine here at school. Ever since kit was invented there's always been a problem of forgetting it.'

'But how can you do that? We've no lockers.'

'I've magic words which enable me to do things most people without these words cannot do. "Maintenance" is one of them. "Administrative problems" is another two that go well together. There's also "insurance reasons" and "work-study allocation". Whatever fits the situation, and "work-study allocation" enables me to keep my kit in a kit-bag in Sealhard's office. You should try it but don't use Sealhard. One kit, one office, I'm afraid. Morrison has an office. You could use his.'

Elliot Morrison also had an uncanny habit of appearing as if manifesting from the power of people's joint opinions. No sooner did Brian suggest his office than Elliot himself popped his head around the door of the prefects' room, few teachers daring to go further than this, and looked at them. There was practically nobody else in the room to look at, although one could hear the slippery shuffle of contraband articles going into hiding.

'I want two strong volunteers. You two'll do.'

Why is it, thought Christopher, that teachers always ask for strong volunteers? Does the word strong mean being able to go ahead and simply be volunteered? Teachers never wait for answers. They just pick the lads they need and invariably choose someone like me who is plainly not strong. May as well ask for someone who's got free time and then pick me who's busy – busy right at the moment getting Brian to tell me what a great lad I am for fighting his cause.

They followed Morrison out of the room, across the yard and into the old assembly hall. There was a filing cabinet close to the emergency exit. It was to be moved to his room at the mathematics billets, a journey almost as far as the distance they had already covered when acquiring the spotlight for their new assembly hall art and crafts display two weeks ago. The cabinet was larger than a spotlight and a good deal heavier. The metal frame was slippery and uncomfortable to hold. Morrison was willing to keep the door open for them as they eased it from its place, and as per his aspired position Brian took the lead, both carrying it with some degree of success off the ground and to where, at the channelled horizon, lay its new home.

'Invaluable piece of merchandise,' said Morrison. 'Facts and figures all to be filed together. I shall have at my fingertips a universe of totally banal but necessary information. One day we'll have computers storing such stuff and taking up a lot less space, but meanwhile. I'll run on ahead and open the door to my room.'

'You do that, sir,' said Brian.

The other door was to be after many billets down a concrete channel of mini-steps and awkward corners. Morrison, of course, did not run. He had no need to and neither did he walk any faster than the rhythm accompanying the jovial hymns he always whistled: in this case John Bunyan's 'To be a Pilgrim'. All the same he was well ahead of them before they were able to clear the extravagant shadows of an un-amused and old assembly hall.

'We're bound to be caught by Emery again,' said Brian. 'This time I'll use "administrative problems".'

'I wonder what type of administration this cabinet represents. Is he going to store information on us?'

'That wouldn't fill half a drawer and there's four piggin' drawers. They're probably the main weight of the thing. Shall we stand it up and take them out.'

'Good idea.'

They stood the cabinet up and Brian almost crushed his fingers. Wobbling frighteningly as he let it go, it stood like a piece of surrealist sculpture commissioned to take its place in that part of the yard between the old assembly hall and the billets. The flat aspect of education and the storehouse of knowledge – they attacked the storehouse first but the drawers refused total liberty. Learning had supplied them with a bond made of metal and plastic rollers and neither of the lads could immediately work out the combination needed between wheels and runners in order to secure release.

'There must be a way of getting them out,' said Brian as he examined the hidden mechanism.

Christopher was conscious of the fact that they were in the middle of the grounds probably being stared at through the silence by a good fifty per cent of the school. It was bad enough being aware of authority without having to entertain its minions.

'What use is it to pull them out anyway?' he asked, changing his mind about Brian's idea. 'We'll just have to return for them.'

'Yes, and then try and put them back in. You know,' said Brian, with a philosophical stare at his witnessed failure, 'perhaps we should just carry on.'

They carried on. Brian took the lead and, for a delicate moment, the entire weight. Christopher, at the back and after a couple of the mini-steps and corners, began to feel the grip of his fingers being swallowed up by the now greasy metal. I'm being tortured, he thought, in order that information can be stored. And suddenly, out of the pain, was derived peace, and on seeing Brian bent and straining before him, there emanated another slice of enlightenment. It lasted no longer than a second, and when that second was up from around the next awkward corner and ready to walk towards them appeared Wilma Carter and Jane Sellers.

'Tweedledum and Tweedledee,' said Brian.

The girls pointed at them and smiled to each other and walked towards Brian and Christopher in a manner which suggested that they were not there to help. Both Brian and Christopher came to the decision that now was a good time to rest. Again the magnificent sculpture was allowed to stand upright, not without frightening all four with its potentially awesome power of falling over.

'What do you think?' asked Jane, who recognized it straight away for what it was. 'Certainly better than your tree, Brian.'

'Yes, I can just see your cat sitting up there,' said Wilma.

'This,' said Brian pedantically, 'is a cabinet. And I can see it quite happily sitting on top of you. In the words of the prophet: "If it was so, it might be; and if it were so, it would be; but as it isn't, it ain't." That's logic.'

'It's logical to assume,' said Wilma, 'that if we post ten house-points in your name you will receive a certificate.'

'You mean he'll be certified,' said Jane who walked around the cabinet, smiled at Christopher and then sat down on one of the steps leading to a science billet.

Christopher sat down beside her. He was thinking how uniformly pretty Jane actually was in her plane blue summer dress offering some sort of shock, as it were, to the grey and brown of the surrounding colours. This girl had actually persuaded Henry to sit for her while she had painted from what she saw of him an imitation of Kokoschka's *Portrait of Adolf Loos*, a print of the original of which hung in the restricted channels of the Art Department billets. I'm sitting in the world of art, he thought. That cabinet, by being with us, is worth thousands. The girl beside me may one day be an iconic shaker of our age. At the moment she was resting from the need to reshape art history, but all the same, in collusion with Wilma, she was thinking about it.

'Do you really have enough house-points in Brian's name?'

'Yes, we really do,' she said.

'And will you really post them?'

'Yes we really will, unless Brian here supplies me with a written apology and an acknowledgement that my cat was superior to his tree.'

'Your cat was a copy of an idea by Lewis Carroll,' said Brian superciliously, 'just like everything you do is a copy of someone else's work.'

'Not everything. The cat was my cat. I may improve on original ideas. I try to advance themes. It's not copying so much as progress.'

'Whereas my tree,' said Brian, 'is the root of everything and branches out into the skies from which there is no progress, just service and an acknowledged stare at the heavens drifting into entropy.'

'What's entropy?' asked Wilma, and Christopher was glad it was she and not he who asked about something which he suspected, being an A level physics student, he should have known. He waited patiently beside Jane for Brian to supply the answer.

'The Second Law of Thermodynamics says that everything is

deteriorating into heat. The universe one day will just be a heat wave. Mind you, by that time, there won't be any more days and so it will be meaningless to say one day, but there won't be anyone there to say it anyway.'

Christopher stood up. It was indeed a pleasure to sit beside Jane, being as this was so far the most he had ever had to do with her, but they had work to do.

'Poor old Morrison is standing by his door, patiently waiting, keeping it open for us and wondering where we are. We better get going.'

'And we better get going too,' said Wilma. 'We have better things to do than waste our time admiring filing cabinets.'

'Don't admire,' said Brian in a more courteous tone. It has been put to him earlier that he was supposed to declare his love for one of them but, maybe due to the excitement of the rugby later on, he could not remember which one. Jane is prettier, Wilma is brighter, both are models of the modern message: we are independent of your passage to happiness but it helps to have us around. 'How about helping us? Two of us cannot take one cabinet too far.'

'Why not? You're both strong lads.'

'Strange,' said Christopher. 'That's what Morrison thinks. I'm as physically delicate as the Little Prince.'

'Ha! You're about as much like the Little Prince as I'm like Winnie-the-Pooh.'

'A fact we won't dispute,' said Brian. 'Come, Christopher, we likewise have better things to do.'

'All right,' said Jane, 'we'll give you a hand. Tell us what to do.'

She joined Christopher at the back and shared the weight from the bottom of the cabinet as it was tipped over to where Brian and Wilma cautiously embraced its weight at the top and on they went.

Christopher had won them over because he had mentioned *The Little Prince*, an experience shared the previous year in lower sixth. Any reference to it now, even when diluted by the likes of Winnie-the-Pooh, was immediately prone to nostalgic enquiry, containing as it did more emotional impact than the other books perused during a minority course on the appreciation of literature wherein, among others, had sat Wilma, Jane and Christopher. He failed to have much to do with them other than share a common experience of reading the same books. No discussion had resulted over and above a collection of written paragraphs about what the readers thought of *The Little Prince*, *The Outsider*, *The Great Gatsby*, *The Go-Between* and *The Grapes of Wrath*. With the exception of the last two, according to the enlightened language teacher who took the course, each book could be read within a couple of days. Steinbeck's epic was granted a week. Christopher read *The Little Prince* in an afternoon, but the final book took three weeks. It was also a given by the teacher that these five books between them said everything necessary regarding twentieth century society. Of Steinbeck Christopher wrote: 'All right – some people had it tough, but what can we do about it now? Was it possible to exist alongside such gross injustice without taking to crime in order to do something considered worthwhile?' He thought *The Outsider* – the only one subject to translation from the original – was saying something he longed to understand but couldn't. 'Why does he not love his girl-friend? The one flaw in his philosophy, although there are many others I'm taking for granted, is his giving up smoking at the one time when he should be smoking more. He is a robot.' He wrote about *The Go-Between* and *The Great Gatsby* as an exercise in comparative literature stating that 'both books probably say all there is to say about love across the classes and in their way unrequited unto death. The farmer kills himself while Gatsby is killed but both endure similar injustice.' Of *The Little Prince* he wrote 'Why did the little prince want a picture of a sheep? It annoys me slightly that this question was never asked and, in my case, never resolved. A sheep would surely have put at risk the livelihood of his beloved rose. The picture of many people lighting lamps one after the other, a wave of lit lamps spreading across the world, is like a dream. I am also pleased by the king. I wish all orders were as reasonable and I wonder overall why we bother when the message is to waste time on something so that it becomes important. The idea of being tamed in order to think golden thoughts of someone who has gone but may return is quite moving.'

He and Jane were now so close together and the pain of their grip being swallowed by the metal edge was such an intense bond in their effort to move, that he should have thought of this desire to be tamed, to be understood, the bottom rung of any artistic ladder. At least he should have thought of Helen. Failing all this there was always the chance of realising that the four of them were concerned with a matter of consequence, moving the cabinet so that it could function as a storehouse for numbers. According to *The Little Prince* it would have amounted to a more important act to allow it to stand as a magnificent example of surrealist sculpture. There was more life involved in the admiring of than the utility encased within its shape. Matters of consequence usually compelled people to betray their ideals. Christopher understood this more than ever. He had defended Brian and in a way gained an act of worship in respect of his desire, caught as it was between total abstention and the need to take part.

They made it to Morrison's room. He was nowhere to be seen. The door had been propped open by text books which got in their way. The cabinet creaked and groaned as if it too was weary and it sang out a distorted series of painful screeches as they tried to ease it against the wall.

'Enough!' said Brian suddenly. 'As Morrison's not here to supervise, enough is enough. Let us rest.'

'What's he want the cabinet for anyway?' asked Wilma. On the other side of the room was a chest of drawers and bookcases stacked with folders.

She walked over into his storeroom and walked out again. She walked to the back of the room and she walked to the front. Walking and looking was Wilma's method of resting. A classroom, she thought, as long as it doesn't contain a class, is as good as any art gallery. 'He doesn't need a cabinet.'

'We just carried it, me and Christopher here, all the way from the assembly hall. I'm not going to question its essential role now. Thank you for your help ladies.' Brian looked at his watch. It was a heavy-looking watch like Louding's and probably just as accurate. 'Christopher, we have to go now.'

Christopher had just started to rest. He was also appreciating the company. He did not want to leave.

'Can't leave now,' said Wilma.

'Why not?'

'We're waiting for Godot.'

This line went over the heads of the other three, and of course they thought she said 'God' and assumed she meant Morrison.

'He'll only give us something else to do,' said Brian. 'We haven't time. At least Christopher and I haven't time. History is to be made this afternoon. You girls, as is the wont of girls, are quite welcome to come and watch.'

'The only history you're going to make, Brian,' said Jane, 'and which we'll love to watch is when you go up to shake Sealhard's hand.'

'So what? Worst things have happened.'

'What, to you? Liar.'

'And besides, it is but a matter of vast indifference to me what may happen in the obscure future. Us two will be bathed in glory. Is that not so, Christopher?'

'Either that or blood,' said Christopher.

'Blood and glory!'

'No, just blood. Like the millions of common forgotten soldiers before us.'

'I see,' said Jane, 'a couple of typical death-before-dishonour boys.'

'In the face of which, dear Jane,' replied Brian, spreading out his hands and pacing the area overseen by the blackboard, 'art has little meaning. Therefore I apologize here and now for disposing of your darling cat over the walls of Canterbury Castle. My tree was but a weed beside it, not worthy enough to have your cat pee upon its boughs. I am a man of action. Have I not my hammer in my hand? Am I not the God of Thunder? Do I not smite down whatever dares to oppose me?'

All three answered all three questions with three variations of the word no.

'I am not waiting for God. I am God. So what of a measly tree, be it one of knowledge, good and evil, life or suspender belts. There are more wonders in my heaven and earth than are ever dreamt of in all your artistic philosophies. It is not beneath me to beg forgiveness and fall at the feet of a beautiful lady who creates cats, but time no longer waits for Gods. Farewell.

Come, Christopher. Rugby awaits.'

The lads left the room and the girls looked at each other.

'We're late,' said Brian, again looking at his watch and breaking into a fast walk which Christopher struggled to match without running. 'What do you think?'

'What? If you say we're late, we're late.'

'No, I mean, do you think they'll post those house-points now?'

'After your great speech? Not a chance.'

'I may have laid it on a bit thick. And the object was for me to write out my apology – not convert it to something out of Marvel comics and Tolkien.'

Brian, still not officially part of the team, was now so certain of his place that he regarded himself as the guest-star, second only to Edmunds, ready to grant the lads time to build up the performance and produce the atmosphere necessary for his entrance, and ready to boost the flagging dimensions of a shagged-out side with all the rescue panache of one-man cavalry. Give them half an hour or so, he thought, then let me take the place of he who can't take the pace and I'll show them what it means to put a champion in reserves.

They were granted five minutes to get changed. Together they entered the changing room with a brisk sense of preparation for battle. Once endured, five minutes later, Christopher was five minutes worse for the experience. Any masochistic, philanthropic, hedonistic, appreciative and honorific delusions he may have entertained since being partially persuaded to play disintegrated in the mundane stretch of a simple swap of clothes – the lacing of his boots being subject to an effort almost beyond previously calculated endurance. Most of the lads had allowed themselves only five minutes to get changed. There was hardly space to claim free from the shared smell of teenage sweat and exhilarated farts. They were all so drastically cheerful. He wondered if gladiators, prior to marching out to face each other in the arena, succumbed to joking and playing and acting in a manner anticipating the prospects of their heaven to be shared and experienced sooner than planned. Before every battle men must have laughed and sang about the consequences of either living too long or being carved up too soon. We are not trained so much to welcome death as to overlook its sting. We are trained to laugh because living wants us to think death is a joke. Yes, he thought, it is a joke, but I'm not laughing.

Neither was Wilfred George. Christopher sat beside him on the only space available along a bench which skirted the circumference of the room. Wilfred was quietly suffering the agonies of a large lad too shy to act with any degree of comfort within the congested heat of getting ready.

'It's hot enough,' said Christopher. 'Do you think the first casualty will be due to heat exhaustion?'

'It'll be me,' said Wilfred, exuding much to do with a big man's hatred of heat.

'Without you we definitely lose.'

'I've played many games this year and I can't remember once touching the ball.'

'Because of you we win every scrum.'

'Because of you, you mean.'

'All I have to do is get the ball hooked under the men behind me. With the push you give I don't even have to do that. That's why I've been given this strange honour of being the school's best hooker. So, it's all your fault.'

'Brian'll take my place,' said Wilfred, assuring himself that he could look forward to premature rest if the heat picked up.

But Christopher had doubts about the scrum being Brian's method of manifesting the glory he had spoken of so eloquently earlier. He looked over to where the tall, wiry framed lad hopped about in his enthusiasm of talking, getting changed, ready to march out and onto one of the waiting buses. Christopher looked for Louding and instead, among many others, saw Stenfield who stood up, fully garbed in his warrior rags of shorts and shirt and well-worn boots, audibly pointing at him, accusing him of having a mighty physique.

'We don't have to worry lads. The mighty Panhandle will save the day. Look, what muscles. What a mighty man you are.'

Everything mentioned was followed by some inane reaction of mirth covering the overall attitude of those expecting defeat. Had Christopher called Stenfield all the names which sprang so easily to mind, this too would have been backed by a peal of nervous, uncertain chuckles.

'Are you jealous?' he asked, remembering a strange hint of the associative wonder hinted at by Colin's revelation last night about his sister. He longed to announce to the imperative brotherhood at Perry's expense: 'It's all because Julie doesn't fancy him. That's why he hates me.'

Perry would most likely strike back accordingly: 'What the fuck you going on about, Panhandle? Julie must cringe having a wimpy brother like you, you little bastard.'

But in the absence of anything more provocative all Perry could say: 'Jealous of a little squirt like you!'

'Hey,' said Bill Grey with the authority so suddenly lacking in Gavin who stood beside him. 'We're supposed to be fighting the staff this afternoon, not each other.'

Everyone laughed and Christopher almost laughed too. He was angry enough now to go out and play and perhaps play as well as he could, but he was also sad, sitting beside someone who was even sadder; sport taking on an aspect of life redolent of those ancient warriors who with their swords and shields ventured forth stripped of any real hope. It was enough to make the most miserable laugh. What was underlying the shame: he was in no mood to appreciate the enlightening irony of all these acquiescent folds (mainly of skin and cloth) going on around him.

'Hey, lads, listen to this, lads.'

Robert Johnson ran to the centre of the room, having emerged from the outside with a piece of news he had picked up from within one of the buses. Two of the three buses designated for the warriors on both sides, and all three still waiting while the rest in their droves had already descended onto Happy Valley taking with them the entire school, was full of the over-frantic whispering promise formulated in mystery behind the scenes, now carried by Rob to those remaining in the changing room.

'Listen, you lot, for Chis'sake,' he demanded, having to shout over the laughter. They all eventually stopped to hear what he had to say: 'The first person on our side to score a try wins a proper kiss from Bev Janek.'

'Hah, thrillsville,' said Perry, still analyzing Christopher's accusation of jealousy, wondering at what point in this accusation Julie had played a part.

'Not just any old peck on the cheek, pratsville. Only the most beautiful girl on the island is going to give any one of you a decent kiss if you manage to get that ball behind the line before anyone else on this side. Doesn't matter which team scores first, it's who scores first in this team that counts.'

'Decent kiss,' said Steve, nodding thoughtfully. 'Any chance of it being indecent?'

'Depends who scores.'

'That's hardly fair on us in reserves,' said Brian, relegated once again and so suddenly into second place. 'The first try could be scored in the first minute with Edmunds on our side.'

'He's not scoring. That's his condition for playing. Maybe that's what she's thinking – she'll get to kiss Edmunds.'

'Probably be Louding,' said Francis, being full back along with Steve and therefore out the odds in favour, and also assured that Louding was out of earshot, having already secured his seat on one of the buses. 'He scores most of the tries being on the wing along with Bill and Gavin here.'

'Doesn't matter. Get in there and score and claim your kiss.'

'Great, okay, come on lads,' said Bill. 'We're playing this to teach the staff a game of rugby. Forget about women and song or whatever.'

Gavin wanted to say something similar and was left at Bill's side to merely agree. 'Peasants,' said Brian, no longer happy, and he left the room. Was it not he who persuaded Miss Janek to become Miss Epi Eagles in the first place?

Poor Brian, thought Christopher, and was it not he ... but what am I thinking? Bev Janek promised no such thing. How could she? She's too shy. She's been put on the spot by fraud, and there's only one person I know who could do such a thing.

He stood up. He was ready to follow Brian.

'How do you think my chances rate for getting that kiss?' asked Wilfred who also stood up, cumbersome but ready, like a willing, hopeless companion volunteering to share a final detail in a vital campaign.

'I doubt if there is any kiss. It's just a joke.'

Bev made no promise but it's no joke. Julie, my beloved sister, does what she does independent of another's horror, appreciation, anger or esteem. She has it in for Bev for beating Sonja, and this is her sturdy method of revenge. She shapes the gossip and in her hands can be the malleable shape of every rumour concerning love and hate.

He thought of Helen. Surely she would sacrifice her pride rather than the big match and turn up to see the teachers play with every desirable risk of meeting me. He loved her still. He had this hollow feeling inside his stomach as a result of being reminded of this love. He was also dreading the match but this hollow did not correspond to such worry. That was a different hollow, a heavy hollow of clenching reluctance.

'Hey, Panhandle,' shouted Perry above the rowdy exodus which followed Christopher. 'Our unlucky day. With you in the team none of us have a chance of getting that kiss.'

'Fuck off, Stenfield.'

And everyone laughed.

The Other Side Of Silence (b)
Concussion and the Cancelled Kiss

It seems to me that novelists often preserve an aloof position in the art by their intellectual analysis of the fundamental cause of human suffering and frailty. They cannot bind themselves to any particular creed or nature less they themselves are accused of the weakness they find so pleasing to write about in others.
Rebecca Panhandle: Books I have Read – *Age of Reason* by Jean Paul Sartre

Word got around that I was to kiss the first boy to score a try at the match. As you can imagine I was horrified and I hoped it would be a white-wash victory for the staff. As it happened the first boy to score knocked himself out. People are making a terrible fuss about me because I won this beauty competition, and really I shouldn't have, but to get knocked out in order to win a kiss is a bit much. Anyway, it must have affected his memory. He failed to claim his prize.
Beverley Janek: Diary

Death loves a crowd!
Captain Nolan proclaimed,
And into this shroud
His sword was well aimed.
And so the 600
Rode into this snare
And took from the valley
Death's loving care.
Stanley Palloway: Diary of Cock Robin.

EVERYONE CHEERED AS THE teams ran onto the pitch, the teachers in blue, the lads in red; Edmunds, also in red, with black shorts instead of white, looking no larger and from a distance no older than the lads, but recognition and fame won him a few screams. Both teams chose their side of the pitch upon which to limber up, kick around, pass and convert a few balls, until eventually they formed two clusters for final captain-led advice. For the lads this would normally have been led by Grey but he deferred to Edmunds who looked at those circling him, and as inspiration was best in brief he said only enough for them to remember: 'Never look behind you until you have to pass but be aware that there is always someone to pass to. Look for the space, never the opponent. Keep moving – always keep moving. We'll win.'

The teams lined up opposite each other on either side of the centre line. For the first and last time before play the lads were able to look properly at what they were up against. Some of the teachers, because they were teachers, looked a bit odd rigged out in articles of war, but others, in particular Fadpeel, Sunspire, Ken McGibb and Crycton appeared fully fit, competently arrogant and lacking in any of the natural sweetness one assumed could be gathered by a life in front of the blackboard. McGibb and Galbraith exchanged in only a second's glance the simple message: 'Okay you Scottish/Welsh bastard. After two years of maths with you…' Warwick looked at Panhandle as if to ask where Innmaker was.

The Beak accompanied the Air Commodore – taking time off from whatever he did to further promote the auspicious occasion and therefore the implied importance of St John's – as he inspected the teams. This must be the real glory, with almost the entire school cheering and the Beak ready to shake each hand and ask each name and introduce each person to this top knob beside him. This should be more for Brian than me, thought Christopher. But the reserves for both sides were sitting over at the main stands, bunched together among the cheering fans with all the innocence of substitute dejection.

'Christopher Panhandle, sir,' said Christopher.

'I say, that's a rather geographical name,' said the AC who looked infinitely friendlier but surprisingly just that bit older than the men Christopher was now facing. 'Part of the island is called the Panhandle I believe.'

'Yes, I believe so, sir. But it's pure coincidence.'

'You do look rather small for this sort of thing.'

'That's why I'm playing sir. They need a small guy for hooker.'

'Yes, looks neater that way, I suppose.'

Christopher had never before figured out why the hooker had to be small and now immediately understood what he meant. He was satisfied with this answer but still not delighted about having to play, feeling more of a sham in the sense of what was offered to him now by way of premature glory. All doubts about being capable of scoring the first try for his side were firmly focused on an enveloping preference to being a hundred miles away, twenty miles even, in Akrotiri, safely tucked up in bed at home, or in an armchair reading a favourite book, or anywhere doing anything but standing here soaking in the excitement of a substantial crowd waiting, perhaps longing, for players to be mashed effectively into the Happy Valley grass.

'Simon Louding, sir,' said Louding.

Christopher looked at him. Saying his first name had caused Louding to blush in the afternoon sun. Score the first try for me, Simon Louding, and spare Bev Janek having to kiss Stenfield.

The formalities took a further five to ten minutes as the Beak and the AC insisted on exchanging brief sentences with each player, Edmunds being on the receiving end of a relatively lengthy conversation which included quite a bit of laughter from both sides. Suddenly both teams scattered. The two captains, Grey and Fadpeel, deciding on the toss of Reverend Galbraith's ten piastre piece who would be playing against the breeze for the first half and which side would take the kick. Christopher had not yet discovered the advantages offered to the side who took the kick as the ball invariably landed in the arms of an opponent who could then, in order to allay the gain in distance, kick it right back. All the same Fadpeel won the toss and he chose to kick against the breeze for the first half. The teams were called to position themselves. Everyone around the entire perimeter of the pitch went momentarily mad, and then the compliance of silence was met as Fadpeel formed a crease with his heel on the centre line, balanced the ball and then with some apparent care walked away from it. It fell over. He walked back amid the hilarity of the joyful tension, and with extra jabs at the crease he repositioned the ball.

Silence again. Even the breeze was calm out of respect for the magic he managed to create.

Fadpeel took the kick. This was followed by a different weight of silence. Dorman took the catch. He ran, kicked, Warwick caught and, a couple of paces, was tackled by Clifton, but the ball sliced through to Ken McGibb and down the line almost to Sunspire. The whistle blew and before Panhandle thought he had taken no more than five or six steps he was facing Warwick in the first scrum-down. Heads locked like teeth in a rusty gear – Edmunds offered a slight grunt as the ball went in and all Panhandle could remember of this awesome experience of being in the middle of the crush was his leg trapped one way, his arm the other, and someone sounding not unlike Kamp the younger calling for the scrum to break.

Seconds later Sunspire scored the first try. This appeared to be too easy. Their sense of unity had advanced long before the lads could overcome the first few nervous minutes of play. Grey shouted for their speed and strength. Edmunds appeared to be socially indifferent, pacing around the spot as Crycton prepared to take the conversion, but then he ran with his arms out as if compelling his front line to keep up by his strength of will. Panhandle was part of the front line and he kept up but the ball successfully sailed over the bar resulting in the teachers gaining their many fans by the sound of the chronic cheering.

The cheering was highlighted by the chanting of individual names and the entire school appeared to wipe from the afternoon any hope the lads may have had in the eighty minutes left of play. But when Edmunds scooped up the ball from a weak link in a well rehearsed chain of passing down the line, followed as he was by Grey, Galbraith and Stenfield on one side, Louding, Peters and somehow Panhandle on the other, a different form of cheering excluded itself to their regime. He passed to Peters who kicked it into the Sealhard's confident and tenderly cradle-shaped arms. Stenfield brought him down but not before the ball went into touch. Then followed a series of what Panhandle regarded as the mysteries of the off-side rule, after which three more scrum-downs and his head began to feel as if it was being slowly peeled from the scalp down. It was beyond him to recall who had actually won the scrums, although without Wilfred by his side there would have been little doubt as to who would have lost. Warwick's speed could only be imagined by each detected bounce of the ball as it trickled in, first from Edmunds and then from Crycton, out from any side as random as particles fired from a sawn-off shotgun.

Edmunds had the ball again. He did a running dance around each opponent and sliced through their wall with the ease of a fly around a wire fence. He passed to Kamp the younger who almost made it to the corner before being hammered into touch, taking with him into the spectators two of the teachers who forced him from his route. This was the second line-out and so close to a try that the lads were frantic about the chances offered to each one of blowing this opportunity. Screw winning, many each thought. I want that kiss. Gavin took the catch, forced the distance by pacing back before handing the ball very generously to Kamp the elder who managed to resist the temptation of kicking it over the bar. He had to pass and so it went to Grey who passed to Galbraith who was downed as if impaled by the power of McGibb's tackle. But not before the ball was picked up by Sunspire who ran back and then to one side and then forward and then before being tackled passed it to what he thought was a passing Warwick.

Edmunds had the ball again. This time he gave it, quite gently – they could have passed the time admiring the fluffy clouds challenging the bullying sun – quite deliberately – he's a good looking lad and he's there to receive the ball and run with it – to Louding. Louding then ran so fast that it was a pity nobody timed him. He was constantly breaking his 100 metre record on the rugby pitch. Maybe the egg-shaped ball tucked under his arm made all the difference but he was willing to put it down to fear. He ran right across the pitch, was going to pass it to a begging, well-positioned Stenfield but changed his mind. There was a space between him and the post and Panhandle. Too many teachers were clustered in a space where any break out would have caused more confusion among themselves and so he took the risk. He ran back along his route and up, and Panhandle, automatically and with telepathic loyalty, followed until he was able to receive the pass.

'Run! Run! Run! Run! Run!'

It was unlikely that Christopher was going to start entertaining alternative ideas. He ran. He had a vague notion of which way he was going. He saw a couple of posts in the distance and knew that Louding, without difficulty, could have made it to this scoring refuge. For Christopher it was a case of balancing on the precipice of possible effort. He did not think of Bev Janek nor did he think of Helen. He was unsure about welcoming the faint view of glory Louding had so kindly offered him. His chest was thumping. His legs were being pulled back by association with failure but he ran on. People were cheering to the rhythm of his legs and this gave wings to his ankles. He actually succeeded in dodging Sealhard and this immediately boosted his confidence. His own team begged him for the ball and the teachers were crowding in but he ran through what Louding had correctly calculated as being the confusion set aside by the mere fact that Louding had actually passed the ball. He followed Edmunds' advice about looking for the space rather than the opponent on each side of his thin slice of life. This is ecstasy, he thought. Who hates rugby now? He ran for one of the posts being the only items of hospitality he could at that moment cope with heading towards. It was white, everything else bar the confused grey of its neighbour was black. And through the cheering he heard: 'For chris'sake pass the fucking ball, Panhandle.'

The word Panhandle was as clear as a camera flash before the black-out. Christopher's legs were completely taken from the speed the rest of him had gathered by the time he was yards before the post into which he sailed. The teacher who tackled him at the last moment, diving for his feet and taking his heels into his chest, sharing the air and the curved exertion of the lad's first ever try, soon realized what had happened. He turned him over. There was no blood on the post and nothing stained the clay. His head, amid the dishevelled hair, appeared to be still in one piece. There was no horrific-looking gash taking the place of what, above the exuberance and the swearing, had been an almost audible crack. Christopher was still breathing. Even while unconscious his lungs churned desperately for the oxygen needed from such a run. A number of players from both sides gathered around. Reverend Galbraith stopped the game and there followed a session of deciding whether or not an ambulance case had been unexpectedly provided as one of the highlights. In his professional capacity of one capable of dealing with every contingent element of rugby-related injury, Gary Edmunds quickly examined Christopher, felt around his head, shook his own, shrugged and asked if they had a stretcher. Reverend Galbraith, professionally attuned to answering deeper questions, asked the same of Fadpeel who looked at Sunspire with the hope that this bit of negligence, if shared, might produce the required article.

At this point Christopher began to wake up. Everything was white and then orange, and then a bit of blue and orange, and then very painful as if his head had caved in to form more colours. He shut his eyes, opened them, saw Louding bending over him and looking as if he was upside-down. He considered the fact that maybe it was he who was upside-down and was therefore gripped by his fear of heights which compelled him to sit up too soon so that what had been his head became a brick wall.

'Easy,' said Louding. 'You've taken a bad knock. Gave us all a bit of a scare.'

'Oh my God, what happened?' Christopher covered his eyes with his hands in an attempt to draw out the agony. 'Louding, I feel ill.'

'It's concussion,' said Colin who crouched down on the other side of him and knew about such things. 'Can you stand up?'

'I don't think so.'

'Let's give it a try,' said Louding. 'We'll help.'

They gave it a try. Christopher could not remember the crowd. He could hardly remember what it was which deserved the applause, and the whoop of fear as he collapsed under his own weight, and then the continuing applause as Colin and Louding all but carried him away from the pitch. They took him to the stands and sat him among the reserves who gathered around to ask him if he was all right and what it was like to be actually knocked out and if he did in fact score that try.

'Was I knocked out? Gosh, I suppose I was. Hey, did I score?'

He looked anxiously at Louding who stayed with him for the seconds needed to include whatever context and rest one could pull from injury time.

'Did I?'

'I think so. You may have won yourself a kiss.'

'I'm not feeling at all well. I think all I want is a bed.'

'Hey, *mon ami*, one thing at a time.'

Christopher smiled which hurt his head all the more and he told Louding to shut up. Louding had to return to the pitch, but before he turned his back on his recuperating friend he reached over and gave him a kiss at the very point between his eyes where he had met the post.

'There you go,' said Louding and ran back onto the pitch. The cheering had ebbed but returned in full force as he made himself available for the remainder of the game.

Christopher, still dreaming and facing the reality of concerned reserves – did Louding kiss me just then – was treated to the administering attentions of the delightful games mistress whom he knew had shapely brown thighs behind her white tracksuit and for whom he and Francis, some weeks ago, had compared carnal desires while playing and watching her play tennis. She examined his head. She parted his hair which was painful enough and prodded the bruise which made him wince. He was not in the mood for being brave in front of her. He groaned and she asked him if he was all right. Did he feel weak? Did he feel ill? Was he able to see properly? He shook his head at the last question and she looked up at Mrs Burlington who was there to represent the school's authority's divine touch at dealing with emergencies. In answer to the games mistresses' concern she offered from her own expression that universal look teachers defaulted to when faced with those cases they considered 'typical'. Christopher would not have been surprised had she asked after his attendance at RC assembly first thing that day. God metes out punishment in similar although, albeit, fewer dramatic doses.

'Yes, I think we better call an ambulance.'

'Is that really necessary?' asked Christopher using the strength stirred now by her voice, wanting to maintain some dignity about his ailment and remembering too that they were in the middle of Holy Week. 'I just received a bad blow. I'll recover. I'll rest over there on the grass.'

'Christopher, you were knocked unconscious. These things don't happen every day.'

He wanted very much to assure Mrs Burlington that he was quite happy about this fact, that he would be satisfied with it remaining a once-in-a-lifetime experience, but at the same time there was no desire to emphasize a need for special treatment, outside the treatment already offered by the games mistress who set about applying to the located bruise a strong smelling ointment which settled the throbbing by attacking the problem with the stinging sensation of ants in his hair.

'I want to see the rest of the match, ma'am. I really don't think I need to go to hospital.'

He was the victim of moral as well as medical priorities. The school was responsible for keeping him alive during school hours, and to delegate this to the military wards of the Episkopi infirmary would lessen the risk of an embarrassment so nearly exposed by their lack of stretchers. Mrs Burlington promptly told Christopher that she was a better judge than he of such matters. For now he was to sit there and suffer further succour from she into whose arms he would have happily succumbed, while she, Mrs Burlington, walked away to arrange his immediate future.

Louding was given the chance to run back to him. He had felt that his space had been invaded by the Burlington onslaught and so had withdrawn from what was causing a heated discussion between Brian and Bill.

'How are you feeling? Bit rough?'

Christopher, still receiving the attention of the games mistress, could hardly tell. If anything, at present, things were very smooth. He nodded.

'Miss,' said Louding, 'aren't you going to bandage him up. He'd look the real hero then.'

'We are taking him to the clinic. They'll do the proper job there.'

Christopher offered Louding one of his well-there-we-have-it shrugs.

'Right, better get back to the game. You did score by the way.'

'How did I do that?'

'You put the ball in the right place before your head met the post. It's funny, you know, but Brian's reluctant to go on to replace you. Says he's far too tall to be hooker and he wasn't expecting to get on quite so soon and hardly expecting you of all people to come off.'

'Well, there's always that other guy, what's his name, Simon?..' and

Christopher shook his head to jolt his memory and immediately wished he hadn't.

'I have to go. Bill says Brian has to play now if he wants to play at all. Too late to decide on anything else. See you. Have fun watching us get killed.'

Louding ran off. The players were settling into their positions. Brian straggled on. This was not the glory road he had been promised, playing in the middle of the scrum where the heroics went unseen. The crowd, stirred by the match thus far but getting ever so slightly restless, had forgotten Christopher. He imagined the Air Commodore informing the Beak that he thought that unfortunate chap had been rather small and thus, injury assured, it seemed a miracle that a try had been scored. Perhaps they'll try and put me back on if I start showing signs of recovery. But what a run, hey? I must have been crazy, possessed, plain stupid or bloody good. Maybe the promise of a kiss from Bev Janek is more powerful than any noble idea I may have had about saving her from having to kiss just anybody – having to kiss Stenfield. Now everybody is back at the match. There's no flavour in being so suddenly forgotten. Even the delightful games mistress has walked away to watch.

But rather than watch them being killed, as Louding suggested, Christopher decided to take advantage of his school oblivion and save himself from perhaps a death equivalent to the embarrassment of being carted away by an ambulance just because he had knocked his head. Had I broken a bone or ruptured a spleen – now that would have been a different thing.

He eased himself from his seat and expecting to feel dizzy and unsure on his feet was surprised to discover that full control had been restored. A pretty games mistress and smelly, stinging ointment – what better medication was there? He walked around to where the stand cast a comfortable shade upon a large enough area of the grass for him to lie out and stay hidden and maybe fall asleep. Perhaps they'll think that an ordinary rest is no more than a hospital can offer, and with this grass offering just the right support tolerable to my pounding head, I will be allowed to rest in peace. Isn't that what they want to avoid, he thought, me winding up resting in peace? He closed his eyes. He tried to imagine the pain operated by an acquiescent fold into the land from which dreams and such stuff were made. He heard his name being called. He so much wanted the caller to sound like Mary-Ann Sheen. The best promise was the female voice it acquired. He was searching for Mary-Ann and a path upon which he now walked to a village in the smoking distance reminded him of the walks taken with Mary-Ann and their much wider route to Treetops in Leuchars.

Two lads – they looked like twins although one had white hair, the other black – stood in his path. They looked at Christopher and betrayed the fact that they had been waiting for him by asking if he was looking for Mary-

Ann. 'How did you know that?' Christopher asked. 'We have a message for you,' they said together. They put their arms around each other, stood side to side and suddenly took on the more grotesque appearance of Tweedledum and Tweedledee. 'A message for you from Mary-Ann,' they said. 'Search for sand along the beach. Such a pity there's so much about. If only it was cleared away then you can see it better like the noise you can hear when all is quiet.' Thus saying the young lads returned to their normal, healthy, twin-like shapes and scarpered, leaving behind them their plastic ball which rattled as it rolled.

Christopher heard his name again.

'Christopher, hello. You're not asleep are you?'

'Hello, Marion. I have been asleep. Is the game still on? Has Louding scored yet?'

Marion was kneeling beside Christopher, having just arrived, and she looked at the crowd which barred their view of the game, and shook her head.

'I don't know. I haven't been watching. Would you look after Simon's watch for me and give me it back at the end of the match?'

She slipped the watch from her wrist and handed it over, dangling it dangerously above Christopher's chest. It was indeed a heavy looking watch. Posing as a contraption containing enough information to save the world from a China crisis it was therefore entitled to look heavy.

'Did you see me score that try?' he asked as he carefully took the watch without having to raise his head.

'I suppose so,' she said despondently. 'Simon could have done it without having to get himself knocked out.'

'That's why he's still out there playing and I'm lying here resting.'

'What was it like?'

'What? Getting knocked out? Like being here one minute and not being here the next.'

'That doesn't sound special to me. I'm always here one minute and then not here the next.'

'I thought you weren't here at all,' said Christopher, enduring more of a moment of *déjà vu* than his delicate head could take. Didn't they have a similar conversation at the dance last Saturday? 'I thought you were off sick.'

'What made you think that? Just can't be bothered to go to school. Bit silly going to school last week of term, but I wasn't going to miss the big match.'

'When you think of what we have to put up with during the term it seems a bit silly not going to school on the last week. Besides which, you are missing the match. You can't see a thing from here.'

'Yes, I know.' She stood up. From where he lay the view of her legs was tantalisingly inconsistent with his present condition and the fact that this was

Marion, not Mary-Ann. 'I only wanted to give you the watch. Be sure to give it back when the match is over – to me, I mean, not to Simon.'

'Naturally. After all, it's only Louding's watch.'

She walked away and that view soothingly decreased. She stopped and looked back at Christopher who, complete with watch, remained where he was. She walked back and he tried not to gaze at her gradually more visible thighs.

'Are you all right?'

'Yes, I feel fine.'

'I mean, are you really all right? You did get knocked out you know.'

'Yes, I know.'

'I saw it happen. I was quite shocked. Louding could have scored but he gave you the ball and you did a great run but it was also a great tackle too. Not many tackles knock people out.'

'Very few,' agreed Christopher, shutting his eyes.

Maybe he wanted her to walk away. He wasn't sure. It would have been nice to continue his dream but the crowd suddenly cheered. Another try had been scored. Marion just had to go and watch but she was reluctant to leave him because he did, after all, get knocked out. She heard that it was not a good idea to let a knocked out person go back to sleep.

'Have you seen your better half lately?' she asked while standing on her toes, trying to peer over the layer of heads to at least ascertain which side had scored, and offering Christopher who had to open his eyes a glimpse of something white but with delicately designed lace, obviously woven with the tension of being seen but kept hidden.

'You mean Helen? I don't think she looks upon me as her better half any longer.'

Marion laughed.

'Whatever made you think she did?'

To Christopher's great relief Marion at this point elected to sit down beside him again, modestly imposing within her cross-legged finesse, the hem of her blue dress between her thighs.

'You can laugh,' he said, 'but I will have you know that there was a time when Helen thought the world of me.'

'Yes, I know. She used to talk about you all the time. But she is a bit of a funny girl. So what happened? Have you two fallen out again?'

'What do you mean again?'

'She's still not angry with you about Saturday is she?'

'I don't know. I haven't seen her since Saturday.'

The crowd cheered again. Some of the younger ones on the fringes were jumping up and down with delight. The reserves were performing a rapturous dance, waving their arms in the air, almost ready to hug each other, all without exception refusing to sit down in their allotted places along the bottom and second row of the main stand. To Marion's horror the name

Louding became an ever increasing chant particularly among the girls. She just had to go.

'Louding's scored and Steve will probably do a conversion,' explained Christopher. 'I don't suppose you've *seen* Helen recently have you.'

'What?' There was another loud cheer. She stood up quickly, wandered away, made a few enquiries and then came back. 'You were right. Louding scored and Steve has just converted the ball. Apparently we're even with the staff.'

'If we lose,' said Christopher, 'I shall never play rugby again.'

Still stacks of time left, still plenty of chances for the staff to pick up their game, gain control, knock out a few more...

I shall never get out of bed again. I shall not deem life worth living outside these sheets. We won. How did we do it? No sooner do I leave the team then they start to win. Bad enough having Edmunds to help us but then Brian goes and starts enjoying his position as hooker and he plays well and proves once and for all that there was never any need for me in the first place. Still, the game lands me in bed. Been here a full day and a half almost. What have I missed? Last day of school before Easter. Can just imagine Helen returning for this one day and wondering where I am and they'll explain to her that I was a hero for an hour and have been rendered bedridden for the rest of my natural days. The unnatural days will probably see me sitting six exams and following some crazy notion that I can make a career out of physics pending results. I've a crazy notion that I can actually pend results, and I do feel perfectly alive lying here. I have no regrets. Each hour is a wonderful arrangement with eternity. They can stand out in the sun and mime to hymns and listen to the Beak drone on about the theme of this morning's assembly which will have been about suffering and redemption, and here I am, free from both, feeling fully fine – a ticket to bliss called concussion. Concussion is where just getting knocked out isn't enough. Your head insists on piling on the experience and your body follows suit. First the legs – I felt faint – and then the stomach – I felt ill – and then everything when I feel so weak I'm ordered to bed where I sleep and dream and sit and read and think and eat – slip out occasionally for the loo and maybe I'll watch a bit of telly tonight. What have I read? Lots of *Charlie Brown*, last three stories from *Winnie the Pooh* and the first chapter of *Middlemarch* (offered for my edification by Angela) making it thus enterprising enough for me to read the last chapter and make up the large bit in between. I'm left in peace to do all this reading and I can indulge in a bit of abstract doodling over a page of yesterday's maths and so I'm ready to write a book about how to avoid life and really start to live. People come to see me though. Family mainly, and a few friends such a Thomas checking to see if I am too ill to work tonight instead of him, and a bit of Colin and some of William Meald who could have brought along Stanley only he's at work enjoying his last day before Easter as well. They all ask what it's like to get knocked out. Had I been shot they'd have had the press around here to take down the answers. Julie didn't bother asking. She was probably searching for the gun at the time I was making my now historic run. How dare I score the first try and upset her little plan of putting Bev in her place? But what if her precious Perry had scored? Then he'd have demanded the kiss and ... maybe that's what she wanted. What *did* she want by putting poor Bev on the spot? And – a question I have not yet asked – am I really owed a kiss? No-one else has asked that question either. They're assuming I may have already received it in secret, but apart from appreciating her beauty on stage, seeing her win the title – and quite right too – Bev has remained for me something of a legend, tucked away in the recesses of her own particular and probably equally bizarre world – a world in which one would find as a companion of conscience: Alexander Beetle. Poor Alexander Beetle. Spent two days with his head buried in a crack in the ground just because he imagined an 'Expotition' party ganging up on him and saying 'Hush!' Then he went to live quietly with his Aunt for ever more.

It was Colin who told Christopher what had happened. The lads only just managed to win. The staff had been tough. Rob Johnson was injured too.

'He was in agony,' said Colin, 'rolling around as if someone had shot him. We had to take him off but he seemed okay afterwards.'

'In that case I'm presuming he didn't rupture his spleen. Did anyone break an ankle?'

'Think I did.'

A slight limp was all there was to suggest that the calf-region of his left leg had taken a beating. Colin was full of praise for Christopher's try. He said that he had never seen one like it in his entire career of playing for and against the school. Was he still ill? Would he be fit enough for tonight?

'Thomas has already been around to ask me that.'

'His brother's over from England. We're thinking of having a party. You may as well turn up. It'll be at his place.'

'I better not. If I'm too ill to work instead of Thomas I'm too ill to turn up for his party. Thomas was wanting me to do tonight's shift although he owes me a shift or two since God knows when. Parties rarely begin before the shift ends and so he can fit in his work.'

'But he wants to join us in the Pigs' Bar.'

'Pigs' Bar.'

'It's where the airmen go. No girls allowed that's why it's called that. If we're no longer able to drink at the Families Club... Can I borrow a few records for tonight?'

'Yeah, go right ahead. I think you'll find some of them are yours. I'm leading a musicless existence at present.'

'Sure you won't be able to make it tonight. It'll be great to celebrate our victory.'

'My head's celebrating it already.'

'What was it like getting knocked out?'

'Can't remember. That's what it's like. You just can't remember.'

Colin left with records and William arrived with tapes, ones that he had borrowed practically from a previous existence. Christopher couldn't remember what he had taped. A bit of Mongo Jerry and lots of Groundhogs. William couldn't stay. He was invited around to the Palloways' for tea and then he and Stanley were off to see *Klute*.

'Wanna come along.'

'I can't. I'm ill. I'm not lying in this bed because I'm tired.'

'A good film would do you good. This film's supposed to be great. Donald Sutherland and Jane Fonda.'

'Wasn't he the guy from *M.A.S.H.* and *Kelly's Heroes*?'

Christopher was tempted but he had already turned down both work and play and therefore was now presented with the moral intrigue of a third, albeit more relaxing, request. It would certainly test the mystery of this strange ailment which had as its accord the illusion of health while hinting at, and from within, death the next moment. Concussion, of course, was independent of ethics. He shook his head.

'I better not get up until tomorrow. Enjoy yourself and say hello to Stanley for me.'

As William left Julie entered.

'How's the intrepid invalid?'

She was in a pleasant mood. There was no sense of emphasis on the implied fact that in her eyes he was neither brave nor heroically in-valid. She asked him if there was anything he needed. She also added that had he been a horse she would have shot him, causing him to wonder whether she had overheard the reference to Jane Fonda.

'What? Before or after I was knocked out.'

Julie sat on his bed. She was indeed a very impressive girl. When she sat on a bed it was an impressive act. No motive from either storehouse of altruism or greed had yet compromised this exacting feature of her faultless attire. She was forever doomed to constantly collect respect, and Christopher could just about perceive her unique form of suffering – the pain of it dehumanising effect. Had he been more capable of acting on impulse, and certainly had not the sibling inhibition imposed its own notion of what was and was not appropriate, he would have taken her in his arms and forced her through a second's overdose of compassion to cry free the aching rigidity of her spirit. But Christopher could not love his sister that much. Closer though he was to her than his other sisters, particularly Rebecca whom he considered a shadowy existence within the household, they were still worlds apart although as near enough now as they could both tolerably manage.

'You scored that try because you knew Janek had no intention of giving anyone a public kiss. It's alright for her to win beauty contests in public.'

'You should have promised the kiss from Sonja. Sonja's a very popular girl, Julie. I wouldn't have gone out of my way to separate her lips from any worthy hero's, even Stenfield's.'

'Makes no difference. It would have been Louding anyway. Kisses are wasted on him.'

'What do you mean by that?'

'I don't know. Don't know what I mean most of the time.' She stood up and she walked back to where the door stood partially open waiting for her exit. 'Good day at school today. Singing *West Side Story* songs at assembly and then in the prefects' room where there was an orange peel fight and Rick Chinner received a nosebleed and from Edmund Whitehead of all people.'

'Really. What made him do that?'

'Who knows? Whitehead gets annoyed easily and Chinner usually has it coming. Could have been nasty but our intrepid head-boy, Gavin Peters, saved the day. He stood between them, ordered Chinner to get his nose matronized, and told everyone that the Beak would be over soon to inspect the premises, and a fight would certainly have the room closed down. They would have to tidy up, he said, and so I left because I'm only lower sixth and not really supposed to be there. And us young ladies had a mini-disco in the arts department, but that got out of hand as well because clay started to fly, and I got some paint on my dress – it was blue paint which didn't match the colour so much as look like a natural stain. Linda Keen kept asking me on the way back: 'Whit ye dun to yeself, hen?' and Russell and Oliver got into this argument on the bus about music and money and some other stupid thing. They nearly came to blows. Russell was swearing away and Oliver kept saying that he can't argue with someone who thinks the way he does. And so they started arguing about the way he thinks until I told them both to shut up.'

'And did they?'

Julie looked at him.

'Where's Angela?' he asked.

'Somewhere on this desolate island going bonkers in love with the place.'

'Does that mean you don't love this place?'

'You know me, Christopher,' said Julie, just before closing the door as she left. 'I don't love places, just people.'

It was there that her irony could be felt airing the room like a breeze from the shutters, making him feel restless. He picked up *Middlemarch* and flicked it open, settling upon Chapter 27 from which he read:

> Your pier-glass or extensive surface of polished steel made to be rubbed by a housemaid, will be minutely and multitudinously scratched in all directions; but place now against it a lighted candle as a centre of illumination, and lo!

> the scratches will seem to arrange themselves in a fine series of concentric circles round that little sun. It is demonstrable that the scratches are going everywhere impartially, and it is only your candle which produces the flattering illusion of a concentric arrangement, its light falling with an exclusive optical selection. These things are a parable. The scratches are events, and the candle is the egoism of any person now absent…

Christopher immediately wanted to ask Gavin Peters if he had read or even looked at *Middlemarch*. I wonder what the chances are of him calling round. Infinity multiplied by zero, which is equivalent to me meeting Helen at any time.

When he fell asleep he dreamt that he had woken up to what he thought was his room, but he was sitting, not lying, and there was no bed but a long white couch. Sharing the couch with him was Angela who was reading a fashion magazine written in French. He didn't know Angela could read French and so she said that she couldn't. She was looking at the pictures. She had to remain aware of what was going on in the fashion world if she wanted to maintain her pose as a dress designer. All around the room was draped materials used to make the dresses illustrated in the magazine. Angela got up and started pulling down the drapes she needed. Behind each was a picture of the place of its origin. Oklahoma, said Angela, after freeing from its grip on the ceiling a length of black denim. She pointed to a house stuck in the middle of what appeared to be a definite brand of American cigarettes. Within the house lived pioneers. Christopher was never sure what actually made a pioneer, but he had a pretty good idea that his own way of life hardly recommended him to the title. The family were by themselves and they etched out their existence by living off the rewards begrudgingly offered to them by various mysterious methods of tendering the wilderness. The young girl of the family had the power to heal cripples, but townsfolk accused her being possessed and so in order to escape being burnt or hung she and her family wandered off to where they now lived. She spent her time healing animals instead and gained a form of happiness unknown to that time in history. Then there were stories from the Ukraine, Nepal, Finland and Ghana. A wise man told a fool to walk a hundred miles for water and two hundred for fire, but the fool only walked fifty and returned with an electric heater and a fridge bought at the local supermarket. Who's the wise man now? But they had no plugs and electricity had not yet been discovered in that part of the world.

I'm getting up. One can only stay in bed for so long. Good Friday was not made for me to languish here and feel sorry for myself but to languish in church and feel sorry for Christ. He looked at Louding's watch. It was still ticking, still full of unprecedented facts and figures. It was not that he had forgotten to give it back to Marion. He had remembered at a time when he was sure the match had finished, only by then he was in hospital being examined by a doctor more interested in the rugby than his head, and Marion was most likely with Louding helping him share the love and glory of the moment, gaining kisses I suppose which, as Julie mentioned, were probably wasted. Christopher had not been carried away in a white truck as feared. Mrs Burlington, who had seen enough, never did like rugby anyway and was subject to extra-maternal feelings of concern regarding Christopher, usually in the form of advice and authority, closely guarded if in any way showing the colours of actual affection, took the concussed lad off in her car. They talked all the way to casualty. She was glad Easter was here at last. The most important date on the Catholic calendar. Herself and a group of friends, plus a few schoolgirls including Savina and Tessa, were off to the Holy Lands for a couple of weeks. Christopher had the impression that the Holy Lands were now owned by Jews and Muslims. He supposed the Islamic-Judaic tourist board catered well for Christians, and Mrs Burlington asked him not to be so flippant. Does Easter not mean anything to him? To give your life so that someone else may live is the most noble act of all. Christ gave his life for us all, but Christopher could not understand with any pressing certainty the danger he himself had been in which necessitated this over-famous and unasked for act of sacrifice from so long ago.

'Anyway,' he said, 'it's easier to give your life for all mankind on the cross than to work hard for a few people year after year.'

Mrs Burlington looked at Christopher the same way Christopher Robin must have stared at Pooh Bear when Pooh proved to be no longer a Bear of little Brain. I keep thinking I'm going to become enlightened, thought Christopher now while he stretched his foot from beneath the sheet which had kept it and its neighbour hidden for more than forty hours. I keep thinking I'm going to realize the truth. He sat up with his legs dangling over the side. He was a new man, somewhat weaker. I'm totally muddled.

'Cheers for the wonderful Winnie-the-Pooh!

'(*Just tell me somebody* – WHAT DID HE DO?)'

Not only did Christopher get up, he got dressed. He went through to the living room and sat down. Everything is gradual. I am about to re-enter life. Angela was making tea and she offered him a cup. That would do for now.

'You should be out in the fresh air,' she suggested with the careless enthusiasm of one who had just returned. 'My God, the beauty of this country overwhelms me. Why do people stay in Akrotiri? We should be out all over the place taking it all in.'

'I didn't know people stayed in Akrotiri,' said Christopher, wondering where within the stillness of sultry, mid-morning heat, fresh air could be enjoyed. 'Everywhere I go I find people going there too.'

'People here lead an RAF existence in a land which is paradise.

'Not many people think Cyprus is paradise. It looks barren and dry with too many people together in a too small a land. We British prefer to conquer vast continents.'

'And remain British.'

'Of course.'

'Therefore you'll always have land which is barren and dry. I hate being British when I'm in another country. I hate being British anywhere but in London. At least in London you think the British have some sense.'

'What do you mean by sense?'

'Perspective on life,' replied Angela without hesitation. 'A direct appreciation for what's going around them. Here we just appreciate what we can eat and drink. What are you doing today?'

'I don't know. Maybe read *Middlemarch*.'

'It's a long book. Take you more than a day to read that.'

'I may have read enough already to finish it off today.'

Angela did not believe him. She only gave him the book to stare at two nights ago on a request for something substantial. He was now able to read to her the passage he discovered. He was not sure whether he wanted her to be impressed by the passage or impressed by the fact that he was impressed by it. One reading was enough to satisfy perhaps both desires. When he had finished she took the book from him saying that it was so true, so true, and she turned to a page which had for her a special passage. It became obvious that such sentences of silk were sown throughout the entire book, perhaps weaving it together into the fictional masterpiece he was uncertain that he would ever actually read.

'Listen to this,' she said, and she sat down and began to read: '"But indefinite visions of ambition are weak against the ease of doing what is habitual or beguilingly agreeable; and we all know the difficulty of carrying out a resolve when we secretly long that it may turn out to be unnecessary. In such states of mind the most incredulous person has a private leaning towards miracle: impossible to conceive how our wish could be fulfilled, still – very wonderful things have happened!" And then there's a beautiful bit about a squirrel – where is it?' She flicked back towards the beginning and forwards towards the middle until she settled where her black pen had scored some months before. 'Here we are. "If we had a keen vision and feeling of all ordinary human life, it would be like hearing the grass grow and the squirrel's heart beat, and we should die of that roar which lies on the other side of silence. As it is, the quickest of us walk about well wadded with stupidity."'

Now that, thought Christopher, is impressive. "That roar which lies on the other side of silence."

'Let's go for a walk to the cliffs,' said Angela.

Christopher walked to the Naafi. It was Saturday and he was now fed up. He went to the book department which offered a few SF titles and the occasional thriller. He was not interested. He looked through the records.

He had heard them all before. Well, not quite, but he felt as if he had. He was faced with two weeks, every day a Saturday. His lack of exuberance was based on a fear of being unable to justify the free time. If the first day (regarding Good Friday as an off-day when illness and sacrifice seemed to plod unwillingly hand-in-hand) was sullenly collecting the minutes, what hope has creation for the next thirteen? Only took God six days to get it together, and Christ achieved more in the space of these three by in effect not doing anything, than anything he, Christopher, was likely to gather by doing everything he could in three hundred. And what can I do? he thought. I can't do maths, I can't do physics and I'm not really that interested in learning about anything else. Yesterday, at the cliffs, when neither did much more than stare at the sea, Angela told him about Paul Klee who, to her, was everything an artist could be – his control of expression within one line etc. Klee had a definite choice. He could follow music and play his violin wherever he went, or study art. He chose art because he could still play his violin wherever he went, but to Angela this was a profound decision. If one was musically talented then surely music was the ultimate; art being too exclusive to risk such devotion if there was a way out.

'Paul Klee,' she said, 'must have been so sure of his work – must have been so sure of his ideas'

'Perhaps playing a violin was too much like hard work,' ventured Christopher, inclined to the obvious by dint of his own mathematical longing for a certainty while lost in despair.

I have no choice because I have no interest. There was a time when I really thought that physics was my redemption, but I was led by the nose. Now I'm being pushed from behind. Well, there's nothing to stop me from choosing art, except that it's all now been chosen for me and it's all now been worked out, and I have no idea what art really is and so I don't suppose that I have much chance in being able to express it. I see work done by sixth formers which excel Picasso and later on they're thrown into the bin. So what's the use?

He walked away from the Naafi and towards a crowd gathered in the sports field. They were surrounding some form of mini-festival as crowds are apt to do when there's nothing better to crowd around, and Christopher now wanted to become part of this crowd. Remaining by himself was bad for morale. March into society and let's see what's going on. It was a special day for cub-scouts. There were two marquees being pitched exclusively to house no more than perhaps a few VIPs and a couple of tables. Packs of cubs from all over the island had arrived to take part in a festival of drama and the preparations were part of the excitement. Jennifer was with Rebecca and Jennifer wanted an ice-cream. Rebecca wanted to go away and see her friends on the other side of the semi-circle formed by the crowd. She did not want to take Jennifer.

'Okay, I'll keep an eye on her,' said Christopher who was in that listless mood which lent a willingness to volunteer for such tasks.

'In that case you must buy me an ice-cream,' said Jennifer.

'You're not doing me a favour by allowing me to look after you and as Rebecca is now gone you're hardly in a position to make demands.'

'Not making demands. Just want an ice-cream.'

'You should buy *me* an ice-cream.'

To Jennifer the very notion of her buying anyone an ice-cream was absurd. As far as she was concerned everybody else did the buying. She did the eating and the playing. They walked towards the ice-cream stand, already layered by people meeting similar entreaties, and there they met Helen.

'Helen!'

'Christopher!'

Helen did not look as if ready to run away. Christopher did not look as if he was ready to make her stay. Jennifer did not look as if she was willing to wait for them to come to terms with their encounter.

'Of course, you're the leader of the pack,' said Christopher.

This definably incongruent reference to an old song, well stated before as a favourite of Helen's, managed to align itself to the present situation. She was dressed like a cub leader, complete with neckerchief and woggle, and she was there to help organize the part her Pegasus pack had to play in the festival. She confessed to having to sneak off to buy herself an ice-cream so as to prevent her minions metaphorically pulling at her hems. Her authority was not worn out by a process of random distribution needed to keep trouble and boys apart. Helen was a happy girl. Christopher saw straight away how it was impossible for her to bear a grudge.

'I haven't seen you all week,' she said as if this was as remarkable as them meeting now.

'Where have you been?' they both asked.

'Where have I been!' they both replied.

'I've been ill,' said Helen, 'and you didn't come to see me once.'

'I've been ill too,' he said, but intrinsic to his recovery was a slice of honesty: 'but only since Wednesday.'

'Not like me. I've been ill all week.'

Wish I'd been ill all week, thought Christopher, then I'd have escaped the mock-heroic way that I literally fell ill. He felt a tug at his pocket.

'I thought you were going to buy me an ice-cream,' said Jennifer well used to interfering in the time-wasting habits of grown-ups.

'Hello, little Jenny,' said Helen. 'How are you?'

'Hot,' said Jennifer who hated being called Jenny, hating Helen on the spot for adding the word 'little' and deliberately assisting her now stupid brother in wasting time. She was not prepared to forgive her either when Helen offered to buy the ice-cream.

'Look, Christopher,' said Helen, pointing to the marquee, trying to wave aside many people in order to provide space needed for the vision of Stanley. 'Stanley – see. He wants you.'

Christopher looked hard among the heads and true enough, there was Stanley wanting him. William stood beside Stanley, and doubtless William wanted him too. Christopher looked at Jennifer.

'I'll look after her,' said Helen. 'I'm not needed yet.'

'I don't need looking after,' said Jennifer. 'I just need an ice-cream.'

Christopher walked away. He would have offered Helen the money, unfair as it seemed to leave her with the only responsibility he had landed himself for the afternoon, but he could not quite grasp the bathetic reality of meeting her now. I should be leaping for joy, he thought, or at least tip-toeing through the tulips, but instead I abandon her in order to talk to Stanley.

'The very man,' said Stanley. 'We've got a job for you.'

'I can't remember requesting one.'

'We're helping with the marquees,' explained William.

'They don't look as if they need help to me. They're not even flapping in the breeze.'

'Come on, we'll show you want we've got to do,' said Stanley, and he led the way. 'You *have* recovered haven't you? You *can* take a bit of work?'

'Thing about concussion, you know, you never can tell when you'll suddenly just have to fade away.'

'Any fading away will be done on a strictly rotational basis,' said Stanley, authorising the procedures by presenting, behind the largest marquee, ropes, pegs, canisters and much to do.

Others were already doing. There were awnings to erect, guys to stretch and peg, flags to fly. Christopher went through the initial stage of feeling reluctant to muck in and then he mucked in. William went away to fetch someone he had just seen. Stanley was not being his usual philosophical self about the work to be done. He relished every effort needed to make the festival a success and yet it would have remained in character for him to belittle the entire institution which harboured such notions as cub-scouts; little boys and serious drama being as implicitly different as cricket bats and mocking birds; it could have been an altruistic plot to discover the pattern upon which the twain would meet.

'So, you're back with Helen are you?'

'Not really. You've just gone and separated us.'

'But you are back to being friends, aren't you, or are you still in love with her?'

Christopher gave Stanley that stare often supplied to those who step upon a truth inconsistent with the human taste for logic and symmetry.

'Are you saying that because I love her it's impossible for us to remain friends?'

'Is that what you want?'

'No, but...'

'Well, there you are then.'

'I don't quite understand what you mean but I never do. But there again I think I do but then I always think I do. I took your advice, you know. I said 'no' to what was needed of me, and now look at me, suffering from concussion. Pass that end of the rope.'

Up a large unstable step-ladder Christopher went, concussion and all.

'What was it like, getting knocked out?' asked Stanley, keeping one side of the ladder steady.

'The most acquiescent thing that's ever happened in my disagreeable life. You know what? It was like being on the other side of silence.'

It may have been part of the more agreeable side of his ailment, victim as he was to some sort of post-comatose conspiracy, to see Louding quite suddenly there supporting the other side, arms stretched across the inverse V upon which Christopher now formed the apex, as the apparition of the magnificent superimposed upon the mundane. In actual fact he had merely walked across with William who persuaded him to help on the strength of a promised share in a crate of canned beer. It helped to see Christopher struggling intelligently with a coil of rope, ready to cast its decorated length across a boundary set by the stage, its initial goal being a similar step-ladder ten yards into the sun.

'Louding, what a surprise! What are you doing here?'

'Helping you work, but, until a moment ago, *mon ami*, I was basking in the sun over there. The price of being available. Should have stayed in BG.'

'God, I'm glad you didn't. Are you really in Akrotiri especially to see the cubs?'

Louding shrugged. Any activity won its appeal if presented as a valid alternative to spending Easter Saturday in the sultry conditions of a lonely RAF married quarters further north. He had thought about going to Buttons Bay and to call by Christopher's *en route* to find out if he wanted to come along. So he was very pleased to see him now as a result of William persuading him to move from his sunbathing spot within the gathering crowd.

'How are things with you?' he asked.

'I'm okay now, I think. I have to keep thinking that or else perhaps I'm not okay. All depends on what I'm thinking, I think. You know Stanley?'

Louding knew Stanley and Stanley knew Louding. This knowledge along with separated, not un-shy, hellos shook the ladder slightly. The four of them, helped by a few others on the other side of the marquee, worked together for fifteen minutes. Only a few people, Stanley included, knew what was happening. The rest had to concentrate. The liquid remuneration consisted of three cans each, and Stanley, quite fascinated by the work achieved, standing back from the empty stage and viewing it as an example of sweat-enticed creation, issued the drink with an air of wealth hardly realized by his contemporaries.

'Yes, I am pleased,' he announced as he shook a can, opened it, and danced the resulting fountain into the air. That's all he said as he walked away with William.

Christopher would have followed, which had probably been expected, but he remembered Helen and the fact that she would soon be unable to keep an eye on Jennifer, coupled to the fact that he was now with Louding and Louding had his reserved place where he said he had been basking in the sun.

'So, tell me about Wednesday.'

'What happened Wednesday?'

'You got knocked out.'

'Oh yes, so I did. Must be part of my concussion forgetting that bit.' He refreshed his memory with a mouthful of beer and then looked at Louding. 'What about Wednesday, though? You were there when I got knocked out. In fact, I could blame you for getting me knocked out, passing me the ball like that. It was the craziest thing you've ever done.'

'No more crazy than you catching it. All the same, *mon ami*, you scored the try and what a try.'

'Did I really score?' Christopher stopped to think about it, having so far resisted any analysis of this mystery. 'I can't see how I could have scored and got knocked out at the same time.'

'But you did. It was not disputed.'

'But how? Did I perform some sort of contortion which rendered both the touch-down and me unconscious?'

'You hit the post. Well, your head hit the post. Your arms, with the ball, hit the ground on the other side. Then off you went and got tended to by that beautiful games mistress. Don't think that didn't go unnoticed.'

'Yes, I remember that bit and, yes, it was nice. She applied her full attention on a spot on my head. I would have happily marched to the trenches or been blown from here to Cairo just to get another dose of that angelic sympathy. Mrs Burlington wasn't very sympathetic. She was annoyed. Very inconsiderate of me to get injured. She wanted to call an ambulance and pack me off to hospital mainly to get me out the way.'

'So what happened?'

'She called an ambulance and packed me off to hospital.'

'Did she? I can't remember seeing an ambulance although all I was really concerned about was avoiding Sunspire.'

'No, there was no ambulance, but she did pack me off to hospital in her car. Before that I met Marion. She gave me your watch.'

'That was very kind of her.'

'I've still got it. It's back at the house beside my bed. I've been staring at it for two days. It won't have it though. Keeps insisting on telling the right time.'

'Aha, you see. Only works for me.'

'Marion thought it was silly of me to get knocked out.'

'I thought it was the most sensible thing you could have done. Wish I had the presence of mind to do it myself. What did the doctor think?'

'I'm not sure. He asked a lot of questions.'

'What type of questions?'

'Who was winning?'

'Winning what?'

'The rugby of course. He was more interested in the fact that I had just come from the game. The kit I was wearing must have given it away. He wanted to know if it was really true that Gary Edmunds was playing for us and what position I played and whether I played a lot. I had to remind him why I was there. He was disappointed it was only concussion. He was expecting at least a broken leg. So we waited, wondering if you would turn up, or perhaps Rob Johnson who's quite an expert and doing himself in. I was secretly wishing it might be Brian because he wasn't happy about having to play hooker. It would have given me the chance to say sorry. I sort of arranged his week more than he would have liked.'

'Actually he played quite well and he went on about what an important and responsible position the hooker is and what a farce it is about having to be small and get your bollocks kicked in and so on and so forth. He had to shake Sealhard's hand next day.'

Christopher stopped walking. He stopped drinking. He was shocked.

'No! Brian had to shake Sealhard's hand! At the Durham assembly?'

'A special one called after the school assembly.'

'Wilma and Jane – they went and posted the house-points.'

'I don't know about that but we all had to go up and shake the sacred hand. All of us who played in the Durham seven-a-side. Sealhard decided to award the entire team with house colours for rugby. You were included so there's a certificate waiting specially for you.'

'You mean I've gotta go up there first assembly next term and receive a certificate all by myself? I don't want a certificate for rugby. I hate the bloody game. If I never play it again it'll be too soon.'

'Ah, it's not that bad. I quite enjoy it, myself,' said Louding continuing their walk.

'That's because you're out in the wing and you're able to prance around quite happily waiting for someone to pass you the ball and then go for glory while we go through hell getting it to you. You can like it all you like. I hate the bastard game. So the more the doctor talked about rugby the worse I felt until he diagnosed concussion and ordered me straight home to bed. So I stayed in bed for two days and I was determined never to get up again. A protest, you see, like John and Yoko, although instead of Yoko I had *Winnie-the-Pooh* and *Middlemarch*.'

'Interesting,' said Louding. 'Why were you protesting?'

'Because life is absurd. We knock seven kinds of hell out of each other all the time and then expected to pass exams, and I was getting fed up.'

'So why did you get up?'

'I was getting fed up with being in bed. Besides, I knew you'd be here.'

'That's more than I knew. Instead of Buttons Bay I was coerced in that gentle fashion known only to Marion and Helen to come and see Helen's precious Pegasus pack perform.'

'That's also interesting,' admitted Christopher.

They were walking back to where he thought Helen would be waiting. It was almost akin to metamorphosis meeting Marion instead, and Jennifer was by her side engulfed in aftermath of a large cone.

'Well, well, well, life is suddenly full of pleasing surprises,' he said, resisting inner-reaction as a nonplussed victim.

'Where? I can't see any,' said Louding, looking about at the surrounding crowd as if surprised himself by so many Saturday people settling down to see a show.

'Shut up you,' said Marion, acknowledging by this demand her part in the company eligible for at least one can of beer.

'How come you've got Jennifer?' asked Christopher.

'Helen dumped her on me,' Marion happily explained.

Jennifer was happy being a burden, preferring Marion who was more in keeping with the occasion while not surrounded by boring looking cubs. Helen was back to being part of her pack which was dressed to play the somewhat frustrating story of King Midas. Christopher did not want to look at her too much. She was not part of the play. He could not imagine her being turned to gold as the catalyst to royal remorse. I still love her all the same, he thought. I have to. It'd be a shame wasting all the energy spent missing her.

'I think you're sister's such a sweet girl really,' whispered Marion.

'Which one?' he whispered back.

'Which one do you think?'

'I collect sisters like one would collect stamps. Have you any swaps?'

'Usually I hate kids and I'm not really here to look after your sister, don't you know?'

'No, Marion's playing the part of Medusa in Perseus and the Underworld,' explained Louding.

'Huh, fat lot you know about mythology,' she retorted not without triumph. 'It's "Orpheus and the Underworld" and it's not about Medusa, but it's about a beautiful woman he falls in love with. Can't actually remember her name.'

'Andromeda,' ventured Christopher who knew even less but loved the name.

'No, wasn't she the woman who gave Theseus the ball of wool?'

'Why did Theseus want a ball of wool?'

'To find his way out of the maze after he killed the mina-wotsit monster.'
'No, his girlfriend was called Persephone,' said Louding.
'That was Odysseus's wife.'
'No it wasn't. That was Ariadne.'
'Rubbish. She was brought back to life by the Golden Fleece.'
'What part does Aphrodite play in this?' asked Christopher, thinking of the rock attributed to her birth where Angela would probably be at that very moment. And upon this rock, he thought, said Jesus to Peter… What's it all about? Did Peter understand what it meant? Had Jesus then said: Pay attention, I'll be asking questions later, how would Peter have fared? Legends stir up history, myths are confined to those areas concerned with the magic of the past, and here I am on a relatively dull Saturday afternoon, part of its occasional intrusion upon our need for staged drama. Odysseus and Jesus shared the same planet as Robin Hood and the Almighty Thor except the latter tended to hang around in Asgard.
'Sorry?' he asked because he wasn't listening to what Marion was saying.
'I said she doesn't play any part. She's a goddess. She just made things happen.' Marion was pleased with her unsophisticated definition of the divine role. 'Wish I was a goddess,' she said, smiling and standing up, not really wanting to move closer to the crowd but forced into a decision somehow stirred by performances about to begin. 'I love making things happen.'
'Stirring things, you mean,' said Christopher, having already partially forgotten what it was he had accused legends of doing.
'I brought you and Helen back together again,' she said defensively.
'Where is she then?'
'Over there. Look. It's starting.'
The lads stood up and followed Marion to where she thought it was beginning to happen. Jennifer tagged along, contemplating the need for another cone while a group of costumed boys, just a few years older and equally in need of cold refreshments, paraded themselves in front of the gathering looking more like a concentrated child's play of superheroes than cultural characters immortalized into one-character habits of fastidious fables.
'You didn't bring Helen and me together – these cubs did,' said Christopher as he looked at them now. 'Helen is in Akrotiri because her Pegasus pack is playing the story of King Midas.'
'They're able to play King Midas without her. She and I persuaded Louding to come along.'
'And that brought me and Helen together again, did it?'
'Somehow it did,' said Marion latching onto a hidden truth shrouded as it seemed to Christopher by persistent irony. 'I knew she was going to Akrotiri today and I wanted to go along just to be somewhere different than

boring BG. I thought, if Louding comes along Christopher's bound to join us.'

'What? Through a psychic power Louding has on my ability to know that he's here?'

'We were going to call on you and then bring you and Helen together but you beat us to it.'

'What are you two talking about?' asked Louding who had wandered further than they because he had more of the quota of disguised inertia which took up the appearance of mass curiosity. He had almost reached the front line before he realized that he was by himself. He felt a bit embarrassed but was able to admire from a different angle the rather bland but visually versatile stage that he and Christopher had helped to erect. It could comfortably accommodate any theatrical wonder while maintaining the parochial distance needed to be British. Louding backed away. It reminded him of an emptiness present in his own life. He returned to the others and asked his question while feeling slightly dazed.

'You of course,' said Marion as if she had informed him of this fact many times before.

'But don't worry,' added Christopher. 'I was putting up a good defence.'

'Didn't we bring Christopher and Helen back together again?'

'Not if I beat you to it you didn't.'

'But it was us that brought Helen.'

'All I know,' said Louding, 'is that it was me who separated them in the first place.'

'Rubbish,' said Christopher but inwardly accepting that that was probably true. 'Helen and I just had an argument which both of us started and neither of us won.'

There was a sudden burst of taped music. Jennifer put her hands to her ears with a start. She also really did now want another ice-cream and so she tugged at Christopher's sleeve.

'The play's just beginning,' he explained.

'I can't see,' she said.

He lifted her up and he realized that he couldn't see either. The cubs were small and their voices low. There were flashes of colour from unusual costumes which pierced the gaps. The occasional lines were shouted by some of the more enthusiastic players. A princess refused to show any signs of joy within her royal and pampered life until she saw a golden duck, attached to which was trail of oddly dressed artisan-based characters. A king turned another princess to gold and lamented his life-long lust for the substance. A magic dragon slipped into his cave and did not emerge again on hearing the death of a young lad called Jackie Paper who had tamed him. A child of the chimneys turned into a baby of the waters, while the magic elf of a wishing well fell in love with the wench who wished for wealth. Another wench, played by a young lad dressed in green leaves, who had the power to control emotions and grant wishes, but only on request, was carried to a transparent palace made by a spider who loved her for her innocence, too innocent to look upon him as ugly, by which time the intrepid three plus young sister had succumbed to a shade of a horse chestnut out of earshot and sight.

And so Helen found them thus, struggling with their difficulty to perform in a dignified manner, under the penetrating and stifling heat, the art of actually enjoying fast melting ice-cream with the gradual intent of making it last.

'You're making a mess,' Christopher informed his little sister to which she replied quite happily:

'You too.'

'Ah but, I'm suffering from concussion and so I've got a good excuse.'

'What cushion?'

'I'm suffering from a dwindling sense of responsibility.'

'Sounds more like fun to me,' said Louding who confined his mess around Marion laying with her head on his lap in a post ice-cream state of afternoon repose. 'Wake up Marion, Helen's here.'

Marion woke up, looked up and then sat up.

'Hello Helen. I'm glad you're here. These lads don't know anything about anything.'

'Yes,' agreed Jennifer with glee, gaining the gist of Marion's message. 'They're stupid just like all boys.'

'Who won out of the plays?'

'I don't know,' said Helen. She looked quite crestfallen and she sat down with what seemed like sadness rather than fatigue. 'I don't think it was us. Little lad playing the king kept forgetting his lines and touched everything in the wrong order. It was supposed to be a sad play and it made people laugh.' She brightened up suddenly because she only just realized something. 'You know they were all a bit on the sad side, except for the golden duck making the princess laugh. I almost cried because of the Walrus and the Carpenter. I think that might win.'

'Walrus and the Carpenter?' Christopher exclaimed. 'Did they perform that?'

'Well, what did you think it was?' But then she granted him the dispensation gained by not having stayed there to watch it.

'The entire poem?'

'I think so.'

He was disappointed. How was it possible, after weeks of being guided by this mini masterpiece of nonsense, that he had missed out on a grand experience of seeing it in action merely because people were in the way and Jennifer had finally persuaded him to buy her another ice-cream? It would not have mattered how badly it was performed, just its essence consulting the barriers of space and repose would have been magic. As it was such quantities of people and heat thwarted what seemed to him to be a final venture before the rest and the ordeal.

'Shit!' he said.

'Ohmm, that's a naughty word,' Jennifer reminded him.

'Your fault for not paying attention,' said Helen, back to normal, sadness having gone its way like a piece of fluff determined while dependent on the breeze. 'Your fault even for not coming to see me during the week while I was ill.'

Amazing, he thought, how the search for justice connects two totally non-related forms of negligence.

'You were ill?' asked Louding. 'So was I. 'Tis the season to be ill.'

'And I'm still ill,' said Christopher, feeling more so by disappointment than a persistent notion of that which kept him low since Wednesday. 'I was meaning to go and see you, Helen, but little things like rugby got in the way.'

He took hold of her stray hand which resisted slightly but without the idea of withdrawing. In fact she improved upon his grasp by slipping her fingers between his.

'I was going to see you on Monday, but it was only right that I went to the final meeting of Mr Eve's tape recorder club. We didn't do much – listened mainly to *Jesus Christ Superstar*. He loves it and thinks the world of it. I quite like it too only it's a bit too emotional for me. I find the whole Easter thing puzzling. Can never understand why people don't remain friends even when compelled to say: "You believe in what you want to believe and I'll believe in what I want to believe and we'll find out later whose right. What does it matter now?"'

The ice-cream melting heat and a general trend to think more favourably of sleep prevented his theologically inclusive argument from being taken up. He was evidently already living within that desired culture.

'What happened on Tuesday, then?' asked Helen.

'What happened Tuesday? I don't know. What happened Tuesday, Louding?'

'God, I can't remember what happened this morning. Didn't the world stand still?'

'No, that was Wednesday.'

'So why didn't you come to see me?' Helen asked, persisting in her pursuit of visitation-based justice and not believing for one moment that it would only take a catastrophe of stationary global proportions to keep him away.

'I can't remember. Yes I can. There was a rugby match here in Akrotiri. Everyone went to watch it, and sometimes, you know, you just have to be like everyone. Gary Edmunds was playing.'

'Who? I don't know a Gary Edmunds. Is he a new lad?'

'No. He's a world famous rugby player, but obviously not famous enough to register on your radar, not having been featured in one of

Popganda's playing lists. Anyway, on Wednesday Louding and I were playing in the same team with him against the staff.'

'Yes,' said Marion, 'and guess what, Helen, they won.'

'Yes, I know. I was told.'

'And these two scored tries. Aren't they clever?'

Equating cleverness with an ability to run far enough with a ball could well have been consistent with Marion's attitude to the way she was now being treated by her immediate male friends, but, having strengthened Jennifer's faith in the universal stupidity of boys, she impressed her sincerity of this contradiction by hugging Louding and making him lose balance.

'Do I get a hug?' Christopher asked Helen. 'I really missed you even if I didn't go around to actually see you.'

'So you scored the first try. Did you get to kiss Bev Janek?'

Christopher had learned long ago never to assume any form of grapevine ignorance on Helen's part, and was therefore not too surprised by her direct and loaded question on a subject he had otherwise thought to be outside her own environmental scene.

'No. I did not get to *kiss* Bev Janek.'

'Why not?' Helen asked with ironic sharpness. 'What's wrong? Aren't you good enough?'

'I haven't seen her yet.'

'Oh, I see. So I suppose you're looking forward to the event.'

'Listen, my sister set Bev up. She's very good at organising rumours, and she was annoyed at Bev beating Sonja at the beauty contest last Saturday night. Despite her many virtues, Julie's a sore loser.'

'And so are you. That's why you didn't come to see me because I walked out on you last Saturday night and it annoyed and embarrassed you.'

Christopher knelt up in order to look down at Helen but her expression was not going to melt into a smile.

'I wasn't angry during the week,' he explained. 'I wasn't even angry on the night. I was just ever so slightly drunk and so I suffered a sore head on Sunday and concussion on Wednesday.'

'Make sure you don't concuss Christopher if you don't want him to go on about it,' said Louding, having recovered his seated position from his hug but still containing a good deal of Marion's weight.

'What cushion?' asked Jennifer.

'It's an illness which allows him to do as he pleases,' Louding explained, 'part of which is reminding people he's got it. There is, or course, only one proper cure for concussion.'

'Oh yes?' Christopher asked, not exactly ready to give up privileges almost exhausted by his decreasing ailment.

'A night out in Limassol complete with kebab, music, wine, discos etc.'

'I thought that was the only known cure for having 'flu, but it didn't work. I still felt bad on Christmas day.'

'I'm not surprised. You had such a good time with the cure. You'll have an even better time tomorrow night. How about it? We'll go out. We'll celebrate Easter. I mean, why aren't we jumping up and down with joy. We've got two weeks off school.'

Louding had managed to disengage himself from Marion and he stood up as he spoke which was about as enthusiastic as Louding was ever demonstrably capable of being. It was just enough to convince the others that he was right.

'Can I come too?' asked Jennifer, convinced.

'Afraid not.' Christopher pretended for a moment that he was looking at Louding's watch. 'Time we were going home.'

Christopher came to the lazy conclusion that Easter Sunday was the biggest non-event on the Christian calendar. Few really believed that rising from the dead was a greater event than the much more common association of 'a child is born', and Christopher had attended mass but remembered none of it. He politely refused too much chocolate thinking now that his health had a valid say. He played a game of scrabble with Peter and lost. He was happily bored. There was no Angela with whom to walk to the cliffs. Barry had whipped her away to yet another Cypriot resort. He walked to the cliffs himself, meeting neither Gavin Peters collecting snakes nor Wilfred George walking to and from the distant lighthouse. There were a few unrecognisables swimming off Copper's Rock. The water looked smooth and therefore warm enough to venture in but he resisted the temptation to go down. He walked over to where he could enjoy the view of Sub-Point and bask in the memory of his first sighting of Stella, but he suddenly felt inexplicably sad, so sad in fact that he had to about turn and walk home. The only immediate explanation for his distress became mixed up with vague images of this still unknown Stella casting virtual promises onto an unrealized future. He relished the lump in his throat and wanted it to sprout tears, but was ashamed at the same time because there was nothing really in his world worth crying over. He thought of Pat Vendle. She had wanted to cry and did so because of the prospect of leaving everything. I'm not even leaving. And he thought of Bev Janek.

So Christopher went home, got changed and caught the bus to Limassol, and by the time he reached Helen's house life resorted once again to being on the right side of splendid. They were still together. Helen was a moment-to-moment girl and nothing in the past concerned her for long. She wanted to enjoy life because that was all she had and each event, even if containing disappointment, could be weaved into a world where situations spread on ahead and did not leave a trail behind. Time, for Christopher, was a powerful foe. He could not appreciate the present because the past thwarted pleasure with its apparent lack of real achievement, and the future held in sway the balancing act between value and dread. For the first time Christopher looked at Helen and shared and understood an indication of her freedom. She was playing her music, consisting of such joys as the Osmonds and Edison Lighthouse, as she made him coffee by clambering all over the kitchen, so it sounded from the noise he could hear her making, while he sat in the living room and browsed through a volume of a colourful encyclopaedia devoted the health and home.

Helen was also in the middle of knitting, an activity which to Christopher was almost as exclusive to women as motherhood. Even to take a prompted interest in the art assumed a false note verging close to infringing some rule from Leviticus, notwithstanding his meagre efforts a week or so ago at cutting up strips of leather for Angela's particular knitting project. Was it not the case that men knitting was an abomination unto the eyes of God? Charm was not interested in details within the realm of masculine ignorance, although Christopher was the first to despise the stereotype male, all-consuming, too fast and over-pampered, but he could not defy various traits and desires nature deployed to his sex with capricious care. It mattered little to him whether Helen was knitting a track-suit or a shroud. All the same, music not rejecting conversation, as she entered with a loaded tray, he murmured above his glossy pages:

'I see you've been busy.'

'Oh yes,' she said and she laughed her shy laugh when attention was focused on her standard but creative means of passing the time. 'It's not very good at all. It's so difficult to do.' Helen's life-long theory conformed to a socialising effect of regarding ease with quality and struggle with lowliness. 'My sister's much better. She can knit the most super clothes in no time, all fancy patterns and lovely wool and it's great.'

Christopher was at odds with being able to think of anything less alluring although he had often been fascinated with Linda Keen's constant needle clicking on the school bus and his sister, Angela's ability to construct a publishable work from wool and leather. He had not yet had the dubious pleasure of meeting Helen's sister, whom he assumed was younger than herself, although he did not know why, by a good eighteen months. She was never in when he was around. They had not been introduced at school; Helen had not even pointed out her presence, and had it not been for Savina's early in the week use of the girl as a limited source of information regarding Helen's absence, Christopher would have felt inclined to go along with the theory very recently adopted by himself that this girl, as Helen's sister, not unlike Helen's mysterious friends, did not actually exist. Helen was never mean with compliments and praise, and the rare times she mentioned her sister helped to shape, more within her own mind, the image of a career driven super-teen. Maybe this super-teen was an alter ego, exposed only to the privileged few, of which Christopher was not yet numbered. But who cared? An efficient side of Helen's being was not the girl he now fancied and thought he loved.

'Your efforts look okay to me.'

All he could see was a rolled up bunch of confined stitches impaled by a pair of needles and pressed down by a confused ball of wool.

'I'm knitting a jumper for England.'

At first Christopher thought this was equivalent to teaching a dog to die for England and then, of course, he remembered the impending event of Helen's departure. He thought of this England as a familiar, docile, dog-shaped map wrapped up in something taken out of St Michael's wardrobe.

'Are you going to England soon?'

And he tried to remember. Is it cold at this time there?

'Yes, I'll be going in June to start in July, for good.'

'Start what in July?'

'Look, I'll show you.' And she jumped up and ran out of the room and ran back in with a letter in her hand. She presented it to Christopher.

'How did you do that?' he asked.

'Do what?'

'Make a letter appear out of nothing.'

'I didn't make it appear out of nothing, silly. It was in the hall. I received it yesterday when I got back. They said I had a successful interview and I can start the course in July. I'm so excited. Only two, three more months.'

'Can't wait to leave me, hey?'

'No, of course not, silly. Wish you were coming with me.'

She sat down beside him, snuggling into his seat, wishing to share his experience of reading her letter.

'I'll probably be in England another three months after you leave,' he said reassuringly. 'But where's this from?' He looked at the letter. 'Bedminster, Bristol. How far away is that from Sheffield?'

It seemed likely that courtship with Helen would now last at least as long as June, which just about covered spring. To share a promise of autumn in England added weight to the prospect of a delightful time together and seemed to dispel, despite depending upon, the dismal affair of A level results in summer.

'Where's Sheffield?' she asked.

'I'm not quite sure. But what's distance for us two, hey?'

'Yes, even when you're thousands of miles away, with me in England and you here, I'll still love you.'

Christopher flushed with sudden joy. It had not occurred to him that Helen still maintained some reflection of his own recently discovered feelings for her.

'Do you really love me?'

'Do you love me?' she asked firmly.

'Would I be here otherwise?'

They kissed. He still held the letter. It crinkled slightly. Helen held herself back and looked at him.

'Yes,' she said without compromising for a second the tenderness she wanted to promote. 'You would be here otherwise. You'd be here whether you loved me or not.'

'I don't think so. Not now.'

But she's right, you know, he thought. And he began to wonder for the first time since he told himself that he loved her: do I love her? Is love solid? Is it definitely there? Is there never any doubt?

He looked at the letter, a proud letter with a formal decoration surrounding the edges. Unaccustomed to letterheads announcing future departures, putting into writing a conspicuous turning point in life, he imagined that he was holding a well-preserved historical document.

> Dear Miss Margate,
>
> I was pleased to inform you that your interview of 8 March 1972 with us was successful. We are therefore happy to offer you a place as trainee SEN, the course commencing Monday, 26 June, 1972.
>
> It would be helpful if you would acknowledge acceptance of the place offered by return, and in this event we would be grateful if you would report to Bedminster Hospital during the week prior to the commencing date in order to facilitate enrolment in our residential block.
>
> Yours sincerely,
> S.A. Lorrel (Mrs)
> Administration Officer.

'Her name's Sally,' explained Helen. 'She's not like an officer at all. She's awfully nice. She actually bought me a drink after the interview. She's very jolly and she laughs a lot. Maybe she put in a good word for me but it was an easy interview anyway. Not like Biggin Hill or anything like that. I knew I'd pass.'

It seemed to Christopher that Helen not only wanted him to be impressed but also assured of her future needs being suitably answered.

'What's she mean by acknowledging "acceptance of the place offered by return".'

'I'm not sure. I'll have to ask dad. He knows all about these sort of business things. The other bit means I have to leave for England a week before the course and get settled in. Gosh, Christopher, it's going to be such fun.' She looked at him meaningfully as if the fun she referred to was present now as a spiritual revelation. She wanted to kiss him but then she had a thought and said: 'Actually I'm quite scared. I'll most likely be very scared – all by myself in Bedminster.'

'Rubbish,' said Christopher, taking her literally. 'Bedminster, like every other place in England is probably packed with people.'

'But I won't know any of them.'

'Well, you know Sally.'

'But I won't have my friends and family with me.'

'Yes, but I have every faith in your shining ability at getting to know people and then you'll have lots of new friends.'

'Tee hee,' she giggled, 'I might fall in love.'

'True.'

'Won't you be jealous?'

'Not if you kept quiet about it.'

'Gosh, I'd never keep anything like that a secret from you, Christopher. I'll write and tell you everything.'

'Hey, you sound as if you're planning to fall in love.'

'I *am* not. I will write to you everything but I couldn't fall in love. Not really. I'd be missing you too much. Won't it be great when we're together in England?'

Her rapture at this idea caused her to sit back and stiffen into an ecstatic pose. He thought it odd that months from now, in England together with her, should see them happier than they were now. But it was true. Mutual happiness tended to cover a broad wingspan into future plans. They were not exactly soaring to the heights at present, although days ago to share a secluded sofa with her appeared to be beyond his immediate dreams.

'At the moment,' he said, wishing to reject present limits, 'we're together in Cyprus and you're not going for a few months.'

'Yes, Christopher, you're so right. Aren't we lucky having each other?' Again she wanted to kiss him but again another thought prevented her. 'If you fell in love would you tell me?'

'You're a silly girl, Helen. Why should I bother falling in love when I'm with you?'

'But you would tell me?'

'Not if it was to make you jealous or unhappy.'

She giggled. She laughed. She leapt upon him, covered his face in kisses and wanted to bite his neck hard.

'Of course it would make me jealous and unhappy,' she gasped. 'You are the silliest boy I've ever known.'

She made an attempt with her tongue and teeth but he resisted.

'No, come on Helen. We're going out tonight, with others, remember?'

Not that he would have to be discreet about such marks of passion. Louding would hardly notice and Marion would be delighted, gazing afresh at the consequences of her new skill at matchmaking.

'So what?' said Helen, jumping up, dancing about the room, as armed as an archer with arrows of impulse in her quiver-full of freedom. 'I want to embarrass you. I want to do everything. Oh Christopher, I'm so happy, I'm so scared, I'm so everything.'

He had a sudden concern about her reminding him that she was still a virgin and perhaps it was within his appropriate powers to do something about it. Virginity was not the all-engrossing subject among the RAF youth, taken as it was a granted impression which allowed an upper level of the ecstasy for necking and petting without further needs. She maybe everything, as she said, but he was not ready to embrace an everything that ventured into a world still beyond his physical imagination, although of course, being the age he was, he had imagined much in numerous acts of self-gratification.

He stood up and stretched and said with a light tone of one wanting the day to move on:

'You are also not so ready. We'll have to think about leaving soon, not to England of course, but to meet Louding and Marion.'

He looked at Louding's watch.

Helen did not like to see Louding's watch on Christopher's wrist. She knew that the awesome object of transglobal information was going to be returned, but all the same it looked like a gift which requested on demand Christopher's loyalty and favour. She had no equivalent treasure to offer. There was nothing to interfere with the symbolic and remote control of Louding's will. She did not resent Louding but she wanted Christopher to herself. Realising how churlish it would be to request, even with the charming mannerism of a child, a last minute change of plan whereby he and she could share their night alone, she stood up and with a mechanical sense of complying to the whims of a group from which it was impossible to extract any isolated sense of victory, she left the room to prepare and gather up what would be needed for her evening out.

She would be staying the night at Marion's and he at Louding's. They had little trouble in catching the two buses between them and BG. On the journey Helen was silent. She smiled a lot. She wanted Christopher to be happy but something which was not happiness helped in her need to rest her head on his shoulders, stifling the words which, from common experience, usually flowed in comfortable abundance.

'Are you tired?' he asked, thinking that she was dozing.

With pleasing difficulty due to where her head now lay she attempted to nod.

'Too much excitement for one little girl in too short a time,' he said. 'But knowing you you'll be wide awake tonight, full of life.'

He left her at Marion's and walked around the corner to where Louding was busy painting in silver the complex lettering on the tyres of his father's car. Christopher had again arrived just in time. He was needed to help push the car into a position allowing some of the letters more access to Louding's steady hand. He explained that this was a new thing, highlighting, like some cryptic design of law, the rubber serial numbers. It would be impossible to think of anything better to do on such a day. Christopher complied by pushing the car when necessary and watching him work when not. This was not a dull job, Louding assured him, looking unusually contorted under the late afternoon sun. He performed each brush stroke with unnerving precision and he guided his craft through the power of his simple sentences about colour, lines and silver against black. Christopher stood behind him and stared at the muscular intensity behind each stroke. What he does isn't art, he thought. It's how he does it. He is such a beautiful young man and the girls all love him and yet he prefers to be with me.

Christopher also stared at the sprinkler watering the front lawn. It made a sound which caressed the moment and the arc of rapid droplets created a rainbow. Each drop went through each colour, a journey dreamt by light and a curtain of green and before reaching within a foot of its destined fall the droplet would vanish as if to be hoarded from sight by sound. It was because of this vanishing point that Christopher enjoyed again the fragrance of enlightenment. One can love everything equally and vanishing within an inch of being touched counts. Of course he had no real understanding at all of what he was thinking about.

At that moment Louding chose to explain the real reason why he was painting the lettering on the tyres.

'I received a letter from Sharon yesterday.'

He stood up. They were ready to push the car again.

'She's okay. She's well, but she says she keeps hating things. She hates school, she hates her parents. She hates her friends. She doesn't know what's happening. Obviously she's very unhappy.'

'Is she doing O levels?' Christopher always attempted at first the facile but direct method of understanding unhappiness in others.

'Next year.'

'Next year?'

Louding did not need to nor did he want to remind Christopher of how much younger, by school-yard standards, Sharon was than himself. He looked at the numbers and letters left to be lashed by silver but did not immediately raise his brush.

'She wants me to fly to England now for the Easter holidays, and I can tell you that's a very attractive idea. I could apply for an indulgence flight and be on the next RAF plane home.'

Using the word 'home' in such a sense irritated Christopher. It was inconceivable for him to think of England as closer to his heart than where he was now. Home was here: BG, Akrotiri, Limassol, all three; a bit of Episkopi perhaps; doing needless tasks in order to formulate the grander prospects of a night around town. Of course England was only an association depending on the whims of love, but this made him jealous. He did not want Louding to go to England for Easter especially as the lad already had plans to spend most if not all of summer there, and to depart on the promise of company more endearing than his own, in particular as an abandoning cure for Sharon's chronic despair, annoyed him intensely. He stood behind his friend intensely annoyed but betraying only a mild interest, swayed as he was by an inclination Louding coloured in his tone which hinted at the idea of such a departure being, in its way, out of the question.

'She says she can't wait for summer for us to be together again. I don't think I can either. Summer's an eternity away what with all these exams and everything, but it's precisely because of these exams and everything that I can't bloody well go now. That's why I'm doing this. I've been moping around the house feeling pissed off since I returned from Akrotiri yesterday.'

Louding very rarely varied his mood to any extreme. It was hard to imagine him moping, but easy to understand why the task at hand was helping. He could flow from that to his evening out in an attempt to temporarily forget about Sharon. Sharon presented a hefty motive for moping, but Marion was here, part of the vicinity, very much at home and totally valid.

'What about Marion?' Christopher asked, knowing behind it all that there was no question of loyalty to Marion. Sharon was the be all and end all of Louding's depth of affection. If she was suffering so was he.

'I'll have to explain to Marion that we can only be friends. I'll take her out tonight and somehow put the message across.'

'Louding, from what I remember, you've somehow been putting the message across for months. How can you and Marion just be friends? The girl adores you.'

'That's not true. She'd desert me at the slightest fancy of another guy.'

'You know you're wrong there. You know you are.'

'Christopher, I know what being wrong is. Being wrong is writing to Sharon and explaining that I can't fly out to see her because of studies and everything and that I'll remain faithful to us being together for summer, but then off I go and cavort with Marion.'

'May I suggest the unthinkable,' said Christopher, staring again at the sprinkler rainbow. 'Give up Sharon for Marion. After all, Marion's here, Sharon's in England.'

Louding stood up. He looked at Christopher as if to check that the concussion Christopher dared not mention again wasn't afflicting his sense of proportion, and then he walked by him and into the house. Christopher followed. He realized that he may have offended his best friend by his obvious lack of understanding but having to defend the rights of Marion had momentarily excited him. After all, he thought, I'd give up Helen in England for Marion here, I think. In order to maintain the humorous standards which usually extolled the virtues of remaining part of the group, in this case the foursome that they would form tonight, he knew exactly how to deal with this crisis.

'I could also suggest that we go to the moon instead of the Moonlight for our kebab tonight.'

'Do they cook decent kebabs on the moon?'

'No, but I hear the dancing's great, especially over it.'

Louding put away the paints. Tomorrow he would finish what he had started. What Christopher had started already finished because of the time. Thirty minutes later they were ready to go out. The effort of choice in Louding's life, in this case shirts and jackets, helped to assimilate reason. He was happier by the time they met Marion; Christopher being as happy as he had been from the beginning, while Helen, looking colourful, smelling sweetly and gently ready to assume her role as his partner, did not look as ecstatic as earlier when, attempting to bite his neck, she had conjured images of a bountiful future mixed up with the frightening task of beginning a new career. Marion, on the other hand, was upset.

'I'm upset,' she said, skipping out of the house in front of them when spying the approaching taxi. Once inside, Louding in front instructing the driver to drop them off at the Andy Capp III, she explained why. She had already told Helen. 'A friend of mine, or rather ex-friend of mine, returned my Leonard Cohen album and it was scratched. She wasn't sorry. She said, if anything, it improved the music. She thought his songs were boring and depressing.'

'And they are,' said Louding, turning around.

'No they're not. They are beautiful. They are so beautiful they … they … I don't know. They do something to me.'

Helen, who had hardly heard of Leonard Cohen, and suspecting that he was beyond her personal sphere of loving the Osmonds and the Jackson Five, thought that the horrible act of scratching a friend's record and not instantly apologising outweighed any matter of dubious taste attempting to justify the abuse. She thought Louding was being unfair and said so. Christopher, meanwhile, had progressed onto an aesthetic level which negated such trivial matters as to who had done what and why. It had been for some time a mystery to him why his sister Angela had waxed so enthusiastically about Cohen's songs, having heard them once himself and confining them to the cryptic realm of 'maybe yeah and maybe no' with the exception of 'Hey That's No Way To Say Goodbye'. Now here was Marion, a trendy girl with her tastes firmly entrenched in the ever-changing but repetitive sounds of the Charts, saying that Cohen did something to her which she was unable to describe. And there was Louding in front wanting to throw her off in order to morally appease the mounting despair he shared with someone he wouldn't see for months.

Their evening did not start well. It continued with lots to laugh about and there was a slice of bitterness adding to the fun in order that each could avoid the truth. To even know of truth was alien to such affairs, but it hung on the side always slightly out of view. The bad start was not their fault. It left a sour taste and perhaps a vow never to use Andy Capp III as a preface to the routine of romance. The presence of UN troops in Cyprus was a subtle reminder of the country's covert plight. Where the soldiers came from, where they went to and what they did was all mixed up in the mysteries of why Cyprus insisted on merely heating the fuse leading to war, with the soldiers now merely appearing as an extra influence on the Limassol nightlife. They could be readily recognized by their uniform and it was therefore assumed that they were always in uniform, a conformity applying to those within Andy Capp III.

'What's happened to everyone?' said Louding, accustomed to arriving at the pub and meeting lads from school. 'Are we in the right place?'

'Let's go somewhere else,' said Marion, feeling less comfortable. Not only were there no school lads but there were no women to be seen anywhere in any form or any evidence thereof.

Helen felt equally vulnerable. The eyes of this part of the peace-keeping force were trained to play their part in any attention-seeking entrance. Christopher did not want to leave because he spotted a spare table and had nothing against this usual variety of what were, on the whole, British, friendly, indifferent and, besides which, he was quite happy that there was no one here he recognized. He was not in the mood for meeting those he usually only saw at school. Forget about school. There were fourteen days of freedom to enjoy, and to start the session off he would buy the first round. He was given space at the bar and a couple of encouraging nods, but as he was gathering his drinks one of the soldiers, so very obviously both Irish and drunk, felt obliged to approach and offer him his opinion.

'You make me sick,' he said, although the amount he had in him and his unsteadiness probably contributed more to this feeling.

'I'm sorry,' said Christopher, slightly amused, walking away, not for one moment expecting the Irish UN soldier to follow him but he did.

The man looked ghastly. His nose was big and red and glistened with a mixture of what could have been snot and sweat. He had a glowing graze on the side of his head as if he had recently taken a bad fall, and the only friendly feature were the turfs of curling hair shooting from around his ears in different directions. He addressed Christopher and his friends with very similar sentiments.

'You all make me sick.'

He stood over them and they looked at each other and then at him, each thinking rapidly about what could happen next.

'But no hard feelings,' he added. He offered his hand to each, starting with Christopher.

'Listen,' said Louding, 'if we make you sick then why don't you go back to your friends over there.'

Over there was where the soldiers sat in cheerful abundance, any one of whom would have been equally as delighted to deny friendship and advise the man to go elsewhere.

'What friends?' he said. 'What fucking friends? They all make me sick. Don't talk to me about friends. This world is fucked because of fucking friends.'

And he staggered dangerously forward towards the table as he laid some stress into his final words, but elected instead to sit down on the spare seat between Christopher and Marion. He continued to shake their hands.

'Liverpool's the best fucking team on Earth,' he announced, which possessed a reassuring note of something positive. Nevertheless Marion felt compelled to disagree.

'Wrong,' she said. 'Man United is.'

'Marion,' said Helen, shocked.

'You tell her to piss off,' the man said to Louding, possibly referring to either girl.

'You're too drunk to know what you're saying,' said Louding, 'and for that reason I'm not going to flatten your face.'

The man stared at him as if ready to demand that he tried. But then he stated a fact which Christopher, although not eligible to enlist such wisdom as a home truth, never forgot.

'It's impossible to be Irish nowadays.'

He thumped the table, made them all jump and very nearly upset the beer and wine.

'I'm Irish,' said Christopher, 'and I don't think it's impossible.'

'You're not Irish. You're just a little fucking pain.'

He reached across the table. He tried to grab the lapels of Christopher's shirt but Christopher stood up, taking Helen's hand, making her stand with him, indicating to Louding and Marion that perhaps, contrary to his earlier intentions of staying for a first drink, it was time for them to leave. A group of soldiers came across, took hold of their erstwhile companion, stood him up and told him in no easy terms to leave the kids alone. One was thumped and another was kicked and so it took a few more to get him under control.

'Come on,' said Louding. 'It's now their war and definitely time for us to go.'

They did not feel that they were deserting a situation which they may have started. The few steps before meeting the taxi which took them to the Moonlight had them analyzing how much responsibility could be put on their ill-timed presence.

'Fancy saying Man United like that,' said Helen to Marion.

'Didn't seem to bother him, not as much as Christopher saying that he's Irish.'

'I didn't call the man Irish. I didn't have to. It was obvious.'

'No, I mean you saying that *you're* Irish. Are you Irish?'

'I am, yes. Born but not bred. My parents are both Irish and I was born in Dublin but it doesn't matter anyway. The guy just wanted to cause trouble and he thought we were an easy target. Had we said nothing he'd have still tried to cause trouble.'

This reminded Marion of what Louding had said and why he had said it.

'Would you really have flattened his face?' she asked.

Louding looked at her, understanding the inference of her question.

'He said what he said out of what is known as diminished responsibility. The wretched man was drunk and miserable which could be worse than sober and miserable. He had just had some sort of accident, so I suppose he was feeling pretty bad.'

'Don't you dare try to defend him. He was a monster.'

'Had he been sober I doubt he would have told you to piss off, although under certain circumstances...' added Louding, thinking about it.

'God, you're a monster as well,' said Marion, half hating Louding's persistent method of being funny. She slapped him over the shoulder while he succeeded in hailing a taxi. 'I don't see why I should talk to you at all.' She entered the taxi first and Helen followed. Once again Christopher found himself in the back with the two girls and Louding in the front needlessly offering directions. 'I don't think we should talk to them, Helen,' Marion continued. 'They really don't think much of us at all.'

'We're taking you out,' said Christopher. 'Isn't that enough?'

'We're not talking to you, are we Helen?'

'No,' said Helen.

'And we're not talking to Louding either, are we?'

Helen once again said no but Louding seemed to distance himself from the semi-friendly conflict in the back. However, he turned around, looked at Christopher and explained how he didn't think much of the chances of these girls remaining quiet for longer than twenty minutes. They failed to include a clause entitling them to talk to each other, and the challenge was taken on.

'I once took part in a sponsored shut-up at my last school,' said Helen. 'I had to stay quiet for twenty-four hours. It was very hard. Twenty minutes won't be that difficult.'

Louding looked at his watch. The second hand reached twelve and he put his finger up for the girls to observe their vow of silence. Less than half-way through they were in the Moonlight. They chose their table carefully, avoiding the eventual squeeze of moving chairs and gaining an adequate view of an increasing number of surrounding customers. Christopher ordered the kebabs and Louding said that the girl who refused to speak in the next twenty seconds would pay the bill. This had little effect. A couple of smiles informed all that neither could afford to pay for one kebab, let alone four. Christopher told them that unless there was conversation from either within the next thirty seconds he and Louding would go to the bar and leave them until the meal arrived. Marion shrugged. Helen looked at her and then she shrugged.

'However, as it happens,' said Louding, 'there's only fifteen seconds to go. So there again, the first girl to talk will be the one with the weaker will.'

Helen didn't really mind if her will was to be considered weaker than Marion's. She was never sure what anyone meant by will when used in conjunction with desire. To her ones will was always directed to what one wanted, and if she wanted to talk so well and good – so will and good. She smiled. What she really wanted to do was go to the loo. Marion may well have accompanied her but she had been thinking while she was so quiet.

'I had been thinking while I was so quiet,' she said as the three of them watched Helen walk away, 'why are we at the Moonlight and not the Britannia? I thought we were going there?'

'My parents are going there tonight,' Louding explained. 'Thought at first they were going here. Both places are just as good.'

'Sure it isn't because of that girl, what's her name, Stella, being here?'

'What?' said Christopher impulsively. He attempted self-control but could not resist asking: 'Where?'

'At the table over there.'

He wanted to turn around and look but his last wish was to seem anxiously doing so, and he was suddenly very anxious. Bad enough having her spotted by another. However, he looked at Louding and was inclined to agree with Marion. Louding, who had actually little time to arrange anything other than being where his parents were not, merely smiled.

Helen returned as the first course was being served. While the vegetables were passed about and the yogurt was spread, Marion informed her about Stella.

'One of our guys is after her,' she added with the malicious rebuke of the scorn implied by their silence challenge.

'One?' said Helen. 'Who?'

But Marion wasn't saying. She seemed equally annoyed at both the man she adored and the man whose loyalty she had regarded as a given.

Helen had no inhibitions about turning around to stare at Stella.

'She certainly strange looking with all those Greeks around her.'

There was a common and not un-racist union among the British girls which regarded the company of Greek men as taboo and Helen was taken up by this conceit in the otherwise careless innocence of her observation, while all Christopher was able to do was to start eating.

'Yes, I think it's stupid being with so many of the natives,' said Marion with the perfect malevolence of one posing above her usual style. 'She puts on a show just to look different.'

'Yes, quite unheard of,' said Christopher, enjoying the girls distracted sense of outrage and unable for a moment to understand why Louding could not adore Marion with the same intensity he used to love Sharon. 'Shall we call her over and save her from herself?'

'There's no need,' said Louding who commanded the best view and had already waved in her direction. 'She appears to be coming over.' He poured out the wine and Christopher cursed his apparently staged control of events. 'Hello Stella. Fancy meeting you here. Would you care for some decent wine? – better than *cockanelly*.'

'I don't think I should,' said Stella as she walked up to Louding's place, thus wiping clean a startling image Christopher had conjured up by the sense of her approach. But reality thumped against his ribs. 'Anyway, we're drinking Australian *Cabernet Sauvignon* and not *cockanelly* and my friends keep filling my glass. It's very nice but too much wine is too much wine. Hello Marion, and hello to you … I'm sorry, I've forgotten your name.'

'Helen,' said Helen as curtly as it was possible to say Helen.

'Yes, of course. Isn't it nice to see you all here? This is my first Limassol kebab, would you believe and so I feel doubly lucky.' This was her way of saying that she had been all over Cyprus having kebabs and up until now the humble locality had been ignored. 'Mind if I…'

Christopher jumped up. He hardly knew what had affected him more: her presence or her apparent ignorance of his. He offered her his seat and he grabbed a spare from a neighbouring table.

'Thank you,' she said softly, still standing and staring at him, issuing her gratitude with an extra coat of fascinated sincerity. 'I don't know you, do I?'

Christopher also had to remain standing and he shook his head, his tongue pinned to the top of his mouth. Louding stood up and came to his rescue.

'Our friend from Akrotiri – has the amazing name of Christopher Panhandle.'

'Gosh, you're not related to Julie Panhandle?'

Christopher relaxed into the resigned familiarity of this question.

'I'm her brother – for my sins.'

'And Christopher,' said Louding, obviously enjoying the weight of this occasion, 'this is Stella Clifton – Martin's cousin.'

Christopher longed to shake her hand but he suspected that the sweat on his palm made him feel offensive to touch. Fortune spared him. She raised the glass she had earlier refused to the sound of his name.

'Christopher. I had to mention your sister. Martin and his friends adore her. She's something of a legend it seems.'

'Not among us she isn't,' said Marion.

'Don't you like her,' Stella asked, noting perhaps from Marion's position that it was she Stella who was busy being disliked.

Marion was suddenly uncertain about the words she should use. After all, it did occur to her that the legendary Julie Panhandle *was* Christopher's sister, and now was not the time to remind Christopher that as such sibling loyalty would be asked to compete with that of known friends, but Stella realized that she, herself, was being unfair.

'Don't answer that question,' she said quickly. 'I'm not here to indulge in gossip. So,' and she sat down allowing Christopher and Louding to do likewise, 'here we are.'

'Won't your Greek friends miss you?' Marion asked.

'No,' said Stella, shaking her head as if wondering why Marion would ask such a question, and Christopher sank further into his abyss of love and worship.

'Are you on holiday?' he asked, not without effort.

'Yes, sort of. I love Cyprus. I just love being here, the land, the people, the food, the goats, the music, the religion, everything. It is heaven on earth here. You don't know how lucky you are living here. So, yes, I suppose I must be on holiday but actually I am working too, so it's not really a proper holiday, is it?'

'Why not?'

'Not really proper to work and be on holiday at the same time.'

'Plenty of people do work during holidays,' said Louding, mistaking the term for time away from school as opposed to a self-imposed break away from the usual routine. 'Us poor school kids work all the time.'

'You mean you boys work,' said Marion with increasing resentment. 'Us girls don't get the chance to work anywhere, except babysitting for a pittance.'

'I don't mind,' said Helen, forgetting her shared grudge while paying homage to what she considered a universal but certainly Mediterranean belief. 'I love not working. Anyway, us girls don't have to pay for so much. My Christopher pays for everything, don't you my sweetheart?'

I pay all right, he thought as he offered her a smile by way of his reply. He would now have willingly died at Stella's bidding had she entertained such a choice in view of the challenge Helen almost consciously made. Stella was not as pretty as Helen. Her skin was pale, her nose could have suffered better shaping and her lips needed care to avoid forbidding expressions, but these physical instances were shaded by the increasing mystery of her glowing eyes. They betrayed an active, vibrant, female brain and he longed to be offered the key capable of unlocking her thoughts. Her glasses, large and pleasingly placed on her oval face grew with the benefit of the translucent view piercing them. They were as much a part of her as the gently laced cloth wrapped around her hair.

'I feel so blessed,' she said. 'Everyone has been so nice to me here, and off I go to Pathos tomorrow, all because I fall in with the right people.'

She then addressed Christopher. Although he was preparing himself for this, her direct voice was enough to physically shake him from his place, and the effort to remain where he was stifled as well as enhanced his worship.

'I presume you're at St John's as well. An A level student?'

'Yeah, well yeah,' he gasped. 'What else is there?'

'Oh, don't say that. You'll give me a conscience. My parents think I gave up school too soon, and, you know, they're probably right. Anyway, you'll all have to excuse me. Enjoy yourselves.'

Her table was being served with the next course on the kebab list and so she had to leave.

'"You'll give me a conscience",' mimicked Marion. '"And, you know, they're probably right". Who does she think she is? Stupid cow.'

'Marion,' said Helen, shocked – shocked also at realising how much she agreed with her.

'I think she's quite charming,' said Louding.

'"I presume you're at St John's as well. I'm so blessed." God, I hate her.'

'Why?' said Christopher. 'What's she done to you?'

He was attempting to hide his deeply smitten state and was also busy loving Marion for her hatred as it justified some of the battle that raged very close to the pit of his stomach. He continued eating, glancing every now and then at Helen to check if she too had in some way been overwhelmed.

Marion ignored Christopher's question or perhaps used it to turn her venom on Louding.

'I hate you too. You knew she'd be here.'

She was so angry that there was a great likelihood she would stop eating, get up and leave. But she continued to participate in something of the jovial union which kept sway on Helen's thoughts. Marion could see that Christopher was blown over, Louding knew about it already and Christopher was blown over. The food was tasteless, the eating process mechanical and Helen was no longer the essence of the evening. She, in ignorance sublime or acting on the present moment which cleared the immediate past, expressed her sudden arrival of abounding joy.

'Christopher, darling, how shall we spend our Easter together?'

'Anyway you want to,' he mused while chewing.

'Do you want to do anything in particular?'

'I cannot think what you are referring to.'

To her this was a compliment. She reached over and kissed him and a strand of oiled carrot hanging from his lips.

'I thought you said your parents were going to the Britannia,' said Marion, being the only one of the four who was able at that time to pick out from the now crowded restaurant the table where Louding's parents, Mr and Mrs Louding, sat.

'I thought they were too,' said Louding. This was not necessarily distressing, but he was not happy about the mix up. He was suddenly unable to remember what his parents had said and therefore which party was at fault.

Helen wanted to talk about her future nursing career in England. She gabbled on with the contented ebullience of one convinced that walls could hear. Christopher tried to listen but he was more interested in Louding's plight. As parents went, Mr and Mrs Louding were totally agreeable people, but being parents they could produce in their only son a unique sense of ill-ease.

'I've spoilt their evening together being here,' he explained as an aside to Christopher, 'and it's dampened our meal them being over there.'

They were many tables away. Christopher could just about see where they were sitting, and only because of a unified sway in either direction of the amount of heads in between.

'Why?' he asked.

'I don't know. I'm just being paranoid. Don't worry about it.'

'I won't. They probably don't know we're here. Let's just act as if we haven't seen them.'

'Problem is, I've just waved to them.'

Christopher laughed.

'This is absurd, Louding. What are we going to get up to which for some reason they present some sort of threat?'

'Everything. The way I eat. The way I stand. The way I might walk over everything if I choose to get up with you now – now, Christopher – and walk over to the bar.'

'Oh, all right. And I've just remembered something. Excuse us ladies,' said Christopher, standing up. 'Come on, Louding. I want to show you something.'

'What, that you can still walk straight?'

'No, but that you can walk straight when you're with me.'

'And in the meantime you desert us,' said Marion who had, until then, been listening to Helen.

'Give you two a chance to talk about us.'

On the way to the bar Christopher showed Louding a receipt, aged and crinkled from being wedged in his wallet for so long, given to him some time by Julie.

'It's for one of the photographs from Pat's going-away do. Remember Pat Vendle? I can't remember there being a photographer about but there must have been.'

The box of photographs was beside the bucket of ice on the bar and Christopher looked at them, not wanting to see too many at once.

'This is stupid and madness,' he said, shuffling through them. 'I'm in love with that girl.'

'Who, Pat Vendle?'

'No. No not Pat. Not Pat. For God's sake, Louding, it's Stella who's sitting over there and succeeded in making me shrivel up like a prune. She said everything in the short time she was with us to make us all feel beneath her. Her snobbishness only helped instead of hindering my feelings, or maybe she did hinder them and I want her even more now because of that. What isn't so funny is Helen. I'm supposed to be in love with her.'

'Well make up your mind, Christopher. Perhaps now you'll understand how I feel about Sharon, with Marion being here.'

'I'm sorry, Louding, but I don't. Sharon's in a different world. Marion is here, and she's more for you than anyone else I know, and God knows I've known a few who thought they were right for you.'

'But not more than anyone else I know. I could say the same about you, Stella and Helen.'

'In that case why did you bring us to the Moonlight knowing Stella would be here?'

'Do you think I planned it? I knew as much about her being here as it turned out about my parents. At the moment my knowledge is pretty low.'

'But Louding, I mean it. I'm in love with that girl and I fully understand why Marion hates her.'

'Shall I tell her that?'

'Oh look, here's the picture, Pat and me dancing. I don't think she danced with anyone else. I look a bit of a prat but not a bad one of her.'

He held it up against the array of lights behind the bar.

'Shall I tell Stella that you love her?' repeated Louding while he too looked at the shot. 'Hey, you know, it's not bad. Didn't know Pat was so attractive. She was quite a character, wasn't she?'

Christopher was unable to reminisce but nevertheless he hummed agreeably being as Pat had been the last girl, other than Helen, he had kissed.

'Shall I tell your parents that you don't like them being here?'

'By all means,' said Louding.

'But I daren't, not if you retaliate with Stella, but would it change much?'

Louding shook his head.

'You're wrong about Sharon,' he said with an air of casting aside caution accordingly as he continued to stare at the picture of Pat Vendle, remembering in his own way that she was one of those girls Christopher had referred to in his attempt to talk up Marion. 'You know, there's more hope in this photograph than in the air we breathe right now.'

'Give it to me,' said Christopher, and he snatched the shot from his friend with a lively conviction that the rubbish he spoke contained just enough truth to be stored within his jacket pocket. He passed over the receipt and kept the picture. 'I don't tell your parents, you don't tell Stella, and also let's keep Pat out of this.' He emitted a short laugh which settled into a sigh. 'Silly, isn't it? Never happy with what we have. What's Stella to me? I hardly know her. Yes, and I do agree with Marion. Who does she think she is?'

'Is that your way of saying, Christopher, that I shouldn't waste time pining for Sharon?'

'If you like, yes. It is a waste of time, isn't it? Did you promise Sharon you wouldn't enjoy life. Look over there, Louding, and tell me truthfully – isn't Marion a delightful lass?'

'Oh come on, Christopher.' Louding refused to be drawn, too stubborn to be consoled by comparison. He looked away from where Christopher was staring and started to examine the other photographs. There were many faces he recognized and all the other faces he didn't looked the same, awaiting their own recognition in order to grant them life. 'Okay, I admit it. While Sharon is not here Marion is good company.'

'You'll always think that. You always have done. Come on, let's go back. They're looking at us.'

'Wait, Christopher. Look. Grace Ford and the Dazels.'

Louding pulled out a picture of Grace from the box. She was with her own family and the Dazel girls. Gale was contemplating her wine while Rosemary was laughing. The others looked ready to offer a toast and Grace was in the centre, her bright smile was for that frozen moment exuding her characteristic mode of complete satisfaction.

'It could be that all of us fancied her at one time or another and she was one girl who didn't care and still doesn't.'

'And another who did,' said Christopher, thinking of Gale but, wanting to avoid a subject containing Rosemary, he pulled Louding away.

He now found himself wanting to enjoy every second with Helen, but always there was a shadow, and that photograph, like a fateful card being pulled from the tarot, introduced the element of the new, vague and nagging. He felt as if he had forgotten something quite important, an area of guilt not properly nurtured.

The four of them drank and ate, talked and laughed and then left. They were all pleased for separate reasons that those they knew from the other tables had left some time before. As previously arranged Christopher elected to pay the bill; Louding would look after the taxis, and he directed this, their third, to the Prison Disco. The place was almost empty: lots of seats, lots of waiters but little atmosphere.

'Shall we go elsewhere?' suggested Louding.

'The Twigger Bar's not far away. We could walk,' said Christopher, anxious not to drop another clanger by assuming that present conditions were suitable. He had always been averse to changes in venue once he had arrived. 'And I've never been to the disco beneath the bar.'

Neither had the other three. They went. On the way Louding raced a stray dog down the street, running very fast, disappearing into the street lights.

'It's far too hot for him to run like that,' said Marion. She was angry again.

'Louding's certainly doing his best to make your evening, if not the best,' said Christopher, 'at least memorable.'

'What's wrong with him, Christopher? He's been acting strange.'

'He can certainly run. Did you see the way he took off?'

'I'm not interested in his running. It's so boring. So he can run fast. Big deal. Everyone goes into fits about Simon's running, but so what? When he walks with me, that's what I love. I really do. I love the way he walks.'

'Christopher and I walk everywhere,' said Helen. 'Remember when we walked all the way from my place to BG to visit your friend – what was his name?'

'Mark. Yeah, but do you know, when we arrived, I don't think he was that pleased to see us.'

Louding ran back sans dog. He was happier now and hardly panting. The poor under-nourished mutt had flaked out yards away. There was still a chance it would follow them and so they entered the disco quickly. It appeared to be no more popular that evening than the Prison, but it was less artificial in its suggestion of being within their consciousness some form of twilight zone, and so, choosing at random a table close to the dance floor they ordered four drinks.

'I don't feel well,' said Helen. She rubbed her stomach. She looked sorrowfully at Christopher. 'Too much food and drink.'

A couple of couples were on the floor. Louding and Marion had gone up to dance. Helen wanted Christopher to kiss her better. Kissing is all well and good, he thought, but one can do that at more places than one can dance, and so after obliging for a few seconds he asked her again how she felt. She was surprised at his lack of sympathy. He was not aware of it, and so eventually, to please him, she said that she felt a lot better. They got up to dance but they were soon sitting down again.

'What's wrong, Helen?'

'I want to go home now. I'm really not well.'

'We've only just arrived. Remember, you're staying at Marion's. We all have to leave together and it won't be fair on them.'

He indicated Louding and Marion with a glance, and Helen could see in that glance the simple elegance of Christopher's greed for the company of more than just herself. Louding came across and said that Marion wanted to dance with Christopher and he with Helen. Helen seemed to regard this as a reasonable cure and Christopher accepted the inevitable statement this entailed as well as the delight in having, for a few moments, the chance of Marion in his arms.

He and Marion were offered this chance by the music and he was delighted to be able to pull her near to him. He quite fancied her now that she was in danger of being thrown aside for this ridiculous image of a depression-filled Sharon, and what had also helped, but he did not know why, was her hasty hatred of Stella.

'Marion, is it really true that you love the songs of Leonard Cohen?'

'Yes. Have you not heard them before? You should listen to the one called "Nancy". It's so sad. Everybody forgets poor Nancy. Every time I hear it it puts a lump in my throat. And "The Butcher" – wow, puts an arrow through me. Just kills me.'

The present music made it difficult for Christopher to imagine any combination of notes forming the killer arrow. It occurred to him that his love for Helen was so shallow that it was not even worthy of a paddle. Last week's remorse had been mistaken for love. But I really can't get Stella out of my mind.

'You're after her, aren't you?' asked Marion with her disarming ability to read the thoughts of one whose present proximity made such a gift seem natural. 'I don't see what you lads see in girls like Stella.'

'I am not after her. It may have escaped your notice but I'm going out with Helen. I just think Stella is charming, maybe in just the way you women, for some inexplicable reason, think those gormless airmen are charming.'

Marion laughed. Now she could be perfectly honest.

'We don't. We just think they're rich. They have money they can spend on us while you school lads just have your bragging and your ridiculous rock music. But I'm not interested in airmen. Yes, I like having money spent on me, but really all I want is Simon, and I won't have some la-di-dah tow-rag take him from me.'

Christopher enjoyed hearing Marion eat into his affections, assuming that she was referring to Stella as the threat to that which in reality Sharon posed. Marion was an expert at complicating what should have been a visible acquiescent fold of loyalties. It can't be possible that Louding will want to give her up now, he thought, but staring at the other two he wondered how close Louding was to thinking the same of him and Helen.

'Marion, kiss me.'

The music certainly suggested this compulsion as being worthy of a request. They were both enjoying the vague promise sprinkled by the dark, but Marion looked at him in surprise. He may just as well have asked her to strike him.

'What? No. I can't Christopher. Not in front of Simon.'

'I'll be kissing you in front of Helen.'

'Don't you think she'd mind?'

'If she doesn't I'll want to know why?'

Marion was probably more scared of Louding *not* minding although needless to say his reaction would have been minimal, Christopher and he being so close. She was close enough to Helen but the combination was weird.

'No, I can't Christopher. It's not that I don't want to. It's just that I can't. Simon is too near.'

'If he was miles away would that make a difference? You'd still be unfaithfully kissing me.'

But Marion was not required to answer. Her smile was enough to console the supposition that was not allowed in any way to influence her decision. Girls don't need to give answers to such questions. Girls have better things to think about and Christopher had to be content with the puzzle he presented being side-stepped by her prerogative. He was not going to get his kiss. How could I want it unless given freely? Like Miss Janek for whose honour I nearly died. She owes me nothing. How can anyone owe anyone else affection? Obligation obliterates – and he thought of the little girl in her back garden who spent an afternoon kissing him when he was equally as little but not equally as willing. And how was I able to refuse her? I'm always paying the price of what I cannot accept. So, Mary-Ann bye bye, and Stella – twice blessed Stella – he shrugged.

Marion misread the shrug, thought it was an act of despair and she hugged him closer. This added weight to the desperate side of her whisper.

'I love Simon Louding. Christopher, I love him so much. People don't believe me. People think I just fancy him because he's good-looking, like all those girls who fancy him because he's good-looking. They all end up thinking he's strange, but what do they know?'

What does anybody know who hasn't experienced the arrow from a song by Leonard Cohen? thought Christopher. Still, dearest Marion, your faithfulness is admirable but you're wasting your time. You cannot really want Louding to owe you his love, and he can't give it freely.

'I'll always be with him,' she continued, 'and do you know what?'

'What?'

'I wish he wasn't so good-looking. I wish he was plain.'

'What, like me?'

'Oh, Christopher. I'm being serious.'

She looked at him. She shook her head, trying to arrange her thoughts around this one point of an explained desire.

'Marion, there is really nothing you can do. If I was to say that I love you the way you love Louding, would it make any difference?'

'Christopher!' She really was looking at him now and she wasn't shaking her head. 'What about Helen?'

'What about Helen? And what a mix-up, hey? Love is as confusing as the telephone network. Say that Helen loves me, and I love you and you love Louding. Where does that leave Louding? Where does that leave any of us? And what can any of us do about it.'

'Christopher, what are you going on about? You don't really love me. You're just saying that.'

He shrugged again.

'What difference would it make?'

'Christopher, what are? ... I mean, you're beginning to...'

Again she shook her head but this time as an attempt to collect her thoughts. The arranging of them would have to wait.

'Marion, I've just been enlightened to a very important aspect of freedom,' but I can also see that if it's not used properly, he thought, it can be disastrous. 'We owe each other nothing. Nobody is in debt to anyone when it comes to love. You cannot win love no matter how loving you are. It can only be given. Not won.'

'That's silly. You win love that's given to you.'

'I don't think so. You just accept it or reject it, and the person who offers it can do nothing either way to influence your decision.'

'You're telling me that Simon will never accept my love?'

'I'm simply saying that his freedom means that there's nothing you can do about it. He may accept, he may reject, but it's not up to you. You're freedom is to give. If you try to force or you try to win you just lose.'

He looked across at Helen who had returned to the table with Louding where their drinks were waiting; the place filling up and the night no longer so young. Maybe she had been telling the truth. She was sitting back trying not to look so miserable. Maybe, he thought, she really is not well.

'I think we'll be leaving soon.'

'You've just upset me,' said Marion which, based on her evening thus far was part of the course. She let him go and walked back to the table. He followed. 'Your boyfriend has just upset me,' she said to Helen.

'I can only say sorry,' said Christopher. 'Didn't mean to.'

He wanted to settled down beside Helen and ask how she was feeling but Marion remained standing. Louding stood up as it to allow her to squeeze by him into her place.

'Perhaps we should go,' he suggested. 'Helen's not feeling so great.'

Marion gave him a stern look and even sterner reply. His entire evening had been a combination of stern looks and replies and this now was the sternest of both.

'What do you care how Helen feels? What do you care about how I feel? You don't care about anything.'

'That's not quite true,' said Louding with a light touch to his betrayal of deeper, heavier feelings beyond those he had for Marion.

'What have you been saying, Christopher?' asked Helen.

'Marion is simply over-reacting,' Christopher replied, trying his best to under-react.

'I am not!' Marion laughed. She wanted to cry. She was quite prepared to accept the extent of Christopher's truth. It had not been a generous day for affection, but who could deny her feelings, now smouldering. She took her bag and she walked carefully but not slowly to the ladies loo.

'Christopher,' said Helen as she stood up. She walked away, following Marion and weaving into the loose crowd as young girls often do while creating the trail of an emotional heat behind them.

Louding appeared to be studying this heat as he watched them walk away. He was more surprised than bewildered as one can always be surprised by either the promised or the predictable. His thoughts were quietly dealing with how to cope with what had to happen.

'Christopher,' he said as he sat down.

'Yes, I know. What have I done?'

'My job for me, perhaps? And in my favour, yes?'

Christopher took up his drink, drank it down and shook his head.

'Depends on what you think is favourable.'

'What did you say to her? You didn't tell her about Sharon?'

'No, of course not. But I doubt if there's any necessity anyway. There can't be much she doesn't know about Sharon, because, let's face it, she does know about her – *doesn't* she? My way of thinking must have added to her misery.'

'Misery. I don't want her to be miserable.'

'Well then, give up Sharon and devote yourself to Marion.'

'I don't think that would work. You see, I don't want me to be miserable either.'

'But you're already miserable. You and I make such a couple of miserables that Victor Hugo has nothing on us.'

'So what is it that Marion is actually over-reacting to if she's already well versed in my situation with Sharon?'

Christopher thought about this. It was not easy trying to build a definite approach to reaction. A not inconsiderable manner of moods and meanings could erupt from one line.

'Freedom.'

'Freedom?'

'Yes, you know, the usual. Freedom and truth and how one is supposed to lead to the other.'

'I see. You offer freedom and truth problems to a girl and you blame her for taking it badly.'

'I offered her the solution.'

'God knows, I've tried to live through your solutions, Christopher.'

'Have you?'

Christopher could not have expected a more startling admission, and so, to calm any urge of expressing the experience, Louding both awarded and cancelled the chance with one of his magnificent smiles.

The girls took a long time to return. Helen was smiling. She was no longer feeling ill. Marion had the appearance of one who had discovered redemption and she joyfully added to the appropriate nature of them all making good their departure. She for one had had enough of this evening.

'Helen and I are going on holiday tomorrow,' she announced as they stepped out into the midnight air.

'Yes, we're going to have a holiday from both of you,' said Helen.

'We're going to Famagusta aren't we, Helen? So there.'

'Tomorrow?' asked Christopher, disturbed more by the rapid planning than the final decision.

'My friends go there all the time. And so does my sister and they all say it's great.'

'Yeah, great beaches, great night life,' said Marion who could well have shared the same friends and sister, the conspiracy stretching beyond that which Christopher actually knew of the two girls. 'Much better than here.'

'Present company not excepted, I suppose,' said Louding. He was both amused and relieved that this solution had not been presented as more of a demand. 'Where will you stay?'

'My sister's already there,' explained Helen, which was her way of stating that where one's sister was one could also be.

'But what about us?' said Christopher attempting to fulfil her hope based on his despair. 'What about our Easter holiday together?'

'You can have your Easter holiday here with Louding.'

What more could he say? What more could they do? Louding hailed a taxi and Helen explained further on their way back to BG.

'My sister has a boyfriend who lives in Famagusta and his family have a big house.'

'Is he British?'

'Of course. Of course he's British. My sister isn't strange like yours.'

'My sister isn't strange, she's just doesn't have any boy-friends, British or otherwise. Part of her place in her command culture.'

'Actually, I've never met him. He's always supposed to be coming here but he never does?'

'Could explain why I've never met her.'

'You've never met my sister?'

'Nor your friends – these friends you always mention who are always giving you advice and now they're taking you away.'

'They're not taking me anywhere. Marion and I need a holiday from you two.'

'Just like that?' asked Louding turning around, having elected as before to sit in the front but listening intently as one who was now conscious of being excluded from the group.

'Yes,' said Marion, 'just like that.'

'So what about us two left to fend for ourselves?'

'After what Christopher told me it shouldn't make any difference.'

'What was it you actually said to her, Christopher?'

'Yes, Christopher?' asked Helen. 'What did you say to her?'

'You mean she didn't tell you? You establish a holiday on the basis of what she didn't say?'

Christopher folded his arms and sat into his corner of the cab.

'If she's not saying then neither am I.'